# Riot, Retribution and Revenge

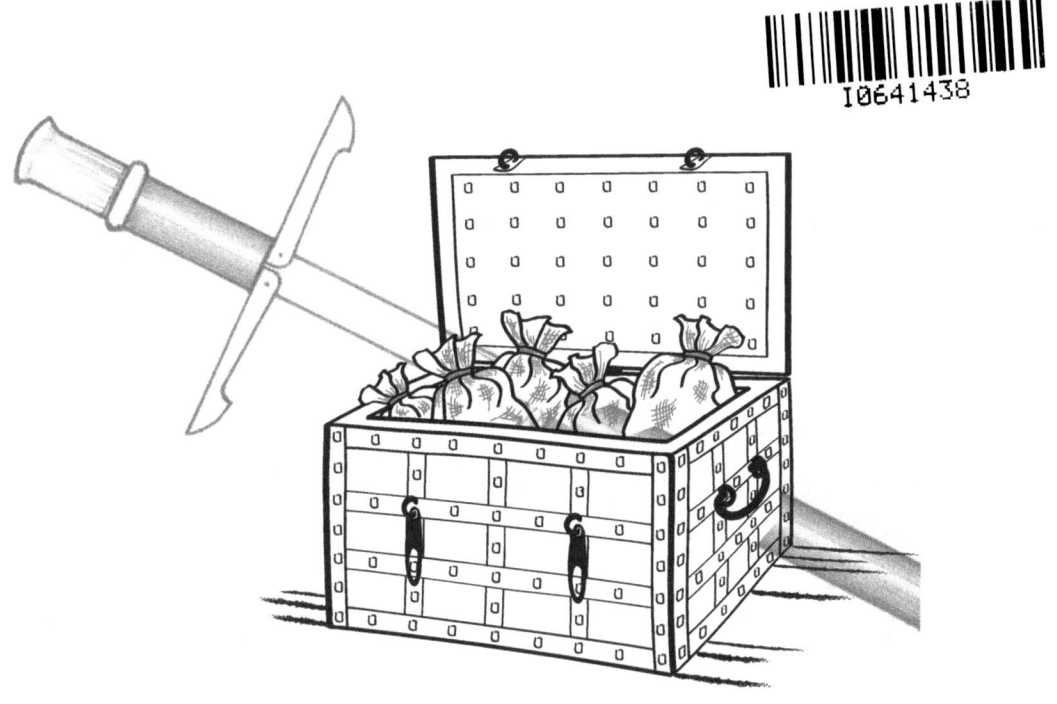

# Alex E. Robertson

Published by:
ALPHA Education Press
9010 93 Street NW
Edmonton, Alberta, Canada, T6C 3T4

Library and Archives Canada Cataloguing in Publication

Title: Riot, retribution and revenge / Alex E. Robertson.
Other titles: Works. Selections
Names: Robertson, Alex E., author. | Container of (work): Robertson, Alex E. Riot and retribution. | Container of (work): Robertson, Alex E. Napoleon's gold.
Identifiers: Canadiana (print) 20210101369 | Canadiana (ebook) 20210101415 | ISBN 9781989024096 (softcover) | ISBN 9781989024119 (Kindle) | ISBN 9781989024102 (EPUB)
Subjects: LCGFT: Historical fiction. | LCGFT: Novels.
Classification: LCC PS8635.O228335 A6 2021 | DDC C813/.6—dc23

# Riot and Retribution

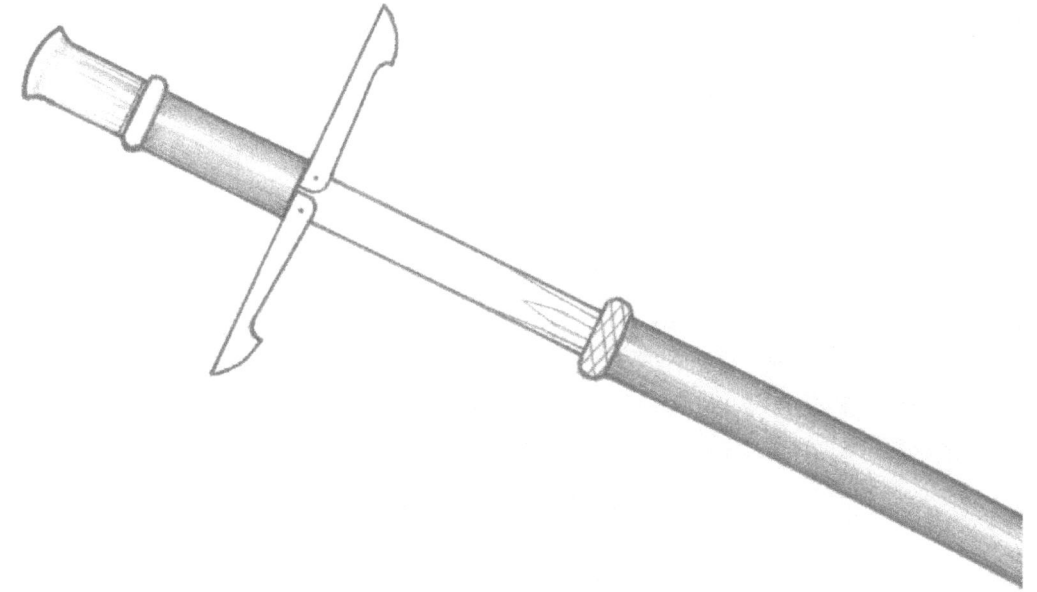

# Alex E. Robertson

# Contents

# Cast of principal characters

## London

| | |
|---|---|
| Nathaniel Parry | gentleman, occasionally employed as a government agent |
| Caradoc | his dog, a Welsh terrier |
| Lord Melbourne | Home Secretary in Earl Grey's Whig government |
| Lord Palmerston | Foreign Secretary |
| Richard Percy | Home Office administrator |
| John Drake | Foreign Office employee |
| Charlotte Drake | his wife |
| Elizabeth Drake | his daughter |

## Bath

| | |
|---|---|
| Dr Charles Parry | physician |
| Emma Parry | his wife |
| Raphael Vere | owner of the New Bank |
| Mathilda Vere | his wife |
| Roderick Wilson | senior clerk at the New Bank |
| Janie Wilson | his wife |
| Henry Blake | clerk at the New Bank |
| Anna Grant | his fiancée and also a governess |
| Captain Oliver Peterson | retired sea captain |
| Lydia Peterson | his wife |
| Emma Peterson | his second daughter |
| Maddie and Ginette | his twin teenage daughters |
| Diarmuid Casey | a political agent |
| Colette Montrechet | a courtesan |
| Martha Spence | landlady of Walcot Street |
| Thomas Spence | her father-in-law |
| Matthew Spence | her son, a sailor |
| Mary Spence | her daughter-in-law |
| Johnty Spence | her grandson |
| Mr Bishop | landlord of the White Hart Inn |
| Frederick Tooson | barman |
| Tobias Caudle | potboy |
| Arthur Jamieson | printer |
| Robert Turner | printer |

| | |
|---|---|
| Captain Charles Wilkins | textile mill owner and captain of the yeomanry |
| Neville Fairfield | member of the yeoman cavalry |
| James Cruttwell | member of the yeoman cavalry |
| Joshua Shadwell | owner of the Green Park brothel |
| Rosie Shadwell | his wife |
| Jabez and Billy | his bodyguards and enforcers |
| Barbara and Abigail | child prostitutes |
| Frances | child procured for sale |
| Mordecai and Declan | bargees, occasionally employed by Shadwell |

**Outlying villages**

| | |
|---|---|
| Howard Dill | gentleman of Norton St Philip |
| Mrs Danby | Mathilda Vere's mother |

**Bristol**

| | |
|---|---|
| Edwin Ravenswood | ship owner, exporter and a principal investor in the New Bank |
| Amanda Ravenswood | his wife |
| Eli Trevellis | captain of Ravenswood's clipper, the *Blue Dragon* |
| Cornelius Fu Lee | guest from China at Ravenswood's residence |
| Mr Kizhe | business associate from China |

# Prologue

**Evening: 29th September, 1831.**
**Cantina Buenavista, Puerto de la Cruz, Tenerife.**

They were almost ready to set sail for Bristol, twelve months after they had left for the China seas. The crew of the *Mathilda* had spent the last three days taking on supplies, patching the torn main-sail and recuperating after the long haul round the African coast. The shabby cantina had been full to bursting since half past seven that evening, when all the crew, bar the last dog watch, had been let loose on their final shore leave. A hiss of expectation coursed through the crowd as a velveteen curtain was pulled aside and a young woman and two men stepped out into the light.

Isabella snatched up two handfuls of her polka-dot frilled skirt, arched her neck, and slowly lifted her sculpted head framed in coiled black plaits. Flashing fire from her eyes, in one swift move she hitched the hem above her knees as the men howled a welcome. Slowly at first, but then gaining speed, her neat narrow feet in the old black shoes began to tap. Juan, sweating into his shirt in the heat of the bar, clapped in syncopation as the metal tips rang on the flag floor and Miguel closed his eyes, lifting his harsh voice in a chanting cry. Faster she stamped, faster, her fingers clicking, her arms moving in the sinuous rhythms of the Andalusian back streets she had left behind.

The sailors were transfixed, the front row brought literally to its knees, largely on the insistence of the men behind. All worshipped at the shrine and competed for a better view: especially of her miraculous bosom which heaved with the drama of the dance over a tight-laced red bodice; but also to see more of her satin skin, glowing like warm honey in the lamp-light, her slicked-back oiled hair glossy as a sea-bird fresh from a dive. Their battered spirits drank in the sight of her, and revived.

"Fine woman that," said a philosophical drinker at the bar, without taking his eyes from the show. "I'd take 'er home for two pins but I can't see 'er fittin' into the general way of things in Compton Dando."

"Too wild, you'd be thinkin'?"

"Exac'ly."

Away from the bar and the dance floor, other women plied a different trade. At a table by the stone stairway a fist flashed and landed square in the slack jaw of a sailor, sending him sprawling back in his chair, but leaving a smiling girl in a yellow frock still perching on his knee.

"Come wi'me mi'dear," said Elijah taking a tight grip on her arm and hauling her off the limp sailor. "He can't hold his drink."

From a dark corner, Matthew watched the scene unfold over the dregs of his wine and his empty plate. He disliked Elijah Berry, a swaggering bully of a man, and was annoyed to see his petty victory. He rose silently and began to edge away. His head had ached too much to join the banter at the bar and he was still nursing a maimed hand, roughly bandaged to protect the two cauterised stumps. They were all he had left of the two middle fingers on his right hand after a clumsy accident in the main-mast rigging. He cursed as he stumbled over the threshold, hoping it was the drink and not the other problem, the recurrent fever which had plagued him since they had made their last landfall in the Gulf of Guinea. He made his way out into the sultry night, passing more overheated cantinas disgorging ragged bursts of music, the buzz of talk, and disordered crashes from erupting fights.

"Too many men, not enough women," he muttered to himself, catching sight of two sailors who had struck lucky and were following a raven haired trollop into a back room. She glanced behind her, swaying her hips, trailing her fringed shawl, lazily amused as they capered after her. One was just a boy, with a reckless grin and high hopes.

A bawling chorus blasted out from the next open door.

"Farewell and adieu, to you fair Spanish la-hey-dies!
Farewell and adieu to you Ladies of Spain.
For we've received orders to sail for Old England
And perhaps we shall never more see you again!"

He passed the fish-wives' deserted stalls and the squat black fort of San Felipe, walked unsteadily along the harbour-side and headed for the quay where the *Mathilda* swayed on the tide. Exhausted, he sat on the low wall and looked back. High above the small knot of the town and towering above the island was El Teide. It had bare scree slopes like the mountains of the moon, and its snowcap glinted cruelly in the starlight. He had thought to climb it, at least to the snow line. It was not to be. He rose and picked his way over the ropes and lobster pots to the ship. Once back on board he took the companionway to the lower deck and the safety of his hammock. He rolled in, gasping down shallow breaths in the close dark.

As his heart steadied, the familiar sounds of the night washed back into his consciousness: the chirrup of the crickets from the shrubs by the harbour wall, the whine of flying insects, the creak of settling timbers, distant voices and snatches of song from the bars. He sank into a confused sleep and his body started to pump out the familiar round of symptoms: violent heats, shivers and drenching sweats, followed by creeping chill and shooting needles of pain in his limbs. Dark thoughts tormented his muddled head: dreams of the voyage, the Indian opium shipments to China, and the secret cargo, hidden in a cabin all the way from Bristol to disappear one night after they docked in the Gulf of Tonkin. The cargo had not rested easy. Young voices had set up keening cries night after night in the early months of the voyage. He had heard their punishments and the mewling after. He woke with a shudder, groped in his pocket for the pellet of opium he had saved for the night and bit into it. As he waited for the deadening rush of peace he prayed for his safe return home, to Bath and his Mary. It would happen: touch wood. He stretched out his good hand to the comforting timbers of the hull.

### Early evening: 30th September, 1831.  Brooks's Club, St James's St, London.

William Lamb, also known as Lord Melbourne, and since the spectacular collapse of the Tory party, the nation's Home Secretary, shoved out his legs to full stretch and arched his back against the comfortable support of the leather armchair. He held himself taut momentarily, before subsiding, hands clasped behind his head. He eyed the side table at his right hand: a plate bearing a solitary biscuit in a sea of crumbs, an empty glass and a drained crystal decanter standing easy by a three branched silver candelabra. This last was lavishly engraved with glimmering festoons, positively awash with them, as he was himself, with the vintage port.

Melbourne was pleased with himself, pleased to be with his own coterie in his club, pleased to be isolated from the harsh world that caterwauled indistinctly behind its sheltering walls. He relished his image as a champion of liberality and sturdy independence, as did most Whigs. More than this, or perhaps because of it, he and his party were eminently better fitted to run the country than the Hanoverian monarchs who squatted on the throne.

"What was said about Johnny Russell's people?" he mused, "just a little greater than God?"

Melbourne gave a brief neigh of suppressed laughter. His people, irreverent and swaggering, inbred and adulterous, were the only ones capable of reforming the country whilst keeping the reins firmly held in their own aristocratic hands. They were in power on a reform ticket, and had to deliver votes, at least to the middle classes. The so-called "coach of reform" had lurched into motion and was now careering wildly into the unknown. It needed a strong driver, holding both reins and whip in his hands. A new government, a new turnip-headed king in the person of William IV, ripe in years, keen for action and simply in need of a steer: a new decade.

Melbourne's bubble of enthusiasm suddenly deflated, pierced by the unpleasant memory that 1830 had ushered in a vicious revival of revolution in Europe and that the Whig reform programme, supposedly bringing a fair voice to the people, was specifically designed to avoid any suggestion of democracy. Melbourne grimaced as he contemplated the next few months, during which the government would have to achieve this miracle, less of a coach drive perhaps than a tightrope walk over a yawning abyss leading directly to hell. Passion, sound and fury were not in Melbourne's repertoire, and all were being traded wholesale by the many warring factions. He preferred to cultivate the image of the dilettante, the man of many parts, effortlessly achieving his purposes with no perceptible effort being expended. He always liked to think of himself as the classic eighteenth century man of reason: civilised, languid, cynical. He turned his mouth down in distaste at the prospect of the trials ahead.

However, just one more problem needed to be addressed that day, and it could be dispatched in the club. This was a happy thought, as the atmosphere in all departments of Whitehall was becoming increasingly hysterical. He sighed at a mental image of Wellington in the Lords' lobby the previous week, puce and glowering at the prospect of giving a few middle class men a vote, hoarsely demanding "the sharpening of swords" for the onslaught to follow when, presumably, the ravening masses would rise and overthrow all that was decent. Whether the people proved to be revolting or not, it was certain that intelligence must be improved in order to forestall any plots which might be hatching. Wellington was certainly right in another of his mutterings, that when planning a campaign one must always be able to see what is on the other side of the hill.

With great reluctance, Melbourne acknowledged his need for more accurate information. Every large town needed efficient government servants of some description to support the work of the Justices of the Peace. These servants needed to keep their ears to the ground to detect the first whispers of trouble.

All major industrial centres had been discussed the previous week, mainly through liaison with the local magistrates, as had the eastern agricultural areas, but decisions needed to be made about intelligence from the south-west. To his surprise, this area was proving to be something of a hot-bed of trouble. Fortunately, the matter seemed to be in hand, and this evening the formalities of engagement would be completed. Lord Palmerston, the Foreign Secretary, fellow club member and Melbourne's unofficial brother-in-law would materialise, bringing with him a solution in the shape of an experienced official from his department. Palmerston had other business to deal with concerning the port of Bristol and had suggested that his man could oversee both foreign and domestic intelligence interests from there.

Palmerston's long-standing affair with Melbourne's sister Emily, conducted with barely the minimum of discretion, was tolerated by her husband Lord Cowper and also by her brother. Melbourne admired Emily unreservedly, despite her being devilish beyond permission, and he liked Palmerston all the more for the connection. At the prospect of the endlessly energetic Pam wading in to solve the remaining problems, Melbourne allowed his mind to stray from those pressing and ugly matters. He detested the concept of surveillance, as did all right thinking Englishmen. Damned shabby occupation for a gentleman in his view: smacked of Continental deceit, but, needs must. Britain stood on the edge of a political precipice with threats to law and order not only from the middle and respectable lower classes, all of whom could rise if the voting was not widened, but also from the terrifying mobs, the residue of society lurking beneath. Misplaced radical agitation could cause them to rise from the depths, an unstoppable tide of scum discrediting the acceptable classes who supported change. His thoughts depressed him and he sighed windily.

"But the port was excellent," he declared, cheering up. "Oh yes.... uncommon excellent." He rolled his tongue over his front teeth and smacked his lips. "Damned fine. Deuced good."

The heavy door opened silently to admit Chislett, Melbourne's favourite club servant.

"Mi'lord, Lord Palmerston's coach has arrived."

"Excellent," said Melbourne, rubbing his hands. "Two non-members will be accompanying him Chislett, so show them all into the Strangers' Room."

Melbourne quit his usual seat and strolled across the hall to the only room in the club where he could deal with the man that Palmerston was bringing to him. He stationed himself in the most comfortable chair with his back to the St James's Street window. The dying rays of the autumn sun shafted through it, ready to do splendid service by illuminating the rest of the party to a detailed scrutiny, whilst leaving him inscrutably shaded. As he smiled indulgently to himself he heard the confused sounds of a party entering the hall. In a moment Chislett ushered them in.

"Mi'Lord: Lord Palmerston, Mr Percy and Mr Drake."

Percy and Drake bowed, murmuring, "Mi'lord", obsequiously from the doorway, whereas Palmerston swaggered in, blared a greeting and flung himself into the seat opposite Melbourne. He exuded confidence from the shock of wiry badger-hair on his head to the tip of his mud-bespattered boots. He was flushed and wind-burned from the exertions of two day's hunting, a picture of rude health. He settled expansively into his chair, eyes darting round the room. Tall and spare, Richard Percy, a recent addition to Melbourne's secretariat, stood awkwardly. He was fishing in his bag to locate paper, ink bottle and pen, pausing to rake his hand through his lank dark hair, sweeping it out of his eyes, then to adjust his gold-rimmed glasses which were in danger of slipping off the end of his nose. John Drake had deftly manoeuvred himself into position for taking the seat to Melbourne's immediate left, which was nearest to the drinks table. He could slide into it effortlessly when the noble lord deigned to invite the commoners to be seated.

However, Melbourne was not occupied with the furthering of Drake or Percy's comfort, but was focused on his own material well being. "More port Chis-lett," he drawled. "Taylor's 1811 mark you, and snap to it. Then away you go. I want this room free from servants until further notice".

"Yes mi'lord," said Chislett blandly. He bowed, retreated and silently closed the door.

"Good evening gentlemen." Melbourne indicated seats for the two guests by sweeping his arm vaguely round the available chairs, the sketchy gesture lifting his rear modestly from his seat, which was as much of a formal greeting as he was inclined to give. Percy sat economically, setting up his writing materials, whilst Drake took his place as he did everything, to maximise comfort for himself. He settled his stocky body into the luxurious depths of the seat, smoothed his reddish-brown beard, narrowed his eyes and prepared to enjoy this unusual opportunity to study two of the most powerful men in the kingdom at close quarters. Chislett glided in with a silver tray bearing more port, and glasses, which he made a move to fill.

"Light the candles first Chislett", ordered Palmerston, ruthlessly sabotaging the

6

carefully staged *mise en scène*. "Let the dog see the rabbit. What!" He continued briskly. "Now then Melbourne, I hear there was renewed rumpus in your place yesterday afternoon. How's the Bill?"

The Reform Bill, the only Bill, and as Lord Brougham repeated endlessly, "nothing but the Bill", was everyone's obsession. It was the first test of fire for the Whigs since ousting the Tories, who had had their marching orders purely because Wellington would not accept any change of any kind in the voting system. Since June the Tory majority in the House of Lords had been in the process of bellowing down the second version of the Bill, a furore outside the hearing of Palmerston whose Irish title kept him in the gladiatorial pen that was the House of Commons.

Melbourne smirked. "The Iron Duke is not enjoying his rustication from office. He is leading the roar to devour our offering, despite our handsome majority in your place and the hateful prospect of the masses rising to murder us all in our beds if we fail."

Secretary Percy had organised himself sufficiently to perfect his attitude of readiness, sharpened pen in hand.

"Damn it Percy! What the hell do you think you are doing?" said Melbourne with unusual vim. Percy blenched and began to shovel his belongings away even more smartly than he had taken them out. "You don't take notes in the Club for God's sake man. You are here to listen and then to take yourself off and do your scribbling back in Downing Street. And what the devil were you going to write anyway? That the people terrify the government? What would happen if such sentiments were read? No, no, no! Wait and listen. You will hear news of a contract if all proceeds well. You will draw it up in your office."

"I am sorry my Lord," blustered Percy, nettled to be criticised in front of Drake. "I misunderstood."

Melbourne's focus of concern had already moved on from Percy who was ignored. He turned again to Palmerston.

"Now Pam," continued Melbourne, "the matter in hand. As you know I am in need of a small number of experienced gentlemen to take themselves off to principal towns during this present period of instability. Apart from the reports from our magistrates we need other streams of information from experienced people who know what they are looking for. We will not entertain free-lance, *agents provocateurs,* ours will be government servants adept at working in the field. Northern, central and eastern centres we seem to have settled, we must conclude with the south-west where I gather you have an interest." He gestured to Drake. "This gentleman is your protégé I take it?"

"Yes indeed, my protégé," beamed Palmerston fruitily. "This is Mr John Drake. Done sterling service in France for the Foreign Office during the recent revolution and before. Three years was it?"

Drake nodded in agreement and began energetically, "Yes mi'lord I was…"

"Son-in-law of Fitzroy. Placed you in the Office under Canning, didn't he Drake? South-west man originally. Some family down Bristol way haven't you? He's the best man for your needs Melbourne, and for mine."

Drake abandoned his efforts to enlarge on his experiences as he was, at long last, motioned to help himself from the drinks tray by Melbourne.

Drake appeared to be giving rapt attention to the noble lords, but had taken to covertly lusting after the distinguished 1811 residing in the port decanter. He reached reverently for his glass, paused to savour the heady nose and sank a generous swig which coursed through him to his very toes. He shivered with greedy delight, cast his eyes round like a ferret and ran his finger round the inside of his shirt collar, a habit betraying his excitement. Drake inspected the decor of the room minutely: brown and green leather, burgundy drapes. Struggling not to grin at the sheer glory of it all, yet intoxicated by his good fortune, he breathed in the heady scents of rich tobacco and a complex bouquet of wines and spirits, which seemed to have seeped into the fabric of the room. He scanned the silver on the side tables and mantelpiece and tried to read the titles on the oil portraits and sporting scenes. This was his first visit, as Brooks's Club was far beyond his social circle and pocket. Key lair of the Whig party since the early days of the old King George III and with shadowy links to the Hell Fire Club and its motto: "Do what thou wilt", the Club exerted an irresistible charm, enhanced by its fearsome reputation for extracting fortunes at the gaming tables as tribute from its elite members. Drake decided, then and there, that he would do almost anything to be part of this tribe: this solid-gold, hall-marked gang of cronies. He wanted it so much that it started to hurt. It was a gnawing emptiness in his belly that soured his enjoyment of the moment and also his considerable successes to date. His hand strayed to his neck again, but his smile was controlled, fixed. Would the Strangers' Room be the furthest he ever got? Surely not, it would make him all of a piece with disappointed money lenders hunting down aristocratic debtors or the doomed Candidates who waited to see if they had survived the Club elections and been deemed fit for membership.

From dull and respectable middle-class origins in the wholesale of textiles, Drake Senior, originally from Frome, had carved out a formidable empire of outlets in South London that had financed the launching of young Drake in the lowest ranks of London society. His ascent had been assured by a brilliant marriage to Charlotte, who at thirty-eight was his senior by two years and had been a mature bride at thirty-two when they tied the knot. Charlotte was a moderately attractive and aggressively stylish woman, sharp-witted and sharp-tongued enough to cut herself, and everyone in earshot when the mood took her. The prospect of marrying into her family and tapping the connections of her influential father far outweighed the periodic discomforts of living both with her and also their small, sulky daughter who was a diminutive replica of her mother. A job in the Foreign Office had enabled Drake to rise meteorically. He had secured a placement in Paris and smoothly transferred to serve the Whigs in the new ministry of 1830. The aching greed that motivated Drake coupled with his questionable morals made him a ruthless and calculating asset to the office. Deceitful, foxy, self-seeking: eyes flicking around the room, assessing, coveting, he wondered what his first move should be to secure membership for himself. On first impressions he gauged Melbourne to be cleverer and more brutal than he pretended to be, not a first choice then as his lever for breaking into the upper-layer of society. He was definitely better off staying in Palmerston's pocket. "Lord Cupid" was bluffer, louder, easier to read.

Palmerston continued: "He could work for you at the Home Office whilst keeping me abreast of affairs. I have a need to deploy some of my staff domestically as our Indian opium trade with China is under increasing threat. The Chinese Emperor has taken against it even more strenuously than before and the authorities in Canton are aiming for the utter destruction of our interest, which is immense. Instead of the 200 chests per year we managed a decade ago we are selling in excess of 20,000, but the amounts impounded are growing weekly as a direct result of this new found zeal." Palmerston thrust out his lower lip in annoyance at the thought of hordes of Chinese officials swarming over British shipping.

"Do I minute that mi'lord when I return to the Office?"

"Certainly not." Palmerston shot an irritated glance at Percy. "Where was I? Ah yes, I need accurate intelligence on the nature of Chinese attacks on our shipping: methods, numbers and so forth. Some vessels are avoiding the usual harbour at Lintin in the Pearl River estuary. I want to know more about these people at the sharp end, off-record. Official channels are not rooting out the truth." Palmerston kicked the edge of the table moodily, showering the floor with a dusting of dried mud. "There are some businessmen, especially in Bristol, who have been most helpful in facilitating the trade and eluding Chinese attentions. We need to know them rather better. I already have a very useful man there. Drake is well aware of him."

Drake arranged his smile into a new one that he hoped looked totally aware, capable and suave, disguising the fact that he had no idea to whom Palmerston referred. He succeeded in appearing sly, but as he was ignored by his superiors, all he achieved was to reinforce Percy's dislike of him, which had been festering since the ride in Palmerston's coach from Whitehall. To Percy's disgust Drake had bragged and toadied to the noble lord throughout the journey, forcing him, Percy, to while away the time inventing fiendishly inappropriate acts of revenge.

"The Emperor will not succeed. We will not allow it." Palmerston narrowed his eyes, a capacity for cruelty was there, again, which none but Percy observed.

"The Chinese will buy our opium with their precious silver," Palmerston declared with a bleak finality. "We will obtain their tea, their porcelain, their brocade and their silk, and the trade will not drain our silver reserves. No, by God it will not," he concluded with a flourish, swigging down his port and slamming the glass down on the tray.

"No indeed," replied Melbourne. "By Gad no. But my urgent concerns, mi'dear fellow, are to nail down radical trouble makers in London, Birmingham, Bristol and all points of the compass. With respect, foreign affairs must take a back seat for now. We must improve our grip on the towns subtly, without the cavalry stampeding all over the show. Reform must go through calmly and to our recipe. Unappetising as it may be, we must bring in the middle classes and separate them from the mobs. The French learned the hard way. Remember 1789." He wagged a warning forefinger and then proceeded to stab the table with it rhythmically for additional emphasis.

"Divide and rule. It must be achieved but it will be as close run as Waterloo, mark my words! The whole land is ready to explode. We must not light the fuses gentlemen, but douse them. Quench them. 'Tis all we can safely do."

Melbourne had ceased to beat time on the table and wiped his brow. The silk handkerchief was already damp, as his brow had taken to perspiring freely as the port did its work in the confines of the closed room. The sea of problems, which had temporarily receded, had returned in fresh waves of torment. "The riots on the land have not yet subsided despite spirited action on the part of the magistrates. Labourers still think they will lose their jobs because of the damned threshing machines. Not that there is much grain to thresh given the poor harvest. Hunger has made them even more furious. Now townsmen are agitating for the vote, uniting the classes against law and order. It could bring us down Pam – bring all to hell! We must bring calm. Naturally the damned French with their Citizen King are giving quite the wrong example."

"A very different situation there if I may…"

"You may not Drake", interjected Palmerston, pouring another port for himself. Fortunately, Melbourne had subsided into silence, exhausted by his uncharacteristic outburst, so did not need to be coaxed down from his high horse. Palmerston continued: "What you will do is go to Bristol for Lord Melbourne, and for me, relay intelligence on the status of the region and make yourself known to the local party men, principal business men, bankers and so forth. You will be briefed, and liaise with our existing contact. If, of course, you are in agreement Melbourne?"

Melbourne, working hard to regain his indolent pose and, pretending to be giving his full attention to recharging his glass, managed a lazy nod in Palmerston's direction.

"Excellent, we agree then. You will also liaise with a junior associate who will assist you. Station yourself in Bristol and we will send him to Bath as the radicals seem to be making the old watering-hole into something of a stronghold. I gather the place is often full of foreigners. Anyway, spas are notorious hell-holes, attract all the refuse of the lower classes who prey on the visitors. Based there he can range over Somerset and Wiltshire cloth towns, if required, and report to you."

Melbourne swilled the port around his mouth thoughtfully. He stared briefly at Drake and caught sight of a ragged scar snaking up above the neckcloth and collar, to reach behind the ear. Drake seemed to sense the scrutiny and ran his finger furtively round the back of his neck.

"Nervous tic," thought Melbourne. "Not really surprising. Wonder if someone tried to slit his throat?"

He could well understand that someone might have been keen to achieve this, as he heartily abhorred greedy middle-class upstarts of Drake's stamp. He also disliked the task Drake had been asked to do. As the Tories had had enormous problems in the past with *agents provocateurs* making false claims to increase their pay, it was a key point of Whig policy to distance government from enthusiastic spying. They chose instead to depend on communications from local magistrates. This was vital for morale, as without London style police forces the provinces depended on the goodwill of the local gentry to ensure the rule of law and they were notoriously resentful of interference from London. The army was a brutally blunt instrument, which he would use only as the very last resort. It was time to play a useful card, ameliorate the influence of Drake and ensure that Palmerston did not conjure up another of his men to act as Drake's assistant.

"We will select remaining personnel for this mission only from agents experienced in foreign affairs and they will be paid a regular salary with no bonus payments. On this understanding my office will finance the venture. As for Drake's assistant, I suggest young Parry. His father, Owen Parry, worked for Castlereagh and Canning for years, took his son with him to France in the late '20s. Died there, poor fellow, son stayed and made himself useful. You said foreigners at spas didn't you? He's good with foreign languages, speaks them like a damned native. Do you know him Drake?"

Drake had heard some stories of Parry senior, who by all accounts was a high-flying, daring and charismatic Welsh charmer who had given distinguished service. He hated him, or rather the thought of him, since they had not met.

"No my lord", he replied blandly, "though his father's name has been mentioned occasionally in the office."

Percy shot a withering glance at Drake, everyone with even the smallest connection to the Foreign Office had heard of Owen Parry, a thorough gentleman and therefore as unlike Drake as the proverbial chalk was to cheese.

"Now Percy," said Melbourne, "you will take yourself off shortly and conclude the necessary paperwork. Just repeat what you have gathered."

Percy answered primly. "Mr Drake to Bristol. Mr Parry to Bath with the remit to visit other towns in Somerset and Wiltshire. All agreed on the authority of Lords Melbourne and Palmerston. Mr Parry to report to Mr Drake. Both to be paid and retained by Home Office. Purpose: intelligence gathering on radical groups and the progress of business contacts with China."

Percy's port was untouched, and was destined to remain so.

"Capital," Melbourne rallied at the conclusion of business and rubbed his hands together briskly. "No delay, no delay. Start tomorrow Drake. Take up residence in Bristol, for the foreseeable. Good to meet you. Back to the office with you Percy, there's a good fellow."

Drake and Percy rose as a Greek chorus and bowed briefly. "Thank-you , mi'lords. Good evening."

To Melbourne's surprise, Palmerston also leapt to his feet. His keen hearing had picked up the beginnings of a familiar ragged cheer from the gaming rooms above. He moved swiftly to the door to alert a Club servant that the guests were to be seen out. "Indeed, good evening gentlemen. Well done Drake. Thank you Percy."

He shot his frilled cuffs in anticipation. "Fancy a hand of whist Melbourne? And if I'm not mistaken the book on next Saturday's match is not yet closed! I fancy the Northern Giant to lay out the Growler in precisely four rounds!" The twin prospects of cards and gambling on his favourite sport of bare-knuckle prize fighting energised Palmerston. He nipped out of the door smartly, breaking into his self-satisfied, metallic chortle, which echoed up the stairwell as he trotted up to join the growing hubbub at the tables. Melbourne hauled himself out of his chair and loped off to follow. Pam's ferocious card play would probably fleece him, again, before the night was through. This he understood: this he loved. Ignoring the muffled cries and peals of obscene laughter from the street which pierced the falling quiet of the emptying room, he turned into the hall and ambled towards the stairs.

# Chapter 1

**10 pm: 5th October, 1831, the City of Bath.**

The grand Banqueting Room of Bath Guildhall was still full to overflowing, with all seats taken and many latecomers standing at the sides of the rows of chairs. Chandeliers smoked blearily in the fug of the overheated room. Vast royal portraits gazed mutely from the walls. The Reform Meeting was entering its third hour and was still commanding the attention of the audience, made up mainly of respectable middle-class men and their wives, be-feathered hats nodding and waving as they craned their necks to gain better views. A dais supported the table of speakers, most of whom were leaning back in their seats, exhausted after taking their turns to address the eager, and now also saddle-sore crowd. The glories of the Banqueting Room did not extend to comfortable seats, and many listeners writhed periodically in discomfort whilst maintaining, at great personal cost, expressions of engrossed attention.

An outsider was delivering the penultimate speech. A gentleman of interest because of his London contacts: Mr Diarmuid Casey was reputed to be a friend of Daniel O'Connell, was widely acquainted with Whig members and a regular terror of the reform circuit. Catholic Emancipation had been gained with spectacular success in 1829, catapulting O'Connell into Westminster as the member for County

Clare. The very mention of his name now scattered the gold dust of success on those he associated with. This particular associate was a tall, loose-limbed and jaunty Irishman, his pale face lit by wild green eyes, his worn frock coat enlivened by a loudly striped rose and cream waistcoat. Words tumbled from his lips in a melodious stream: justice, decency, the rights of man, the voice of the people and the voice of God. He slipped in the unacceptable phantom of democracy so cleverly, so fleetingly, that most of the assembly did not register that they had actually heard it. What they did hear was fulsome support for the Bill and devotion to the Whig cause and the "£10 householders" who would gain the vote. When he spoke of the people surely he meant them? Their ripples of applause punctuated his beguilement of their ears and eyes, and Diarmuid smiled.

Standing by the door half-way down the left side of the room, scanning the assembly meticulously through the smoky whirlpool of heads, searching and gauging them, a tall, dark-haired man, still wearing his dusty travelling cloak, relaxed slowly against the door jamb, resting his aching back. He balanced part of his weight on the swordstick he held in his right hand and smothered a yawn. The mail-coach journey from London had been the nine-hour marathon courtesy of the Pickwick coach company, perhaps it would have been better to settle for an overnight stop. He and his fellow passengers had been more than ready for a longer break at the Crown in Reading, but it was not to be. The half-dozen inside passengers had time only to unpack themselves stiffly from their narrow seats, creak to the coaching inn, quaff a noggin and wolf a few biscuits purchased from the enterprising Mr Huntley's girls, who could be relied upon to bustle across the road from the bakery as soon as any coach came to a halt. Then it had been up and away. He suddenly smiled broadly and tapped his stick at the memory, attracting glares from those sitting nearest. Diarmuid Casey's theme did not require grins or taps as he was in the grave early stages of generating wholesale condemnation of the beastly Tory opposition. Nathaniel Parry coughed quickly, disguised the unseemly smile and allowed his mind to wander.

Summoned by Lord Melbourne's Office last week and briefed on his mission, he had spent the intervening days preparing to quit his London rooms for a lengthy stay in the West Country. Not an unpleasant prospect. He remembered many childhood visits, in happier times when with his father, and on one faded, dream-like occasion with his late mother, he had visited family connections in Bath. He remembered Dr Caleb Parry's house as a boisterous and luxurious haven of delights, full of music and laughter. Later, in his teens, there had just been himself and his father seeing Charles, Caleb's eldest son and successor to the famous medical practice. He liked

Bath's antique charms; the bowl of hill-sides; the rolling Mendips beyond and further still, the lure of the salt-caked coasts of Devon and Cornwall. He was a Romantic and it all seemed dashed Romantic to him. His cashmere stock, turquoise and tied in a draped Byronic knot, advertised his sensibilities. There was nothing starchy about Nathaniel, unless occasion demanded.

His thoughts returned abruptly to his journey. Caradoc had been a volatile traveller over the later stages. His constant companion and friend for over two years, Caradoc was a wiry black and tan Welsh terrier who normally travelled without complaint, but after Reading he had taken exception to a new passenger's basket, which proved to house a live chicken. In one mighty leap, after a brief warning spell of throaty growls, Caradoc had dived into the dame's basket, dragged out the fowl and shaken it like a rat over the other five passengers in a riot of feathers, cackling, snarling and trampling. All terriers are tenacious hunters and to ignore a bird in such close proximity would have been a dereliction of duty. Strangely, the bird had survived to complete its journey to Bath, banished top-side to the cheap seats. Meanwhile, money had changed hands and Nathaniel had bid the stout dame a courteous farewell when they alighted at the White Hart. But she had not forgiven Caradoc, who for his part had treated her with the lofty disdain quite proper from one of the oldest breeds in the land. Nathaniel and Caradoc had time only to ditch their travelling trunk at the Hart and find the venue for the night's meeting. Despite the White Hart's comfortable attractions, or probably because of them, intelligence would not be so readily gained at that address. He needed to shift to a more rowdy and possibly republican roost before the night was over. Caradoc, though politically minded and a champion of liberal independence, had been left outside, guarding the Guildhall, lying low by the railings which fenced "the area", the deep drop affording light to the lower floors. Caradoc's signature behaviours: excessive barking and digging, would be calmed, the former as he knew he was on duty, and the latter as there was no earth. Nothing else would have prevented excavation to an epic depth.

Nathaniel became excessively hot as the evening progressed, and clearly he was not the only one. Fans were being employed briskly by the old and young bonnets in the audience. He enjoyed looking at women, and his practised eye had selected a good half-dozen strikingly pretty ones, a couple disarmingly so, amongst the expected majority of the plain, the dull and the dutiful. This was a bonus, as lengthy and late reform meetings seeking to win votes for middle-class men did not often draw many beauties. It was predominantly a male gathering, and the lines of chairs were filled with them in their dark frock coats, with beaver top-hats held damply on laps, lace cuffs and heavily ringed hands on stick handles.

Rank after rank, with the women between like gaudy birds, pale faces shone and the air had grown foetid with the press of humanity: powdered women, whiskered men, the odd one with an eye-patch covering brutal military wounds.

Suddenly, he found himself gazing at someone altogether different. Close to the back, at the end of a row, poised and oddly calm in the restlessness of the crowd, not deigning to add to the regular flurries of applause but watchful, impassive, was a foreigner, a man from the Far East. He seemed about Nathaniel's own age and build, twenty-six and muscular, but he was dressed more soberly. His garb was of severe black, which, apart from a gleaming white, unruffled shirt, was entirely unrelieved. It was some years since, in France with his father and before the latest revolution, that Nathaniel had met with a man from Cathay. He had been a businessman, a stuffed shirt loyal to the Emperor with no words of his own. This man did not have the appearance of a diplomat. A prolonged surge of applause greeted the end of the speech and Nathaniel was briefly distracted, flicking his eyes to the dais in response. When he looked back, the stranger was looking directly at him. Nathaniel felt a frisson of energy as they held each others' eyes for a silent second before both swivelled away, feigning neutral glances over the company. A dangerous customer, thought Nathaniel, allowing his eyes to remain on the dais where a short, earnest man was begging their attention.

"I am sorry, Ladies and Gentlemen. So sorry to inform you, that Mr Crisp has been delayed." Subdued groans and a wave of chatter broke from the audience. The little man raised his voice quaveringly. "But he will be with us within the quarter-hour to conclude our meeting." He wrung his hands in anxiety and continued, "I beg you to take advantage of the break and perhaps take the opportunity to walk in the lobbies and meeting rooms adjacent whilst we await his arrival."

Before he had finished speaking scores of chairs scraped in unison and hundreds of legs stretched to the rustle of silk and brocade, voices rose with the tide of reformers, as they made their way to the exits. Nathaniel glanced back quickly, but the foreign gentleman had gone. In the next instant, as Nathaniel had been by a side-door, he was borne away by the crowd to the landing and into the first meeting room on the right. Once there he billeted himself by the window, shot it open and breathed in a deep lung-full of the sharp autumnal air. Fire-smoke, horses and a clatter of traffic rose from the street. He leaned out and spied Caradoc foraging in a cart whilst the carter paused to halloo a greeting across the road to a man standing outside the Greyhound. Nathaniel quickly dodged back behind the curtain before he was in turn spotted and unleashed a barrage of barking. He turned to be confronted by a friendly, beaming giant.

"Mr Nathaniel Parry?"

"I am sir, the very same," Nathaniel bowed briefly.

"Well now! How do! It had to be you young Parry. So glad to receive your letter my boy and have you back in Bath. Spotted you earlier idling by the door, spitting image of your father. How the devil are you and why aren't you staying with me?" Bluff and tall as a tree, Dr Charles Parry in full evening-dress had cleaved a path through the throng, trailing a quartet of followers and pumped Nathaniel's hand in hearty welcome. "Damned sorry about your father, fine man. Quite understand your wishes for a quiet funeral, hope you received our condolences in time. Impressive to hear that you worked with him in France. Well done sir! Now let me introduce you to my friends: Mr Raphael Vere and Mrs Vere, Mr Nathaniel Parry, a relative we have seen far too little of over the last few years."

Sixty and sleekly immaculate, Raphael Vere shook hands and inclined his head in greeting. Nathaniel's powerful grip surprised him and he stared directly, fascinated by the travel-stained young man who looked at odds with the surprising credentials recited by Charles. Piercing blue eyes met Vere, but they were not challenging, they twinkled with amusement, so Vere assessed him as an affable young sprig, worth cultivating in honour of the Parry connection which still wielded great power in Bath society. Nathaniel recognised Vere's wife, who apparently was called Tilly, as he had spotted her earlier as one of the more beautiful bonnets of Bath. She was of an age with Nathaniel and greeted him shyly, leaving her delicate white hand in his for just a moment longer than was necessary. She was a vision in peach silk, pearl trimmed and topped by a misty waterfall of blonde curls, sumptuously corkscrewed, caught up behind in a pearl clip and floating in glimmering clouds around her face and shoulders.

"Any member of the Parry family is warmly welcome in Bath," boomed Raphael Vere, "Dr Parry and his esteemed late father are widely acknowledged as the most distinguished medical men this city has ever seen."

Charles Parry bowed at this. "Thank you my friend, though I am as yet merely following in the footsteps. You remember father don't you Nathaniel?"

"Of course. Also your famous brother, how is William? Or should I call him Edward, does he still prefer his second name?"

"He's well thank you, exceedingly well, and he's still Edward to us! Commissioner of Agriculture in New South Wales. Australia bi'Gad!" exclaimed Charles.

"Sir Edward," chimed Vere unctuously. "Knighted these last two years. You did know? The Parry Sound in the Arctic should now be the Sir William Edward Parry

Sound. Who would have thought we would have a Bath man recognised as one of the greatest explorers of all time!" Vere preened in the reflected glory and smiled conspiratorially with Dr Parry.

"I'm afraid I was in France in '29. My father's illness." Nathaniel had a nightmare vision of his father, sinking with a sweating fever in the heat of Paris: the chaos of the impending collapse of Charles X's government, the stench of the river, his sense of utter despair.

"Let me introduce you to Mr Vere's companions Nathaniel," interrupted Charles smoothly.

"Delighted to meet you, Mr and Mrs Vere," said Nathaniel, turning from them to the other couple in their cluster, which was now almost unduly intimate as the surge of people from the Banqueting Room had forced them, hugger-mugger, into the corner, backed-up to the window. He recognised the man as typical of the retired officer class, hawk-eyed, craggy faced and direct, with none of Vere's urbanity, which Nathaniel found refreshing. Severely clad in clothes of a cut more at home during the French Wars, Peterson was decidedly boots, not shoes.

"This is Captain Oliver Peterson, with his daughter Miss Emma Peterson."

"Captain Peterson, Miss Peterson, good evening."

As he studied the worthy Captain's face, Nathaniel conjured up an image of his own father in the last days, reminiscing from his sick bed about his missions. He recalled a long story of derring-do off West Africa, an Atlantic voyage on a frigate, captained by one Oliver Peterson. The mission had been hard, with scant success, but sweetened by the wisdom and companionship of this man.

"Captain Peterson! Former Captain of the *Renowned*? Hunted slavers in '14?

"I did, forsooth!" replied Peterson warmly. "As Dr Parry observed, I should have known you immediately. You are indeed so like Owen. I remember your dear father with great affection. A man of exceptional daring and skill: a thorough patriot. Yes, an honour to serve with him." The Captain shook Nathaniel's hand with both of his. "Visit us in Marlborough Buildings my boy. My wife will be delighted to meet you. We would all be delighted, wouldn't we Em?"

Nathaniel took the hand of the willowy young woman at Peterson's side. She had not caught his eye earlier, but he now saw that she was attractive enough, but eccentrically dressed to his eyes, which were used to London fashion. Like her father she shunned the extravagances of the *beau monde*. She favoured an Empire style reminiscent of the early 1800s. It was still common to see poorer women decked out in the simple high-waisted gowns of thirty years ago, but rare to see it amongst the middle-class. As she stepped away from her father he saw she was unusually tall, towering over the petite Tilly Vere, and had coppery-red hair caught in a thick plait, and topped with just the narrowest of jewelled bands.

"Good evening, Mr Parry," she said, quietly, hiding to perfection the embarrassing confusion she felt to be confronted with this man. He was unsettlingly, insupportably attractive and she was shocked by the response she felt as she looked into his eyes. She felt her heart miss a beat and a flush rise to her cheeks. She dropped her head and looked away. The merest suspicion of her interest in the visitor would be spotted by her doting father and instantly communicated at home where it would unleash a tirade of questions from Mama. Emma would be doomed to dwell in a misery of embarrassment for Mr Parry's entire stay in Bath.

At twenty-four years of age, it had been made very clear to her that she needed to marry. Her tiresome elder sister Celia had settled triumphantly near Cirencester with her farmer. Brother Robert was in the navy and out of range, so, like the tall poppy that she was, Em presented the next target for Mrs Peterson. The twins were still trilling round the house like overgrown sparrows and provided no alternative distraction whatsoever. Burying herself in books and needlework was not all she expected to do in life, but it suited for now, and there was a degree of freedom. She loved empty afternoons, which she was at liberty to fill with strolls and lectures and visiting. Evenings were leavened by seasonal balls and soirees, and of late by attending endless reform meetings with her father, whom she adored. A latent thirst for knowledge had been awakened and politics was becoming an absorbing interest for her: another thing to keep well hidden from Mama. She arranged her face as a study of engaged politeness and concentrated on the conversation.

Captain Peterson was continuing his monopolisation of the visitor: "Did your father speak much of our adventures on the *Renowned*? Rum times, close calls, but what comradeship! Ever mention my officers Grant and Tomlinson? Eh? You think so! Splendid. Your father became fast friends with them both. Grant's girl Anna is here in Bath, Great friend of Em's. Poor Grant's dead though. Did you know of it? Damned'st thing. Went to bed. Never woke up! But here's the coincidence, Tomlinson's nephew fetched up here too and became the gentleman friend of Anna. Isn't that so Em?" He beamed at his daughter and, sensing her reluctance to speak, continued. "So you have also worked for the government, Mr Parry?"

"Yes Captain, I had that honour in France," replied Nathaniel neutrally. "Now I am here to renew my family connections, to rest and sample the famous waters."

Charles Parry suddenly turned and peered over the crowd as he became aware of a new sound from the Banqueting Room, an unwelcome cacophony of hoarse, accusatory shouts, scuffling feet and the unmistakable crashes of over-turned chairs.

"Perhaps it might be politic to withdraw without the edification of Mr Crisp's speech. It was not perhaps the wisest of choices to feature that gentleman so late in the evening."

Worried glances were exchanged between Vere and Peterson, who needed to consider the ladies. Mr Crisp the radical hatter had been a controversial choice in any case, and his other commitments had compounded the situation by necessitating a late appearance. It sounded as though a Tory welcome was brewing to greet him.

Raphael Vere took control. "I propose that you all join me in the Pump Room tomorrow morning at ten o'clock where we can continue our conversation in greater comfort. Captain Peterson and I had planned to meet and I would esteem it an honour for the Parry family to join us."

Growing sounds of chaos from the meeting and the drowning calls of the convenor for calm demanded a hasty decision.

"Delighted," concurred Dr Parry hurriedly.

"I look forward to it," smiled Nathaniel.

Moving swiftly to the staircase, Mr Vere and Captain Peterson chaperoned their ladies past the crowds now overflowing from the Banqueting Room and the two Parrys followed closely as rear-guard.

"So Nathaniel, we meet tomorrow at the Pump Room. You are sure you won't come home with me? My carriage is waiting. Mrs P will be delighted to have you, ample room and all that." Charles beamed, avuncular, gracious, casting a friendly arm round Nathaniel's shoulders. It was churlish to refuse, but it had to be done.

"Perhaps in a few days Charles? Just need to be in my lodgings for a while and conclude some business."

"If you are sure?"

They swept through the double doors and out onto the street, whereupon a wiry black and brown missile launched itself, yapping, into Nathaniel's arms.

"Steady as you go Caradoc," he warned, as the flailing paws deposited a number of muddy prints on the arm of Dr Parry's best evening coat.

"Down sir!" Caradoc was dumped unceremoniously on the pavement. "Sorry about that Charles, he is overexcited. Wanted to come to the meeting. See you tomorrow."

Nathaniel and Caradoc sauntered across the High Street as Dr Charles Parry raised a bemused hand in farewell, flicked absentmindedly at the fouled sleeve and then waved his coachman over from where he hovered in the doorway of the Greyhound.

The noisy crowd leaving the Guildhall filled High Street and the Market Place in a trice and Nathaniel and Caradoc disappeared from view. They skirted the corner of Cheap Street, dodging groups of gentry, carriages and horses, and small ragged knots of beggars, which fluttered and swooped like coveys of bats in the dark corners. Nathaniel walked briskly now, using his swordstick swagger perfected in London and Paris to open a way through seething crowds. Caradoc trotted on his left, acting as out-rigger, strengthening their flank, shooting steely glares and warning yaps. They made their way through Abbey Churchyard, past the Great Pump Room and under the colonnade to emerge into Stall Street, which they crossed to enter the bustling White Hart Inn. Even at this hour, the inn blazed with light and beer-fuelled gusts of noise broke intermittently from the lower rooms. A patchwork of guest-bedroom lights shone from the upper floors and shadowy figures could be picked out in some windows, looking out on the West Door of the Abbey which reared up, enormous against the night sky, the twin lines of stone angels frozen on their ladders in the long climb to heaven. The eponymous White Hart in the form of a handsome statue stood alert above the main door, antlers raised, gazing not to the church but to the dark trees on Beechen Cliff which framed the city boundaries to the south. Nathaniel ducked into the narrow passageway of the inn, dodging the press of visitors spilling out of the doorways of the rooms to left and right. Coffee room, coach office, snugs with leaping fires: he wound his way through to the principal bar, behind which stood a dapper and magnificently moustachioed barman, with a bearing both peremptory and military. He was polishing glasses and whipping the room to order: directing potboys and barmaids, chafing regulars and greeting newcomers.

"Mr Parry! Your pleasure sir?" He was quick to spot Nathaniel as he shouldered a path through the throng to the bar.

"Brandy and hot water if you please, and one of your excellent cold pies. Beef and oyster? Small beer for my companion and a succulent bone if one can be found."

Nathaniel winked at Caradoc who was already reclining comfortably by the fire, emitting a low, appreciative growl.

"Straight away sir!" Ceasing to polish the gleaming rummer the barman called behind him, "Tobias, Tobias!" and at once a young potboy trotted obligingly into the bar from the kitchen corridor. He was clad in a long white apron, liberally smeared with gravy at the hip, oversized boots, battered leather breeches and a scarlet waistcoat, the hand-me-down rig of a Hart postillion. He smiled broadly, blankly, eyes searching for advantage, skin tight over the cheekbones, greasy blonde hair anchored behind the ears and arms loose by his sides.

"Yes sir!"

"Beef and oyster pie for the gentleman and a bone for his terrier. Double-up, double-up!"

Nathaniel settled by the wall at the end of the bar to survey the ebb and flow of customers as he waited. Blasts of heat and clattering came from the kitchen corridor to mingle steamily with the sporadic guffaws and hum of chatter. A tired barmaid poured foaming beer from the jug by the barrels behind the bar. Nathaniel appraised her swiftly, sore red hands, damp apron, somewhat drab and dishevelled but the kerchief crossed over her breast was clean and white and she had a gentleness of carriage and expression. Her movements were considered and her smile was surprisingly sweet. Nevertheless, he reflected, glancing at the flushed, bristling face of the barman as he bellowed additional orders over his shoulder to the kitchen, she would be lucky to keep her place. The other maids were blowsy, defiantly wearing their demure White Hart dresses off the shoulder: dash and fire, crowing laughs.

"Have you decided if you will be wanting a room Mr Parry?" enquired the barman as he poured the brandy and a bowl of beer for Caradoc. "I can offer one for tonight but every last one's taken tomorrow."

Nathaniel smiled, taking his plate from Tobias, who had shot from the kitchen corridor at a half-run with the plate of pie and a bone which he had thrown to Caradoc. "No thank you, I have business elsewhere in town. But I would appreciate the help of a man to handle my trunk and play the link-boy. Can you spare one for a couple of hours?"

Scenting the prospect of easy money, Tobias puffed himself out and drew himself up to what he imagined was the strength and height needed for the trunk handling Nathaniel had in mind. "Sir, Oiy could help Mr Parry sir!" He looked steadily at Nathaniel in silent entreaty, it had been a particularly long day and he had two hours remaining of his usual shift. Spending half an hour pushing a wheelbarrow in the fresh air and selling information to a toff from London was too good an opportunity to miss.

"This boy will do very well if he can be spared," said Nathaniel, amused.

"Tobias, ask leave of Mr Bishop. He's in the office." The barman turned to Nathaniel. "He's hired to you for two shillings sir," he said warily, mentally pocketing one shilling. "Including the loan of a barrow."

The tired barmaid quietly set down Nathaniel's steaming glass then brought over the bowl of beer and a hunk of fatty meat she had snatched from a discarded plate on the bar. She knelt by Caradoc to give him his supper, run her hand over his wiry fleece and smooth his head.

"He likes you," said Nathaniel, "It's a mark of high favour as Caradoc isn't

23

generally keen on new acquaintances."

She smiled, her sweet face alight. "I do love dogs sir. 'Specially unusual ones like him with 'is beard so grand and 'is coat so curly," she laughed softly in delight, scratching Caradoc's ears as he amiably set about his supper.

Tobias pushed through the crowds to stand by Nathaniel, twisting his apron, breathing hard. He had been obliged to scour the stable-yard to track down the proprietor, Mr Bishop, who was dealing with the ostlers and had not wanted to listen.

"Oiy can 'elp you sir. Mr Bishop gives me leave to bring y'r trunk out and see you to y'r lodgings."

"Well done young man. I'll see you by the front door in half an hour."

Tobias fled back to the kitchens, reckoning how much of his shilling he would have to share with the cook.

"I guess you know this city well ma'am," said Nathaniel quietly to the young woman who still crouched by Caradoc, muttering endearments. "I need to find myself some liberal conversation tonight. Can you recommend a tavern with rooms? I've just been to the Guildhall meeting and fancy hearing some more reforming talk."

"Well sir," she said, screwing up her nose in concentration and rocking back on her heels. "I take it you will be wanting a respectable tavern. You'll do well to stay in the upper-town."

"Oh yes," he answered gravely. "Respectable if you please."

"Try the George and Dragon in Walcot Street. There's a regular school of reformers there most evenings and there's clean rooms. If any's to be had at all that is."

In half an hour Nathaniel found himself following in the footsteps of Tobias, who was trundling his belongings in the borrowed wheel-barrow. He wrapped his travel cloak around him more tightly, as a searching wind got up and chased skeletal leaves down Union Street. Caradoc trotted alongside Tobias, guarding the trunk by darting at the piles of ordure in the gutter and challenging passing coaches, shadowy cats and stray dogs. The crowds were thinning, but regular policemen on night-watch passed by, swinging their lanterns and making a show of keeping a look-out for trouble.

Tobias seemed impervious to the cold and kept up a stream of chatter. Like a hound on the scent he could almost smell money. More stories, more laughs, more knowledge. Like the new paper said: "Knowledge is power". Tobias clung to that: it was inspirational. He had listened to the men in the Dragon reading aloud from the

24

new paper which had materialised like a call to arms that very summer. *The Poor Man's Guardian* it was called, selling at one penny, though it was illegal to be caught selling it. Even now, so the men said in the Dragon, Mr Hetherington the editor was jailed in London because his paper was cheap enough for the ordinary people to read and he dared to publish without the government stamp.

Any critical talk of politics was seen as sedition, and it was full of such talk, and full of heady dreams for all poor men. Dreams of voting, of being heard, of having a better life, a fair day's pay for a hard day's work which would fund a decent life: a respectable life with rooms of your own, a place to live in like a proper person. Tobias slept at the back of the stables at the Hart. He was usually grubby, uncomfortable and cold, but his new and temporary kitchen job had at last brought him the steady fuel of scraps which banished hunger. From his craven state of powerlessness and want, Tobias was looking up and wanted to rise. Nathaniel glanced over the thin back, bent over now and stretching the stitches on the patched shirt as Tobias plied himself to his task. The gentle slope caused him to falter, the banter dried up and his breath came in sharp gasps.

"How old are you Tobias?" enquired Nathaniel gently.

"Twelve sir. Oiy know this city like the back of mi 'and. Worked at York House Oiy did last year. Oiy seen the Duchess and Princess Victoria an' all."

"I think you should walk ahead now. Make sure we have a clear path." Nathaniel took the handles of the barrow and pushed Tobias forward. "Go ahead with Caradoc."

The boy stumbled forward. "You sure sir? Thank'ee sir. Oi'm goin' to take you along the Borough Walls and up Northgate to Walcot. The Dragon ain't far. You're wantin' the Dragon ain't you? Mary, Mrs Spence, you know, the barmaid you talked to, she said it was where you'd 'ear some reform talk. She lives in Walcot Street and knows the taverns. Not that she's a drinker mind. She lives with her 'usband's mother, she's a great Methodist is old Mrs Spence. She be not that pleased with Mary workin' at the Hart."

As they made their way up Walcot Street the pavements became more crowded again, warehouses, small manufactories, houses and taverns jostled the street, the black backs of the houses on the Paragon terrace climbed up, mountainous, ahead and to their left, and snatches of music floated into the night from open doors. The George and Dragon was a well appointed tavern, full of drinkers and disputes which grew in volume as they approached the front door. Tobias stayed outside with the trunk and Caradoc took up a perch on top of it whilst Nathaniel made his way in. A hubbub greeted him, coming from the right hand parlour where a hoarse voice was struggling to read to the company from a newspaper, above a growing tide of barracking from his listeners. Nathaniel passed by swiftly to the main bar.

"Do you have a room for tonight?" he enquired, raising his voice above the row from the parlour to attract the sweating barman.

"Just tonight sir," said the barman hurriedly dispatching potboys with ale jugs. "Will that interest you?"

"Seems this city is expecting a landslide of visitors tomorrow landlord!"

"Season's in full swing by next month and preparations are a-foot, but we have market-men here regular. 'Course what with all this Re-form lark we've extra public meetings and assemblies and grand balls and the like. Reform groups are laying on all sorts of entertainments left and right."

"You are a keen reformer then?"

"Keen businessman sir. We likes a bustle in Bath but big crowds are rarer than in the old days. Then we was thronged and jam-packed with the quality. My old father came here fifty years ago to run a tavern and he saw the falling off when the French wars started and damned Boney put paid to the rollickin' times. Glad to see that villain get the beatin' he deserved."

The night was sliding away and Nathaniel was acutely aware that he needed to attach himself to the voluble reform crew in the parlour if he was to earn his keep. He hired the room without further a-do and went out with the waiter who had been charged with taking up his trunk. The urchin Tobias also needed to be paid off. Tobias accepted Nathaniel's florin gratefully but was loath to lose his new patron and made a pitch for more business. "Oiy don't start 'til breakfast tomorrow sir and Oi'm not workin' all the day. Do you need showing 'round town? Oi knows a lot," he faltered at the last, wilting under Nathaniel's steady gaze.

"I thought you had a regular job at the Hart."

"Oi do 'elp out when they're busy in the kitchen," he said, rubbing his face to stave off the leaden fatigue which rolled over him in waves. "Joseph's laid-up wi' a broke leg and Oi've a few hours a day 'til 'e's on 'is feet."

Nathaniel took pity, again. Small boys were famously good at watching and noticing, Tobias might just come in useful.

"Tomorrow before breakfast then young man. Keep your ears open for lodgings for me. Somewhere along this street would suit."

"Yes sir," Tobias nodded his head and turned back towards the centre of town, smiling to himself in weary triumph.

Nathaniel, with Caradoc at his heels, plunged back into the Dragon and ran lightly upstairs, following the waiter and his trunk. The dark staircase wound upwards to the first floor, where they took their temporary possession of a room directly above the front parlour. Wasting no more time, he flung his cloak and stick on the bed as Caradoc stretched himself out in anticipation on the rug, watching the waiter light the fire which was lying, ready-made, and sprang obediently to life, "Right, you're off duty," he said ruffling Caradoc's head, "catch a wink of sleep. I'm for a back-seat below." Nathaniel ushered the waiter out, locked the room and made straight for the reformers. He slipped in to take a place in the shadows by the door, well away from the roaring fire which, unlike the dainty casket in his room, was a heroic affair whose tongues of heat were roasting those near it. A couple of dozen men were jammed into the bar, artisans, small proprietors, all with hats off and eyes alight with notions of the rights of man, fuelled by beer, but also with the intoxication of being in a world on the edge of change. The press of bodies and agitation of the men had generated a sour stench, partially masked by the fumes of drink and greasy smells of roasting meat from the main bar.

The reader, a stout middle-aged artisan, clad in the customary fustian jacket and drab breeches, was rubbing his perspiring forehead with an outsize paisley patterned handkerchief.

"Wait now lads. We'll 'ave it again to get the sense of it."

"Sense is clear Arthur. The *Guardian's* givin' us warning. Just like Mr Hunt did and none o' us listened. The Bill should be demandin' votes for all us men, not just them as pays high rates. £10 householders be damned! Who 'mongst us has the pleasure of payin' £10 in rates?" said a thick-set man, balding and angry, who snatched the paper and waved it in accusation round the table.

"Oiy 'ave," piped up a man by the door, "Oiy pays over £10 and so do other businessmen 'ere. Got to start somewheres Robert. Them as pays 'ighly should get a vote first. We need to see 'ow it goes, and folk in small 'ouses can be brought in later."

"Why," shouted Robert Turner, flinging the paper down so hard it slid away from him over the blackened, beer-ringed oak table. "It wasn't what was to 'appen. Tom Paine said it in our father's time. 'Nat-chu-ral roights' we 'ave. We're not criminals. We're working men who makes this country run. We does the workin' and the fightin' when fightin's to be done. We pays taxes. Like the Yankees said, no taxation without representation. Universal suffrage is what we've a-been after since they Frenchey wars ended in '15. Why shouldn't Oiy vote 'cos moiy 'ouse is rated at £6. An' why shouldn't a man vote just 'cos 'e lives in his father's 'ouse?"

"Ye 'ave representation and ye'll 'ave more when us £10 'ouseholders vote."

"I want to vote mi'self!"

"Ye talks like a blackguard republican! Don't go a-quotin' Yankees to me! His Majisty ain't been crowned more 'an a few month and ye're a mouthin' republican sentimints!"

"Now lads, easy now. No one's a mouthin' loike a Yankee as I 'ear," blustered Arthur Jamieson, regaining control of the *Guardian*, and carefully, respectfully, smoothing it down over the table top. "Bob Turner sit down, Oiy knows ye'll support the Bill and ye're a patriot through an' through." He smiled encouragingly at Robert who took a steady pull at his drink and sighed, deflated.

"I'm not sayin' as I want to see the Bill fail," said Robert, sad and disgruntled. "Tis a mighty thing to make any change. I know it."

"An' it's not just votes is it?" Arthur continued. "They great cities 'aven't even got Members of Parliament of their own as they weren't built in the old days when seats were give out by King John."

"'E never give out no seats," shouted an irritable voice behind Arthur whose owner was trapped too close to the fire.

"Well 'oo did?"

The dispute rambled into historical speculation. Most paused to swig their beer and some decided it was time to call for more. Pints of cider seemed the best solution to the imponderable questions raised, but Arthur, weary from his stint as chairman called for gin and beer: it was "the dog's nose" and nothing else would do.

### Bedford's Billiard Rooms, Milsom Street, Bath.

At about this time, as Nathaniel was thinking how much he had missed the soft burr of the Somerset accent and deciding that his first Bath reformers were far less dangerous than many he had heard in London, a well-fed and fashionably dressed gentleman, fifty, superficially handsome and somewhat the worse for drink, was lolling back in his usual chair in Bedford's Billiard Rooms, Milsom Street. He watched the play with unseeing eyes, indifferent for once as he had bigger business on his mind.

Despite the hour the usual crowd of local businessmen and military types was still out in force: half-pay officers, old generals from the Indian Army, Captains and Commanders, spirit soaked, wreathed in tobacco clouds and intent on the games as they crowded round the baize tables. The evening at the gaming rooms had been longer than he had anticipated, which was not usually a problem, quite the reverse in fact, but his wife Janie had been particularly unpleasant and pressing about the time of his return. Was it already midnight? He heaved a sigh and squinted at his pocket watch. It was indeed midnight. Not ten o'clock, when he should have been leaving

Bedford's, according to Janie. He swilled back the remnants of his brandy and attempted to banish the vision of that sharp little face which awaited him in the bedroom, hideous mob-cap pulled unattractively over her hair, which would be bristling with papers, thin fingers grasping the sheets in a paroxysm of silent rage which would be given full voice as he inched the door open.

Better to sleep in the dressing-room. He nodded bitterly to himself. Janie had been spoiled as a child in India, waited on hand and foot and indulged by her fond mama. No matter how many servants they employed, it never seemed to be enough to make her content in Bath. He had worked steadily through her inheritance, which, with his miserly pay, barely sufficed to allow him a few gentlemen's pleasures. His credit was still good at Bedford's: just. His wine-merchant too was supplying the essentials: just. He took a considered pinch from his silver snuff box and inhaled deeply, steadying his breathing.

Roderick Wilson did not dwell on his current financial short-comings, instead he dreamed of the future, a rosy future coming ever closer to make a glorious present. Tonight's negotiations should improve his position no-end. What a stroke of luck! He was about to apply just the right amount of pressure to extract a tidy settlement, and who knows what it might lead to? He gazed unseeing as the final frames of the night were played out. Final bets were taken. Waiters lounged, sleepy in the corners. He cared not a fig for the play, but dreamed instead of money, and position, and the irresistible Coco, his exquisite Colette. As French tarts went she was superior in every sense. With his new riches he could install her in some rooms of her own, prevent her from entertaining other clients. He had never really liked that aspect of their relationship. He wanted a mistress, all to himself.

"Mr Wilson," an urgent voice at his elbow, "Mr Wilson, your chairmen are here."

Roderick smiled, immensely gratified. "Yes Jones, thank you." He heaved himself out of the chair, took the proffered caped greatcoat, his hat and gloves, and rolled out into the cold air. Occasional gas lamps illuminated the footpath of Bath's principal shopping street. Pools of light relieved the dark and candles and lamps shone from upper windows. Standing in the shadow by the wall were two burly chairmen, swathed with shawls against the growing cold and wind.

"Mr Wilson sir? Gentleman you want to do business with sent a note earlier saying as you were to come to a meeting."

"That's correct," Wilson had been delighted to receive a message from the barman at Bedford's earlier that evening. He had been waiting for his man to make a move for the last few days and now, at last, a private meeting. No names needed of course, this was a delicate matter. They would meet, settle, and then see how things progressed over the next few months. Wilson climbed into the sedan chair and one of the chairmen closed the door behind him. He felt the chair lift as the men seized the poles, fore and aft, and moved off smartly. Curtains had been pulled over the windows and it was snug. He covered his legs with the rug and sensed they were setting a cracking pace, downhill in the direction of the river. This was surprising as his man lived in the upper-town. But naturally, he could never have a meeting such as this at his home. Perhaps they were to go to the office? Wilson tried to lift the curtains but found they were secured at the sides, not so unusual in the cold weather. Chairmen were having to make special efforts to ensure comfort now that flys were licensed to operate as hackney cabs in the city. Many chairmen claimed they were ruined, but hundreds of them still operated, lumbering up and down the hills of Bath, into the houses if necessary to convey their passengers right to their own bedsides.

The steps of the chairmen had accelerated to a half-run, jogging over the cobbles, always downhill. Wilson tried the window to see if he could lift it behind the curtain. Screwed shut. He tried the door. Locked. Through his drink be-fuddled wits pin-pricks of anxiety began to stimulate concern.

"Stop!" he called. "Stop now I say!" Their steps thudded onwards. Wilson began to beat in the door. "Confound it I demand to see our route! Stop!"

The chair came to a sudden halt and landed heavily on the ground. The door clicked unlocked and grasping hands reached into the chair, dragging Roderick Wilson out into darkness. Before he had time to call out, before he could take a breath, a cosh whistled through the air and slammed a sickening blow onto his head. Wilson's body, limp as rag, collapsed back into the chair. His slack legs were folded and shovelled in. The door was slammed and locked, the dark figures took up the poles and headed to the river. More cautiously now, down to the lower-town they stole, by the Hetling Pump House, far past the fashionable quarters to the maze of courts and faded terraces broken up to serve as either lodging houses at three pence a night or as squalid dens for prostitutes, beggars and thieves. Past warehouses they hurried, past stables, leather-works and corn-factors to the quay.

The chairmen idled as they approached the river, downstream from the Old Bridge was the ideal spot. Lower down river from the Broad and Narrow Quays, the wall petered out and was replaced by sewage outfalls and marsh grasses, middens and overhanging trees. Floating bodies in Bath often fetched up at such a berth after the wretched suicides had flung themselves from the bridge or slid into the shallows and waded into the green-blackness of the Avon. Just the spot for their burden. Orders had been clear. This was the night that Wilson was going to end it all. He just needed to be shown the way. They found a quiet place in the dark shadow of the corn-factor's warehouse.

"Thank God for that. Bastard was 'eavy."

"Quiet. Get 'im out." Wolfish eyes gleamed above the shawl wrapped round the lean, bearded face.

His fellow conspirator, broader, stolid and with an ill grace, clicked open the lock, swung the catch and made to pull the body out, but was flung backwards to roll in the filth of the quay. A frenzied figure, bloodied and desperate, broke free and set up a terrified howl, partly blinded by the force of the blow which had stunned him but not rendered him insensible for quite long enough, Wilson took off in a wild career. He stumbled past the first assailant who was scrambling drunkenly to his feet, slithering on the slick cobbles, trying to gain a purchase sufficient for him to charge after Wilson and smother his cries. The other man was on Wilson's tail, pausing only to pick up a stone and hurl it after his prey. The wounded man zigzagged like a hare before the pack, two sets of running steps now pounding on his trail. His breath came in tearing gasps and his strangled yells died as he struggled, but failed, to give voice to a coherent cry. His lungs seemed to be collapsing, his legs failing to move faster. Faster, faster: he willed his aching body to move and instinctively headed for shelter. He cornered sharply as an alley loomed to his right. He fled down it and crashed into a door, it gave way and he fell into a silent workshop, colliding with a bench and scattering a hail of tools as he burst through, tripping and stumbling into the pitch-dark. He turned to look behind and almost at once the grey of the doorway was darkened by the shapes of the two men. Wilson gasped in terror as they advanced on him. His arms raked the bench behind him, grasping for tools, throwing them in mad desperation at the advancing figures. All but one from the shower of missiles fell helplessly, but a screw driver made contact with one of the heads of the chairmen and gouged a runnel down his face. Bellowing in rage and pain the injured man narrowed the gap in seconds and flew at Wilson, raining blows on him and beating aside arms raised feebly in defence. He caught his victim round the waist, hauled him up and flung him across the bench, into the wall. Wilson's body twitched as it landed on a tool rack and then moved no more.

"Ye've skewered 'im Mordecai. 'E's stuck through the 'eart on an awl. Ye crazed bugger. 'E was meant to have done 'imself in an' now 'e's stabbed!"

Mordecai glowered, stood hesitant for a moment, then from force of habit leant over the body and ran his hands over the pockets.

"Leave it!" pleaded Declan. "The watch might think the stab was from some junk in the river and 'e's a suicide, not done over in a robbin' clear and simple! Safer for us for sure! Let's get 'im away." He patted Mordecai uncertainly on the shoulder and moved to the door.

Mordecai paused, ready to pull back, but the diamond in Wilson's ring glinted in the moonlight. He wrenched it from the fingers, flabby now, inhuman, pocketed the ring and braced himself to lift Wilson's body from the spike. He grunted with effort as he flung the dead weight over his shoulder and turned to leave.

"Not a word more, matey. Not one soddin' word."

With a glare of murderous intent, Declan was silenced and Mordecai led the way out. The two conspirators paused in the doorway to check the night and saw only a pair of homeless dogs, snuffling over the refuse by the warehouse. Eddies of laughter and music broke distantly from some of the taverns on Narrow Quay and Avon Street but all else was still. They made their way swiftly to the edge of the river wall, and Mordecai let the body down into the greasy flow, kicking it free from the wrack of leaves and detritus by the margin to float freely along the edge of the river. They picked up the poles of the chair and slunk off towards Green Park. Once in the mews they located the correct shed and surreptitiously replaced the unlicensed chair which they had temporarily stolen earlier that evening from a bankrupted chairman, victim of the flashy horse drawn flys which had poached his regulars.

**The Bath Road**

By three o'clock, in the dead centre of that autumn night, a lone horseman picked his way along the turnpike road from Bath to Bristol. The night in Bath had been unrewarding in terms of intelligence gained on the party he was meant to be stalking, but revealing in many other ways. His orders had revealed that his new employer, the Bristol trader Mr Edwin Ravenswood, was a subtle one, an intricate planner, relentless in his pursuit of his purpose: utterly ruthless. This he could understand, in view of the business they were in. The journey to Bristol had started at the end of the previous year when he and his men had joined the crew of Ravenswood's ship, the *Blue Dragon*, in the harbour south of Canton. He had sailed to Bristol and delivered the sealed boxes of currency and bullion, as expected, and had spent the months of the *Blue Dragon's* refit serving Ravenswood before the return to China. The service had been singularly instructive.

He glanced up as a distant light caught his eye. He was nearing a toll house and had no inclination to rouse the keeper to pay his dues. The night's journey was close to its end, as his destination was his employer's home which was acting as his own temporary residence. Arno's Tower, Mr Ravenswood's new manor-house in Arno's Vale, was a short gallop over the field and through the wood, beyond the other mansions of the *nouveau riche* which had sprung up on the outskirts of Bristol by the old medieval village of Brislington and now overshadowed its own modest manor.

He gathered his horse for the leap and soared over the hedge, disappearing from the road and setting his course for the distant Ravenswood mansion. Soon tiny lights glinted into view like shards of glass and the tower stood dark in relief against the stars. He picked up the broadening path, cantered along it for half a mile, called out to the watchman to pull the gates back and swung his horse down the drive to the pillared entrance. The protruding stone tower, crowned by crocheted spires, was pierced by arches and flanked by stone griffins as high as a man, illuminated from below by gas jets, which also shone out from stone and iron settings below the yawning mouths of gargoyles, which shot from all the crowded battlements and turrets of his employer's Gothic fantasy. The Chinese guest, the mysterious stranger who had caught the eye of Nathaniel Parry in the Guildhall meeting a few hours before, leapt from his horse and surrendered the reins to a stable-boy who had appeared as Ravenswood's servants always did: unbidden, discreet, attentive.

"Cornelius!" called a deep, resonant voice from the hallway as he climbed the steps and entered the open doors. "A fruitful night I trust?"

"Interesting sir, but not as fruitful as we wished," replied Cornelius Lee. "Our quarry was not at his usual pursuits but retired home quietly after a political meeting. I will attend his gaming club on the next high stakes evening and proceed with our original plan." He bowed briefly. "And now sir, if you have no further instructions I will retire."

Edwin Ravenswood fixed his newest employee with a searing stare, taking in the powerful physique and cat-like calm of the undoubtedly dangerous Mr Lee. Ravenswood smiled his cold, dead smile and inclined his fine dark head. "Yes, Cornelius, goodnight. I await an important guest so instructions can wait for tomorrow."

Cornelius moved gracefully to the huge winding staircase which coiled round the central tower of the house like a serpent, connecting its arcaded floors and culminating in a high dome of stained-glass, blind now, with not even the wan light of the moon to light it and shower the stairs with colour. He moved silently onto the second floor landing, opened and closed his bedroom door firmly and stood silently on the open landing, watching the hall below. Within ten minutes his patience was rewarded as the rush of carriage wheels on gravel sounded in the drive. Confused footfalls, carriage doors: Ravenswood's greetings followed and Cornelius stole forward to the edge of the arcade, concealing himself behind a pillar.

"Honoured sir," Ravenswood sounded reverential. "A pleasure: a great pleasure to welcome you to my home."

Cornelius registered the unusual level of deference, the desire to please. It boded nothing but ill.

"My servants will take your luggage to your suite. Your valet will have the adjoining room. Would you care for refreshment?"

Cornelius leaned forward just enough to catch sight of the guest, one sighting being ample, he did not wait to hear an answer but melted back into the shadows and soundlessly entered his own room and comparative safety. He took off his hat and riding coat, his boots, waistcoat and jacket, laid them out precisely and sat, cross-legged, before the open window, looking far away, over the tree tops to the stars. He breathed deeply and placed his hands on his knees. The newcomer was important indeed, a man whose face he had come to know over the last few hard years, a man known by repute to all those who sailed the high seas on the dangerous side of the law. This man was feared by all who even suspected one iota of his capabilities, of his brutality and of his capacity for calculated cruelty. He was the emissary of the Count and seemed untouchable, operating on a level beyond reach. He was Kizhe.

"Kee-jay," repeated Cornelius to himself: in Russian it meant "others". "How many others? How many guises and stratagems of destruction stemmed from his fertile brain? How many deaths had he conjured to gain his fortune and that of his shadowy master? This man, this important man, the Mongolian-Russian who held the Count's steel chains of power which linked the Russian Empire, China and all the East. Their reach was long, through the opium fields of India and Afghanistan, through the brothels and harems of the Levant and the governments between. And now Kizhe is here."

As an optimist, Cornelius Lee had no option but to consider the new advantages of his position. As a realist he moved swiftly on to the latent threats and dwelt on them until the first fingers of dawn crept over the sky, and he had no considerations left.

# Chapter 2

**Dawn: 6th October, 1831. The George and Dragon, Walcot Street, Bath.**

"Thank you, that's all I need."

The pert chambermaid had to accept that no more services could be rendered or tips cajoled from the handsome guest, so she gave up, made a sketchy curtsey and flounced off along the landing. Caradoc took the opportunity to slink out behind her in search of some exercise and breakfast, whilst Nathaniel padded over to investigate the washstand in the dark corner, which leaned askew against the oak panelled wall. Earlier the maid had laboured up the stairs with a steaming jug of hot water that now waited, cooling, by its matching porcelain basin. Both were elegantly restrained, Dresden style, but had seen better days.

He poured a generous measure, sluiced his face and rubbed it dry on the linen towel, before shivering involuntarily and wrapping his dressing gown closer to combat a sharp and persistent draught that had set up through the ill-fitting window as the morning wind rose. It was not surprising that the chambermaid found him unusually attractive: he cut a dashing figure in his Damascus silk-velvet robe, intricately patterned in rich chestnut-brown, tawny-gold, maroon and deep sea-green. It had been his father's, a souvenir of a mission to Turkey when Owen had been in the entourage of the envoy to the Sublime Porte. The provenance appealed strongly to Nathaniel's taste for the exotic, and without doubt, Lord Byron would have approved of it.

He took a seat at the table by the fire, which was slowly flickering into life after being rattled up by the maid when she had returned to deliver his breakfast. He surveyed the spartan fare of beer and bread which sat, uninspiring, before him, and sighed, inwardly declaring that the morning should not pass without him sampling Bath's famed sugar buns, and maybe the local brioche, "a Sally Lunn". All could be washed down by something tasty, maybe creamy hot chocolate or a tiny strong coffee. With those delectable thoughts he could almost smell Paris. Sparely built, powerful, and with a martial passion for exercise, he was usually hungry and it seemed a very long time since the pie at the Hart. Nathaniel yawned, ran his hands through his tangle of black hair and moved to the window to get a clear view of the street below as it came to life.

The Corn Market was opposite and a few men were hovering in the street by the doors. Horse-drawn carts rattled by with milk-churns and cheeses, mountains of vegetables for the daily provisions market and straw for the livery stables. A scavenger's cart moved, noxiously, away from the beasts' pens by the market stalls, the men chivvying each other, clumsily struggling to quit the street before the watch spotted them. He looked higher to the undulating line of green hills that bounded the city, broken by the valley of the Avon. To the east lay London and the new rooms in Lambeth which had recently become his home, to the west, the port of Bristol and a pressing engagement with one John Drake. He heard some heavy movements above as other guests started to rise.

Nathaniel stirred himself to find clean clothes and repack his trunk. He crossed the room and knelt on the floor to raise the heavy lid and survey his belongings. He deliberated on his movements for the day. New lodgings must be had, and preferably nearby, as Walcot Street seemed a canny billet, stationed as it was between the upper and lower towns. He would visit a few more taverns to gauge the mood in the city, tap Dr Charles Parry and his circle, the amiable Captain Peterson and the voluble Mr Vere. That should suffice to allow a scratch report to be made to Drake on the 8th of the month in his lodgings in Clifton: a rendezvous arranged when they had met in London. The Home Office briefing by one of Lord Melbourne's staff, a Mr Percy, was quickly done as it required him merely to report on attitudes to reform and the level of threat to law and order. The posting had been complicated by Drake's involvement and his additional instructions. He was to be stationed in Bristol and was charged with the task of negotiating with an entrepreneur involved in the shipment of opium from India to China.

That Britain illegally shipped considerable amounts of opium was common knowledge. India provided a ready source and the East India Company had been a major player for years. What was new was that the Emperor of China had started to apply a more effective embargo and his men were busily impounding British ships and cargoes. It seemed that Drake's man in Bristol was adept at maintaining his trade, flouting the Company's monopoly, and evading the attentions of the Chinese navy. The Foreign Office was keen to know the secret of his success, or at least to assist him in continuing to achieve it. Drake had outlined the importance of his own role and the necessity for Nathaniel supporting him hand and foot, which Percy had not made much of. Drake had also spoken, at length, of his service in France and Nathaniel had idly studied the edge of a wound on his neck which itself spoke of action, but Drake had seemed uncommunicative when Nathaniel raised the names of his old contacts in the diplomatic service at the court of Charles X. He shrugged at the memory. No doubt he would learn more of the doings of Mr John Drake at their Bristol meeting.

Mechanically, Nathaniel continued unpacking: linen, stacks of shirts and jumbles of coloured waistcoats, coats and neck-cloths, his mind left free to speculate on what might be learned in Bristol. Opium was a necessary drug for everyone, from fractious babies in their cradles to the dying on their deathbeds. It brought them all the same blessed tide of sleep. Some fell victim, and craved it to distraction, as the Chinese seemed to be doing in increasing numbers. They had joined the opium eaters. He thought of Coleridge and De Quincey, both of whom had let it eat their lives away. Opium, it seemed to him, was like most things in life, two great opposites, neither existing without the other: Good and Bad, God and the Devil, Heaven and Hell. Both part of the whole: both ever present. He checked his own leather-cased bottles of medical supplies, especially the Kendal Black Drop, his Lancashire cure-all. It contained at least double the strength of laudanum in ordinary doses with the best Turkey opium, saffron, cloves, spirit and acetic acid. Nathaniel had never allowed servants to prepare his travelling case; his life could depend upon it. Not that he put all his trust in medicaments. As Byron said, "Always laugh when you can, it is cheap medicine." He smiled at the memory, it was cheap and it did no harm.

This particular trunk was his father's sea-chest, a sturdy oak carcase with metal bonds, still faintly painted with the family name "Parry". It was a relic from Owen's first voyage to the Levant in the early stages of the French wars, when he was a young man new to the service of his country. In the base, and also in the lid, there were hidden compartments, Nathaniel moved the lining and pressed the lever in the corner of the trunk to raise the base. Snug in the felt lining lay his makila, the Basque walking stick, which had been the companion of both Parrys on walks in wild places, or places where use of the customary swordstick was unwise. Less of a gentleman's accoutrement than his favourite silver-headed stick, it was a shepherd's staff, cut in the living wood of the medlar tree that had seen great service as his quarter-staff and bludgeon. He lifted it out, running his hands over the rich wood, and, grasping the pommel, slid it off to reveal a deadly, glinting spike. Sharp as a spear and deadly, it could run a man through. He examined the point minutely, and, satisfied, replaced the pommel and returned the stick to its place in the base of the trunk. He quickly repacked his belongings, layering them with the grey stems of brittle lavender that still released the faint aromatic scent of summer.

He was distracted by the unmistakable sound of a terrier scurrying along the landing, followed by the unruly steps of a child's boots. He closed the trunk and rose to open the door.

"Ha! Caradoc, in you rascal! How-do young Tobias! What news?"

"Good mornin' sir. Oiy got plenty!"

"Well sit down to tell the tale, and you can eat my breakfast if you want it," said Nathaniel, throwing himself on the bed and dislodging Caradoc who had already buried into the mound of blankets.

"Thank you sir," said Tobias, dragging the chair tight up to the table and falling on the bread and beer. "Good news is," he spluttered, mouth full, "Oiy got you a grand lodgin' in this very street. When Oiy got back to the Hart last night Mary was still there and Oiy told her as you were only in the Dragon a night and needed to stay longer. She straight away upped and said you was welcome to ask old Mrs Spence, her 'usband's mother that is, as y're now after private lodgings and not a tavern. She had taken a likin' to you sir and said you should walk down with me now, afore she leaves for work, and ask Mrs Spence yourself."

"Excellent, and I sense there's more."

Tobias swallowed hard and then paused for effect. "Body of a gentleman 'as bin found in the river!" he said conspiratorially.

"Scavengers saw 'im a-floatin' 'ead down and he's been laid out in the Duke of York on Narrow Quay for to be inspected."

Nathaniel had had the misfortune of seeing a number of dead bodies, gentlemen and others, and was not as moved as Tobias had hoped.

"Do you get many accidents here, or suicides?"

"Accidents are mainly kids fallin' in sir. Suicides is norm'ly poor folk."

"Any idea who he was?"

"No sir. But the city police are investigatin'."

Nathaniel nodded sagely, but knew exactly how effective that was likely to be. London's new metropolitan force of "Peelers", set up a couple of years ago by the formidable Sir Robert Peel had yet to be spread throughout the country. Some parish

38

police forces were aping the smart uniforms and rigorous systems of the Peelers, but most still dithered on with night watchmen and patchy day patrols. Not one provincial city had yet got a force to coordinate detection of crime over all its parishes. There was unlikely to be much progress made with that particular investigation.

"Good work Tobias. If you've finished with the breakfast, hop off downstairs and I'll meet you in ten minutes."

Nathaniel, forsaking his travel cloak with an eye to the morning rendezvous in the Great Pump Room, turned out in shiny shoes, a worsted frock coat, white ruffled shirt and plain white trousers, burgundy waistcoat and a high beaver-hat, Anglesey style. He and Caradoc followed Tobias up Walcot Street to the beginning of the sharp rise in the road that led to London Street. On the left was a terrace of neat houses in the customary cream-coloured Bath limestone, designed to the customary strict classical proportions decreed when the city was rebuilt as a temple to modernity. For over a hundred years gracious Palladianism had been the only style for Bath, terrace after faultless terrace, making it difficult for visitors to figure out exactly where they were, unless of course they stumbled onto one of the great crescents or the uniquely odd King's Circus. Mrs Spence's house was in a short terrace which proved to be the exception to this rule as all the houses sported pretty Venetian windows. Tobias hammered on the door knocker and Mary answered quickly, less tired now and more comely, but with the same gentle grace Nathaniel had noticed when she served at the Hart.

"Good morning to you sir. Tobias gave you my message! Come in and welcome. Mother!" she called upstairs and bid them walk ahead of her to a bright kitchen at the rear of the house. A large fireplace and cooking range took up most of the far wall, and, sat before the grate in a rocking chair, was a very old man. He lifted his rheumy eyes to the visitors and wheezed a greeting, slapping his hands on the arms of the chair.

"Ha-ha! Ye come forward young men. Come forward I say. But mind the Johnty now! Don't go a-tramplin' the babe though 'ee do get sore underfoot. Come, come!"

Nathaniel and Tobias picked their way, as bidden, over a small child who was managing to maintain an unsteady sitting position whilst occupying himself by exploring a wooden clothes peg. As they moved to take in turn the shaky hand thrust out to them from the folds of the old man's woollen blanket, Mary joined them in the kitchen with a powerful looking woman of about sixty years of age.

"Mr Parry may I introduce you to Mrs Spence my husband's mother, my husband being at sea."

"Good morning madam," said Nathaniel, smoothly and with a bow. "Nathaniel Parry at your service. I gather that I might be so fortunate as to rent rooms here. I am visiting town this month and have some business to complete."

Martha Spence was a commanding woman, dressed in severe high-necked black, strong, big-boned and of late much given to Methodism. Widowed after her husband's death in the winter of 1808 on the retreat to Corunna she looked after her sweet and simple daughter-in-law, the grandson, as yet too small to be indicating if he was to be an adventurer like his father or another little "weak and wan" like Mary, and also the ancient father in-law Mr Spence Senior. Old Tom, normally as cussed as you please did patchy service as baby-minder and vegetable peeler. She eked out her modest income from prudent investments but additional income in the shape of paying guests was vital to keep the family afloat, and the best room and dressing room on the first floor needed a new tenant. Such thoughts prevented her from ousting the truculent looking terrier out of hand and shooing the urchin Tobias Caudle out of her kitchen. If she had told him once it was twenty times about the state of his boots.

She smiled tightly. "Follow me sir."

By the time Nathaniel came back downstairs, deal clinched, money having changed hands and praise having been lavished on the plain and spotless rooms above, other relationships had moved on significantly. Mary had provided Caradoc with a bowl of Tom's beer and plate of hardtack biscuit which he was enjoying whilst listening to the old man talking about hunting dogs and permitting the Johnty to tap him rhythmically with the clothes peg. Mary and Tobias were by the doorway, anxious to leave for work.

"Madam, many thanks, I will return later with my belongings. Now Tobias direct me to the nearest reputable stables. I need to hire a horse."

"That'll be Mr Tasker's Livery sir, Pulteney Mews. Oiy'll point the way as we walks to the Hart," said Tobias, eyeing Mrs Spence suspiciously and hoping she would let him leave without a rebuke. He was cultivating a powerful image of efficiency with Mr Parry and could do without an ear-wigging.

Caradoc, swallowing the remainder of the biscuit, capered after the party.

"Good morning to you Madam, Mr Spence," said Nathaniel.

"Good morning to you," said Martha as she followed them to the front gate. "And you Tobias Caudle," she declared as she slammed the gate shut and glared at the spotless foot scraper. "You can stay at the door if you turns up with boots as caked as that again, ye young besom."

Nathaniel and Caradoc spent a pleasant few hours on the canal path, hacking from Bath to the village of Bathampton and the fields beyond. Tobias had directed them to a well run and busy stable where a fine pale gold stallion had been hired. He proved to be mettlesome and Nathaniel enjoyed the challenge in the freedom of the morning. Dew glistened on the hedgerows, and sprays of the last ripe blackberries shone lustrously as the sun found its way through the morning mist. They galloped along the dusty path, scattering drifts of leaves and the last glowing chestnuts loosed from their green-spiked armour bounced from the pounding hooves. Rabbits thumped away at his approach and the air was alive with bird song. Caradoc ran extra miles circling the fields, chasing the rabbits, hares and once, most unfortunately for him, a sheepdog who proved to be masterfully proprietorial. Shortly after nine they reined in again at the stables, returned the horse to livery and hastily transferred Nathaniel's trunk from the Dragon to the rooms at Mrs Spence's. Caradoc showed no enthusiasm for the tryst at the Pump Room and Old Mr Spence permitted him to lie at his feet by the fire.

Just before ten o'clock as planned, Nathaniel entered the Great Pump Room in Abbey Church Yard and looked about him for a sighting of last night's Guildhall party. The room was grand, and broadly as he remembered it from a previous visit, though the brocade was a tad more tired and the company a good deal more mixed. Middle-aged dames marshalling compliant husbands with gawky daughters in tow had increased in numbers. They were predatory, scenting fresh males to harvest in their drag-nets as potential bridegrooms for the girls and fortunate connections for the families. Musicians played discreetly, providing an atmosphere both cultured and festive. Brutal economic necessities were played out, fastidiously, to Mozart.

The rush of the mineral water and the clink of glasses dispatched by the Pumper could also be heard from his alcove overlooking the medieval King's Bath and knots of people chatted in standing groups or sitting together. Vast glittering chandeliers caught the morning sun and reflected rainbows on the company below. There was constant movement as newcomers arrived and competed to attach themselves to the most fashionable group. Others freshly disentangled from unwise choices milled around the room, eyes darting to find a happier landing. The commanding height of Dr Charles Parry enabled Nathaniel to steer himself to his company with ease. Charles was again free of "Mrs P", who Nathaniel remembered was averse to crowds, but was talking hard to Captain Peterson who stood with a lady and the young woman he recognised as Emma Peterson. There was another gentleman in the group: a small barrel of a man, with a comical smile and bright flush on his cheeks, the latter possibly generated by his unfeasibly tight high collar.

The barrage of introductions and greetings provided the information that Captain

Peterson was accompanied by his wife as well as his daughter, and that the rotund party was a Mr Howard Dill who, like Captain Peterson, had business with Mr Vere that morning. Both remarked that it was unusual for that gentleman to be late.

"If you recall Nathaniel, you met him and Mrs Vere last night. He is the proprietor of the New Bank," explained Dr Parry. "He is a shrewd businessman and no mistake. Profits and investments are soaring."

"Yes, yes," added Mr Dill delightedly, his bushy eyebrows leaping above his tiny glasses. "I have known him for years and it has been perfectly astonishing to see the growth of his banking interests of late. I gather you are only here temporarily Mr Parry, so perhaps we will be unable to persuade you to invest in the city!"

"Yes Mr Dill," said Nathaniel. "I am here for a few weeks, enjoying a break from London."

"Tired of London, tired of life!" breezed Charles Parry. "Johnson could not have been further from the truth. You may be tempted to spend longer here Nathaniel. You will be invigorated man! Fresh air, fine waters, and family ties. Mrs P says you are to come to dinner tomorrow, no excuses!"

"With pleasure," murmured Nathaniel.

"And don't forget new acquaintances!" said Captain Peterson. "You are also welcome to dine with us at your convenience, perhaps next week?"

Mrs Peterson had been prepared for this, as her husband had regaled the family over breakfast, at considerable length, with tales of his exploits in the company of this young man's father. It would be distinctly more diverting to listen to such tales in the company of the young gentleman himself, so she had encouraged the offer of an invitation. Annoyingly, although she had met Mr Parry the previous evening, Emma had been non-committal, but that was hardly unusual where young men were concerned. Lydia Peterson glared covertly at her daughter, willing her to look up and smile. Had all those years of expenditure on governesses and tutors been totally wasted? Failing to animate Emma, she beamed encouragement to Nathaniel and was not disappointed.

"Thank you sir, and thanks to you madam, most kind."

Nathaniel liked the Captain and looked forward to the dinner. Madam seemed friendly, but he was amused to notice that Miss Peterson avoided his eye.

"You're deuced lucky to be in a health resort. As are we all," said Dr Parry portentously. "You will no doubt have heard the latest on the spread of the new fever, the cholera morbus?"

"How is it different from our present fevers pray?" asked Captain Peterson. "We have enough of them already to know them fore and aft I would have thought."

"Ah" said Dr Parry, warming to his theme, "this is very different I can assure you. This "Pest from Bengal" is a swifter killer than we are used to. Seems to spread like any other fever through foul airs or contact with sufferers, if you will pardon the mention of such indelicate matters ladies."

"I read about this in the paper, Dr Parry," said Emma Peterson, her face suddenly alight with interest. "It is almost at our door is it not, having ravaged the Far East and Europe? There was some recommendation to prepare brandy and rhubarb for sufferers and to keep them warm, but there was also talk of confining victims and their families to their homes with a sign telling of the sickness painted on their door. Wasn't that done in the fourteenth century in the time of the Black Death! Haven't we moved on? The symptoms are different from that plague, but seem almost as frightful. The violent sickness and clawing of the hands and feet, the discolouration of the bodies…"

"That's quite enough Emma," interrupted her mother firmly, placing a warning hand on her daughter's arm. "I certainly do not wish to hear of such abominations: especially in the forenoon. Dr Parry, perhaps you could expand on the value of our mineral waters in the pursuit of health? Our visitor is perhaps not fully aware of the signal values of the Bath waters for all types of indisposition."

Emma blushed with frustration, as she had particularly wanted to hear Dr Parry's views on the impending epidemic. She tossed her head moodily and looked away, only to catch Nathaniel's amused smile as she did so. She almost laughed aloud, for he winked at her, so quickly, so shamelessly, and, as he had intended, only she saw it. It was so utterly unexpected, so disarming: shockingly delightful and discomfiting in equal measures. She froze in the struggle to compose her features and wondered if she had imagined it.

Fortunately for her, Mr and Mrs Vere arrived at that very moment and Raphael Vere immediately monopolised the conversation. Vere, no longer the complacent burgess, was harassed and anxious. His wife Tilly, resplendent in a sapphire-blue hat and coat with the most exuberant sleeves yet seen in the Great Pump Room, seemed exasperated.

"Good morning ladies, gentlemen," said Vere unhappily. "Do forgive our lateness, it has been occasioned by a most perplexing occurrence. Nay, worrying I have to say. I received news from the bank this morning that my manager Mr Wilson had not arrived to open for business, an unparalleled occurrence. I went myself to admit the clerks and when Mr Wilson's assistant checked his desk and the safe, he discovered that a considerable amount of money, cash and bonds and various papers had disappeared." He paused to catch his breath. "There was no forced entry," as he added this last, his heavy features sagged at the inevitable construction which might put upon it. "I have known Wilson for over ten years. I cannot believe he might have knowledge of such depredations. Excellent man. Though I have worried about him over the last few months." Vere left his worries undefined.

Whilst partly listening to the fluttering of well-mannered concern generated by this disclosure, Nathaniel privately recollected Tobias's tale of the body in the river and decided to dig more deeply, but was obliged to wait for the opportunity. Thoroughly tired of the conundrum of Wilson, Tilly Vere had set up a fluting monologue on the coldness of the wind, moving inconsequentially on to the impending season of events and in particular the inclusion of various reform soirees, for which, apparently, she could not wait. Under cover of the polite responses to Mrs Vere, Nathaniel saw his chance to move in and have a quiet word with her husband.

"Mr Vere, could I ask you, what worries did you have about such a trusted employee? Forgive me for enquiring but I have some experience of investigations and might be able to offer advice."

"Yes indeed Mr Parry, most kind. Charles has often spoken to me of the impressive successes achieved by you and your father." He paused to ensure the company was well occupied and lowered his voice. "I am sorry to say that Mr Wilson has of late been indulging his habit of gambling to a more significant degree than his means allowed. I must admit he had approached me for help over the last few weeks. I did as much as I could, as a friend. But also as a friend I had to council him to change his company and seek entertainment elsewhere. I pray that he has not taken dire steps to resolve a personal dilemma."

The aside had been noted by Captain Peterson and Dr Parry, who were less than absorbed by the consideration of the soirees that continued to divert the ladies and the jovial Mr Dill.

"Well," said the Captain brusquely, "no doubt all will be resolved speedily. Did any of your employees shed further light on the problem?"

"Mr Henry Blake, Wilson's assistant, is still helping police with their enquiries."

"Henry Blake," said Captain Peterson with renewed interest, "Commander Tomlinson's nephew! Excellent young man, excellent family."

"Ah yes," said Vere, with lukewarm enthusiasm, "young Blake is at present explaining his whereabouts last night. He attended the same gaming rooms as Wilson you know."

Captain Peterson bristled at the slur but was prevented from making a rejoinder by Dr Parry.

"Can't think of a red-blooded male in Bath who hasn't attended gaming rooms!

What! Let's hope your Mr Wilson makes an appearance and solves the mysteries before the end of the morning! Now Nathaniel you are determined to remain in lodgings by the river I take it?"

"Yes Charles, for a few days, but I look forward to dining with you tomorrow at Sion Hill."

A burst of joyous laughter distracted the party and they turned to see a bevy of young women swirl into the room surrounding a rakish young man with a brazen mop of red hair and a rose and cream striped waistcoat, who was delivering what appeared to be a rattling good tale. A circling rearguard was formed by a group of mamas and papas, anxious chaperones poised to pluck their charges away.

"Isn't that the speaker from last night," said Howard Dill, craning his neck for a better view, "Good Lord, he seems to be a regular Pied Piper for the young women!"

"Diarmuid Casey," said Dr Parry. "He spoke well, and seems to be unwilling to stop!"

"Introduce me Raphael," demanded Tilly Vere, pulling at Vere's arm and flashing her brilliant smile. She added mendaciously to strengthen her case, "I so enjoyed his speech and have a mind to ask him some questions."

"Certainly my dear," said Vere wearily. "Do excuse us."

From force of habit, Emma Peterson avoided glancing at the captivating Mr Casey and kept her eyes resolutely lowered. Her mother despaired of her and focused on preventing Nathaniel from evading the dinner invitation.

"Well Mr Parry, perhaps you will visit us in Marlborough Buildings and we can arrange a dinner?" said Mrs Peterson.

"By all means," said Nathaniel. "I bid you good morning ladies, gentlemen."

He made his escape and skirted the excited group surrounding Diarmuid Casey. The Irishman was playing up to them with consummate skill and they were drinking in his charm wholesale. But perhaps not all were so easily entranced. As Nathaniel passed by he caught sight of a striking dark-haired woman with an almond shaped face of exquisite beauty. She was dressed in spring-green and had a small corsage of delicate white flowers on her lapel. Smiling archly, not so much at Mr Casey but at the rest of the girls, she posed, holding his arm: cat-like, enigmatic, one bold dark eyebrow raised in quizzical amusement. There's a minx, thought Nathaniel, as he strode out through the doors to Abbey Church Yard and threaded his way through the gathering crowds to the Hart.

A number of enquires needed to be pursued in the afternoon and a little local knowledge would help him start. The Hart was settling down after the recent arrival of a coach, guests had disappeared upstairs or into coffee rooms, parlours or dining-rooms, orders had been barked out and from the kitchen came the answering clatter of pots. Horses, foamed and steaming after ten miles hard labour, were being led to stables by the scarlet-coated grooms. Nathaniel made his way to a familiar seat. The burly barman recognised him immediately, settled him down with a mug of local cider and provided all he needed to know to draw up a plan of attack.

He would start at the York House in the upper town, inn of choice for many London coaches and the venue favoured, as he had already been told and sensed was doomed to be told daily, by the Duchess of Kent and her daughter the heiress-apparent Princess Victoria. The Chequers in Rivers Street was a haunt of chairmen so should give an insight into the attitudes of a disgruntled sector of Bath's workers. The lower town seemed a mixture of the respectable and the reprobate. He decided to tackle a couple in Avon Street, though a disguise would be required by the sound of it if he were to escape rough-handling. The Duke of York on the Quay also seemed a good bet for scurrilous news, he remembered it from Tobias's tale that morning. Surprisingly, the Crosskeys seemed to have a notorious reputation and it was just a few steps from where they were talking, across the High Street in the shadow of the Abbey. That would also do for a start.

"Thank you sir," said Nathaniel, finishing noting the venues in his pocketbook. "There is one other question I have. Where can a man find some fencing practice in the city?"

The barman drew himself up to his full and not inconsiderable height. "You sir, 'ave come to exactly the right place to find out about sword play! I am assumin' you have been in the military?"

"I have served with the army," said Nathaniel cautiously.

"Apart from regular annual trainin', quite regular a group from the North Somerset Yeoman Cavalry meet on Captain Wilkins' land at Twiverton. Real gentleman is Captain Wilkins, he owns a factory there and encourages any gentleman who owns a sword and is keen to keep their hand in. You never know with times as they are. The damned Frenchies a-winding up the Belgians, and the Poles hammer and tongs at the Ruskies. Not to mention the I-talians!" His moustache bristled vigorously, ready for anything. "You can catch the Captain here. Bath Yeomen use this inn as their headquarters for meetings."

"Thank you for the information," said Nathaniel shaking the barman's hand. "Most helpful."

"You are welcome," said the barman. "Frederick Tooson at your service sir."

As Nathaniel prepared to leave, Tobias loped out from the kitchen corridor at his usual half-run, bearing steaming plates of roast beef, which he delivered before doubling back to Nathaniel.

"Find a good 'orse sir? Do you need any more 'elp?"

"Not specifically young man. But I'll tell you what you can do." He lowered his voice conspiratorially, "Now keep this quiet, but I might spend more time in this town and I need to know if it's safe. See if you can find out where the people live in this city who tend to make up the mobs when there's trouble. Do you know what I mean? Who would be likely to cause the magistrates to read the Riot Act?"

"Oh yes sir. Oiy knows what y're after. Crowds that go a-breaking windows at election nights or go amok at the weekends when they're in drink?"

"Exactly."

"There 'aint no secret 'bout that Mr Parry. Over the river in the Holloway and the Dolemeads and all the lower town round Avon Street and Milk Street 'as most packs of troublemakers. H'immigrants and such as well. When mi ma was alive we lived down by there in Little Corn Street, Little 'Ell it's sometimes called sir. Oiy still knows some o' they lads there."

"Have a chat with them, see how things lie Tobias," said Nathaniel, pressing a half-crown into the boy's hand. "Lot of unrest at the present time with the next reform vote coming in a few days."

"To be honest sir, Oiy don't really know exac'ly what this new re-form vote is about. Oiy thought being as 'e's in charge and 'e wants reform, Lord Grey would tell all they parliament men what to do and they'd jump to it. But Oiy'll tell you if Oiy 'ear anything of int'rest."

"Tobias, can you read?"

"No sir, Oiy ain't never bin to school."

"Not even Sunday School to learn your letters?"

"Mother didn't hold with religion sir," muttered Tobias, his eyes slewing away in embarrassment. "Anyways, she said you had to have shoes and clean clothes to be let in, and that was not always so for me sir."

"But you know the reform of parliament will give the vote to more men who deserve it don't you?" Tobias encouraged him with a nod so Nathaniel continued. "It has to pass three readings and discussion and voting in the House of Commons, then the same in the House of Lords to become law. The Lords are the sticking point. They do not want more voters."

"Lord Grey's a lord though and he wants it."

"Yes but the majority of the peers are against him."

"Oiy can't read but Oiy can listen," said Tobias, inspired to raise his head. "Mr Turner in the Dragon reads from the new paper to everyone. The poor man's paper says all men 'oo work 'ard and are true Britons deserve to vote. It made you feel you could be something, you could be somebody." Suddenly his face lost its animation, "But them at the top never want others to 'ave anythin' do they sir? They're a-feared for their power."

Nathaniel looked closely at the boy, whip thin, the same patched shirt hidden by the over-sized scarlet waistcoat borrowed from the hook in the kitchen, the borrowed flapping boots, the same tired and grimy trousers reaching his mid-calf. Impulsively he drew a ten shilling note from his pocket.

"Tobias, buy some clean clothes and shoes. There is a dealer I saw in Walcot Street where you can get a second-hand suit complete." The boy looked uncertain. "I can't have you working for me looking like that," said Nathaniel sternly. "And Mrs Spence will bar you from reporting to me in my rooms if you haven't better boots to change to when you're not wearing Joseph's."

"Oiy'll be loike a new pin sir," said Tobias, his lip quivering. Before the tears fell he managed a lop-sided smile, then dodged back down the kitchen corridor.

### The Peterson Residence, Marlborough Buildings, Bath.

After lunch the customary dull quiet descended on the Peterson residence in Marlborough Buildings. Emma sat in the sitting-room sewing a new pelisse in lavender grey, killing time until her friend arrived, whilst the sound of her twin sisters enduring their French lesson wafted down from the schoolroom. Ginette and Maddy were identical, thirteen years of age and given to private jokes, explosive bursts of giggling and general tiresomeness. It was a relief for the whole household when they were brought to order by Mademoiselle Junot. Emma's elder sister Celia had been relatively good company until she made her great match with her farmer. Now short bouts of socialising with the lovebirds went an extremely long way.

Emma continued to run a neat seam down the shimmering fabric, mulling over the surprising events of the morning. Skimming over memories of the usual gossipy small talk that characterised sessions in the Pump Room with her parents, she let her mind return to the most interesting fact. Mr Nathaniel Parry was probably the nicest looking man she had ever seen. Not probably, definitely. The mere thought of him was enough to, what had Anna said that was so funny? Enough to "come over all unnecessary". That was it. She smiled at the memory, but was instantly downcast at the thought of the gruesome embarrassment that awaited her at next week's dinner. Her mother would sense her interest, sniff it out like a pointer and worry it to death, frightening off the outrageously handsome Mr Parry and humiliating her as she did so.

She stabbed her needle into the seam balefully, how ridiculous life was sometimes. Then she felt ashamed and conjured up visions of dead cholera victims piled in blackened, twisted stacks. Her thoughts veered away to drift back to last night's meeting and the impassioned pleas for change. What was the point? Were the mighty Lords in London listening? All would be clear in, she thought carefully, in two days. Just two days: then the vote. There could be MPs for the new industrial towns and cities and ordinary middle-class gentlemen voting in every constituency. It couldn't be wrong, surely? There were other things she was slowly coming to think were not wrong either. Some people spoke of women having a vote as well. No-one at the meeting did though. First things first, she could see that. But if this change went through, who knew where it would end? She breathed deeply, it seemed unimaginable but maybe one day she could take any job she chose, not just governessing like Anna who had little choice, but perhaps a man's job, like a solicitor, or a doctor. How dearly she would love to do that! She could have her own money. She would not be obliged to get married. But then she remembered Mr Parry.

She was interrupted by distant sounds at the front door and Anna's voice in the hall. At last, her visitor. Anna Grant's afternoon off was an oasis in the week. Her childhood friend and boon companion of the years in Portsmouth, when both their fathers were at sea, now worked in St James's Square. It was not five minutes walk away. They had taken to spending an hour or two together once a week, the only time she had Anna to herself now she was engaged to Mr Blake.

Emma rose to greet her friend, but her welcome froze on her lips.

"Anna what on earth is the matter!"

Tear-stained and pale, Anna fled to her side and grasped her hands.

"Oh Em we've got to help Henry. The most awful thing has happened."

"Sit down Anna. Give me your bonnet." Emma rang for the maid, pulled up another chair and held her friend's hands tightly.

She dispatched the maid as soon as she appeared. "Bring some tea Enid. Now, Anna, slowly, from the start."

"Henry and I did something wrong last night Em," agonised Anna, her plump face a picture of misery. "No, not too wrong," she said, catching Emma's stunned expression. "Well I didn't think it would be so. I asked him in to take a glass of wine with me at my employer's house. The family's out until later today. I was left to look after the baby and Henry and I thought it would be a good opportunity to have some time together alone." She screwed up her face in pain at the recollection. "Oh Em when they find out I'll lose my job."

"But why should they Anna?" said Emma briskly. "You are hardly going to confess."

"Henry is in Grove Street police station Emma. Last night money and bonds and papers disappeared from the office he shares with Mr Wilson and," she continued with a sob, "Oh Emma! Mr Wilson has been found murdered. He was found in the Avon and he had been stabbed. In the back!"

"Murdered! I'd heard he was missing. Mr Vere told us at the Pump Room this morning. Are you sure? Anyway what could possibly connect Henry with this?"

"He will not tell them where he was last night Em! But much worse. Oh so much worse. His rooms have been searched, all the employees have had searches, but some of the missing bonds have been found in his! There is no possible explanation. What can we do? What can we do? There was even talk he might have killed poor Mr Wilson! Never, never, Em. Not Henry!"

Anna gave herself up to sustained sobbing and succeeded in creating sufficient noise to summon Captain and Mrs Peterson from their housekeeping conference in the study.

"Good Lord, Anna," exclaimed the Captain. "What on earth is going on?"

"Sit down Oliver," said his wife, pouring the neglected tea. "Again Anna please."

Anna subsided. She sniffed and hiccoughed her way through the woeful tale for a second time.

"How do you know this?" enquired Captain Peterson.

"Mr Vere was so kind as to send a message. Henry had asked him to let me know and I have been to Grove Street. I have told him he must say where he was last night. He says he won't, but even if he does it won't be enough will it! It doesn't explain the bonds." Her lower lip began to tremble afresh and her eyes swam.

"Right young lady," said the Captain firmly, rising to pass her the discarded bonnet. "You will return with me now to Grove Street. We will speak with Henry together. We will then go to your employers' home to await their return. You will explain what you did last night and I will plead your cause. Let us simplify this toil, one step at a time."

"Father I will come with you," said Emma, glancing at the miserable Anna.

"Yes," said the Captain, not relishing the prospect of walking the streets of Bath alone with a weeping female. "Capital idea Em. We'll be back as soon as possible Lydia."

As they left, Mrs Peterson poured herself a cup of tea, reflecting on the fact that fiancés were not always an asset. It offered some comfort. She pondered how best to inform Mrs Grant of the misfortunes of her daughter, such a pity, and he had seemed such a nice young man.

## Arno's Tower, Arno's Vale, near Bristol.

As the Petersons escorted Anna Grant back into town, a private coach drawn by four perfectly matched greys made its way past Totterdown and the last tollhouse of the City of Bristol on the Bristol-Bath road. As it entered Arno's Vale it took a sharp right down a newly metalled road towards the woods. Amanda Ravenswood had made herself extremely comfortable, her feet in their shining patent slippers thrust up on the opposite seat under a fur rug and her hands folded inside the capacious muff which dangled from a silk cord round her neck. She wore a large hat with fur trim, rather excessive for early October, but it had to be done. It was the first of its kind, direct from Paris for the new season. Her mission that afternoon had been satisfactorily completed and it had included impressing Mrs Lottie Drake, the London matron, and also her husband who was apparently of exceeding importance, working directly for Lords Melbourne and Palmerston. To Amanda, used to the commanding and chilling presence of her husband Edwin, Drake had appeared banal and nondescript: not imposing enough to impress with his ferrety-foxy face, his smug complacency. She had made a normal lady's afternoon call on Mrs Drake and had also been rewarded by an introduction to the husband. She had plenty to relay to Edwin on her return home. He would undoubtedly make short work of Mr Drake when they met, whatever his purpose with him might be.

Amanda had the low cunning to realise that it would be of no advantage to her ever to pry into her husband's business. She lived in awe of his power, his rage and his subtle cruelty which marked every aspect of their lives together, even the most intimate. She shivered at the thought of him, even now after two years of marriage he was a fascinating stranger: perilous, potentially deadly. She smiled parting her red lips over strangely pointed, dazzling white eye-teeth. Not features to attract the average man. Edwin Ravenswood was far from average. It had been interesting to see that Lottie Drake was also far from a dull London matron. The Drakes had taken pleasant and fashionable rooms in Clifton. They were well situated in Cornwallis Crescent, on the slopes above Hotwells. After initial pleasantries, John Drake had taken them out for tea to the Bazaar. They had provided a head-turning performance for the provincial *beau monde*. Amanda and Lottie had sat opposite each other like two birds of paradise squaring up for battle: two brilliant egg-timers of style, broadest leg o' mutton sleeves competing, vast skirts billowing below and tiny waists between. She had had the better of it. Mr Drake was to dine with Edwin to discuss their business and she was to meet again with Lottie, who offered not only a clothes-horse duel in extravagance, but also the most deliciously spiteful conversation to be had in Bristol.

The coach pulled up in a flurry of gravel at the forbidding griffin-flanked entrance to Arno's Tower, the Ravenswood mansion. Footmen sprang to let down the steps and Amanda descended haughtily, dispensing her habitual cold glare to the servants, striding up the steps to the echoing stone hall. Her hat and muff were dropped into the hands of waiting maids and she made directly for Edwin's study.

"Mi'lady," the footman caught up with her and bowed low. "Mr Ravenswood is in the Oriental Salon, with his guests. They have only just returned from a tour of the wharf."

His guests from the Far East were clearly still in residence. Amanda glowered as she walked down the west-wing corridor to Edwin's *pièce de résistance*. Of course he had to show it off to them. To impress? To dare them to criticise? Edwin enjoyed living dangerously and she knew instinctively that the two guests were providing much dangerous enjoyment.

But how long would he live to savour it?

She knocked briskly and entered. The salon glowed in the low light of the afternoon sun. Here were Edwin's laquered screens, his paintings and ceramics, his carved dragons, his erotic prints, his weapons of exquisite workmanship and deadly intent. Suits of Eastern armour with winged shoulder-banners and barred masks, swords curved, long, short, sheathed and bare, winking evilly from wall hooks and cradled in ebony stands. Edwin sat on a high-backed chair facing the two men. Cornelius Lee, young and feline, sat as usual, quite still, serenely watchful. Last night's arrival, a Mr Kizhe, was older, more squat, more massively powerful with seamed skin and the eyes of a snake, mesmerising, poised to seize its prey.

"Well my dear," said Ravenswood, with an unspoken warning in his voice. "I'm sure you have plenty to do. I hope you enjoyed your afternoon with the Drakes."

"Yes Edwin. I think Mrs Drake and I had much in common and Mr Drake sends his compliments and looks forward to your meeting."

"You have much in common?" remarked Edwin unpleasantly. "How surprising. I look forward to meeting Mrs Drake at some point."

"Would you like dinner at six?" said Amanda, keen to leave the room which had quickly become oppressive: the suffocating, brooding silence generated by the two men made her deeply uneasy. Her usual barbed exchanges with Edwin were impossible: she did not dare.

"No my dear," said Ravenswood his dead eyes smiling in pleasure at her discomfiture. "Eight. We are going out to shoot."

After an hour bagging Ravenswood's ducks the three men made their way from the water meadow across the parkland immediately surrounding the house and approached the wood. They were accompanied by two of Ravenswood's men with a pair of gundogs, extra ammunition and guns. Edwin Ravenswood and Kizhe walked ahead and Cornelius Lee followed, still in black, unlike the others who had donned elaborate shooting gear. He was also different in that he carried a bow slung across his back and a quiver at his hip. As they reached the outskirts of the wood Ravenswood's henchmen were dispatched to the tree line to act as beaters if required, which also kept them out of earshot.

"I prefer to introduce serious business in the open air when away from home, and in alien territory," said Kizhe watching Ravenswood narrowly, then shifting his gaze to the henchmen who were dipping out of sight and into the trees. "So let us take the opportunity and be brief. The Count has been pleased with your success in keeping the supply lines of opium open to the major Chinese cities and with his continued support that side of the business should continue to prosper. The meeting with your Mr Drake will secure the collaboration with the British government and therefore with the indispensable British navy." He cocked his gun as he spoke and caught a hare as it bounded from cover, the dogs scattered as they vied to retrieve it. "What we need to develop is the new business line that has been developing so well under your guidance Mr Ravenswood. We will have a new triangular trade all of our own my friend." His deep-set eyes glinted at the studied reference to the foundation of Ravenswood's wealth. Edwin's family had grown fabulously rich on the bounty of the infamous triangular slave trade which shipped out of Bristol bound for Africa. British guns, gewgaws and cheap metal goods had been exchanged for African slaves, which were in turn sold on as human cargo to the steamy plantations of the New World to finance the purchase of rum, sugar, coffee and cotton. The abolition of the trade in 1807 had brought little in the way of protest from Bristol slavers, as by then Liverpool had long eclipsed them in the trade, and families like the Ravenswoods had invested wisely in West Indian estates and diversified into less controversial goods.

"It is fortunate indeed," continued Kizhe, "that the British authorities are so dependent on maintaining the opium sales to balance their trade with China. You British do so like your Chinese silks, your brocade," he laughed unpleasantly, "and of course your tea! Which you drink so barbarously. And you Mr Ravenswood, your Chinese art is so important to you, yes?"

Ravenswood stood silently, indulging his guest.

"However, it is the cargo we have found to replace the British pots and pans and mirrors that the Count's interest is now focused upon. We do not need pots and pans and mirrors Mr Ravenswood."

"Sir, there is no problem of supply. Let us speak plainly I have the greatest interest in increasing our supply of the females your customers need. I have two chosen for delivery to fulfil the requirement of the Count. They will sail with the *Blue Dragon* which is completing its refit and will be delivered to the usual harbour."

"The Count wants a continuous supply of children Mr Ravenswood. He has clients with particular tastes in East Africa and the Levant, as well as India and the Far East. I have an urgent order not just for the two ten year olds but also for two small English girls, fair and under three years of age. They stay on board when the next opium shipment is collected in India, then go overland from the Chinese port to be transferred to the customer on the Russian border. Do not fail." He paused, taking aim as a string of birds broke from the woods. The gun roared and a black shape and fluttering feathers cascaded from the sky: the dogs, slavering with flying tongues and pounding feet strove to outrun each other and catch it as it fell.

"I have a supplier Mr Kizhe," said Ravenswood calmly. "The needs of the Count's customers will be met."

"They need to be prepared before delivery," said Kizhe, fixing Ravenswood with a steely glare. "Ensure they are compliant."

"It will be done," said Ravenswood shortly and moved to the attack. "Bristol has a long and formidable record in the business of, shall we call it 'white slavery' Mr Kizhe. For over a thousand years we have been past masters in the trade. Do not think our African blackbirds were our only commodity."

As Kizhe raised his next gun in response to a bird rising from the edge of the wood, Cornelius Lee drew an arrow which he loosed to spear it, silently, before Kizhe had levelled his barrel.

"Ah, ha. The ancient arts are alive and well in Somerset I see," said Kizhe appreciatively.

"I like to keep in practice," said Cornelius.

"It is well that you are here Mr Lee," said Kizhe. "The Count particularly wanted a Chinese courier for the next voyage, not just to check prices with the opium broker but more particularly, to deliver the other goods. I hope I have made clear that it is of the utmost importance that the delivery is made. The customer is a valued colleague of the Count."

Suddenly, a shout went up from one of the men in the wood and a dark figure broke from the trees, encumbered with a bulging bag and trailing a snare, running haphazardly left and right, clearly with the aim of evading shots from the pursuing men and from the hill. Without pausing, Kizhe raised his gun and shot, the distant figure crumpled, fell and rolled to a stop, his bag bouncing down the slope, disgorging a pair of rabbits, bloodied, necks askew.

"Damned poacher," said Ravenswood laconically. "Good shot Mr Kizhe."

Cornelius was already sprinting down the rise to the twitching body. It had been a head shot, a lethal and brutal choice entirely typical of the marksman. The man lay in agonised death throes, half his face blown away to leave a morass of blood and bone, too shocked to cry out, too wounded to rise again. Cornelius knelt and slid his knife mercifully between the man's ribs. He rose and made his way back to the shooting party.

Ravenswood had already called his men over. "Take the body to the lime-pit and the game to the kitchens," he ordered. "Gentlemen, time to change for dinner."

Later that night, Cornelius Lee changed from his evening wear into a close fitting silk jacket with mandarin collar, wide ankle-length pants with room to move and flat black leather pumps, all black as pitch. He limbered up briefly: head, arms, legs, then slowly raised each leg in turn above his head, holding it, holding it, heel turned out to land a blow. He then stood straight and motionless for a heartbeat, turned a standing somersault, landed silent as a panther and slipped out of the window to bound over the balcony and disappear into the night. He stole away like a wraith over the park, vaulted the wall, ran lightly down the metalled drive and passed like a shadow towards the Bath Road. He skirted the grounds of Mount Pleasant, the copper baron's mansion, which until the building of Arno's Towers had been the grandest pile in the Vale. He trod softly in the darkness past the Neo-Gothic archway, past the black bulk of the stables and laundry, brutally built of copper slag and dubbed "The Devil's Cathedral".

"How little they seem to know of devilry here," he thought to himself. He recollected the cruel head shot delivered by Kizhe, the man's shabby clothes, the painful thinness of the flesh under his hand as he steadied the body for a quick release. If that is the Cathedral, Arno's Tower is the gilded throne of the Devil. He chose a narrow path through the undergrowth and sprinted on to his favourite spot: St Anne's-in-the-Wood. He had learned of the old holy well from his reading before he arrived in Bristol and it appealed to him. Long neglected and surrounded by derelict buildings, he had chosen it for his temple. He halted in a dell suffused with moonlight, silent but for the soft sounds of night creatures: the downy beat of owl's wings, the snuffling of hedgehogs, the distant bark of a fox. Here he began his regime, breathing deeply. He bowed his head in the silence of the night and prayed. The Taoism of his childhood had left Cornelius Lee with a residual spirituality. He took comfort through his prayers to the cleansing wind in the trees, to the shafts of moonlight, to the dappled shade and the black well by the ruined wall. The crumbling foundations were all that remained of the proud medieval shrine, visited by kings and made holy by the whispered prayers of the anchorites. He prayed to St Anne, wherever she was, whoever she might have been.

# Chapter 3

**7th October, 1831, Walcot Street, Bath.**

Martha Spence ran a tight ship. By first light she was a-bustle: fires were ablaze and water boiled briskly in the kitchen kettles. Old Tom had been rooted out of his malodorous alcove bed. His chamber-pot empty and rinsed, he had been cleansed, freshly wrapped and anchored into his chair for the day. Mary had been roused to scour the Johnty, soak his napkin and any offending bedding, and lay the breakfast table. The crackle of the fire; the clatter of pots, pans, purposeful feet and busy hands; squeaky chirrups from the Johnty; Mary's soft murmurings and Tom's squeezebox cackling floated up the stairs and through the cracks of the door to Nathaniel's room, and all were overlaid by a mighty blast from the Church Militant.

"Forth in Thy Name, O Lord, I go!" Martha belted out, mercilessly, from the garden.

"My daily labour to pursue.

Thee, only Thee resolved to know," she paused to rustle up more wooden pegs from an apron pocket and finish attaching the flapping wet washing to the line.

"In all I think, or speak, or do."

She smiled, eyes glinting and slightly breathless, watching the steam rise from the sheets and dissipate like a ghost at cockcrow into the cold steel-blue of the October morning. She breathed deeply and gave voice: "Thee may I set at my right hand!"

Nathaniel had taken cover at the first trump, sliding under the blankets for defence, whilst Caradoc had leapt to attention. He had one ear cocked, the other sagging below the vertical and had set up a deafening volley of yapping, energetically trampling his master in time to the fusillade. Driven from bed, Nathaniel pulled on the silk Damascus gown, ejected Caradoc to find the garden and made for the window to inspect the day. He dragged back the central curtain to expose the graceful arched Venetian window and the room flooded with light. Bright and sharp, the sun was rising over Bathwick, lighting up the cream stone of the terraces and the thousand chimneys, dispelling the mists which clung to the treetops. "Keats weather," said Nathaniel out loud. "Autumn and the sun conspiring: 'how to load and bless with fruit, the vines that round the thatch-eaves run.'"

"Are you awake, Mr Parry? Are you alone?" asked Mary, tapping hesitantly at the door. "I've brought your water and breakfast up, sir."

Nathaniel prepared himself for a day on the town, perhaps a canter along the river path, perhaps over the hills and far away. He was in high good humour and, having recovered from the rude awakening, felt inspired enough to attempt a tune as he dressed. He did not select Charles Wesley, but lined up uncompromisingly with his Welsh forbears and struck up his favourite version of *Men of Harlech*:

Da-di-da, di-da-de dadee. Da-da-da-da-da-da da-dee,"

even managing to break into full song for the finale:

"There I mid the swords thick gleaming, Cymru follow me!"

Sadly, this promised to be a day of limited sword-play. He made a mental note to take up the suggestions of Frederick Tooson, the barman in the Hart, for some practice with the local yeomanry. He took his swordstick from the corner, drew it and bent over to inspect it, which brought another vivid memory of his father and the hours they had spent pouring over his heavily wrought eastern blades. He swung the slender sword in a perfect circle, lunged once, then ten times more with the right hand. He swapped hands and lunged twenty times with his left before temporarily sheathing the blade. He took out one of his shabby disguises, a threadbare and rusty frock coat, and hung it on the door, man height. Standing still before it, he tamed his breathing, sank to a stance and in a moment drew the sword to lunge precisely.

Heart. Draw back, re-sheath. Throat. Draw back, re-sheath. Again, again, again. Reluctantly, he put it away and resigned himself to a day of comparative idleness. The only fixture was the dinner with Charles at Summerhill, his Sion Hill mansion. This left the morning and afternoon for recreation and a brief check through his report for Drake, with whom he would spend the next couple of days. In terms of location, Clifton offered some interest, though there was potential for tedium in the meetings with Drake himself. In any event, there was no deferment possible. The Lords' decision on the Bill had yet to be made, so his current surveillance assignment must bide its time. He dawdled over his bread and coffee, reflecting on yesterday's trawl through Bath's inns, taverns, beer-shops and markets. It was as well that he had taken the precaution of disguise for the lower town venues, or he would have attracted unwelcome attention. It had definitely been a makila day: the stout walking stick had proved extremely useful for forging a path through groups of toughs and fending off stray dogs. To his chagrin, Caradoc had been left behind. His appearance was too distinctive and his demeanour of yesterday afternoon had been too combative for covert operations.

Although one of the daintiest cities in England, Bath still offered plenty in the way of villainous alleys, middens, rooting pigs, dead horses, cats and dogs whose bloated bodies wallowed, grotesque and putrid on the lazy flow of the Avon. The river to the west of the old bridge had presented the appearance of an open sewer, with small birds picking their way across it dry-foot from one island of floating detritus to the next. The populace in the lower town had varied between the respectable and the dubiously employed, the desperate, the indigent poor and the clearly criminal. On the quays, raddled prostitutes lurked in door-ways by evil smelling courts. Coarse and blowsy in the harsh light of day, softening as the gaslights were lit and night fell, they turned on their wily charms:

"Buy me a glass o' beer sir?"

Thin waif-like girls, still comely but with old faces, had their feral lines wiped by the dark. Chameleon-like they turned into the "nightingales" and "nymphs" of the lower town, ready to part eager men from their purses. So much, so predictable, he had heard nothing to alarm the powers in London. Enthusiasm for reform was general and was even expressed with some vim in the local Tory newspaper *The Bath Chronicle*, which he had read whilst consuming an unusually fine joint of roast lamb in the Full Moon, the haunt of men of commerce by the river. Support for the Whig government, loyal addresses to the King and an atmosphere of excited anticipation seemed to characterise the whole city: for now.

He made his way to the kitchen, planning to round up Caradoc and bid good day to his hosts before taking a turn on the Parades. That was, after all, what one was meant to do in Bath with the famed season poised to take off. He would stroll in the rarefied air of the upper town and watch the world go by, as it in turn watched him. There had been some pretty sights already. As he jogged down the stairs his mind wandered over his new acquaintances of eligible age: the mild, lovely and work-worn Mary, the earnest Miss Peterson turned out like the Empress Josephine in her house-coat, the ravishing Mrs Vere, the bunch of beauties in the Pump Room, especially the bold almond-faced vixen hanging on the arm of the Irishman. She had looked particularly fine. It was good to have time to think of such things.

"Good day Mr Spence," he said, loudly and slowly as he thrust his head round the door. "Is Mrs Spence here? I will bid her good day before I leave."

Tom looked up from his rug cocoon.

"Ha ha! Come ye over young man! Come over and take a seat along o' me for five minutes." He beckoned erratically. Nathaniel hesitated, then pulled up a chair, preparing to do his duty.

"What tales young man? What has Bath brought thee so far?"

"I spent time in the Pump Room yesterday. A very fine building sir."

"Not all day ye didn't! What else?" demanded Tom, hungry for news, fixing his indeterminate and watery gaze in the vicinity of Nathaniel's shoulder, where the white light of the morning sun shone from the windowpanes and glossed the white wall behind him to a nimbus of light.

Good naturedly, Nathaniel allowed Tom the sport of extracting information from him whilst he manufactured the persona of a well-to-do London gentleman unused to these parts, a martyr to recreation and novelty, anxious as to the likelihood of riot and revolt in these unsettled times. He felt he pulled it off rather well. Tom grew confidential.

"Don't ye be a worritin' y'self sir," he said dismissively. "When great Lords like Grey and Russell are a-wantin' reform, and the ordinary folk are a-wantin' it, and the middlin' folk are a-wantin' it. They's likely to get it! If it be worth 'aving," he muttered, then shot his head out, tortoise-like, and fixed Nathaniel with a glare in the very image of Coleridge's Ancient Mariner. Nathaniel struggled, but failed, to keep a straight face and block the lines bubbling up in his memory: "He holds him with his glittering eye …..The Mariner hath his will…"

Tom continued: "You were but a child in '15 when the people were a-cryin' out for reform. Then it were different. All the Lords were agin' it and reformers were grievously beaten down. Why, Mr Hunt 'imself spoke 'ere in '17. Oiy 'eard 'im. Though it were difficult to get near for the damned cavalry. Dragoons packed round 'im tight as peas in a pod. All they wild talkers like Richard Carlile and they crazed Spenceans, them re-publicans, they got government to take fright they did. With their ve-hement talk and a-flyin' o' the Frenchey flag and a-wearin' they damned red caps. It frightened grand folk." He paused to gather a rasping breath, "Spenceans be all dead now young sir. Wildest of our re-formers now claims they just wants votes for £10 men. £10 bi'God!"

Nathaniel smiled encouragingly, watching, fascinated, as Tom seemed to sink deeper into the wreckage of his long life. Bizarrely, the claw-like hands which emerged from the rug were mechanically knitting a blanket square, the clacking needles marked time and provided a semblance of animation as he struggled to marshal his memory. "When Oiy were strong and workin', before Oiy went to sea, most men 'ad a copy of Tom Paine, we thought 'e talked sense. *Common Sense* he wrote mind! Wrote it for the Yankees he did. And *The Rights of Man*! Lord we did think we knew the road. But then…but then…". Tom shook his head and screwed up his aged features to re-order his thoughts. His face became a mask of taut wrinkled lines as he inwardly struggled to banish the ghouls swirling to the surface of memory: a fiendish mask of Robespierre, the shadow of the guillotine's blade, headless corpses, the shells of men returning from interminable war. "They Frenchies did for reform they did," he growled. "Now we think we 'ave another chance." He gave a wheezy chuckle which collapsed into hacking, tumultuous coughing.

"This is not France, Mr Spence. It will be different this time," said Nathaniel, bending to retrieve the ball of wool as it rolled across the spotless scrubbed floorboards, to snatch it from possible destruction in the jaws of Caradoc who had returned to lounge by the fire, and also from the porridge smeared fist of the Johnty, who was in his customary position, wobbling by Tom's feet with his sturdy legs thrust out before him. "The Bill is through the Commons with a strong Whig majority. This has never happened before. It could be the start of slow and peaceful change which will in the end bring the suffrage to all men." He inspected Tom closely and felt oddly ashamed as he delivered the platitudes to the old man. Mrs Spence had said Old Tom was over ninety years old. For him the firebrands of the 1790s were wild young men and those days of antique horror seemed more real than 1831.

"Reform brings riots and rebellions which loose wild beasts in men," said the old man sonorously. "Critters you never knew existed in the quiet days. 'Twas ever the same! Mi' old grandf'er told me tales. He was alive in old Noll Cromwell's day! Noll 'e knew the danger of they Levellers and he finished them. But we must 'ave reform. No fear of the wild beasts should stop us."

He sighed and smiled wanly: "'Ave ye heard of the Lollards young man? Do'ee know of they far off days when the poor English all rose up and they said: "When Adam delved and Eve span who was then the gentleman?" Well now we do 'ave gentry, I thinks us all should 'ave a chance to be gentrified. But us 'aven't. They gentry is all going to get the vote, as is the shopkeepers, the middle folk. What chance will the lower sort of people 'ave then to improve they selves? Do ye think the Whigs 'ave forgotten the mistake they made in cheerin' they Frenchies in '89? They is twice shy now sir. Twice shy. They will keep down the common man."

Nathaniel listened in silence, confronting an image of his own early youth, his devoted love for the libertarian Romantics which lingered still. But mad Shelley had drowned and dashing Lord Byron in his Albanian rig had been knocked out by disease as soon as he raised his head for Greek independence. They lived for reform, for change, poetical hearts on their sleeves for the common man. Did they really know what wild beasts their dreams unleashed? He thought of Shelley, standing by the scaffold as the Pentrich conspirators dangled in '17. Shelley famously had no pity for the ringleader, Jeremiah Brandreth, incited by a government spy to raise the Midlands in the name of the people. Shelley, recalled Nathaniel, had written primly that he had no sympathy for Brandreth, as he had killed a man. Then off went Percy with his Mary, off to Italy to sail to his reckless death, so sure he could manage the rising wind. But he couldn't.

A rapid knocking roused them from their thoughts and summoned Martha to the front door from her washing. She came into the kitchen, still rubbing her hands dry on her apron. "Gentleman to see you Mr Parry. I've shown him into the parlour." She shot a suspicious glance at Tom, but he had subsided into his rug and was knitting peacefully.

Nathaniel followed Martha into the front room, which was sepulchrally cold after the warmth of the kitchen. Standing in front of the window, arms behind his back, legs astride, as if in full command of the fore-deck, was Captain Peterson.

"Sir! Good morning to you. How may I be of service?" said Nathaniel smoothly, though his spirits were marginally dampened as he suspected that the worthy Captain had been dispatched by his wife to entrap him into agreeing to an early dinner rendezvous, chez Peterson.

"Mr Parry, I am sorry to disturb you, but I have come to request your help." Captain Peterson swayed back and forth, uncomfortable in the confines of the small room and with the urgency of his errand. "This is not on my own account, but for the sake of two young persons embroiled, I am sorry to say, in a criminal investigation. These two are related to old comrades of mine, both known to your father. Henry Blake is nephew to Commander Tomlinson and Miss Anna Grant's late father also served with me. To be blunt, you know of criminal matters and of London ways of detection. I fear a gross miscarriage of justice could occur. Nay, is occurring! I have little faith in the powers of the local authorities and desire to lay the facts before you to learn your opinion."

"Do sit down sir. I am at your disposal."

The grim discovery of the stab wound in Roderick Wilson's back, the investigation of Henry Blake, the discovery of the bank's property in his rooms and his subsequent incarceration pending trial were communicated to Nathaniel swiftly and sparely.

"Blake was a young fool, Mr Parry. He spent the evening in question with his fiancée, Miss Anna Grant, at her place of employment, in the absence of her employers or any other chaperone, and was loathe to admit as much when questioned. This has been rectified." Oliver Peterson frowned at the memory of the strained interview at the residence in St James's Square. "Rumours of his connections with the late Mr Wilson and gaming establishments have surfaced. Fanciful theories have emerged of either some joint nefarious scheme of robbery cooked up between Wilson and young Blake which ended in murderous dispute, or that Blake chose to intercept Wilson after he had committed a crime and made off with the proceeds." Captain Peterson's kindly face puckered with lines of anxiety. "Miss Grant, who is a close friend of my daughter, came to our home with this sorry tale and sought her advice. I had to intervene! Our connection is close sir. Since the death of her poor father I see myself as in some respect *in loco parentis*. Her mother remains in Portsmouth and her position here was taken partly as I might keep an eye on her. I am fond of both of them Mr Parry and am convinced of Henry's innocence. Could you possibly review the case? Perhaps you might see guilt where biased eyes such as ours cannot, or more hopefully, see a way to exonerate the boy? I have already spoken with Mr Vere the proprietor of the New Bank. He fully supports the idea of my request and insists that your fees and any expenses will be paid in full by the bank."

Nathaniel mentally shelved his plans for the day.

"Not my usual type of enquiry sir, but it will be a pleasure to offer whatever help I can. As you must know, my father held you and your officers in the highest regard. I know what he would have done in my place."

They shook hands and made some preliminary plans. Captain Peterson offered to escort Nathaniel to the Paragon to meet with the widow Wilson. They had some social acquaintance through the Captain's dealings with the New Bank, where he was poised to make considerable further investment in the near future. This might ease a difficult interview. Nathaniel opted to visit the unfortunate Henry Blake at Grove Street police station alone, catching him that afternoon before his inevitable removal to Shepton Mallet Gaol. Having been introduced to Mr Vere, he could deliver his card to the Vere residence in Lansdown Crescent later that day, and if possible meet with him, before the dinner engagement with Charles.

They made good progress down Walcot Street towards the centre of the city, Caradoc loping behind, and took a sharp right turn up a narrow run of stone steps

63

connecting the street with the main road to London, along which the houses of the Paragon were ranged. The Wilson residence was part of that impeccable Palladian terrace and easily found.

"Caradoc, guard duty sir!" commanded Nathaniel as he pulled the doorbell.

A pallid maid answered the door and ushered the two men into a restrained and elegant drawing-room. Paintings of Indian landscapes dominated the walls, gold framed but not lavishly embellished, and the fire was well shielded by a screen discreetly decorated with dried flower arrangements beneath glass. The piano was closed and a clock ticked, loudly, on the mantelpiece. Mrs Janie Wilson had once had a fragile, desiccated attraction, which had withered under the duress of life with her husband. The face turned up to them in weary greeting was sallow with a peevish mouth. It was as if the life had been slowly dried out of her, like the captive flowers on the fire-screen. She sat ramrod straight in a black gown, wrapped in a once exotic but now faded fringed shawl with worn tassels, which she ceaselessly wound around her dry fingers. They were seated and partaking of morning coffee before the subject of the murder was broached.

"So, Mrs Wilson," the Captain began, "Mr Parry, who is well versed in matters of investigation and has worked for the government in London and abroad, has consented to investigate the untimely demise of your husband. Mr Vere has engaged him officially."

"Abroad you say? Have you been to India Mr Parry?" she said. "Happy days I spent there as a child, and as a young woman before my marriage."

"I have not had that pleasure as yet madam."

She pointed listlessly at a large painting of a grand mansion in the English style, surrounded by palms. "My home sir. And those portraits, my dear parents. I will be candid with you sir. My late husband Roderick Wilson squandered my dowry and was frequently away from home indulging his penchant for gaming. I was not wholly surprised to learn that he had met with a misfortune, in the lowest part of the town. No doubt you noticed the lack of a footman in this establishment?" her voice quavered and almost disappeared. "The shame of it."

"So Madam, you are able to bear up at this time of your loss with," Nathaniel paused, inspecting the tight little face, the hard stare, "with equanimity?"

Could she possibly have the contacts and determination to have had him murdered?

"Our family life has not been as happy as I would have wished Mr Parry," she said coldly. "My husband had a mistress, a French doxy. I do not wish to discuss that further. Forgive me."

"Do you suspect that your late husband was involved with dangerous characters madam? Or that those he mixed with might have involved him in criminal activity?" enquired Captain Peterson gently.

"He was an attractive man Captain, he made friends easily and enjoyed the pleasures of life. I really could not say where his conscience would have drawn a line. However, I have seen gaming slips and receipts from all the principal gaming establishments in the town scattered in his dressing room. Mr Bedford's Rooms in Milsom Street were a favorite haunt of Roderick's, but so were Lock's and Hall's."

Nathaniel rose to leave: "Mrs Wilson I would appreciate the opportunity to see Mr Wilson's room if I may and to make some other enquiries here in your house, perhaps I may speak with your servants?"

"Not today Mr Parry. I am awaiting instructions from the magistrate concerning searches by the local police. You may do so later. Also, you are welcome to attend the funeral. It will be at the Abbey on the 11th of this month and afterwards, here."

Mrs Wilson drew the interview to a close and Nathaniel and Captain Peterson found themselves returned to the pavement.

"Austere woman Mr Parry," said the Captain ruefully, "evenings round the fire would have been long for Wilson. Dashed long. Not excusin' the blighter, but, well, dashed long."

Nathaniel smiled, despite his annoyance at losing the opportunity to search Wilson's house. "Damned bad luck I'm in Bristol for a couple of days. Trail will be cold here. However, I will bid you good day sir. This afternoon I will see young Blake and Mr Vere as we discussed and I'll see what I can suggest." He whistled up Caradoc, who had been inspecting the railed area leading to the Wilson's kitchen, and strode off towards Milsom Street.

By early afternoon Nathaniel was stationed at his usual seat in the Hart. The visit to Grove Street police station had proved to be precisely as Captain Peterson had predicted. A woebegone Henry Blake had been by turns despairing, indignant and desperate, pleading for any assistance possible if it were to save his neck. He appeared to be a callow youth, devoted to Anna Grant, a young woman who was also a featherhead of the first order to think she could entertain a young man in her employer's home and successfully evade detection. It appeared that there had been at least three other servants at home that evening who had spied on the governess's assignation and could vouch for the presence of her fiancé. Henry Blake was unable to explain the appearance of the incriminating bonds, cash and papers at his rooms and he claimed he was a model citizen with few outstanding debts, which, Nathaniel decided, he could verify at least to some extent. However, the depth and breadth of

Blake's greed would also need to be known to ascertain whether he was capable of committing the desperate deeds. Nathaniel prodded his dish of West Country faggots with a moody fork. They were rapidly becoming as cold as Wilson's trail and he was pleased to be distracted by a familiar voice.

"Mr Parry, Oiy gat somethin' to tell you!"

The accents of Tobias Caudle were instantly recognisable, and as Nathaniel turned to greet him he was pleasantly surprised to see that the ten shillings had been wisely invested. Polished boots, gaiters and brown trousers were topped off by a clean white shirt, neckcloth and striped waistcoat. There were also signs of him having had his head under the pump to complete the transformation.

"My word young man!" exclaimed Nathaniel whistling appreciatively. "Smart as paint!"

Tobias glowed with pride. "Oiy got two shirts now sir. Mary said she'll wash 'em for me if Oiy'll keep mi face clean."

"Well, what news you young popinjay!"

"Well," said Tobias sidling closer, "Oiy did speak to the boys in Little 'Ell like you asked. Two of 'em 'eard a racket on the night that gentleman went in the river. Lot of runnin' an' roarin' an' that. They was up in a loft lookin' down on the Quay and saw two hefty lookin' men handlin' a body down to the river. One did 'ave a bleedin' face. They passed under a lamp sir and could be seen clear. And that's not half of it," he added clandestinely, "mi friend Tom was in the Duke of York an' 'eard talk of a break-in at the leather-dressers in Hucklebridge Court that same night. The workbench was all over blood sir! Leatherman wouldn't tell no police or watch though, a-course."

"Well done Tobias," said Nathaniel, reflecting that Henry Blake could in no way be described as "hefty".

"Tobias!" bawled the barman. "Plates a-waiting, front parlour. Double-up, double-up!" Nathaniel slipped a sixpence into Tobias's hand as the boy took off and was about to whistle up Caradoc when he was hailed by the barman Tooson.

"Mr Parry! Are you still after some fencing practice sir?"

"I most certainly am!" said Nathaniel.

"If you'll step along to the coffee room you'll find Captain Wilkins himself. He's meeting with some of his officers but I asked him if he would break off to talk with you and he said he would."

Frederick Tooson's expectant gaze was unmistakable. Nathaniel pressed a shilling into his hand and made his way to the coffee room, ducking the beams as he went.

In the comfortable saloon, Captain Wilkins was sitting at a private table tucked into the corner, talking earnestly with two men. All three had the familiar military bearing, were sharply dressed and purposeful, the coffee remained untouched.

"Captain Wilkins? Sir, may I introduce myself. I am Nathaniel Parry, a visitor staying locally for a few weeks. The barman suggested you had been kind enough to offer a few moments of your time to discuss fencing training. Though I suspect it is not entirely convenient now?"

Captain Wilkins looked up, though clearly privileged and blessed with a massive frame, he was lean and had an exhausted air about him. Nathaniel remembered he was a substantial mill-owner, reputedly employing over a thousand operatives, men, women and children, and treating them all with unusual patronage. Such philanthropy would have been dispensed at substantial personal cost, creating a bed of nails for his profits in the trade depression.

"Do sit down and join us Mr Parry, Bath is not such a large city that I had not heard of you. Dr Charles Parry is an acquaintance of mine and I know he was looking forward to your arrival. I am afraid my fellow officers and I have urgent business but can certainly spare a few moments. May I introduce Mr Cruttwell and Mr Fairfield. We use this hotel as our headquarters for the Bath Troop of the North Somerset Yeomanry and have some tactics to discuss." Nathaniel warmed to this brusque man, his searching eyes, his controlled, elegant bearing.

"Apart from occasional training with the men, a few of us have taken to fencing once a month privately at the tennis court in Morford Street. The 10th falls next Monday and it's our next meeting. If you come there at five o'clock in the afternoon we will be delighted to see you. You will bring your own weapon I take it?"

"I will be delighted to do so," said Nathaniel enthusiastically. "If you don't mind I'll bring this." Lifting his stick, he drew the concealed blade a hand's breadth from the hilt and the quillons sprang out to form a slender guard. The metal blade gleamed wickedly even in the dark corner, the burnished cutting edge curiously patterned and with a cold blue sheen.

"Be it on your own head to fence with such a flimsy weapon," said Fairfield dourly.

"But that's a rare edge you have there," said Mr Cruttwell, leaning over to catch another glance as Nathaniel slid the blade away. "I haven't seen such strange markings before."

"It isn't English," said Nathaniel tersely, cutting the enquiry short. "I'm sorry to have interrupted your planning gentlemen."

Captain Wilkins smiled wearily. "Contingencies sir, contingencies. The Lords' response to the Bill is imminent and they have a Tory majority. We need to be ready."

"Do you expect trouble here?"

The Captain looked grimly at Nathaniel, "We have no idea what to expect sir. But the blades are sharpened."

Nathaniel rose. "I bid you good-day gentlemen. Until next Monday then." After brief bows were exchanged Nathaniel made his way out.

Caradoc spotted him, pausing only long enough to dispatch the abandoned faggots, and padded out at his heels. They made their way to Mrs Spence's *via* the livery in Pulteney Mews where Nathaniel hired a post-chaise for the trip to Bristol, haggled over the pair of greys and then detoured round Sydney Gardens to take the air before making their way home to Walcot Street. Charles had invited him to dine at an unfashionably early hour, so a late afternoon visit to the Vere residence *en route* to Sion Hill would fit nicely. Nathaniel took care over his appearance, remembering the lingering touch of the beautiful Mrs Vere's fingers on his hand at the Guildhall that first night. She was a susceptible and pretty woman, and it never did any harm to make an ally. He laughed to himself as he ran a brush through his unruly hair, dodging his head left and right, trying to find a part of the mirror free from the leprous spotting of age. No doubt continual provision of the good life would keep the pretty filly trotting by the side of Raphael Vere. Sixtyish and running very slightly to fat, Vere was comfortable, indulged and self-satisfied, no doubt all of a dither at the scandal rocking his bank and willing to shower money on anyone likely to make it go away. He tied his turquoise neckcloth in his favoured Byronic draped knot, chose the turquoise, green and white silk waistcoat, keeping the trousers and coat to black. Cloak, top-hat and for the upper town, the swordstick: he was ready.

The walk to the top of Walcot followed by the climb up Guinea Lane was a sharp pull, with even Caradoc slowing to a walk. They issued forth onto Lansdown and soon turned to take a breather. The view had grown to a grand vista. As always, far away above the Abbey Tower and lining the horizon, were the green woods. Below that forest rim, the Bath stone of the sinuous parades and terraces now glowed honey-warm in the late sun. His eyes, scanning the distant trees, stopped to admire the Prior Park mansion which stood out amongst the green of Widcombe, pedimented and columned, its landscaped gardens rolling down the slopes. He turned abruptly on his heel and continued the climb, soon rounding the bend to Lansdown Crescent and following its curve to the Vere residence. He jangled the bell-pull and turned to view Palmer's perfect pastoral vision. There in the midst of the urban crescent was nature. Sheep grazed by the railings and down the steep drop of rough grass to the descending curtains of terraces. At once more domestic and graceful than the Royal Crescent, Nathaniel reflected firstly that Vere had done extremely well for himself, and secondly that he could live there himself with very great pleasure indeed.

"Good afternoon sir." A powdered footman opened the door and unbent himself just sufficiently to usher Nathaniel into a spacious hall with a black and white chequered marble floor and white classical statues standing sentinel along the walls. The curving stairway wound its way up and ahead stretched a long, echoing corridor.

"Mr Parry! Upon my word I am delighted to see you!" Raphael Vere appeared at the first landing and accosted Nathaniel from there. "Bring him up, Tanner. Drawing room."

"Could my dog go to the garden Mr Vere?"

"Oh bring him up! Do!" Tilly Vere had joined her husband, her eyes shining in delighted welcome. "He can join us can't he, Raph? Tanner bring tea."

They settled in a bright pink and green room on the front of the house, with a sumptuous view, batteries of beeswax candles already lit and a fire in the hearth. A harp, pianoforte and violin were in evidence, but no sheet music could be seen. Tilly busied herself initially with dispensing the tea and feeding the rapacious and shameless Caradoc with pastries. He lounged, most lordly, by her feet and occupied her whilst Vere unburdened himself, at great length, of his miseries.

"So you see Mr Parry, it is imperative that justice is served. I am saddened by the implication that two of my employees might have been involved in some desperate scheme to rob the bank but I will not shrink from the publicity. Blake must pay the ultimate penalty." In the over-heated room he was sweating and wiped his brow. "Such a blow to think that Wilson would deceive me. I had tried to help him as you know Mr Parry but he was sinking ever deeper into the mire of debt. His addiction to gaming had run out of control. I hope Captain Peterson has informed you that your expenses will be met if you could spare the time to look over this matter. It would be a comfort to know that an experienced investigator was involved." Raphael Vere smiled encouragingly.

"Oh yes Mr Parry," said Tilly Vere. "Such a comfort to know you are helping us. But first, do tell us of the work you have done in London. We hear that you have travelled for the government all over Britain and abroad. It sounds so exciting doesn't it Raphie?" She gazed enraptured, turning her shining blue eyes on him and beaming. The low autumn sun lit her cascade of blonde curls and glittered on the pink diamonds of her jewellery. Chosen to match the upholstery, thought Nathaniel idly but appreciatively. She did not seem to require an immediate answer to her question, but continued to enlarge on the excitements of travel. She moved closer, a rustle of silk as she leaned towards him, enabling Nathaniel to be fully aware of her: her skin, creamy and flawless, the rise and fall of her breasts, her scent, intoxicating and honey-sweet. She was a rare beauty, lusciously vibrant: expensively and fashionably dressed as she had been when he first saw her at the Guildhall. For the afternoon she played the Van Dyke courtesan: vast slashed sleeves, a neckline plunging precipitously, edged in foaming lace.

He suddenly became aware that she had stopped talking and expected an answer. He struggled to haul his thoughts back on track.

"Yes Mrs Vere, travel is a great adventure. It has been a privilege to work in Paris and elsewhere in Europe. Though the travel was not for pleasure alone, wars and revolution do bring their discomforts. I have also been to America, where I have some interests."

A distant peal on the doorbell intervened and presently Nathaniel was surprised to find Mrs Janie Wilson ushered in to join them. The widow was duly greeted, seated and furnished with tea and pastries.

"Mrs Wilson has kindly consented to dine with us this evening and we hope she will stay until tomorrow," said Tilly, stroking Mrs Wilson's arm sympathetically. "So important to be looked after at this terrible time."

Janie Wilson smiled tartly, delighted that the invitation could be accepted on the basis that she was alone and required "looking after", though the idea of the vacuous Tilly caring for her was ludicrous. She wrapped herself more tightly in her shawl, despite the heat of the room and edged away from the attentions of Tilly.

"Madam," said Nathaniel. "I was disappointed not to be able to investigate at your home this morning. A sight of Mr Wilson's room and belongings will materially assist my enquiries," he paused as her frown deepened.

"Oh I'm sure there is plenty time for that Mr Parry," said Vere quickly. "You were to allow the police in weren't you Mrs Wilson, then Mr Parry could perhaps visit?"

"Yes, we had already agreed that," she said pettishly.

"But if Mr Parry knows all about investigating couldn't he go now whilst Mrs Wilson is resting here? The police will not be searching now will they?" said Tilly.

"Mathilda," said Vere warningly, "I suggest that you do not attempt to direct operations. Mrs Wilson and Mr Parry have come to an agreement." Nathaniel was interested to see how swiftly the pose of doting husband dissolved. Vere switched in an instant from swain to elderly father, or even, an unpleasant speculation,

70

grandfather. How old had Tilly been when they married?

"Yes indeed," said Nathaniel, glancing at the clock on the mantelpiece. "And if you will excuse me I have an engagement and should take my leave. Thank you for seeing me. I will be in Bristol for two days but will resume my enquiries when I return."

Nathaniel left the trio to their early dinner and struck off up the hill at a lively pace, looking forward to his rendezvous with Charles.

"What do you make of that then Caradoc?" he said as they rustled through the leaves. Caradoc, unconcerned, barely glanced behind him, over-full with pastries and over-heated, he had enjoyed the attention, felt he had played his part, but was pleased to be out. Nathaniel strode on in silence, not entirely sure what he made of it either, and willingly shelved the matter for what should turn out to be a rather pleasant evening of family gossip and a little business in the form of taking the political pulse of a select group of Bath society.

## The Shadwell's Residence, Green Park Buildings West, Bath.

Whilst Nathaniel and the gentlemen round Charles's table at Summerhill House settled into their third bottle of claret and the moon rose white over a low bruise of purple clouds, Rosie Shadwell closed and locked the door of her front parlour in Green Park West and took a strongbox from a cupboard by the chimney breast. With a lithe, cat-like grace she swung the heavy box onto the table and sat down to work. Deftly she unlocked it and began to count the wads of notes and slithering mounds of sovereigns, dividing them into a dozen small piles, four larger ones, and two others of far greater size. Her coppery hair caught the light from the candles and the bright fire, her green ear-rings rattled as she worked and her eyes shone as they always did when she was counting the week's takings.

The room was well appointed, the paintings, sensual and erotic, were in ornate gold frames, the furnishings were opulent, decadent. Madam Shadwell, tightly corseted and casually robed in emerald silk took out a tiny pair of gold spectacles and a notebook. She began to enter the sums in her neat, practised hand, and from the upper rooms, a faint chorus of sounds could just be heard. From the drawing room above her came a lazy buzz of chatter, three female voices, the clink of tea cups and snatches of a tune played idly on the pianoforte. Higher, from one front bedroom came the crack of Mitzi's whip, applied to good effect judging by the groans of pleasure extracted from a plump, white customer trussed naked at her feet. Next door the sounds were fainter still, restricted by the silken gag over the mouth of a hirsute customer shackled to the bed, the rhythmic creak dictated by the spirited

71

attentions of Letty. Volcanic wrestling instigated more conventionally by Clari brought a more erratic cacophony of crashes and bangs from her apartment. The final and higher pitched thread of sound came from the attics. One room was decorated as it always had been, as a nursery. There a customer dangled a girl of thirteen on his knee whilst he sang nursery rhymes in a warbling falsetto. He pawed her restlessly whilst she gazed mutely forward, counting the stripes on the wallpaper.

A soft knock on the front door. Rosie carefully placed her spectacles and pen on the table, moved swiftly to the door, unlocked, then locked it behind her and slipped the key on its long chain into her pocket. Her face assumed a fixed smile, she smoothed her robe over her hips, pulled the neckline lower and opened the door. A sedan chair was quietly spirited into the hall for the customer to emerge, entirely discreetly, in the very confines of this most orderly of disorderly houses.

"Good evening sir. What a pleasure it is to see you again, Josephine has been asking after you and is so excited you have made time to visit us this evening."

If the customer had not been cosseted by Rosie, relieved of his coat, ushered upstairs to meet the girls and plied with drink, he might have wandered down the corridor, out to the back door and down the steps into the cold garden. Down the shadowed path, by the rose bushes and arbours, past benches and dark trees he would at length have reached a two storey building at the rear of the property. This was a coach house which still housed a coach, horses, stable boys and Shadwell's two guards, who could be found standing at the foot of the steps holding bludgeons. On the upper floor was Joshua Shadwell's office, and in that apartment the owner was engaged in conversation with two men. They had upon them the smell of the streets, though their garments were not poor. They sat facing Joshua across his desk, both wary, but one more truculent than the other and sporting a deep, partially healed cut down one side of his face. Joshua himself, as was his wont, had his top drawer open as he spoke, displaying his pair of pistols, ready primed. He was dressed, as usual for business, in sober grey, with immaculate white linen and neckcloth and midnight blue satin waistcoat.

"You have partly redeemed yourselves after the unfortunate skewering of the suicide," he said darkly, his brown eyes glinting dangerously under his heavy brows. "As you know your original fee was reduced to three-quarters of that agreed because of the unfortunate consequences. The placing of the goods in the Kingsmead rooms was done well, most fitting. But placing tackle in rooms when you already have the key provided by me, the obliging landlord, does not exactly make you bloody master criminals. Now does it?"

Joshua was always at his most dangerous when he appeared reasonable.

Mordecai and Declan took care not to meet his eye.

"To earn the missing one quarter you had hoped for, my client needs you to be busy tonight. You will go to the Paragon and enter on the quiet," he passed a small piece of paper with a number written on it. "This house. No bloody other. Do a thorough search for papers referring to any business affairs in Bristol or anything looking business-like that you don't understand. Take whatever else you want in the way of general burglary which is what this is meant to be. Come back here to exchange said goods for payment. Let the dust settle. Make it mid-week."

"Will it be an empty house you're a-sending us to then Joshua?" said Declan, anxious, his beady eyes narrowed.

"It is empty tonight, guaranteed." Joshua smiled unpleasantly. "Now about our other business, where the real money lies."

Mordecai sat up straighter, licking his lips. "What've we got on the next sailing?" his voice was harsh, his teeth exposed, yellowed and sharp.

"We have a small but important cargo for a special customer in the Far East. There will be two kids under three years and two of about ten years old to go in your barge as usual to Parker's Wharf on Redcliffe Back. Your contact is Eli Trevellis who is the captain of the *Blue Dragon*. You will pass on the goods tomorrow."

"Where exactly are they now?" asked Declan.

"The two older ones are in the Avon Street stew, drugged and quiet. The others will be purchased tomorrow and moved directly. The deal's going through with their mother, there's no father. Mother's got nine other brats and can't make enough on any game to keep 'em without charity, and anyway, she has no likin' to being known by the authorities. She needs more money for herself and her habits."

"We want no trouble with 'em on the barge," said Mordecai glowering. "Last lot needed more dosing before we made Bristol and we had to knock 'em out."

"Don't you ever mark 'em Mordecai," threatened Joshua, pointing a finger accusingly, "or it will be the last mark you make so help me God."

Mordecai shifted restlessly in his seat, fingers itching to seize Shadwell by the throat and squeeze the life out of him.

"Right-o Mr Shadwell," said Declan. "We will go directly. Come on Mordecai now." He pulled at Mordecai's arm urgently. "We'll be off sure we will."

Mordecai slammed his chair against the table swearing under his breath and made his way out behind Declan. Joshua glared after them and rose to watch his men escort them out of the coach house, through the back gate and onto the path leading to the river.

"Bloody amateurs."

The fact that they ran a regular and entirely legal barge service between Bath and Bristol had initially recommended them to him. His most recent commissions had stretched them to their limits, and if he had not been pressurised himself he would never have risked asking them. He cursed fluently: cursed himself for being beholden to anybody and for trusting anybody, and he cursed his block-headed, cack-handed bargees who had claimed so bravely they were expert murderers. "I should have them do what they do best," he muttered to himself.

Over the last five years they had managed to convey unwanted girls from his brothels in Bath to Bristol for shipment to the lucrative overseas market. The game had become increasingly dangerous over the last two years as ever younger girls had been demanded, girls from the gentry too. Kidnapped girls, and infants, had been shipped with increased regularity. He had a bad feeling about it. Regular tastes he understood, but not this. Rosie never took under twelve's to keep in their houses. No point breaking more laws than necessary. He took one pistol from the drawer and closed it before locking up and heading for the house.

"Goodnight boys," he said to the men as he passed by them and emerged from the dark into the pool of light by the door.

"Goodnight sir."

He walked back to the house slowly, pausing only to check the upper windows. All seemed in order, as usual the lights in Clari's room were on and would continue to be so until dawn. As he reflected that there were worse places to live than a high class knocking shop, a cold wind rose spitting dead leaves into the air and rattling the creeper on the walls. He shivered and hurried on down the path, taking the steps two at a time to make the door and pass into the warmth of the house.

## 8th October, 1831, Walcot Street.

Nathaniel had a late start the next day. The evening had extended into the night and it had been almost dawn when he returned down Lansdown Hill to Walcot. Talk had ranged comfortably over Bath doings including Charles's new society for creating work for the poor, family news and other trifles until the ladies left the table. It had then quickly descended into national politics, law and order and the inexorable onward march of the cholera. Charles expected it any day now. They had talked up medieval spectres of the Black Death and then banished them with a good dose of inconsequential ribaldry and yet more claret. He reluctantly heaved himself out of bed to prepare for the trip to Bristol to visit Drake. He pulled on his robe and brought in the water and breakfast left some hours earlier by Mary, plodded to the washstand and table, then opened the window to clear his head. A peal of bells rolled over the town from near Southgate: mournful, funereal. He called down to a passing gentleman.

"Sir, why the muffled peal? Who's died?"

The man looked up sadly. "The hopes of the people sir. They are dead. The papers are out with black mourning edges, most shops are shut and St James's is sounding the peal. The Lords rejected the Bill yesterday and London is in a roar. Yesterday's editions have just arrived and the news is all over the city. It's a black day sir, but they'll not get away with it. The people will not stand it. There will be retribution!" His anger animating him, he flushed in confusion, raised his hat and moved off.

In a low mood, Nathaniel left peremptorily with a small bag and Caradoc, to collect the hired post-chaise in Pulteney Mews. He mounted the nearside horse of the pair, bundled Caradoc into the coach and rode postillion for the twelve mile drive to Bristol.

### The Drake family's rooms, Cornwallis Crescent, Clifton, Bristol.

By the time he arrived in Clifton and found Cornwallis Crescent he was in better spirits. Footmen sprang out to deal with the post-chaise, the horses and Caradoc, whilst Nathaniel was shown to a grand drawing room to meet John Drake.

"You have found some magnificent rooms here Mr Drake," he said, smiling and eyeing Drake closely, trying to decide why he had taken such an instant dislike to the man.

"Yes," said Drake cautiously. "Need to maintain the image of the service Parry. Also my family are here, so bachelor accommodation is out of the question."

"Are they enjoying their stay?"

Drake reflected for a few moments. Lottie was now enjoying herself immensely, fraternising and competing with Mrs Ravenswood. Drake had encouraged this to further his relationship with Mr Edwin Ravenswood who was proving to be an even better contact than hoped, and definitely one he wanted to keep away from the dashing Mr Parry.

"Who would not be enjoying a few weeks at Clifton Spa? The village has plenty of diversions for the ladies. The waters can be taken and there are ample assemblies and private soirees," he said, airily waving them away with a languid hand. "It's not London, but it serves for a season."

They spent a few dutiful hours discussing Nathaniel's report on Bath and his contacts, omitting the full details of the murder enquiry but including his intention to pursue leads in Bristol. This was followed by Drake presenting his views on Bristol, omitting his burgeoning friendship with the suave and monied Ravenswood. Drake mentioned obliquely that Lord Palmerston's hopes for developing contacts with local ship-owners on the Far East run would be fulfilled, and pontificated on the value of the same for some time, until Nathaniel became restless and encouraged Drake to agree to a walk. Once out of the house, they strode purposefully and in silence up the steep streets to the Downs. A few groups of gentry were taking the air and animals grazed peacefully. Rabbits hopped and the Downs rolled away to the distant line of trees. They passed a ruined mill and Drake exchanged a few words with its owner, an engaging man, bespattered in paint and plaster.

"He's leased it from the Merchant Venturers," said Drake, more relaxed and less annoying. "He's making a studio and a camera obscura. I come up here each day to see how he is doing. It was an old snuff mill, burned down years ago. Great project."

They continued along the crest of the Downs and then made a small descent to where the grass was interrupted by a stretch of broken ground and piles of stones.

"This," said Drake excitedly, "is the start of a suspension bridge which will link the two sides of the Gorge. A young engineer has faced down Thomas Telford himself and carried the laurels in the competition just this year. He's called Brunel. He'll be about your age."

"French is he?" asked Nathaniel, interested.

"Father is. You must know of him. He's the Thames Tunnel engineer."

The tide was out and far below broad mud banks shelved steeply to the brown flow of the Avon. They looked circumspectly, cautiously craning their necks over the sides of the gorge which was cruelly rocky with stunted trees clinging to toe-holds on the sheer sides.

"St Vincent's Rocks," said Drake, keen to share his newly learned knowledge. "There's still a hermit's cave in the cliff side."

Away from work and the jockeying for position, the ceaseless self-seeking and greed, Drake seemed a more interesting man, a better man. Two sides to everyone Nathaniel reflected: both part of the whole.

In a rush of good nature, Drake decided to extend the walk to take advantage of the day. They descended the steep incline from Clifton and pushed on to the centre of town. They made their way to the wharves at the foot of the red cliffs for a session in the Ostrich where they consumed a large quantity of local cider before making their way round the pub to a back yard to treat themselves to the spectacle of bare-knuckle boxing.

"Lord Palmerston would appreciate this," shouted Drake animatedly. "Great sporting man is Lord Cupid you know!"

"So I hear," said Nathaniel.

"Do you box, Mr Drake?"

"Not personally," said Drake.

"Sword-play?"

"Not now."

Drake's hand strayed to his collar and his finger instinctively ran along the side of the ragged scar. His head swimming from the flagon of cider, his mind raced back unbidden to Paris in '25. The yells of the crowd receded. He could hear again the terrifying whistle of his opponent's blade as it sliced the air to land with bone-jarring force on his feeble guard. He re-lived the desperation of being driven back, his spine crashing on the stone wall. He felt the hot breath on his face as their blades locked and the screeching ringing by his ear as his opponent pulled his sword free for the final flurry. He had sagged to the ground, spent and craven beneath the renewed fury of strokes when the shots rang out. He had survived: his second, as treacherous as himself, had brought two primed pistols. Not the most gentlemanly end to a duel of honour. His challenger and his second lay in seeping pools of blood whilst his own man had spirited him away.

When they returned to Cornwallis Crescent, Nathaniel had a pang of remorse to see the indignities to which Caradoc had been subjected in his absence. The child Lizzie, a small and imperious termagant, had attached ribbons to him and a doll's coat. The sturdy beast was tolerating it in view of her years, though an older torturer would have been fought off long before. The evening passed slowly. The abrasive Lottie had returned from town and encouraged Lizzie to recite poetry before dinner. She herself provided a musical interlude on the pianoforte after the lengthy meal and Nathaniel had retired early. He was mildly surprised the next day to find that Drake was occupied with an afternoon and dinner engagement with Mr Ravenswood, which would limit their final meeting to the morning. He was clearly not to be invited to the session with the ship owner, as Drake was of the opinion that Palmerston's business could be discharged very well without him.

"I will take myself off to the docks this afternoon," said Nathaniel over breakfast. "I'll dress for the occasion and have a look at the vessels, just to familiarise myself with the traders. Where does Mr Ravenswood keep his ships?"

"King's Wharf, down the Floating Harbour at Redcliffe," said Drake, pausing in his assault on the toast and raspberry preserve. He smothered his reluctance and added: "His next ship for the east is the *Blue Dragon*. You can't miss it. It's a clipper. Raked masts and ends sharp as a rapier, built for speed. It's got a carved dragon as a figurehead with Bristol blue glass eyes. But I wouldn't poke around too much Parry," he said patronisingly. "He's got some Chinese crew this year. They don't take kindly to strangers and you'd better look out for yourself pretty generally around the docks."

"Thanks for the advice," said Nathaniel.

That evening, in the darkening twilight, a dishevelled man and his dog made their way along Marsh Street, side-stepping the refuse and beggars, eyeing the inns and beer-shops. Gales of laughter and singing blew out of the bars, Irish fiddles scraped tunes and the stamp of dancers' feet beat time. It was a rackety quarter of the docks, brimming with sailors, immigrants, itinerants, swindlers, murderers and thieves. Nathaniel wound his scarf higher and pulled his hat lower. The latest additions to his wardrobe, acquired from a local pawn shop, stank of the previous owner. Caradoc had growled a protest, but the rank odours of Marsh Street soon eclipsed both the smell and his early objections. In truth, anything was preferable to being sought out for entertainment by Miss Lizzie in Cornwallis Crescent. They sidled into a rowdy tavern called the Three Sugar Loaves. The swinging sign sporting a painting of three white conical loaves was a common sight in the city where sugar refining still boomed on the back of the West Indian molasses trade. He had seen other taverns with the same name, but none was so brutishly unappealing.

The air was stifling, a miasma of beer and spirits overlaid with the smoke of a hundred tobacco pipes and the rancid puffs from the fire sulking under a pile of vegetable peelings. Nathaniel bought brandy and water and edged his way past the crowd at the bar, past the fiddlers and a pair of raucous quarrelling whores, being egged-on to settle their differences with a fight by the growing crowd that seethed around them. Through a low doorway he saw a quieter room and made for it. Men were hunched over shove ha'penny boards, some played cards, some chess. Backgammon held a bunch of punters by the fire but away in a corner alcove he spotted a small, intense group of Chinese sailors making preparations to play a different game. He stood by the fire, warming his hands, listening and watching. He recognised Mandarin, but the accents were strong and the men made few comments as they settled.

Their approach to the game was reverent and controlled. The two players bowed gravely, this was a game the like of which he had never seen played before, and would not again until the century was old. But he knew of it. He recalled his father's gentle voice spinning a web of mysterious tales from his travels: battles, swordplay, dragons, emperors and the subtle game of stones. As he rubbed his hands before the flames, he watched covertly from the corner of his eye. A cloth had been laid on the table, marked out with nineteen lines in both the horizontal and the vertical. Two piles of counters were emptied from leather pouches: white stones of clam shell and the others small rounds of black slate. The older player took a place with his back to the wall and the white shells were pushed towards him. The younger took the slate pieces, held the first one between his index and middle fingers, and placed it, carefully, on an intersection of the lines in the upper right hand corner. The atmosphere was calm, yet with underlying tension, the rowdy guffaws and shrieks of the bar faded into insignificance with the muted slides of the ha'pennies, the shuffle of cards and jests of the other players around them.

Nathaniel felt impelled to draw nearer. As the players silently took turns to place their stones, they contested the territory provided by the squares. Pieces were sacrificed, taken prisoner, territories ebbed and flowed but inexorably the older man playing white gained the advantage. Nathaniel watched as the game unfolded, leaning on the chimneypiece, entranced. Quarter hours had grown to an hour when he became aware that he was being watched. There was a still figure at the far end of the bench whose eyes were upon him and he sensed that they had been so for some time. He turned to look directly into the eyes of a man of about his own age, powerfully built. He was the man he had seen at the Guildhall on his first night in Bath. Again, dressed entirely in black, even his shirt now covered by a dark scarf, he bowed slightly, acknowledging Nathaniel. He was recognised, despite the stinking rags from the pawnbroker, despite the passage of days. Another memory flashed unbidden, the stories of black-clad mercenary soldiers in feudal Japan: the ninja, murderous, secret, invincible. Nathaniel made a bold move and took a seat by the spectators. Within another quarter of an hour the game ended with the victory of the older man. Surprisingly, no money changed hands, but the players bowed to each other, aware of the other's skills, the younger man bending significantly lower than the elder.

"You know the game?" inquired the man in black, moving closer to sit by Nathaniel and speaking with only the slightest trace of a foreign accent.

Nathaniel hesitated momentarily, then decided on a degree of honesty, as he still felt the same latent energy and danger in this man he had sensed on first sighting him. "My father travelled in the East before his death a few years ago. He explained this game to me, but I had never seen it played. I take it this is by way of a travelling set. Is it not conventionally played on a wooden board? And am I correct in suggesting that it is strategic rather than tactical in the sense that chess is a tactical contest?"

"Yes. The game is called Wei Ch'i, and was invented in China thousands of years ago. It is an art of encirclement in which strength and final victory depend on the highest levels of strategic competence. The man who played white is a master. His tenacity allowed him to achieve ultimate hegemony in the field. You noticed, I know, as I was watching you. You admire such tenacity?" He smiled. "Perhaps we should be introduced? I am Cornelius Fu Lee. I am here on a business trip and I'm sailing for the east shortly. These men are from the ship's crew. We're probably the only Chinese in Bristol. I have not seen one other despite the so-called Cathay Wharf I found by Redcliffe church."

"I do admire tenacity sir, and here I saw strategic calculation of the highest order. I am Nathaniel Parry. Like you I am on business here, visiting a colleague, but intend to return to Bath shortly and stay for a few weeks. I am visiting my family and I have rooms there. I recognise you Mr Lee, and I know you recognised me. We attended the same political meeting at the Bath Guildhall."

Cornelius Lee smiled: *"Touché."*

Nathaniel decided to ignore Drake's advice. "The main shipper to the east from here is Mr Edwin Ravenswood. I believe his *Blue Dragon* is preparing to sail. So I suspect he is your employer. He seems to be making an excellent trade in opium whilst others are falling foul of the Emperor's searches."

Cornelius Lee stared impassively at Nathaniel. "You are well informed Mr Parry. What might your business be?"

"I am an associate of Mr John Drake."

Cornelius nodded. "As I expected. And tonight he dines with Mr Ravenswood. We both have the evening off my friend."

Nathaniel glanced over the now completed game. The two players were discussing the match, re-setting the early positions, the master explaining some weaknesses in black's opening play. Cornelius followed his gaze, "You see how the master teaches his opponent? Next time, perhaps, his game will improve and white will have a bigger challenge. Both will improve as a result. Even though they are opponents, by cooperating they each achieve a higher objective."

Nathaniel eyed Cornelius speculatively for a moment. "May I buy you some refreshment Mr Lee?" They made their way to the bar.

"Brandy?"

They sat facing each other over the steaming pewter mugs of brandy and hot water.

"To successful trade," said Nathaniel, raising his mug.

"To success, Mr Parry." Cornelius continued, "The opium trade to China is of great importance to England is it not?"

"Of the greatest importance," answered Nathaniel. "It is essential if we are to balance our trade there."

Cornelius reflected without speaking, then looked directly at Nathaniel, holding his gaze and seeming to look into his very soul. "You seem to appreciate the subtleties of Wei Ch'i Mr Parry. We consider that it is a reflection of life, and is a game of harmony and balance. In your opium trade, do you operate a moral balance or just an economic one?"

"In what sense?"

"A balance of the greater evils: the relative threat to Chinese lives and the danger of degeneracy through opium addiction versus your reluctance to spend your silver?

"Men have free will Mr Lee. Opium is not seen as an illegal substance in England, in fact it is a principal medicament. Taken as laudanum here, the poor call it their "penn'orth of elevation". And why not? It kills pain, improves health and raises their spirits. God knows that many of them need that. There's little joy for the poor in any land. "

Cornelius continued, unmoved. "Foreign sales to opium dens are illegal in China. Did you know that nine in every ten young men in coastal areas are now addicted to opium? There is no harmony in such a condition."

A silence grew between them. Cornelius Lee might well be a danger to the trade that the British government was at such pains to promote. Nathaniel looked at the face opposite him, which was closed, unreadable.

"Are you playing devil's advocate Mr Lee?"

"All games are potentially deadly Mr Parry. I like to be on the side of the light rather than the dark."

Nathaniel, perplexed and making a move to leave, suddenly noticed that Caradoc had stretched himself out on the floor by Cornelius Lee and, most uncharacteristically, slept with his head on Lee's feet.

"My dog likes you Mr Lee. It is rare for him to lower his guard and trust a stranger."

"We are no longer strangers."

He held out his hand to Nathaniel, who grasped it and was surprised to find the hand he shook to be extremely hard, yet heavily calloused only on the knuckles, not the palms. The hands of a fighter he thought: no businessman and certainly from his demeanour, no sailor.

"Goodbye Mr Lee."

"Mr Parry. Until we meet again."

# Chapter 4

**Mid-morning: 10th October, 1831. Cornwallis Crescent, Clifton, Bristol.**

Nathaniel's leave-taking of the Drakes was pleasant enough. He had breakfasted leisurely, and was pleased that Caradoc had been spared a return bout of annoyance from the infant Lizzie, who was tormenting her governess by the time they started work on the ham and kidneys. Lottie had also finished at the table and swept off to a morning assembly where she would meet Amanda Ravenswood. His hired post-chaise and pair had been well groomed in the stables to the rear of Cornwallis Crescent and the horses were stamping to be off by the time he made his way to them with Caradoc and Drake. Nathaniel threw in his bag and hoisted Caradoc onto the seat.

"Thank you for your hospitality Mr Drake. Shall we travel to London together on Friday?"

"I don't think so, Parry," said Drake. "I don't want to be tied to a set time. I'll see you in Percy's office at Whitehall on Monday the 17th for the meeting, as planned."

Drake waved Nathaniel off courteously enough, well pleased to have that particular player off the field and safely returned to the pavilion, to be dealt with in due course. He turned on his heel and marched out of the stable yard, but instead of returning to the house made for the Downs. The evening with Ravenswood had raised possibilities, some of them alarming. He felt a cold sweat break out on his skin as the autumn wind raced up from the Severn and cut through the fine material of his coat. He needed thinking time.

## Back to Bath

The road to Bath was well metalled: efficiently turn-piked along its entire length and thick with every category of traffic. Nathaniel set up a cracking pace, stretching the hired chaise to its limits. He entertained himself weaving round the wagons and the trails of pack horses, racing a mail-coach and a couple of young bloods in gigs. Caradoc bounced like a cork beside Nathaniel on the driver's seat and yapped relentlessly, pouring scorn on the lesser canines racing their wheels as they passed farms and villages and be-rating collectors at turnpike cottages. Even after they had returned the steaming horses and filthy chaise and walked back to the rooms in Walcot Street, dusty, spattered with mud and aching in every muscle, they were both in triumphant high spirits. Caradoc flung himself at Tom's feet by the fire whilst Nathaniel managed to persuade Martha to undertake the lengthy business of boiling up water for an unusual mid-day wash in his room. He climbed the stairs and settled to write a report for Lord Melbourne. He and Drake had planned to return to London for a meeting with Melbourne and Palmerston to acquaint the noble lords with the progress of events, but on the personal front he needed to return briefly to his rooms in Lambeth. He stripped off his stained travel clothes, donned the Damascus robe and assembled his writing equipment. He hauled his travelling desk out of the trunk and balanced it on the bed, arranging himself behind it on piled up pillows, cross-legged like a Caliph. His meeting with Cornelius Fu Lee had intrigued and concerned him. He took out his knife and sharpened his pen. Cornelius could usefully stay out of the report.

Nathaniel had felt disturbed since the previous night in the snug at the Three Sugar Loaves and was assailed by nagging doubts. He had never before questioned the ultimate morality of the opium trade. Why should he? It was a normal assumption that all men's choices could lead to good or evil. That was the nature of free will. Damn it, milk could kill a man and often did, most town water could be lethal, especially for strangers. Opium was a precious commodity, and it could drive the most brilliant to craven beggary and madness. He dipped his pen in the ink-pot and began to write his report, carefully, in his immaculate script. The sound of the soft repetitive scratching of the pen on the paper filled the silence of the room. He covered a side, sanded it, and blew away the excess. As he paused, a vision of Coleridge flickered before his inner eye. *Kubla Khan* would never have been written without opium. He recited aloud:

"In Xanadu did Kubla Khan
A stately pleasure-dome decree:
Where Alph, the sacred river, ran

Through caverns measureless to man
Down to a sunless sea."

He loved those lines: they were the zenith of Romanticism. He repeated them slowly, relishing them, and then, as it seemed for the first time, he was alive to their overwhelming threat, the sinister horror eclipsing the beauty.

"But oh! that deep romantic chasm which slanted
Down the green hill athwart a cedar cover!
A savage place! as holy and enchanted
As e'er beneath a waning moon was haunted
By woman wailing for her demon lover!"

Coleridge's brilliance and his physical miseries were part of his family's mythology. Charles Parry and his late brother Fred had been friends of the famous poet and his father had treated him in the grips of his addiction. On the way to speak in Bristol in 1813, Coleridge had rested in Bath, and got no further than the Greyhound in High Street, where Caleb Parry had attended him. Coleridge had been sunk in torment, his pains tearing him like a caged leopard devours its prey: his sanity, his precious "I-ship" slipping away. Slipping away, thought Nathaniel uncomfortably, on the "sunless sea", through the yawning abyss. He saw again the grave face of Cornelius, heard his voice, low and relentless, relating the sorry tale of destitution and misery. He conjured up to mind an image of desperate and degenerate youth in China, coastal towns laid waste by the relentless march of British trade: a trade he was employed to further by masters who required him to see Cornelius Lee as an enemy; a dangerous one. He grinned wryly as he finished his report. There was no doubt that Cornelius was dangerous, but he was finding it hard to see him as an enemy.

By half past four that afternoon, with swordstick jauntily employed and setting a brisk pace, he was striding up Walcot Street towards the London Road, Caradoc frisking at his heels. It had been too long since he exercised his sword and he looked forward keenly to the session at Captain Wilkins's fencing club. He had had a gloomy conversation with Mr Tasker and the grooms at the livery when he returned the post-chaise. It had reminded him of the frustrated rage of the people at the Lords' rejection of the Bill and Old Tom's mutterings about the "wild beasts loosed" had followed him out of the house. Perhaps it was more than exercise he would be needing. They climbed the steep hill of Guinea Lane and crossed Lansdown to make their way to Morford Street and the Tennis Court which accommodated the gentlemen and their fencing. Nathaniel settled Caradoc at the door and sought out

Captain Wilkins to make himself known.

Wilkins was with his friends, the morose Fairfield and a corpulent, jovial man who looked familiar. All three were busy, clad in white shirts and breeches with stiffened padded waistcoats, limbering up as effectively as their respective constitutions allowed. It was a lofty room, well suited to purpose, with the nets stowed and half a dozen other teams of gentlemen in separate groups, un-sheathing weapons, fixing blunting tips to their points, laughing, excited.

"Welcome Mr Parry!" said Captain Wilkins, striding over and wringing Nathaniel by the hand. "Stand on no ceremony! We form up in fours and you will be occupied directly as Mr Cruttwell is delayed. May I present Mr Howard Dill, the fourth member of our usual quartet."

"Good day sirs," said Nathaniel. "Mr Dill, I recollect I have had the pleasure of meeting you last week, in the Pump Room. You were with my relative, Doctor Parry."

"Capital!" declared Dill, his circular glasses both flashing white as they caught the light. "What a memory Mr Parry! Indeed we did meet exactly as you say!"

"I see you have brought your weapon of choice," said Fairfield dismissively. "We fight with duelling swords first tonight sir. Whole-body target: tip to score. I see you are determined to fight with a thin cross-guard lacking even a knuckle-bow to protect your hand. We cannot be expected to make allowances."

"I can assure you sir that I do not seek allowances of any kind."

Nathaniel's mouth offered a friendly smile but his eyes did not. He threw his cloak to the wall, grasped the silver hilt of his stick and unsheathed the sword, a weapon previously admired by the absent Cruttwell and dismissed out of hand by Fairfield. The Japanese tempered blade flickered grey-blue in the light, along the rolling curves of the water-mark and on its shimmering edge. He fixed a false tip to the end of the sword, stepped back lightly, placed the hollow cane aside, and swung the weapon one-handed in a tight circle, flicking it over his wrist, catching it smoothly. "Shall we begin?"

"Very well," said Captain Wilkins with a sudden snort of laughter, "Champing at the bit what! Fairfield, first bout with Parry here."

Mr Dill passed his wire-mesh mask to Nathaniel then moved aside, surprisingly briskly, to stand by the Captain who directed the combatants to starting positions.

Nathaniel raked his left hand through his hair, clearing his eyes, then slid the mask over his face.

"*En garde.*"

Fairfield, also masked and ready, shifted on his feet, settling his weight on the

85

back foot.

"*Prêt.*"

Wilkins lowered his hand simultaneously with the verbal signal to start.

"*Allez!*"

The fencers dropped into strong stances and circled warily. They feinted again and again. Tap, tap, tap, sword met sword: weighing each other's potential, quartering the floor, feeling the responses. Padding, slow moves forward, then "*appel*" – stamp, stamp – startle, circle again: wary, waiting; biding their time.

Fairfield suddenly sensed an opening and made a mighty lunge followed up with a barrage of blistering attacks. Nathaniel, true to his name was swift with the parry, deflecting, weaving away. His economy of movement astonished the watching pair, Dill chuckled in appreciation.

"*In quartata* and *passata-sotto*! Princely Mr Parry. Princely!"

Fairfield breathed hard, sweat starting to run on his face. Nathaniel had turned and ducked and dodged away, he had been led a dance. A shameful one. He gathered his strength and attacked with renewed ferocity. The clash of blades rang and rang again. Clanging, faster, feet slithered and stamped. Back and forth: back and forth.

Nathaniel sensed his opponent was tiring and delayed, delayed, delayed. Then as Fairfield roared in like a bull with a hefty lunge, Nathaniel's characteristic mercurial parry was followed up instantaneously with a devastating riposte. He deftly switched sword hands as he turned and threw his opponent off balance. Fairfield staggered backwards in disarray: one, two, three, four, five blows, and on the last theatrically disarmed, his sword flew from his hand to skitter across the floor and crash to the wall.

"Bravo!" cheered Dill and Wilkins.

"Bad luck Fairfield."

Neville Fairfield held out his hand, blowing hard, trembling with the after-shock, but he was a soldier, able to swallow his pride.

"Pleasure to spar with you Mr Parry."

"And I with you sir."

Nathaniel's initiation over, the atmosphere lost its charge of aggression and the evening unwound happily enough. The rotund Dill survived, his dignity intact, and even acquitted himself well in some of the competitions. They paired up for alternate bouts, accommodating Cruttwell when he arrived and moving on to sabres. By the end of the evening, sweating and garrulous, they begged turns with Nathaniel's blade.

"The balance is rare," panted Wilkins as he returned it after he finished sparring with Nathaniel, who in turn handed back a borrowed sabre. "Very different from anything I've used before."

"The blade is Japanese, specially made for my father. He brought it back from the Orient and had it dressed in England. I have had cause to be grateful to it," said Nathaniel examining it carefully, "and I still follow my father's advice to train with both hands. Sorry if it surprised you Mr Fairfield." He smiled, meeting Fairfield's eyes and was rewarded with a rueful grin. Fairfield steered the conversation onto more neutral ground.

"Where did you learn to fence?"

"With my father, but also in London. I was fortunate enough to attend Master Domenico Angelo's club, the "School of Arms" in the Haymarket. It moved just last year to St James's Street, but it is still the same, and the best. The founder's traditions live on to the third generation. Old Mr Henry instructed me, and Mr Henry the Younger. He still works at the club when he has time but he's busy training the army."

"Impressive," said Fairfield. "But if I were you Parry I would keep up the practice. Times are dangerous. There's to be a reform demonstration in this city on Thursday this week. Thousands will be mustered and we just don't know what will happen. All the magistrates are under starter's orders to read the Riot Act at the first signs of trouble."

"Towns may soon be even unhealthier places than they already are," interjected Howard Dill with undue relish. "I myself, Mr Parry, live in a charming village, just seven miles from Bath. I invite you, nay, I entreat you to visit me!"

"Why thank you very much," said Nathaniel, non-committal.

"I live in Norton St Philip," persisted Dill. "My cook is on leave. Compassionate you know. Aged aunt is ill, needs seeing to, so I'm taking lunch daily in the George Inn. Join me one day sir! Soon!"

Nathaniel could not resist the infectious cheer of the little man.

"Many thanks Mr Dill. It is a kind offer."

The club broke up before eight p.m. and the gentlemen dispersed. Most made their separate ways home, but Nathaniel was restless after the sword-play, his body still coursing with energy, generating a ravenous hunger. He tracked down Caradoc who had taken to excavating a neighbouring garden.

"Report here Caradoc "instanter" if you have any interest in beef and beer!"

The terrier cleared the wall, dragging wisps of vegetation behind him, and skidded to a halt at Nathaniel's feet, yapping, head to the side, one ear raised high.

"Yes, beef and beer sir!" said Nathaniel. "We shall track them down."

He gave Caradoc an affectionate pat and they bowled down the hill to town. They made their way past the darkened windows of Martha Spence's house in Walcot and continued until they arrived at the George and Dragon, where Nathaniel had spent his first night in Bath. As before, heated political dispute was raging in the front parlour and after ordering a pint of porter, a saucer of small beer, and a beef and oyster pie with two plates, they joined it.

Roderick Wilson's funeral service in Bath Abbey was held the next day and was well attended, as were all functions that were held in that hub of society. The Abbey was attended daily as an arena for public promenade: gossip and show. Funerals added a frisson of gothic melancholy, morbidly exciting for visitors and locals alike. The black-clad congregation filled the nave below the soaring Perpendicular Gothic tracery that created "The Lantern of the West": their low whispers swashing like an incoming tide round its walls. The Abbey walls had been pierced so thoroughly they provided a better original for the saying "more glass than wall" than Hardwick Hall itself. The great Abbey windows shone, their muted rainbows of stained glass lit by the lowering afternoon sun and their shafts of light catching the multitude of settling dust motes.

The mourners had taken their places in small groups in the half-hour before the arrival of the coffin and Nathaniel had come early, placing himself at the back of the church to gain a better view of the company. Raphael Vere and Tilly had come in ostentatiously. She managed to shoot him a sly smile, unbeknown to her husband, before clattering along the pew, her jewellery tinkling as she went, her whispered asides sounding just too loudly to pass unnoticed. Captain Peterson, Mrs Peterson and the three girls had taken their places discreetly. The twins made a pretty picture as they fluttered in, identical in every aspect and turned out in lilac with black ribbons. Emma Peterson had ignored him on entry but he had noticed a blush on her cheek. She had a dignity and elegant beauty which he observed idly for a while. Miss Peterson reminded him of a roe deer, chestnut brown and glowing, hesitant and fragile, ready to run. But then he remembered her from the morning in the Pump Room: feisty, clever, and admonished by her mama for her unseemly interest in the cholera. His eyes wandered away to roam over the massed ranks of Wilson's associates: gentlemen of business, of his clubs, customers from the bank and representatives of the assorted social hierarchies of the city with their wives and families. He saw Charles and Mrs Parry at the front, Charles's massive bulk towering over the other mourners. They caught each other's eye and nodded.

Behind him the main doors opened and a cold draught brought a blast of autumn into the church. He turned as the organ struck up a funeral march and watched the coffin borne aloft down the central aisle, followed by the veiled, crabbed figure of Janie Wilson and assorted distant relatives. Most eyes followed them as they trooped dolefully towards the altar, but Nathaniel paused to watch the ushers as they began to close the heavy doors. A slim figure clad in shimmering black silk slipped in between the robed Abbey servants and took a place opposite to him, on the back pew to the left of the nave.

The service wore on, predictably. They listened, they prayed, they stood, they sang, they sat, they listened, they stood, they sang. Towards the end, Nathaniel noticed a slight movement to his left, the woman on the back row raised her veil to dab at her eyes, and he was rewarded by a sighting of a familiar almond shaped face, creamy skin and cat-like eyes: a little paler in the face, a little redder in the eyes, sadder but unmistakable. It was the minxy girl from the Pump Room who had dangled on the arm of the Irish politician. She felt his curious stare and met his eyes boldly before dropping the veil into place and turning to look resolutely ahead. He decided to question her as they left. It was too good an opportunity to miss and for the remaining half-hour he looked forward to a useful exchange with the most entrancing woman he had yet seen in Bath. Gathering intelligence on Wilson had never seemed quite so engaging. But he was doomed to disappointment. As he watched the coffin disappear through the doors on its way to the waiting coach, and prepared to make his move, his arm was grasped by Mrs Charles Parry. She had made her way, clandestinely, down the south aisle in the closing minutes of the service.

"Nathaniel," she scolded, tightening her grip on his arm and turning him to her.

"You really should have come up to sit with Charles and me! You shall now accompany us to Mrs Wilson's reception at the Paragon. The carriage is in Orange Grove and we can catch up on all your news of your friends in Bristol! Come on, no delays!"

As they made their way out through the great doors, he glanced to the opposite pew and was in no way surprised to see that it was empty.

They were decanted at the Paragon by Charles's servants, and made their way to the drawing room on the first floor. The apartment became crowded and hot very quickly. Small groups formed and extended their elbows to carve out standing space for themselves as they juggled glasses and plates which were constantly replenished by a footman and two maids.

"Is that Tanner, Mr Vere's footman," asked Nathaniel covertly of Captain Peterson as they sank a welcome goblet of wine by the open window.

"Vere's paid for the whole affair and lent a couple of servants to wait on. Damned decent of him," said the Captain.

Nathaniel pondered this. "Last week I called in on the Veres, as we'd planned, after I saw young Henry. Mrs Wilson arrived at Lansdown Crescent for dinner. Vere seems to be keeping a very kindly eye on her."

"Typical of the man, as you see. By the way, have you seen Wilson's rooms yet?"

"No, I was rather hoping to remedy that shortly."

"You've heard of the robbery? No? The very night you saw Mrs Wilson at the Vere's this house was broken into. Wilson's dressing room was ransacked by the sound of it, quite a bit is missing."

"Damn. I should have insisted on a search last week. Our killers are evidently closer and less casual than might have been the case. All good evidence to help clear Henry Blake, but we need something more concrete."

"Killers? Plural? Where did you learn that Parry?"

"Local source," replied Nathaniel.

Further discussion was impossible as the Veres and the rest of the Peterson family broke from the crowd in a cluster to join Nathaniel and the Captain.

"Mr Parry, at last I meet with you again!" Mrs Peterson fixed him with a look that brooked no argument. "We do hope you can come to us for dinner on Thursday, Thursday 13th yes?"

"With pleasure," said Nathaniel graciously.

"Mr Parry, Papa said you live in London!" piped a small Peterson female.

"How exciting!" bizarrely, two identical pipes sounded.

Nathaniel was forced to laugh out loud as the other twin chimed into the conversation. Her voice was identical to her sister's, as was her intonation, and her clothes, and her wide-eyes, and the precise angle of the set of her dainty jib. They giggled in unison, identically.

"Ladies. It has its excitements, as has every city including your own! I have not had the pleasure of being introduced to you and fear I shall disgrace myself by confusing your identities!"

"I'm Maddy and I'm the oldest by five minutes."

"And I am Ginette."

"Now I will never make a mistake," said Nathaniel seriously, whilst surreptitiously noting that Maddy's efforts to pluck her eyebrows had shortened her left brow just enough to create a difference from her sister's. That should be enough to give him the edge over them for the next couple of weeks.

Pink with embarrassment, and keeping to the outskirts of the circus entertainment provided by her sisters, Emma hoped that the exchange with the dashing Mr Parry would end before she betrayed herself. She still found him too attractive to look at if there was any danger of him meeting her glance.

"Miss Peterson, how very nice to see you again, though under sad circumstances. I assume you knew Mr Wilson quite well."

"Oh, yes, I mean, no, I did not know him very well," she stammered, looking reluctantly into the amused gaze of Nathaniel. "Father knew him better than I did Mr Parry. But it is nice to see you again."

"Stupid! Why did you say that?" she said to herself as she clenched her hands tight on the black reticule she found she was holding before her like a buckler in battle. She lowered it instantly.

"Your mother has been kind enough to invite me to dinner on Thursday. I do hope that you will be at home that evening." Nathaniel smiled at her broadly. "We will have more opportunity to talk."

"I look forward to it," said Emma, willing herself to relax and hoping that the pounding of her heart was not noticeable through her gown.

"Though how could it not be?" said the inner voice of reason.

It was not necessary to dwell on the possibility that she might look as though she were having a heart attack, as she found herself elbowed aside. Tilly Vere leaned into their conversation, disentangling herself from her husband's arm as he continued to talk animatedly to Captain Peterson.

"So pleased to see you again Mr Parry," she said breathily, looking up at him with her shining, limpid eyes through fluttering lashes. "Tell me all about your visit to Bristol."

Emma looked down, affronted to see a drift of Tilly's blonde curls resting on her own arm. She discreetly brushed the tendrils away and forced herself to listen attentively, and with grudging admiration, as the accomplished flirt displayed a master class in teasing and coaxing, plying her wares, soliciting Nathaniel's smile, all within reach of her husband's neglected arm.

The arrival of the widow curtailed the conversations and changed the dynamics of the group. To avoid the necessity of repeating well-worn condolences, Mrs Charles Parry launched into a monologue on the short-comings of the forthcoming season and held forth powerfully, engaging the Veres and Petersons *in toto*. Briefly, Nathaniel found he had Janie Wilson to himself.

"I was sorry to hear of the robbery Mrs Wilson. Although there is little chance of finding any clues I am still hoping for your permission to conduct a search."

"Certainly Mr Parry, you may do it now. I care not," said Janie Wilson, with an acid smile. She lowered her voice to a conspiratorial rasp. "Though it is amongst the low-lifes and bawds of this city that I recommend you pursue your investigations. You could not fail to notice the creature sitting by the door opposite from you in the Abbey! How she had the audacity to attend I cannot imagine."

"The young woman who arrived late?"

"The very same. I saw her on the way out. Colette Montrechet is the French baggage I told you of. Known to my husband in every sense of the word and no doubt hoping for money. She shall not have a penny. Though who knows when the estate will be settled. This house was robbed last Friday, and the thieves rifled Roderick's papers. I know he had been redrafting his will. His solicitor was awaiting it but fortunately does not have a copy of the new version which might just have rewarded the trollop for her services. We shall have to wait and see."

Janie Wilson seemed entirely unaware that she had not only informed Nathaniel of a motive for murder on the part of the mistress, but also managed to place herself prominently amongst the possible suspects.

"So sorry to hear of the burglary Mrs Wilson, but if you will permit me I would still like to see your husband's belongings."

"Then do so now." She beckoned a maid over from where she fidgeted by the door. "Show Mr Parry to my husband's dressing room."

The search proved fruitless, as expected. He rejoined the Petersons and the Veres and drew off the men for a private word out of earshot of the rest of the party.

"Mr Vere, I have conducted a search here but as you will know there has been a robbery and the trail is cold. However, the good news is that it seems increasingly likely that Mr Wilson was killed by two men, one of whom sustained a face wound during the assault. I believe your employee Henry Blake to be innocent and I strongly suspect the incriminating papers were planted in his rooms. I am following a lead at present which could provide witness evidence to identify the perpetrators."

Raphael Vere flushed red.

"Mr Parry, this is remarkable!" he gasped. "Who gave you that information might I ask? I sense a reward in the offing!"

Nathaniel observed his excitement with interest. Perhaps Mr Vere knew more of Wilson's foibles and their possible effect on his business than he admitted.

"I'm afraid it is too early to discuss that, but you could help me with another aspect of Mr Wilson's affairs. Were you aware that he might have been preparing a second will? Did he ask you to act as witness perhaps?"

Raphael Vere seemed surprised, but also more collected. "No, certainly not."

"No matter," said Nathaniel. "I will present the facts when my investigation is complete. A few days should suffice."

Raphael Vere bowed and moved back to Tilly, allowing Nathaniel to manage a private word with the Captain.

"I think an interview with Wilson's mistress would be useful. Apparently he had a liaison with a Miss Montrechet. I am persuaded she was the woman accompanying the young Irish politician when we met in the Pump Room."

"Yes, that's Diarmuid Casey, he has rooms in Queen Square, in the house on the corner of Gay Street. You could have a word with him first rather than seek her out. Better form don't you think?"

Nathaniel decided to leave Caradoc where he had left him before attending the funeral, stretched out before Mrs Spence's fire by Old Tom's feet. He made his way thoughtfully down Milsom Street, determining to visit Queen Square and present his card at Casey's rooms. He was picking his way past the exquisite shops decked with a profusion of clothes, shawls and every toy an inventive and commercial mind could design, avoiding dogs on leads and women's parcels, ballooning from the arms of their beaus, when he heard a shout and caught sight of a familiar face.

"Mr Parry!" bawled Tobias a second time from across the road. He was waving from a large shop-front opposite and was partially obscured by bristling scaffolding and advertisements for its grand opening the following month. "Mr Parry! Wait for me sir!"

Tobias skipped between the carriages and jumped the dung piles to present himself at Nathaniel's side.

"Oiy gat some intelligence sir," he said confidentially. "Oiy saw a man with a scarred face, fresh wound an' all on one o' they Bristol barges late last Friday. Might be the man mi boys from Little 'Ell saw the night Mr Wilson got murdered."

"There's probably a few bargees fit that description Tobias," said Nathaniel.

"Maybe," said Tobias, thinking hard to ensure he did not miss a tip. "But it's somethin' ain't it? And Oi'm still askin' mi boys to keep an eye out for you sir, riverside and up-town. Some do crossing sweeping up 'ere."

"Not very successfully," said Nathaniel eyeing the mole hills of dung.

"Well I'd better be off then," said Tobias disconsolately. "I'm deliverin' a message to Mr Jolly."

Nathaniel took pity on him.

"You've done well Tobias. Keep sharp. And don't say too much to the boys from Little Hell. They may serve two masters."

Nathaniel pressed sixpence into his hand and Tobias dodged back across Milsom Street, ducking under the scaffolding to disappear into the dark interior. Nathaniel made his way via Quiet Street to Queen Square and the temporary residence of Mr Diarmuid Casey.

The concierge instructed a maid to see Nathaniel upstairs to Mr Casey's rooms. He was ushered into a small entrance hall as she disappeared with his card. He glanced around, swiftly appraising. It was dingy, paint peeling, but with a riotous bunch of dahlias firing the side-table with colour and the scent of autumn. The tired rented rooms were lit up by their presence: short-lived, evanescent. They reminded him of his first sighting of Casey, the fiery speaker in the Guildhall, and the second sighting, when he was surrounded by the swarm of girls, the satin gad-flies of the Pump Room, drinking him in, a wild draught of Ireland. A dark brown velvet curtain swept aside with a clatter of brass rings, and Diarmuid Casey presented himself with a bow.

"Well hello Mr Parry! Welcome. Come in sir."

Nathaniel could not have been more pleased to do so, for as he entered the room he was greeted by the mocking, smiling, feline eyes of Miss Montrechet. She was reclining on the brown velvet chaise longue, dangling elegant ankles and dainty feet, evidently recovering from her mourning by consuming substantial glasses of Casey's spirits.

"Sit down here sir directly and make yourself at home!" Diarmuid Casey beckoned him over, placed a glass in readiness and offered him a comfortable seat by the fire. "Let me revive you before you launch into your business. And let me introduce you to my friend, Miss Colette Montrechet."

Nathaniel took her outstretched hand briefly, then settled into an armchair opposite Diarmuid.

"I am delighted to meet you both as it is with both of you that my business lies. I am investigating the death of Mr Roderick Wilson on behalf of his employer Mr Vere."

"Are you now," she said, putting her head to one side and narrowing her eyes, sharpening her features. "And you are here, hot-foot from the Paragon I suspect? Your poor head bursting with venomous details of my affair with poor Roderick? Did the formidable black widow poison you with her bite?"

She laughed softly, and continued, her voice melodious and surprisingly sweet: with just a breath of her native France remaining, lifting it in an entrancing lilt.

"Poor silly man!" she raised her shoulders and pouted. "He deserved her, but he didn't deserve to die. He was so excited the night before his death. Ooh, la, la, was he excited! He said he was to become rich. He said his ship was coming in. Which would have meant that mine too was likely to make a safe haven!"

"Will you be taking a dram of my *uisce beatha* Mr Parry? From the oldest source of whiskey in all of Ireland."

As Diarmuid poured a generous measure into a heavy, fluted tumbler, Nathaniel noticed that the bottle was only half-full, its wrappings discarded on the floor. A few remaining slices of seed cake sagged awry on a plate, which itself balanced uncertainly on a pile of papers spilling from the side table.

"'Tis from Ulster. Established well over two hundred years, but the distillery is smart as paint, built in my father's days."

The three of them raised their glasses which glinted tawny gold before the warmth of the leaping fire.

"A *votre santé* Mr Parry. And since we're sharing a drink you can call me Coco."

Bold, self-possessed, yet wary, she challenged him, still in her black gown, but with a rose pink shawl draped over her slim shoulders, softening the light on her skin.

"*Slainte*" said Dairmuid gravely. "To freedom, Mr Parry, and you can call me Diarmuid since we're sharing a drink."

"Thank you both for your hospitality," said Nathaniel slowly, weighing their mood, watching the sly smiles exchanged between them and savouring his drink before he continued.

"I have no doubt that Roderick Wilson was murdered by someone other than Henry Blake who has been arrested on suspicion of the deed. Papers and money were probably planted in his rooms and Wilson's papers have been stolen. Mrs Wilson certainly bore her husband ill-will. The marriage cannot have been entirely happy," he glanced at Coco, waiting for reactions. "Perhaps she had the capacity to plot his murder?"

Nathaniel left the question in the air and continued to watch Coco. Almost as likely as Janie to have profited by the death if the second will materialised, and with contacts amongst the low life of the city, she could have played more than a small part.

"Janie Wilson is a lady Mr Parry," said Coco, chiding him. "Do you know nothing of Bath ladies of a certain age? Possibly the slow drip of poison over months or years, but certainly not a contract for killing! This is not Naples!"

Nathaniel smiled, "Mr Wilson probably left you something in his will Miss

Montrechet."

She shrugged. "Possible but unlikely. I doubt there was much to leave!"

Nathaniel tried again. "Mr Wilson's employer, the generous Mr Vere, certainly has the welfare of Mrs Wilson at heart and perhaps seeks to preserve her reputation." Outside a coach creaked by, wheels clattering and harnesses jingling, inside the fire settled with a crack, sending sparks racing up the chimney, but Nathaniel got nothing in reply. He turned to Coco and tried a different tack.

"What do you know of Roderick Wilson's recent good luck and his relationship with his employer?"

"Roderick was always generous," said Coco, draining her glass and automatically refilling it. "But he had started talking of setting me up in an apartment at his expense. That was new. He still gambled, but I don't think he had won substantially. As to Raphael Vere, I suggest you speak to Howard Dill. You were with him at the Pump Room last week. Little fat man. Sweet man." She yawned, briefly displaying perfect white teeth.

"I do know him," acknowledged Nathaniel. "I spoke to him last night. Why might he be helpful?"

"He is one of the original depositors in the New Bank. He knew Vere's first wife and her husband who started the bank in the first place. Visit him. Do you know where he lives?"

"The village of Norton St Philip I believe."

"Lovely house," said Coco, as she suddenly sat up on the chaise longue and dusted the seed cake crumbs from her lap. "Diarmuid, you rascal, you've let me drink too much whiskey. I must go. I'm on duty with a new gentleman tonight. I need my beauty sleep." She eyed Nathaniel closely, studying his reaction.

"Good afternoon Miss Montrechet," he said, standing and bowing.

"Good afternoon, Mr Parry." She looked at him, offering a challenge and repeated slowly, "Good afternoon, Nathaniel. You're very handsome. Find out who killed Roderick and come and see us again."

She gathered her shawl about her, drained the remainder of her whiskey, and kissed Diarmuid who took her arm and led her to the door. She paused as she passed Nathaniel, and in one graceful movement, gently shook off Diarmuid and slid her arms round Nathaniel's neck to hold him close, brushing her lips slowly against each of his cheeks. She pressed her warm, supple body against him, her soft breasts against his chest, staying just long enough for him to breathe in her perfume. A surprise: the clean fresh scent of lavender, not the heady spice of a tart. He felt it a matter of some congratulation that he had not wrapped his arms around her to enjoy more of the same, but had managed to sit down and remind himself she was a whore. He finished his tumbler of whiskey before Diarmuid returned after seeing Coco out.

"She has rooms upstairs. Gorgeous creature! We've been friends for years," he said breezily as he refilled their glasses. "Poor thing was upset when old Wilson passed. She is too soft-hearted for her own good so she is."

"Have you both lived in Bath long?"

"She's been here a couple of years, but I've just fetched-up for the season to do the rounds with reform speeches in this corner of the south-west. I'm in Mr Daniel O'Connell's connection and hoping for a seat at the next election." His green eyes flashed in delight and he flung off his jacket to reveal a none too clean shirt and the same striped waistcoat he had sported when Nathaniel first saw him. "There's a new world round the corner Mr Parry. Nathaniel is it? Yes for sure," he screwed up his eyes to focus on Nathaniel's card which lay on the side table. "The freeing of the Catholic Church in '29 opened the flood gates. All Danny's doing mark you! By God the man's a saint. The Liberator he is to us all."

He raised his glass solemnly and rose for a toast, "To the sainted Daniel O'Connell. God bless him!"

Nathaniel raised his glass. "To Mr O'Connell! Good health!"

"That's the spirit!"

"You think the Bill will pass soon?"

"Got to. Got to happen," said Diarmuid, sitting forward, the picture of boyish energy, gripping his glass, his thick thatch of chestnut-red hair on end like an unruly ploughed field. "You know the trades are rising this Thursday do you?"

"I heard there was to be a march," said Nathaniel. "Do you sense trouble?"

"Who knows!" Diarmuid's eyes gleamed, relishing the possibility.

"Is Miss Montrechet a reformer?"

Diarmuid roared with laughter and slapped his thigh. "Coco! She hasn't a political bone in her body! Her family lost everything in the Revolution. Grandparents were murdered in 1790, everything confiscated, so her father was ruined. He muddled along, got married, made a life of sorts but got killed in a riding accident in '19. Coco was about ten. Her mother just faded away, dead in a year. Coco wasn't the fading type! She lived on the streets and survived. By God did she survive! She was a grand courtesan in Paris when I met her. We met up again in Ireland, in Dublin. She'd followed some fella there but it didn't work out well. Couldn't be more pleased to see her here. I rolled into the Pump Room a few weeks back and there she was. She'd been fairly steady with Wilson, but had a couple of other customers. Mr Howard Dill being one of them. She found me rooms here, she's just upstairs and here we are!"

Diarmuid drained the last of the bottle of whiskey into their tumblers.

"Why don't we make our way out for a bite to eat? I have a powerful hunger!" he declared.

"Why not," said Nathaniel. "Whilst we are about it, could we make our way to Wilson's sporting haunts? I have a mind to find out a little more of his reputation."

"No sooner said than done!" declared Diarmuid, leaping to his feet and grabbing his coat. "'Twill be a famous evening. I feel it in my bones!"

The next morning Nathaniel picked his way on his hired horse through the steep valley of Limpley Stoke. Caradoc darted in and out of the deep drifts of leaves, worrying sleepy mice out of their nests and taking detours to dig ferociously in promising holes by the road side. The trees were alive with a rustling wind and snatches of bird song, the straggling flight of a migrating flock marked the wide blue above as one undulating black arrow. Startled deer lifted their heads by the tree line in answer to Caradoc's yaps and the drone of a late bee zipped by the horse's head causing him to start and stumble on the stony way.

"Easy, easy now boy."

Nathaniel swung himself out of the saddle as the horse laboured up the steep rise and tramped along beside him as they climbed above Monkton Combe, heading out on the Frome road for Hinton Charterhouse, the last village before Norton St Philip.

Only a slight headache remained above his left eye, which was surprisingly lucky considering the long evening spent with Diarmuid Casey. They had started in Bedford's Billiard Rooms in Milsom Street, Wilson's premier haunt, and had quickly established that, although a heavy gambler, Wilson had redeemed the larger part of his debts and had left there on the night of his murder in good spirits. He was collected by chairmen commissioned by a gentleman he wished to meet, but there the story had dried up. The waiter seemed to think the chair was a private one, as he recollected no licence plate and the men were not familiar. They had made their way via the Hiscox Rooms in New Bond Street, where Wilson was partial to a flutter on backgammon, and thence to Lock's in Union Street. They had then supped magnificently in the Hart before concluding the night's investigations in Kingston Buildings at Hall's. The story had been the same at every port of call. Wilson was not in precipitous debt, was unlikely to have been slain because of his habits and had been well pleased with himself in the week before his untimely death. The small hours had found him back at Diarmuid's rooms, where his genial host had produced a fiddle and proceeded to play like a demon, coaxing his guest to roar his way through an hour of Irish drinking songs followed by a voluntary of every favourite Welsh ballad he could muster. He had returned to Walcot Street in the dead of night, crept in through the kitchen window, ousted an outraged Caradoc from his bed and slept the sleep of the just. He had slept through the dawn rousing of the household, catching only Martha's final offering of the morning. At the signal, "We plough the fields and scatter, the good seed on the land," he quit the bed and made ready for his rural expedition.

He had managed to leave by mid-morning and had been spared rigorous questioning from Martha as she was fully occupied in exclaiming with Tom over a communication from Mary's seafaring husband. An a.m. start had been vital in order to negotiate the hire of a horse and arrive in Norton St Philip in time to catch Howard Dill at his lunchtime stall in the George. Nathaniel had made excellent time on the quiet roads, the most time consuming obstacle had proved to be an unreasonably large flock of sheep in Hinton, herded at a snail's pace by an elderly sheepdog. Despite this he managed to rein in shortly after noon and hand over his horse to one of the George's stable boys. He made his way through the flagged medieval courtyard to a wood-panelled dining room at the front of the inn where it was an easy matter to locate his quarry. Howard Dill sat behind a robust portion of pie and a pewter mug of cider, smiling beatifically and watching the smoke rise against the metal fire-back to lose itself in the cavernous chimney.

"Mr Dill, I hoped to find you here. May I join you?"

"Well, if it isn't Mr Parry! Delighted, delighted my dear fellow! Sit down, let me order your lunch directly." He shouted to the barman, "Here my man, I have a guest! In fact," said Dill cheerfully, "two guests. I spy a thirsty terrier."

The innkeeper made his way smartly to the table with a bowl of water for Caradoc and took the extra orders.

Nathaniel had seated himself by Howard Dill on a high backed oak settle, which kept out most of the draughts, and looked round the room. The lime-washed walls were grimed brown with generations of pipes and fires and the worn tapestries rose gently with the warm currents of air from the fire and periodic cold blasts as the door opened to let in new customers. The room smelled of forests, of wet wool and dogs, smoke, beer and spirits overlaid with the sweat of working men. Four or five huddles of customers now populated the room. Prosperous farmers were talking pay in low voices with their labourers, who were bare-headed and clumsy in their work-worn linen smocks and gaiters, the dogs sleeping in the dark by their feet below the tables.

"It was a good ride, but I'm weary after it I must confess," said Nathaniel, relaxing into the worn velvet cushions stacked against the wooden back of the settle.

"This is an intriguing place."

"It was built for the monks long ago. Did you ride through Hinton Charterhouse and see the ruins? It was a Carthusian Priory founded in the thirteenth-century. This was the monks' wool-store. It did duty as an inn for the wool fairs after the monks were disbanded at the Dissolution and it wasn't all plain sailing afterwards, it's had a bloody history. Monmouth's rebels used it for their trysts in the seventeenth-century and Hanging Judge Jefferies tried them here and hung them high on the green for their taking of the liberty!"

"You're well versed in local history sir!"

"I'm a single man. I have no family to fill my time," said Howard Dill, a broad smile belying the melancholy of his words.

"You're happy here?" enquired Nathaniel.

"As a bug in a rug sir!"

They ate in companiable silence, draining their cider, pushing back their plates and stretching out their feet under the trestle table towards the fire. The resident dog, a vast German boarhound, lumbered over and rested his black muzzle on Howard Dill's shoulder, lent over to mop up some scraps of meat from the plates and moved on. Caradoc, worn out by the morning's run, slumbered unopposed in the inglenook amongst the logs.

"A digestif Mr Parry?"

"What do you suggest?"

"We must make a gesture to the Carthusians," said Howard Dill gravely. "The Green Chartreuse if you please sir!" he shouted to the innkeeper.

"The distillation of hundreds of years of holy skill Mr Parry! One hundred and thirty varieties of herbs and plants suffuse this blessed liquor. It is a medicament of the highest order."

They raised the tiny glasses of bright green liquid to the light.

"Your very good health!" declared Howard Dill.

"And yours sir. *Slainte*!"

"Ah, ha! *Slainte* is it! You have spent a merry evening or more in the company of the estimable reformer, Mr Casey I presume!" said Howard Dill, his spectacles flashing their characteristic opaque blankness in the light of the fire.

"Indeed," said Nathaniel, watching his host closely. "I spent yesterday evening in his company. And I met Miss Montrechet in his rooms before we took ourselves off into town."

"Oh! The delectable Coco! Nathaniel, may I call you Nathaniel? Good. She is a joy sir! But one to be rationed," he screwed up his face in concentration, "to be taken with care. Very like the Green Chartreuse. I avail myself of her charms on occasions. High days and holidays my boy. Unlike the egregious Wilson. Burned at the flame you know. Wanted to fund her entire as his mistress. A doomed venture, but he never found that out. God rest his soul!"

"Coco said you knew a great deal about Mr Raphael Vere, who is employing me to investigate Wilson's death."

Dill's good-natured face clouded. "Raphael Vere is a very wealthy man, despite some calamitous losses sustained in the early canal boom. He has tight dealings with some shippers in Bristol which must have been his salvation. One investor in particular is the key to the bank's new investments. He's called Edwin Ravenswood and he is an exporter, operates out of King's Wharf on the Eastern run. He has a town house in Redcliffe Parade overlooking his vessels. Vere is busy with him on a new project in which Captain Peterson and I might become more closely involved. A new vessel is needed."

He sank into thought, his cherubic mouth for once turned down, his jowls sagged giving a fleeting vision of Howard as an old man. The drowsy warmth of the parlour and the kindly effect of the pie and drinks loosened his tongue further.

"Strictly in confidence!" He glanced round for prying eyes and ears, and satisfied that the other customers were absorbed in their own affairs, continued in a low voice, inclining his head towards Nathaniel.

"He married a lady well known to my family. Mrs Patience Meredith, the widow of Elijah Meredith who founded the New Bank. Patience was five and twenty years older than Vere when they wed. They seemed happy enough, but the year after she died in '18, Vere married Tilly. Fourteen years of age and pretty as a picture, not that she isn't still. They travelled abroad for a time to quieten the scandal, living on the proceeds of Elijah's bank. Her mama was responsible for the match, bundled poor Tilly off as soon as she could. Last of six girls you see and the mama tired of the courting game. She sealed a bargain with the first to offer. Always did like them young did Vere."

"But his wife was by far his senior?"

"Patience was seventy-two when she died but she could have made her century. I do not believe she died naturally!"

Nathaniel pressed his advantage.

"I understand. But what about today? What do you think he is capable of Mr Dill?"

The desolation in Howard's face gave eloquent answer.

### The Shadwell's Residence, Green Park Buildings West, Bath.

As night fell in Bath, all was not well at the Shadwell's residence in Green Park West. A casual observer would have noticed nothing, as the house presented its usual respectable face to the street: fresh paint and clean stonework; foot scraper standing to attention, footpath neatly swept and the deep area behind the railings scrupulously free of leaves; chimneys smoking busily. But Madam Shadwell was not on duty in the front parlour and her door stood ajar. Up the elegant staircase on the first floor, the formal rooms were ablaze with flattering candle-light. Snatches of conversation, the clink of glasses, giggles, and the deeper bass voices of two happy customers could be heard floating through the door to the landing. Higher still, on the second floor, the application of Mitzi's lash could be heard distantly from her bedroom. The other doors were also firmly closed, muffling the sounds of pleasure. But higher still, up the winding, narrow stair to the attics and nursery, a different sound. Rosie Shadwell bent over a thin child who squatted, bare-legged over a bowl of water, dyed red with blood which flowed from jagged cuts on her lower body. The girl held a cloth to her face, which had also been laid open by a savage blow. She moaned, rocking back and forth to comfort herself.

"In the name of God Babs, how did it come to this?" said Rosie as she rinsed the girl's legs which were already purpling with bruises. "You look like you've been run over with a coach wheel!"

"I feel like it," Barbara muttered indistinctly, but raised a lop-sided grin.

"What did he hit you with?"

"His hands Ma'am. He had such rings on him. He's ripped my skin all over."

"So I see."

"'E came in like a thunder cloud. Normally all very nice, 'Where's my baby girl?' and all that. Not today Ma'am, he was cruel to me, mocking. Said I was too old and hardened. I should be on the streets." Her eyes welled with tears, "You wont let me go Mrs Shadwell will you? I can serve the men like the rest of the girls. I'm nearly fourteen. I'm not a child now! Per'aps someone else should do the nursery?"

"You will do nothing for at least a week 'til you heal up," said Rosie briskly. "Then we'll see."

She sat on the edge of the bed and looked Barbara firmly in the eye, holding her hands, "We don't hold with customers damaging girls in this house, you know that. But this particular customer is a very important man Babs. Do you know who he is?"

"I know he is a banker, he told me once." She hesitated, "Pardon me for repeatin' it, but he said that he controls Mr Shadwell's investments and holds the future of this house in his hands!"

"Enough Babs. Don't repeat it again. Now hold these wet cloths on the wounds. I'll send Josie up with some honey to dab on when they stop bleeding and she'll bring you fresh towels." She stood and wrapped her robe around herself, tying the sash tightly. "She'll bring up a drink for you. Make sure you get it down, then get some sleep. There'll be no one else in here tonight."

"Thanks Mrs Shadwell."

As the door closed, Barbara's white face crumbled. She covered her mouth with the soaked cloth, rolled over on the bed in a ball and was still. Rosie Shadwell closed the door and descended the stairs slowly, her face livid with rage. The lost earnings would be extracted from that particular customer, in full, with interest. She paused at the landing window and looked down the dark garden. Past the arbours and lawns the lights in Joshua's office above the coach house winked through the trees. She would discuss the matter with him later. He would know what to do. As she turned to make her way back to the parlour, two men came silently through the back gate and made their way to the stable stairs.

Joshua sat opposite the customer in question, letting the waves of abuse break over him and waiting for the blustering storm of anger to wear itself out. He glanced at his clock on the mantle, it was almost an hour since he had dispatched his men to sort out a spot of trouble in one of his Avon Street brothels. They should be back soon, he reasoned, breaking the heads of that class of customer was not a lengthy or elegant business. And, as it was mid-week, before the night was out, Mordecai and Declan would also be round to be paid. He would not be alone for much longer.

"And then," roared Vere, "in front of Captain Peterson, Parry talked about having evidence. Evidence! From witnesses, mark you Shadwell! Witness evidence that your incompetent moronic assassins were seen killing Wilson. Not only did the suicide turn into murder but the perpetrators were seen, one wounded on his face which makes him a marked man for months to come. If Parry links your men to you, the consequences will be catastrophic!"

"For us both," said Joshua quietly.

"So what do you intend to do about it?" hissed Raphael Vere, his plump cheeks trembling. He gripped the edge of the table and rose to his feet, challenging Joshua Shadwell.

Joshua lent back in his chair, sliding open his drawer to catch the comforting sight of his pistols. Vere was not normally a man of violence, not at first hand, not at his own hands, but tonight he was almost deranged. The findings of the investigator from London had alarmed him and he was now realising the foolish stupidity of his clumsy tangle with Wilson.

"Sit down Raphael," he said, with a steely calm. "Keep a clear head. You've made mistakes already through hastiness. If you hadn't been so desperate keen to have little girls you wouldn't have exposed yourself to blackmail. But accepting you are, desperate keen that is, you should have kept your activities off your own doorstep. Letting a likely character such as Wilson be with you when you were both well gone in your cups, and letting him in your house amongst your papers when you were both the worse for wear were serious errors. My men tried to get rid of him for you, quietly. There were complications. Death can be complicated. And now we have a different problem. Our associate in Bristol will not look kindly on any public unpleasantness. He needs absolute efficiency. Absolute confidence."

Vere's face hardened, becoming mulish. "Do you think I am not aware of that? Why do you think Wilson had to go? I want this to stop here. I want them dead," he growled. "Both of those clowns. I want all evidence gone. Do you understand, Shadwell!" Vere's voice suddenly rose to a crescendo as he lurched across the table to grasp Joshua by the lapels. But Joshua saw him coming, leaned back, snatched a pistol out of the drawer and levelled it at Vere.

"Sit down!" he roared. "Don't you ever try to touch me! Calm down damn you Vere! Pull yourself together!"

As Vere pulled back, transfixed by the sight of the pistol, the door burst open to reveal the dark bulk of Mordecai Fletcher, eyes blood-shot with fury.

"You want it to end do you?" he shouted hoarsely, striding across the floor and launching himself at Vere. "It will end, you bastard!" He wrapped both hands round Vere's throat and they crashed to the ground. Declan had been on the stairs behind Mordecai as they had first listened in mute incomprehension to the ravings of Vere, demanding their deaths. He raced to pull Mordecai off his victim, as Joshua also ran to the struggling men, pistol reversed to provide a butt with which to rain down blows indiscriminately on them both.

"Stop! Stop you bloody fool! Take his collar Declan, pull him off!"

In the rolling, roaring melee Declan was flung off like a nine-pin. He pitched heavily into Shadwell and scattered the flaring candlesticks, papers, quills and ink from the desk. At the same time the pistol discharged a thunderous retort and plume of smoke. Three men staggered to their feet, but Mordecai Fletcher, face frozen in a snarl of fury, lay in a widening pool of blood as treacherous flames from the fallen candles licked up the curtain linings, firing the window with a lurid light. In that one moment of silence Declan fled. He made it through the door, slid down the stairs, flew across the flags of the coach house and paused swaying at the entrance. Hearing the voices of Joshua's two men at the gate, he threw himself behind the shrubs and into the shadows. Raised voices in the office above and the flicker of rising flames in the window drew the men in to investigate, which gave Declan a chance. He made it to the gate as they entered the coach house, calling for their master, and tore off down the black lane to the quay. Heart beating fit to burst from his chest he hammered on, zigzagging through the courts, making for his barge, but as he neared it, he shied away.

"Safety in numbers. God help me!"

He slowed to get his breath, sat shivering on the ground, back pressed to the Corn Factor's wall, then stood, unsteadily, and made his way to the Full Moon. He slid into the packed bar with the other bargees, bought a drink, voice shaking, and pushed his way to a seat by the fire. In his world, there was only one authority higher than Mr Shadwell. He would rouse his horse and leave for Bristol that night.

# Chapter 5

**Mid-day: 13th October, 1831. The White Hart, Stall Street, Bath.**

Nathaniel sat over a steaming plate of ham and potatoes, warming his hands. He had excised the prime knuckle-bone from the platter and given it to Caradoc, who was at his usual post amongst the logs in the inglenook of the fireplace. The dog also had his customary saucer of small beer, but Nathaniel had taken brandy and hot water, downing much of it on the spot in answer to the growing chill. During the high winds of the previous night, the trees had shed many of their leaves, which lay in sodden piles of brown and maroon, inert and slimy in the sharp, dank air. His short walk down Walcot had been a cold one. The early touch of winter had bitten through his travelling cloak and into his bones and he had been glad to arrive at the Hart. The bar was over-crowded, dark, and hot as a cauldron, with men bulked out in caped greatcoats fortifying themselves for the afternoon and booming politics into the foetid air. Aping the regular demonstrations in London and the large industrial towns, this afternoon would see the liberal-minded in Bath take to the streets in support of the Reform Bill and Nathaniel was duty bound to watch them at it. The plan was for the demonstrators to convene in Queen Square by one p.m. then march in good order with bands and banners to Sydney Hotel, where the doyens of Bath's reform world would greet them from the hustings on the front lawn. General Palmer the liberal representative of the city would be the main speaker, with Captain

Mainwaring acting as Chairman. There was support from an assortment of imported speakers, including Diarmuid Casey, who were to add their own loyal addresses to the King and promote Bath's petition in support of the Bill. Many speeches would be made, songs sung and loyal declarations made before a peaceful conclusion: if all went according to plan. But the spectre of riot hovered, and, just in case it managed to land as it had already done in the Midlands, he needed to secure a reasonable vantage point in Pulteney Street.

The Whig lords in London were on a knife edge, as they needed mass agitations to alarm the Tory lords into accepting the Bill, but those demonstrations must fall short of uncontrollable riots which may lead to revolt. It was a fine and uncomfortable balance. The last thing they wanted was a united working class roused to a mob and demanding the Bill as a stepping stone to universal suffrage: the vote for all men, the Holy Grail of democratic reformers and anathema to the Whigs. It was a dangerous game, as the people, potentially the new Leviathan of power, might just rise in defiance of Commons, Lords and Crown alike to demand individual rights for all men. The gaol at Derby had been attacked earlier that very week and the castle at Nottingham was all but razed to the ground. Nathaniel comforted himself with the fact that both disturbances had been quenched fairly briskly by a deployment of troops. He glanced round the parlour. There did not seem to be any good reason for denying the franchise to any of the men assembled there, though some would fall short of owning a house of the required annual value of £10. He speculated as he watched them feeding, drinking, wearing out the arguments they had been rehearsing since the end of the French Wars. Should all male householders vote? What about the slum owners, should they lose the vote if they neglected their property? He watched the potboys about their business. Should they vote? They owned nothing, many flitting from rented room to rented room with no responsibilities. Many were illiterate and could not read a ballot paper. Some could not follow a simple line of argument. Surely they could not seriously expect the vote to make its way down to them?

Since June, well before the Lords' rejection of the second version of the Bill, the meetings of massed thousands had started. Hetherington's *Poor Man's Guardian* had acted as a unifying organ for the movement in the capital: enthusing, cajoling, marshalling. Henry Hetherington himself was a founder member of the new National Union of the Working Classes, which revived old fears of united labour. Nathaniel had caught up with the mood in the George and Dragon on Monday night. Excitement had been high, as had been expectations for the success of the demonstrations. But what would success bring? He frowned at the prospect and dug into his mound of potatoes.

Most of the men, waiting now in the cold in Queen Square, not lunching in the Hart, would still be denied a vote. Many houses in the lower town were worth only a half of the value pegged for access to the franchise. Lord Grey himself, Prime Minister and the champion of the Bill, wanted reform only in order to preserve. The rich and powerful would continue to rule, Bill or no Bill. So how long would it be before even the most law-abiding amongst liberals realised that polite protest stood for nought and their patient hopes for gradual, continued improvement were doomed? His mind returned to France and the collapse of Charles X and his cronies. The supposedly bloodless revolt had inflicted three days of mayhem on Paris, enough to remind the locals of the terrors of 1793. The British seemed to have forgotten 1649 and the execution of their king, forgotten the Civil War had happened at all, or at least the government hoped they had.

But on Monday night, aflame with desire for change, Robert Turner had spoken of 300,000 at a meeting last week in London. The whole of the army would be dwarfed by such a force if called to meet it. The language was also changing. Turner had read out from the penny booklet of the National Union, quoting the *Rights of Man*, describing law as the expression of public will and resistance being a sacred duty if that will be violated. More than this, he read Hetherington's invocation of Lord Nelson's message before Trafalgar: "England expects every man will do his duty". Perhaps "England" meant the workers and the populace was becoming battle ready? Whatever the upshot today in Bath, he knew Monday's meeting in London would be a fraught one. He checked the long-case clock in the corner: he needed to leave within the quarter hour to make his tryst with Robert Turner and Arthur Jamieson, the lynch-pins of the political club at the George and Dragon.

He continued to chew steadily on the ham, suddenly becoming aware that he was making little head-way, despite having been working on it for some considerable time. Perhaps Tobias had had a hand in it in his capacity as trainee cook. He shielded his plate from the elbows of boisterous customers jostling for attention and observed Frederick Tooson at his usual post behind the bar working up a glistening sweat, toiling to meet the unaccustomed demand. Potboys and barmaids were weaving through the press of customers, delivering precipitously stacked plates of food, foaming jugs of ale and sloping tankards to the tables. Nathaniel managed to catch Mary's eye as she passed, laden with four piled platters, and gave her a smile of encouragement. She paused briefly on her way back to the kitchen, fishing a piece of fatty meat from her pocket as she did so.

"There you be Caradoc. You sha'n't go hungry," she smiled, throwing it to

Caradoc's lair by the fire. He caught it and gulped it down.

"Glutton," said Nathaniel. "You spoil him, Mary."

"Sir I'm that happy! A little bite o' fat will make the dear creature happy too! All I can think on is my Matthew returning." Her face had lost its strained melancholy and was alight with joy. "Just a few more days. Probably. I keep telling the Johnty that Daddy's coming home!"

A flicker of anxiety crossed her face, after over a year away, to be so near, yet still at the mercy of the seas and fickle, bitter misfortune. Her stomach turned over, the familiar bucking sensation of terror and imminent loss.

"It's wonderful news, Mary," said Nathaniel. "It's put a spring in Martha's step too."

"She dotes on him sir. He's her only son; even though she's none too pleased he's chosen the sea. Anyway, she'll be glad of more help in the house."

"I hope she would ask me, Mary, if her need was urgent."

"Oh sir you're a paying guest, she couldn't. But Old Tom is getting heavier to lift as he's losing what strength he has left in his limbs. We need regular aid. I will think of something. Do not consider what I said sir, I spoke out of turn."

"Could you ask Tobias to come over to me when he can?"

"I surely will sir."

An unusual presence materialised behind the bar in the shape of the landlord, the brooding and magisterial Mr Bishop.

"Now Frederick," he admonished the barman, whose strident moustaches had escaped their waxing in the heat and the hairs stood out at angles like a bristled hedgehog. "We should've anticipated the rush today with the march imminent. We are almost dry of cider and the cellar-man's damned near ruptured with the number of barrels he's raised. Send a boy to the brewery to place an extra order. Delivery this afternoon mind or we'll lose the business."

"Yes sir Mr Bishop," said Frederick, as his employer marched down the steps to do battle with the remaining barrel.

"Tobias!"

Tobias Caudle hallooed an indistinct reply and broke cover from the corridor, scudding to a halt by Frederick and winking to Nathaniel. "Speak to you later Mr Parry sir!"

Once Tobias had been dispatched to the brewery Frederick took advantage of a lull in the orders.

"Could go either way today sir. Mark my words," he said gravely. "Captain Wilkins and his men are equal to anything, but between the two of us, the rest of the

Somerset Militia's a joke. Laughing stock they are!" He leaned conspiratorially over the bar. "Trained in the Sydney Gardens over the summer they did, you never saw anything like it, no not in all your born days! 'Specially if you was in the military." Nathaniel smiled encouragingly.

"Plough boys most of 'em," scoffed the barman. "Their gear's just left-overs from the Frenchey Wars! Guns'd prob'ly blow up and maim the lads before they'd shoot accurate at the angry man! Laughed out of the Gardens they was! By the by, did you enjoy your session with the Captain's fencing club?"

"Capital evening," replied Nathaniel. "Thank you for putting me on to it."

As Frederick seemed inclined to swop confidences, he decided to fish for more. "I also met a Mr Howard Dill again yesterday. We lunched together. Very pleasant gentleman. Do you know of him?"

"I should think so sir. Mr Dill's family were regular merchant princes in Bristol. Slavers y'know. Not that we talk so loud on that subject these days. Wealthy gentleman he is still. A lion in Bath society sir. Notwithstanding his mild appearance if you take my meaning." He gathered together some of the empty tankards which had grown like a forest on the bar as they talked. "Not exactly a benefactor here though, not like the Captain who's a saint! His workers have good wages and get treated every Whit to a fair and a feed. It's a red letter day on the Twiverton calendar I can tell you. And it's well known his youngest workers get off very lightly. You know, under nines. The Short Time fellas are always shouting about them little 'uns. Well they do no more than about six hours a day. It's a regular holiday compared with field work. There's nothing a damned Factory Act can do to better the Captain's regimen I can tell you! Anyway, the government will give the Short Time agitation short shrift. Ha! Short shrift, not short time! That's what they'll get. Whigs have their hands full with the Reform Bill. There'll be no interfering in a man's independence in his own business. Not in our life times at any rate!"

Having put the world to rights to his immense satisfaction, Frederick Tooson puffed out his cheeks and deigned to raise an eyebrow to invite an order from the most insistent of the customers who were densely packed and parched, behind the new and flourishing growth of empty tankards on the bar.

Nathaniel whistled for Caradoc and they made their way out into Stall Street. A brittle, watery sun had broken through the flying clouds, lighting the tops of the buildings and sharpening the shadows. The wind whipped at his cloak and threw the leaves up in squalls. He could hear the multitude as he reached the Upper Borough Walls. The crowd had swelled to fill Queen Square to overflowing and it took some time to locate the printers' delegation where Robert Turner and Arthur Jamieson had said they would be. There were dozens of silk trade banners, riding a man's height above the mass of heads and hats, and flags on poles flapping and cracking in the fitful gusts of wind. Robert, assisted by a puffing Arthur, was struggling to anchor one of the wooden supports of the printers' banner into a leather holster which dangled from a lanyard round his neck.

"Easy Arthur now. Easy! This damned thing'll do me a mischief if it slips. Got a mind o' its own!"

"There you be. Safely stowed."

"Thank God for that. You all roight wit' other end Eddie?"

"Ooh arr," grunted his fellow bearer. "Oiy got 'er 'oisted perfect 'ere!"

The banner was a veritable sail of silk bearing the lavishly embroidered arms of the Printers' Union. It was more usually aired on church walking days and there was some anxiety about it getting wet. Eddie had a bolt of cloth over his shoulder to fling over the banner if the heavens opened, as they seemed poised to do.

"What a crowd!" exclaimed Nathaniel. "You must be pleased with the turn out."

They looked about them, triumphantly. The square was solidly packed with a mass of respectable humanity. Men, and even a few women, all in their best clothes thronged together, talking loudly and excitedly, eyes bright with visions of victory. Who could withstand such numbers? Such a show replicated in all the principal towns of the land must alter the minds of the Lords and win the day, or so it seemed. From Nathaniel's vantage point he could see that the printers were matched by the waving banners of the cabinet makers, plasterers, masons and sawyers, with other trades out of full sight on the other side of the square. Placards bobbed above the heads of the crowd ranging in sentiment from the loyal: "Long live the King!" to the more combative; "We are all agreed" and "The Bill and Nothing Else!"; to the extravagantly inflammatory call of the American rebels; "No taxation without representation."

"Will the authorities let the tax claim stand do you think?" asked Nathaniel.

"They want no trouble," said Robert Turner gleefully. "We own the town today!"

A few constables stood in groups round the outskirts of the crowd, but did indeed seem to be in as good a humour as the marchers, and not a dragoon in sight.

As Nathaniel swept Caradoc up from the ground and tucked him under his arm to avoid him being trampled, he caught sight of a rare scuffle. A group of the notorious "boys of the town" had entered the square from Barton Street and were jostling a group of marchers.

"Ye young demon!" bawled a man, dropping his placard and seizing the nearest

111

boy. "Pick my pocket would you!"

"Wasn't me. Search me! Search me!" The urchin pulled out his torn pockets as the constables closed in, grasping him and the collars of any other boys within reach. As a body, all the marchers in the area rounded on the scene and made grabs for ears, arms, necks, or rags, whatever came closest to hand.

"Search them all!" roared the victim. "This scallywag will have passed on my wallet to another. We're wise to you, ye young devils."

Blows and cuffs were liberally administered and in moments the wallet was recovered from the floor and the boys where shooed away.

"See what I mean," laughed Robert. "Even them varmints can be tamed when we all act together!"

Nathaniel noticed Tobias on the corner of the square, exchanging rapid words with the boys as they made off for the lower town. Nathaniel made his excuses and caught up with him.

"Oh 'ello Mr Parry," said Tobias. "They're some of mi'boys from Little 'Ell."

"So I see. Mind you don't get too fond of their company Tobias. You seem to be doing well at the Hart."

"I am sir," he smiled. "I got a proper room in the stables now and I'm doing more in the kitchens."

"Yes," said Nathaniel, "I thought you might be. Now what can you tell me about the chances of a riot?"

"There'll be no trouble today sir. All town's calm as a mill pond. See, there's no soldiers and no magistrates. You don't need to worry. The lads just wanted to see what the crowd might 'ave to offer, so to speak."

A mighty blast on trumpets, massed shrieking from the fifes and the booming of bass drums interrupted them.

"Look Tobias, the procession is moving off. I think I'll follow them. It looks safe enough."

Tobias peered at Nathaniel through his straggling fringe and smiled knowingly.

"You're not really frightened at all are you sir?"

Nathaniel flicked him a sixpence, dropped the wriggling Caradoc to make shift as best he could and merged with the thousands as they followed the drums towards Pulteney Street. Cheers and waves from the windows round the square drew his eyes upwards. Most windows were filled with the smiling faces of elegantly dressed ladies and children, safe above the maelstrom of the crowd and enjoying the spectacle.

"The Bill the whole Bill and nothing but the Bill," bawled a young boy amongst

112

a clutch of infants leaning from a first floor window-sill. He followed up with a delighted shriek of laughter and was promptly dragged in by a governess. Nathaniel waved back to the other children and then sought out the windows of the corner house. Diarmuid's apartment was dark as he expected, but above it, a bonus, Coco in a rose silk dressing gown, her dark hair flowing over her shoulders, a glass in her hand. He waved wildly, surprised by how pleased he was to see her. She blew him a kiss and raised her glass as he was swept on by the crowd.

Nathaniel found himself exhilarated by the experience of marching with so many, the tread of thousands reverberating on the ground, the calls and the snatches of song lifting their hearts and the crush threatening at times to lift him off his feet. He felt the mighty power of the people and tried again the sound of phrase that had come to him so forcibly, the new Leviathan. But it was not a despotic beast on today's showing. It was a creature entirely benign and the atmosphere of good-humoured carnival persisted. As they made their stately progress down Bridge Street towards the broad concourse of Great Pulteney, he raised his head to look to the distant hustings and flags in front of the Sydney Hotel. All before it was now a solid river of reformers. It was unlikely that he would be able to get close enough to hear the speeches and decided it was better to rescue Caradoc, take him home and then approach the hotel from Bathwick Street, short-circuiting the crowd. He caught sight of his dog, whistled him over and scooped him up, so he could make his way back to Walcot against the flow, keeping close to the buildings.

He managed to double back to High Street relatively quickly and hurried down Walcot Street, setting Caradoc free to run ahead. They passed the deserted George and Dragon, the silent markets and shops, many closed in honour of the demonstration and some, like the premises of James Crisp the hatter, festooned with reform banners urging solidarity. As they closed in on their lodgings, he caught sight of the figure of a woman pacing back and forth in great consternation. Caradoc evidently recognised her and raced over, yapping a greeting. She turned quickly, startled, and bent to pat the dog. Looking up anxiously she saw Nathaniel, called out in relief and rushed to him.

"Oh Mr Parry I am so pleased to see you! I knew you had rooms somewhere hereabouts but had no idea where. I must speak with you. I left Tanner waiting outside the dressmaker's."

The young woman had a veil over her bonnet which fell to her shoulders, obscuring her face, but the voice, the loose bun of golden curls at her neck and the richness of her apparel left him in no doubt as to the identity of his visitor.

"Mrs Vere, follow me, my rooms are here."

He ushered her before him to Martha's front door, observing her distress, betrayed by her trembling hands and stiff back. This was a Tilly he was unfamiliar with. No longer the beautiful, selfish wife with her habitual air of entitlement, but more like a younger sister: gauche, vulnerable and afraid. Nathaniel let them in and they paused in the narrow hall, shutting out the street, creating a moment of proximity and intimate silence, which was instantly to be broken. From behind the door at the end of the passage sounded a high reedy voice, raised in song, and accompanied by an erratic beating of metal percussion on the flag floor.

"We'll rant and we'll roar,
Like true British sailors,
We'll range and we'll roam,
O'er all the salt seas,
Until we strike soundings.....

No, no young Johnty! Thou shalt not beat thy great grand'fer with that ladle! Ye besom!"

Caradoc raised his tail high and trotted straight for the door, pawing it open and making a bee-line for the ancient man and infant by the fire. Tilly Vere stood uncertainly in the dark hall and Nathaniel strode before her to the kitchen.

"Hello Mr Spence. Is Mrs Spence at home?"

"She be out in the back garden sir but will be in directly! Bring in your guest, the Johnty and me could do with a diversion!"

Nathaniel sensed the reluctance of Tilly and spared her that.

"That is a kind offer, but I will speak with Mrs Vere in the parlour if I may, as she has urgent business. Please tell Mrs Spence. Tea would be very welcome if she would be so kind as to make some."

"A truer word was never spoke," said Tom. "Oiy would welcome it like a brother mi'self. Powerful thirsty work conversin' with this young sprig 'ere."

Johnty had occupied himself with a close scrutiny of Caradoc who had appropriated the ladle and was worrying it.

"Just a'fore ye go to be closeted in the parlour," said Tom slyly. "What news of the march? There's been a mighty throng of folk a'goin' down the street this morning."

"It is going very well," said Nathaniel, as he followed Tilly into the front room. "Very good humoured."

"It'll come to nought then!" called Tom after them triumphantly.

Tilly settled herself in a high backed mahogany chair by an occasional table which was draped in a red crushed-velvet cloth and supported two porcelain figures:

114

a coy shepherdess and her shepherd. Tilly slowly lifted her veil to reveal a face grotesquely changed. It was distended down the right side, swollen and reddened, with the bloated and bruised eye-socket closed up like that of a new-born pup.

"Good God what happened to you?"

Tilly's open eye swam with tears and she held the edge of the veil over her injuries, ashamed.

"My husband struck me. As you see, not just once but repeatedly. Mr Parry I am so afraid."

Unannounced by any audible footfall, the door fell open. Tilly struggled and failed to pull the veil back over her face, her hands coming to a premature halt under the silent scrutiny of Martha who stood, framed, in the door-way.

Nathaniel sprang to his feet and introduced the women.

"Mrs Vere, " said Martha, scrutinising the damage to Tilly's face, "as you are seated in my parlour may I ask what has happened to you?"

"I have had a fall madam," blustered Tilly. "Mr Parry is engaged on business for my husband and I need to speak with him privately."

"You may speak in comfort here madam," said Martha stiffly. "I will bring tea and cake for you directly. Mr Parry I hear that was your wish?"

"Very kind of you Mrs Spence," said Nathaniel.

All three of them knew that Martha had to chaperone the meeting. Propriety, religious duty and her unconquerable curiosity made it entirely unavoidable. Nathaniel had to buy time.

"Mrs Vere is feeling unwell and has had no lunch. Perhaps we might also have some cold meat and bread?"

Martha silently accepted the deal and withdrew.

"She will probably give us ten minutes," he smiled encouragingly as the door closed behind Martha.

"Mr Parry! Oh, Nathaniel! Raphael has hurt me in so many ways. I will never trust him again and I'm not staying! I must leave him!" She moved swiftly to the seat next to Nathaniel and seized his hands in hers. "I've known it now for over a year but I guessed it before. My God, I thought I could change him!" her voice broke to a sob: she breathed deeply and continued. "I don't know how to say this. He's not normal, he likes little girls, children. Not women. He married me when I was fourteen years old, but still looked a child. For some time he has baited me," she struggled to articulate the bitterness of her defeat, the first encountered in what had been a singularly charmed life. "He said I had lost my bloom, my freshness!" Unable to resist, she instinctively attempted to flutter her eyelids and gaze into his eyes. The effort caused her to wince in pain. It was pitiful and he felt a stab of sorrow for her, the beautiful, girlish wife, whose existence was valued only for her beauty and whose real self, whose mind and soul, counted for absolutely nothing to anyone.

She continued in a monotone, as though once started, as in a confessional, she must not stop. "He stayed out at nights, sometimes all night. I know he has been with others. Harlots. I could smell them on his clothes. Last night he came in very late and in a wild mood. He was so cruel. That is when he started to mistreat me, he hurt me, abused me." She shook her head, shivering, repulsed by the memory. "Afterwards, in his sleep he was raving, cursing. He called out, 'Babs, Babs, my lovely girl!' I woke him and asked him – who was this Babs? He was in a fury. He struck me about my face with his hand, and beat me with his belt. I will never allow him to do that again but I can't fight him. I'll run away. He was talking to our footman Tanner about business in Bristol tomorrow. Help me Nathaniel!" Tears ran in rivulets down her cheeks and her hands shook convulsively in his.

"Tilly be calm. Listen to me. I agree, you are in danger, but running away won't solve this. You need to extricate yourself more carefully and be able to live a reasonable life without him. It is possible that the law might accomplish this for you. I have been told that your husband's first wife may have died in suspicious circumstances. Keep still and listen! Furthermore, I have a suspicion that he knows more of the murder of Roderick Wilson than he has admitted. At this moment, a young man is in gaol and might suffer the ultimate penalty for that murder, which he did not commit and in which your husband might have been involved. It is vital for many people's sake that we find out the truth. Now, do you know of any reason for your husband wanting Mr Wilson dead?"

Tilly steadied her breathing, thought for a moment and then began.

"Roderick Wilson was an employee and also of late a boon companion of his. They frequented the same gambling clubs and billiard rooms. Probably brothels as well for all I know. One night at the end of last month they had been out very late and came back together to our house. They carried on drinking in Raphael's dressing room and Mr Wilson stayed the night there. When Raphael went to dress the next morning there was a furious argument. I think truly he had forgotten that Mr Wilson was there, he never usually allows anyone else to spend time there alone. Mr Wilson was baiting him over something he had seen. I know Raphael keeps things secretly in there, but usually under lock and key. Tanner supervises the maids as they clean there and the housekeeper doesn't have a key."

"I want you to try to gain access to that dressing room. See what you can find. Anything that Wilson might have seen which would give him a hold over your husband. Anything to tie him to brothels: or to young girls. I am also interested in your husband's relationship with a Bristol ship owner called Edwin Ravenswood. What exactly do you know of that man and their business dealings?"

Tilly moved closer. He tightened his grip on her hands.

"Nathaniel," she breathed. "I know a lot about Mr Ravenswood and I will search the room, but I am so frightened. Please look after me. I am not a poor woman. I think you find me attractive." She kept her good side towards him and leaned in to rest her head in his shoulder. He found their entwined hands pressed between her bosom and his chest as Tilly moved in even closer. Salvation came in the worthy shape of Martha and the tea tray, which struck the door insistently demanding entry. Nathaniel was on his feet in an instant to let her in and Tilly jumped up in confusion, turning her back on the room and studying the view from the window to explain her move from her visitor's seat. Martha bustled round arranging high backed chairs, placing the dishes and cups on the table.

"Now Mrs Vere perhaps you would like to pour whilst I bring the rest?"

Tilly abandoned the veil and set about the task.

Cold lamb and red currant jelly, bread, tea and a cake had been presented, the cake centre-stage.

"This is from a special batch, You are welcome to try it." said Martha proudly. "My son will be home soon and this is one of the plum and treacle cakes he is powerfully fond of."

They worked silently through a preliminary plate-full of meat under Martha's watchful eye. She continued, "He will sail into Bristol any day now!"

They continued to eat in the silence, smiling in encouragement for Martha to fill the void.

"He's on the *Mathilda*."

"That's my ship!" announced Tilly, suddenly animated. "Mr Ravenswood named it for me! My husband's bank has financed a number of Mr Ravenswood's voyages. His shipping company is an important customer and his vessels are an investment for the New Bank." Tilly looked meaningfully at Nathaniel.

"He sails for Mr Ravenswood then Mrs Spence?" said Nathaniel.

"I think so," said Martha. "Yes, I think he did mention that. But it is so long since he went on the voyage." Her face softened and sagged, the sharp features relaxing into a network of wrinkles, and her eyes crinkled with love. "Thank the Lord he will be back soon! At least it's not a warship, just trade you know. Just the seas to combat. No more Bonapartes just yet! God rest his soul but Boney was a hellhound!"

117

Nathaniel determined to see Tilly off on her way and brought the tea party to a conclusion as fast as he could. She would be unlikely to achieve much in the way of snooping until tomorrow at the earliest, the last working day of the week and with the possibility of Vere being away from Bath. Maybe she would get a chance to search the dressing room then. He ran his hands through his hair, focusing his thoughts. The chances of finding anything of use were slim. His next move would be to follow up Vere's under-age weaknesses, and there was one woman he was decidedly keen to see again who probably knew all there was to know about Bath brothels.

By late afternoon Nathaniel had positioned Caradoc on guard by the bushes surrounding the gardens in the centre of Queen Square and was in the entrance hall of Coco's building. He had barely an hour before he needed to return home to change for dinner with the Petersons and was relieved when the concierge instantly secured the services of a familiar pasty faced maid to usher him up the stairs to Coco's rooms. As he paced behind her, Nathaniel wondered idly how many clients trod this same worn blue carpet hoping to bargain for Coco's time. The condition of the stairwell deteriorated in direct proportion to its height. By the time they reached Coco's floor it was shabby, with dusty corners and chipped paint, which made the contrast with the interior of her apartment all the more startling. He was shown into a sitting room at once restrained and elegant. The Age of Reason ruled in the salon of Miss Montrechet. No clutter, no riots of stuffed birds or chintz festoons, just smooth gilded surfaces, calm pale hues, cold marble tabletops, a classical statue in one corner and a mahogany Louis XV clock on the mantelpiece. But as he looked more closely at the timepiece he laughed to see that the gilt bronze base sported the figure of a partially clad woman frolicking with two chuckling cherubs in a forest arbor. Suddenly he was aware of her, standing motionless by the window, inspecting him.

"Good afternoon Miss Montrerchet. What a beautiful room you have here."

Coco tripped lightly to him from her vantage point and planted two chaste kisses on his cheeks.

"Welcome Nathaniel," she said, adjusting her light wool shawl, soft cream and fine as a cobweb, and steering him to take a seat by her on one of her three green and white striped sofas. "I was intrigued to see you walking over the square to see me. So purposeful, so intent! What do you want?" She smiled challengingly, coiling her arms around him and staring into his eyes. "I wondered how long it would take you to return."

Nathaniel took her hands firmly, bringing them down to her waist.

118

"Coco, pleased as I am to see you, and wonderful as you are looking, I am dashed short of time and I need your help with some rather specialised local information."

She widened her eyes boldly in mock amazement and pursed her lips. "Well?"

"I have spoken with Howard Dill as you suggested. He was most helpful. I now need to speak with some people on the other side of the law. Have you any idea which of the bawdy houses here deal in young girls?"

"Which don't!"

"No, I mean children. Unusual tastes?"

"I am disappointed in you Nathaniel," she said, winding her arms around him once more and whispering in his ear. "So unworldly: so hot in your pursuit of wrongdoers, so vigilant, yet so dismissive of your poor Coco."

She kissed him lingeringly, her lips soft and warm against his. He felt the flutter of her heart, breathed in her gentle scent of lavender, now overlaid with the richness of lily and rose, and took her in his arms. To resist was more than flesh and blood could realistically withstand. More than that, it would not be gallant: it would not be what Lord Byron would have done.

"You taste nice," she said, sitting back suddenly.

"So do you Coco," said Nathaniel. "but I am here on my business, not yours."

"I didn't intend to charge you," she retorted, too quickly.

"Seriously," said Nathaniel, showing her a kindness by ignoring the weakness, "where should I look for such information?"

"I know where Vere went if that is what you are after."

He nodded in reply.

"Then go to Green Park West, the house with the pink drapes. It's run by a couple called Shadwell, Rosie and Joshua. But take care. Joshua doesn't like to be questioned and he has a couple of men on duty most days. They run some of the Avon Street stews for him, dealing with the rough trade. He is no stranger to violence Nathaniel, but he only allows gentlemen to Green Park." She laughed shortly. "Gentlemen! A contradiction in terms. You can go there if you want a girl so young she looks like a child, or if you want to be punished." She paused and he was surprised to read uncompromising disapproval in her face.

"I've never worked there, of course," she continued. "But I've heard the stories. You are no parochial yourself Nathaniel, you must know these things. Atrocious deeds are committed in our civilised society which all the King's forces and all Peel's policemen care nothing about at all. As well as the work in the houses, children disappear from the slum areas of towns and don't even make it to the brothels. Poor parents and bad ones sell unwanted children. You must know that there is a white slave trade. They are sent abroad. Some so small they are drugged and sent out in coffins to avoid questions. Some aren't even for sex. They are tortured to death, Nathaniel, by those who enjoy inflicting pain on the helpless. There's a cause for you, for the government which seems to prefer to work itself into a fine frenzy about voting or preventing children earning wages in factories or the difficult lives of black slaves on the other side of the world."

"Do you think the Shadwells or their customers are involved?"

"Why not?"

"What have you heard of Raphael Vere?"

"Nothing specific, but ask a girl called Barbara at the Shadwell's. She's been working in what they call "the nursery". Try her."


Despite his forebodings and the restrictions the event placed on his investigation at the Shadwell's, the evening at the Peterson's turned out to be a surprising and jolly one. It brought good, if puzzling news, and defused the combined effects of his interviews with Tilly and Coco, which had both been distracting in very different ways. Nathaniel had dressed with care for the evening, selecting a bright blue necktie, tying it in his favourite draped knot and matching it with his blue striped waistcoat. An evening round any family hearth was a rare experience for him, and the bonus of a conventionally happy family such as was provided Chez Peterson was rarer still. He brushed his unruly black hair back from his face and grinned broadly. He was rather looking forward to it. The barbed and querulous sessions with the Drakes at their rented rooms in Bristol had not been the same thing at all. Tonight would be for relaxing.

He wore his double-caped greatcoat to guard against the sharp west wind, but was still cold by the time he and Caradoc arrived at Marlborough Buildings. After extended periods with Tom and the Johnty in the kitchen, Nathaniel had felt the terrier might be in danger of overstaying his welcome so he had prised him from the flags by the fire and marched him up the hill and round the back of the Crescent. Again, despite his own blackest forebodings, Caradoc had an unexpectedly excellent evening. Instead of being left "on guard" in the area by the basement kitchen, he had been elevated to the dining room on the insistence of the twins, who had proceeded to fete him flatteringly and relentlessly, placing him under the dining table so he could be fed surreptitiously throughout the evening. As they had led Caradoc away, Nathaniel was delighted to be greeted not only by Captain and Mrs Peterson and Emma, but also by a beaming Anna Grant and Henry Blake.

"I cannot adequately express my relief," insisted Henry later, as they started work on their first course at Mrs Peterson's grand table overlooking the back of the property and the shadowy woods and lawns of the park. Dodging his head round an exuberant table centrepiece of silver gilt nymphs, fluted vases and nodding ferns, he had at length managed to fix Nathaniel with a look of ecstatic relief and proceeded to re-tell his tale.

"I could barely believe it when the officer came and simply said I was free to go. All charges dropped! The body of a man was found in the lower town this very morning," he paused theatrically for effect, "shot to death!" The rest of the party had heard this fact, and a recitation of its significance, a number of times before Nathaniel had arrived and the sensation, for all but Anna, had worn rather thin. She remained enraptured as he continued but the cutlery was very busy at all other place settings. "When the body was inspected bonds from the bank were discovered on his person, from the same issue as those found in my rooms! And," in preparation for this last clinching detail his eyes blazed in triumph, "around his neck on a chain was found Roderick Wilson's gold and diamond ring. Mr Wilson's name was engraved for all to see which indicated the wretch as at least a thief. Thank God the officers finally decided to believe me. As well as Anna's word, others had testified that I had been seen in St James's Square late that fateful night. My visit was far from being the secret I had planned! The dead man was recognised as a bargee, a rent collector and known scoundrel. He had been seen near my rooms in Kingsmead on a number of occasions and it has been decided that he was cunning enough to have tried to disguise his crime by implicating me. It is common knowledge that Mr Wilson and I were the only two clerks in the main office at the New Bank and were known in town."

For Nathaniel, the news was good in so far as that it released him from his duty to investigate the murder for Vere and the Captain. Henry was free and bumptiously happy, viewing the case as closed: though of course it ought not to be. Nathaniel busied himself in playing the charming guest, congratulating Henry and the efficiency of the constables and responding when necessary to the waves of chatter emanating from the twins. They were both sure they had made a superb impression on the visitor and the exchanges had allowed the solitary Emma time to relax and observe him.

As the banter flowed inconsequentially, she managed to release partially the cruelly tight pins that secured her hair in an intricate bun at the back of her head, whilst leaving the trailing curls at the front. The construction of the extravagant hair-style had been overseen by her mama and radical change would have attracted too much attention. Her fearful anticipation of the evening had created a headache of monstrous proportions and she had been forced to hide in her room to avoid her mother for most of the day. Sadly, it had been impossible to ban her from the final stages of dressing for the evening, and Mama had made herself most tiresome. The hair-dressing, the gown, the choice of jewels and a conversation plan to ensure Emma presented herself congenially to Mr Parry had exercised her considerably. Emma had managed to keep her temper, and practised deep breathing exercises as the remorselessly excitable voice had bleated ever on, as indeed, she suddenly realised it still did.

"Your poor dear mother Anna!" exclaimed Mrs Peterson. "I warned her in my letter that you had very bad news you were preparing to convey concerning your fiancé. What torments she must have endured knowing that he was incarcerated on a murder charge! You must write to her directly to ease her mind."

Anna had been preparing herself for this, her lines were rehearsed and ready, "I decided to spare her the full details Mrs Peterson. I felt it would be too cruel. I simply informed her that there had been an unfortunate death at Henry's place of employment, which was being investigated and he was upset by it."

"Oh," sighed Mrs Peterson, disappointed.

Anna's heart banged unpleasantly, preparing her for another of Mrs Peterson's protracted eruptions, and she glanced over in mute appeal to the Captain.

"Much the best my dear," said the Captain, patting his wife's arm to discourage the voicing of extended dissatisfaction. "Very wise of you, Anna. All over now." He turned to Nathaniel, "Mr Parry, we hope that our little affair has not diverted you too much from your family and other business. I hope your visit to Bristol went well."

"It did indeed," said Nathaniel blandly. "I met my colleague, all very satisfactory."

"I have not been to Bristol for years," declared Emma suddenly. "I enjoyed it so much. So many ships, the masts like forests. So many strange cargoes, the air smelled so rich, so exotic!"

"Would you like to adventure abroad Miss Peterson?" said Nathaniel. "I must confess I feel restless if I stay in one place for too long."

"Oh Mr Parry," simpered Mrs Peterson, who felt Emma's conversational gambit had been unusually promising and provided an opening to play a particularly good, but dangerously high stakes card: hope sprang in the motherly bosom. "Do not say you will be leaving us. You hardly know the company yet and the season is just beginning. Why, a Masked Ball has been announced just this week. It will be at the Upper Rooms on Saturday the 29th. Mr Parry," Mrs Peterson, eyes a-gleam and exerting a vice-like grip on Nathaniel's arm, went for broke, "say you will be of our party!"

On the edge of a regretful refusal, Nathaniel paused, glanced at Emma and almost laughed out loud. She looked horrified, eyes wide in disbelief. Her rich chestnut hair in a glorious profusion of curls, her usual discreet gown replaced by one sweepingly low necked, in apricot satin with a richly laced falling collar, she blushed deeply. She was clearly appalled by her mother's move, but in an instant accepted it with a charming grace and managed to smile at him. He liked her bravery; it was entrancing. Emma Peterson was a very attractive, self-possessed, intelligent woman, different in so many ways from the two other women who had presented themselves to him that day: Tilly, eager for a new shoulder to lean on, another prop for her to coil her beautiful, needy body around and Coco, urgently desirable, dangerous, but her image confused by overlaid visions of the French docks lined with brothels, the worn out, diseased prostitutes lolling at the doors.

"I would be delighted to join your party Mrs Peterson," he said. "And to escort Miss Peterson to the Ball if that would be suitable. I am afraid I must return to London this weekend, but will return after I conclude my business."

Mrs Peterson, almost bursting with delight, had to restrain herself from embracing him and wondered how long it might be before she could bring the newly launched affair to a proper matrimonial conclusion. "We will have the tickets ready and meet you at the Rooms at six on the evening of the 29th! A date to remember! We will be six in our party. Six at six that evening."

"Yes, my dear," said the Captain, hastily. "If it is convenient for you, Mr Parry, we would all be pleased to entertain you. The least we can do. So kind of you to help with our little problems."

The evening continued to pass off well as they worked their way through the fish, meats and desserts. Emma drank more wine than usual and was talkative, feeling that the arrangement for the ball, though grotesquely humiliating at the time, gave her permission to speak to him. It could be seen as a social duty. Anna and Henry were engrossed in each other and the Petersons encouraged the twins to perform on the piano and sing after the meal, loudly commending them and providing cover for her to dally very pleasantly with Nathaniel. They talked of travel and adventure, of London, of sickness and health, of poetry. They warmed to each other as they swopped verses from Keats and clapped enthusiastically as each song ended, encouraging more. They sparred in whispers, duelling with verses from *The Eve of St Agnes*. Emma lost, blushing furiously she pretended she had forgotten the lines, as she was next when the story reached the place where Porphyro stole into

Madeline's room. It was too much in mixed company, even if the others were pretending not to hear. She would never have started without the wine.

Finally, as the twins were hoarse they were relieved of their duties, which prompted Anna to make a move to leave. Henry was to escort her to her employer's in St James's Square and the party broke up. Nathaniel took his leave formally, bowing over the ladies' hands, expressing thanks and was out through the door and on the front step in the cold night when the Captain stepped out after him.

"Satisfied with the Wilson business?"

"No sir. I will continue to gather intelligence. In particular I would like to know more of Mr Raphael Vere. I know you are of his circle in Bath and gather you have considerable investments in his bank."

"I have, and am poised to pump more into it. His ventures have been pleasantly remunerative I must say. What's your caveat sir?"

"I think he is under severe strain at present and I would like to know the cause of it. I'll let you know as soon as I make progress."

Caradoc sidled up and Nathaniel held out his hand to his host. "Thank you Captain for a really enjoyable evening. I will return to Bath towards the end of the month."

"In time for the Masked Ball!" said the Captain, raising a bristly eyebrow. "I'd regard it as a personal kindness if you would."

"I intend to."

Emma watched from her window to see Nathaniel and Caradoc walk up Marlborough Buildings to the Royal Crescent, she watched them pause to look at the lights in the vale and saw Caradoc rush yapping at the shadows thrown by the trees. She watched as they pushed on, round the curve of the buildings and out of sight. She held the curtains tightly, blessing and cursing her mother, hardly daring to believe the possibilities offered to her, on a plate, by that foolish, intolerable woman.

The following evening Nathaniel made very different preparations for his excursion into Bath. He took from his trunk a small bag of mixed coins: shillings, half-crowns and sovereigns, and a frock coat he had not yet worn in the city, a bulky one which did away with need for a greatcoat or his cloak. He tried it on, checking the buttons, all there. It was important, as this was a reversible coat, brown on one side, green on the other, and it would spoil the illusion if it flapped open and displayed the colour hidden within. He had poachers' pockets in the skirts, ready primed with a collapsible top-hat, flatter close-fitting cap, spectacles and white muffler. With the judicious addition of a limp, enough in the way of a disguise for one man to swagger from the upper-town, cut down an alley and emerge for the trek to Green Park as someone different. The makila was selected as a walking stick in preference to the swordstick and Caradoc was relegated to the garden, though Tom, who had been shaping-up as Caradoc's sworn friend and ally by late afternoon, would no doubt order Martha to let him into the kitchen as soon as she returned from her Methodist meeting. Tom and Caradoc had had a tiff earlier, a matter concerning an attack on Tom's knitting, but all now seemed forgiven.

Nathaniel marched off jauntily down Walcot, sporting the top-hat and swinging his makila, practising a few sweeps, adjusting his grip as he went. The street was subdued, with just the odd carter completing his rounds. A ragged boy stood forlornly by the opposite gutter.

"Sweep you a crossin' sir?"

But Nathaniel's way was to the west and he shook his head. He made good time, passing the Saw Close and pushing on to Kingsmead, the frontier of the lower town. By this stage of his walk the noises of the night had risen to a cacophony around him. Ale houses and inns, garish with gaslight, were rammed with raucous customers, the streets were busy with people dodging the fly carriages which trotted their passengers along the cobbles, rattling and swaying as they picked up speed on the straight. A few sedan chairmen padded like silent ghosts on the pavements in the shadow of the buildings. He side-stepped them and slid into a dingy, deserted alley, safe from the eyes of the street and effected his disguise in seconds. He took off the hat, collapsed it and swapped it for the cap, reversed the coat and donned the conspicuous white muffler and spectacles. He checked that he was unobserved and sidled out, crossing the top of Avon Street. Here the crowds spilling from the assorted drinking dens blocked the pavements and the stench of the slums wreathed around him like a poison gas, gagging in his throat. Lives were lived more on the street in proportion to the unpleasantness of the dwellings, and from here to the river were some of the worst the city could offer. The debris underfoot had become thicker and more noxious, the black mud now glutinous and sucking at his boots. The roaming dogs were more numerous, sharing the detritus with foraging chickens and a rooting, grunting pig, obscenely daubed in filth, a bizarre remnant of rural life, clinging on in the city like an obese ghost of the past. Nathaniel's tapping makila had helped clear the way thus far, but the thickening crowd and its increased volatility had made it unwise to continue flourishing it. Suddenly, to his left, a door flew open and a boisterous knot of drinkers over-spilled from a tavern, shouting wild encouragement to two women who had clearly been fighting for some time and had attracted such partisan support that the landlord had ejected the lot of them.

A blowsy harridan, hair descending in lank rods from a misshapen bun, mouth wide and snarling obscenities was shaping up afresh to her assailant, a handy looking young woman with a rapidly blackening eye and greasy torn bodice.

"Go on moiy love!" bawled a man, jostling others back to allow his pugilist of choice more space. "Land 'er another right 'ook!"

The fat woman obligingly swung her ham of a fist, but as if in slow motion. The handy woman, less drunk and bulky, moved in to block the blow with her left and delivered a powerful punch to the protruding stomach, an open and vast target. Her fist sank in momentarily, but she was clearly experienced and pulled back smartly to miss both the toppling upper body and fountain of vomit which preceded it to the roaring acclamation of the crowd. Nathaniel also dodged, as the back row of spectators billowed towards him. He slowed his gait as he did so and concentrated on developing a pronounced limp, leaning heavily on the makila.

The elegant terrace of Green Park West soon came into view, rearing up out of the dark before the shaved and tree fringed lawn which lay before it across its private road: so close to the river slums, yet it could be miles and worlds away. A patrolling constable nodded to Nathaniel as he made his way to the Shadwell's door. It was more elegant that he had imagined, the drapes Coco had mentioned were a pale dusky pink and grey striped. The house appeared seemly, muted, well appointed, with immaculately clean steps and neat boot scrapers on guard against defilement at each side of the door. He pulled the bell and was ushered into the hall by a comely woman in a green gown, with flaming red lips and stone cold eyes.

"Welcome sir. How may I help you?"

"Thank you Madam. I am visiting your house on a recommendation," he had decided on a recklessly mendacious ploy, as he never intended to darken the doors again. "Mr Raphael Vere suggested I come here for entertainment this evening as I am a visitor to Bath and enjoy exactly the same type of recreations as he does himself. I would particularly like to meet Barbara of whom he speaks so highly. Is that possible Mrs Shadwell? You are Madam Shadwell I presume?"

She took his coat, muffler and cap silently. His makila he retained, still leaning on it and listing to the right as he walked.

"I'm afraid that is impossible sir. And your name is?"

"Mr Jack Drake."

"Well, Mr Drake, Barbara is not available at present. However, Abigail will be delighted to meet you. I assume you know our arrangements here?"

"In terms of?"

"In terms of remuneration, Mr Drake."

"Oh certainly," he lied confidently and well.

After being led upstairs to a salon and plied with drinks and conversation by a bevy of assorted whores, which he rightly guessed was a ruse to increase his bill, he was at length taken to the attic nursery by the girl introducing herself as Abigail. The girl looked about fourteen but was clad in a child's dress with a short skirt falling only to mid-calf. When they reached the nursery she sat him in a chair and placed herself on his lap.

"What would like your little girl to do?" she simpered, head to one side like an inquisitive robin: a practised gesture, arch, pert, and to Nathaniel, surprisingly repellent.

"Abigail, I don't want your usual services. Sit on the bed and listen."

Eyes wide with alarm, but keeping her face compliant, she sat opposite him, hands clenched to small, bony fists.

"I need to speak to Barbara. Babs. Can you manage to bring her in here to speak to me?"

"She's ill sir."

"This is extremely important Abigail." He took the bag of coins from his pocket, judged her price, the time available, Madam Shadwell's obvious suspicions, and knew he had the smallest window of opportunity. He could not afford to offend her sense of worth, so he offered a sovereign.

"Bloody 'ell! Is that for me just for bringing Babs in?"

"Yes. And before you do, tell me how customers pay Madam Shadwell."

"You never been to a knockin' shop mister?" said Abigail, pityingly. "Regulars have a drink with Madam every month or so and settle up. Some gentlemen give us extra for ourselves, but we're not meant to keep it. New customers have to pay on the nail."

"How much is usual for you?"

She eyed him suspiciously but, swayed by his unusual good-looks, blurted out the truth before she had chance to think of anything cleverer. "Depends what we do. For half an hour, just basic, ten shillings." She looked at him hard. "Seein' as you're not a regular, do you understand that if you tell on me to Madam I'll get flayed?"

"Of course I do. Now will you help?"

Abigail paused, her eyes darting as she weighed up the odds. Then she blinked, took the sovereign and left, he heard her walk along the corridor and knock at a door. She returned with a smaller girl who had a swollen face, healing scabs and two purpley-black eyes.

"Sit down Babs," said Nathaniel, motioning to the bed. "Let me guess Raphael Vere visited and left you like this. I've seen other examples of his work."

Babs looked to Abigail briefly for support. "Abi said you know not to breathe a word of what I say outside o' these walls? And you're payin'? Yeah? Right then: it was 'im."

"Babs. Here's a sovereign for you. There's another if you help. What do you remember of Vere's last visit?"

"It was two nights ago. He was wild. Never seen him so afore" Her voice faltered, her accent broadening as she stifled tears. "That night I 'ad to stay alone in my room after 'e went. I've not earned since. Any'ow, I 'eard voices when 'e left, from down the garden, in Mr Shadwell's office. The coach house. And I 'eard a big bang, it was a gunshot sir. Just one, then nothin'. But I looked through the window later and I seen the men carrying out a burden. I'm guessin' it was whoever got shot."

"Do either of you know anything about girls, children, disappearing, being taken for trade?"

"Not regulars 'ere," offered Abigail. "But you must know it 'appens. Sometimes girls come and stay a night then go off, don't they Babs? Suppose you don't want to ask Mr Shadwell?" She giggled, high pitched and nervous. Even in jest, the thought of questioning Joshua Shadwell made her flesh creep.

As she was speaking Nathaniel had stood up and moved to the window. There were lights in the coach house and he saw Madam Shadwell by the door, starting to make her way back to the house accompanied by two men.

"My time's run out," said Nathaniel tersely. He adjusted the unfamiliar spectacles on his nose and fished out two more coins. "For you girls. Good luck. Now hide them. Babs get back to your room. Abi, to save you from unpleasant questions about what we were doing get me two belts, or sashes, whatever you have. I need to tie you up. Quickly! Tell Madam I over-powered you and made off."

Barbara crept back along the landing and Abigail took two sashes from the drawer. He gagged her swiftly with one and tied her hands to the bedstead with the other.

"Wait 'til you hear the front door close after me then start a disturbance."

He left the nursery door wide open and descended the stairs, just in time to meet Madam Shadwell who was entering the passage from the garden door.

"First rate Madam," he said, pressing a sovereign into her hand. "Must fly. I hope to return very soon."

Immune to the threat in her icy smile, he took his belongings and limped out into the night.

The two henchmen had some pursuit skills, but it was obvious to Nathaniel by

128

the time he reached the end of Green Park that they were on his tail. He decided against the busy route back *via* Kingsmead and deliberately turned towards the quayside. It was likely to be quieter, with fewer partisans to enjoy whatever might be required to rid him of the unwanted attention. He also preferred more space. He slowed down, allowing the two sets of steps to gain on him. They neared, then separated, one to his left, one to his right. He was approaching Broad Quay, close to where Wilson had met his death. There were workshops, alleys, plenty of space to manoeuvre and few people. He turned suddenly.

"Can I help you? You seem eager to catch me up."

They closed in: both powerfully built, though not as tall as Nathaniel, one bull-necked, slow moving, the other quicker, sharp-faced, more of a weasel, the smell of the street on them both. He caught the glimmer of knuckle-dusters in place on their hands to loosen his tongue.

"You didn't pay all yer dues mister. You owe a little in the way of explanation," said the bull-neck on his right, stepping towards him as he spoke. "Callers at Madam's usually come with their sponsors for a first visit. Seems strange don't it, you being alone? Madam doesn't like too much "talkin'" at the house," he leered unpleasantly, enjoying his wit. "Prefers we "talk" elsewhere."

"There is nothing to talk about," replied Nathaniel smoothly. "Mr Vere isn't available to accompany me this evening. Surely his name alone was sufficient introduction!"

As Nathaniel spoke the silent weasel on the left moved in sharply, aiming a right punch at Nathaniel's head. The bulging spiked metal covering his knuckles just nicked Nathaniel's cheek as he stepped back, swinging the makila upwards to deliver a double-handed blow to the man's head, flooring him, insensible, in a second. Simultaneously, bull-neck to the right launched an attack of his own. The makila swung round, again double-handed, delivering a bone-numbing strike to the punching arm. Nathaniel leaned in to bring the heel of the stick down into bull-neck's face. The nose split with a sickening crunch and gushed a fountain of blood as he staggered backwards as if drunk, howling in pain and pawing at his injured face. As he slammed backwards against a workshop door, Nathaniel sprang forward, drew the bladed handle with his right hand, shot up his left elbow below bull-neck's chin and pinioned him. He plunged the deadly makila into the man's exposed belly and bull-neck froze, nose still gushing and eyes pouring. Nathaniel held the blade an agonising quarter-inch into the flesh.

"You want to live?" he demanded, his voice low and menacing. Bull-neck's head nodded, loose like a puppet's. "Keep very, very, still and answer me. Do you know

Raphael Vere?"

The man paused, gathering breath, the blade burning in his belly, blood coursing from the face wounds into his mouth. He spat feebly.

"Yes, he's a customer," he gasped. "Seen him often. Owns a bank. Meets with Mr Shadwell in the office. That's all. Take out the blade for Christ's sake."

"I want to know about a dead man with scars on his face, newly marked."

"Mordecai," he said faintly, holding himself rigid. But the swimming eyes in his ravaged face were fighting still, struggling to focus on his assailant, struggling to memorise every feature. He comforted himself, retribution would follow as night followed day. "Works for Mr Shadwell. That's all you bastard. Take it out!"

"That's all I need," said Nathaniel. "Glad to have met you. I didn't want you and your friend skulking behind me all night like two lost dogs."

With that, he pulled out the reddened blade, leaving bull-neck to collapse shuddering and whimpering to the ground. Nathaniel wiped the blade clean on a pocket handkerchief, carefully, unhurriedly, and slid it back into the stick as he slowly backed away. He was pleased to see the weasel now twitching and groaning, to have killed him would have been excessive. At Little Corn Street he turned and disappeared into the shadows, peeling off his muffler, spectacles and cap, stuffing them into his pockets as he went. Glancing behind, he assured himself they were not following, and padded along silently towards the upper-town, weaving round the drunks, the whores, the dogs, the baying cliques of men and lone tramps. As the tide of low life receded and began to be replaced by respectable pedestrians, he became more aware of his ghoulish appearance. He decided on an impulse to make his way to Queen Square. Blood streaked his hands and sleeves and he could feel that the cut on his cheek had opened further. He would need more than an alleyway to render him fit to return to his rooms and, reviewing the possibilities for a port in this particular type of storm, only one name sprang to mind.

Within fifteen minutes he was standing by Coco's building. Lights shone from her room so he flung a stone at the window. She pushed up the sash, ducked her head under it and smiled as she recognised him.

"You don't need to attack my property to get my attention!"

"Coco, if you are alone can I come in?" he called urgently. "I have had a spot of bother and need to clean up." He turned up his face in the halo of gaslight so she could inspect him. "Most of this isn't mine."

She looked down at him appraisingly. "One minute," she said, flitting back into the room and returning with a key. "Catch! And don't make a row on the stairs. I have my reputation to consider."

130

# Chapter 6

**Early evening: 14<sup>th</sup> October, 1831, on the Bath Road.**

Joshua Shadwell regretted that he was becoming familiar with the high road between Bath and Bristol. The last five years had seen his visits to Bristol increase in frequency as his business connections with Ravenswood's mercantile empire had grown. Familiarity had not in this case bred contempt, but something far more unpleasant, an unsettling, corrosive fear. It was not wise to be too close to Edwin Ravenswood.

Joshua shifted uneasily in his seat at the unwelcome memory of Ravenswood's displeasure, but was shaken out of his morbid thoughts as the coach swerved sharply into Keynsham high street. He braced himself briefly against the violent lurch, then relaxed and stared morosely at the other passengers occupying inside seats. A drawn, exhausted couple faced him: she with a sleeping child on her lap, both red faced and chill-blained, raw fingers swollen and noses pinched; he, sallow and haunted, his frock coat shiny and eaten by last summer's moths. A sharp stench of urine wafted from the swaddlings of the child as they rattled over a stretch of cobbles, adding to the stink of old clothes and unwashed bodies. Joshua, who was surprisingly fastidious for a man in his profession, shot them a venomous glare and looked away, glancing instead to his right to weigh-up a rich businessman whose well-fed bulk jostled him on every bend. Joshua inhaled the welcome scent of cologne water. The man was olive skinned, the fabric of his coat lustrous and unusual: a foreigner. The port of Bristol brought in many strangers and Bath's spa drew them inland. What else might he be? Card sharp; quack; prospective customer? Joshua's thin lips drew back in a leering smile, alarming the sad mother opposite who had caught his eye and immediately thought better of it, hurriedly busying herself with the child.

The call to visit Ravenswood's residence in Redcliffe had been peremptory and, in view of the events of the previous night, had caused even his hard heart to thump

131

unpleasantly in his chest. The Ravenswood coach had swept up to Green Park Buildings and out had jumped two of Ravenswood's footmen, bold as you please, carrying barely concealed weapons. They had demanded to see him, and Rosie, like a raw girl, had shown them to the office. He had been marched to the coach and driven off, but had not, he noted for the hundredth time, been driven home as readily! He cursed Ravenswood as the coach lurched on a Saltford bend. *Shifting for myself once the great man has done with me!* He seethed inwardly, his mouth clamped in suppressed fury: then he relaxed, reflected. It could have been very much worse. The idiot Declan had run like a hare after Mordecai was shot, and by noon yesterday was on board the *Blue Dragon*, spilling his guts to Eli Trevellis. Joshua glowered at the thought of how badly it might have gone. By late afternoon he had been climbing the steps to Ravenswood's elegant town house in Redcliffe Parade to offer his explanations.

The house was used as a residence, an office, store and vantage point, as all the life of the wharf could be seen spread out below. The parade ran along the top of the red sandstone cliff, which was itself honeycombed with caves, passages and store-rooms, a number of which could be entered from Ravenswood's basement. At the foot of the cliff was one of the many moorings which stretched down the Floating Harbour from Redcliffe to Baltic Wharf by the Cumberland Basin. They were all forested with naked masts, swaying lazily, the vessels pulling on their ropes with the gentle swell of passing boats. Drying sails billowed out like clouds above the crowded dock-side with its teeming anthills of men labouring on the ships: repairing, painting, loading. Bales, sacks, drums and packages of every conceivable size and shape waited to be trundled in barrows over the undulating gangplanks and stacked in the bowels of the vessels where they waited to be blown over the seven seas. The smells of the trade goods, the pitch and the brine beckoned to him, overpowering the filth of the city. Men shouted, some sang in a demented chorus with the caged birds on the foredecks. Joshua, as usual, had been intoxicated by the scene, but on this occasion could not enjoy it. He had waited, hanging on the bell pull, a cold sweat breaking out on his back, prickling like a rash.

He had been shown to Ravenswood's headquarters on the first floor, his office *cum* dining room occupying what had been the drawing room of the grand house. The walls were lined with bookcases housing immaculately bound records of transactions, reference books and map collections. The long dining table for meetings and meals occupied the centre of the room and resting against one wall was an elegant bureau, unusually, a volume lay open upon it. Ravenswood's desk faced the window to allow him a view of his ships, the wharf and shipyards and, across the river, the tangled buildings of the Grove, backing onto the elegant Queen Square mansions. Papers rested on the tooled brown leather desk top, set out in severe piles, each sheet meticulously initialled with the master's characteristic flourish. A gold and jewelled paper knife winked cruelly by his right hand. Joshua winced at the memory of the start of the interview. He had been motioned to stand by the desk, a bad sign. Declan had been hauled in to repeat his sorry tale, which he had done, eyes glazed and staring straight ahead, well schooled. But the messenger was not unscathed, the swollen mouth crusting into fresh scabs and blackening eye sockets showed that the first telling of his story had not been a comfortable one.

"So you see," Ravenswood had smiled, eyes ice-cold, as he sat motionless, a predator preparing to strike. "We seem to have a problem, Mr Shadwell. Your employees, who also work indirectly for me, have been sub-contracting their labours profligately. Via your mediation they attempted to perform as assassins on behalf of a certain banker, subsequently broke into locked premises and planted evidence hoping to secure the execution of an innocent clerk. In an unseemly scuffle on Wednesday night, at your premises, this man's accomplice was shot during a brawl with the said banker. This man is now afraid for his life and through the offices of Captain Trevellis has sought my protection." Edwin Ravenswood rested the fingers of both hands on his desk. Joshua noticed with surprise and alarm, that his knuckles were raw.

"Sir," he paused, steadying his breathing. Never in his life had he been so glad to have not just one ace up his sleeve, but what he hoped was a royal flush. "Declan here has nothing to worry about." He tried a reassuring smile in Declan's direction. "If he had stayed long enough he would have been able to help set all to rights. Him and Mordecai have worked for me for years, as well as running the barge they took in rents for me when my men were busy. Generally made themselves useful. Trouble only started when Mr Vere had a personal problem." Joshua felt he had boxed very clever indeed at this point. Any undue indiscretion about Ravenswood's business in front of Declan could have been fatal. "A senior clerk at the bank by the name of Wilson was blackmailing him and tightening the squeeze. I knew you were a customer at Mr Vere's bank sir, so I wanted to smooth his way." Joshua gambled on the fact that Ravenswood did not trouble himself to inspect the details of other New Bank accounts and was ignorant of his growing debts and mortgages, underwritten by Vere. "Mr Vere was rattled sir. His tastes at my house were expensive and, unusual. Also, he was losing more at the gambling and when he was deep in his cups he talked freely about his business. Maybe there was more. Wilson spooked him and he took fright. Wednesday night, after beating my youngest girl cruelly I might add, he came to the office and Declan and Mordecai showed up," he flickered another reassuring glance to Declan. "He set about Mordecai and a pistol discharged."

Allowing the half-truth to settle, he looked at Declan directly, consciously slowing his words, allowing time for them to sink in.

"Then, Declan, for your information, my men dumped Mordecai where the watchmen would pick him up smartly. We searched him, destroyed the papers you two had taken from Wilson's and left a wad of bonds on him to match them hidden at the young clerk's place. I'd kept a few back, for insurance so to speak. Then, when the boys moved him, what should we find! Wilson's ring on a string round his greasy neck! Diamond set and engraved with him and his missus' names clear as day. Keepin' it like a damned sailor's ear-ring for his funeral mebbe! So, that should tie him fair and square for the murder and it'll take the boil off any connection between Mr Vere and your good self, or to me. Mordecai's been taking rents for me in Kingsmead Street for over a twelve month, and what with his face wound from the night with Wilson, he's been easily recognised. Word is he's squarely blamed for planting the bank bonds at the young clerk's."

Ravenswood remained impassive. "Mr Shadwell, Declan here fears Mr Raphael Vere. I am personally disappointed with the performance of our banker friend and am not sorry to inform you that his work in Bath is over. He will be calling to see me later today and will be transferring his attentions to a new business opportunity." He fixed the tormented Declan with a stony stare. "Declan, look at me." The woebegone face turned. "Mr Vere will not be returning to Bath, or indeed to Bristol. Do you understand?" The battered head nodded as Ravenswood turned to Joshua. "Declan will continue to run his barge, he will serve me also in Bristol. He will not undertake any further activities for you, so pay him off. I gather he fled before he was paid. I am gratified to learn that you have been able to neutralise the unnecessary publicity Vere's activities have attracted." Josuah bowed briefly, without lowering his eyes and reluctantly gave Declan two sovereigns. "Declan, go down to the *Blue Dragon*. Report to Captain Trevellis." Ravenswood motioned to Joshua to sit opposite him and poured them both a generous measure of rum as Declan blundered down the stairs, two at a time.

"Now, what more do you have to tell me?" The silence grew as Joshua took a gulp at his drink, mechanically reworking his story, looking for any weak link which needed a bulwark. Ravenswood noted the pause, and continued. "Vere was a loose cannon which had grown increasingly wayward over the last few months. I sent a new operative of mine to Bath over the last few weeks to investigate Vere's gambling and drinking habits which, as you know, had developed to the point of indiscretion. I did not like what I heard, Joshua. I hope you have no hidden habits of which I might disapprove."

"No sir, I have not. And I am glad to hear it was your man prowling round Vere. Some of my informants, the Broad Quay boys, let slip there's a man asking questions. He's made a regular pet of one of the potboys at the Hart."

Ravenswood looked puzzled. "I doubt my man has done so. Is the interrogator they spoke of a foreigner?

"Not as such. Got a Welsh name though. Parry."

Ravenswood's black brows lifted momentarily. "Keep a weather eye on Mr Parry, Joshua. Government man. I will deal with him if necessary, but we have other matters to occupy us today. Who was Vere buying time with at your house?

"Barbara sir. Nursery."

"No loose ends Mr Shadwell. Send her here on the barge. She can go with the next consignment. We'll likely lose one or two before they make the east, she can be, as it were, reserve stock. You must have realised we have held off sailing."

Ravenswood rose and walked to the window to look down on the *Blue Dragon* idling at the wharf. "There's a problem with the victualling. Bloody peasants firing haystacks and fields." His mouth worked in suppressed fury, setting in a harsh line, though his voice was deadly calm. "Melbourne has arrested perpetrators pretty freely but he's weak on sentencing. I would have had their limbs off." He sank briefly into a reverie before continuing. "The Normans had a way with revolts. Are you a historian Mr Shadwell? Are you familiar with our medieval predecessors?" He turned back to Joshua, his face animated at the thought of retribution. "Their methods were similar to those of the tribes of the Middle East. Death itself is too easy. A deterrent is required, to deter others from sin and encourage them to tread the paths of righteousness." The light died in his eyes. "Send the girl to me. Vere will not be telling any tales and neither will she. As for you and your pitiful employee, I will not tolerate any future weakness or failure."

They had been interrupted, much to Joshua's relief, by sounds from the hall. Visitors were being shown up to the office by the maid and the door opened to reveal two figures. Joshua sprung to his feet and made hurried moves to leave. It was some time since he had been in the presence of danger so palpable, and his throat dried in fear. The shorter man, an Asiatic, squarely built with little in the way of a neck and huge hands, radiated evil. His demeanour was coldly hostile, his reptilian eyes darted over Josiah as if sizing him up for the kill, his tongue flickered over his lips. For reassurance Joshua moved to touch his pistol butt through his coat, but froze in the act as the man's eyes tracked his every move, crinkling in silent, derisive

135

glee. The other was also from the east, but looked to be more from the south, more typically Chinese with sleek black hair brushed back from his ivory brow. He looked powerful, vigilant.

Ravenswood was speaking, so Joshua strove to smile. "Mr Kizhe, Mr Lee, may I introduce Mr Joshua Shadwell, he serves our business in Bath, the famous city spa. Mr Lee I know you have spent a few evenings there recently in pursuit of the errant banker Mr Raphael Vere. His career will be curtailed tomorrow. You will wait for him on the *Dragon*, where he will be arriving for a meeting with me very shortly."

Joshua pushed the stiff curtain aside to peer into the dark through the stage-coach window. He was relieved to see that they were passing the Weston toll house. He sighed. Never had he been so pleased to leave Ravenswood's office, though God knows he was never keen to loiter. He almost felt sorry for Vere, but not quite. As he had moved to quit the office, Ravenswood was offering to show the two visitors the under-cliff store rooms. Again, an unfamiliar twinge of pity. As the *Blue Dragon* was not ready to sail, the captive girls would still be incarcerated below ground. The infants wouldn't last long after they reached their destination, if they made it that far, but the two others might. And Barbara: she wasn't a bad girl. The men would have to see her off, he hadn't the stomach for it. He dropped the curtain, extinguishing the view, though he continued to gaze, unseeing, as they entered the town.

That same night Arno's Tower was ablaze with light. The Ravenswoods were entertaining, and, as usual, pleasure was intimately bound with business, the mansion stage-set to enthral and overawe. A chain of flambeaux lit the drive, flaring into the night, and culminating in two vast cauldrons of fire on either side of the great doors. The lights caught the stone grotesques, making them leap to life in relief against the inky-black darkness, and as John and Lottie Drake approached in their hired coach, they purposefully avoided catching each other's eye. Both were determined to outdo the other in delight in their new found friends, neither could let themselves admit that the overall effect was alarming rather than welcoming, neither acknowledged the sulphurous whiff of the Inferno. Once inside the formalities proceeded more conventionally and they relaxed, basking in the excessive show of hospitality. Preliminary drinks and tidbits were enjoyed in a salon of hedonistic baroque rather than gothic splendour, though there was a fire crackling fiercely in a cavernous fireplace, relentlessly stoked by one of Ravenswood's legion of servants. Inconsequential conversation drifted harmlessly between them.

Edwin Ravenswood looked breathtakingly handsome to Lottie: so tall, so darkly attractive, especially when compared with her vulpine husband who seemed diminished by Edwin's presence. John's eyes did not light on his wife's to catch the unspoken criticism, but were busy gleaming in delight and envy, swivelling from crystal chandeliers to luscious silk upholstery, and again to towering oils of ancestors perched on benches in pastoral Gainsborough poses beneath leafy trees. Though not Gainsboroughs, and not ancestors, at least not Ravenswoods, thought Lottie shrewdly. Not that she cared over-much, she just hoped John could manage to stop short of obvious sycophancy. He was the government man after all. It was Ravenswood's job to do the wooing. And she would most definitely like to be wooed. She turned to respond to Amanda Ravenswood's unusually polite question about Lizzie. Amanda had no interest of any kind in children, and was playing the chatelaine to perfection, reining in her acid tongue, layering graciousness over her characteristic viciousness. Lottie was amused. Her frequent meetings with Amanda were the high points of the week. They dawdled over tea on at least two mornings and one afternoon, sharpening their conversational talons, shredding the reputations of the rest of Bristol's *bon ton*. How delicious that Amanda was afraid of her husband!

The dinner was served in a magnificent dining hall. The flunkeys were immaculate, a liveried footman behind each place, and the food sublime. However, the jollity so carefully constructed and launched was lost, abruptly shipwrecked, as they were joined by two foreign gentlemen. Lottie sensed the menace in the air and found it thrilling. The older character was a thick-set man reminding her of a sketch she had once seen of an Esquimaux tribesman butchering a whale, his face battered and bitten by the Arctic wind, transfixed by his purpose. The guest, however, was free from furs, scrupulously turned out in evening dress and with the air of a patrician: a tyrannical one. Edwin's manner towards him was careful, studied, at one point almost deferential. She was fascinated. The younger one was clearly subordinate, though held in some respect by the other men. He was attractive and elegantly muscular, but he took no trouble to flirt with her, or even to observe the niceties of polite conversation. Preliminary overtures to Edwin and the older man, a Mr Kizhe, conjured up the expected responses: interest, flattery, encouragement, and gentle sparring, as gentlemen's ripostes should be. The younger one would take considerably more work, which she looked forward to. She consoled herself by observing John, who was acquitting himself surprisingly well with Amanda, offering conversational gambits, admiring the house and the table without misplaced gush. Her observations were interrupted far too soon for her liking as Amanda rose from her chair in response to a piercing glance from her husband. They were obliged to quit the table and withdraw to leave the men to their cigars and spirits. Their skirts whispered, coldly sibilant along the stone floor of the colonnaded landing as they made their way to the drawing room. A triumphant smile played around Lottie's lips as she selected her next barb. "Do tell me more of your experiences in Paris my dear," she said to her friend's retreating back. Amanda was very proud of her time in France, but was furiously disappointed that she had been unable to break into the highest society. "I so loved the evenings John and I spent at Versailles."

As soon as the door was closed behind the ladies, the gentlemen were settled to their port and smokes and then the servants were dismissed, Edwin Ravenswood moved swiftly to business.

"Mr Drake as we have discussed earlier, I am deeply flattered that His Majesty's government has seen fit to honour my company by showing interest in my Far Eastern trade. My vessel, the *Mathilda*, is due to dock within days and the news from her last port is very good. The opium realised 20% more than our maximum forecast. Demand continues to grow in the coastal Chinese cities and our contacts amongst the, shall we say, "privateers" of the China Seas have enabled us to continue using our secure harbours for the foreseeable future. I know how important it is for Britain that this trade continues to flourish. A necessary support of the business is our additional freight, marketed through Mr Kizhe's contacts. We have discussed this briefly, have we not Mr Drake? The additional income raised is not just substantial, but prodigious."

He dwelt on that last word, savoured it and allowed it to rest in the silence that followed, allowing Drake in his greed to swallow it whole. Ravenswood next inclined his head to Kizhe, who acknowledged it with a nod, allowing only his gash of a mouth to offer the faintest ghost of a smile before he replied.

"My employer has been extremely pleased with the females and your service record, though the recent unwelcome delay in sailing will have to be made good during the voyage. Our customers do not like to wait, Mr Ravenswood. I will accompany the *Blue Dragon* on its outward trip at least as far as India, where I have other business." He lifted his massive hand, a meaty bear's paw, and drew deeply on his cigar, breathing out slowly to wreathe himself in aromatic smoke.

"Mr Drake," he said slowly, turning to him, eyes narrowed in scrutiny. "My compliments to your government. I also am gratified to know that our mutual affairs are so strongly supported by the mighty British Empire. Mr Ravenswood tells me that you will convey good news of our opium trade to the noble lords of Whitehall. He also tells me that you will accept our humble thanks, awarded annually I understand, for your continued support?"

John Drake's jaw tightened and he clasped his hands hard to prevent his fingers straying to his neck wound. Lottie had warned him about that, he had never realised before just how often he did it.

"Thank you sir. I am delighted to accept. As you know your opium trade is vital to our Chinese interests and anything we can do to further your successes will be our pleasure."

Even as he spoke the words seemed to stick in his throat. "Anything we can do?" How could he say that? He fixed a rictus smile, and fought to rid his mind of a grinning image of Dr Faustus, selling his soul to the devil, as Kizhe in the role of Mephistopheles was nodding his acceptance and the deal was done. Palmerston would be jovially delighted to hear of the opium runs, the safe havens, the piratical support, and would no doubt be pleased to lend the guns and sabres of the Royal Navy if they ran into serious trouble with the Chinese. Lord Cupid might even understand the trade in prostitutes. But that was not all it was. He felt a stab of pain in his heart as he thought of his Lizzie and the privileged, carefree infants he saw on his walks, dancing over the Downs and clucked after by their nurses. The "additional freight" was human, and to his horror it had become clear that there was no lower age limit for the trade. He had worked with enough perverts in the service to have a clear idea of the range of tastes that unlimited money could cater for. Over a few long alcoholic nights, Ravenswood had drawn him into the web. Yes, he wanted money. Yes, he was furnished with the necessary good news to convey to the Foreign Office and his star would rise. The price had to be paid and the cost would be borne by his savaged conscience.

Drake relaxed his tight smile and reached for his port. "Just one other matter gentlemen. As I have already discussed with Mr Ravenswood, the Office has sent out another gentleman to work with me, a Mr Nathaniel Parry. He is based in Bath with instructions to report on radical agitation, but he has family and contacts there which have developed his interest in Bristol affairs. I have to go to London tomorrow as we both have a meeting in Whitehall next week. Needless to say, I will work to reduce this interest and suggest you reject any advances he might make or any of his attempts to investigate. Let's say he is not amenable to negotiation. His father served before him and he has archaic notions of duty." Drake raised a conspiratorial eyebrow, acknowledged by Ravenswood and Kizhe. Cornelius, silent thus far, appeared to remain implacable, but for the first time that day his inner eye sensed a break in the clouds.

Until Drake's venomous little show, the day had been uniformly depressing for

Cornelius Lee and as the table conversation had drifted to a consideration of Ravenswood's extensive wine cellar, he permitted himself a mental review of it. The day had first suffered during extended sessions with Kizhe, checking and re-checking the details of the outward journey to China, and reached its lowest point when he had been obliged to view the clutch of wretched prisoners in Ravenswood's stone vaults. They were quiet enough in their plush cell, drugged and hollow eyed: the infants dozing fretfully, the teenage girls lolling on a sofa under the eye of a powerful woman in a drab apron, assisted by a tight-laced whore with a mane of blonde hair, filing her nails by the fireside. The room had smelled sickly, heavy with perfume and drugs, and his stomach heaved at the memory of it. After Kizhe had inspected the girls to his satisfaction, the men were directed to quit the room via a narrow spiral stair cut into the living rock that wound its way down to the wharf. They had to pick their way slowly as the stairs were dark, steep and irregular. Each carried a flickering candle cupped in their hands to guard the light from the damp blasts of air gusting intermittently from side passages which pierced the wall every ten steps, offering diversions into utter blackness. As they had emerged, blinking, into the raw light of the quay, Kizhe, who was gruffly pleased with the day, had bidden Cornelius farewell before making off into town for a solitary drink.

Cornelius had another duty to perform, and had side-stepped the coiled ropes and paint pots to make his way to the *Blue Dragon*, where he must supervise the meeting with Vere. He had made his way over the gang-plank and into the tarry darkness of the ship to meet Trevellis emerging from the ladder leading to the lower deck, laden with ropes and canvas sheeting. Cornelius had followed him to Trevellis's own cabin, stooping low to keep his head below the spars. He sat in the Captain's chair in the squared-paned bow window and waited. In little more than an hour Raphael Vere had entered the cabin, grotesquely out of place in his silk top hat and lavender gloves, angry not to see Ravenswood and demanding an explanation. Trevellis had shadowed him in, and within seconds he was overpowered and bound. The interview had been predictable. Vere blustered wildly to justify the murder of his senior clerk, all in the worthy cause of protecting the reputation of his valued client and business partner, Mr Ravenswood. Wilson had stolen items from Vere's home, which linked directly to sensitive aspects of the Ravenswood shipping interests and so he had to be removed. Furthermore, at the first sign of betrayal, Vere had fearlessly killed the failed assassin and continued to manage the affairs of the bank with the utmost efficiency. He was Bath's puppeteer, his hands pulling all the strings. Furthermore, he had single-handedly shaken off a London investigator, who was now in the palm of his hand. His plump face reddened as he struggled to unburden himself of the tale, and also of Trevellis's vice-like grip. His mouth had become flecked with spittle, his eyes watered with tears of outrage. Unsurprisingly, Trevellis had tired of the performance before Cornelius did, and had dealt Vere a crushing blow to the back of the head. The indignant voice was abruptly silenced and the plump body had crumpled, concertina-like to the ground to be smartly sheathed up in the canvas by Trevellis.

"What are your instructions?" Cornelius had enquired, idly re-arranging the papers on the desk.

"He's going to board the steam packet to Cork, but 'e might not be there to disembark. It's powerful rough in the Irish Sea this time of year."

Cornelius had left Trevellis shouldering his burden, whilst he walked back to Redcliffe Parade to reclaim the horse he had borrowed from Ravenswood's stables and to make his way back to Arno's Tower for the dinner party with the man from the Foreign Office.

### 5 a.m.: 15th October, 1831, Arno's Tower, Arno's Vale.

As was his habit, Cornelius dressed for training and slipped out of his room before dawn, silently crossed the terrace, then gathered speed and sprinted through the park to St Anne's Wood. It was a good start to the day, the starlight was bright, limning the trunks and tangled boughs in silver, silhouetting a dog fox slinking off the path ahead of him. After he crossed the deserted Bath road he slowed his pace and concentrated, wondering if he had sensed a minute change behind him, a different sound. He turned and ran backwards for a step or two but there was nothing new to see or hear: just his soft footfalls and the rustling surge of the wind in the trees. He skirted the old stables and headed off through the wood. He kept up a steady pace until the last few hundred yards when he accelerated and leapt to clear the last huddle of bushes before slowing to a stop in his usual place by the ruined wall and the well. He bowed his head and placed his hands together, focused on his place, his purpose and his soul. Calmly, he breathed deep, and began. Warming his chilling body, he stretched, reached, prepared each limb, arched his neck and stiffened his hands into knife-hard blades, thumbs in and fingers taut, bent slightly inwards. Slowly he moved through the sinuous and deadly dances: rehearsing the ancient battle moves of his art. Some moves he performed agonisingly slowly, precise and perfect, some exploded into a mesmerising flurry of blows against the phantom army: every punch, every kick designed as a final one. Each sequence was practised exactly as he had first been taught, outside in all weather on the dusty square, or in the wooden temple that had once been his home. Twenty years of training had forged Cornelius Lee and his art was his soul: the two indivisible.

After his first hour, he stopped and closed his eyes, to focus on his breathing. In the stillness he immediately sensed another presence, close by in the dell. From his right had come an infinitesimal sound, and soft disturbed wings flapped in the dark. He launched himself into a complex series of forward kicks which moved him across two-thirds of the open space, gathered himself up and soared into the air, somersaulting once, twice, three times to disappear in the shadow of the wall. A dark shape separated itself from the shelter of an oak tree and followed, rounding the wall to an enclosed semi-circle, open to the sky. The burly figure glanced round silently in the pale light, watchful, suspicious, his head turning sharply left and right.

At the moment when he decided that he was quite alone and his quarry had disappeared, Cornelius leaped down from a high perch on the wall behind him. At the soft sound of his landing, the man's surprise was instantly overtaken by instinct: in one smooth circling movement he reached with his right hand for his hidden weapon, drew it ringing from its sheath, and brought the crude blade whistling down to Cornelius's head. Simultaneously, Cornelius had stepped forward, leaning towards his opponent and catching his sword arm in a double-handed cross block below the wrist. Spinning clockwise on his left foot, his right hand gripping his assailant's wrist, he pulled the man down hard, his left hand slamming into the back of the exposed elbow. With a grunt of pain the man loosened his grip on the weapon, which slid away over the damp grass, but with astonishing speed he used the momentum of Cornelius's attack, dropped his left arm to cushion the fall and curled into a double-roll. He was on his feet in seconds, ten feet distant, facing Cornelius. The familiar dead eyes crinkled: "Well, Mr Lee. We seem to have the same plans this morning. A little outdoor training is always congenial at the start of the day."

Cornelius gave a short bow. "Good morning, Mr Kizhe. I was unaware you favoured this place."

"I have been watching you. You have an interesting style, a soft one if I might say so." He glanced round, thinking, surprised at Cornelius's versatility. "It is still early. Would you care to test a few more of your techniques?"

"By all means."

Kizhe shed his heavy cloak and scabbard, rolled his head round, snapped a few punches and dropped into a stance. First they circled each other, assessing each other's height and weight, feeling the ground with their feet, and as they did so, their faces drained of all animation, sinking into the gaze of the warrior: mask-like, unfocused yet all-seeing. Suddenly, Kizhe launched a lightning blow at Cornelius, which was elegantly side-stepped and countered, the return blow stylishly pulled, quarter-inch impact only, just enough to bruise.

Again and again Kizhe rained down swingeing attacks, and every one was used against him. Cornelius had decided on his first meeting with Kizhe that when it came to this, he would spar entirely in defensive mode. He had no wish to injure or kill Kizhe, yet, and had no wish to reveal his spirit to this man. Strategy for Cornelius was The Way, the ultimate craft of the warrior. Every encounter, every moment, was for learning, for reviewing strategic choices: to this there was no beginning and no end. He waited until he sensed his assailant tiring, then chose his moment. He tensed his torso for the impact, allowed Kizhe to catch him with a direct body-blow, stepped back and bowed.

"Shall we walk back together?" he said.

Kizhe allowed his mouth to smile in return.

"You fight well, though I still say your style is a soft one. It seems to have too much of the Buddhist about it!" He gave his harsh bark of a laugh. "You failed to strike me with any power Mr Lee."

Cornelius smiled in return. "My style is a mixture of many disciplines. This was one," he said quietly.

By the time they approached the house, dawn had broken over the black woods and the sky was barred with iron-grey. A ragged chorus had broken from the bedraggled birds perched on the naked boughs, their wet feathers ineffectually failing to fluff up against the cold.

"It is good to practise with an opponent," said Kizhe, "we should spar again."

"I am sure we will."

Cornelius made his way to the kitchens to search for breakfast but Kizhe made straight for his suite. As soon as he locked the door behind him, he began to peel off his damp clothes before one of the full-length gilt mirrors that Ravenswood provided in such profusion. The satisfaction he had gained by landing the decisive blow on the elusive Mr Lee swiftly evaporated. Stripped naked, he looked carefully at the tight pattern of red bruising on his body. The sight of so many blows, so well placed, so politically pulled, infuriated him. His face darkened to a scowl as he mentally replayed the final moment of their bout. Lee had sustained a punch and retired, but he should have gone down. Kizhe had the unappealing suspicion that he had been played.

He lumbered into the bathroom, and glared balefully at the brimming bath-tub, left steaming and ready by his valet, the mound of warm towels waiting by the fire. He climbed in and reflected: he had learned more than one good lesson this morning.

The vulgar luxuries available at Ravenswood's mansion must be rationed, they sapped the strength and must be recognised for what they were. Small doses and regular training would neutralise their influence. He breathed in deeply, allowing his body to sink beneath the surface of the water, and as he rested, shark-like in the depths, he toyed with the thought that there might also be a need to neutralise his new sparring partner. And on the instant, he surfaced: refreshed and revitalised.

## Back in Bath

Later that morning, a female figure disguised in a hooded blue travelling cloak clattered her way along London Street and thence to Walcot. Her dainty pale blue satin shoes were strapped into high wooden pattens which succeeded in raising her feet above the slurry of the roads but slowed her gait to that of an unsteady geisha. As she travelled in the same direction as the crowd of smocked labourers and farmers with their herds and dogs heading for the market, her progress was swifter than it might have been, but it had still taken over half an hour to make the descent from Lansdown Crescent. Fortunately, she found Nathaniel's lodgings easily, closed the gate behind her with some relief and pattered up to the door to beat on the knocker.

"Come in, come in!" shouted a quavering voice. Tilly's face hardened in disappointment.

"Hello Mr Spence," she called, reluctant and sulky, as she entered the hall and made her way to the kitchen.

The rack above the fireplace was laden with steaming sheets, shirts and boiled pudding-cloths, hoisted aloft by the rope secured on the wall. Bread was cooling on wire trays and a pungent meat broth simmered in the cauldron over the fire. Every surface had been scoured, cleanliness being next to godliness, as a wall text reminded her. Old Tom was in his usual seat by the fire, peeling turnips and grinning in toothless delight at the arrival of reinforcements.

"Jus' take a firm 'old of yon Johnty missus. Grab 'im now!"

The rotund baby Johnty had spotted the open door and taken off with surprising speed in a curious shuffling crawl, pulling himself forward on his pudgy hands like a young seal. Tilly made a grab and managed to secure a firm hold on one leg.

"Ye young demon!" cackled Tom. "Jus' look at that missus. This very week the Johnty 'as taken off! 'E'll need to be tethered now when 'e's out o' they crib. Pick 'im up! I likes to see such spirit in the young but we can't 'ave 'im dashed under a carriage wheel can us? That's it 'old 'im tight. Like a greased eel 'e be! Where wast a-goin' my 'andsome?" He gazed in unfocused delight at his great-grandchild, shaking his head in wonder.

Tilly managed to restrain the Johnty who obligingly settled in her lap, took her velvet cloak in both sticky hands and rubbed his grimy face in it crowing with delight.

"Martha will be in directly missus. Was it Martha you was after?" said Tom, attempting innocence. "Or might it be Mr Parry perchance. Fine young buck 'e is. Back after dawn 'e was this mornin'."

The back door opened, and to Tilly's relief Martha entered with a bowl of bruised apples.

"You're looking better Mrs Vere," she said, examining Tilly's face. "Now these would have been useful last time we met! Did you use rotted apple and rose conserve on the eye? No? Well, you'll know next time. Will you be wanting to speak with Mr Parry?"

As Martha made her way upstairs to fetch Nathaniel, Tilly gave up trying to wrest the handfuls of cloak from Johnty, who was now totally absorbed in testing them, possibly to destruction, and listened half-heartedly to Tom's views on the snail's progress of the bill, livestock prices and the weather. As his eyesight was poor, she was able to read the other texts on the wall as she listened, without giving obvious offence. Finished in cross-stitch and hanging on strings from the picture rail were numerous legends, including: "Whatever thy Hand findeth to do, do it with all thy Might," and, "Order is Heaven's First Law." A small worm wriggled out of the apple nearest to her on the table and she glared at it, annoyed that it reminded her not only of Martha's unappetising concoction for black-eyes, but also of Raphael's treachery.

"Eve and the apple! Arrant lies," she thought crossly. "Adam would have demanded it and wondered why it was not served sooner."

She was distracted by sounds of the party coming downstairs. A woolly black and tan tornado was first to the kitchen, launching itself through the door to land paws and panting head on the Johnty in her lap.

"Oh Caradoc! And Mr Parry! I am pleased to catch you at home. I need to speak with you urgently concerning my husband's business." Tilly had shed her ill-humour on the instant, and concentrated on twinkling prettily, conscious that her pose with the Johnty was not unappealing. As she inspected Nathaniel more closely she noticed the cut on his cheek and continued. "Oh Mr Parry, I see it is your turn today. Have you been in a fight?"

Nathaniel beamed from the door, his Damascus gown tied at the waist over his frilled shirt and trousers. He touched the healing cut gingerly. "Footpads madam, the merest trifle. It is of no account. Down Caradoc! Mrs Vere he is delighted to see you. Shall we talk in the parlour? Mrs Spence, could you kindly bring tea?"

Martha lifted the reluctant baby from Tilly's lap and nodded meaningfully. "Yes Mr Parry, I will be in with it shortly. Will you be needing the rotted apples as well?" But they had already gone.

As they closed the parlour door Tilly gabbled her news, *sotto voce*, grasping Nathaniel's hands between hers as she did so. "Yesterday I got into Raphael's dressing room. I couldn't believe my luck. He was called over to Bristol at short notice. Edwin Ravenswood sent a coach to convey him. He had been expecting a visitor but had to leave anyway and Tanner was instructed to see to him. The maids were busy providing refreshment and I went into Tanner's room. He had left his keys on his desk! I went in and searched Raphael's bureau. Oh Nathaniel, I found some shocking publications. They were disguised under plain covers, but I looked! Such obscenity!"

"Did you bring them?"

"Certainly not!"

"What else?"

"I found a cash-book in the very bottom of a box in the wardrobe and copied out some pages," she said, flushed with her own daring, as she handed him a sheaf of papers from her reticule. He flipped through the pages.

"A great deal in a personal code, needs work to clarify it. But I'd say it looks like your husband had some substantial outgoings of a personal nature Tilly. Also, plenty references to a certain ER." He said, running his eye down the figures rapidly. "And plenty going for "B". Payments from a Mr Shadwell. I know a little about him. Do you know him?"

She shook her head drawing a trembling breath. "And Raphael did not return home last night. Thank God. I don't know how I would have faced him. I think I would have run. I could have come here couldn't I? No one saw me leave today, and I don't want to go home." She edged closer. "And what can the figures from his book do to help me? Can they rid me of him?"

Caradoc put a warning paw on her skirt as Nathaniel heard Martha's tread in the hall and simultaneously disengaged Tilly's hands from his.

"Sit down," he whispered quickly. "Have some tea, then go home and pack. Return to your family for a visit. Leave a note explaining that you are needed. I have to go to London today but will be back soon. Write your family address for me so I know where you are. Now shush." He smiled encouragingly as Martha's ample rear bounced the door open to admit her and the tea tray.

Nathaniel walked Tilly to the door as she left, full of tea, cake and advice from Martha on baking, home remedies and the latest location of her namesake vessel the *Mathilda*, which even as they spoke, was speeding on a fair wind round the north Devonshire coast to the Severn Estuary to return her son to domestic duty in Walcot Street. Tilly scribbled her family address on a scrap of newspaper he had brought from the parlour. She pressed it into his hand and after only the briefest of glances up and down the street, wrapped her arms around Nathaniel and lifted her face to his. "You will help me won't you Nathaniel," she breathed, "don't desert me after all I've done. I need you to support me. I'll wait at my mother's home for a week, until I hear from you." She brushed his lips with hers. "Until next week," she pressed her hand to her lips and blew a parting kiss. Confident now, she turned towards London Street with the light of triumph in her eye. She was too pleased with herself to notice the small figure of a governess hurrying up the street after collecting ribbons and silks for her mistress whilst her charges had extra lessons from a dancing master. Anna's dancing skills were far inferior to her offerings in languages, arithmetic, drawing and music. Additional tuition had been sought and she was relegated, much to her delight, to running errands in town on Saturday mornings. Anna, however, was not too occupied to turn her head on hearing an excited yapping across the road, or to miss Tilly embracing Nathaniel in plain sight on Martha Spence's front path. Anna's main problem now was how, and when, to inform Em that her escort for the Masked Ball was probably not quite as available as she had thought.

## On the London Road

Night had fallen, but Nathaniel's coach continued to make good time over Hounslow Heath. He had taken the precaution of keeping his swordstick with him in the coach and held it, at the ready. Though the gibbets and their swaying bodies of hanged highwaymen had been down for over twenty years and there were Peelers and mounted patrols in the more populous areas of the toll road, old habits died hard. The heath, long the most dangerous stretch of road in the country still held its reputation. The odd "high tobyman" was still arrested there for trying his luck, along with the more common footpads and thugs who usually infested town roads but sometimes strayed further afield. The guard was well armed with a blunderbuss, what he called his "new-fangled" pistol, and a sabre for good measure. Admirable as this was, Nathaniel preferred to have his own arrangements. Which, he reflected with pleasure, were shortly to be augmented by a pair of new-fangled pistols of his own. He had inherited a fine pair of Ulrich flint-locks from his father, who had bought them in Stuttgart shortly before he died, from none other than the famous

Bernese gunsmith, Franz Ulrich himself. They were pretty little pieces, ultra-compact, like the pocket-size American Derringers, and his London gunsmith had pronounced them easy converts to the new percussion mechanism. They had been sitting in the shop for a week, waiting for him. Owen would have loved to try the new mechanism, which promised virtual immunity from misfires, the curse of the flint-lock. Nathaniel laughed to himself as he conjured up a scene. It would have been on some deserted God-forsaken heath, hour after bone-chilling hour, plugging away at piles of stones, probably in the rain or howling wind, Owen laughing, eyes flashing in delight. His smile was long-lived at the thought of his father, though it carried with it the familiar stab of pain at his loss.

He felt the stagecoach slow down and he looked out to see the lights of the Bell Toll House approach. He bent down to pat Caradoc as he stirred amongst the hay laid down to warm their feet. They would both be glad to arrive at Lambeth for pie and mash, and he was keen to collect his pistols. The week had not been without interest and he was impatient to dispatch the meetings with the noble lords and return to Bath. There was little to report in terms of radical unrest, the reform groups having retreated to their caves, seemingly fully occupied in licking their wounds after the Lords rejection of the Second Reform Bill. Bitterly disappointed, but digging in stoically for a long campaign, they were quiescent and he saw no signs of agitation or incipient riot. The government could perhaps have done with a little more in that department if the Lords were to be frightened out of their resistance to reform by the greater threat of revolution. Drake had kept his business in Bristol jealously to himself and would no doubt be in a position to reassure Palmerston on the health of the opium running business. Nathaniel had decided that Drake's displeasure was a small price to pay, and he would continue to pursue the links between Raphael Vere, Edwin Ravenswood and the unsavoury Shadwells, who seemed to be up to their necks in trading under-aged girls. With regard to the Bath ladies, there was even more to recall him to duty. Tilly's scribbled notes needed closer study and he felt a degree of obligation to her after setting her up to filch evidence from her husband's room. To be honest, it could not be seen as a hardship to have to spend a little more time in Tilly's company. He was also game for the evening at the Masked Ball with the Petersons, the chaste attractions of Miss Emma would act as a distraction and divert him from the charms of the delectable Coco.

Meanwhile, in the heart of the city, Chislett drew the drapes at Brookes's Club in St James's and checked that the Strangers' Room was ready in every particular for Lord Melbourne and his party. He re-positioned the glasses, the favourite port and the biscuits, lit the candles and withdrew as he heard the patrician tread of members on the corridor.

"Good evening Chislett."

"Good evening my Lord."

Melbourne led Palmerston and Drake into the Strangers' Room and took a comfortable armchair by the fire. "Dashed cold what!" he drawled, rubbing his hands and reaching to the flames.

"More exercise needed sir!" said Palmerston flinging himself on to the sofa and pouring himself a drink. "The blood should be agitated daily."

Melbourne pulled a face. His afternoons had in truth been rather less exciting of late, as his boon companion, Caroline "Norty" Norton, was about to be confined by the birth of her second child. The thought of the ravishing, witty Caroline brought a genial smile to his lips. They had been all but inseparable for over a year, since her ass of a husband had encouraged her to befriend Melbourne in the hope of preferment for himself. Preferment had been obtained to the tune of £1000 per annum, but Norton's greed was unassuaged and she had been allowed to continue her dalliance with the rakish Home Secretary. She was twenty-three years of age to his fifty-two, but the attraction was mutual. Melbourne had a weakness for young women, had adored her grandfather Richard Sheridan, and was entranced to see she had inherited some of his literary genius. His stormy, brilliant, blindingly beautiful Norty distracted him from dwelling on the ancient wreckage of his love life. His wife had finally died over two years ago and his fling with Lady Branden was reduced to exchanging written snippets with her from their latest perusals of French erotica. His sad handicapped boy was out of sight, if not out of mind, and darling Norty really was the spice of life. Dear Richard had understood how essential women were to one's happiness. He absent-mindedly hummed a snatch or two from "Here's to the maiden" from Sheridan's *School for Scandal* before giving up and sighing windily, as he had been doing increasingly often.

"Banish the world-weariness dear boy! Go hunting!" ordered Palmerston.

Melbourne poured himself a port, reflecting ruefully that Palmerston's blood would have been agitated by more than the hunt. When his beloved sister Emily was not orchestrating the action at Almack's Club with her delectable troop of followers, she was still warming Palmerston's bed. At least two of her four children had a look of him.

Drake sat quietly, observing his betters, biding his time. His news was good, so he had no discomforts on that score, but he needed to plant some traps for Parry.

"Well Drake," said Palmerston, smacking his lips noisily. "Have a port man and bring us up to date. We gather you needed to see us privately before the meeting in the Office on Monday."

"Yes indeed," murmured Drake unctuously. "I have some excellent news my Lords."

As Melbourne kicked the fire lazily, sending renewed showers of sparks racing upwards, and Palmerston basked, arrogant and supine, like a rogue elephant at a watering hole, Drake poured himself a drink and spun his tale. Ravenswood, accomplished, connected and supremely successful was eager to continue helping the government and was as putty in his hand. Drake had details of the privateers of the China Seas who would continue to facilitate the opium trade for Ravenswood and had assurances that Ravenswood would cooperate with other traders to ensure that the Chinese navy continued to fail in all attempts to frustrate business. Drake himself would broker any talks if additional help were to be needed by the traders.

"It is important my Lords, that Mr Ravenswood's business is not impeded and I have one concern on that score." He leaned forward earnestly to add weight to his words. "Mr Parry, sound man as he is, lacks experience. He has become embroiled in some local affairs in Bath which could cause unnecessary publicity for Mr Ravenswood's shipping company and is loathe to approach his findings in a," he allowed himself a superior snigger, "in shall we say, a politic manner."

"Dampen the blighter down Drake. Good man," rumbled Palmerston, reaching for the biscuits. "Gad Melbourne," he declared as he shovelled them down, "we need to move on to dine, haven't eaten since dawn."

Although Melbourne was nodding amiably and making encouraging noises, Drake's treachery had not gone un-noticed and served to intensify Melbourne's existing scorn for that particular bounder. He congratulated himself anew on the appointment of young Parry and looked forward even more to his reports, which with luck would be not only informative, but also extremely impolitic indeed.

### Evening: 17th October, 1831. Carlisle Lane, Lambeth, London.

Two days later, Nathaniel was back in his lodgings in Lambeth with Caradoc, mulling over the day's work as he contemplated the deserted grounds of the Archbishop's Palace which provided his only view. Setting aside the triumphant collection of his pistols from the gunsmith, the visit to London had not been a particularly successful one. He had spent half a day at Whitehall, first waiting by Percy's office, as planned, for a meeting to discuss progress. The amiable Percy had taken his report on Bath and radical activity, scanned it through without comment, and placed it in an overflowing tray on his desk. Nathaniel had then told Percy of his discoveries and suspicions concerning the opium traders of Bristol, the links with the kidnapping of girls and the unsavoury nature of the banker he had been directed to contact as a reliable and promising Whig supporter in Bath. He had produced a detailed report of his findings and to his disappointment, had seen it take the same route as his first offering.

Despite waiting for most of the rest of the day, he had not seen Drake, who apparently had arranged to meet the noble lords separately. He had managed the briefest of exchanges with Lord Palmerston and they had been far from satisfactory. The Foreign Secretary had breezed into Percy's office, glanced perfunctorily at Nathaniel's reports, returning the first one to the tray and beckoned for him to follow. He had been allowed a quarter-hour in His Lordship's office to outline his findings, then been told to keep his eye on the radicals and leave all Bristol business to Drake, who had everything in hand. Lord Melbourne, according to Palmerston, had an urgent appointment and was not available, but would be informed of all Nathaniel's findings in due course. Nathaniel knew he had been out-manoeuvred but, fortunately for his peace of mind, had been spared the indignity of seeing Palmerston carelessly crumple his second report, ball it, and then hoof it unceremoniously into the bin.

"Well Caradoc," said Nathaniel, reaching for a bulky package of mail he had collected at the Office. "It rather looks as though we might be on the Bath coach a little earlier than billed." He spread the correspondence on the table, separated the most inconsequential from the formal and homed in on a communication from his family's solicitor in Wales, which he scanned quickly, his mood lightening with every line. "Not the Bath coach, by the look of it!" he said, leaping up and striding to the window for better light. "We are summoned, my little friend. Pack your bones!"

The solicitor's familiar crabbed hand needed some interpretation, but the gist was that his father's cousin had died, a will was to be read, and it was in his best interests to come to Anglesey to listen to it. It was filthy weather for cross-country coaches, but as yet there was no frost, ice or snow. He flung himself into his writing desk chair and dashed off a letter to the Petersons.

## Afternoon: 18th October, 1831, Marlborough Buildings, Bath.

Anna Grant had managed to contain herself until Thursday and her scheduled afternoon tea with Em. Not that she wanted to be the bringer of bad news, but there was such a thing as duty. She set off with a spring in her step from St James's Square and made straight down the hill to the Peterson residence in Marlborough Buildings. She was shown in by a maid, paused briefly by Captain Peterson's study

151

to exchange a few pleasantries with the dear man and then entered the drawing room to let Em settle her into her usual seat.

"You look radiant!" said Em fondly. "You must be so happy now Henry is," she paused, unwilling to dredge up bad memories, "well, out and about let's say, and back at work." She beamed at her friend. "Enid will be up with the tea and the Bath Buns presently. We are still celebrating!"

"Well," said Anna. "To tell you the truth, Henry is more out and about than he should be. The bank has closed for a week as Mr Vere has disappeared!"

"No!"

"Yes!" squeaked Anna. "Not seen since last Friday, and Mrs Vere has gone away."

She bit her lip, the opportunity could not be missed. "Actually Em, I need to say something about Mrs Vere." She struggled momentarily, but decided she would burst if she kept it to herself.

"Em I saw her at Mr Parry's lodgings on Saturday. She was talking to him at the gate. And she kissed him. I'm sorry to say it Em what with you going to the Ball with him. I just thought you should be told."

Emma felt her stomach lurch, but fought to keep her face entirely expressionless. She had thought of little else but the Ball since last Thursday's dinner and Nathaniel's letter from London had been hidden away in her sewing bag as a treasure, kept within reach and re-read a dozen times a day. It had been addressed to her parents but gallantly explained, for her benefit, that he was detained by business matters. He pledged to return at the end of next week, in plenty time for the Masked Ball, which he was looking forward to, eagerly. So he said. She had visited the dressmaker, designed her mask, started making it and even shown off her ideas to the twins. She blenched at the memory of her gales of confident laughter, and felt not only foolish, but acutely ashamed. Anna's tale had dealt her a body blow, but really, how could she have been such a fool? Why else would he have agreed to escort her, but to oblige her family? Why wouldn't he want to kiss Tilly Vere? What man wouldn't? She had to salvage some self-respect.

"You say she kissed him Anna?" said Em. "They are friends you know."

"Oh yes, I know," said Anna. "And it was in public, quite above board."

Enid knocked and brought in the tea. The snatch of conversation and the strained silence were fascinating surprises. Like a good servant, she could not react, but relayed the scene in detail as soon as she made it back down to the kitchen.

"Miss Emma has gone white as a sheet," she said, sinking her teeth into a bun. "And that Miss Anna looks like she thought she'd won a sweep-stake then realised

152

as she couldn't quite put her hand on the ticket!"

"Why?" asked Cook, looking up suspiciously from her tea. "What were they sayin' when you took in the tray?"

"Somethin' about kissin' and it all bein' in public and above board."

"Who was kissin'?" demanded cook, refusing to be interested before the story showed it had legs, and shapely ones at that.

"Well," reflected Enid, steadily crunching her way through the sugar cubes which infested the base of all authentic Bath buns. "Stands to reason it can't be Mr Henry or Miss Anna would have been bawling. Must be that Mr Parry who came to dinner last week. Miss Emma must be after 'im and 'as been beaten to it."

"Did you see 'im?" said Cook. The tale had taken off and accelerated to an acceptable canter.

"Oh that I did," said Enid, rolling her eyes. "Tall, dark and 'andsome!"

"Now ladies, less of the gossip and more of the service if ye don't mind! Make mine a steaming brew and a couple o' they buns."

"Keep your wig on," grumbled Cook, pouring out the required brew to the footman, who disobligingly removed his wig, deposited it on the table, poured his tea into his saucer and flexed his elbows in preparation for pouring it down his gullet.

Once Anna had gone, Emma had time to come to terms with the news. She was infatuated with a man she did not know. He was a Londoner, well-travelled, an adventurer on foreign service, who quite possibly might never return to Bath after his next visit. He might be in Africa, or India, or Paris, again. She threw herself into her chair and took up her sewing in case her mother came in. Didn't she want to stay at home and not marry for a while? No, she thought to herself, taking out the letter and gazing at his signature again. She did not. She wanted to throw herself into his arms and recite the rest of *The Eve of St Agnes*. And act it out. And run off with him into the storm. She managed a laugh at the ludicrousness of it. How old was she, sixteen? But somehow, just to think of such things made her feel a bit better. One must be pragmatic. He was outrageously handsome. To land a man like that would incur far more in the way of competition than fluffy, beautiful Mrs Vere. Tilly might be a good flirt, but she wasn't clever in other ways. And it had been a kiss bestowed by Tilly, not himself. Emma thrust the letter back into her bag, took up the needle and began to sew. Her breathing steadied and she reached a state of calm. She too had a strategy.

153

# Chapter 7

**Early afternoon: Friday 21ˢᵗ October, 1831. Green Park West, Bath.**

"You've no idea what you're talking about woman. Ravenswood has a long arm, and so have all the men working for him. And there are more of them than ever. I saw some Oriental coves at Redcliffe Parade. New men, not his usual gang. Handy lookin' bastards they were."

Joshua Shadwell paused, chewing his lip and glaring at his wife, who sat, cross and exasperated, struggling to out-face him across her table in the front parlour. With a Herculean effort she allowed her face to smile encouragingly.

"Bristol is far enough away," she said, quietly but urgently, unfolding her arms and leaning over, reaching out for his hands. "With Vere and Mordecai dead and Declan in Bristol the link to Bath is broken. He can get his cargo elsewhere. There's hardly a shortage of Bristol trollops willing to sell their children, or a lack of laudanum soaked whores who'd sell their souls for the next bottle. Tell Ravenswood you're out of business. And," she added bitterly, "it's likely to be no more than the truth!"

Joshua shifted in discomfort at the reminder. "It depends what happens to the bank," he said gruffly. "Depends who takes over. I don't know how Vere showed our debts. A lot of our business was private. Anyway, there's nothing happening for now, they're still closed."

"It's not just your debts Joshua! I've warned you about our girls. They don't believe your tale that Babs and Abi are stayin' freely in Bristol and they want to know when they're comin' back. There's a mutiny brewin' and the regulars will play merry hell if the girls aren't workin'.""

"There's more where they came from," he said, viciously defiant.

"We've customers booked in today for Babs and Abi. What are we going to do? For sure, you'll find more girls like them, and you might find a Josie, and maybe a Clari, but I doubt it. But Mitzi and Letty?"

The savage lines of his face began to sag, and it gave her the nerve to press her advantage.

"Do you think high-class tarts will work for us if word gets out? They see themselves above the Avon Street service as well you know. You can't treat them like drabs, Joshua! You're out of your depth. You're drowning for Christ's sake! That Ravenswood is evil. Break from him!"

Joshua struggled to absorb the reality of the week. How could his affairs have sunk so low in such a short time? When he had reached home last Friday night, he really thought he had papered over the cracks, smoothed things over and plucked victory out of disaster. The Vere episode had been resolved. Babs would go: sore point, but necessary. Declan was dealt with. Last Saturday, Joshua had risen late to recover from the mental exhaustion of being interviewed by Ravenswood. By the time he had appeared in the breakfast room he had felt quite the debonair businessman, sure of his story and burnished, just a little, with a golden glow of triumph. The colour had been leached out of him in an instant, as if he had been pushed under a cold pump. She had been waiting for him, crouched in her chair like a whipped cur, blurting out her pent-up tale before he'd fully opened the door. His boys had been humiliated, beaten by one rogue punter: Jabez was still in his bed groaning with a belly wound and a shattered beak, whilst Billy was nursing him and his own broken pate. Worse than that, the punter had given Vere's name as his sponsor and asked for Babs. Even though he'd got Abi, Rosie swore the two of them had been conniving with the punter. Rosie's description of him had been unsettling and Joshua smelled a rat, but of far greater importance was the laying-off of his men, and that had only been the start.

"No loose ends." The words of Ravenswood had haunted him. With Jabez and Billy unable to work, he had no one else he could trust with Babs, and after hearing Rosie's tale he knew he had to be rid of Abi as well. It had taken most of the week to negotiate the transfer of the girls with Ravenswood. It had been distasteful. He had taken them to Redcliffe Parade himself in his own coach, pretending they were going to see some special clients. Dosed drinks had laid them out, and he had left hurriedly, guilt-ridden, as they were taken down to the caves by Ravenswood's men. Rosie didn't dare ask too many questions, as she could guess the answers.

"Do you hear me Joshua! Break with him!"

He glared at her, inchoate, impotent rage welling up from his guilty soul. He tore his hands from hers and strode to the window.

"He'd hunt us down. We'd have to sell up. Move away."

Strangely, just saying the words was like catching a rope thrown to him over a void. When he turned back to her the despair in his eyes had died away, smothered by a new light, cunning and feral, a flash of his old self.

"Perhaps we can do it Rosie. That would ditch the debts to the New Bank and get us out of Ravenswood's reach. And well away from these clammering whores," he shot a venomous glare to the rooms above. "What did you say was likely, a mutiny? They can mutiny on their bloody own."

"Leave our home! Run away! No Joshua. Please, no, I love this house." Rosie shouted, shocked and fearful, now that her goading had spurred him too far. "And I won't throw away the business!"

A rapid knocking at the door prevented him from answering or delivering the slap in the mouth she was clearly asking for.

"Come in!" said Rosie, standing to face the angry figure of Clari which now filled the doorway, arms akimbo and spoiling for a fight. Crowding behind her were the other women in a body, faces set hard, standing shoulder to shoulder. Together, as though a dam had burst, they launched a wave of furious complaint at Rosie's head. Joshua dropped into the armchair by the window, struck by how closely Rosie resembled a lighthouse in a stormy sea as it took a battering from the elements. He sank deeper into his chair, mentally retreating to a better place.

## The Danby residence, Tilly's family home, Beckington.

Approximately ten miles distant from Joshua Shadwell's discomfort, Tilly Vere was sunk in a slough of dejection of an entirely different type. Rather than feeling pursued, she felt abandoned, a new and most disagreeable emotion. She had endured almost a week at her mother's house and the strain had begun to tell before her bonnet was off. Mama had been of the opinion that Raphael had simply gone on an extended holiday, which was not surprising as Tilly had not made home sufficiently attractive. Without elaborating in any useful way, she had intimated that wives should ensure that all the needs of their husbands were fully catered for, as she had so expertly catered for those of her dear late husband. Tilly had listened and sulked, as her mother had returned to this favourite theme on a daily basis, until Wednesday, when she had ruthlessly acquainted Mama with the sordid details of her husband's sexual preferences. After taking snuff, Mama had proved to be unusually fertile in

156

expedients. Tilly would have to go home, make of it what she could and allow a husband his latitude, as many great women had done before her. By Thursday Tilly had enlarged on Vere's attacks on her person, her fear of more of the same, and her appeal to Nathaniel Parry. This last had been swept aside as a recourse of the flimsiest usage. A lodger in Walcot Street was not promising as a provider and Mama had occupied her waking hours since this last confession in calculating exactly how quickly, and onto whom, she could off-load Tilly.

Meanwhile, Tilly had taken to sitting on the white seat in the orchard at the bottom of her mother's garden, wrapped cocoon-like in a voluminous green and brown cashmere shawl. That Friday afternoon found her there. She had drawn up her feet and rested her head on her knees, listlessly watching energetic blackbirds foraging in the hedge and envying them. The sound of voices caused her to look up and she was surprised to see her mother making swift progress over the lawn accompanied by a maid and a visitor, a portly one, who was beaming a greeting to her, his spectacles flashing opaque in the sun's low rays.

"Mr Dill how very pleasant to see you again," she called.

"Oh madam, the pleasure is all mine. 'If the heart of a man is depressed with cares, the mist is dispelled when a woman appears!' How true! How true! The sight of you dear lady, so beautiful, like a dryad, a spirit of the trees."

"Mr Dill has been to Bath, Mathilda," said her mother meaningfully. "He has called at your home and at the bank. He has some propositions." She could not have dwelled longer on the term, and followed up by smiling coyly at Howard.

"Sir, please do come in for some refreshment. I'm sure you can encourage Mathilda to return to the house, it's far too chill to remain outdoors." She shot a glance at the maid and snapped out an order: "Tea for three in the drawing room. Biscuits and cake." She bestowed a doting smile on Tilly and Howard before following the servant indoors.

Howard Dill extended his hand to Tilly, but instead of relinquishing it after she rose, tucked it instead under his arm. Tears of gratitude flooded her eyes and she turned to give Howard her most shatteringly beautiful smile.

"How very kind of you to visit me Mr Dill."

"Not at all my dear lady. It is always a signal pleasure to see you, but I also need to speak to you of other matters. I need your collaboration. Tanner informed me of your whereabouts." His voice became serious and he slowed to a halt before continuing more urgently. "Mrs Vere, the bank cannot remain closed. As you know I am a major depositor and it is important to me that certain issues are resolved. I propose that we open again under the temporary supervision of young Henry Blake who will recall his subordinates and the other servants of the bank. We will advertise for a senior clerk to replace Mr Wilson. I have contacted Captain Peterson and Dr Parry, the other major depositors living in Bath, and they are in agreement."

She continued to beam at him, so Howard pressed on.

"You may know that we have a significant investment underway at present, as we are arranging the financing of another vessel for Mr Edwin Ravenswood of Bristol. He is also intimately concerned with the bank and much of our corporate investments hinge on his business. My family have known his for generations. You may know of our involvement with Bristol shipping. And you also have interests in the bank, organised by your husband," he smiled benevolently, "of which you might be entirely ignorant dear lady. We need your help in gaining access to relevant papers and there is the trivial matter of some signatures. Will you return to Bath with me? My carriage is at your disposal."

"Mr Dill, I fear for my life if Raphael returns. Things have occurred," she paused, lamely, unsure of how much to say.

Howard Dill wrapped a protective arm around Tilly. "Come in with me, Mrs Vere. May I call you Tilly? I will protect you from all comers, including your husband. Tell me at your leisure what has occurred. You are not alone my dear lady."

As they stood, Tilly entwined in Howard's bear-hug at the edge of the orchard, her mama dropped the curtain she had been peering round, deposited herself on the watered-silk chaise longue and heaved a sigh of utter relief. Howard Dill was a bachelor of enormous resources. His mansion at Norton St Philip was but one of his holdings, which spread as commodiously over the hillside pastures of Mendip as they did over the quays of Bristol. If Vere proved impossible, he might be quite easily replaced, and bettered, in wedlock or out, with this most promising companion.

She reached for her fan, so annoying these sudden rushes of heat in one's middle-age. It had been a sore trial disposing of her numerous daughters, and even the best laid plans could be so easily thwarted after victory seemed entirely secure. She had considered Howard Dill for one of her brood years before, but had always wondered if he liked women at all. She had pegged him, at the very least, as a perpetual bachelor, a dilettante, happy with his books and his enthusiasms. The type who, centuries before, would have been, perhaps, a prosperous Abbot or an ascetic academic immured in his ivory tower. However, confirmed bachelor or not, the acquisition of Mr Dill into her social circle, in any capacity, would be a coup indeed. Perhaps her giddiest daughter would be of some real use after all. The liaison with

158

Vere had been triumphant in its way, but she was not a city person. To shine in one's own parish, on one's own stage! Well, that had to count for more. She leaned over the table which the maid had stacked for tea and chose one of cook's delectable millefruit biscuits: almonds, citrus peel, angelica, crisp and light, no flour, delicious. She was still dispatching it as Howard and Tilly entered.

"Oh come to tea you young people! You must have had so much to talk about. I had quite given you up!"

## Late evening: 27th October, 1831. The White Hart Inn, Stall Street, Bath.

It was the following Thursday before Nathaniel returned to Bath. Night was falling as he made his way back to Walcot from the Hart, Tobias trundling his bags by his side and Caradoc capering and yapping alongside, invigorated at the sight of a friendly face and the smell of familiar streets after the hours of glum jolting in the straw of the coach foot-well.

"You look taller Tobias."

"Good livin' Mr Parry. There've been a few changes over the last couple of weeks. Mrs Spence 'as let me take an attic room in the house. I can pay a bit in rent, but really it's as Old Mr Spence's been laid up in bed. She needed more of a lift with 'im. Also, now I've boots and a set of clothes she says I'm fit to be in her kitchen. And, I do go to the Methody Sunday School now, so as I can learn mi letters. I know half the alphabet already. You can't go unless you've shoes. And I speaks better."

"Yes, I remember you told me that, but it seems odd to me Tobias. Why do you need to be able to afford shoes?"

"Don't know. 'Suppose it shows thrift. Mrs Spence is powerfully keen on thrift."

They arrived to find Mrs Spence and Mary, with the Johnty on her lap, sat in some state round the table in the front parlour. Unfolded before them, lovingly smoothed out to lie flat on the red velvet cloth, was a letter, and before Mary was a glass of Tom's small beer.

"Mr Parry!" exclaimed Mary as he looked round the door to greet them. "We've a letter from Matthew and it's from Bristol! He's going to be home in a couple of days now. They're just sorting the pay and a few jobs on the ship before it's re-fit. We're drinking to his health! Mother has the elderflower. Come and join us for a minute sir if you will." She jumped up to bring over a chair for him, and characteristically swept her own excitement aside. "What news from London sir? We've missed your company."

"I'll join you with pleasure," said Nathaniel, taking a seat at the table as Martha sprang up to take another glass from the dresser.

"I can offer you some bread and meat loaf to go with it Mr Parry. And you young Tobias," she said, the good news getting the better of her judgement. "As it's an extraordinary occasion, sit ye down with us and have some elderflower cordial. Or indeed the small beer." As she placed her glasses on the table with a reverent flourish, her lined face shining, sudden unexpected tears coursed down her cheeks. The party looked on, embarrassed to see Martha's austerity dissolving before their eyes like surface starch. "Oh Mother!" exclaimed Mary. "Are you alright?"

Martha rubbed her cheeks vigorously. "My son is coming home! Thank the Lord! I'll bring your food."

"It's unusual to find you ladies in the parlour," said Nathaniel to Mary, smoothly filling the silence as Martha hurried out.

"Mr Spence has been poorly and not sleeping at night. He's been dozing in his box-bed of an evening and we didn't want to disturb him. He's on the mend I'm pleased to say, and Tobias has been a saint helping this last week."

Tobias swelled with pride and held up his glass. "It is my pleasure," he said grandly, in conscious imitation of Nathaniel.

"Now," said Martha, fully recovered, sliding her laden tray onto the table and slipping the treasured letter under the toes of the pot shepherd. "Less of the toasting. Our joy is in plain-sight of the Lord and needs no more buttressing in beer. Mr Parry, how was London Town?"

Nathaniel ran his hands through his hair and leaned back in his chair. "Where to start Madam? I spent a few days in London and concluded my business, but travelling to Wales accounted for most of my absence. It wasn't a planned trip."

His listeners leaned in, agog. Martha filled his mug with more beer and Nathaniel launched into an edited version of his journeys.

"I received notification that I had inherited some property near Beaumaris, my father's home-town on the Isle of Anglesey, and I had to go immediately to conclude the business."

"The Isle of Anglesey!" said Mary sighing. "It sounds so romantic."

"Oh it is," said Nathaniel laughing. "It is a beautiful place to the far north of Wales, beyond the misty mountains of Snowdonia. There be dragons, Mary! It was a beast of a journey. At times we thought we would never get there at all. It was long and very slow. We took five days from London, most of the time in the teeth of a gale that threatened to blow us away. To spare the horses all the gentlemen passengers walked many a mile once we were off the good roads, even on the flat."

"But 'twas to an island you went? Were they running the ferries in such foul weather?" asked Mary. None of them had ever been to Wales, had not even crossed

160

the Severn. He might as well have spoken of crossing the East China Sea to the Land of the Rising Sun.

"No need for ferries," said Nathaniel, excited by the memory. "We rode over Mr Telford's mighty bridge across the Menai Straits. When your Mr Brunel has finished in Clifton you will have another such closer to hand."

"I'm going to see it," said Tobias. "I shall walk upon it when it's done! When is it to be done?"

"I saw the stones where the foundations will be when I went to Bristol last," said Nathaniel. "But the talk in London was that Brunel has only raised half of the funding at present, so you will have a few years' wait Tobias."

"Did you see your family?" asked Martha, offering Nathaniel the brown brick of meat loaf and a carving knife.

"I saw some distant cousins, and lawyers, Mrs Spence. Many lawyers. Most of my time was spent with lawyers. But it was worth it, as I'm now the proud owner of a property near my old childhood home, though that was sold long ago. And Caradoc had a grand time, didn't you boy?"

Mary reached down to pat Caradoc's wiry back. "Did you love it boy? Did you like the sea then?"

Unusually, Caradoc ignored her and continued his unequal struggle to bolt down an over-generous portion of meat loaf.

" Beaumaris is where he came from. I brought him away with me two years ago, after I had taken my father's body back to Wales. He's my link to the homeland."

Reluctant to say more on the subject, Nathaniel raised his glass. "Ladies, to home-comings! Now we must leave you to enjoy the rest of the evening. Many thanks for the supper Mrs Spence. You are a paragon amongst women."

"Well Mr Parry," said Martha, smoothing her apron in pleasure, "you're welcome I'm sure."

That night Nathaniel lay on his back, watching the stars through his open curtains. The journey to Anglesey had been nostalgic and painfully beautiful, as well as stunningly remunerative. His private means had hitherto stemmed from a legacy left by his late mother, which was substantial but unlikely to last a lifetime. Government pay was erratic, making the new stream of income from property in Wales extremely welcome. Moving between the inn at Beaumaris and the homes of various distant cousins, he and Caradoc had seen much of the island. They had walked the coast round Red Wharf Bay where he had declaimed Byron to his heart's content, in particular a favourite couple of lines about beaches. He recited them again with relish, briefly startling Caradoc.

"There is rapture in the lonely shore,
There is society where none intrudes,
By the deep sea,
And music in its roar."

He grinned with pleasure at the memory of the rolling fields and sitting for hours on the ancient mound of the burial chamber at Bryn Celli Ddu. Later, in the board-hard bed at the inn he had dreamed disturbed dreams, narrated in a torrent of Welsh. He had conjured Druids, oak-groves and Roman slaughters in the cold nights and sung himself hoarse by the sea at daybreak, with no-one but Caradoc to hear as he perfected his rendition of William Williams's *Sea of Glass*.

*"Arglwydd, arwain trwy'r anialwch."*
Lord, guide me through the wilderness.

He sang again, but quietly, for the pillar of fire, and the pillar of mist and the manna from heaven and resolved to try it out on Martha to see if she knew it. He had not heard her sing it as part of her regular morning repertoire, but his cousins claimed that it was the only Welsh hymn translated to English and sung regularly by English Non-Conformists, especially the Wesleyan Methodists.

He would not, however, try her out with the other accomplishments he had worked up. He had plugged away with the pistols on the headland to perfect his use of the new percussion cap mechanism, at first narrowly missing Caradoc, who had insisted on trying to beat him to the target. The worthy fellow had, perforce, been tied up. Generally speaking, his personal training regime had flourished. He had pounded along the beach before breakfast and managed some boxing and sword-play with the local yeomanry in the evenings. After Caradoc's first misunderstanding over the target shooting, he had also buckled down to some training and had, on occasions, been startlingly obedient.

The return to Bath required him to resume his enquiries and make good on some outstanding promises. In lieu of counting sheep as he tried to fall asleep, he considered his list of obligations. At the start of November he was duty bound to make another report to London on local radicals, though the luke-warm reception of his last efforts had killed his enthusiasm for the assignment. Of greater interest was the case of Wilson's murder. The verdict still rankled and he would like to get to the truth of it, though the likelihood was slim. He had spent a few evenings in Beaumaris dissecting the details of Tilly's notes from Vere's private cash book and it was clear that he was a person of interest. He had been moving large sums, presumably from the bank, to fund his gambling and other recreational interests.

Sight of that alone, without any additional evidence on the details of his more unorthodox tastes, would have given Wilson ample material to blackmail his employer. His connections with the Green Park brothel and its possible links to kidnapping muddied the waters further.

He needed to see Captain Peterson to share thoughts on the progress he had made, such as it was. Speaking of which, joining the Peterson party on Saturday and escorting Miss Peterson to the Masked Ball was something else he needed to do. The ball was the day after tomorrow. He made a mental note to ask Martha to prepare his evening wear. He also made a mental note that Emma Peterson had been surprisingly good company at the family dinner: charming and pretty. The ball should be no hardship. More urgently, he needed to know where Vere was, check Tilly was safe, and disentangle himself from her as painlessly as possible. It would probably also be wise to remember not to call on Miss Montrechet again. He fell asleep wearing his Damascus gown and a beatific smile.

He woke to Mary's gentle knocking on his door. "Mr Parry sir, I've got your hot water and there's a letter for you."

Nathaniel repaid Mary the fee she had given the postboy, settled back in bed and broke the seal on the note. It was anonymous, but needed no signature. As he scanned it rapidly it was clear it could be from no-one else but the mysterious Mr Lee. He sat up cross-legged in bed and read it again, carefully.

*Dear Mr Parry,*

*We met some weeks ago in Bristol. You may remember we watched a game of strategy together and we talked. From my connections it is clear that a violent demonstration is likely to be made here in Bristol against the City Recorder, and probably also the Bishop, on Saturday the 29th October. As you will know, the Recorder has made himself notorious, particularly in this City, through his continual attacks on the Reform Bills in the House of Commons. The Bishop has also spoken against it in the Lords. On Saturday the Recorder visits the City and the mob is making ready. I am writing to you as I know you are charged with the reporting of such incidents. I also have some other matters to discuss with you and would appreciate your presence here. From early evening on Friday the 28th October I will be at the inn where we first met.*

*In the hope that this finds you in time,*

*From one who aims to serve the light.*

### Afternoon: Marsh Street, Bristol.

Nathaniel had dug out his reversible frock coat, collapsible top-hat and a long black scarf for the trip to Bristol. Marsh Street was decidedly insalubrious and a degree of anonymity would be politic. In case of trouble, he had settled on taking the makila and the pair of pistols, tucking one into each of his poacher's pockets. He had every intention of returning by Saturday morning at the latest, so toyed with the idea of leaving Caradoc behind, but the loyal creature baulked. He grumbled when Nathaniel ordered him to stay on guard. He growled when reminded of the relevant lines in Byron's Don Juan about the sweetness of hearing the honest deep-mouthed bay of the watch-dog, welcoming the master home. So, it was the man complete with his dog who made his way to the Three Sugar Loaves in the late afternoon.

Marsh Street proved to be very different in daylight hours, with more respectable working women and children in evidence. A few matrons in aprons were chatting in the entrance to an arched alleyway that opened onto the street, arms full of damp linen from the washing lines they had rigged up to zigzag the crooked lane. Some young girls balanced water crocks on their heads, giving them surprising grace as they walked, swaying slowly home from the conduit, laughing together. Chickens pecked in the gutters and a gang of infants chased down the street, pushing each other and shouting wildly.

Nathaniel's purposeful walk, the sight of the makila and the glowering Caradoc, were sufficient to discourage the jostling pack from closing in to beg or pick his pocket. Nathaniel glanced up to the high floors and the attics, down to the areas and the basements. Through the dust-streaked windows he spotted shadowy figures moving in the rooms or pale faces looking out like ghosts. Marsh Street was populated by flocks of poverty stricken tenants, from the sound of them, mainly Irish, who roosted in the gaunt remains of the houses in squalid rented rooms. It was not all housing, the tenements were interspersed with warehouses, mainly for sugar, and drinking dens catering for the dregs of Bristol's drinking public. Most of these seemed deserted, doors closed against the daylight, but in a few hours the wharf rat trade would spill down the street from the quays, unrolling a grimy tide of rackety music and bellowing voices, profanity, vomit and fighting. Amongst the swaying inn signs he finally spotted one sporting the three white triangles of the sugar loaves and pushed his way through the door.

It was dark inside, but a surly barman was on duty talking to a brawny customer in an offensively checked waistcoat and greasy frock coat who lent over the bar towards him, swopping tales with an air of exaggerated confidentiality.

"Brandy and hot water if you please."

The barman moved off reluctantly to get Nathaniel's order.

"Welsh terrier," grunted the man. "Good little dogs they be. 'Ad one once. Scrappy little fighter 'e was, but characterful if you take mi meanin'."

"I do sir," said Nathaniel. "Do you keep a dog now?"

The man gestured to the fireplace, where a hulking Staffordshire lay sleeping, his twitching ears bitten into scallops round the edge like a tea-time doily, skin sleek over tight sculpted muscles.

As it slept, Nathaniel risked a few more moments in the bar.

"I guess the city will be up in arms tomorrow."

The man hawked and spat with furious precision into the spittoon which squatted on the sawdust floor between them.

"Wetherell won't know what 'it 'im. Bastard as 'e is. On 'is 'igh 'orse 'e were in London, railin' against the Bill, a-sayin' 'e speaks for Bris'l! Booed out o' the city 'e was at the openin' of the Assizes, in April that were. Damn him, says Oiy. Our Members are both reformers and the city's be'ind 'em. We'll show 'im and the bloody Tory councillors. Do you know Bristol friend?"

"Only been here once before sir," said Nathaniel. "It seems a great city."

"It were great," said the man savagely. "Though we've bin a-losin' out to Liverpool sin' moiy ould dad were a boy. Dock fees are sky-high 'ere and if the West Indies sugar plantations loses their slaves, as seems most likely Oiy might add, our refinin' fact'ries will be sunk as deep as the rest o' the trades. Business is bad 'ere. Men are 'ungered sir! But we're not standin' fer it! We've 'ad our own Political Union since last year and there's fightin' talk there Oiy'll tell ye. It's not just Frenchies with the heart to rise up," he added darkly. "And look at what they done." He leaned over to Nathaniel, prodding him in the chest to add good measure to his words. "Drummed out their king again didn't they, an' this time, pops in another without invitin' Madame Guillotine! Anyways, even if there's gore, what's a riot or a revolution eh! We'll prob'ly be dead of the cholera before anything else gets us! You know there's been deaths? In Sunderland they were. The Pest from Bengal! It's on its way alright!" He drank deeply, with a macabre satisfaction.

"I've been up-country in Wales," said Nathaniel. "I didn't know."

Nathaniel had liked what he had heard, but sensed customers were starting to trickle in and he needed to keep his eyes open for Cornelius Lee. He turned round to lean on the bar with his elbows and survey the rest of the pub. A few Chinese sailors had entered and were making their way towards the door of the rear bar where he had watched the Wei Ch'i players. Nathaniel made his excuses and followed them. The room was dim and smokey, the fire sulky and reluctant to flare, but he could see that Lee was already seated in the corner, waiting.

"Good evening Mr Lee. I received your note this morning."

"I am pleased to see you," said Cornelius, smiling at Nathaniel and rubbing Caradoc's ears in welcome. The dog had made a bee-line for Cornelius and put his head on the wooden settle next to him.

"I told you of the likely troubles tomorrow to provide a reason for you to travel here. That news is public enough to allow a note, though it had to be an anonymous one." He dropped his voice, motioning Nathaniel to move closer, and glanced round to ensure the sailors at the next table were well out of ear-shot. "There are other matters which I can only speak of. Mr Parry, I know that you and your colleague Mr Drake are here to support the opium shipments of Edwin Ravenswood for the greater good of the British Empire. You know my views on the trade. I want you to know now that my reasons for joining the crew of the *Blue Dragon* are not to assist. I do not wish them well."

"One man against a crew of," Nathaniel paused, calculating swiftly, "would it be about sixty?"

"There are forty men. The *Blue Dragon* is four hundred tons, so it has the usual size of crew for a regular vessel: ten per hundred tons. However, I do have some friends amongst them, maybe ten at most. Four to one: not bad odds as it happens. It could be much worse. The *Blue Dragon* is about a third of the size of a regular East Indiaman but clippers tend to have larger crews than normal, because of their line of business."

Nathaniel nodded. "Ready to fight off unwelcome interest."

"Yes, but I do not intend to fight for the ship Mr Parry. I shall gather intelligence and, as you say in England, keep my powder dry."

"It is rare for a man to cross the world for purely altruistic reasons," said Nathaniel, watching Cornelius closely.

"I agree. My mission has personal motivations. Suffice to say my brother died recently, and miserably, to the great sorrow of our family. He was a hopeless opium addict. His dependence on the drug corrupted him and brought him to his ruin. Truly, he was consumed by the darkness and the opium den he frequented was supplied by none other than Edwin Ravenswood." Cornelius paused briefly, as if closing a door on his secrets. "However, Ravenswood has other interests which I hope you will help me to curtail. On the *Blue Dragon* will be some kidnapped females, two infants and four young girls. They have been especially chosen to be shipped abroad and used as the creatures of an evil man known as the Count. He has English girls taken to the East to be abused in any way he or his associates care to

166

devise. The supply is regular as the girls do not survive long. This is not an isolated instance and Ravenswood is not the only exporter, but if we can save these few, it will be a deed well done. Just before the *Dragon* sails on Sunday they will be moved aboard from caves under Ravenswood's house. The ship is late already and no further delays are possible because of arrangements for the opium collections."

"And you want me to help you release the girls?"

"I want you to effect the release Mr Parry. I cannot do it myself as I cannot risk losing my position on the *Blue Dragon*. I must remain on the ship for the voyage east in order to achieve my own objectives. If you will not help I might have to let them sail. No attempt to bring in help from the watch or other officials will have any chance of success. They will not be able to enter the house against Ravenswood's wishes. He is a man of great power in this city and has the local magistrates, how would you say? In his pocket?"

Nathaniel's eyes searched the impassive face but as before sensed no treachery or threat, just an immense latent power, a compelling force. His mind conjured up, unbidden, a vision of his father, telling his stories in the dark by his bed: tales of eastern warriors and mythical battles, the titanic struggles of the elemental forces of good and evil which would go on throughout all time. He must have smiled, and Cornelius sensed, as well as saw, the relaxation of tension.

"Tomorrow night I dine with Ravenswood at his house. It is in Redcliffe Parade at the top of the red cliff itself. Also there will be a man called Kizhe. He is a very dangerous man, an envoy of the Count himself, sent to pay a courtesy visit to Ravenswood and inspect his business. My friends amongst the Chinese crew have told me that half a dozen of Kizhe's personal guards have been planted amongst them to keep him informed. Kizhe will also sail with the *Blue Dragon*, so tomorrow's dinner is by way of a farewell."

Cornelius paused to take a pencil and notebook from his pocket. He bent over the table in the uncertain light from the fire and the spluttering tallow candles and hurriedly sketched as he continued: "Here's where we are now. Here's the dock. The prisoners are being kept here, in caves below the house in Redcliffe Parade. Ravenswood uses them as cellars. There are dozens of rooms and passages hollowed out in the cliff, some can only be reached from the quay, but many of them are directly below the houses in the Parade and used by the owners. Last time I was in Ravenswood's house I saw the prisoners. I know exactly where they are kept. They are only guarded by two women who drug them if they struggle or complain. A stairway leads down from the caves through the rock to the quayside, just here, where there is often a sailor on guard. I propose a rescue plan for tomorrow evening.

167

It cannot be earlier. If there is sufficient time between the girls' removal and the sailing, Ravenswood will order the kidnapping of more girls. We need a diversion to allow you time to get them out and I have an idea. Ravenswood has another ship at anchor on the quay called the *Mathilda*, docked here. He likes to keep an eye on both vessels from his windows. By tomorrow night the *Mathilda's* crew will have been discharged, so if it were to be set alight there would be no-one to deal with it. He would be drawn down to the quay to rouse the sailors from the *Blue Dragon* to fight the fire. Such a distraction could allow a rescue. We need to have a coach waiting, which could be hired from the stables round the back of the Ostrich."

Cornelius shot a searching glance at Nathaniel as he tore the sketch map from his notebook, crushed it and flung it to the back of the fire. It flared and sighed as he pocketed his belongings. Involving this man had been a calculated gamble which, if he had judged him aright, would be more than justified, and if he had not would have created yet another problem.

"I know the inn," said Nathaniel. "And I also knew of the trade in the children. It's villainous, and in principle I agree that the girls should be released, but I have some affairs to put in place. I really should be in Bath tomorrow." Despite an unwelcome vision of disappointed Petersons, he rose and clapped Cornelius on the back. "Come on let's look at the house where they are held. You say it's close by?"

When they emerged from the Three Sugar Loaves it was full dark and the life of Marsh Street had ignited. Sounds of frenzied fiddling and the stamp of feet blew out on gales of heat from gaping inn doors. Revellers staggered before them, seeking challengers or partners for their random drunken dances, but all instinctively steered clear of the two tall men with their faces muffled against the buffeting noise, the stench and the chill. Cornelius and Nathaniel walked silently down Prince Street towards the harbour and turned left into the Grove, making for the ferry to Redcliffe. As they levelled with the Coach and Horses a noisy group left the bar and stepped onto the path in front of them. Four sailors, loudly drunk and keen for everyone to know it, were baiting two women and their slightly-built male escort. They had moved in to surround them, chaffing and pawing at the women, spoiling for a fight. Nathaniel and Cornelius automatically gave the party a wide berth.

"Leave us alone! Let us pass!" shouted a feeble male voice, the delivery agitated and strained. "These ladies need to go home."

"I think they could answer for themselves. Couldn't you moiy 'andsomes!" roared the foremost, rubbing his hands against the cold. "Oiy needs to warm myself and fancies a dance with one o' these shapely pieces 'ere! 'Specially you missus.

You've a fine figure on you and you seems a man or two short in your party!"

"A night on the town along of us is what they have a fancy for I'll be bound," chipped in another.

"An' we know just the place don't us lads?" said the boldest sailor, taking one of the women in his arms. "Look! She likes a dance. Don't you missus!" he yelled, twirling her round, at which the woman set up a piercing scream, wriggled an arm free and slapped him full in the face.

As Nathaniel registered that the woman bore a striking resemblance to Mary Spence, Caradoc had already snarled a brief warning and rocketed across the pavement like a black and tan comet, flinging himself at the man and embedding his fangs in his arm. The man went over like a bowling ball, outraged and yelling in pain with Caradoc hanging on like a limpet, whilst the woman, newly released, sprang away to the arms of her companions.

"Get off! Get this mutt off me!" bawled the sailor, rolling on the ground and beating at Caradoc with his free fist, as the man behind him produced a knife and closed in. "Caradoc!" shouted Nathaniel "Here sir!" closely followed by: "Stop! Come here!" to no response whatsoever. As he covered the intervening ground in two strides he tried it again in Welsh, *"Rhoi'r gorau i! Tyrd yma!"*

But Caradoc was lost in the red mist of battle and there was no time for more words. Nathaniel swung the makila up to grip it quarter-staff style in both hands and slammed a blow from the right into the knife-man's middle. As he folded up Caradoc regained control of himself and neatly transferred his attentions to the buckling knife man. The bitten man rose from the ground roaring in fury, to be floored anew by Nathaniel's left-sided follow up, as the female party and timid minder scuttled away into the shadows, the latter calling in desperate gratitude, "I'll rouse the watch! Thank you! Thank you!"

Cornelius had noted the stick work approvingly and was pleased to see that Nathaniel was instinctively aware that there were two more potential assailants. Nathaniel had turned deftly to face them after dropping the second man to the floor. The makila whirled again: right, left, then a crushing blow to the head of the bitten man who had not learned his lesson but, like Lazarus, had risen again. The other three began to pick themselves up ruefully, grumbling but not offering more and Caradoc returned to heel.

"Good man!" said Nathaniel. *"Dyn da!"*

He grinned at Cornelius and made a move to leave. Cornelius nodded, but even as he did so two more burly men sidled out of the bar and decided on the instant to revive the ambitions of the fallen.

"Now lads," hollered a new voice. "What's the game 'ere! Up an' at 'em bully boys!"

Nathaniel dropped back to where Cornelius stood on the quayside. Side by side they had more of a chance against a possible six.

"I'll take the fore-most," said Cornelius quickly, as the fresh men ran for them from the door. The first cannon-balled forward to throw a punch at Cornelius's head, and managed only a wild uncomprehending yell as he found himself up-ended and flying though the air. Cornelius had stepped aside to block and throw his assailant. Head over heels he flew, over the quayside, to crash into the black waters of the dock. The second man, stunned by a blow from Nathaniel blundered towards Cornelius and in seconds had followed the first diver over the side.

In seconds their gasping heads broke the filthy surface. "Help! Help us! Can't swim! We're goin' under!'"

Nathaniel drew a pistol from his coat and motioned to the two men who had escaped the ravages of Caradoc's teeth and had been advancing for more of a share in the fight. "Pull them out," he ordered. "Or do you want to test my aim?"

They did not. Nathaniel, Cornelius and Caradoc left them to it, scrabbling for lengths of timber to hold out to the floundering men, who were still cursing and begging, beating the water with their flailing arms.

"You fight well," said Cornelius, to Nathaniel as he led the way along the quay to the Grove ferry. "Where did you learn?"

"I spent much time with my father and he instructed me," said Nathaniel. "He was a man of wide experience. He travelled in the east and found there a great deal to admire. From being a child I have enjoyed western style fencing but I also know something of your ways of the sword. And I can still manage a basic conversation in Mandarin. Though it doesn't match your skill in English. Where did you learn?"

"My mother was born in America."

Nathaniel stopped in his tracks. "My mother too was American. I should have known. Cornelius can hardly be a popular name in Cathay!"

"And your name is not as common in England as in the United States I guess."

They smiled to each other across the dark. Two men: both dark-haired, of almost identical build and age. Nathaniel instinctively held out his hand to Cornelius, who paused momentarily, then took it briefly in his.

"We have some feeling of brotherhood between us, you and I," said Nathaniel. "May I call you Cornelius?"

Cornelius bowed and then stood straight, his hands loose by his sides, watching Nathaniel.

170

"So, Cornelius, one more question. Your fighting style is unlike that of most Chinese sailors I have seen. Can you tell me where you trained?"

"In China I spent many years at a temple with a master there. I am not a sailor."

"Were you to be a monk?"

Cornelius did not reply, the one question had been answered. They walked in silence to the ferry, he took two ha'pennies from his pocket to pay the ferry-man and they settled on the wooden bench to scan the opposite bank. Redcliffe Wharf lay to the left with its tangle of cranes, barrels and planks, the *Mathilda* and the *Blue Dragon* to the right, rolling gently at anchor at King's Wharf, apart from the other vessels. The *Mathilda* was worn from her long voyage but the *Blue Dragon* was as smart as paint, "Bristol Fashion". Above them was the towering red cliff, topped by the neat palladian terrace of Redcliffe Parade. On landing they took up a vantage point out of sight of the solitary sailor on guard at the entrance to Ravenswood's caves and plotted again how a release could be engineered.

"I know a little about explosives," smiled Cornelius. "It is a simple thing to cause a localised fire on the *Mathilda* and a surprise for the man on the door if he lingers. I can provide these things, and will ensure that Ravenswood and the rest of the dining party are alert and encouraged to intervene. Though I doubt I could stop them. The fear of fire spreading to the *Blue Dragon* after all the delays to her sailing would be insupportable. Do you have other weapons?"

"One more pistol. But my makila is quieter and more reliable."

"Yes, it is a well made stick. You also have Caradoc. Do not underestimate the power of a fighting dog."

Nathaniel drew the handle from the sheath and the dagger blade glinted in the starlight. "And do not underestimate the Spaniard's stick my friend."

"Come," said Cornelius, "I would like to look at it more closely in the light. We'll make our way through the yard and round the back of the Parade to the mews. We can find the nearest livery and get into the inn by the side-entrance. There we can talk of weapons, and eat, and make decisions about tomorrow."

"I've been here before, with John Drake," said Nathaniel as they entered the bar of the Ostrich. Caradoc made for the inglenook, tail up and well-pleased to see Nathaniel making straight for the bar. He settled amongst the logs, panting in anticipation of a pie and a bowl of beer.

"Not a man to trust far," said Cornelius, taking their pots of cider from Nathaniel. "I know you work with him, but beware, he knows of the trade in girls and is already in the pay of Ravenswood. He will not allow such matters to interfere with the opium runs. Furthermore, I sense he will compromise your reports if it suits

171

him. He is not a man of honour or of loyalty."

"But you are?"

"To death." Cornelius smiled. "As I think are you. Nathaniel, may I now ask you one question? Can you tell me of your business in Bath?"

"As you know I am reporting on radical unrest, if there is any, but I have also become involved in a murder case on behalf of friends. A bank manager by the name of Raphael Vere has disappeared. I am sure he holds the key to the murder of his senior clerk. He is a cruel and unscrupulous husband, and a gambling man of perverted tastes, this I know already, and I suspect he is involved in the traffic you seek to disrupt here."

"I can help you there. Vere should be dead by now. He was to be lost overboard on the Cork steam packet, and you are right, he was deeply involved in the trade. I can also put your mind at rest on the other matter. He bragged to me that he had commissioned the death of his clerk and dispatched the murderer, though I doubt the truth of that. The man was a silken slug used to ordering, not doing. Your colleague Drake seems to me similar, greedy but cleverer, still sharp enough to rise a little further. I am surprised he brought you here. I would not have thought it sufficiently luxurious."

"He has some interests, apart from himself! He likes boxing and he surprised me by his passion for engineering and for history. He also has a taste for beauty. Perhaps he is not entirely irredeemable. He was fascinated by this place. It was apparently the haunt of notorious pirates."

"Perhaps his namesake?"

"No, Drake the privateer lived in an earlier time. The pirates of the seventeenth century were here by all accounts. It was Blackbeard's local, or so Drake said. But I know it must have sea-faring connections. I have often seen an ostrich carved as a figurehead on the prows of ships. It is an African creature but also a sign used by ship owners. I know of one Welsh family, the Probyns who use the ostrich in their arms, but there are others. The Africa trade was important here in the past."

"To return to my question about Bath, why must you be there tomorrow?"

"I have promised family friends that I will be of their party at a Masked Ball. It seems a trivial matter, but the Captain was a friend of my late father's and I am to escort his daughter. It would be discourteous to let them down without a word."

"Then send word! There is still time. There are dozens of coaches daily to Bath from Bristol."

"Postboy deliveries are erratic. But I have been plotting an idea as an insurance measure. Is the *Mathilda's* crew still in dock?"

"They are all to be paid off tomorrow before the vessel is moved to the yard for re-fit."

"Excellent. My landlady in Bath has a son on board. If I could catch him with a note to take he could ensure he sees Miss Peterson in person."

Cornelius looked amused. "So it is not just for the estimable father that you are concerned? Tell me, do you lodge in Walcot Street?"

"Yes. How did you know?"

"I have a good memory. I only need to read papers once and remember them well. I have seen the crew rosters for Ravenswood's ships. There was only one Bath man on the sheets I saw. A man called Matthew Spence who lived in Walcot Street."

Nathaniel looked at Cornelius quizzically. "A skill such as yours would come in very useful in my line of work."

"So, Nathaniel," said Cornelius finishing his cider. "Will you play our little game tomorrow?"

"Yes. I will send a message *via* the mail coach and also a personal note *via* Matthew Spence if he is to be found. You dine at six you said? Meet me tomorrow morning with any materials you have and a plan of the caves. I will encourage the *Mathilda* to flare into life a quarter hour after you start and then I will enter the caves. I'll organise a coach, and if the girls are willing to be rescued I will do my best to rescue them."

"It would be better to take them to Bath. They have all come from there through the efforts of a character called Shadwell."

"All of them? Then the links in the chain are clear. I have contacts in Bath who would enjoy a crusade to break it. And I have a few ideas as to where the girls could be taken if no one claims them. There are public institutions in Bath which will take them in. As for tomorrow night, I have some friends I could call on. They might help."

They sat on in silence, gazing into the singing fire and, despite their confident scheming, each considered the foolhardiness of the project and how extremely unlikely it was to succeed. Each ran over alternative possibilities and rejected every one.

## The caves in Redcliffe

Theoretically within shouting distance of the fireside of the Ostrich, but embedded deep in the red sandstone cliff, two girls sat close together on a camp bed. They spoke in low whispers, ensuring the two bawds sharing a drink by the door could not hear.

173

"Babs, you must do as I say," pleaded Abigail, stroking her friend's arm, trying to calm her. "You must not complain or cry out again. Appear happy, smile, say you are looking forward to the trip."

"Oh Abi I'm so a-feared. God save us! An' I've such a pain in my head."

"Shush, you fool, shush," hissed Abi. "They'll drug us again if you start and we must keep clear heads. If we get one chance to get away we'll have to be fit to take it. Do you understand!"

Barbara nodded, her eyes staring in horror, her hands shaking.

"Once we're on the ship it'll be like the press-gang. We'll be gone for years, maybe for ever. From now we'll take turns to sleep so we're always ready. I heard them say we're sailing on Sunday. It's Friday night now. We can do it."

Even as she spoke, Barbara rested her head on Abigail's shoulder and began to slip away.

"So tired Abi. I've such a pain."

Abigail put her arms around Barbara and started to rock them both. Rhythmically to and fro: trying to heal the fear, trying to stay awake. She did not dare sing; must not draw attention to them. She stole a glance over to the door, the two women were laughing softly together, swigging in turn from a bottle and swinging back on their chairs. The little girls were asleep and quiet enough but the babies were sleeping fretfully in a truckle-bed, sometimes calling out, drugged beyond wakefulness, each descended into a nightmare world, a passive infantile hell of their own dreaming. They were comfortable after a fashion, the cave was warmed by a system of hot pipes and a fire, but water dripped down one wall. It was a strange place of limbo, piled with diversions: toys, sweet-meats, clothes to try on. And there were books. Abigail thought she knew most things about men but some of the sketches had sickened her to the core. She had no doubt what their fate would be and she prayed for strength.

"Lord, any chance there might be, any whisper of a chance, I'll take it. I'll get away from here, be a better girl. Help me God if I ever get the chance I'll be different. I'll leave Madam Shadwell's. Oh God, you know Joshua Shadwell betrayed us! Please God strike him down!"

She let her mind run over the betrayal for the hundredth, or the thousandth time. She had lost count. The order to dress in their best, the drive in the best carriage with the prospect of two days in Bristol, the tales of rich clients: all had been excitement and adventure, a welcome change from the routines of Green Park. They had been given a dinner in a smart dining room in Redcliffe Parade. Lots to drink: too much, more than she had ever had. Then the terrible awakening in the red cave: the realisation that they were trapped, the struggling, the shouting, beatings and slapping, foul drinks and unconsciousness. They had been tied at first, until they had promised to obey and be nice. Days had melded into days. She had been hanging onto the snatches of conversation between the guards and had slowly pieced together all she needed to know. They had been sold, their lives thrown down as tribute to the master of this house, a man even Shadwell served. Why had they been chosen? How could he have done this? They'd both been good girls for him and Madam. She had feared him, but life had been better in Green Park than in her squalid home in Avon Street, so she had taken what there was to enjoy and suffered the rest. Perhaps God would answer her prayer and strike him down. But if he didn't, perhaps she, Abigail, would strike instead. Wild schemes of retribution cheered her up and she spent the night devising increasingly brutal punishments for Mr Joshua Shadwell. It was empowering. By dawn her devices had taken on a life of their own and she felt she had something else to live for.

# Chapter 8

**Late morning: 29ᵗʰ October, 1831, Welsh Back, Bristol.**

Nathaniel pushed open the black studded front door of the Llandoger Trow and stepped into the seething welter of King Street, thronged with traders and sailors, loud with the clatter of carts and sounds of the quay which stretched away beyond the gabled press of seventeenth-century houses and inns, down the Floating Harbour to Redcliffe. He paused to whistle a reluctant Caradoc out of the warm bar, and turned to head off towards the Grove ferry. The morning could not have gone better. From first light when the chambermaid at the Ostrich had lingered in his room, game to dawdle away a half-hour, he had been able to edge the rescue plan a little closer to success. The maid was a comely Welsh girl, dark as himself, with hair like black silk and eager to talk.

"Mr Parry is it?" She had said, in her soft Celtic lilt, smiling as she turned from placing his hot water jug on the wash-stand. "Are you a Welshman then sir?"

Then they had talked of Anglesey and her home on the Lleyn Peninsula, which she missed with a passion but did not seem to have ambitions to return to.

"Mud it is here!" she had exclaimed, gesturing down the harbour towards the coast. "Have you seen what they call a beach out 'yer at Weston? Our sand's soft and gold, like sugar it is. And the sea! As clear green as an emerald."

"Like your eyes."

"Oh sir!" She had blushed, very pleased and keen to be helpful. "If you're stayin' you'd like the Wednesday Goose Fair. It's up the harbour and the Welsh traders'll all be there, all the slate men and the coal carriers. Plenty to eat and drink.

176

Their boats and the trows are berthed at the Welsh Back just along the quay," she said pointing now in the opposite direction, past the Grove and up towards Bristol Bridge. "Most of the Welshmen drink at the bottom of King Street in the Ship or the Llandoger."

The information had been more useful than she knew. Before he left and realised its full potential she was more useful still. Paper, pen and ink and sealing wax were magicked up from the bar with his breakfast and within the hour he was out and about. He had found the mail-coach office, left a letter for Captain Peterson and hired a hackney carriage for three days. The driver's only task was to be waiting to hand over the reins in the mews behind Redcliffe Parade by six in the evening. Nathaniel had then found the Llandoger and taken a seat in the bar near the loudest group of Welsh traders he could find. A quarter-hour of listening and a few shared jokes in Welsh had moved him onto the table. Despite the centuries of shared trade, the Bristolians and the Welsh were still not brothers. Canny listening had enabled Nathaniel to isolate a roguish boat owner and a few more drinks had secured the hire of his jolly boat. Nathaniel had spun a fair tale of needing to move some goods at dusk, hinting at illicit trade, hinting too of profits at the expense of a Bristolian rival. A guinea sealed the deal and a couple more were promised if the man met him as planned, at twilight on the Welsh Back.

Nathaniel reflected on the progress. The plan was a good one but it hinged on Cornelius's explosive surprises being small enough to hide on his person and allow the crucial shinning up the anchor cable that he had planned. As he shrugged the thought away and buttoned up his coat against the cold, a deep and mighty bellow of rage sounded from behind the pub in the direction of Queen Square. It was the unmistakeable roar of an enraged crowd about to turn into a mob. He turned on his heel and made his way towards the disturbance. Rounding the corner from King William Avenue he found himself on the edge of a chaos of running fights, swirling in isolated paroxysms of fury within a shifting crowd which covered most of the square. Bystanders had gathered on the periphery of the battles, standing back by the houses, most watching, drawn to the violence and the spectacle, but, as the case of the group of men in front of Nathaniel, some were egging on the combatants, bawling encouragement and suggestions. He moved nearer to the men, moving his hand down the stick of his makila, ready for his next move, as he closed in to speak to them.

"What's caused this?" asked Nathaniel to the man beside him. The thick-set sailor, a quieter man on the edge of the group, had the time and inclination to talk.

"They've chased up here to catch 'old of Wetherell. You a stranger? Well, 'e's the Bris'l Recorder. Chased 'im up 'ere they 'ave. He's 'ad to postpone the openin' of the Assizes and is 'oled up in the Mansion 'ouse over by there." He gestured to the corner mansion of a gracious eighteenth century terrace. Nathaniel glanced around and noted that Queen Square was gracious all round, stately, vast and shady, with trees, gravel walks and an equestrian statue of William III held at a rigid prance in the centre. It seemed more than double the size of Bath's Queen Square and big enough for an army to have mustered in it. The houses were occupied by a mix of residents, businesses and grand municipal offices, but had nothing in the way of civic defences, apart from the scattering of officious looking bludgeon men sporting Council armbands. Armed with wooden staves, they were energetically setting about the livelier demonstrators, breaking heads and beating backs, causing the mood of the crowd to turn ugly.

"Been after 'im from 'is first showin' comin' over Totterdown," continued the sailor. "'Is coach 'as been stoned good and proper. That ain't 'is you're seein' now, over there by the Mansion 'ouse, an' 'e's not farin' so good either by the looks on it."

It was not faring "so good". The coach bore the signs of an enthusiastic pelting and some of the crowd were rocking it, straining to tip it over as they watched.

"Are the troops called out?" enquired Nathaniel.

"Suppose so. Some 'o they Bloody Blues, you know, Light Dragoons, 'ave been quartered in Clifton all the week. They're at the ready and there's Guards about somewheres. Mayor Pinney tried to get three hundred specials but 'e 's short o' decent men. He's made up numbers wi' a hundred or so of these rough buggers. Itchin' for a scrap they are, as you see. Seems to me they're just rilin' everybody up. I'm tellin' you, this ain't lookin' too good. Pinney asked us sailors to 'elp as well, sent word for us all to enrol as specials. 'E knew first sight of Wetherell would rouse people up, but almost to a man we told 'im to be off. Jack Tars are no cat's-paw for the bloody Council. Pinney should 'ave told Wetherell to stay away from Bris'l. 'E's no business 'ere. We're a reformin' city we are and the sooner the bloody Council realises it the bloody better says I!"

"So the Recorder and the Mayor are still in the Mansion House," said Nathaniel, surprised. "Looks like they might have a longer stay than they bargained for."

As crossing the Square was impossible, he and Caradoc retraced their steps, followed the quay round to the Grove and joined the queue for the ferry. Once across and on his way back to the inn he ran over the events in the square in his mind and, just in case the demonstration ran out of control, he made a snap decision to send an interim report to Lord Melbourne. He made his way to the nearest mail-coach office, borrowed writing materials and dispatched a warning note. Within half an hour he was entering the Ostrich again and spotted the familiar figure of Cornelius Lee, sitting as usual with his back to the wall, well placed to see whoever entered or left the inn. Caradoc went straight to him, ready to take exception to a lean, suntanned figure sitting close to Cornelius on the bench. The stranger was unmistakably a sailor back from a long voyage. He appeared exhausted, his demeanour haggard and apprehensive. On the floor by his feet was a travel-stained bag, a rolled hammock and a bird cage in which perched a brilliantly plumaged red and grey parrot. Spread on the table before them were steaming plates of mutton stew, mugs and a jug of beer.

"May I introduce you to Mr Matthew Spence from the *Mathilda*," said Cornelius. "I managed to persuade him to wait until you arrived, but he is anxious to be home."

Caradoc stretched out on the floor under the table, after deciding to accept Matthew but keep a weather eye on the bird. Nathaniel took a seat opposite them and drew a letter from his coat.

"Mr Spence thank you for waiting to hear me. I am lodging at your mother's house in Walcot and knew you'd docked on the *Mathilda*. I would be much obliged if you would take this letter to Bath for me. It is essential that Miss Peterson receives it. I should be at the Assembly Rooms with her this evening but am delayed here. Another lodger at your home, Tobias Caudle, will take it to her once you arrive in Walcot, if you would be so kind as to instruct him to do so." He took two guineas and a sixpence from his pocket. "Please take this. It will help you catch a fast coach and give a few pence to Tobias for his part."

"I will sir," said Matthew slowly. "To tell you the truth our pay is not what we had been promised. Any extra will help. I'll take your letter."

As he reached out for the sealed note Nathaniel noticed the hand Matthew proffered was short of two fingers. Recent wounds by the looks of them, the fingers probably severed by a cable, and the arm bore signs of infected bites. He looked Matthew full in the face and read there the miseries of his voyage. He was a man in shock, still with one foot in his old life, plagued by whatever nightmares he had endured, desperate to be home but unable to imagine his homecoming. Nathaniel postponed his preliminary plan to question Matthew Spence about the cargoes on the *Mathilda*.

"You have a fine family Mr Spence," said Nathaniel. "A sturdy son who will cheer your heart and your mother and your wife are counting down the days and praying for your safe return. They can think of little else."

Matthew's eyes glazed as he stood up clumsily, eager to be gone. "I've never seen him yet sir. Your letter will be delivered, depend upon it. Good day to you gentlemen."

As Matthew made his way out, bundling his luggage through the door and raising an outraged squawk from the parrot as he did so, Cornelius slipped a small sack into Nathaniel's hands. "Here are the charges, half a dozen balls of fire: smoke and firecrackers followed by the flames with a slow-match time delay, but you won't have to place them yourself. Two reliable men have agreed to meet you and lay the charges, you might recognise them from when you watched the Wei Ch'i school. You can keep a look-out for them whilst they are aboard. With my encouragement the results should be enough to draw Ravenswood and Kizhe down to the quay."

"Good, that should improve our chances. Ask your men to be on the Welsh Back near the *Pride of Avon* trow. The skipper's renting his jolly boat to me and we can approach the *Mathilda* from the waterside. I had planned to row over myself, tie up the boat and climb the anchor cable to get aboard, but your men can do that for me with pleasure. Furthermore, there has been an interesting development," said Nathaniel, pulling over an untouched plate of stew. "The potential for riot has grown over the afternoon as the Council's special constables are busy antagonising the demonstrators in Queen Square. I'll go down again later this afternoon to see if it's possible to siphon off a few to Redcliffe. The lock on the grill door to the caves should be easily picked if I get the chance, but I'd also like a sledge-hammer nearby, in case it isn't, and I need to break the stone work. The coach is hired and will be waiting in the mews behind the Parade."

"Good. And now, the route to the cave." Cornelius sketched the stone stairway, its sequence of side tunnels and hollowed out vaults. "You should quit the cliff the same way as you entered, but this is what you look for if you are driven up the steps to the main house. Here's a way out through the kitchens." He paused, deliberating. "Are you taking Caradoc?"

"I was going to leave him with the stableboy until I come with the girls, or without them," answered Nathaniel guardedly. "Why?"

"It might be easier to encourage them to leave with you if you take him. That part of the plan might be difficult. They might be reluctant. Also he could help with the guards. I'll tell the two men who lay the charges to stay on the wharf and wait to help you when you get out of the caves."

The two men drank silently and considered the possibilities. The prospect of transferring brutalised young girls and infants, possibly under fire, was daunting. It was unhelpful to acknowledge it, but, unlike the Vere's of this world, they had

180

between them no experience of under-age females whatsoever. The beer did not last long.

"For good or ill we may not see each other again," said Nathaniel. "You will sail on the *Blue Dragon*, presumably tomorrow?"

Cornelius nodded. "Thank you my friend for agreeing to attempt this and bring some degree of confusion to my enemies. Am I correct to say that it is a typical English toast? In your case: confusion to the French?"

"It was our toast for many years," laughed Nathaniel, "but we are meant to be allies now."

"As we also are allies?"

"In this case, yes. Confusion to our enemies Mr Cornelius Lee, may they be one and the same."

## Afternoon: The Peterson Residence, Marlborough Buildings, Bath.

The atmosphere in the Peterson household had risen to fever pitch over the preceding week, largely whipped up by the twins and Mrs Peterson. Saturday luncheon had been particularly shrill and the Captain had sought refuge in his study immediately after the fruit pudding. Door closed, facing the park, he settled to the newspaper with only the occasional distant shriek and pattering of steps up and down the stairs to disturb him. It wasn't that he was a kill-joy in any way, he reassured himself, he knew he would enjoy the Masked Ball, indeed he had a fondness for charades and disguises. Started in the tropics he recalled, the sailors had always got up a comedy masque of some ilk as they crossed the Equator. Brave shows, damned good! He played Neptune himself pretty frequently. Dashed monster of a grey wig, horsehair beard, tin crown. Liked it. It was the domestic preliminaries he found somewhat tiresome, though the women loved them. Well, Lydia and the twins did, he was not so sure about Emma. Dear Em! Lydia had been investing rather a lot in the prospective company of Mr Nathaniel Parry whom she had as good as engaged to the poor young creature already. The trifling matter of the courtship and proposal had been entirely overlooked. Captain Peterson pursed his lips and then blew out his cheeks speculatively. Couldn't bank on government men being in Place A if national affairs dictated a swift removal to Place B, but he had not breathed a word of his misgivings. Better to let affairs run, the sails were full and they were under way, nothing to be done. Though he did glance at the carriage clock on the mantelpiece. Mid-afternoon and no indication that young Parry was even in Bath.

On the landing by the school room Ginette and Maddy were moving into the climax of their play. They had set up Papa's gilded Venetian mask on a chair wrapped round with his red cloak and topped with his black tricorn. They were prancing round it with damask curtain cloaks, Ginette in her mother's mask and Maddy in Emma's.

"Now we have the sword fight!" squeaked Maddy. "Get the swords Bad Columbine!"

Ginette ran into the school room and fished out the raspberry canes they had hidden in the cupboard.

"Here catch! *En garde* Good Columbine!" she threw one to her sister as she adjusted the mask which had slipped down her nose.

They lashed at each other happily until they tired of it and flung themselves on the floor.

"I want to be Good Columbine now."

"No," said Maddy instantly, then narrowed her eyes, calculating which reason to offer to achieve the desired effect. She plumped for flattery. "The black mask suits you better."

"But it's the Bad one, I want the Good one. It's got the crystals and feathers and you've had it long enough."

Maddy rolled over, playing for time.

"It was very tedious of Papa to refuse to be Harlequin. Why did he want this beastly mask with the beakey chin? It's so plain!"

"Better than being Pantaloon. He would have looked ridiculous and he does like ridiculous things sometimes." Ginette was fond of the word ridiculous, it was almost as good as her favourite, "hideous", which she used all the time. "He is old enough to be Pantaloon though. But maybe he wanted the full face mask so he can dance with some beautiful ladies and they won't know how old he is."

Both girls set up shrieking laughs and rolled on the floor.

"Funniest thing would be if the doctor wore one of the plague masks. You know the really, really beakey ones with the pointy, pointy white noses," said Maddy. "He couldn't get near any beauties with that sticking out! Wouldn't it be scary though if he did wear it? Now we've got the new plague coming and we're all going to be dead! Bring out your dead," she growled sonorously, rolling her eyes until only the whites showed. "Bring out your dead!"

"Stop it Maddy," said Ginette. "It's not plague, it's called the Cholera Morbus and it's a fever and only poor people die of it."

"Are you sure?"

"Anything else would be too hideous."

"It would. Now, begin again, I shall be Em and you can be Mr Parry," said

Maddy. "Put on the gold beakey mask!"

"No I want Em's mask, you can be Mr Parry." Ginette made a grab for the delicate confection of cream velvet, green silk, crystals and amber feathers. Maddy dodged and set up a yell, so Ginette dived to grab her instead and the two rolled over in a ball of curtaining and cannoned into the chair, which toppled over, sending the grand gilded Bauta mask, the red cloak, and the black tricorn over the banister. Two heads shot over the rail to watch their progress. The red and the black fluttered down to make safe landings, but the gold papier mache did not fare as well and landed with a crack, dividing up smartly into two.

"Hideous," said Ginette.

"Too hideous."

## Afternoon: Queen Square , Bristol.

By late afternoon Queen Square in Bristol bore an even closer resemblance to a battle ground, with railings ripped up and flung aside or brandished as spears. Piles of rocks and bricks had appeared ominously in the square, though most ground floor windows had already been smashed and interior shutters had been slammed shut to try to protect the residents and their property. As Nathaniel and Caradoc arrived they felt renewed restlessness in the crowd. There had been a call for the Mayor to show himself.

"Give us the bloody Recorder," bawled a wild voice, cracked from an afternoon of yelling. "We'll murder 'im!" The crowd roared approval and was rewarded by the hunched figure of Mayor Pinney, sidling round the door with an aide who placed a chair on the flags for his Worship to stand on. When he did, there was a slight lull in the noise.

"Serve 'im up to us!" bawled one. "Go on, you can do it!"

The Recorder was not served, but the Riot Act was. Pinney gabbled it out, stuttering over it in his haste to be gone. The howling from the mob grew to a tide of fury and as he ducked indoors a fusillade of bricks and stones broke over the Mansion House front. Armed with spars of wood the mob battered the door down and flowed inside laying waste to the furniture and glass, mirrors and paintings as they surged upstairs in hot pursuit of the fugitive mayor. Nathaniel stayed on the edge of the square, but it was clear that the whole lower floor had been taken by the mob. One man came out laden with fruit and a leg of meat from the kitchens, one rolling a barrel of beer, others lugging crates of wine to the tumultuous approval of the mob.

"They're locked in on the top floor," shouted a man with a roasted chicken under his arm. "Let's smoke 'em out!"

"Smoke 'em out! Aye!" answered the baying crowd and immediately set to shoring up the Mansion House with combustibles, many dragged from inside the house itself.

"Burn it down!"

"Who's got a light here?"

Nathaniel's eye was caught by a movement on the ridge tiles of the roof, a dark figure was scrambling along it and working his way across the terrace. At least one of the mayoral party seemed to be slipping away. He could not follow the unsteady progress further as at that moment a troop of cavalry galloped into the square and scattered the rioters before the Mansion House. They reined in to a majestic stop in a swirl of gravel, peppering any who remained within ten feet. The commanding officer rose in his saddle and shouted up to the barricaded upper windows to tempt the mayor down for parley. The mayor stuck out his head, which stimulated a renewed groaning from the crowd, but his elevation had bolstered his shredded courage.

"Clear the square sir!" he demanded, his voice high pitched as piano wire and close to breaking.

The officer stood his ground, seemingly reluctant to act and started to engage the nearest rioters in conversation, but behind him his men were comprehensively stoned by the mob. Railings and bricks were flying and it was at this moment that Nathaniel noticed a detachment of rioters making off towards Welsh Back. He followed them, dodging the plunging horses' hooves and brickbats in the growing dark. It was getting close to his rendezvous with the skipper and his jolly boat, he had to hurry. Leaping a smashed coach-wheel, he ran across the intervening battle ground and followed the small group of half a dozen to King Street. They were just disappearing into the Llandoger as he caught up with them.

"Lads," he said urgently, suddenly inspired. "The Recorder's escaped and headed off to Redcliffe Parade. There's supporters of his there and Bishop Gray's men. They won't be expecting a rousing yet. We could be first there!"

"Redcliffe Parade, aye there's some stinkin' rich enemies of the people there alright!"

"Aye and the Bloody Blues won't be up there to stop us havin' a fair share. I could 'ave done with a leg or two o' that beef I seen carted out o' the Mansion 'ouse afore the troops come."

"Us'll wet our whistles here and be up directly for a regular soakin' after. Depend on it!" declared the man nearest to the bar. "Now lads a jug o' cider to get us goin'."

Nathaniel disappeared into the night as they refuelled. He skirted the corner of the street and made his way to the shadowy bulk of the trow. Standing on the quayside was the skipper, who pocketed the sovereigns and shot Nathaniel a warning glare. "Right boyo, return this 'ere boat by midnight like we arranged and tie her up tight y'ere." He seemed reluctant to leave. "Would you be needin' any 'elp with they Brist'l boys?"

"None at all," said Nathaniel levelly. "Your boat will be back, tied snug and before the hour. Good night to you."

Caradoc set up a menacing growl and the skipper glanced from one to the other. Between the two of them they more than convinced him to return to the Llandoger. Nathaniel looked round scouring the harbour-side for a sighting of Cornelius's men. As he turned back to the little boat, considering his next move, two figures materialised at his side. Dressed entirely in black as Cornelius would have been, they had also black hoods and scarves obscuring their faces. Over their shoulders he spotted ropes and short strung bows, at their waists, short blades. There was no need for words, they bowed and followed him and Caradoc onto the boat, settled into the sculls and pulled away soundlessly into the Float. In a matter of minutes they had pulled level with the *Mathilda*, tied up and taken the sack from Nathaniel. They slipped on black fingerless gloves with viciously spiked palms, and then swarmed nimbly up the cable to land silently on deck.

Nathaniel waited in the tense cold of the jolly boat. From above him on the *Mathilda* he heard, and that only once, the singing whirr of two bowstrings and saw some shining fuses soar up to the rigging. A slight shuffling noise and soft fall as if of a body collapsing on deck, then nothing more. He listened to the distant tide of noise from the square, the confused pounding of hooves, and ragged yells. What he could not understand was the absence of gunfire. But whilst he pondered this fact he had a sudden and unwelcome vision of an enraged Mrs Lydia Peterson, who must by this very moment have realised that her demand for six to convene at six had been denied. It could be a difficult and unpleasant night for Em, and he regretted that.

## 8 pm: The Assembly Rooms, Bath.

"So we've decided to have the wedding in Spring. We'll wait for better weather won't we Henry? It will have to be St James's as he's taken to it. Admires the vicar no end don't you Henry? He's worshipped there every Sunday without fail, since, well since the incident. Who would have thought just a few weeks ago that our wedding would be possible at all! What with the awful murder, I could quite faint at

185

the thought of it. Couldn't I Henry! Haven't I often said I just felt like fainting away! Of course it's been such a blessing to have him back at work and on his increased salary. He is really indispensable at the bank. The new senior clerk only came on Friday and is quite dependent on you, isn't he Henry?"

Lydia Peterson tried to stop herself grinding her teeth and failed. Even the effort required to maintain a semblance of interest in the subject matter on offer was almost too much for her. She was willing the ineffectual Henry to stem the flow, even to interrupt by offering some feeble responses to the fatuous rhetorical questions. It would have offered some relief. It was clearly too much to ask that he would sweep her off to the dance-floor and not come back. Anna Grant had blossomed into something quite detestable now that Henry had been reinstated. This miraculous re-appointment stemmed originally from the good offices of Mr Howard Dill. Lydia briefly and silently cursed him. Of course, Oliver and Dr Parry had supported it. And it was the right thing, of course. She sighed. It really was insupportable. The Ball had been a disaster and it was nowhere near over. She would by choice have prostrated herself, howled the house down and abandoned the evening, but couldn't, and now to add insult to injury, she had to endure Miss Grant. Oblivious to the ill-wishing, Anna prattled happily on, a buxom meringue in pink and white, with cat mask to match, whiskers a-quiver. The cat has got the cream, reflected Lydia bitterly, but for me, bitter aloes. It had been jinxed from the start. First the girls smashing Oliver's mask so carelessly. The only one they had purchased. How wasteful! Perhaps an omen? Then just as they were to climb into the carriage, Emma looking quite radiant, and her own gown, really, exceptional, Enid running out with the note from the postboy. Damn Mr Nathaniel Parry! Detained in Bristol! Detained forsooth! Nothing should have been permitted to detain him. So sorry, unavoidable, hope to have the pleasure of apologising on his return etc. She would certainly like to see him. Oh yes, she could happily box his ears all night and not tire of it.

"Lovely," boomed Oliver good-naturedly. "Lookin' forward to your nuptials my dear girl. St James's 'ey. Excellent. Yes indeed, and the bank young man? All well?"

"Yes thank you sir, our new clerk, Mr Sanderson, seems to be settling in well. Thank you for helping get everything going again. It was quite a worry." Henry Blake's thin face betrayed the strain of the past weeks, he had lost weight and his eyes glittered unhealthily, but his face had the glow of salvation about it, a wild smile of ecstatic relief usually seen on a drowning man as he catches the life-belt. "But it is odd without Mr Vere sir," he said earnestly. "Is there any news?"

"None whatsoever," said the Captain, pulling his bushy brows together.

186

"Nothing sir. Dashed odd." He glanced round the ballroom fiercely, but his eye softened as he caught sight of Tilly. "Look over yonder! Marvellous to see Mrs Vere. Lovely girl, lovely. Dill's looking after her. Good man. Splendid what!"

Howard was certainly looking after Tilly, and much to her obvious delight. He was shoe-horned into his best dancing suit for the occasion, his characteristically tight shirting up round his ears and finished off with a magnificent magenta neck-cloth. The country dance set currently being called from the dais had obliged him to gallop down the dance-floor with enormous verve, twirling Tilly all the while, and they both seemed to be loving every minute of it. The Captain also enjoyed the spectacle of Tilly capering: her sparkling eyes and flushed pink cheeks, her utterly magnificent bosom straining against her tight-laced evening gown as she gasped for breath and threw back her head, laughing loud and long. Remarkably lovely he thought, remarkable, but he did reflect that this was not the public face of the anxious and bereft wife. She seemed so very glad. Raphael Vere's inexplicable absence was a confounded nuisance as far as business was concerned, but it was obviously pleasing his lady wife. Oliver's kindly face clouded. Nathaniel had not been satisfied by the solution of Wilson's murder and neither was he. Perhaps Vere had something to hide. Howard Dill had sown even more serious seeds of doubt in their meetings the previous week. Vere could very well be shaping up as a monster. Could he have been so wrong in his assessment of the man? For more on that alone he wanted to speak with Nathaniel urgently. He had his own reasons for regretting the absence of the dashing Mr Parry.

Anna and Henry rose to dance and he realised that he would have to gather his wits to solve the most pressing problem caused by Nathaniel's absence that evening, the conspicuous lack of an escort for his daughter. If he did not ask his wife to dance presently there would be trouble of another kind, but he could not yet find it in his heart to abandon Em. The dear girl seemed calm enough, much more so than Lydia who had beaten down hysteria and disappointment just sufficiently to allow her to stay. But there was something rather too silent in Em's demeanour, something too icily correct and accepting. It did not bode well. This was shaping up to be a long night for all of them, a damned long one. He drained his glass of claret, and was in the act of gingerly replacing his fractured mask when Tilly and Howard burst upon their table having spun dangerously out of sequence and abandoned the set.

"Good evening Mrs Peterson, Miss Peterson, Oliver," panted Howard. "May we join you?"

Howard and Tilly's arrival broke the tension and postponed the vexed question of the dancing. "With the greatest of pleasure," said Oliver, who really could not remember when he had been quite so pleased to see the dear fellow.

"I fell into conversation with Mr Casey," said Howard. "Very bad news from Bristol. Have you heard?"

"What's happened?" said Emma sharply.

Her disappointment she had conquered. Long games of strategy must not fall prey to temporary set-backs. Her biggest problem had been how to cope with the reactions of everyone else. To be pitied was a shaming thing: demeaning. She had wondered if a feigned illness would be the only way to draw the sorry enterprise to a halt, and was considering throwing a faint. The Ball that she had been foolish enough to dream about for weeks had turned out to be an endurance test for all of the family. But all of those thoughts evaporated in a second as she heard Howard's words, which brought home to her just how much she loved Nathaniel Parry. The thought of him in danger made her heart lurch and tied her stomach in knots: noose-tight.

"What do you know Mr Dill?"

"Only what Mr Casey has told me dear lady," said Howard, looking closely at Emma. "News came with the mail-coach. A riot has broken out in Queen Square and the troops are out. The mob's after the Recorder for his attacks on the Bill."

"Good God!" exploded the Captain. "If it's anything like Nottingham the destruction will be terrible. Are the Yeomen out?"

"Captain Wilkins hasn't had the call yet but is at the ready. Or so says Casey," added Howard.

"Mr Parry is in Bristol on urgent business!" squawked Mrs Peterson, a ray of light shining up from the abyss of her disappointment. "He is a government man you know. He should be with us this evening but he must do his duty, Mr Dill." She clasped her hands as if in prayer. "He is doing his duty to keep us safe in our beds!"

If Emma had had any emotional energy left she would have saluted this manoeuvre as it signalled a new maternal interpretation of the evening, a triumphant, self-sacrificing and flattering one.

"Here is Mr Casey," said Howard, as Diarmuid cantered into view at the end of the set, whirling his partner round for the return.

"Mr Casey!" shouted Howard. "Mr Casey, do join us when you've time sir!"

Diarmuid grinned widely and made his way over immediately, hauling his dancing partner behind him, seemingly utterly unaware of the stir he caused. Matrons' fans were fluttering at every table with a view of his progress and the young girls were preening, hoping to catch his eye, but when the spectators recognised the identity of his partner the reactions were somewhat different. The matrons hissed behind the fans and the girls' faces fell: it was the gentlemen's turn to preen.

"With pleasure, Mr Dill," called Diarmuid as he closed in on the Petersons' table. "We're just about done in so we are! Ladies and gentlemen may I introduce Miss Colette Montrechet. Coco my dear, Captain and Mrs Peterson, Miss Peterson and Mrs Vere," he smiled wickedly between kissing the ladies' hands. "I believe you know Mr Dill."

As Coco went about her greetings Tilly suffered, she had barely consolidated her recovery after the news of Nathaniel when this new blow fell. Her eyes glinted rock hard as she recognised the enhanced level of threat to her precarious revival. Coco was far too familiar with Howard, and it was apparent that Nathaniel had promised to escort Emma Peterson. The evening had taken an exceedingly disagreeable turn.

Emma, however, was not captivated by the new arrivals and let her attention wander from the party. Her eyes searched out the main door again, as they had done a hundred times that evening. The sea of peacock colours, the gaudy costumes topped by their masked heads continued to revolve, the fiddlers in the gallery sawed away, the fires roared and the heat haze continued to rise, but over the heads, by the door, she caught sight of a tall, muscular figure his gold mask topped by a mane of black hair. She gasped for joy and slipped away from the table, flitted over the polished floor, wove her way through and round the crowd to catch him up.

"Nathaniel!" She caught his arm and he turned.

"Yes madam?"

The realisation of her mistake was like a blow. Her hand flew to her mouth in consternation.

"Oh! I am sorry. So sorry sir. I thought you were someone else."

She recoiled to collide with a couple behind her: his mouth was wrong, his face, his smell, all wrong. Desperate to be out of sight of the stranger she fled, out through the doors and the Octagon, into the card room, behind the door, to take refuge at a neglected table, her heart pounding. She breathed deeply to steady her nerves and put her head in her hands.

"Miss Peterson. Emma?"

She looked up, embarrassed, into the concerned and watchful eyes of Coco Montrechet.

"He would not stay away unless he had no choice. He is a man of honour: he's my friend. You don't need to say anything Emma, no need to explain. It's easy for me to see what's happened."

She solemnly handed Emma her handkerchief to mop up the treacherous tears that had appeared unbidden, soaked the silk base of the mask and trickled down her cheek. Emma pulled off the mask in disgust and mopped her eyes.

"Thank you," she said haltingly. "I thought I saw him, I don't know what possessed me to bolt across here. Quite ridiculous." She looked up at Coco in despair. "I am afraid for him. A riot is an ugly thing. Anything could happen. People die."

"Emma, this is not France. There will be no heads on pikes, so pull yourself together. He is a strong man and a clever one," said Coco smiling. "Now, no point wasting the evening. Come with me; I want you to do me a favour. I need to speak to a lady about some jewellery and I need to abandon Diarmuid for a while."

Coco led Emma back to the ballroom, round the edge of the dancers who were floundering their way to the end of the set, and made a safe landing at the Peterson table. Since they had left the numbers had been boosted by the addition of Dr and Mrs Parry and Diarmuid held sway over them all. The table was captivated and even both the matrons were laughing.

"Diarmuid," said Coco meaningfully, touching his arm, "I must see a friend of mine briefly and Miss Peterson has very kindly agreed to dance with you. Ah! I hear a waltz. Good luck Miss Peterson and thank you."

"You have saved these good people from another tale, Miss Peterson," said Diarmuid bowing and taking her hand. "It's an angel you are, as any man can clearly see."

Lydia Peterson's lips pursed in annoyance.

"Oliver," she hissed in her husband's ear. "Do you realise who that woman was?"

"I don't think I do my dear," he replied, chuckling with indulgent delight at the sight of Emma waltzing away with one of the most eligible men in Bath.

"She was Roderick Wilson's mistress!"

"Was she by George," he said amiably.

"She was, Oliver, and she has manoeuvred our daughter into the arms of her latest beau. He is an Irishman, Oliver. We do not know his family."

"Mrs Peterson," interrupted Dr Parry. "May I have the honour of this dance?"

"Oh Dr Parry," said Lydia, indecisive for just a moment, until the prospect of dancing with one of the richest and most popular men on Sion Hill eclipsed all else. Berating her husband could be postponed, but a close waltz with Charles Parry most definitely could not, so she smiled instead. "With pleasure."

Simultaneously, Tilly took the opportunity to whisk Howard out of harm's way against the imminent return of Coco, leaving Mrs Parry and Captain Peterson at the

190

table.

"Would you mind terribly staying here with me Captain and talking awhile?" she said. "I'm not terribly keen on being trampled by the herd."

"My thoughts exactly," said Oliver, breathing a sigh of relief. "Allow me to bring you some refreshment, Madam."

He waved over a waiter and they drank a toast together.

"To better times Mrs Parry!"

"Yes indeed. It's sad isn't it Captain. Only last year we had such high hopes. The new government and the new king. So much promise! Dear Earl Grey and his great plans for reform. Now life seems to be plunged in difficulty and quite fraught with danger. Europe seems to be in turmoil and our own people are rising in the towns and the country. They are hungry you know Captain," she said urgently. "Charles has seen people starved to death in the villages. And the terrible news of the cholera morbus! Charles was very dreary about it this morning. It will be here in a matter of months and there is nothing, nothing whatsoever, that can be done about it!"

"We'll lime-wash the walls and isolate the cases. Been done before madam, we'll do it again."

"Yes Captain, but Charles told me that people catch it without being anywhere near other victims and even if they are not in unhealthy air. Miasmas and sufferers are not the only bearers of it."

"Perhaps it is God's punishment for the sins of the world!"

"You don't believe that do you?" said Mrs Parry eying him doubtfully. "Charles sees enough saintly folk dead and villains walking to disprove that old saw!"

"No," said Oliver, "I do not. But I believe in good and evil in this world, and your husband is a good man. Here's to him and his like!"

## Early evening: Beneath Redcliffe Parade, Bristol.

Crouched on a double bed in the corner of the cave, face to the red stone wall, Abi held Babs even tighter as tears streamed unheeded down her face. She rocked them both, to and fro, and could not fathom for the life of her why she was doing it, for it could no longer bring calm or sleep. Still she rocked: rocked to keep her sanity, to soothe the pain in her heart and keep her from wailing aloud. After a brief hour of sleep in the early hours Abi had wakened to find Babs stone-cold dead beside her, a trail of vomit down her chin. Poisoned by the drugs, she had suffocated and slipped away. Abi felt sick to her core with pity for the stiffening corpse in her arms, and for herself. Babs had made her escape, no more worries, no good-byes, but what now for herself? She stole a glance over her shoulder, nothing had changed. She still banked on one possible chance to bolt. It would be at the moment they left to get on the boat, and that would be soon. She had kept up the pretence all day. Babs was tired, Babs had finished her food when they weren't looking. Babs was fine.

A small hand grasped her shoulder. "You'll 'ave to put 'er down Abi," whispered Frances, who had slipped over quietly to sit by her. "Tuck 'er up in the corner so as they'll not know." She inclined her head to the doorway. One solitary whore was dozing in her chair, back to the door and feet on the low mantle-shelf of the fireplace. Fortunately for Abi, one of the younger girls had become an ally. Frances, who thought she was probably twelve, and not ten as her mother had insisted when she shovelled her onto the Bristol barge, had the feral survival instincts of a pye-dog. After giving up her initial plan of fighting her way out, those instincts had re-asserted themselves. Playing the game was the only way to avoid further drugging, which was essential if she was to keep sharp. Give or take some aches and pains, she felt she was probably as sharp as she was going to get. Her fellow "ten year old" had proved to be an enemy. Tess either lacked a sense of self preservation or was a born whore. She had fallen in with the guards, especially Tibbs who was scratching herself in the doorway as she snored. Tess had taken to combing her brassy hair for her, creeping around her like an alley-cat and at this very moment was curled up by her feet. Frances had kept well away from both of them, tending the babies if they needed it, but it had to be said her efforts hadn't done much, tonight they were in a poor way. Their eyes didn't look right, swimming in their heads, but they were quiet. The whores had overdone the Godfrey's Cordial, a trick of her own mother's that Frances had seen too many times before. She had grown fond of the infants over the weeks of captivity. She called them Poll and Moll as they didn't seem to have names for themselves. They were twins and delicately beautiful when they had arrived at the caves, fair as two rosebuds with hair blonde as spun gold. Not that they looked so good now, she thought. Their skin was blueish, almost bruised, their faces pinched.

Frances was helping Abi tuck up Babs, when a crazed clattering of feet sounded down the stone stairway. Tibbs's assistant burst through the door and shook her awake.

"Quick, quick! Rouse yersel' there's real trouble 'ere. There's a mob in Queen Square layin' waste an' the troops are out. There's gangs roamin' in the town an' there's some buggers a-comin' down the Parade and smashin' all the glass. The *Mathilda's* a-fire an' the Master's out on the quay with they Chinese! I'm not being trapped down 'ere if there's fire!"

Even as she pulled Tibbs to her feet, they heard the crashing of masonry from the dark pit of the stair-well. The metal grill door slammed open against the rock-side with a hollow clang, followed by the unmistakable sound of running footsteps, and more, a low, growling snarl and the swift scratching of dog's claws as it bounded up the stone steps. As the tarts gawped in horror down the void, Abi and Frances took their chance and sprang from the bed. Wrenching a fire-iron apiece from the companion set on the hearth, they covered the distance between them and their targets in seconds and landed crushing blows on the backs of their heads. Again and again, they swung their arms 'til they ached, mercilessly belabouring their captors with blows hard enough to stun oxen. Tess, startled out of her sleep, set up a wild howling and backed up to flatten herself against the wall in terror. Abi and Frances were oblivious, still beating, beating with all their pent up fear and fury, relentlessly beating, blow on blow until the floor was slick with blood. The women still twitched as Nathaniel and Caradoc reached the doorway, Caradoc leading the way, smelling the captives, the blood and the fear. Tess dodged round them screaming like a banshee as she fled up the stairs, swerving into a narrow side alley, plunging away into the blackness.

"Oh God save us!" said Abi, slowly lowering the bloodied poker as she stared at the tall dark man who had burst into their prison. "Is it Mr Drake?"

"Abi!" Nathaniel stopped in his tracks, his mind racing back to the distant night at Shadwell's. He smiled in recognition: the alias could still do good service. "Quick now girl. And you," he shot a warning glance at Frances who still brandished a fire-shovel. "I won't hurt you. I'll get you out." He glanced round the cave, taking in the sleeping infants in the truckle bed, the sprawling bodies by the doorway.

"Now move fast. Lift the babies and follow me."

Dazed by the speed of events, Abi and Frances moved automatically, wrapping the infants roughly in their bedding as they snatched them up.

"And take those fire-irons. We'll go the way I came but we might be challenged."

Suddenly, fresh sounds broke upon them from above and lights shone from the top of the stairs. "Quickly now, down these steps," commanded Nathaniel. "Follow my light."

"Stop! Or I'll shoot you down!"

Nathaniel spun round as a powerful figure in Ravenswood's livery rounded the turn in the steps, lifting his pistol to fire.

"Drop down!" shouted Nathaniel, pushing back up the steps past the confusion of girls and trailing bedding, simultaneously drawing a pistol and firing into his assailant's body. Even as the man's own weapon fired wide and he slumped over bellowing in pain, a nimble footman wielding a bludgeon leapt over his stricken body to be met head-on by Caradoc. He had leapt at the man's throat, a blur of black and tan, claws and teeth. Nathaniel flung aside his lantern to swap the spent gun for the loaded one as the man yelled out in agony and beat wildly at Caradoc with the bludgeon. Nathaniel levelled the weapon but in the flickering light from the cave there was no clear shot.

"Caradoc! Here! Leave him!"

As the footman and Caradoc fell, struggling in a death roll on the shallow landing before the cave door, Nathaniel leaped forward, stowing the pistol and drawing his makila from his belt to block the flailing bludgeon. Caradoc jumped clear, yelping in pain from the blows as Nathaniel grasped the wooden sheath, drew the dagger and plunged it deep into the heart of his adversary.

He tore out the weapon and rose to his feet. "Follow me!" he said, pushing past the girls to plunge down the dark steps to the waterside. Down they careered after him, hands skinning on the stone as they steadied themselves, round and round the spiral, dreading the sound of pursuit. As they neared the door, lit from without by a red glare, the confused sounds of the quay grew to a crescendo, Nathaniel held up his hand.

"Stop! Go carefully now. Keep close together and don't be alarmed, someone might still be here to help us."

They looked out onto the garish chaos of the Back, edging behind a stack of barrels to put a barrier between them and the crowds of labouring men on the quay. The *Mathilda* was well alight and the crew of the *Blue Dragon* were plying their buckets and pumps to douse it. The air was lit by stark white moon-light and the licking flames, it was full of the acrid smell of the fire and billowing smoke, the yells of the sailors and the crashes of falling spars on the *Mathilda*, all playing out to the distant din of riot from Queen Square. They needed to quit the harbour and work their way round the Bathurst Basin to the mews behind the Parade. One of Cornelius's men was waiting with the coach and the other had offered to stay on the quay. Unsurprisingly Nathaniel could not see him, but took the chance to pause briefly, turning at the sound of an angry voice raised above the tumult. Ravenswood himself, for it could be no other, was standing on a cart directing the fire-fighting operations, his face a mask of fury. Close by him he saw the lone figure of Cornelius, watchful and withdrawn, and over by the fire, his implacable bulk silhouetted against the rage of the flames was Kizhe, his reptilian gaze searing the quay.

As Nathaniel dodged out of sight, turning back to motion Abi and Frances to follow him, the infant in Abi's arms suddenly writhed, made to wriggle free and set up a high-pitched wail. Like lightning Abi clamped a hand over the infant's mouth but fell back against the cliff as the bucking legs caught her in the belly and the flailing head shot back to slam into her face, making her head ring and her eyes pour. Instantly a black figure materialised from the shade of the barrels and in one smooth movement gagged the infant with a cloth.

"He's with us," said Nathaniel tersely to Frances, blocking the raised fire-shovel she had managed to swing up in her free hand.

The man pinioned Poll under one arm and hauled Abi to her feet with the other, propelling her forward towards the Basin. Nathaniel looked round for Caradoc who had limped down the steps to his side and was struggling to raise his tail at the sight of his master. Nathaniel automatically bent down to lift him up and recoiled as his hand slid on the fur, Caradoc's coat was wet with blood. Caradoc allowed himself to be lifted but whimpered piteously, his body wracked by shivering in his pain and shock.

"Is he alright mister?" said Frances, her face showing white as paper in the dark, her thin arms still clinging on to Moll's limp body and her fire-shovel.

Nathaniel could not answer, but managed a quick smile of encouragement. They made what speed they could with their burdens, following Abi and the sailor into the sheltering confusion of the stacked provisions on the quay to be swallowed up by the dark.

## Midnight: Marlborough Buildings, Bath.

The short coach journey home had been a better humoured one than the Petersons had dreamed possible. Oliver was content, reflecting on his surprisingly enjoyable talk with Mrs Parry whilst listening with half an ear to Lydia, who was continuing to regale them with a highly satisfied commentary on the dancing. He had been mightily relieved to see Em enjoying herself and would have personally presented Miss Montrechet with a medal for engineering it. After such a night he even felt strong enough for tomorrow's inevitable conversation with Lydia about that particular young woman. Emma herself could not remember a stranger night and, against the odds, it had been a remarkably good one. She recognised that she must really love Nathaniel, as opposed to just saying that she did. The savage pain at the prospect of losing him had taken her breath away. She was also pleased to find she was extremely partial to Mr Diarmuid Casey, who had danced her off her feet. It was more surprising to find she had kindly feelings for Coco, her gratitude for the invitation to dance with Diarmuid eclipsing instinctive pangs of jealousy. They were handed down from the carriage by the footman and were in high good humour waiting for Enid to open the door when a slight figure emerged from the steps leading down to the area and the kitchen.

"Miss Peterson, I've a letter from Mr Nathaniel Parry. I've 'ad to wait Miss and your cook was kind enough to let me sit with 'er. I promised I'd put this in your 'and."

In her bedroom that night she re-read the note from Nathaniel. It was not so much what he said that delighted her as the manner in which it came. He clearly did care for her, or at least cared for what she thought of him. It had been more than a good night. She snuffed out her candle and slipped into her nest of sheets, blankets and eiderdown, turning over the events in her head, looked at them this way and that, but she did not sleep. As the night ebbed away, as they so often did, small insidious worms of doubt intruded, snaking their way into the comfort of her thoughts, laying their sour trails. Before she finally slept, she saw the beautiful elfin oval of Coco's face and heard her lovely voice, strong and sure:

"He's my friend."

One worm of doubt had raised its maggot head, but in the long watches of the night when reason loses its way and small ills cast harsh shadows miles high, one was enough to ruin all.

Coco has his friendship. What else has she of him?

The noose-tight knots regained their grip.

## Midnight: The Crown Inn, Keynsham.

The onward journey from the cliff's foot to the coach took on a nightmarish confusion in Abi's memory once she had the leisure to reflect on it. Her knees under her chin, she pressed herself into the depths of the wing-chair before the fire. Poll had damn near knocked her out before the sailor came to help. Perhaps that's why she couldn't recall it straight. She'd almost collapsed with relief when he'd taken Poll, her knees had buckled and the sounds around her had died, but the man had pulled her up, dragged her on, half stumbling, half running over the wharf. As they fled the cold air had seemed to slap her stark-staring awake, her eyes had felt they were bulging out of her head. He'd dodged her round the barrels, up steps, round the corner to the mews, into the coach and somehow, somehow, they had got away. Crammed inside, doors shut, she had had Poll back again on her lap, gagged but kicking like a mule. She'd had to slap her hard. Frances had Moll, who was conscious before the first toll-house, retching and sick. She looked down at the sleeping dog on the hearth and leaned over to smooth his head. He was Caradoc, she knew that now. She checked the bandage round his leg and body, but the red patch seemed no bigger. Mr Drake had had to carry him because of the fight with the footman and then the dog had been rolling in pain on the floor of the coach, whining and crying. So what with the whining and the vomiting and the kicking, she'd had to stick her head out of the window and get Mr Drake to stop. More than that, they needed the privy and Poll and Moll hadn't waited: they reeked to high heaven. They'd got no further than Keynsham, though she knew Mr Drake wanted to get them back to Bath. They'd stopped at the post-house where there was only one room free, so here they were.

She looked over to the big bed with its horsehair mattress and coarse sheets. Frances was lying on the edge, corralling Poll and Moll into the shallow basin in the centre. Later she would have to edge over to the wall and squeeze in there. It wasn't an attractive option, she was tired to the bone but did not want to sleep. Mr Drake had dressed Caradoc's wounds before he'd gone downstairs. There was hot water, clean cloths and supper for them all and he'd left them to their own devices. Somehow she and Frances between them had cleaned down Poll and Moll. Poll had quietened, thank God, worn out after her performances and the two children had spent some time playing with the bread and meat, eating their fill with their fingers, between breaking off and babbling at each other in their peculiar squeaky little voices. She could hardly believe that even part of the ordeal was over. Would Mr Drake tell about the whores and the poker? Would she be hanged? She folded her arms tight, hugging herself in fear, seeing beaten, bleeding heads, seeing Babs white and dead in the bed. Tears ran down her face, blurring the dancing flames and the clouds of wood smoke as they fled up the chimney. She knew where Babs came from, but no-one there would care if she was dead or alive. And no one cared for her. There was no one to tell. Mr Drake had said he had heard they had been kidnapped and would return them all to Bath. She hadn't said anything, but she could never, never return to the Shadwells. At the thought of Joshua Shadwell mouthing his lies she remembered other things, remembered the depth of her despair. After all, there was one good reason for going back to Bath. But after that? Caradoc whined in his sleep, she leaned over to him again, rubbed his wiry head and threw another log on the fire. Tonight she'd sleep in the chair, or better still, stay awake. It occurred to her that it was her turn to be a guard and that idea alone offered some comfort.

Downstairs in the bar Nathaniel stretched out on a settle in the corner, he had no choice but to stay there all night. He'd bring Caradoc down in an hour or two when the bar cleared and check on the girls, who with luck would be asleep, then he'd see it out in the bar until dawn. He'd seen to Caradoc's wounds and been able to leave the infants to Abi and Frances. He had checked out the drinkers and had seen nothing to suggest they had noticed his irregular band enter the inn. The room was crowded and the talk was all of Bristol and the riot. He let the speculation wash over him as he stretched his aching neck and put his feet up on the fender. It could have been worse, he might have perished himself or been captured and failed to save anyone. But such comforts did not banish his regret for Barbara, left entombed in the cave. And the next day would bring its own difficulties.

He pulled his hat over his eyes to discourage conversation and, as usual, ran over his commitments instead of counting sheep. The mood of the older girl, Abi, was uncertain, but he had decided she wasn't a positive danger to the others and would be better left in charge to give her something to do. They were too disorientated to run and seemed to believe he would return them to Bath as he promised: though why the older girls would trust any man surprised him. Probably the absolute lack of a choice had a lot to do with it. He shelved the problem of his first port of call on returning the girls to Bath, deciding to sleep on it and he moved to more predictable outcomes. Good news for Captain Peterson on the investigation front would be followed by fulsome apologies for the Masked Ball debacle. Followed perhaps in turn by an afternoon with Miss Peterson? As the fire collapsed with a sigh and the sounds of the room petered out as the last guests moved off to their beds, sleep suddenly came in stealthy ambush, rapid as the Severn tide. He slid away, down into dark dreams of fire and blood, black-hooded Chinese sailors and Cornelius, in sharp profile against the glare of the *Mathilda*. Then the fire disappeared and there he was in Mrs Spence's parlour with Tilly herself, her head on his shoulder.

"I am so frightened. Please look after me."

Then she was gone, and in his arms was Coco.

# Chapter 9

**Morning: 30th October, 1831, Redcliffe Parade, Bristol.**

"Can you hear it?" demanded Edwin Ravenswood, throwing up the sash window violently and letting in a blast of damp autumn air. Surging in with the draught and filling the stale apartment were the confused yells and crashes of renewed battle in Queen Square. "The God damned *canaille* has roused itself again!"

John Drake looked up wearily from his seat at the dining table, cleared now of the debris of last night's abandoned dinner and waiting for whatever scratch breakfast the servants could muster. Last night had figured with some of the very worst experiences he had endured in the worthy cause of self-advancement. It had been so promising: a farewell dinner celebrating the imminent departure of the *Blue Dragon* and its cargo; and, certainly not before time, one final bout of stilted conversation with the unsettlingly sinister Kizhe and Lee; as a finale, the prospect of cementing his relationship with Ravenswood, job done and a handsome remuneration as good as pocketed. It had started well enough, but the oysters had barely been shucked before the simmering riot across the river had erupted into chaos. His mind wheeled back to the demonic concerto of shattering glass and rending timbers, the howling of the mob, the tattoo of hooves on cobbles as the troops moved in. They had felt safe at first on their high cliff top, the river seeming to provide a *cordon sanitaire* between them and the events across the water. Then, almost simultaneously, came the yell of "Fire!" from the quay and running footfalls drumming on the parade. A splinter group from the square had rampaged towards Ravenswood's house, hurling brickbats systematically against all exposed windows and screaming vengeance on the Recorder, all councillors and all their supporters, whilst below them, inexplicably, the *Mathilda* burst into flame.

Ravenswood had been on his feet in seconds, his chair flying back unheeded, his face furious and terrible. They had been on the parade in minutes: Kizhe wielding the vicious, squat blade that lurked at his belt, in an instant belabouring three men to their knees as Lee effortlessly cut a swathe through the rest of the dozen or so rioters with his bare hands. Drake counted four sprawled on the ground before turning to see Ravenswood mercilessly beating another bloody. He himself had stood, immobile, watching the carnage unfold and feeling strangely removed, until one rioter ricocheted into him from a stunning blow delivered by a footman who had run out with them to the road. Drake had punched the body, jarring his arm and scraping his knuckles, then ducked, but failed to avoid, a right hook. It had caught him squarely, lit up his head with flashing lights and set up a throbbing pain in his jaw, which still pounded dully. He fingered it, letting his fingers stray to the old jagged scar before forcing his hand back down to the table. The fight had petered out quickly with the rioters beating a retreat from the onslaught, those sound of wind and limb gathering up the wounded as they went. He had followed Ravenswood and the others down the stone steps to the quay to join the fire-fight to save the *Mathilda*. The smoke and flames bathed the assorted stores and men on the quayside in a fierce, lurid glaze and the night was clamorous with the fearful thunder of the fire, clanking buckets and alarmed rough cries. Ravenswood had dominated the proceedings: marshalling, admonishing and frequently striking the remnants of the *Blue Dragon* crew who were within reach or hailing distance. They had all been entirely absorbed by the battle on the parade and the fire on the quay until the sickening realisation dawned that the night had an even graver consequence.

Drake shuddered at the memory. Two screaming maids had careered down the steps and broken the news of the catastrophe in the cave. Both infants gone, two girls gone, one girl dead in bed, another stark staring mad and keening like a lunatic, the two tarts on guard, dead, two male servants, dead. More carnage. All that remained of the carefully selected human cargo was the mad grieving girl who was quickly drugged insensible and secured on the *Blue Dragon*. Kizhe's wrath had been truly terrifying. In the aftermath, with the *Mathilda* still smouldering and the *Dragon's* crew hastily reassembled, he had ordered immediate sailing. Captain Trevellis had dealt a surprisingly optimistic card by suggesting that although they should leave at once, they could anchor in North Devon near to his home town where he had contacts with the local poor house. As they were now desperate he could look over the baby-farm there and, if any blonde girls were available, offer to take the infants off their hands. It had been done before but was a hit and miss affair.

"Needs must when the devil drives," Trevellis had said dryly.

Drake remembered Kizhe's face. The Captain had never spoken truer words.

It was a bitter dawn, and the *Blue Dragon* had sailed on the ebb tide, along with Kizhe and the inscrutable Lee, who had borne the reverses with his usual taciturnity. Ravenswood had ordered the removal of the corpses, the boarding up of the windows and the securing of the cave. It had been a gruesome few hours and Drake was dog-tired. Every one of his bones seemed to ache as an accompaniment to his throbbing jaw.

"It is astonishing that they have the energy for more," he said wearily, waving a hand towards the swelling tumult sounding across the river. "Perhaps they are performing in relays."

Ravenswood shot him a look of utter malice. "Their "performances" as you call them need to be curtailed. If I ever find out who targeted my house and my ship I will flay them alive. I lost too many dependable servants in last night's work. Trevellis informed me before they sailed that he had discovered two bodies on the *Mathilda*, charred but recognisable as the watch he had seen on deck in the afternoon. We have lost Elijah and Reuben Berry, they had puncture wounds as if they had been stabbed through the throats, or even shot with arrows. How could that be?"

Drake felt himself wilting under Ravenswood's implacable glare, but decided that to smile politely would be a singularly bad move. He contrived instead to sit, dour and motionless, until Ravenswood marshalled his silent fury, took a seat at the table and resumed his monologue.

"It is very unfortunate that these events occurred at all, and even more regrettable that Mr Kizhe was here to observe them. My contacts with the Count are not my only ones, but they are lucrative. Your share of the proceeds could dwindle Mr Drake, if Trevellis fails to augment the cargo to Kizhe's satisfaction."

Drake smiled thinly as a chasm seemed to open beneath him. Was this a judgement? He had had misgivings about the girls, but had allowed the scheme to run, reeling him into its murky depths where he now seemed in danger of drowning. This was a gloomy thought. He swiftly decided it did not vouch dwelling on and chose instead to throw a life-belt to a far more worthy concern, his self-satisfaction. Had he simply had a lucky escape? He could still claim to have ingratiated himself with Ravenswood and report favourably on the flourishing opium trade, which would satisfy Palmerston. Perhaps he had merely singed his fingers rather than sustained a burn.

"Financial reward is of peripheral concern to me Edwin," he said, with apparent

201

ease. "What is important is the safeguarding of the *Dragon* and the opium trade, which in the view of the government is of principal interest and attracts the goodwill of His Majesty's ministers. You can be assured of full support for that aspect of your business."

Ravenswood did not reply but rose again peremptorily to return to the window and seemed to be absorbed in his study of the opposite river bank. He turned suddenly, "Drake do you have a pistol?"

"Not with me. I never imagined the night would take the turn it did."

"I have a spare brace. Come with me to the square."

Ravenswood's eyes were black pools, his face deathly pale. Drake was struck again by its mask like quality and his memory flashed back to a private discussion he had had in 1819 with Leigh Hunt. Swearing him to secrecy, Hunt had let Drake have sight of a suppressed piece sent from Italy by Shelley, which he was holding back from publication. It was a long poem lampooning the authorities after the so called "Peterloo Massacre" of the crowd at St Peter's Field in Manchester. He had only seen a snatch of it, but it had haunted him for years: "I met murder on the way, he had a mask like Castlereagh." He had seen Castlereagh before his suicide. The man was a positive ray of sunshine next to Ravenswood. Drake adjusted a smirk that threatened to lift the corners of his mouth: it would not do, Ravenswood might strike him down where he stood.

Within the quarter-hour they were equipped with pistols and were on the ferry making their way towards the hubbub of the square. Once they reached the entrance it was as if they had descended into a circle of hell. The square was packed with rioters, now drunk and roistering. Hundreds if not thousands of bottles of the best wines, the best champagnes, the best ports, sherries and rums that the square dwellers could buy had made their way down thousands of greedy throats and were continuing to do so. The revellers staggered, singly and in groups, cursing, brawling and vomiting, oblivious to Riot Acts and troopers, an unstoppable bacchanalian tide. The statue of William III, besieged in the centre, now sported the red cap of liberty and a tricolor. A tipsy reveller hung onto the horse, defiantly chanting snatches of songs, incapable of climbing down. Others fought over bottles or haunches of meat, neither thirsty nor hungry, but frenzied, insatiable and bestial, feasting as if at their last meal, oblivious to the past and the future, the Recorder and the Bill.

Ravenswood smote two men down with his pistol butts, kicking their supine bodies aside as Drake looked round anxiously for an escape route. It was not to be. A dragoon rode over and pulled his horse in savagely by them.

"We need more men like you gentlemen. Go to the Council House and swear in as special constables. The Mayor's sent out an appeal to the churches to get the congregations out. Go on! That way!" He gestured wildly towards Corn Street before spurring his horse away to avoid the shower of stones that the crowd had commenced to rain down on him. Reluctantly Ravenswood abandoned the search for his next victims and took the advice. Drake followed him out of the square. In the side-streets the action was muted, small groups of rioters and dragoons skirmished and a few groups of battered men sat on the ground leaning against the walls. Ravenswood and Drake were able to make their way to join the growing throng outside the Council House. Men of all types were gathering to be sworn in and take the official white linen armband and wooden stave of the Mayor's service: gentlemen, merchants, tradesmen, shop workers, labourers. Drake was reluctant but curious and began to look about him in the queue.

"I'd have thought that the dragoons would have charged before now," he remarked to the man next to him in line.

"And so do we all," he replied. "Are you a stranger, sir? You don't sound like y're from these parts."

"I am from London."

"Then I will tell you something sir. This is a Whig crowd. If you're Tory you won't find many of your fellows along of here. We've Tory Councillors and they've fanned these flames to do the reformers down. Why was the mob not scotched last night? Hey? One sabre charge from the dragoons and they would've been finished."

"No one wants another Peterloo," said a solid man to their right. He lifted his massive head to glower at the speaker. "Would you like to give the order and have women and children run through? There's whole battalions of females and boys in the thick of it in the square and 'ave been since it started there. Would you like the country excoriating you sir! Talk's cheap!"

As the Whig champion rose to the challenge, Drake slipped away to take his place by Ravenswood. Ten more minutes of queuing and they were within earshot of the Mayor's officer who was enlisting the last two men in front of them. Drake gauged one of them to be in his mid-twenties and middle-class, with a cosmopolitan air about him. The other was a substantial gentleman of about forty-five and looked familiar.

"Name?" enquired the officer mechanically. As he looked up, the top half of his body instantly stiffened as if in salute. "Mr Roch sir. Sorry sir."

"Yes officer," said the man urbanely as he took his armband and stick from the officer's assistant. "Nicholas Roch."

"Yon wretches seem to be leavin' the docks be at present sir, but I have had the honour to sign up some of your fellow directors who have volunteered in the public int'rest."

"Good news officer. Excellent."

The man laboriously entered Roch's name on the roster and turned to the younger man.

"And you sir?"

"Brunel. Isambard Kingdom Brunel."

The officer sat back to stare. "You're the bridge man, then! Glad to make y'r acquaintance sir! Don't you go a-falling down the gorge now! I've a bet on you survivin'. Damned fine odds Oiy might add, beggin' your pardon for mentionin' it. Here's your band, stave and a pair of handcuffs." He resumed his official tone, taking in Roch as well as Brunel. "Now don't be shy in using your sticks gentlemen. Lay on with a will and we'll trounce these ruffians, in quick-sticks you might say," he added encouragingly.

As the friends turned to move off, Ravenswood impatiently shouldered his way to the desk whilst Drake hung back to step out neatly in front of the young man and capitalise on cornering a celebrity.

"Sir, forgive the intrusion, but I heard your name. You must be Brunel the engineer. Congratulations on winning the bridge competition! I look forward to seeing it completed."

Brunel was a very short man and seemed a troubled one, particularly after the chaffing at the desk. He pushed back his high top-hat to look at Drake and bowed briefly.

"Thank you sir," he said. "Though if this foolishness continues we might both have a long wait. We've launched the construction project but we need more investors. Riots have a nasty habit of frightening more than just the horses. Investors panic at the first sight of a mob. Are you an investor yourself?"

"No, but I'm lodging at Clifton and have seen where the footings will be started. I might well decide to venture a stake."

Roch consulted his pocket watch and appeared restless. "Well I'll be off to the square."

Brunel grinned wryly to Drake. "Do it quickly my friend, and keep safe."

He turned to follow Roch and was swallowed up in the crowd, leaving Drake with no further excuse to delay. He reluctantly stepped up to the desk and volunteered his name.

**Walcot Street, Bath.**

A steady drizzle was falling on the roof of the carriage and a chill had crept into every corner of the cramped interior. Abi sat huddled by the window, rocking herself absently as she looked at the front door of the neat terraced house which had closed behind the man she had thought was Mr Drake and his dog Caradoc. The man had had little to say to any of them since they had quit the Crown. When they had finally fetched up in Bath he had hurriedly charged them to stay put, then disappeared into the house, carrying the wounded dog with him. She hadn't really been surprised when she had heard the old woman at the door call him Mr Parry. New customers at bawdy houses often gave false names. She was not surprised, but unaccountably she had felt an aching sadness in her chest and had struggled to keep back tears which threatened to spill over her cheeks. A boy who looked about twelve had come out to sit on the driver's seat and hold the horses. Should she get out to talk to him? Find out a bit more about "Mr Parry"? Frances was preoccupied with Poll and Moll who were revived after the meals at the inn and were playing an interminable game of peeping round a cloth which Frances was holding up. The pastime had given Abi a break from the three of them and gave time for her to consider her future. The options were not attractive.

"Penny for your thoughts?"

Frances was looking at her, and had probably been doing so for some time. Her sharp eyes bored into Abi like gimlets, raking her thoughts and demanding a response.

"Oh, just thinking what to do next. I've no home now and I've no livin' but I'm never working for the Shadwells again, or anyone else like 'em," she finished fiercely in a hurried flush of anger. The loss of Babs coursed through her afresh like vitriol, making her feel sick, almost dizzy with helpless rage. "I'm stayin' in Bath for a while. I've things to do," she ended abruptly, unsure of everything except a burning need for a visitation of judgement on Shadwell.

"I'm not goin' 'ome neither," said Frances confidently, lifting the toddlers down onto the floor of the coach where they immediately set to wallowing and chuckling to each other in the grubby straw.

"I'm never goin' back to mi ma. I'm goin' to look after Poll and Moll for a bit. See they're alright."

"You can't. You've no money, nor any job, nor any prospects neither, and no place for any of you to sleep."

"Well Mister 'll prob'ly put us all in the poor house for now. I've been in plenty times before. It'll do for a while."

205

Abi recoiled at the thought, after earning an income and living in what she thought to be some style for a couple of years she could not reconcile herself to being a pauper.

"Not me Frances. I'm older than you. I can get serving work somewhere."

Frances screwed up her nose as she thought. "As you've been on the game and don't want to go for it no more you could go in Ladymead Penitentiary. It's just down the road here, we come by it," she pointed down the street towards town but Abi would not look. "You could stay there for quite a bit for nothing. They'll teach you things about working and things like that," she finished vaguely.

Abi made no answer so Frances tried again.

"There's an asylum for girls up Margaret's Hill. They would take us two, but I'm not goin', Poll and Moll are too little. All three of us could go in the poor house."

"You can't take care of them," said Abi, exasperated she raised her voice as if Frances were deaf. "They're not yours and you're too little."

Frances suddenly swung her hand round and slapped Abi hard on the face.

"Don't you say that!" she shouted. "Stop it!"

Abi gasped with pain and flew at Frances, making a grab for her hair, Poll and Moll, distracted by the violence, set up shrieks by way of a chorus and the coach rocked.

Tobias leaped down from the driver's seat and threw open the door.

"Stop your scrappin' you two! You're making a devil of a din and if Missus Spence hears she'll be out to you and then you'll be sorry."

They sprung back, guilty and stinging.

"Mr Parry told us he brought you all the way from Bristol to help you. You're not goin' to please him carryin' on like fishwives!"

Tobias was a good looking boy, similar to Frances in many ways with his delicate features and blonde hair. She blushed furiously.

"Sorry. Sorry Abi, but you made me mad."

Abi rubbed her face. "Yes. I know," she said, and added grudgingly, "Sorry Frances." She shifted her attention to Tobias. "How do you know Mr Parry then?"

"I work for him," said Tobias, puffed up with a swagger of conceit and stressing his newly learned aitches. "He's from London. Been here a few weeks on and off. Come up for the Season he did. He's lodging here with Mrs Spence."

"Is there room for me?" said Abi. "I could be a chamber maid."

"No. Missus' son's come back from sea and he's not that well. 'Part from him there's Mary his wife and Johnty and old Mr Spence and I lodge here too. Mr Parry's got the big room and a dressing room."

Abi looked crestfallen.

"But if he's taken the trouble to bring you back from whatever coils you was in he'll not leave you on the street. He's a gentleman. He told me not to ask you anything so I won't, but I know the both of you by sight. I come from Little 'Ell myself. I'm Tobias."

"Frances."

"Abigail."

Nathaniel came out to find them shaking hands gravely and, despite his preoccupations and exhaustion, was struck by their beauty. Three handsome children, aged beyond their years by abuse, of one form or another, at the hands of adults. He knew, despite their beatific looks, they were capable of acts of the utmost depravity. "Surely", he reasoned to himself, "they must be retrievable? Aren't we all retrievable? Human nature was a mixture of good and evil and the good must be capable of growing, if only it could be found and cultivated a-right." He was much taken with Robert Owen and his theory of the perfectibility of human nature. Abi was dark and pretty. Tobias and Frances had the fair looks of fallen angels, with Poll and Moll rolling at her feet like cherubim. Tobias seemed a changed creature since his first sighting of him at the Hart. A set of clothes had made an unimaginable difference, and not just to his appearance but to the health of his soul.

Finding billets and occupations for the girls would be a taller order than buying a set of second-hand clothes and would no doubt prove to be wearisome, even more so than the interminable night at the Crown in Keynsham and the crawl back to Bath in the coach. He had not dared whip up the horses for fear of hurting Caradoc more than he already was. Against the odds, after the various skirmishes in Bristol, the terrier seemed to be returning to his old self. The whining misery had ebbed, his eyes were sharp again and he had allowed himself to be settled by the fire to lick his wounds, a task made sweeter by the honey Mary was lavishing on them. Nathaniel shook his head to dispel the memory of the last twelve hours and had the flash of a memory of Cornelius Lee. He would be glad they had won the game. Light versus dark: light four, dark nil. But then he thought of Babs, her body left stiffened on the bed in the cave and the mad screaming child bolting down the tunnel. Dark: two.

He forced a smile. "Out with you girls. Pass Poll and Moll over Frances. "

The toddlers stood uncertainly together on the footpath, as usual exuding a whiff of stale urine. Martha Spence strode down the path and opened the gate.

"Bring them in Mr Parry. Now then who have we got? Polly and Molly is it? Frances and Abigail? As the Lord said, suffer the little children to come unto me! The first morning service starts presently so we can do no better than to cleanse these mites and take all four of you to the church. The Minister will guide us, and the master of the workhouse will be there with his wife, they'll help us place these wee ones. There's a baby-farm connected with the Walcot workhouse and they can bide there for the meantime." She looked searchingly at Abi and Frances. "And you two girls could go in the casual ward for tonight. We might get a serving place for you, but it will take time."

She added, *sotto voce* to Nathaniel, "Seeing, Mr Parry, as you're determined we can't take the lot of them to the officers of the watch there's nothing more to be done."

"Not advisable to involve the watch at present, Mrs Spence," said Nathaniel. "Thank you for your kind offer to take them to the church."

Even as Frances smiled boldly at Martha, Abi had begun to back away.

"Not for me thank you Madam," she said, her eyes wide like a trapped hare. "I'm grateful sir, but I'll shift for myself."

There were other options. Nathaniel quickly calculated them and settled for the least censorious port for this particular storm.

"Wait Abi! You can help me take the coach to the livery. The horses need stabling, then we can talk."

She wavered, uncertain, but took the lifeline and climbed back in the coach.

"Thank you a thousand times Mrs Spence," said Nathaniel. "Your kindness will not go unrewarded."

Martha smiled, content she was doing the Lord's work, and on the Sabbath! With an infant hand in each of hers, she shepherded Frances before her into the house whilst Tobias hung back to catch a word with Nathaniel.

"I took the message to Miss Peterson last night sir. Matthew gave it me and I took it like you asked. 'Ad to wait hours I did." He put his head on one side, sizing up his chances of an extra sixpence. They were good.

"Lady was right glad to have your note sir."

Nathaniel flicked him a coin. "What was her mood, Tobias?"

"They all came back in rollickin' high spirits after the masquerade Mr Parry. All a-talkin' at once and laughin' fit to bust."

Nathaniel was surprised to feel a pang of regret. What had he expected? Grateful tears? Misery after a wasted evening? He felt oddly discomfited.

"Thank you Tobias, very well done. I'll see you later. I need to come back and clean up before going round to Captain Peterson's. Ask Mary to have some hot water ready in an hour or so."

"Can't see you later sir as I'll be at work at the Hart, but Mary has the Sunday off. Mrs Spence won't have her in work on the Sabbath but she'll let her do the water, seein' as you got filthy whilst you were about good works." He dawdled, unsure whether to speak. "I know them two girls sir. I've seen the little one in Avon Street. The other," he paused, unsure of his audience. "We'll she's a whore sir."

"Not anymore," said Nathaniel. "Thank you for not asking questions Tobias. It would be good to forget you saw them."

"Can't remember anythin' about 'em sir. Oh but Mr Parry, before you go there's one other thing might int'rest you. There was merry 'ell in town last night. Hundreds were millin' round the coach offices hangin' on the news from Bris'l. It got a bit rowdy."

Nathaniel flicked him a second coin and climbed up to the driver's seat.

"I might catch you at the Hart then, I plan to dine there."

Within the half hour Nathaniel and Abi had left the coach and horses at Tasker's livery in Pulteney Mews, the stables Nathaniel had used on his first day, and were rounding the corner of Queen Square to Coco's lodgings. Before leaving the livery he had secured his plans for Monday and taken the opportunity to book out the same pale gold stallion he had ridden before. He would tie it to the hired transport and ride it back from Bristol after he returned the coach and horses. He made desultory attempts to talk to Abigail on the walk from the livery stables but made little progress. She seemed to have retreated into herself and was calculating plans of her own: watchful and ready to bolt if any noose threatened to slip over her head and tighten. After rapping a summons on the door the usual maid let them in and they climbed the stairs together.

As they stood waiting at Coco's door Nathaniel turned to Abi. "Remember, this lady is a friend of mine. She will do you no harm. It was she who first told me about the Shadwells and the trade in girls like you. I'm sure she will help if she can."

He was not. He was not sure at all, and had no real idea of Coco's possible reactions, other than guessing that a visit to the Methodist minister or Walcot poor-house would not be her first thoughts. After some delay, Coco opened the door with a flourish to reveal herself in an apricot silk dressing gown, awash with foaming blonde lace. She took his hands and pulled him over the threshold.

"Nathaniel, where have you been! Neglecting your social duties and skulking about Bristol by all accounts."

She paused to cast an appraising eye over Abi. A pretty child standing awkwardly on the landing, over-dressed in flashy silks, thin coat, indoor shoes, haunted eyes. After her last conversation with Nathaniel whilst scrubbing him free of blood and dirt after the tussle with Shadwell's men, she was sure she knew exactly what type of child young Abigail was.

"Come in Nathaniel darling. And you sweetheart."

She ushered them into her sitting room, its usual restrained calm made hectic by the addition of Diarmuid sporting a loud tartan gown, fiddle in hand, squinting at a sheet of music propped against her clock.

"Would you look who 'tis!" he declared delightedly. "If it isn't the very man! Come over here Nathaniel, I've a new air in this collection before me, and divilish awkward he is to play."

Coco drew Abi over to her. "Come with me to my kitchen *ma chérie*, we'll make some tea."

As they left the room Diarmuid cocked his head in their direction. "Been kidnapping?"

"Quite the reverse. I can't give details and don't want any police interest, but I guess Coco has told you how I found out about the trade. This girl, and another five, had been taken against their will and were going to be shipped as prostitutes to the Far East. They weren't expected to survive long. One was dead when I found them and one ran off, so I brought four of them from Bristol last night and I'm trying to get temporary billets for them in Bath, but I have other business to see to. I was hoping Coco might have some contacts to get this one a servant's job, perhaps in this building or somewhere else in the square?"

"She might well," said Diarmuid speculatively. "I can't say your tale surprises me. I'd heard the like often enough, but I salute you my friend for taking trouble over it. By the by, you might have got out just in time, the mails brought news that the rioters are out again in Bristol. It's worse than yesterday by all accounts. "

Coco returned, closing the door quietly behind her.

"She wants a few minutes to herself. I've given her a drink and some dry slippers. She can keep them." She stretched herself luxuriously over her striped chaise-longe. "You did a good deed for her Nathaniel, I heard what you said to Diarmuid. You can leave her with me for a day or two and I'll see if I can place her. She seems to be in a state of shock but is certain enough she wants to stay in Bath as long as she's well clear of Shadwell's cat-house."

Diarmuid abandoned the fiddle, set to rifling Coco's drinks cabinet and made himself busy pouring whiskey for them all. "To the magnificent escapees! *Slainte*!"

Nathaniel drained the fiery liquid and felt better. The plan was slowly coming together, it might even succeed, and could now be shelved for other matters.

"Coco, were you at the Masked Ball last night?"

"She was the belle of the ball!" interrupted Diarmuid. "And executrix of all affairs! She coupled me with the most charmin' girl I've danced with all week and set more cats amongst the pigeons with all parties than mortal man could keep up with."

Coco purred and held out her glass for more. "Nathaniel, young Miss Emma Peterson was distraught for your safety once she heard of the riots in Bristol. If only she'd known you were breaking and entering, stealing and murdering she could have rested easy!"

Nathaniel shot her a warning glare, which was ignored.

"Your little Abi told me the details over the tea. Nice work," she raised her glass lazily. "*À votre santé*!" She arched her back in a feline stretch; Nathaniel could not look away from her lithe body, and was not meant to. "Emma is a sweet girl," she continued. "I wasn't going to let her languish all night, so I encouraged Diarmuid to take care of her for the evening. They are now the best of friends, aren't you?"

"The very best," said Diarmuid pouring another whiskey. "She handles well in the dancing, light as a will-o'-the-wisp."

"I'm pleased you all had such an agreeable evening, "said Nathaniel laconically.

"You would have loved it," said Coco. "Your divine cousin Dr Parry managed to romance Mrs Peterson out of her temper at your unaccountable absence and Howard's gallant kisses for me almost reduced Tilly Vere to scratching my eyes out."

"Tilly?" said Nathaniel. "With Howard?"

"But of course. She has quite given up on the absent Mr Vere. Who for my money must be either dead or shipped out to the Far East himself by now."

"So Howard is looking after Tilly," said Nathaniel, surprising himself by the vast relief he felt on learning this. "And," he continued, hardly believing his good luck. "Miss Peterson did not have a wretched evening, which she would not have deserved and would have been entirely my fault." He threw back his head and laughed, for what seemed the first time for days. "Coco, to make my morning complete, say it again, can I really leave Abi with you for a day or so whilst I see to some business? Yes? Capital! I'll see you later. Excellent whiskey Diarmuid."

Nathaniel kissed Coco, shook Diarmuid by the hand and left with a considerably lighter heart.

Washed and brushed up Nathaniel presented himself at the Peterson residence in Marlborough Buildings later that afternoon. He had left Caradoc comfortable and slowly improving by the fireside in the company of Old Tom who was still nursing a hacking cough, the Johnty with a running nose and Matthew who had developed a low fever since his return and was wrapped up in a red flannel blanket. Apart from the addition of the exotic parrot, the kitchen resembled a male hospital ward, with Martha and Mary in lieu of nurses seeing to the needs of the patients. Fresh linen and a sky-blue neckcloth had helped Nathaniel rally, though he still felt his experiences over the last days had roasted him somewhat. He needed to draw away from the fires, take it easy. He might even take the waters: not an appetising thought. Maybe tomorrow.

"Yes sir?" Enid the maid opened the door, her eyes widening.

"Good afternoon. I would like to see the Captain."

"Captain and Madam are out driving sir. Would you like to leave your card?"

"Is Miss Peterson at home perhaps?"

Steps sounded behind Enid. "She is. Thank you Enid, that will be all. Mr Parry, please come in." Enid pattered off to the kitchen, eager to relay the information to Cook.

Nathaniel and Em faced each other, motionless, in the silent hall. She was smiling to greet him, her thick auburn hair coiling over her shoulder in a rich plait, which snaked down to her waist. Her gown was a luminous pearl silk, sprigged with flowers, her shawl a delicate sage green. He looked at her and saw Botticelli's Primavera, fresh and radiant, her beauty staggered him.

As always in grand strategy, the first to move is usually at a disadvantage, but Nathaniel was a true Romantic, so he took her hand and kissed it.

"I am so sorry to have failed to be with you last night," he said, lifting his bright blue eyes to hers and keeping hold of her hand. "I heard you received my note and sincerely hope it helped to redeem my behaviour. Only the gravest emergency kept me from being with you." He had not really meant to go that far, but the words were out before thoughts could interfere.

"I was frightened for you, Nathaniel, and was so grateful to have your letter. Please do not concern yourself about it. Mama recovered, especially when we heard of the terrible events in Bristol. It was not surprising you were detained. And, I have to say, the evening was not all bad. I made some new friends."

How long did they have, she wondered? Papa and Mama had driven out, Papa was to visit Mrs Vere and Mama would have more of a drive alone. The twins were sewing in the drawing room upstairs and with continued good luck would remain so. The hall was the only option. She found she was gripping his hand as though her life depended on it: maybe it did.

"So I gather," he was saying.

"Do you? From whom?"

Wrong move. Instantly she wished she could bite back those words. She really did not want to know if he had seen Coco before calling on her: it would not help her cause but was worse than that, it was a slippery slope to misery.

He let her words hover in the air. No mention of Coco could be allowed to intrude, and it would not be gallant to suggest he had discussed her with Diarmuid.

He fell back on flattery. "I have been told you are a beautiful dancer Em. I regret missing the chance to hold you in my arms."

"Don't miss another one."

She had shocked herself rigid: she could not believe she had said that.

It was the work of a moment. Nathaniel pulled her to him and kissed her, breathing in her scent, burying his face in her neck, whilst above them, muffled shrieks burst from the first floor. Startled, they broke away from each other and looked up directly into the red faces of Ginette and Maddy, frozen in delighted guilt as they hung over the banister rail. Emma surprised herself for the second time.

"Come down directly girls to greet Mr Parry. He has survived the riot in Bristol and come to see us. Come down now!"

Ginette and Maddy trotted downstairs, shame-faced.

"Good afternoon Mr Parry."

Their chorus had lost its edge, they were wrong-footed.

Nathaniel gravely kissed both their hands. "Miss Maddy, Miss Ginette, how delightful to see both of you again."

"How did you remember which one I was?" demanded Maddy.

Since the eyebrows had grown to uniform shape and length he had fallen back on the fact that Maddy always pushed in front of Ginette, but that would not do.

"You move differently. Both equally beautiful, but in your own special ways."

"Do we?"

Em took Nathaniel's arm. "Papa will be at the Vere residence by late afternoon, why not take tea with us then walk up the hill to join him. Maddy and Ginette have a masque of their own they made up to entertain us."

She rang the bell for Enid.

"Go and change girls. I'm sure Mr Parry would love to see your play."

"I can't wait."

The rush of soaring elation in Em's heart threatened to burst it. Perhaps she was becoming a master strategist after all. Should it be mistress? No, that really would not do.

**Late afternoon: Lansdown Crescent, the Vere residence.**

"So you think Raphael is dead?"

Tilly was animated by a new strength. She had been very busy re-inventing herself and shrugging off the used-up skin of her old life. She had hoped he was dead: the best possible result. Her assets would be substantial, her independence from her mama assured, and just to under-write her triumph, a new safety net had been secured in the comfortable shape of dear Howard. It was extremely important that Raphael was as dead as a coffin nail.

Nathaniel felt sufficiently martyred for all remaining guilt concerning the previous night to be totally expunged. Damned near drowned in tea after viewing and applauding the twins for a good hour and then marching up Lansdown Hill to endure more of the same he was within an ace of completing all duty calls, with just Mrs Peterson remaining to be dealt with in a future bout. Tilly seemed a different creature, basking in Howard's attention and showing no inclination to set about him whatsoever. Despite her exquisite beauty, that had to be a bonus. Even those stunning looks now seemed so unsatisfying after his recent embrace with Em. Tilly's beauty was on a diminutive scale, doll-like, contrived and unreal.

"I'm afraid so Mrs Vere," he said, maintaining the necessary sombre tones. "Though no body has been recovered you must prepare yourself for the worst."

She lowered her eyes and manufactured a small sigh as she grasped Howard's arm.

"Capital, Nathaniel, capital" boomed Captain Peterson. "Dashed unpleasant to hear it though, dashed unpleasant. We must all now look to the future."

"Indeed we must," said Howard unctuously, patting Tilly's hand. "The affairs of the bank have stabilised. Sanderson has proved to be an asset and we intend to move forward with our plans to finance a new vessel for Mr Ravenswood of Bristol. His returns from his other vessels are impressive." He squeezed Tilly's hands now, proprietorially. "Mrs Vere is entirely in agreement with this."

Nathaniel rose to leave. "Well Madam, Gentlemen, I should allow you to complete your discussions in peace. Thank you for your hospitality Mrs Vere."

"There won't be much peace Mr Parry!" said Howard as they rose to take their leave of him. "The centre of Bristol is once more in the hands of the mob, the gaol and toll-houses are on fire and the commanding officer, a certain Lieutenant-Colonel Brereton, has sent the 14th back to Keynsham under Captain Gage! Captain Wilkins has received an order from the magistrates to muster the Yeomanry to help the forces in Bristol. I might join them."

"Oh Howard I beg you not to go!" wailed Tilly, alarmed by an unwelcome vision of her new champion being robbed from her by the Bristol mob.

"I shall go directly into town to see what's a-foot," said Nathaniel.

"Allow me to walk to the door with you," said Captain Peterson. "Do excuse me Howard, Mrs Vere, I will only be a moment."

Once they had quit the house and stood outside together, overlooking the deserted green bowl of fields below, Nathaniel quickly acquainted the Captain with most of the details of the previous night. The omission of Ravenswood's name was a glaring one, but Nathaniel had to play that card close to his chest, in view not only of Palmerston's demands for the opium business to prosper, but also of the urgent needs of the investors in the New Bank.

The Captain nodded slowly. "I respect the necessity for you to keep some aspects of the affair to yourself as persons of note are involved, though the news of the kidnapped girls is grave indeed. You have helped them enormously, admirably I might say, but I have a household of girls of my own and I feel sorry for the young one of working age. Sent to the poor house you say? Perhaps I could offer her a place on my staff? Unblemished character you say previous to her abduction?"

"As far as I know Captain, but what I do know of her is limited. It is generous of you to consider such an offer."

It was very generous, and by saying no more he also chose to be so. Frances might well be unblemished in terms of convictions, but that was probably all. In line with his faith in Owen's theory on the value of nurture overcoming nature, he decided to give her the benefit of the doubt.

"So you're thinking of going back to Bristol? Take care of yourself," said the Captain, giving a bark of a laugh. "Mrs Peterson is very keen to see you in the near future. It would be tiresome if she were disappointed!"

Nathaniel set off down Lansdown Road, jauntily swinging his swordstick and not displeased at the prospect of renewing his acquaintance with Charles Wilkins. He liked the man, and the rest of the fencing club at Morford Street. Despite the leaden exhaustion which had been growing on him after a virtually sleepless night, he felt invigorated and optimistic. Could he settle here? Regular sessions with the Yeoman fencers? Bath buns and balls, walks over the Mendips? Would he miss London? Not really: though he could be there within the day if he did. As he crossed George Street to Milsom Street, its fashionable drapers and toy shops shrouded in blinds for the Sunday observance, he had another thought. Should he do the decent thing and put in an offer for Em? Did he want a wife? She was certainly the type to marry. He felt vaguely discreditable after the kiss in the Peterson hall when the Captain was out. He cheered up at the thought that it would have been more to his

215

discredit if the Captain had been in. He sighed inwardly as he made his way down Union Street. One did not marry the Coco's of this world, and Em's kiss in the hall had been delicious. Lost in contemplating her virtuous delights he was brought up sharp on the edge of a large and potentially volcanic crowd which was seething round a nucleus centred on Pickwick's coach office in the White Hart. Hundreds of people, mostly men and boys and almost all shabby and boisterous, were feeding on news bulletins from the Bristol stage coaches.

"What's happening?" Nathaniel asked of the first respectably dressed man he could find. It was instructive that it had taken a good few minutes to locate him.

"New Gaol's in flames!" he said gleefully. "They done away with the tread-mill and the gallows complete! Prisoners are loosed and there's tales of the crowd moving on the Cathedral. That bugger Grey won't be safe with or without 'is Bishop's hat. They'll teach 'im for goin' agin' the Bill!"

Nathaniel moved away briskly, weaving his way through the crowd to close in on the coach office. He pushed his way to the desk and penned a swift message to Lord Melbourne. From the exponential increase in volume he judged the crowd outside to be shaping up into a mob, a metamorphosis likely to be accelerated as the daylight died. According to Tobias there had been some disturbances last night and the news from Bristol would undoubtedly fuel more. As he re-emerged into Stall Street he could sense that the mood of the men had hardened. Savage faces leered, feeding on Bristol's second-hand anarchy, restlessness flowed like a tide through them, searching for a focus. Ruffians, thieves, the boys of the town: all the refuse of the underclass had risen to the surface and was on the move, looking for a target. Unluckily for Charles Wilkins and the handful of yeomen who accompanied him, they chose that moment to walk round the corner from the White Hart stables in their full uniforms: blue jackets with red fronts and lace, grey trousers with a red stripe and white feathers nodding from their helmets. The mob circled them, blocking the way, isolating them as if in a pit for baiting. Charles motioned to his men to stop trying to move forward and challenged the crowd.

"Out of the way now. We're on the magistrate's business."

"It's our business now," snarled a swarthy man in a fustian jacket and cap directly in front of him. "You're goin' nowhere without explainin' yourself."

The men within earshot bayed their approval, shouting to those behind to spread the word on who had been snared.

"Well Captain, we've 'eard the troop's gathering in Queen Square," said the man, loud enough to entertain the crowd. "Not thinkin' of joinin' 'em were 'ee?"

"I am charged by the magistrates to assist the troops in Bristol. The city is under

216

attack. Homes and businesses are being destroyed and it's our job to protect the citizens. Men, you know me as a reformer. I've every sympathy for the Bill and the feelings of the people of Bristol, but we cannot have the rule of the mob. We must keep the King's Peace. It is our duty!"

His last words were drowned by a barrage of insults. The nearest men shook their fists, some landed half-hearted punches and the crowd began to close in. Nathaniel had seen the way the scene was playing out and had moved swiftly to a position behind the soldiers. They were very close to the front door of the Hart and he had seen Frederick Tooson looking anxiously through the windows, he would be ready to let them in and bar the door behind them.

"Captain Wilkins, this way!" shouted Nathaniel, lifting his stick as a barrier and putting himself between the front line of men who were squaring up and the sanctuary offered behind the iron-clad door of the Hart. Nathaniel glanced at the men warily, ready to draw his blade, but it was not needed. The soldiers did not need a second telling but moved well, and with Frederick's help they were all inside the door in seconds. As it closed fountains of glass exploded into the entrance hall as the mob showered stones at the windows.

"Get those shutters up!" shouted Frederick, red with fury. "Damned vermin! On a Sunday as well! Guttersnipes!"

An auxiliary force of inn servants, including Tobias, burst from the kitchens and spread through the inn to secure the rear and then the upper floors. Nathaniel, Wilkins and his men tackled the front windows which were under the fiercest attack, slamming and barring the wooden shutters, one after another, heads down against the continued showers of glass. An insistent pounding had been set up on the door as a dozen shoulders laid into it, heaving for all they were worth. Fortunately the door seemed to be worth more and held up.

"Mr Bishop sir!" called Frederick to his employer who had emerged, horrified, from his office. "They tried to manhandle Captain Wilkins and his men, they've taken refuge here. Captain needs to muster the Yeomanry and they won't let him pass. They'll do him a mischief if he tries to go out."

"Don't worry Mr Bishop," said Captain Wilkins, making a move to the door. "I won't skulk in here as your inn is brought down around you. I'm going out."

"Not now Charles," said Nathaniel, grasping his arm. "Don't be in a hurry to make yourself the first victim of the Bath Riot. You've a job to do in Bristol."

"You stay put Captain Wilkins. I'll have no killing on my doorstep," said Mr Bishop dourly, before raising his voice with magisterial resolve to bellow upstairs to the servants. "When the shutters are secure get yourselves down here and barricade

217

the doors and windows all round with the settles and benches."

Captain Wilkins dispatched his yeomen to help the inn servants and they all set to hauling furniture against the entrances as the cacophony outside rose to a crescendo. It was heavy, frenzied work. With most windows now broken and the shutters up, the mob took to orchestrated cat-calling and chanting, which grew in volume and menace.

"Have you any weapons, Mr Bishop?" said Captain Wilkins, taking out his pistol and unsheathing his sword.

"I'll open the gun cupboard, but we've only three firearms all told, and they haven't been shot for an age."

At that moment a horrendous rhythmic beating began against every door, front and back.

"They've cudgels!" shouted Tobias, squinting through the shutters on the first floor. "And the bastards are piling up faggots. They're goin' to set fire to us!"

A splintering crash sounded from the front parlour, then repeated heavy blows, sharp now and clear, cheered on by the braying mob.

"They've breeched the parlour!" shouted the Captain, charging through the door to meet them.

"More benches to reinforce," yelled Mr Bishop, grabbing a warming pan from behind the bar as he went.

Nathaniel was ahead of the Captain to meet the first arms and legs that thrust through the smashed shutters. He drew his blade and smote each limb as it presented itself, nicking the flesh to encourage a speedy retreat, as four stocky potboys joined him to shore up the breech with wood, nails and a wardrobe that had been slid downstairs like a ship launching to sea. Nathaniel, no longer tired, felt a professional satisfaction as the front row of assailants pulled back yelping to give way for the next wave. No deaths, no one permanently maimed, easier by far than sparring with the waving curtain at his rooms in Walcot Street.

"Bravo!" shouted Captain Wilkins, pistol-whipping the first head with the butt of his gun, as it thrust through the broken shutter.

As they held the front the side window shutters gave way and two thin youths slid in like eels, laying about them with cudgels, breaking the glass on the paintings, smashing the mirrors, bottles and jugs. Tobias shot in and flailed about him with a metal skillet, landing severe blows to their heads.

"I know you Silas Maynard," he shouted at one youth so all could hear. "It'll be Botany Bay for life if you hurt anyone here. Be off with you whilst you can, you stupid dolt."

Semi-conscious and reeling from the attentions of the skillet, Silas and his accomplice scrambled back out of the smashed shutter, splinters biting into their hands and shards of glass slicing their skin as they went.

"Excellent work Tobias!" shouted Nathaniel as he stopped for breath and the potboys heaved a cupboard into place, covering the shattered window and muffling the din.

"Charles why don't the Yeomen move in here from the Square? They must hear what's a-foot."

"Beg your pardon sir," interrupted Tobias, "but I've seen what's doin' from the first floor, the mob's blocked the end of Stall Street. Only way the Yeomen 'll get here is to ride 'em down and they can't do that without Captain's say so. Also," he said importantly, "I seen a clutch of rioters movin' off to'ard the Abbey. The're goin' to stop any police comin' from Walcot. They can easy do it, there's 'undreds and 'undreds of the buggers sir. And there's somethin' else."

"What for God's sake!" said Mr Bishop, pan at half mast and the light of battle dying in his eye as he surveyed the destruction in the parlour.

"One of 'em is flyin' a red flag sir."

Nathaniel and Charles exchanged grave glances as outside the beating on the shutters sounded ever louder and faster as new men replaced those worn out by the first assault.

Meanwhile, on the landing of the first floor in the corner house of Queen Square, Coco tied her bonnet ribbons and buttoned her grey pelisse methodically. "So you will listen for Abi won't you, Diarmuid darling?"

"Your wish is my command my Lady of Tara," beamed Diarmuid, flinging down his pen as she spoke to him from his doorway. "The slightest touch on my door and I'll be right there ministering to the need of the young. Don't worry. She'll probably sleep all night and not know you're gone."

"I told her I won't be long. It's quite likely Constance can find a serving job for her, so it's in her interests to wait patiently."

"I'm more concerned about you," said Diarmuid moving to the window and lifting the curtain as he already had done fifty times that night. "There's trouble in town and about a dozen of the Yeoman Cavalry have set up quarters in the square."

"Is there a cab at the stand?"

"Two champing at the bit."

"Then I'll love you and leave you."

Upstairs, Abi crouched at the door listening as Coco's clear voice echoed up the dark stairwell. She slipped back to the dining room where a truckle bed had been rolled out for her to sleep on, and put on her shoes, her coat and the shawl she had purloined from Coco's drawer. The shawl was thin but it would do well. She wrapped it round her face and head to effect a disguise, tapped her right pocket to feel again the hard shape of the small gun she had found in a wardrobe, then the left, feeling gingerly for the slender, curved outline of the knife she had taken from the sideboard. Silent as a ghost she tiptoed down the stairs, past the Irishman's room, and out into the cold night.

"Thank God! There's some officers coming through from Abbey Churchyard!" hollered Tobias from his first floor vantage point. "They're layin' into the lads nearest to them. Oh they're givin' 'em what for!"

"Not a moment too soon," muttered Nathaniel to Charles as the soldiers, potboys and cooks assembled for a crisis meeting in the hall.

"What I need is a diversion," said Charles. "I've made a decision. I'm going out alone to meet the rest of my men. I must complete the muster and ride to Bristol. Mr Bishop, the loan of one of your coachmen's greatcoats if you please. It goes against the grain but I'll cover my uniform and climb out over the roof."

"They need red 'ot pokers up their arses so they do," grumbled the cook.

Even as he finished, every face lit with a wild surmise.

"Are the fires still in?" asked Nathaniel.

"They'll be blown up to do credit to a blacksmith," said the cook in joyous wrath, heading to the kitchen like a man possessed.

"Come on," yelled Tobias. "There's enough fire-irons in this place to arm us all. I'm goin' to the first floor."

They scattered, galloping through the rabbit warren of ancient rooms that lurked behind the elegant exterior of the Hart to search out the ideal poker, tongs, shovel or toasting fork to plunge into the maw of the kitchen fire. Bellows were brought into play expertly by the cook and an ostler who had been caught drinking tea in the kitchen when the battle broke out. Captain Wilkins was waiting impatiently by the skylight when they emerged below him into the hall, with their hands wrapped in wet towels and their weapons of choice before them glowing a rich, satanic red.

"Ready," said Nathaniel. "Captain Wilkins make your move when you hear the front door open. Everyone else, as we open the door, give a battle cry and lay into their legs, we want no maiming of hands or faces from this night's work. When they're on the run, as the cook so rightly said, tan their behinds!"

On the count of three, the iron bound door was flung back and the White Hart battle party howled out of their fastness like furies from hell. Nathaniel and the yeomen led the charge followed by Tobias, Cook and Mr Bishop, with the ostler and assorted potboys bringing up the rear. The surprise visited on the besiegers was total and unmanned them entirely. Their own battle cries melted into wails of terror and a rout began. From his position on the roof Charles Wilkins was gratified to see not only the small band of flailing red weapons making slow and steady progress against the dark mass pitted against them, but also inroads being made on the periphery where an answering halloo came from the fresh throats of dozens of special constables, beating exposed heads with their staves as they swept on towards the Hart.

In the dark, behind a low shrub in the garden of Shadwell's brothel, Abi silently stretched her cramped limbs. She was very cold and had no real plan, apart from staying alive long enough to accomplish her objective. She had taken the spare key from behind the ivy and left the gate undone, but doubted she would survive to pass through it again. At first she thought she might march straight into his office in the stable and confront him, bawl him out and not let him say a word, then shoot him like a rabid dog. On second thoughts she abandoned this. It was a poor idea. Jabez and Billy would more than likely be skulking in their quarters at the back of the stables like guard dogs in kennels. They'd be out and do for her if they heard any disturbance. So she needed to wait, as she kept explaining to herself. He was definitely in there. Candlelight played on the curtains and the lantern was hanging on the outside door to light the path leading to the house. Lights streaked out from behind her, through the chink in the drapes from Clari's room on the second floor and below her the salon was ablaze, but the nursery above was plunged into darkness. It seemed fitting. She and Babs hadn't been replaced quite yet. The distant din from the centre of town ebbed as she waited. The harsh calls, crashes and yells, the staccato clopping of horses' hooves, all seemed to have worn themselves out. It seemed quieter now, but the world was watchful, still a prey to violence, disorder and death, waiting for the next onslaught.

Suddenly the lights in Shadwell's office were extinguished and she heard steps descending the stairs. A dark figure emerged and paused by the lantern, elegant and lean, he fastened up the buttons of his silver-grey frock coat against the chill, seemed to listen to the faint sounds of the distant crowd and sniff the air, then made his way to the path that led to the house. As he approached, she rose silently to her feet, took out Coco's gun and stepped in front of him. He gasped, his hand flying involuntarily to his heart.

"For God's sake! Abi? Is it you?"

She saw him run his hands down his sides, hoping he had left just one weapon concealed, giving him just one chance of killing her where she stood. He had not.

She lifted the small pearl handled gun, straight armed to shoulder height.

"You betrayed us!"

She was alarmed as her voice sounded alien, it trembled and almost died. She saw it gave him hope, he opened his mouth to reason with her.

"You gave us up and Babs is dead. She died in my arms in that rat hole of a cave! You gave us up!"

Strength came to her, but as she squeezed the trigger Shadwell had already lunged at her with a wild yell. The gunshot exploded but the charge went low, missing its mark and embedding itself in his thigh. Her arm kicked back, the gun flicking out of her hand. She snatched the knife from her pocket and slashed wildly at him as they fell together in confusion on the flagged path. Bleeding heavily, Shadwell struggled to capture her hands, forestall the mad cutting blows, but after the first seconds of numbness, pain suddenly leaped into his leg, his vitals, his arms, like a ravening wolf. As he groaned and loosened his grip she wriggled away and crawled out of reach. Moaning in fear, Abi grabbed the gun, scrambled to her feet and made for the garden gate, as behind her Rosie Shadwell reached her husband, screaming his name, and Jabez and Billy's hulking shapes broke out of the stable entrance.

Abi couldn't seem to make her legs move, as in some terrible nightmare she tried to pump them back and forth, but they moved as if under water. Jabez and Billy, seeing Rosie kneeling over Joshua, both turned to pursue Abi. She wrenched the gate open and staggered out into the dark lane where she almost collided with a slight figure in top boots and a riding coat.

"Run Abi, run," a familiar voice, a woman, and a push towards a waiting carriage. The boyish figure whipped out a long pipe and blew it straight into Jabez' face as he rounded the gatepost. A fine orange mist enveloped his head, he clapped his hands to his eyes, loosed a most terrible scream and dropped to his knees. Billy, two steps behind, ploughed into him and was brought up short. He lifted his hands in anticipation to protect his eyes, only to have them brought down again as he sustained a ferocious kick between his legs, opening the way for his own dose of cayenne pepper from the blow pipe. They looked up in their bleary torment into a blunderbuss levelled at them by a man leaning out of a post-chaise, heard a light female voice command the horses and the chaise disappeared into the night.

"Billy," said Jabez, grabbing his comrade's sleeve, his eyes blinded by coursing tears "we was outnumbered. There was three men, do you hear me boy?"

At the upper window, open to the night and all its sounds, Clari continued to stand transfixed by the scene which had unfolded below. The thin girl, her shape and voice so familiar, bringing Shadwell down as he so richly deserved. Then the clincher, that woman's voice: "Run Abi, run!" Clari smiled down on the shrieking Rosie and bellowing Joshua. So Abigail had returned. She pulled down the sash, more satisfied than she had been for many a night.

# Chapter 10

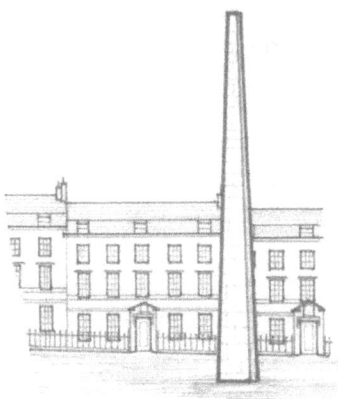

**Midnight: 30<sup>th</sup> October, 1831. Queen Square, Bath.**

"Pasty sir?"

"By all means," said Nathaniel, wrapping his handkerchief round his hand and selecting one of the burning hot pastries from the tray. He picked it off by the heavy crimping and rested its searing bulk on his knees, where it did additional duty as a hot brick and kept out some of the cold. "You, young man, are a life saver," he said as he combed his pockets for a couple of pence to give to the boy. "Could you rustle up some beer to go with it?"

"Oiy will be back directly," he said, his eyes lazily swivelling over the crowd, his delivery, measured and bordering on the bovine. "Once Oiy've shifted these pasties sir."

He had been unlucky in his pasty seller. Grateful and opportunist shopkeepers had been sending out regular squads of boys to ply the yeomen with refreshments as soon as it had become safe to walk from the centre to Queen Square. The Walcot police force and a host of specials had combined to scatter the mob as it was ousted from Stall Street and the former battle grounds were now calm. The horde had fragmented into splinter groups, fleeing the city centre to salve their pride by inflicting piece-meal destruction elsewhere. There had been a cry amongst the boldest to sack other inns owned by Mr Bishop and his partner Mr Cooper, but now their blood was up, any likely target *en route* would be lucky to escape. The square was thick with soldiers, potboys and waiters, traders and other respectable men, carts and horses. Some of the Yeoman Cavalry had lit small fires and some were huddled on camp stools, waiting for the order to ride for Bristol. The siege of the Hart had caused some breaking of ranks and misinformation, some had heard the muster was delayed and had not set out, whilst some had arrived only to go home again. The

224

scene was shambolic, and if Bristol was depending on Bath for an early raising of its siege it was doomed to disappointment. Nathaniel was in the centre of the square, sat on the damp ground and resting his back against Beau Nash's obelisk in the company of Neville Fairfield. They looked up as the familiar figure of Charles Wilkins emerged from the crowd and hurried over to sit by them.

"It will be near to dawn before we can complete the muster," grumbled Wilkins, wrapping his cloak around him and taking a pull of brandy from his hip-flask. "Will you ride with us Nathaniel?"

"I wish I could Charles, but I've got a hired coach and pair from Bristol and they need to be returned before the day's out. They're stabled in Pulteney Mews and I need to settle up for the livery before I leave. The stables open at dawn, but there could be some delay. Perhaps I will see you in Bristol?"

Wilkins nodded despondently after draining half of his brandy. Fairfield looked haggard but he managed a smile. "Take something with a bit more weight than your swordstick! You'll need to be in one piece if we're ever to spar again. Will you be joining us at Morford Street next month?"

"I hope to be in Bath, and in one piece," said Nathaniel, breaking the meat pasty into two so he could pass one to Charles.

"Much obliged," said Captain Wilkins. "I'm famished." Once the sharp edge of his hunger was dulled, he felt convivial enough to pass round the rest of the brandy but his brow was still furrowed with anxiety. "I hope we are all in one piece come next month. I caught the news from an incoming Welsh coach not ten minutes ago and it's bad. The centre of Bristol is still aflame and they said you could see the glow across the Severn. The Bishop's Palace has fallen now, as well as the Mansion House, Customs and Excise Houses. The warehouses are broken open and the mob's thieving from private homes. This mayhem isn't for the Bill, it's for devilment. It's a damn shame we were held up here, but we'll go as soon as we can. I'll leave it an hour or so, make sure Bath's quiet, then go home to check the mill. My workers are protecting the buildings in shifts, bless their hearts! I'll be back here before dawn."

Nathaniel rose to leave. "So perhaps we will meet in Bristol? Good luck to you gentlemen."

He glanced up at the corner house as he made his way through the horses and scattered camps of men: all was in darkness. Coco and Abi must have retired. Perhaps Diarmuid was out, getting the flavour of the night, maybe he was beating out retribution on some guilty heads as a special constable? Nathaniel felt dazed and his walk slowed almost to a stagger. Delayed exhaustion was flooding his body and without the adrenalin rush of battle for sustenance, it threatened to drown him. He stopped a passing potboy and bought a mug of rough cider. Its acrid burn revived him and he set his course along George Street for Walcot.

His first tap on the door awakened a familiar torrent of barking from Caradoc, but Nathaniel was grieved to note its hoarseness and also that the familiar scrabbling of paws on the flags was slower than it ought to be. Martha was immediately behind Caradoc and opened the door a cautious crack to allow an inspection of the visitor. "Mr Parry! Come in sir!" she said, visibly relaxing and letting the door swing wide. "I feared it might be some scoundrels! Tobias is here and we've heard all about the set-to at the Hart. Come in, come in!" She stuck her head out to check the road up and down. Satisfied she retreated and slammed the door shut behind them.

Nathaniel bent to greet Caradoc, who had defiantly torn off his bandage, but had little strength and was wobbling unsteadily. He swept up the dog and, leaning away from the welcoming licks, he managed to take Martha's hand and plant a swift kiss of his own upon it.

"Thank you Mrs Spence. Thank you from the bottom of my heart for caring for Caradoc, you had more than enough to do with your own family and the girls I inflicted upon you this morning."

Martha was momentarily lost for words, astonished at the rush of pleasure generated by such a piece of gallantry. She could not remember when a gentleman had last kissed her hand. No wonder, she thought, it was the first time. Her husband had done so once or twice, but he had not been a gentleman. A good man: but not a gentleman. She smiled, confused, but managed to mutter, "My pleasure Mr Parry," as she led him into the kitchen.

Mary was pouring beer for Old Tom, who sat looking perkier than Nathaniel had seen him for some time, and also for Matthew, who was on the settle, removed from the fire and without his flannel blanket, but looking gaunt, with the Johnty asleep in his arms. Tobias, clearly in the midst of his tale, or some repetition of it, was leaning with affected nonchalance on the mantelpiece, holding court.

"Mr Parry! Mr Bishop said he was that proud o' me he'll increase my wages. I'm goin' in tomorrow to help him get the parlour straight enough to open. We kept 'em away from the beer and the wines and spirits didn't us sir!"

"You certainly did him proud," agreed Nathaniel, landing himself abruptly on a hard, stiff-backed chair by the kitchen table.

"Oiy 'ave never 'eard the like since Mr Hunt's meetin' in '17," crowed Old Tom. "Though there was no battlin' from the people's side on that occashun." He poked out his head from his shawl, restored to his usual pose of an ancient and scaly tortoise, eyes beady, thin lips parted in anticipation of a morsel. "What's doin'

226

now?"

"The yeomanry will ride to Bristol at dawn," said Nathaniel. "Stall Street and the Square are almost quiet now, the specials are still patrolling."

"They came 'ere for to enrol us but we was too crocked!" said Matthew, shame-faced. "Grandfather too old and me still with the fever. But I have some good news. Arthur Jamieson and Robert Turner came round, a-sportin' their bands and staves and they said there was a press of business down by the barges. One bargee hasn't done a stroke of work for a fortnight gone and he's a man short. I'll go down the quay tomorrow and see if he'll take me on."

Mary's face shone as much with delight as the clammy exhaustion which had enveloped her the whole day in the over-heated sick berth of a kitchen. "Matthew says he won't be goin' to sea for some time now," she said, wiping her forehead on her apron. "Will you Matthew! Maybe he will find regular work in Bath."

Nathaniel accepted a mug of beer from Martha. "Perhaps you need more space here," he said thoughtfully. "I can move out to the Royal York."

An outburst of complaint assured him he could not, and settled the matter.

"You have your room as long as you need it," declared Martha.

"We are snug in Mary's room and need no more," insisted Matthew.

"You are a good tenant," wheezed Tom. "Pays on the nail, 'e do," he continued to himself. "Better food by a long shot since 'e's bin 'ere."

"Tell me Mrs Spence," said Nathaniel, embarrassed. "What happened this morning on your visit to church with Frances and the infants?"

"Well, they're in Walcot Poor-house for the time being," said Martha. "The girl Frances seems a bright little body. She insists she's their cousin and wants to visit them regular. I have asked the Minister if he can help place her in service."

"I might have an earlier offer Mrs Spence. I saw Captain Peterson and he is willing to employ her at Marlborough Buildings."

Martha nodded once and narrowed her eyes. "What about the other girl? Abigail?"

"I took her to a friend's home where she is settled for the night and I have hopes that she will find her a place soon."

"A bad business Mr Parry," said Mary. "The times are perilous. What with all the bother up north, and now with Bath up in arms and Bristol over-run and a-fire. Lord help us, such bloodshed!"

"Bloody hell! Damnation!" squawked the parrot suddenly from the cage in the corner. "God's blood shipmates! Blood and sand! Blood and sand!"

With the righteous battle cry: "Blasphemer!" Martha leaped from her chair, snatched a cloth from the drying rack and flung it over the cage. "That will silence you! You evil, prating bird! I'll wring its neck if this carries on Matthew."

Matthew glowered. "Leave him be Mother, he'll learn. He's an innocent creature brought up in bad ways."

Martha's good humour was put out.

"Mr Parry," appealed Mary. "Don't you believe the creature can be trained?"

"I'm a great believer in the power of the good example," said Nathaniel wearily, "and where could he get a better one than here?" Glancing at the clock on the shelf, he forced himself upright from the chair. "Do excuse me, I need a few hours sleep if I'm to return to Bristol early with the coach and pair." He bent to pick up Caradoc and made for the stairs.

"I'll be about by five sir," said Tobias eagerly. "I'll bring you your water and a bite o'breakfast."

"I shall be up and about in my own kitchen Master Caudle by that hour," said Martha sternly. "Now we all need to retire and pray for God's mercy," she added piously. "There have been calls from the pulpits for a day of repentance for the evil deeds done in this land. We can start with our prayers this very night."

**The early hours: 31st October, 1831. The King's Arms Inn, Malmesbury.**

Diarmuid poked the remnants of the fire into life before returning to his unfinished supper at the table. It had been an unusual evening: a rare and reckless one. Coco never ceased to amaze him. He poured another glass of claret and watched the winking firelight play through its richness. He swirled it round the body of the glass, watching it cling and roll slowly down like a translucent receding wave. Malmesbury had proved to be a wise choice. The dark panelled room offered an antique comfort, warmth, a clean bed and plentiful food and drink, even at this god-forsaken hour. The coaching inn was an old but efficient one and he had felt sanguine about leaving his coach and pair in the stables. Despite appearances, Diarmuid Casey was finicky about his personal possessions. He had not always had many and valued those he had acquired. But he did like excitement and a modicum of danger. Squiring Mademoiselle Colette Montrechet round Bath for the last few months had been a joy, all the more delicious for it being unlooked for. "But", he reflected, taking a deep draught of the claret, "all good things must come to an end: just one more trip and the current fandango will be complete."

He picked up the chicken leg and tore at it with his teeth. The Pelican Inn at Gloucester did not sound as commodious as the King's Arms but they need not stay. It should only be a matter of delivering the girl and they could head straight back to

Bath: and not before time. His own work had been languishing and he was expected back in London as his lectures in the west had been over for a week and Mr O'Connell had need of him. He would, however, keep his Bath rooms. The bonus of meeting up with Coco again would not be squandered.

The current caper had all gone rather well. By some flash of womanly intuition Coco had known where the girl had gone and what she was up to. They had scooped up the crazed Abigail and whisked her out of Bath avoiding all let and hindrance, putting a good few miles between her and the Shadwells, and with an ounce of luck should settle her in some make-shift employment before noon tomorrow. She could keep her head down until any resulting brouhaha in Bath blew over. He chuckled to himself as he pictured Coco's respectable pose as his relative with her serving maid when they fetched up at the King's Arms. It had been a fortuitous choice. Coaching inns always had advertisements in the stage offices, and although they had not found any vacant positions for her in the forest of notes on the board, a jovial cove travelling from Gloucester over-heard their requests and had given them the break they needed. He had come from the Pelican in St Mary Street, where the landlord had most negligently allowed three chamber maids to slip away over the last week. His bad luck should soon become their doxy's salvation.

His thoughts were interrupted by a soft creak as the communicating door opened to admit Coco. "How now fair cousin!" said Diarmuid amiably.

Coco sat down with him and poured herself a drink. "*Slainte*! So far so good. She is grateful for the chance of work in Gloucester and has fallen asleep. There should be no more escape bids tonight."

"Congratulations to you my dear one," said Diarmuid. "You're a woman of great resource and I keep discovering more. Where will it end? I have to know! With any tale I am a regular terror and always read the last page first, so indulge me and confess all now!" He watched her, teasing, yet as always with her, he was not in full control. He felt the thrill of the chase: would he ever manage to uncover all of her charming deceits? Would the firelight help him do it, the exhilaration of the past danger, the undoubted romance of the night? For Coco to rise, dance, sing him a song, throw off her clothes and tumble into bed with him was commonplace: it was her secrets he lusted after, as they had, to date, been unattainable. The fire collapsed, singing, in the hearth and he rose to throw on another log. It could be a time for confidences.

"What exactly would you like me to confess darling?" said Coco, entertained by his interest.

"I've known you for a good many years, so I have," said Diarmuid slowly. "I've seen you charm men, women and the birds out of the trees. I've seen you plenty times before in men's riding gear, and I've seen you drive a pair, but I've never seen you fighting, my girl! Let's start with that. Where did that particular skill originate might I ask?"

"I've not had a sheltered life Diarmuid."

"Neither have many women, but they still can't fight. Go on, tell me more!"

Coco put her head to one side, weighing up the merits of divulging some tantalising half-truths against spinning a few outright lies. "You know I was orphaned. I had older brothers and we fended for ourselves after our mother eventually died. I spent some formative years in *arrondisements* which were far from genteel, Diarmuid! I was also in Marseilles," her face clouded and closed, he really didn't need to know that, but she continued: without the names, without the gothic tales of misery. "I learned savate," she smiled, appearing pleased with herself. "Have you heard of it? No? Such a sheltered life *cherie*! It is a good way to defend yourself if you need to. I will train you! You will be a force to be reckoned with."

"What did you do to their eyes? What was in the pipe?"

"Just pepper. Cayenne. Most effective and better if you target it. So remember, don't throw it, shoot it directly. A man I knew had so many treasures from the East. He had a beautiful collection of lacquered boxes holding different concoctions of stinging pepper. They were used as weapons. Some had mouth-pieces for blowing a cloud at his enemies. Small blowpipes work just as well. Just one charge has very desirable effects."

"As I saw," said Diarmuid, watching her intently. "Fortunately those are not the only desirable effects you have Coco."

She smiled, her eyes opaque, watchful, and leaned over to kiss him.

## Mid-morning: Bristol.

As Nathaniel passed the Wells fork in the Bath road, and descended the incline to follow the south bank of the river to Redcliffe, he could hear the ominous rushing of distant flames and taste the smoke in his mouth. Black clouds edged in an angry red billowed up from the direction of Queen Square and he could hear the distant tumult of battle, briefly outmatched by a thunderous crash and confused cries as another building collapsed, reluctantly giving up the ghost after two days of torment. Isolated groups of ragged men were dodging the traffic and fleeing from the centre, some laden with booty, who would rue their greed when the troops began their sweeps of the arterial roads and the surrounding fields. For now they staggered on unmolested, most rolling drunk, blackened and wounded. One man ran crazily at the horses' heads brandishing what looked like a communion goblet.

"I got silver matey! Give us a sovereign! Give us ten shillings then!"

Nathaniel whipped the horses on and the man fell cursing into the road. He drove alongside the mud banks of the Avon, pleased that the buildings on the south side of the river seemed whole enough. Some had shattered glass, many had boarded up their ground floors, but the flames had not spread here. Nathaniel hurried on to Redcliffe and was relieved to find the livery was also intact. He bullied a reluctant groom from the office where he lurked behind make-shift barricades, settled his debt and after bargaining for water and a rub-down for the stallion, decided to try to ride into the city over Bristol Bridge to see the action for himself, then make his way to Drake's rooms in Clifton.

He made slow progress along the Welsh Back to Queen Square, as he had to pick his way as if over a battlefield. With the whip left behind at the stables, he drew his makila from his belt and held it with the reins, ready for service. Fires were still flaring from King Street and in the square beyond, but it occurred to him that without the intermittent drizzle the furious destruction would have been even wider spread. Wailing cries rent the air, groups of women knelt by some of the ruined houses, rocking and praying, hands clasped in desperation, eyes closed on the desolation before them, prayers unanswered. Charred bodies lay like rough-barked tree trunks where they had fallen or crawled to as they made their escapes from the infernos, some were impaled on railings after losing their footing on higher floors, other corpses were dismembered or disfigured by gaping wounds, cut by sabres after falling victim to earlier charges from the roaming cavalry detachments. Groups of dragoons continued to search the streets, Gloucester men and other Wiltshire cavalry detachments, men of the Somerset yeomanry including some familiar faces from Captain Wilkins's troop, all clattered past to mop up remaining cells of rioters still bent on plunder, or simply too befuddled with drink and lethargy to escape. Loosed pigs grunted as they rooted in the corpses, chickens picked at abandoned caches of food and dogs howled for their masters. His horse stumbled on pavements forced up into ridges by the burning in the vaults below and shied away from shimmering rivers of molten lead which snaked down walls from the melting roofs, enamelling them with a demonic sheen. Nathaniel unwound his neck-cloth and wrapped it round his face to protect it from the searing heat and choking smoke: the overwhelming stench of liquor, rum and brandy, burning, blood, and death.

With reckless daring, given the heavy military presence, some rioters were still trying to sell their booty on the streets. Feather beds for a shilling, gold and silver plate, furnishings and bedding, all on offer from ragamuffins stuffed out like bolsters, wearing so many layers of waistcoats and topcoats in the heat that they resembled nothing so much as three-bird Christmas roasts. Occasional gangs of young boys still rampaged wielding burning brands, though they scattered as they caught sight of any of the avenging detachments of troops, their reluctance to miss any last opportunity for pillage outmatched by a feral sense of self-preservation.

Sickened by the sights, Nathaniel decided to skirt the square, make for the drawbridge at the far end of St Augustine's Reach and thence to the Cathedral precinct. The destruction there had blazed a trail as far as the Bishop's Palace where fires still burned, though the precinct itself seemed quiet. The Cathedral doors hung open and a rearguard, all weary and soot smeared, some bandaged and bloody, stared out like sleepwalkers as they heard fresh hooves approach, then fell back to their miserable task of clearing debris and sorting the spoil. The ground was littered with torn pages of manuscripts, which lifted occasionally to swirl in the fitful gusts, briefly revivified, to die again amongst the charred books, hassocks and abandoned flags as the wind dropped. Nathaniel pushed on through Clifton Wood towards Drake's rooms in Cornwallis Crescent, relieved to see fewer signs of the depredations as he climbed higher, though the streets were eerily quiet for a Monday morning, the houses closed and barred.

He rode round to the stables and left his mount with a groom. Drake's horse was missing, which was not a good sign, but he was resolved to go in, Drake or no. The horse needed more of a rest and he might at least learn something of Drake's movements, even if he were missing. He was shown to the drawing room to meet Lottie, but did not find her alone.

Amanda Ravenswood and Lottie Drake had spent an increasingly fractious morning in each other's company. Normally they drank tea, wine, Bristol sherry or gin, depending on the company or lack of it, and divided their time between Lottie's drawing room, the Assembly Rooms and walking the crescents and the Downs. They gossiped, they dissected the reputations of the rest of Clifton's finest, they competed and they generally enjoyed, but today had been very different. In fact it had been uniquely unpleasant. Amanda had arrived, sulky and cross, after being driven from Arno's Tower to Redcliffe Parade, as planned, only to find it empty of all but the most menial of servants. Edwin had not waited to entertain her for luncheon, as arranged, but had instead gone to town, determined to enrol as a special constable according to the gibbering maid who had come out to speak to her. Only a boorish under-footman was available to help her coachman with the horses and the house had an uneasy, neglected air. There had been some calamitous misadventure that no-one seemed willing to speak of. The *Mathilda* was a smouldering ruin and apparently some servants had been killed, there were certainly no arrangements made for her reception whatsoever. Unaccountably, and despite the rumoured sabre charge at dawn from assorted dragoons, she had still seen some marauding gangs of the lower classes roaming the streets as she had been driven to Clifton. Three days of mayhem. She pursed her lips peevishly. What on earth was the military for if it could not keep order?

The arrival of a visitor offered a promising diversion, as Lottie's anxiety over the whereabouts of her husband had become tedious well over an hour before. Amanda had no fears for Edwin's safety whatsoever, in fact, apart from her annoyance about luncheon his extended absence was something of a bonus. His mood of late had been alarming, and at times of any type of difficulty he tended to vent his frustration on her in a variety of ways. Most of which were unpleasant. She had been looking forward to the departure of the Chinese visitors and the *Blue Dragon*, which had clearly occurred, but otherwise the day had fallen far short of her expectations. A visitor, any visitor, would have relieved the ennui, but this one was diversion indeed. She extended her hand to greet a tall, powerfully built young man in his mid-twenties, a good decade her junior, with thick black hair swept back from his face, sparkling bright blue eyes and something else, there was a dynamic energy about him which she found compellingly attractive. It was a life-force of a different quality from Edwin's, who was also tall, darkly handsome and undoubtedly energetic. This man, this Nathaniel Parry, had a wholesome appeal. He even smelled of the open air. With a pang of discomfort she compared it unfavourably with the spiced unguents and scents that Edwin had favoured of late. She felt a physical response as Nathaniel took her hand, a charge of passion, which even as it rose within her was almost instantly extinguished by a cold flush of fear. How could she even think it? Edwin had an uncanny ability to read her thoughts. Even an attraction to another man would be seen as a betrayal. She withdrew her hand abruptly. Edwin was a monster, but, she reminded herself, as she had so often before, he was wealthy and devoted to her, the two attributes necessary for her to remain with him. But even as she rehearsed the familiar mantra of justification, another voice, whispering and insistent, corrected her. "He is wealthy, the prime and only attribute necessary". It had often surprised her, despite her vanity, that she had not found him to have a mistress or other occasional women.

"Any day, any time," whispered the voice, "it could happen. It may already have done so, and you are powerless."

Nathaniel was settled on a high backed chair with a glass of sherry, opposite the two women who perched on a striped sofa, their fashionably padded sleeves and full skirts competing for space, their jewels vying. He could see the similarities between Charlotte Drake and Ravenswood's wife, both enjoying their riches, both brittle and haughty. They were beautiful, in a harsher, more studiedly elegant manner than the fluffy Tilly, though they were decked out in a similar style, the extravagant leg o'mutton sleeves, the plunging necklines, the yards of lace and ribbons. He had a fleeting vision of Coco, she would not have poised herself like these two harpies, ready to pounce and dissect him, but would have stretched herself out languorously, invitingly, kicking off her shoes. He smiled at the thought of her and her generosity of spirit. Neither of the two society women would have wasted one moment's thought on such a pitiful creature as the child-whore Abigail.

"Well Mr Parry," said Lottie, the anxiety in her voice overlaid by the sharpness of frustration and a growing anger. "Do you have news of my husband? He went to dinner with Mr Ravenswood last night and we gather they have gone to join the special constables. What possessed him I cannot imagine!"

"I have come here to ask you the same question Mrs Drake. I need to discuss business with him and hoped to find him here."

"They will probably return to Redcliffe Parade after they have finished performing as constables. We have a house there," said Amanda, watching Nathaniel stonily. "Tell me Mr Parry, what exactly is going on in town?"

"It is in ruins," said Nathaniel shortly. "It still burns and the mobs are not entirely banished, though the military have the upper hand. I would advise you ladies to stay indoors. Where is your main residence Madam?"

"Arno's Vale," said Amanda. "I have my coach waiting. The driver will take me home later. I shall try Redcliffe Parade on my way and see if Edwin has returned. I know he will not quit the city as a ship of ours has been damaged and we have some trouble at the Redliffe house. I gather the mob attacked it, we are some servants short."

Nathaniel watched her closely, relieved to hear that his deeds had been palmed off on the mob. It was a good moment to try to disengage Drake from Bristol as they were both due to make their reports to the noble lords within days and, unlike their last trip, he was determined to keep Drake with him for the journey as the long hours on the road could be put to good use.

"Mrs Drake you might be wise to remove to Bath. I gather your husband's business with Mr Ravenswood will conclude shortly and it will be safer there. There was some trouble last night but it is trivial in comparison to the events here. Mr Drake and I need to travel to London urgently and it would be wise to go to Bath before he leaves."

Lottie reviewed her situation. The adventure in Bristol had soured. Amanda was far less diverting than she had been and the city was too volatile to vouch keeping Lizzie there any longer. It was all too tiresome and she was ready for a change.

"The Bath Season is well under way is it not?" she said, fixing Nathaniel with a cold interrogatory stare. "I read there was to be a Reform Soiree at the Assembly Rooms on November 5th. We are rather tired of random bonfires but a little *feu d'artifice*, a little sparkle, might not go amiss. It seems the Whig campaign still has life in it despite the Lords' judgement, and provided the miserable populace will conclude its roistering and allow ordinary life to continue, the evening might well be an interesting one."

"I would like to go," said Amanda, feeling suddenly unwilling to lose her new companion. "Charlotte, you could ask John to encourage Edwin to attend."

"Well ladies," said Nathaniel, rising to leave. "Thank you for your hospitality. I think my best move will be to go to Redcliffe Parade and wait for the gentlemen to return."

After he had been seen out, Amanda said. "He never asked for the number of our house. He seems a resourceful man. And he is rather handsome."

"Is he? I suppose so," said Lottie absently, turning down her mouth in disapproval. "He's a subordinate of John's. He might well be right though. I might insist we go to Bath." And, she thought to herself, she might do well to encourage Amanda to insist that she and her husband follow suit. She had not quite abandoned her designs on Edwin Ravenswood, and the waltz was the most convenient invention imaginable, providing as it did an unrivalled opportunity to be close, very close indeed, with other women's husbands. Her anxiety for John had become tedious and she allowed herself to move on to far more stimulating possibilities. Assuming a smile she liked to think looked brave yet vulnerable, she picked up the sherry decanter and poured two generous measures into the empty blue glasses.

Nathaniel rode back through the shattered town, easily avoiding trouble. The dragoons had grown in number and there were literally thousands of special constables seeking out rioters and looters, dispensing brutal summary justice before hauling them off to the magistrates. He made his way to Ravenswood's residence in Redcliffe Parade, tied his horse to the railings and climbed the steps to the front door. Additional make-shift shutters had been attached both to the door itself and to all the windows on the front of the house, though the piles of broken glass in the area and on the side of the steps showed that these had come too late to forestall the first wave of vandalism he had generated in the Llandoger. He was admitted to the house and shown into a dining room on the first floor where he found Ravenswood standing by the window, deep in conversation with Drake. It was Nathaniel's first sighting of him since the hectic night on the wharf and as the ship owner turned to shake his hand, he was struck by the brooding menace of the man. He was of a similar height to Nathaniel and black-headed like him, though of Drake's age. Ravenswood's eyes were dead pools, allowing no emotion or expression, his hands, though immaculately manicured, were bruised and swollen.

"Mr Parry, what can I do for you?"

"I have need to speak with Mr Drake on matters of business sir. I came here after visiting Cornwallis Crescent. The ladies directed me here."

Drake flinched at the mention of his wife. "How is Lottie? How's Lizzie? Has the Crescent escaped harm? I have been too occupied to return!"

"They are safe in Clifton as the mob spread no further than the cathedral precinct, but I did suggest Mrs Drake might be more comfortable in Bath."

Nathaniel sensed an unpleasant tension between the men, and he had no desire to prolong his stay. His dealings with Drake needed privacy.

"Mr Drake, as our meeting in London is imminent and we have much to discuss, perhaps you might change your usual plans and travel with me?"

Drake brightened visibly. "Oh yes indeed Parry. We must return urgently, given the circumstances. I will come to Bath tomorrow, with my family, and you and I will leave directly for London. I gather the situation in Bath is better than here!"

"Well, don't head for the Hart. There was some disturbance in the city but the York House is untouched."

"Capital," said Drake unevenly. Even the unattractive prospect of hours of cross-questioning by Parry was preferable to one extra day, or one extra minute with Ravenswood. After the disastrous night and endless day in the town battling with looters he was exhausted. He felt filthy, his mouth gritty and sour. An early removal to London would also reduce the time spent explaining himself to Lottie, which was another important aspect to be borne in mind. "Well Ravenswood," he continued. "I thank you for your hospitality. It was unfortunate that all did not fare as well as it might."

"You had a ship ready to sail I gather," said Nathaniel innocently. "Not the one lying at anchor I hope."

"No, not that one," said Ravenswood, with an unpleasant smile. "No doubt we will meet again at some point Mr Parry."

"No doubt sir," said Nathaniel bowing, and intending to postpone that threat if he were ever allowed the choice. Turning to Drake he said, "Tomorrow morning then, at the Royal York," turned on his heel and left.

**Evening: Queen Square, Bath.**

That evening, Nathaniel and Caradoc were standing in the twilight on the landing by Coco's door: Nathaniel convincing himself that he was glad to hear Diarmuid's voice as he waited. After dealing with Drake he had spent plenty of time soul-searching on his ride back from Redcliffe. He knew it was far from wise to spend more time alone with Coco, but needed to find out how her good deed for Abigail had gone. Coco opened the door with her customary flourish, arms wide in welcome like a burlesque dancer emerging from a stage curtain.

"A man and his dog! Come in, come in! Take a seat Nathaniel, darling. We have settled your little girl in Gloucester. She is waiting on tables in the Pelican and vows she will stay put. You could visit her if you like."

"Why should she not stay put?"

Coco screwed up her nose at Diarmuid who was fastening himself into a greatcoat and seemed ready to leave.

"Stay for the tale Diarmuid. Sit down Nathaniel, your little miss was up to mischief last night."

"Coco, she is not my miss," complained Nathaniel mildly, but took a seat whilst Caradoc made a bee-line for Diarmuid, who seemed a more likely ticket to the outdoors. Caradoc had spent too long cooped up after the exploit in Bristol and sensed the call at Coco's could be a long one.

Coco briefly explained how they had rescued Abigail after her failed assassination attempt on Shadwell and spirited her away by coach, whilst Diarmuid embroidered Coco's role, shamelessly flattering her, as they both watched the effect on Nathaniel. His obvious admiration for her entertained both of them, good-natured sybarites that they were.

"So you see, Nathaniel, our beautiful Coco is a force to be reckoned with: a force of nature sure she is. Cross her at your peril sir!"

Nathaniel was tired of the jokes. Evenings with the pair were rather like consuming absinthe, the green drink of Maison Pernod Fils: *la fee verte*, the lethal green fairy. The first sips were magical, but the wormwood inexorably rose to eclipse the magic as the long night wore on. A little went a very long way.

"You have worked wonders," he said, rising to leave.

"Walked on water," chimed in Diarmuid. "Your debts are off the scale and you will be in our thrall for ever!"

Nathaniel managed to raise a laugh. "That may be the case, but I must leave you for now. I'm truly grateful that you gave the girl a chance to redeem herself. Are you in Bath much longer, Diarmuid? I'm away to London tomorrow but will return

237

shortly. I gather there is a Reform Soiree and speaking of redemption, I need to redeem myself with Miss Peterson."

"We will be there," said Coco. "But I expect you to dance with me, Nathaniel. Diarmuid will abandon me for your Miss Peterson as soon as he sets eyes on her."

Unaccountably vexed at the chaffing, Nathaniel needed the walk to Marlborough Buildings to clear his head. He did not know exactly what he would say to Em, but knew he needed to see her. He felt a physical ache of loneliness and wanted to slide into the warmth of her embrace, and that of the whole Peterson household if they would allow it, they could do him sterling service as an emollient bath. He felt he needed to cleanse his spirit in their familial nest. He had not been used to such a retreat but had started to value it. He would not mind seeing the twins, or even Mrs Peterson, and in that respect his luck was in, if it could by any stretch of the imagination be called that. Enid informed him that the only senior Peterson available was that very lady.

Nathaniel was shown into the drawing room to greet Mrs Lydia Peterson, who was standing by the fireplace wearing a gown of pale blue silk moiré and an expression that could only be described as forbidding. "Well, at last, Mr Parry," she said acidly.

"Mrs Peterson, how glad I am to see you!" Nathaniel turned on the tattered remnants of his charm: ate humble pie for his lamentable failure to attend the Masked Ball; enquired after her health and that of the Captain; the fortunes of the twins; the situations of Miss Anna Grant and Mr Henry Blake; the progress of Miss Grant and Mr Blake's wedding plans; and of course, he wondered where Miss Peterson might be. The chill in Mrs Peterson's demeanour lifted, reluctantly, and by degrees. This was a game he played well and he was rarely resisted.

"We realised of course that you were unavoidably delayed by the unfortunate occurrences in Bristol. A place I always regard as demonstrating the most shameless vulgarity I might say. It seems to me to be the fount of all evil-doing in this part of the world." She smiled thinly, he could almost hear the ice break. "We did appreciate your letters of apology. And I know that some poor girls were saved, Mr Parry. I fully appreciate the need for discretion, my husband has explained that matters of national importance are involved. Quite heroic, I can see that now." She had not seen it at all a mere hour ago and had remonstrated volubly as Oliver and Emma had prepared to go to the poor-house to appoint one of them as a kitchen domestic. "Even as we speak the Captain and Emma are in Walcot, negotiating employment for a child, I believe by the name of Frances."

There was no point in staying longer. Catching Em alone today was going to be

238

impossible. Better delay it until he returned from London.

"I gather there is a Reform Soiree at the Rooms on the 5<sup>th</sup> November." He hurried on despite a new ice-age tightening its grip on Mrs Peterson's features. "I intend to return and attend, hoping to redeem myself somewhat and escort Miss Peterson."

"Perhaps it would be wise not to make too firm a declaration Mr Parry," said Mrs Peterson, surprising and also profoundly depressing him, by arranging her face in a poignantly rueful smile.

## 1st November, 1831, the Bath-London Road.

The coach journey to London was a sore trial for John Drake. Parry made it abundantly clear before the first change of horses that he knew as much as he, Drake, knew of Ravenswood's opium runs, the illicit trade in females and the nefarious methods employed to obtain the same. He also knew of the calamity in the caves, and worse than all of this, he knew of Drake's complicity in all aspects of the venture and his connivance in the suppression of Parry's reports to Melbourne. To add insult to injury, these painful home truths were imparted in gruesome discomfort on the roof of the coach to ensure privacy, and on their return to the inside seats, after a change of horses, he had to endure Parry's cavalier exchanges with the other passengers and the attentions of the dog Caradoc, who had taken an entirely unwarranted interest in him. It was a trying and miserable day.

Nathaniel's spirits had risen with every mile they covered. He managed to let Drake know that his plotting was discovered without divulging the identity of the informant. Cornelius Lee remained anonymous as Nathaniel's confederate. He was free to deliver whatever retribution of his own he wished to visit on the heads of the crew of the *Blue Dragon*, the shadowy Count, or even, in the fullness of time, Ravenswood himself. Though, reflected Nathaniel, it would probably take more than Lee, talented as he was, to bring down such a well-connected scourge as Edwin Ravenswood. Drake's experiences with him must have been severe indeed, as he seemed entirely unmanned by them. There was no trace of the greedy, swaggering braggart, the bumptious and callous superior, just the empty shell that had housed him. Drake had even tormented himself, in the long silences between bouts of home-truths, with the suggestion that Ravenswood had abandoned him so utterly that he had himself taken Nathaniel into his confidence and revealed all. By the time they reached Reading, Nathaniel had even been moved to sympathy and encouraged Drake to relive his more positive experiences as special constable. The chance meeting with Mr Brunel was expanded upon and enlarged, to become glorious, recasting Drake from casual conversationalist to Brunel's confidante and friend, his brush with a looter would have given the Bow Street men a run for their money. By the time they rattled over the London cobbles Drake had retrieved some semblance of self-esteem and it was not a moment too soon for his emergence from the pit, as the meeting with Melbourne and Palmerston was scheduled for the following day.

## Morning: 2nd November, 1831, Carlisle Lane, Lambeth, London.

Nathaniel had had a good sleep at his lodgings in Carlisle Lane. Fortunately his letter had arrived in time and the housekeeper had been able to make herself busy on his behalf. He had been greeted with a dust and bug free apartment, a bowl of clean water and an aired bed: nothing not to like. Apart from the silence. He had risen this All Souls Day with no morning chorus from Martha, no chirruping from the Johnty or Mary's soft steps on the landing. No crashes as Tobias careered down the stairs, no wheezing cackle from Old Tom. Caradoc too seemed to feel bereft and was reluctant to be left, but eventually saw the sense of it. Nathaniel stoked the fire, bade him good-day and stepped outside in his three-caped greatcoat, glanced up and down the deserted road, then swung his swordstick full-circle and tapped off smartly towards Westminster Bridge. November had come with a vengeance and there was a vicious east wind cutting up the Thames estuary from the North Sea. He missed the wild west wind, the softer breath of Autumn, Shelley's enchanter scattering the ghostly leaves. But there was no time left to dwell on his loss; he pulled his hat down hard and hurried on to Whitehall. He was heading for Downing Street, the current head-quarters of both the Home and Foreign Offices and as such official lair of both the noble lords.

Melbourne lounged, rather than sat, opposite Nathaniel and Drake, but there was nothing relaxed in his mood. He appeared testy and eyed them bleakly across his desk. Percy was busy arranging their various reports before him so Melbourne could remind himself of them at a glance. Nathaniel noted that one was distinctly more battered than the others, creased and curling at the edges: it was one of his. Percy caught his eye and risked flashing a conspiratorial grin in his direction. The two employees sat in silence as Melbourne ran his eyes over the reports again, eye-lids half closed, but one tapping finger on the desk signalling his displeasure. Melbourne tapped with increasing resolve: tap, tap, tap, remorseless as a clock, until Drake could bear it no longer.

"My Lord, I hope you were pleased with my," he paused unwillingly, "that is, our reports from the south-west. My Lord Palmerston has expressed his pleasure in the links I have forged with Mr Ravenswood, the Bristol ship owner. He will be a

240

reliable source of information on the status of the opium trade to China and is a man of powerful influence in the area. He is a loyal Whig supporter."

Melbourne glared balefully. "Valuable as that link may prove to be Mr Drake, we must focus our attention on your other duties in the area. Parry's early reports of the trouble fomenting in Bristol were of particular utility. And," he added in a theatrical undertone, "his cautionary comments regarding Ravenswood's enterprises did not go unappreciated."

Drake felt the sweat trickle down his back and he tugged at his neckcloth for relief.

Melbourne continued: "The rash of violent outbreaks since the Lords rejected the Bill has been greatly disturbing and it was only by the swiftest action on the part of local magistrates that it was contained. The disgraceful scenes in Bristol show that action was in that case far from swift. The commanding officer Brereton and the Mayor are being questioned for their lamentable failure to order an immediate cavalry charge on Saturday the 29$^{th}$, as soon as the Mansion House was attacked. Arrests are likely." He sighed as if exhausted already by the prospect. "Brereton's was potentially a capital crime. Capital crime damn it!" He seemed suddenly animated, and repeated the charge fiercely, the energy of it rousing him to lean menacingly over the desk, before slumping back. "Law and order, gentlemen, law and order: it relies on swift and efficient action from our Justices of the Peace. The yeomen cavalry are our backstops. Come the day when there are police forces in all towns and counties we will be better informed and better able to control the mobs. That day is a long way off and will no doubt bring with it problems and annoyances all of its own." He waved a weary hand towards the pile of reports. "Bristol is now over-run with detachments from every county of the south-west. And there's the Welsh brigade from Cardiff. We've even sent damned frigates to patrol the Severn!"

Melbourne ruminated for a while, then, seemingly satisfied he looked up, and Nathaniel decided to build a few bridges.

"Mr Drake is probably too modest to tell you my Lord, but he enlisted as special constable in Bristol whilst I was engaged in my work in Bath."

He sat, impassive, as Melbourne grunted a few enquiries and Drake bleated a few words in response. It would not do any harm to offer a life-belt to the drowning man. It would act as a reassurance that Nathaniel was unlikely to inform on him and pave the way for future work, converting Drake from an active enemy to a more humble and congenial colleague.

"Well then, the immediate dangers seem to be over. What!" continued Melbourne, "But I require you both to return to the West Country to keep a weather eye open. I gather that one of our up and coming supporters has disappeared. A Mr Vere of the New Bank? I had considered appointing him to the magistrates' bench. It would appear that the existing bench has at least a quorum of imbeciles singularly ill-equipped to deal with the ferocity of the populace. Lord Palmerston is keen for Mr Ravenswood to be appointed and I intend to appoint my other close contact, a Captain Peterson, who has kept me informed throughout. Excellent man. Speaks highly of you Parry."

Nathaniel could not disguise his surprise. "Captain Peterson? Your contact in Bath?" To see Parry wrong-footed gave Drake another crumb of comfort. He hadn't seen that bloody man so comprehensively baffled since he'd met him. It wasn't much, but on a barren day such as this it did a little to raise his game.

## Evening: 5th November, 1831. The Assembly Rooms, Bath.

The Rooms were full to bursting with Bath's *beau monde* and a fair sprinkling of eminent Bristolians, briefly escaping the ruins of their own city for a Reformers' fund-raiser. A string quartet was performing the country sets, lathered in sweat with the effort, faces like the morning sun, armpits chaffed and raw as they sawed away in their embroidered livery. The dance floor beneath the sparkling chandeliers was thronged with lines of dancers, some puffing down the lines, some prancing, some quite lost a full four beats behind and scrambling to catch up. There was an air of defiance in the revelry and a sense of triumph. Though the Bill was not yet through, the victory of law and order over the dark forces of riotous revolt was something to celebrate. On this Bonfire Night, unlike other reforming cities, Bath had not resorted to burning effigies of the Lords and Bishops in the place of Guy Fawkes. The city had bandaged its wounds and was, by and large, open for business. They were ready for the next bout.

Captain and Mrs Peterson, Anna Grant and Henry Blake, Tilly Vere and Howard Dill, Dr Parry and, a very rare sighting indeed, Mrs Parry, made up one set and were cutting reasonable figures in the *Sir Roger de Coverley*, the grand finale of the country dances.

Further down the floor, Coco and Diarmuid were stepping out with a group of younger dancers, two giggling girls in their first season, two raw-boned young men from the country set and an aspiring politician and his wife down to see Diarmuid and accompany him to London after the week-end revels. "Bi'Jaysus," whispered Diarmuid in Coco's ear as they met again after the furious section of strip the willow. "These two young bloods are fox hunting men and cutting a fine dash. It's goin' to do for me! Drinks at the next halt!"

"Drinks it is!" shouted Coco as they capered down the line.

"What ho!" hallooed one of the young men as he tore by. "Don't mind if we do! What!"

At a table in the corner sat a quartet in close conversation. One man seemed sunk in thought, the other paying relaxed attention to a handsome, brittle woman in her late thirties. His wife seemed tense, attempting to break into the conversation between her husband and her friend but not quite managing to do so. The exchanges did not go unremarked. Both women were decked out in sumptuous gowns of the latest fashion, eclipsing the boldest of Bath's beauties, including the sparkling Tilly Vere. Their finery, and in particular their flashing jewels had drawn much attention, including a sharp glance from Coco who had made it her business to scrutinise the pair as she sped by.

"Perhaps we should dance, Mr Ravenswood," said the handsome woman, her hauteur exchanged for a beguiling smile. "I seem to have some dances free."

"Perhaps we should," he answered. "But not a country romp, surely Mrs Drake."

"Oh no Mr Ravenswood, I think they are finishing, perhaps a waltz?"

"And Mr Drake shall dance with me," said Amanda, her eyes glittering with fury as she turned to him. "Let us not sit idly on our hands sir."

Away from the hurly-burly, Emma Peterson had taken refuge in the ladies' cloakroom. She stood before a mirror, expressionless. Nathaniel had not yet arrived and she was summoning the courage to return to the ballroom. She had spent a trying afternoon in Anna's company listening to wedding plans, to tales of the progress of the trousseau, which was formidable, and to monologues on the excellence of Henry Blake. She was certain she could take no more of the same. She had exhausted most avenues of conversation with Dr and Mrs Parry, her mother having forbidden her to touch on the subject of the rapid advance of the cholera, as well as any mention of the peculiar circumstances of the arrival of their new kitchen maid. Not that she would have discussed Nathaniel's business in public. She felt herself flush at the thought of his name and leaned closer to the mirror. She would not cry, but did she look as though she had? She had had another note from him it was true, telling her of his rooms in Lambeth and his walks by the Thames. It rested in her reticule even now, but she prevented herself from taking it out. Her new found self-assurance was in grave danger of shipwreck. Like Shelley. After their game with *The Eve of St Agnes* she had prepared by re-reading more Keats, more Byron and much more Shelley. Poor shipwrecked Shelley. She recited to herself:

"And the sunlight clasps the earth, and the moonbeams kiss the sea; What is all this kissing worth, If thou kiss not me?"

And one tear slowly welled up to roll down her cheek.

**Off Cape Finisterre, aboard the *Blue Dragon*.**

Cornelius had been able to ensure that his four principal allies amongst the crew shared his small cabin with him. He had his two most trusted friends, the sailors who had fired the *Mathilda* and covered Nathaniel's escape from Redcliffe as well as two others, both regular players in the Three Sugar Loaves, men who had proved their worth. The *Blue Dragon* had floated on the ebb tide, down the Avon to the Severn Estuary without mishap. Luckily for them all, given the mood of Ravenswood and also of Kizhe, both pilot and tide were ready to see them out when Ravenswood issued his commands. Delay would have been painful for everyone concerned. Also to his surprise, Trevellis's ploy had managed to succeed and assuage Kizhe's temper. They had anchored off North Devon as planned and the Captain had secured the purchase of four blonde paupers from a secluded rural poor-house, all under ten years of age. They had been added to the cache in the secure cabin to travel with the other child brought from Redcliffe Parade. There had been no noise from the cabin, which boded ill, but Cornelius was powerless to relieve their condition. A hulking woman with suspiciously muscled forearms was in charge of them, all guarded by two of Kizhe's most loyal men.

Kizhe himself had been allocated a superior cabin near Trevellis, protected by a couple of his men and it was only at mealtimes that Cornelius had guaranteed access to it. That particular night, both of them, Kizhe's henchmen and the Captain were at supper in Kizhe's cabin.

"We will anchor at Lisbon," said Kizhe, his sharp eyes piercing Trevellis as he tore a knuckle of ham apart with a snap. "I need to see a Portuguese trader for a few more girls. The transatlantic trade still runs well there. A few more exotic birds will spice the dish." He laughed shortly, a harsh snort, briefly displaying his discoloured teeth. "After Madeira, we'll aim for Guinea. More exotic still!"

"I don't have the instructions from Mr Ravenswood for extra ports," said Trevellis gruffly, too sure of himself to notice the deadly glint in Kizhe's eye. In seconds Kizhe had lunged from his seat, drawn the short ugly weapon he habitually carried at his hip and pinned Trevellis to the back of his chair, the dull blade with its vicious hook rammed against his throat, the chair leaning back crazily, Trevellis's feet dangling clear of the floor.

"I am giving you instructions Captain," he said, quietly and slowly in the paralysed silence of the cabin. "I assure you that I take full responsibility for this," he tightened his grip making Trevellis flinch, "shall we say, this "deviation" from your preferred route. Mr Ravenswood's arrangements fell short of the Count's requirements. That was a pity," as he continued a thin trickle of blood began to seep from Trevellis's neck as the hook bit into it. "A great pity: but it will be remedied. The requirements will be fulfilled. The extra ports will be added to the journey. I remind you Captain that I have not only my own group of men on board, but a sizeable portion of the rest of the crew is also more than ready to follow my instructions. Those loyal to me will not go unrewarded. I advise you to do likewise. Do you understand me Captain?"

As Trevellis managed a strangled assent, Cornelius could only assume that the performance had been as much for his benefit as the Captain's. He let his mind roam back to the start of his assignment in the Autumn of 1830, when through his timely ambush of the crew sent from Canton, he and his men had managed to replace them and travel to England on the *Blue Dragon*. The following summer had been profitably spent embedding himself into Ravenswood's operation, but the arrival of Kizhe had made his position precarious. Since the shooting of the poacher and their fight in the wood, but especially after the discovery of the sailors with arrow wounds on the *Mathilda*, he had known that Kizhe mistrusted him. He must warn his men as Kizhe could move against them at any time, but probably would not do so yet. The meal concluded raggedly, Trevellis slinking off to his cabin leaving Kizhe and his men to finish the food. Cornelius found he had little appetite.

Alone in his own cabin after supper, Kizhe stripped off his shirt and carefully wiped his hachiwari: the helmet breaker. The squat blade with its hook was his signature weapon. Just to hold it gave him a savage, elemental pleasure. He returned it to its ornate sheath and flung himself into his hammock, holding the case up to the swinging light of his lantern and running his blunt fingers over the scroll work. He remembered every moment of the night when he first took it for his own. The dark Tokyo streets, the shrill whistles, the running feet of the police. Many of them carried a hachiwari for street fighting and to combat swordsmen, but few could match this beauty. It had battered his back and his skull as the policeman beat him to the ground, it had bruised his body and fractured his arm, but he had broken that man's neck. He laughed at the memory. Snap! Like a ham knuckle-bone! Perhaps some other necks would need to be snapped. He scowled at the thought of the rat-like Trevellis and the blundering crew, but also at the thought of Cornelius Lee. As planned, three men had sailed from China to Bristol with the *Blue Dragon*, transporting the payment from the opium and paying off Ravenswood. Three men had been expected and three had appeared, as had the sealed money chest but there was something unusual about Lee. He wasn't the usual type of envoy sent by the opium bosses in Canton: crude, venal men with men's normal appetites, men after Kizhe's own heart. Lee was abstemious, zealous: there was something strange. Kizhe paused, scouring his memory. Yes, the soft fighting style, deceptively useful, there had been something of the monk about Lee: a whiff of incense. Kizhe's scowl relaxed and he snorted out a harsh bark of pleasure at his own wit. He was resolved that any remaining mysteries would be unravelled before much longer. Enquiries would be started as soon as they put into Madras, and if his suspicions were aroused before that time, well, so much the worse for Lee. He put the helmet breaker beneath his pillow, and like the other dark creatures of the deep he drifted away, at one with the treacherous rolling of the sea.

### Martha Spence's house, Walcot St, Bath.

Nathaniel had spent considerable time preparing for the evening. He had decided on the blue neck-cloth, tied in his favourite draped Byronic knot, and his blue and white striped waistcoat. Mary had starched his shirt and Tobias had brushed his evening coat. He left Caradoc sleeping in the kitchen and after closing the door behind him, stood for a moment, undecided, on the path. Tonight he would make a decision about Em, but not quite yet. Instead of going straight up Lansdown to Alfred Street he detoured along the London Road, walking behind the houses near the river. The sky was periodically lit with squibs and he caught sight of fires burning in back gardens. Some families were out together, arcs of children squealed round fathers as they lit their small stores of fireworks against the garden fences. Some children stood like statues, silent and mesmerised by the fizz of spinning Catherine Wheels, others danced and screamed with delight as the bangers and crackers exploded. He raked the bushes with his stick as he walked, deep in thought. When he reached Grosvenor, he turned left to regain the highway. He had out-paced the pedestrians of the town and the road had become solitary. As he turned to make his way back, the odd private coach rattled by, with powdered couples making for the Rooms. He overtook two old people, strolling on the pavement, arm in arm and bundled in shawls. "Nothing in the world is single," he quoted to himself. "All things by a law divine, in another's being mingle. Why not I with thine?"

He felt pretty sure she was game for mingling. The embrace in the hall in Marlborough Buildings had been surprisingly warm, he could feel it still. But making an offer was a step further. He needed to see her. Still feeling troubled, he hurried on, but still arrived late for the soiree. The Rooms were brilliantly lit and crowded, as if society was flaunting its confidence, facing down the darkness that prowled still in the haunts of the destitute, the starving villages and the miserable city slums. Those who could afford to celebrate were resolved to do so. He made his way down the grand entrance hall of the Rooms and almost reached the entrance to the ballroom when he was waylaid by a group of revellers catching a breath of air outside the press of the dance floor.

"Mr Parry! Well met!"

Nathaniel paused reluctantly at the greeting and found himself surrounded by a group led by Neville Fairfield, his right arm muffled in a sling.

"What happened!" exclaimed Nathaniel.

"Injured in Bristol so I had to come back. Sword arm don't you know!" said Fairfield ruefully. "Thirty-six hours in the saddle we had Parry. The Captain and the rest of the troop are still under orders. Should be there mi'self."

Before he could extricate himself he had to extend pleasantries to Mrs Fairfield, to Mrs Cruttwell and all the others in the party, even before Neville began to enlarge on the deeds of the yeomen in Bristol. It all took some considerable time before he could make his way to the ballroom. He arrived at a lull in the dancing and immediately he caught sight of Coco's graceful back, instantly recognisable, and Diarmuid, talking and laughing as usual, and as usual not just to Coco, but also to a crush of young women, with their men ranged behind them, doomed to play second, third and fourth fiddles until Mr Casey had done. Nathaniel made to beat a retreat, but Diarmuid hailed him.

"If it isn't himself! Colette my dear, it is himself Mr Nathaniel Parry and just as we'd given him up for dead!"

As Nathaniel walked unwillingly towards the group he saw Em approaching. She looked pale and beautiful, in a fitted gown of cream muslin, her hair piled up with a diamond clasp, shining strands curling to her shoulders.

"Em! Miss Peterson!" he said. "I am so pleased to see you."

"Miss Peterson has come to claim me Nathaniel," said Diarmuid. "I had the divil of a job tracking her down and we are promised for this dance."

"Nathaniel you will dance with me," said Coco smiling.

From a safe seat by Howard, Tilly watched the crowds of dancers closely. She had already spotted a man she had known from her youth. John Drake had gone up in the world since their early fumbles at Frome Assemblies. But of more immediate interest, she had not missed the warmth of Nathaniel's smile as he saw Emma Peterson, nor the frisson between the two of them, Mr Casey, and his detestable partner. Earlier that Autumn she had herself kept an optimistic eye on Mr Casey but had given up when she realised the parlous state of his finances. She watched the two couples waltz out of view and turned to Howard.

"Mr Parry is much struck by Miss Peterson don't you think? But he dances with Miss Montrechet, and there is definitely something between the two of them. I can sense it."

Even as she said it she regretted it. A far-away look came into Howard's eyes.

"Ah yes my dear, Miss Montrechet." He caught sight again of Coco's whirling skirts, and Nathaniel's head close to hers as they talked. "There is most definitely something, but it need not interfere with Miss Peterson's plans."

As the music stopped Nathaniel disengaged himself from Coco's embrace, took her by the arm and steered her towards Diarmuid and Em.

"Thank you Mr Casey," Em was saying, as Diarmuid bowed low over her hand and kissed it tenderly.

"Like a will-o'-the-wisp you are to be sure," he said smiling into her eyes. "Didn't I tell you before Parry. She dances like a fairy so she does."

"Yes you did," said Nathaniel shortly. "Miss Peterson, may I have the next dance."

And even as Diarmuid complained that he had booked that dance as well, Nathaniel took her in his arms and they moved swiftly out of reach.

"Did you get my note Em?" said Nathaniel smiling, breathing in her scent and tightening his hold on her waist.

"Yes, thank you. I have them all. How long can you stay in Bath, Nathaniel?"

"Certainly a few days. I need to speak to your father."

At the light leaping in her eyes he bit back his next words. He had been going to say he had some business to discuss after his meeting with Melbourne. Instead he held her even closer.

"Em, I'm sorry."

"For what?"

"For not being here."

"You are here now, Nathaniel."

"Em we have only known each other for a month, but I've missed you whilst I've been away. Do you think you could be happy with me?"

"I have been reading Shelley," she said suddenly. "He had more of love than Keats, and I want more of it, Nathaniel. I have loved you from the first time I saw you. You must know what he said: "And the sunlight clasps the earth and the moonbeams kiss the sea," she faltered, unable to go on.

But Nathaniel could, putting his lips to her ear he whispered, "What is all this kissing worth, if thou kiss not me!"

# Epilogue: One year later

**Late afternoon: 5<sup>th</sup> November, 1832.  Brooks's Club, St James's Street, London.**

"Gad! Deuced fine this 1811!" Lord Melbourne stuck his legs out to rest them on the raised fender. Heels together, he clapped his feet smartly, three times on the trot, as coda to his enjoyment. He was ensconced in the depths of a wing-backed chair, drying out from the brief drenching he had sustained whilst moving from his coach to the club's front porch. A passing post-chaise, furiously driven by a young blood, had dashed through a deep puddle and splattered most of its contents onto his trousers. Opposite him on the other side of a low table and with his back to the main door, sat Palmerston, deep in thought, lower lip at the jut. He swallowed a mouthful of the port absentmindedly.

"Tell me if Charles comes in. I need a word."

"Doubt if you'll be in luck," said Melbourne, amused. "Poor fellow looked damned seedy earlier today. Wouldn't surprise me if he threw over the whole damned business and retired to Howick to immure himself in his library."

Palmerston narrowed his eyes, "And then who else but your good self could possibly be in line to step into Number 10?"

"Well my dear fellow," said Melbourne, lazily. "Quite so, *noblesse oblige* what!"

Palmerston was acutely aware that Lord Grey could abandon his post at any moment making his brother-in-law in waiting even more valuable to him than he already was. As the most senior Whig he was clearly the Prime Minister in waiting. After the titanic struggle with the Lords had ended in crowning success with the passage of the Reform Act in June, Charles had seemed to wilt before their eyes. Job

249

done and his place in history secured, he had faded and most days appeared as a wizened old man. The death of his favourite grandson and continuing tussles with his son-in-law had contributed to his decline. It was a matter of time, maybe a few years, or a few months, before his final retirement. Palmerston knew he must alert Melbourne to the growing threat to the Chinese trade.

"I have had a disturbing communication."

Melbourne smiled amiably. Palmerston pressed on: irritated.

"The harbours which Drake assured me would be continuously useful for opium shipments have been blockaded by Chinese troops. By some means the Emperor's forces in Canton have been made aware of the route and have taken steps to close it. Ravenswood's interests in the opium growing in India continue unmolested, but his little wheeze for landing the goods discreetly will not be running so smoothly in the future. He might have to take his chances with the ships running Company opium," He dropped his gaze and glowered into the fire. "There might come a day in the near future when the Emperor will need to be taught a lesson."

Melbourne allowed himself a sustained sigh. The prospect of expending time and energy on such an adventure was not enticing.

"My dear fellow, things might not be so bad. You know that our intelligence gathering is, well, rather hit and miss. You may not have the full story, or even a quarter of it. You're better off reading *The Times* than listening to our own people. Damned reliable those *Times* fellows. Dashed well informed." He allowed that to sink in, then continued. "We need to be alert to domestic matters Pam. Speaking of the press, it was drawn to my attention by Percy that *The Poor Man's Guardian* has seen fit to fulminate against the Act and is stirring up the lower classes for all it's worth. Which won't be much if I've anything to do with it! They're after lowering the bar on the household value for the townsmen's vote. Damned ink's barely dry on the dashed Act! Furthermore, I need hardly remind you that the day of fasting and humiliation for the cholera, demanded so vociferously by the Church, made no appreciable difference. The air, even here in London, remains foetid despite all efforts and apparently panic is setting in. Even the hackney cabs are damned near ruined as people fear using public facilities!" From the glazed expression he sensed a faltering in Palmerston's resolve and pressed his initiative home. "And quite apart from existing trials, the Factory and Education Bills must command our attention at present, not to mention the Slavery Bill. They must all be pushed through next session well before we finish our review of the Poor Law. Root and branch reform we've promised! Election promises my dear fellow. The rate payers will not stick such high poor rates for much longer. Damned stratospheric!" He looked slyly at

Palmerston. "It will be another generation in the wilderness for the Whigs if we don't deliver the goods on our watch. Younger men's careers might founder on the back benches 'til they're put out to grass."

Palmerston shrugged his shoulders. "Yes, yes. I know. First things first. The China trade is inconvenienced but has not as yet entered a critical phase. We will bide our time." Temporarily out-manoeuvred he rose abruptly and shot his cuffs. "Now my dear fellow, are you in form for gaming? I told Russell we'd be at the tables before we dine."

## Nathaniel's lodgings in Carlisle Lane, Lambeth.

Across the Thames in Carlisle Lane, a tall young man was seated by the fireplace in his top floor rooms. A wiry black and tan Welsh terrier was lying spread-eagled by the log box and, apart from the wind rattling the window-frame and the juddering lick of the flames, all that could be heard was the steady ticking of the clock on the mantel. Nathaniel Parry searched his pockets and placed two letters on the table. The one from Em had been read and re-read. He now had a collection and would add this latest one. Perhaps tomorrow he could leave for Bath. The Season had started there and his work had reached a pause: it was a good time to go. Occasional bangs and cracks outside reminded him of the day. It was twelve months to the night since he had proposed to Em. The Captain's relations with Lord Melbourne had been a surprise. He did not know if he had been manipulated, but did not really care. Byron, he decided, had a few things right. "Each kiss a heart-quake" he liked that, he'd grown attached to Em's kisses and looked forward to some more. But was Byron right about a man's love being different from a woman's, being a thing apart from the rest of his life? Perhaps, in part. He laughed and felt happy. The future seemed bright.

He took out the second letter which he had read once, clandestinely, at Whitehall where it had been delivered some weeks before and had been sitting waiting for him on Percy's desk. He had been lucky it had been scooped up by Percy, which had allowed it to remain unread before his return. Guarded though it was in tone and content, it could have been more illuminating than it intended to be if Drake had managed to cast his eyes over it. It was worn and marked from its long journey, heavily creased, the ink faded. It announced in neat italic script that it had travelled from the British Residency of Singapore, in the sub-division of Bengal, and after the first polite salutations, had much of interest to tell.

251

*"I am well set up in lodgings by the harbour,"* wrote his correspondent, *"which are serviceable despite being as sweltering and airless as you can imagine, as our latitude is virtually on the equator. I hope this news of my voyage reaches you at your London office as now, with my task complete, my thoughts frequently return to you. I want to tell you the tale of the journey we spoke of before I set sail. Also, I am curious to know how you fare. In particular I would like to hear of the undertakings you made last Autumn and trust they met with success. For my part, you will be interested to know that after leaving Bristol we added to our cargo in Devon, in Lisbon and Guinea, much to our visitor's satisfaction, and all rounded the Cape safely. We spent some time in Bombay, where significant transactions were made, before we followed the coast and rounded the extreme south of India. Our visitor disembarked in Madras but I will ensure my path crosses his again. Depend upon it. Despite heavy seas in the Gulf of Bengal and the Malacca Straits and some episodes of disturbance and discomfort aboard ship, the cargo remained in fair shape and we made landfall here in Singapore. The town had grown since I last saw it ten years before and is a thriving entrepot. No signs remain of the Dutch masters and the British reign supreme. From here we journeyed on up the Gulf of Tonkin until we reached our designated harbour. All survived and the cargo was disembarked. I did not continue north with the cargo, but left my men to fulfil that task and went alone to Canton where I reported to my employer. I have now returned to lodgings here in Singapore, awaiting my passage back to Europe where I have further business to attend.*

*So, my friend, my mission met with some success, as did yours, though the works of evil men still thrive and spread, as you say in England, like the green bay tree.*

*Until we meet again, I have the honour to be,*

*Your most humble servant, CL."*


Nathaniel smiled to himself: "And I yours Cornelius Lee: and I yours. May our paths also cross again, and in happier times."

He pocketed the letters and stood up, turning to look out at the darkening sky. The patchy clouds, wreathed with smoke from Guy Fawkes' fires, blurring and haloing the harsh white moonlight, were suddenly pierced with gold. A fizz of sparks shot up; high, wild and bright, followed by a battery of multi-coloured geysers of rich red, green, blue and silver, flying up in a fiery rainbow. He felt a surge of elation, grabbed his greatcoat and swordstick, roused Caradoc with a call of: "Mutton-chops and beer sir!" and within the minute they were down the stairs and out into the gaudy night.

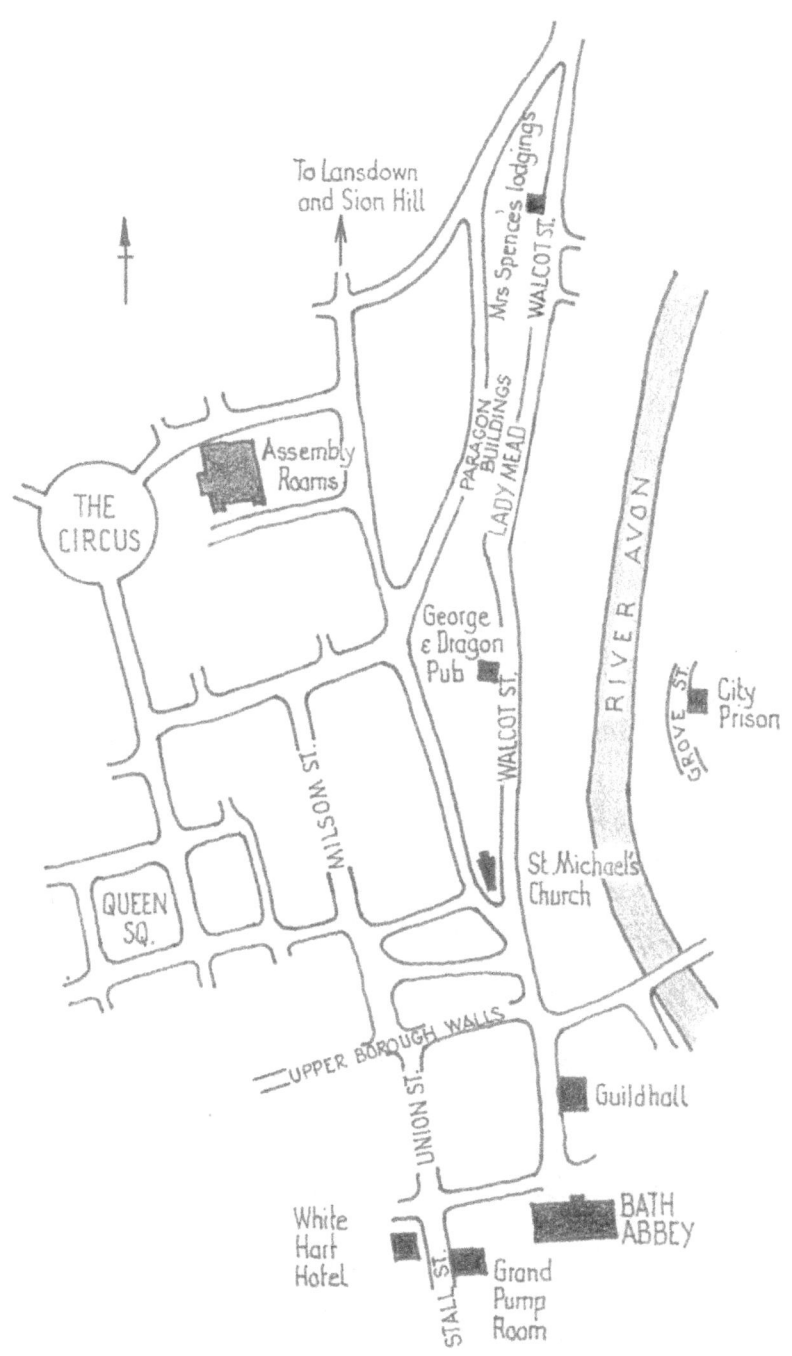

The Upper Town, Bath

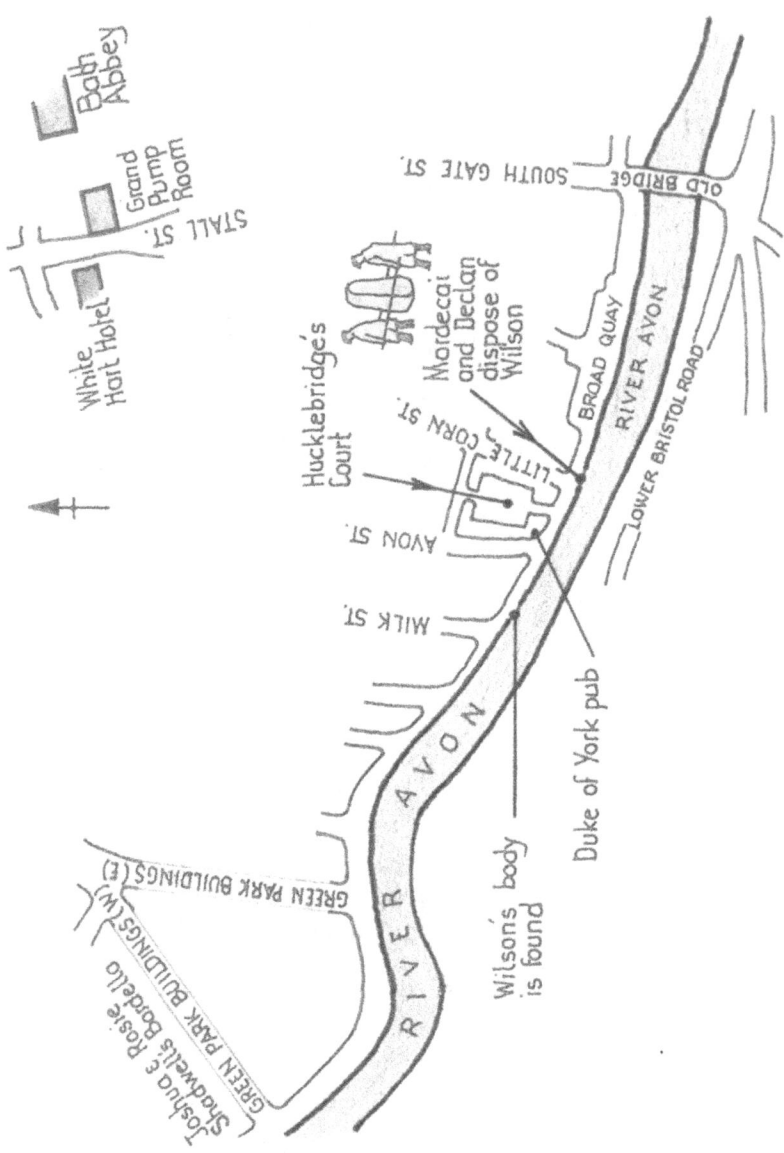

The Quays, Bath

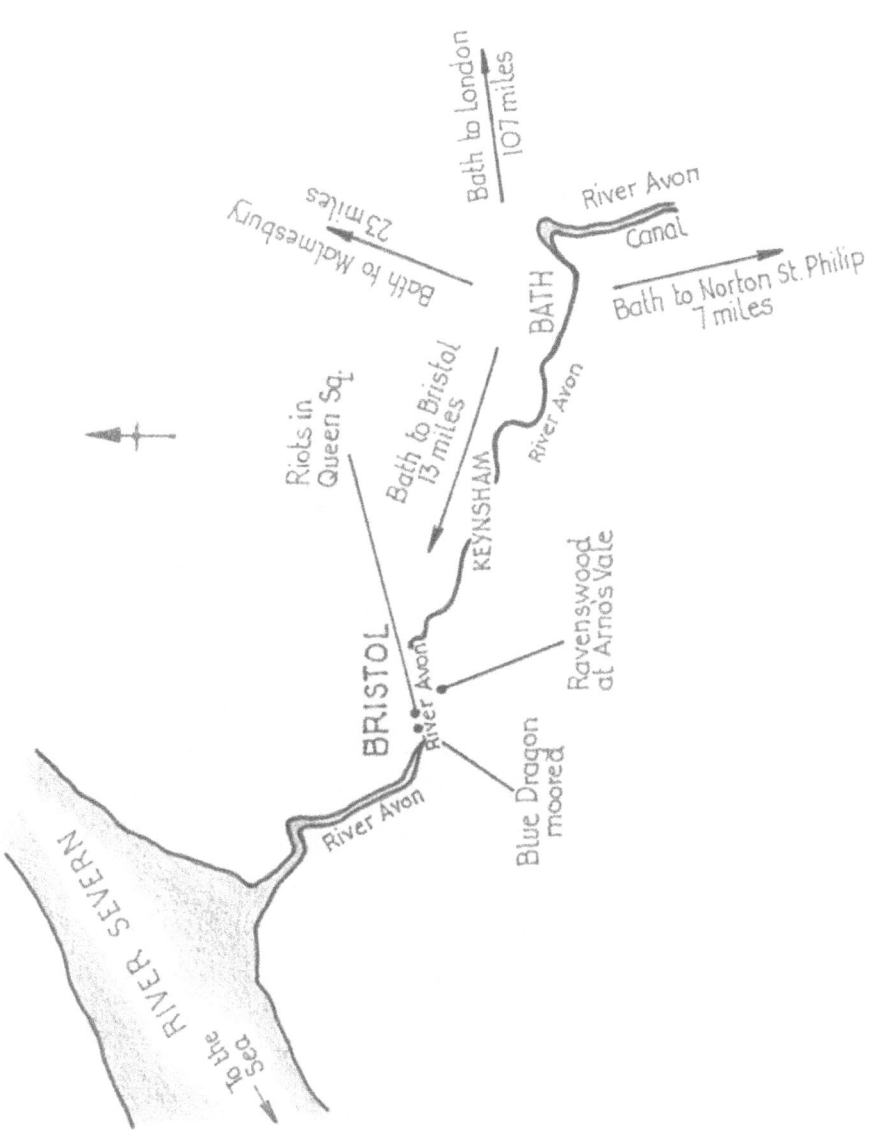

Bristol and Bath

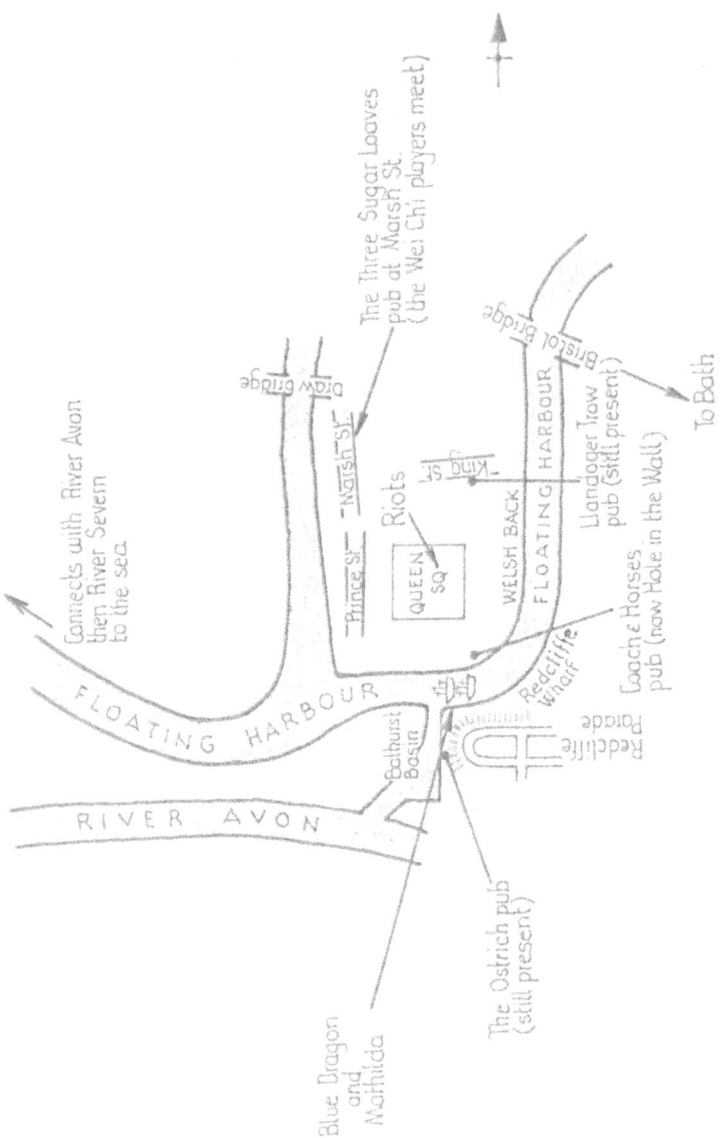

The Centre of Bristol

# Voters and Political Parties in 1831

## Voting qualifications

Approximately 10% of adult males in England and Wales were entitled to vote before the Reform Act of 1832. These men made up less than 3 % of the total population, yet even they were often unable to use their vote. Only about one third of the constituencies were contested in an "election" and open ballots were the rule. Having to declare a vote in public allowed the intimidation of voters by landlords and employers. As the right to vote was often connected to property ownership, owners of multiple properties could vote more than once.

Rural (county) constituencies had different voting qualifications from urban (borough) constituencies. All county seats observed the same rules. Adult males owning land valued at two pounds or more for the land tax were allowed to vote.

## Whigs and Tories

The two main political parties in 1831 were called the Whigs and the Tories. The party system was not as rigid as it is in the 21st century. Individuals moved more frequently between parties and approximately 60 MPs remained independent of both these groups. The party names date from the 17th century when the party more loyal to the wishes of the monarch were insulted by being called Tories. This Irish term suggested that they were encouraging the King in his support of Catholics, despite their own loyalty to the Church of England. Those who were more critical of the King became known as Whigs, a term referring to rebellious Scots.

## Authors' Note

Although this book is a work of fiction, the disorder which took place in Bristol and Bath in 1831 was all too real. The events in Bristol were notorious on a national scale as the worst of the Reform Bill riots that broke out after the rejection of the Bill in the House of Lords. Apart from Lords Melbourne and Palmerston, Doctor Parry and Captain Wilkins, all major characters are fictional, though many peripheral characters have the names of real Bath personalities of the time e.g. Mr Bishop and Mr Cooper were the landlords of the Hart, Mr Tasker ran the livery in Pulteney Mews and General Palmer was Bath's reforming MP. Also fictional is the idea that there was an organised and covert plan between the Home and Foreign Secretaries to develop surveillance during the 1831-2 Reform Bill crisis. However, as activities of that nature were not scrupulously documented we allowed our imaginations to speculate.

Whilst there was a brisk and illegal opium trade, on a triangular route from England to India to collect the drug, and then on to China for sale through brokers, the activities described in Bristol are wholly fictional. This being the case, it was very pleasing to discover that the clipper *Sea Witch* (1846) had a dragon figurehead similar to that described on the bow of Ravenswood's ship, the *Blue Dragon*. The first opium clipper was the *Red Rover*, launched in 1829 to beat the north-east monsoon and establish three opium runs per year instead of the usual one. In the 1830s the clippers came to dominate the trade. The first vessels in this class, built for speed with "rakish masts" set at an angle and sharp streamlining, were the Baltimore Clippers first used in the late 1770s during the American War of Independence. Clippers alarmed other vessels, as they were the chosen craft of privateers and pirates. Sadly, kidnapping and the trade in young girls flourished at the time. The campaign against it only gathered pace in the 1880s when it resulted in the raising of the age of consent to sixteen years.

Although the doings of the noble lords are more widely known, as both of them survived long enough in politics to become Prime Minister, the Bath characters, Dr Parry and Mr Charles Wilkins, are not familiar even in Bath. Dr Caleb Parry and his famous son William Edward were real Bath characters, as was Caleb's eldest son Dr Charles Parry. Charles and his wife lived in Bath at the time of the novel, though their characters have been imagined. Charles's gregarious nature was developed from evidence that he and William Edward grew up in an enterprising family. Caleb Parry was nationally important as a physician, and occupied his leisure time with music, painting, literature and experimental sheep farming. William Edward was a successful Arctic explorer and Charles was well known for his medical and history writing. He was active in Bath society and established an organisation to provide jobs for the unemployed. Charles Wilkins can be seen in the local newspaper reports to be not only a rich and successful mill owner, but also a kind employer. His exploits with the local Yeomanry can also be discovered in the news and letters sections of the local newspapers. Unlikely as it may seem, he really did escape in disguise over the roof of the Hart during the riot and the staff fought off the besieging mob with red-hot pokers. The regular fencing training in Bath is an invention, though Nathaniel's reference to the London club is accurate. The Bath Season of 1831 ran regular balls and the Reform Soirees were popular, though not necessarily on the nights designated in the story.

All the inns and habitations referred to, apart from Arno's Tower, were actual locations, some of which survive. Arno's Vale was a popular place for the *nouveau riche* of Bristol to build their mansions at this time, the most notable being Mount Pleasant, which is the present Arno's Court Hotel. The black stables remain beyond the Bath Road, as does the holy well of St Anne, though in a park as opposed to a wood. Detail concerning the weapons is also accurate. Nathaniel's swordstick with spring loaded quillons forming a hand-guard was based on nineteenth century examples, though his version has a special Japanese blade. The makila, a Basque walking stick, is still manufactured. In the nineteenth century it was common for one variety of makila to have a short concealed blade. The hachiwari referred to in the story is believed to be the forerunner of the jutte weapon, and was used by the Japanese police when they were unable to carry swords as they were not members of the Samurai class. Coco's use of a pepper spray was also a technique borrowed from the Japanese police of the Edo period (1603-1868). A policeman would have a small lacquered box called a gantsubushi which had a mouth-piece and pipe for directing the flow of cayenne pepper into the eyes of individuals resisting arrest. Expertise in Savate, French kick-boxing, was current in the early 1830s. This allowed Coco to have experience of this style of fighting. The fighting skills demonstrated by Cornelius reflect the well-respected Chinese martial styles, often taught in secret, which underpinned and influenced further developments of martial arts and weaponry on the island of Okinawa in Japan.

*Acknowledgements*

Accurate details concerning the locations, the political situation, the characters of the politicians, events in the Bristol Riots, and the disturbances in Bath have been researched by Alex over many years and adapted for the purposes of the narrative. The staff of Bath and Bristol Reference Libraries and Colin Johnston and his staff at

Bath Record Office were extremely helpful, as was Graham Snell, Secretary of Brooks's Club in London, who was most kind in sharing his expert knowledge of the history of the Club. We extend our grateful thanks to them all. We would also like to take the opportunity to thank our friends and family: Jane and Malcolm Thick for the time they have taken to read draft chapters and advise us of any historical infelicities they discovered. Any remaining errors rest with the authors. Thanks also to Sarah Sawyer, Richard Hill and James and Claire Kolaczkowski for their time spent in reading the draft chapters, for their comments and their encouragement. Thanks also to Stan Kolaczkowski, for his advice on martial arts, plotting and presentation, and also to Max Schonbach who assisted with the preparation of the illustrations and maps, and drew the swordstick on the cover. We also thank Ana María Espiñeira Luksić for preparation of the rest of the cover art, and Hilary Strickland for the cover layout. Finally, we appreciate the patience of Bob's wife Marina during the preparation of this work

Watch out for Nathaniel's second adventure:
*Napoleon's Gold - The Wages of Sin.*

Bath, January 2016
Dr Alex Kolaczkowski
Professor Robert Hayes

## The Authors

The nominal author of the book, Alex E. Robertson, is a pen name, incorporating the names of the creators of the work. The text was written by Dr Alex Kolaczkowski, based on an original idea from Robert Hayes, who is also the research collaborator, producer and editor of the project.

**Dr Alex Kolaczkowski** has taught history at schools in Bath and Bristol, as well as in Wiltshire, Oxfordshire and Surrey. Her B.Ed degree was awarded by the University of Bristol and her Ph.D by the University of Bath. A dedicated teacher, passionate about all aspects of her subject, she took her pupils on frequent field trips, making ancient, medieval, early modern and modern topics alike come vividly to life. Bath and Bristol are cities very well known to her having lived, studied and worked in both of them. Her expertise in Bath history stemmed from her years spent researching the city as a case-study for her doctoral topic on the development of municipal socialism and the civic ideal in the nineteenth century. By invitation from the Dictionary of National Biography she provided the entry for Sir Jerom Murch who was Mayor of Bath on seven occasions, and wrote a paper on aspects of Bath Non-Conformism for the Unitarian Journal. These research activities helped provide her specialist background knowledge of the period and places in which the novel is set.

**Professor Robert Hayes** is a full-time academic at the University of Alberta in Canada. Apart from his distinguished research and teaching in chemical engineering, he is a calculating thinker with an interest in mystery and intrigue within a historical context. As a PhD student at the University of Bath in the early 1980s, he developed an interest in the game of Go (which originated as Wei Ch'i in China), often travelling to Bristol to play at the Go Club in Hotwells, and later was a founder member of the Bath Go Club at the Crown Inn, Bathwick Street. During the 1990s he was a frequent visitor to Bath and Bristol. In addition to his passion for historical mysteries, he is a lover of fine wines, single malt whisky, and of course whiskey.

## Brief introduction to the use of local dialect

To convey the atmosphere of the region, some conversations with people native to the area are expressed in a phonetic version of a south-west English accent. There are many varieties of this gentle rural accent, and the version used in this novel is typical of the accent that could still frequently be heard in Bath well into the twentieth century.

The accent tends to exclude letters at the beginning and ends of words, to shorten words, and alter grammar. In the nineteenth century it was normal for the lower classes in all areas to exclude the "h" at the start of words, and if they wished to sound very polite to include an "h" at the beginning of words where there was no such letter. To help the reader, we have provided explanations of selected phrases as they first appear.

This will help visitors, particularly those from abroad, to identify and appreciate the local accent, which can still be heard occasionally today.

| Phonetic version | Meaning |
| --- | --- |
| **Prologue** | |
| I'd take 'er home | I would take her home |
| I can't see 'er fittin' in | I cannot see her fitting in |
| Exac'ly | Exactly |
| Come wi'me mi'dear | Come with me my dear |
| | |
| **Chapter 1** | |
| Oiy could 'elp | I could help |
| 'is beard | his beard |
| y'r lodgings | your lodgings |
| mi' and | my hand |
| Thank'ee sir | Thank you sir |
| The Dragon ain't far | The Dragon is not far |
| Not that she's a drinker mind | She does not drink heavily you understand |
| She be not | She is not |
| then we was thronged | then we were crowded |
| rollickin' times | exciting times |
| beatin' | beating |
| Oiy don't start 'til breakfast | I don't start until breakfast |
| til 'e's on 'is feet | until he is able to work again |
| givin' us warning | giving us warning |

| | |
|---|---|
| not just them as | not just those who |
| who 'mongst us | who amongst us |
| Oiy 'ave | I have |
| Oiy pays | I pay |
| somewheres | somewhere |
| Them as pays | Those who pay |
| see 'ow it goes | see how it goes |
| what was to 'appen | what was to happen. |
| 'Nat-chu-ral roights' we 'ave | 'Natural rights' we have |
| the workin' and the fightin' | the working and the fighting |
| they Frenchey wars | the French wars |
| Oiy vote 'cos moiy 'ouse | I vote because my house |
| 'cos 'e lives | because he lives |
| Ye 'ave representation | You have representation |
| ye'll 'ave more | you will have more |
| mi'self | my self |
| Majisty | Majesty |
| more 'an | more than |
| ye're a mouthin' | you are expressing |
| sentimints | beliefs |
| No one's a mouthin' loike a Yankee as I 'ear | No one is speaking like an American that I can hear. |
| ye're a patriot through an' through | you are entirely a patriot |
| I'm not sayin' as I want | I am not saying that I want |
| Tis a mighty | It is a mighty |
| They great cities | The great cities |
| 'E never give | He never gave |
| 'oo did? | who did? |
| Bastard was 'eavy | The bastard was heavy |
| Get 'im out | Get him out |
| Ye've skewered 'im | You have stabbed him |
| done 'imself in | committed suicide |

**Chapter 2**

| | |
|---|---|
| She straight away upped and said | She immediately said |
| afore she leaves | before she leaves |
| 'as bin found | has been found |
| saw 'im a-floatin' 'ead down | saw him floating with his head down |
| is norm'ly | are normally |
| go a-tramplin' the babe | treading on the baby |

263

'ee do get sore underfoot

Ye young besom

Frenchies a-winding up

Poles hammer and tongs at the Ruskies.

Find a good 'orse sir?

go amok at the weekends.

H'immigrants

When mi ma was

Little 'Ell

Oiy ain't never bin

loike a new pin

annoyingly he is often under your feet

You young rascal

the French annoying

the Poles attacking the Russians

Did you find a good horse sir?

become violent at the weekends

Immigrants

When my mother was

Little Hell

I have never been

like a new pin (shining and clean)

## Chapter 3

Come ye over

take a seat along o'me

ye didn't!

Don't ye be a worritin' y'self

are a-wantin' it

were a-cryin' out

were agin' it

All they wild talkers

and a-wearin' they damned

thought 'e talked sense

Critters you never

'Twas ever the same!

Do'ee know

to improve they selves?

Oiy gat somethin'

Two of 'em 'eard a racket

Lot of runnin' an' roarin'

Come here

sit next to me

you did not!

Do not worry yourself

are wanting it

were demanding

were against it

All of the aggressive speakers

and wearing the damned

thought he spoke sensibly

Creatures you never

It was always the same.

Do you know

to improve themselves?

I have something

Two of them heard loud noises

There was a lot of running and shouting

## Chapter 4

Per'aps

Perhaps

## Chapter 5

Plough boys most of 'em

Slavers y'know

Got a mind o' its own!

You all roight wit' other end

Most of them are plough boys

They were in the slave trade you know

It has got a mind of its own!

Are you alright with the other end

Ooh arr
Oiy got 'er 'oisted perfect 'ere!
Ye young demon!
mi'boys from Little 'Ell
Oiy would welcome it ike a brother mi'self
Thirsty work  conversin' with this young
sprig 'ere
Just a'fore ye go to be closeted in the
parlour
folk a'goin' down the street

Sweep you a crossin' sir?

Go on moiy love!
Land 'er another right 'ook!

outside o'these walls?  And you're payin'?

Any'ow, I 'eard voices when 'e left
regulars 'ere

Oh yes
I have hoisted it perfectly!
You young demon!
my boys from Little Hell
I would welcome it like a brother
I feel thirsty after talking with this
young child
Just before you go for a secret
conversation in the parlour
people going down the street
Shall I sweep the road so that you may
cross sir?
Go on my love!
Hit her again with your right fist!
outside of these walls? And you are
paying?
Anyway, I heard voices when he left
regular customers here

## Chapter 6

his funeral mebbe!
Yon
Jus' look at that missus
when 'e's out o' they crib.
'e be!

Where wast a-goin' my 'andsome?

young buck

his funeral maybe!
yonder (over there)
Just look at that madam
when he is out of his cradle.
he is.
Where were you going my handsome
child?
lively young man

## Chapter 7

Methody
But 'twas to
'Ad one once.
if you take mi' meanin'

a-sayin 'e speaks for Bris'l!

Though we've bin a-osin' out to
Liverpool sin' moiy ould dad were a boy
men are 'ungered
Up an' at 'em bully boys!

Methodist
But it was to
I once owned one.
if you understand my meaning
saying that he speaks on behalf of
Bristol!
We have been losing trade to Liverpool
  since my old dad was a boy
men are hungry
Up and attack them my fine boys!

## Chapter 8

| | |
|---|---|
| Been after 'im from 'is first showin' comin' over Totterdown | They have followed him since he first appeared from Totterdown |
| but 'e's short o' decent men. | he has not enough good men. |
| itchin' for a scrap | wanting a fight |
| rilin' everybody | annoying everyone |
| Jack Tars are no cat's paw | Sailors will not be used |
| Serve 'im up to us! | Present him to us! |
| Aye! | Yes! |
| I could 'ave done with a leg or two o' that beef | I wanted a leg or two of that beef |
| Us'll wet our whistles here | We will have a drink  here |
| y'ere (Welsh accent) | Here |
| You'll 'ave to put 'er down Abi | You will have to put her down Abi |
| Rouse yersel' | Rouse yourself |
| smashin' | smashing |

## Chapter 9

| | |
|---|---|
| Leavin' the docks be | Leaving the docks unmolested |
| Glad to make y'r acquaintance sir! | Glad to meet you sir! |
| I'm not goin' 'ome  neither | I am not going home either |
| Well Mister 'll prob'ly | The man will probably |
| Come up for the season he did | He came up for the Bath season |
| No. Missus' son's come back. | No. The lady's son has returned |
| in rollickin' high spirits | in extremely high spirits |
| Hundreds were millin' round | Hundreds were crowding around |
| Not thinkin' of joinin' 'em were 'ee? | You were not thinking of joining them were you? |
| Rioters movin' off to'ard the Abbey | rioters moving off towards the Abbey |
| givin' 'em what for | attacking them fiercely |

## Chapter 10

| | |
|---|---|
| Oiy 'ave never 'eard the like | I have never heard anything like it |
| on that occashun | on that occasion |

# Napoleon's Gold -
# The Wages Of Sin

# Alex E. Robertson

# Contents

# Cast of principal characters

## Agents and officials of the British government

| | |
|---|---|
| Nathaniel Parry | gentleman, employed as government agent |
| John Drake | Foreign Office employee |
| Lord Palmerston | Foreign Secretary |
| Lord Melbourne | Home Secretary |
| Richard Percy | Home Office administrator |

## Agents of the Imperial Chinese government

| | |
|---|---|
| Cornelius Fu Lee | undercover agent |
| Fong and Chen | his retainers |

## The Parry household

| | |
|---|---|
| Emma Parry | Nathaniel's wife |
| Caradoc | his dog, a Welsh terrier |
| Frances Price | Emma's maid |
| Tobias Caudle | manservant |
| Mrs Rollinson | housekeeper |
| Harriet Pullen | kitchen maid |

## The Peterson household

| | |
|---|---|
| Captain Oliver Peterson | retired sea captain |
| Lydia | his wife |
| Maddie and Ginette | his twin teenage daughters |
| Céline Junot | their governess |

## The Vere household

| | |
|---|---|
| Mathilda Vere | lady, resident of Lansdown Crescent |
| Howard Dill | her gentleman friend |
| Mrs Danby | her mother |

## The Spence household

| | |
|---|---|
| Martha Spence | landlady, resident of Walcot |
| Thomas | her father-in-law |

| Matthew | her son |
| Mary | her daughter-in-law |
| Johnty | her grandson |
| Benjamin Prestwick | tenant and comrade of her late husband |
| Declan O'Dowd | tenant |
| Finn O'Malley | tenant |
| Jimmy Congo | Matthew's African parrot |

## The Shadwell household

| Joshua Shadwell | owner of the Green Park brothel |
| Rosie | his wife |
| Jabez and Billy | his bodyguards and enforcers |
| Clarissa Marchant | prostitute, known as Clari |
| Letty Watson | prostitute |

## Bath characters

| Dr Charles Parry | physician, related to Nathaniel |
| Mrs Parry | his wife |
| Diarmuid Casey | Member of Parliament |
| Colette Montrachet | courtesan, known as Coco |
| Robert Turner | printer |
| Arthur Jamieson | printer |

## The Ravenswood household in Bristol and contacts

| Edwin Ravenswood | ship owner and merchant |
| Amanda | his wife |
| Eli Trevellis | captain of the *Blue Dragon*, Ravenswood's clipper |
| Mr Kizhe | Ravenswood's Russian-Mongolian business associate, (pronounced: Kee-jay) |
| Mr Qiang | Kizhe's servant,    (pronounced: Chahng) |
| Jerry Tiler | Kizhe's associate and "shadow" |

## The Drake household in London

| Charlotte Drake | wife of John Drake, known as Lottie |
| Elizabeth | his daughter, known as Lizzie |

**The Mortimer-Buckley household in London**

| | |
|---|---|
| Sir Giles Mortimer-Buckley | baronet and Member of Parliament |
| Lady Leonora | his wife |
| Prudence Battersby | his daughter |
| Lulu Battersby | his granddaughter |
| Maisie Trickett | Lulu's nanny |

**The Montrachet household in the Medoc, France**

| | |
|---|---|
| Jules Delgarde-Montrachet | Coco's brother |
| Claudette | his wife |
| Marc and Simone | his children |
| Pierre Valdez | his foreman |
| Antoine Lacaze | his labourer |

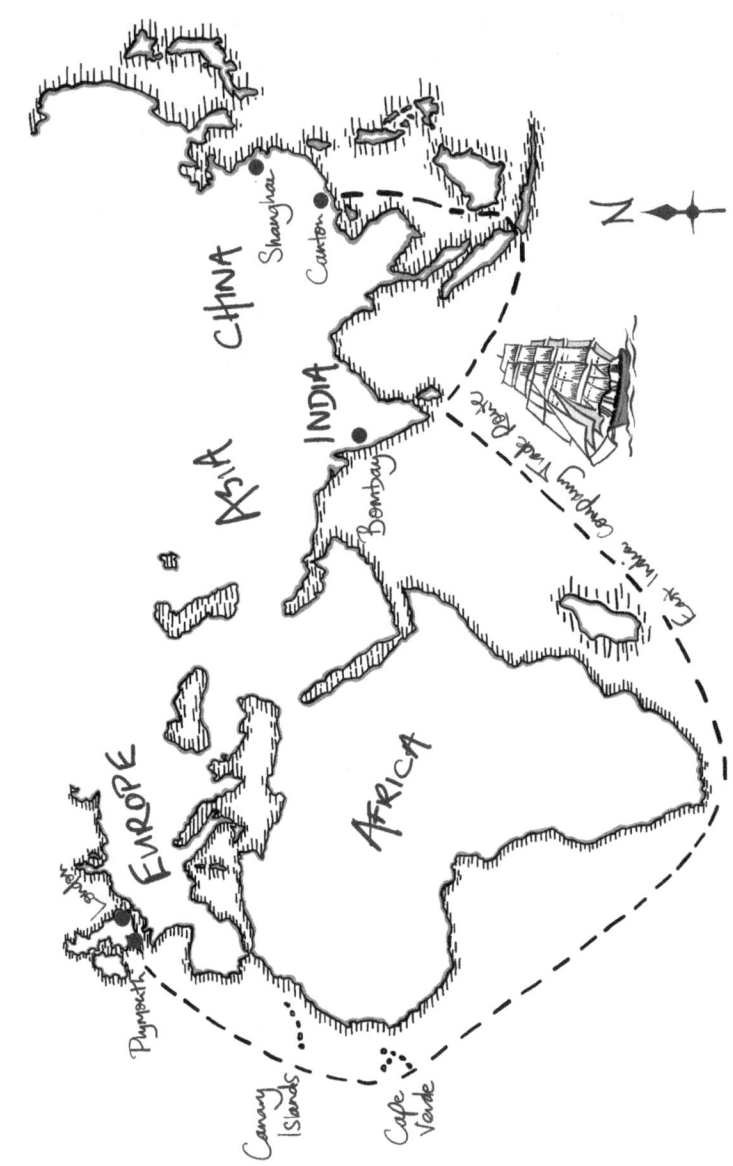

The Trade Route to China

# Prologue

**Twenty-five years before the events related in this book.**
**Evening: 20th December, 1808. Beñat's *Posada*, the Spanish Basque country.**

They sat motionless before the fire, intent on the flames and the seething mixture in the pot. At first you would not notice them; they were so still, one on each side of the hearth, like caryatids, the stone maidens of Karyai. Then on an instant their heads lifted and they looked into each other's eyes, the one a mirror image of the other, both flesh and blood, with the same sharp beauty. Izar's bracelets rang and flashed as she reached for more of the gritty powder in her pack and sprinkled it into the broth. She smiled to her other self with satisfaction as she stirred the mixture and it smoothed and cleared. Her sister took up the bellows, gently squeezed a rush of air under the logs to make the sparks fly and then reached for a handful of seeds. Her hand circling, she murmured a low chant and cast the dry husks into the flames. Aromatic smoke wreathed up to fill the ingle-nook of the rough stone fireplace and crept out into the room, flowing round the wooden tables and rising in clouds, crowding the blackened ceiling. The girls crouched lower, mesmerised by their task, absent-mindedly hitching up their skirts as the heat built, running their hands over their legs as they felt the fire burn.

The tall fair man at the bar had eyes only for them. He took another slug of the local spirit, searing his throat with the heat, and let his eyes roam over their bodies.

1

They had arrived an hour before and set to work. As the fire had beaten hotter, they had shed their fur-lined cloaks and woollen shawls; shaken out long manes of black hair which snaked down to their waists. They had lithe brown arms, high sculpted breasts showing above tight-laced bodices and they moved like wild cats. He felt more than equal to taking the both of them that very night and sniggered to himself at the thought of it. But even as his mind played with the idea, savouring it, a cloud of denser smoke billowed out into the room and for a moment he thought he saw in its depths the shade of a third woman, a white sister, turning cavernous eye sockets on him and a gash of a smile. Alarmed and confused he turned away, fingers fumbling for the silver medallion at his throat. Rattled out of his lust, he fixed his eyes instead on the capacious rump of the innkeeper's wife, which wobbled busily as she hacked up cold meat for the supper.

Izar spoke softly as she rose from the hearth.

"The wagon has left the valley. It is time."

Without a word, the silent sister wrapped her shawl round the pot handle, lifted it from the fire and followed Izar round the side of the bar and down the dark corridor to the kitchen, out of sight of prying eyes.

Owen Parry had paid off the innkeeper and brought the twins down from the mountain to play their part. They needed little persuasion to join in any plan designed to torment the French invaders, as he had discovered earlier that year. Shot and beaten, he had been retrieved from the mountain by the pair of them and patched up in their hut. His wounds had healed quickly and neatly, so he had proof they had the touch to cure, but he also knew they could wreak destruction. There was no need to worry about their part in the night's work. Most of his experiences in Spain had been in these mountains and he was used to their discomforts, which was fortunate. He sat perched on top of the stable roof, braced against the side of its stone chimney, his eyes locked on to a distant peak of the Montes Vascos, scouring it for the tell-tale glimmer of a lantern. He had not slept for two days and his eyes burned as he peered into the gloom, willing himself to stay awake. It was dark and murky, and as usual, ruthlessly cold, with a hard frost petrifying every surface and piercing through his cloak to his bones. An iron silence gripped the mountain and the grey shred of road that hung on its slopes like a cadaver's tattered bandage, marking the way to the isolated inn. Not one peasant, beast or bird had ventured abroad, not even one creature of the night, not a fox, not one hunting owl. It was unfortunate that he could not trust the jovial Captain, or either of his raw assistants, to take the watch. But that was probably as it should be. Life, in his experience, never offered good fortune without a balancing dose of bad. It was in the nature of things. Owen grimaced as

2

the inn door swung open, shedding a spear of light and snatches of talk across the courtyard. A powerfully-built man, over-tall for his role as a Basque shepherd, strode towards the stable.

"Fancy a mug of brandy and water? Hot as hell and kicks like a donkey!"

Waving a full mug, Captain Giles Mortimer-Buckley grinned up at Owen, carelessly slopping some of the hell brew over his boots as he did so. He appeared bland and affable, but Owen was not convinced. Captain Buckley's antics over the last week had suggested he had the potential for much more than his face offered and most of it would be unwelcome. Conventionally handsome, but with early signs of dissipation blurring his features, Buckley had an eye to the main chance. His war was being waged to fill his pockets, rather than for personal or national glory. He was not a typical recruit for the intelligence corps, in which Owen had served throughout his career, but these days his masters were in no position to be particular. Most of the best agents were either dead or imprisoned and pickings were scanty. An effective swordsman, quick with his fists, Giles Buckley had hastily volunteered himself and two of his more biddable men for this mission, this desperate little show of defiance. Madrid had fallen over two weeks previously, victim to Napoleon's "avalanche of fire and steel" and the Emperor's brother Joseph was safely installed as King of Spain in the *Palacio Real* for his Christmas celebrations. It was not a bad time for Buckley to absent himself from his regiment. Bar the consolation of besting the French in a skirmish here or there all that waited for them was a retreat to the coast, likely to be followed by an inglorious sail home.

Owen did not feel like a drink. "No thanks. Go back in, Buckley. They can't be much longer." Seeing the slack smile spread further on the Captain's face, he added: "And remember, now you've had a few drinks, don't try to talk to the innkeeper in Castilian Spanish. Don't put his back up. Do you understand?"

Captain Buckley bowed briefly, not lowering his eyes, turned on his heel and made for the comfort of the bar, but even before he had crossed the yard Owen caught sight of the warning from the peak a mile away. One after another, five unmistakeable twinkles of light shone out. The prey had passed his man and was heading for the trap. Owen slid down the roof and the wastewater chain, sprinted lightly over the frozen yard and caught up with Buckley as he reached the door.

By the time the sound of hooves, the faint clinking of horses' harnesses and the grinding of wheels had reached the approach to the inn, Owen, Buckley and their two men were waiting in the dark corners of the stable to dispatch any guards who might be left to watch the wagon. Their breathing had slowed, taking in the stale scent of old hay, mules and horses. Their hearing strained above the muted rustles from the beasts, and they watched the cracks in the door, picked out in stark white by the moonlight and the guttering flicker of the yard lantern. Owen held his Basque shepherd's stick, the makila, double-handed and at a slant, its brutally solid handle raised whilst the others tightened their grips on makeshift cudgels from Beñat's store.

Following the receipt of an intelligence report warning of a British attack, the French soldiers had been detailed to drive the covered wagon out of the valley and away from the armed column. They had started their detour a couple of kilometres before the rest of the baggage train reached the site of the expected ambush, a pinch-point where the river wound in a blind bend and the valley sides steepened. They were to proceed up the mountain track and complete a circuit of fifteen kilometres before rejoining the armoured division as it made its way to Madrid, laden with the royal supplies for Christmas and the next campaigning season. They were to halt at the only inn along the track, which they could now see, bulky but indistinct, in the gloom ahead.

"I'm so starving hungered, I could probably eat your nag," grumbled one of the rearguard, loud enough for the ears of the man who rode in frozen silence alongside, but low enough to avoid the notice of the officer leading the detail.

"And I could probably eat you as well you fat bastard. And drink this stinking apology for a *posada* dry as a bone."

The stocky cavalryman pursed his lips then countered.

"Could you now? I could eat my horse and yours, and you, you worm-eaten skeleton. Not that you're worth the eating! Did you see the vultures circling when we left the column, François? One sight of your stringy carcass and they took off!" His shoulders rose in a wheezy chuckle.

"Dismount!"

They reined in with relief, eager for a more comfortable roost for the banter or at least for some foetid warmth and whatever else the inn could offer, but their hopes were not high. It was uninviting, a squat, dark huddle by the wayside, which became further obscured by a fresh belch of smoke from its chimney as they prepared to dismount. It could never have sustained the column, but it did not need to. They would not have to fight for their rations, as there were just six of them: the officer and the sergeant at the front, two regulars in the wagon and the two bringing up the rear. The officer barked out his orders and the words loitered out of his mouth in freezing clouds.

"François, Alphonse! Take the wagon into the stables, see to the horses yourselves if there's no help, then come and eat. You two stay inside the wagon, we'll relieve you in two hours."

The French masters were not suspicious. They did not expect the Basques to love them. They did not seem to love anyone, certainly not their old masters the Spaniards, or any other alien power seeking to interfere with their race or their land. The officer and his men closed the door on the night and made for the settles round the fire. He called for food and drink in passable Gascon, which he had been assured the locals would recognise, but expected no more in the way of cheer than he got. The massive figure behind the bar nodded sourly and growled an order to a bundle of a woman, swaddled in shawls. The couple looked like a pair of Pyrenean bears in their brown homespun, he with his rough pelt of chestnut hair and irritable, reddened eyes, she waddling and submissive. The two soldiers watched her progress as she padded out towards the kitchen, cracked jokes in French at her expense, and then lapsed into silence with the others, thawing out, eyes adjusting to the leaping firelight and the smoke which gusted from the hearth with every swing of a door.

Within minutes, their piled plates, wide-bowled glasses and jugs of drink appeared, but they were not brought in by the bear-woman of the inn, but by the sisters. In they came, all bold smiles and swaying hips, laughing now, trailing their hands over the men's shoulders and leaning close as they poured each one a generous drink. The tired men's faces lit up, then fell slack with desire, drunk already as the crafty smoke fumes worked on their exhaustion, unravelling their defences as their bodies relaxed in the warmth.

"Sup your fill, gentlemen," teased Izar, her Gascon was rusty and halting but her smile seemed to ring true. "Long life to the Emperor!"

"Amen to that," replied the officer, lifting his glass and reluctantly taking his eyes from her. "Well men, you probably caught the gist. To the Emperor, then, and a quiet night followed by a successful day!"

The four raised their glasses to each other, drank deeply and in seconds gasped their last. Clawing at their throats, shuddering to their knees, their choking cries lasted only moments before the four bodies were still, bent in tormented death throes amongst the straw and the filth of the floor, whilst from behind the bar bounded two huge white shapes, rough-coated mountain dogs with fangs bared, pushing past the women, bearing down on the bodies, growling and snarling.

"Leave them!" ordered the innkeeper. "I'll not have you poisoned!" As the dogs backed away he rolled out from behind the bar, lifted the platters of meat and flung

5

the food onto the floor. "It was going to be your supper anyway, my beauties. All comes, in time, to those who wait."

"I hope that is also true for all your people in *Euskal Herria*," said Owen, in perfect Basque and with a smile, as he led his men into the inn and motioned for them to haul the bodies away.

"*Ongi etorri!* Welcome again, my friend. I thought you might have frozen to the roof before now," growled Beñat, but his bushy moustaches and eyebrows rose to show he smiled as he reached for the bottle of Txakoli. "A glass for you all before you clear this vermin?"

The sparkling white-green wine lent an air of celebration and their spirits rose. Giles Buckley looked round the bar expectantly.

"Where are the sisters?" he asked.

Owen smiled. "Gone. You will not see them again tonight."

"I liked the look of them," said Buckley, reluctant to let it go. "What was Izar's sister called?"

"Her name is Amaia," said Owen. "In Basque it means: The End". You would do well to leave them for your next life, Buckley, whatever that might be. For now, all of you set to work and take these corpses out. Leave the other two in the stable as they are, strip and bury these four. Bring all their belongings back here." He bowed briefly to the innkeeper. "Beñat, we have left the two corpses clothed, armed and under sacks and guarantee they have no knife or gunshot wounds. They are ready to be planted in the ravine. Remember, leave them partly in the river but trap them with boulders. The French should believe the wagon and the rest of them were swept away. My friend, *eskerrik asko*, we are truly grateful for your help tonight."

"It was a pleasure," rumbled Beñat, as he carefully lifted the used glasses and the jugs with their lethal charges. "Don't worry about the French, it will be done. But don't imagine we wouldn't deal the same hand to every last Englishman who plans to overstay his welcome!"

"The entire British army will probably quit Spain before the spring," said Owen, running one hand through his unruly black hair, concentrating his thoughts. "But we will return. Napoleon will be kept out of Portugal and driven from Spain before we're done. We have sworn it."

Beñat shrugged as he made his way to the kitchen. "Good luck with that oath, Englishman." He paused, looking back slyly. "*Eskerrik asko etortzeagatik!* We'll look out for your return. You're good for business. You paid well for help to kidnap a supply wagon and give it a lick of paint to change its loyalty, if that in truth is all you've done tonight."

"We always do fair deals," said Owen, easily, "and you are welcome to your wages. We'll be off smartly, as planned, when we've finished the burial and we'll take the rest of the paint and the brushes, if you don't mind. We might need them again before we make the coast. You are welcome to the rifles, and the uniforms. The clothes will do for fuel if nothing else. But hide them well for now. The attack on the main column will be a token gesture. It will only hold up the French briefly, but you should still have at least a day before the search parties arrive. And Beñat," said Owen pausing as he made his way to the door, "I'm not English. I'm Welsh. As a Basque, you should make it your business to understand the difference."

"*Agur*, Welshman," said Beñat, his eyes crinkling into a smile. "Until the next time."

The descent from the Montes Vascos was uneventful. They drove the wagon in its new muddy-green livery in the opposite direction from that taken by the column and pushed on north to the coast. They snatched sleep in rotas and disturbed nothing more challenging than a few herds of mountain goats. Above them the blue sky was studded and seamed with the black shapes of hunting birds. Vultures soared over the peaks and closer to hand an inquisitive raven flew down alongside them as they reached the coastal plain. Avoiding the walled port of San Sebastian, they made their way towards a sheltered harbour where Owen had a rendezvous with a Royal Navy frigate, the *Renowned*. On their last night together, sitting by the campfire, Owen told them how they would divide the night's watches and a companionable silence fell.

"So d'ye think the rest of the Frenchies will 'ave given up waitin' for the wagon by now?" asked Benjamin Prestwick suddenly.

"For sure," said Captain Buckley. "Don't fret Prestwick. They will have swallowed the tale of the accident in the mountains and be trailing down the Madrid road by now, mourning their losses and polishing their excuses. They will need them to ring true when they fetch up at the court of Joseph I, *Jose el Primero*," he paused to add heft to his newly acquired Spanish. "It will take some nerve to admit they've lost his Christmas boxes. Mind you, as the claret is going to make it he will be pleased enough. *Pepe Botella* likes his drink."

"He is probably no more of a drunkard than the next man," said Owen, as he lifted the fire with his boot, letting a rush of air feed the flames. "No one said a bad word about him when he ruled in Naples."

They sat in silence, staring into the fire, until Captain Buckley's self-interest surfaced.

"So we're to be cut loose to make our own way back to the regiment?"

"Yes you are, Captain Buckley," said Owen, "but not empty handed. In the best tradition of the British forces, prize money will be awarded."

Buckley remained guarded but his eyes gleamed in the firelight, and the two soldiers stole a quick glance to each other. Benjamin Prestwick's hands slowly commenced to rub in anticipation.

"We need to check the goods anyway. I don't want to debouche at Plymouth and get a nasty surprise when I reveal the loot to my superiors," Owen laughed.

"Sir, what if it be just regular stores, or ammunition?" said Prestwick fearfully.

Owen rose and flung back the tarpaulin on the back of the wagon.

"I have it on the best information that British gold can buy, that we have a haul of coin here to make Croesus himself flush up and his eyes water. Fouche's spies are not above double-dealing and apparently Napoleon does not even trust the spymaster himself. My contact is one of them. He infiltrated the armed column, convinced the officers that they were going to be attacked and lined up the detour. He gave me his personal guarantee that this is the most important consignment of the Emperor's Christmas bounty to his beloved brother Joseph. There was enough for *Pepe Botella* and the aristocracy of Madrid in exchange for their unconditional love and loyalty, or so Boney thought. Enough to convince Jo he is better off struggling in Spain, where he is despised, than lolling back in comfort in Naples. It is also enough to provide finance for whatever the new campaigning season might bring. My contact will already be on the *Renowned*, and he returns to England with me. Now, help me get these down!"

The men hurried over, clumsy with excitement. A dozen strongboxes were dragged out and lined up. Owen drew out hammers and chisels and the work began. The first was forced open and proved, as billed, to be full to the brim with canvas moneybags. Buckley lifted one, grunting with the effort, and set it down between the four of them. Owen loosened the ties and folded down the sides to reveal a shimmering cache of gold napoleons. His men stared at it dumbfounded for a moment, then fell on their knees before the mound. Gibbering in wide-eyed delight they plunged their hands into it, lifting waterfalls of forty-franc pieces, which slithered and winked like a thousand suns in the dancing firelight. As their cries died, Owen took charge.

"Close it," he ordered. "Let's get on. We must check them all."

And they did, methodically forcing open each chest in turn to reveal its hoard of gold. But the penultimate box yielded even more than gold napoleons. In this they found a king's ransom of jewels. Boxes of brilliants flashed in the starlight, necklaces of sapphires and diamonds, rubies and emeralds, every woman's gaud they had ever imagined and bags of other duller, but even more useful rocks, anonymous and austere. Pack after pack of uncut stones, nestling like withered seeds which, when cut and faceted, would bloom to sire a forest of wealth. And beneath them all, stranger still, a hoard of ancient talismans set in gold and dark stones: birds, beasts and staring eyes, exotic loot from Napoleon's Egyptian campaign.

"God's teeth!" breathed Buckley. "We've found the Crown Jewels!"

"Oiy never did see the loike," muttered the normally silent Philip Spence. "In all me born days! No, Oiy never did so, nor ever thought to." He was ashamed to discover that he had tears in his eyes and dashed them away roughly. "Ben, what say you?"

Benjamin Prestwick, thunderstruck, could only nod.

"As senior officer I authorise the division of spoils," said Owen briskly. "Fifty napoleons each, same for all ranks, and one item of jewellery. Take your pick."

Prestwick and Spence hung back to allow Buckley first choice and then reached out with trembling hands to lift their own prizes. Owen left the coins, but when they had finished he made his choice from the jewels, a necklace of blue stones, in a curious antique gold setting. Each man's booty was tied into his handkerchief and packed into his knapsack before they began the task of securing the boxes.

Owen and Spence took first watch, each with a pair of pistols and a Baker rifled carbine primed and ready, whilst Buckley and Prestwick bedded down by the fire. The hours slipped by quietly and now they had descended to the coastal plain it was not so numbingly cold. They also had their thoughts to keep them warm. Owen pulled his cloak tighter. He kept his eyes sharp, but his thoughts drifted to London and Sarah, his wife. He pictured her laughing with delight, and their son, Nathaniel, holding her hands and standing uncertainly on her lap. In his mind's eye the grave toddler let go of his mother and held out his arms, and as Owen reached for him he looked into a mirror of his younger self, the same blue eyes and dark looks. They did not need the money. They had all they needed. But would she like the sapphires? She was a wealthy woman in her own right, it would be a welcome bauble, but his return would be the jewel.

Sitting by him, but a world away, Philip Spence's heart still beat with a joy it had never known. The money and the jewels would transform his life. How much would he get for the foreign money? It was a windfall of years of wages at one go! How many years? Four? More? And the precious stones! Nothing would ever be the same, and he prayed as he had never done before.

"God 'elp me make it back to Martha! No more soldiering, Lord. I'll get a steady job and buy a place of our own. Back to Bath for me for good, and plenty victuals every day for all of us. God bless Mr Parry. God bless Martha!"

He conjured up a vision of his ramrod straight wife. The windfall should put him in her good books for life, let it be long! He grinned widely, then suddenly remembered the child, the bawling red-faced bundle he had kissed goodbye.

"And God bless little Matthew, and Father. Amen, amen!"

Captain Buckley and Benjamin Prestwick took over in the middle of their short night. They would complete the journey to the coast before dawn, at which point the three soldiers would be released to strike out west and return to their regiment to face whatever hell awaited them in the next battle with Emperor Napoleon and his *Grande Armée*. Buckley had slipped one of his napoleons into his pocket, and felt it now with his cold fingers. He could feel the heavily embossed head of the Emperor and the wreath on the reverse. As he turned it over speculatively, he made a decision.

The following day marked the parting of their ways. Equipped with new horses, rations and directions for the return to the base at Corunna, the three soldiers bade farewell to Owen Parry and their brief careers with intelligence, saddled up and made their way west. After nightfall, when they had made camp and Captain Buckley dozed by the fire, Benjamin Prestwick had the opportunity to acquaint his friend with the events of the previous night.

"So 'ow much did you take Ben?" whispered Philip, warily. He felt a sinking sickness in his stomach at the thought of the betrayal of Mr Parry. They had been given a handsome pay-off; more seemed like theft from their own.

"Captain Buckley said as 'e ought to have more than us as 'e is an officer. Oiy wasn't going to argue. Then 'e upped and said Oiy deserved more too. Oiy said Oiy would share mine with you. 'E was not so pleased, said Oiy was not to tell a soul, but that didn't seem fair to you, moiy old mate." Ben eyed Philip cautiously, weighing his responses. "Any'ow, 'e loaded up with napoleons and jewels. Oiy filled moiy knapsack too, Phil, but 'alf 's yours Oiy swear. It's going to be alroight for the both of us." His brow darkened and he shot a glance over to the fireside as Buckley moaned in his sleep. "It'll be fine and dandy," he said, gripping Philip's arm and shaking it to stifle his doubts. "There'll be no trouble. There's plenty left and we closed the sacks up perfect. Nobody will know."

Benjamin Prestwick was right in many ways. They heard no more of the wagon and its fate. Neither Owen nor his superiors reported any problem with the sacks. The government registered only pleasant surprise, and welcomed the haul as a bonus for effort after a poor year. Benjamin himself escaped with his share, but there his prophesies fell short, as Philip Spence did not. The fate of the rifle regiment turned out to be a cruel one and he was one casualty in the deluge. As Owen had foretold, in company with the whole British Peninsular Army they were in full retreat through Northern Spain by Christmas Day, heading for Corunna and escape on Royal Navy transports. By January they had reached their destination but thousands had already perished. Constantly harried by Napoleon's army they had also suffered a chaos of vile weather, alternately sodden in rainstorms then frozen in blizzards. Time and again discipline had collapsed and the British soldiers had avenged their despair on the miserable villages they passed through. Before Napoleon lost interest in the pursuit and left Marshal Soult to finish off, he noted gleefully that the cruelty of the British soldiers had made them hated by everybody in Spain and he could think of no better way to neutralise resistance to French control. To compound the misery, most of the promised ships had not arrived in port. The British fought like madmen as they waited, making time to bury their commander, Sir John Moore, who perished amongst the thousands of men from the ranks. During the retreat Philip had been made up to Sergeant for conspicuous bravery, but there was no time to bury him with respect. His body was left, broken and bloody, on the road into Corunna. As shot had whistled past them and the thunderous French cannon roared, Benjamin had held Philip's head and sworn on his knees to take his share to Martha. It had salved his conscience to promise this and made it easier to take his leave of the pitiful body on the road. It seemed to make what they had done fitting. It was repayment for loss. Making this last promise to a friend proved to be a stroke of luck for Benjamin Prestwick, though at the time it seemed to bring nothing but bitter misfortune. As he knelt on the frozen road, intent on his last words to Philip, he caught a blast from exploding ordnance and fell, unconscious, by the body of his friend. It was another day before he entered the city, without his boots, battered and deafened, but cradling his bulging knapsack like a sick child, far behind his unit and with men unknown to him.

"Captain Buckley. Report on the roll call, if you please!"

The few remaining officers in the rifle regiment had gathered in the Captain's cabin on board their transport vessel for a final review of losses. The broad-based decanters stood their ground on the table as the ship rolled in the heavy January seas and there was no desire to postpone dinner any longer than necessary. Captain Giles Mortimer-Buckley scanned the regimental roster very closely, efficiently suppressing his delight. Spence and Prestwick had not survived to embark. He had seen them both felled on the road, and the others in their platoon were accounted for.

It had not been necessary to help them on their way, but it had been unfortunate that their share of the loot had to be left for the Frenchies. Magnanimously, he accepted this small set-back.

"Fortunes of war," he said to himself, as he arranged his face for the delivery of his valedictory on the virtues of all the missing men.

**Five years before the events related in this book.**

**Evening: 20th December, 1828.**
**The Restaurant Le Grand Véfour, Palais Royal, Paris.**

Colette Montrachet gathered the folds of her furred cloak over her arm, reached out for the gloved hand of the footman and stepped daintily out of the carriage, exactly as she was expected to. The Marquis was waiting to put a protective arm around her, steer her past the Louvre and through the pavement crowds to their rendezvous at the Palais Royal. The old palace reared up before them, massive and sparkling in the darkness, alive with lights and flares. The noise of the revellers hit them like a wave as they hurried forward to be enveloped in the swirling cream of Parisian high society. Richelieu's old lair had been built close to the royal residence so he could serve Louis XIII whilst keeping a close eye on the deceits of his queen, Anne of Austria, and the Palais had been a centre for intrigue ever since. The Dukes of Orleans had commercialised the place, capitalising on the secluded gardens and profusion of charming arcades, which now housed the theatre, cafes and restaurants, billiard parlours, perfumers, jewellers and stores of every type. You could buy food, furniture, toys, truffles, every toy and trifle under the sun, or so it seemed.

Two of the arcades were dedicated to the provision of prostitutes for gentlemen clients, and as Colette and her Marquis sauntered by, she spared a glance for them as they flaunted their louche gaiety, painted faces and trilling laughs. She thanked God she was not with them, plying her trade. Securing the Marquis de la Blanquefort had been surprisingly easy. Her Marseilles Count had brought her to the capital, and when business had called him away she had quickly transferred herself to a new patron. Most nights had been satisfactory, but tonight promised more than the usual round of dining and cards followed by the enthusiastic attentions of the Marquis. She nodded absent-mindedly as he pointed out his favourite eyeglass shop, his favourite snuff merchant and, in his view, the most distinguished purveyor of cologne, but as she did so, she felt beneath the shawl collar of her cloak to run her fingers round a hard gold edge. Lying blind beneath the fur was a miniature, and apart from some scattered tales and memories, it was her only link with her family's past. She often found herself touching it, as a talisman, a guarantee of good fortune.

The brooch held a tiny painting of a young woman in a high white wig and low-necked ball gown. She wore a heavily-wrought gold necklace, studded with diamonds. This was just one set, so she had been told, of the famous suite of Montrachet jewels commissioned by her grandfather from Maison Bapst, court jewellers to Louis XV and his doomed grandson Louis XVI. Like her grandmother, whose likeness it was, the jewels had all been lost, as had her grandfather and all their people, their lands and chattels. The enduring family myth was that the collection of jewels had been acquired by Napoleon himself, though the rest of the estate had been broken up into hundreds of lots and sold separately: a commonplace fate for the aristocratic families of the *Ancien Régime* and their fortunes. The Revolution had claimed many heads and ruined many lives. It had been unfortunate for the Montrachets that they had failed to catch the tide of compensation which had flowed after the defeat of Napoleon and Louis XVIII's coronation. By the time Charles X had taken the throne it was too late. France was in no shape to compensate more of the old aristocracy; on the contrary, another revolution was more likely than not.

In her current career as a courtesan, Colette was used to playing for high stakes and she had felt that she lived a reasonable life, as far as it went. But only the previous week she had glimpsed the hope of something much more. At the *salon* of Laure, Duchesse d'Abrantès, she had caught sight of an English woman wearing a rope of gold and gems that was unmistakeable. Not her grandmother's diamonds, but emeralds, set in the same heavy tell-tale links, each shaped as a capital M. Over the intervening days the idea of recovering them had grown to an obsession and, against his better judgement, she had manoeuvred the Marquis into accepting a dinner invitation to a party which would include the Duchess. Colette had no plan as yet, apart from finding out more about the woman, but she knew she would stop at nothing to reclaim what was rightfully hers. The necklace represented more than money, it was a link with all that she lacked, and all that her family had lost before. There had been three of them left after her mother followed her father to the grave. One brother had picked up the strands of a new life in the south, the other lay two years dead in an American grave. She felt that she had found a new direction for her life and saw it as a quest. It was going to be a religion, a purpose. The Marquis glanced at her and mistook the gleam in her eyes.

"Don't expect too much, Coco my darling," he said, tucking her arm through his and pressing her hand to his lips. "The Duchess was on good form last week but can often be far from engaging. Some of her followers are dull dogs and her latest beau, young Balzac, is an opinionated puppy, who monopolises the conversation abominably. She dotes on him as he is working through a Napoleon fixation at present. He is capable of spending all evening teasing tales out of her about the imperial glory days and he is coaxing her through scrawling endless volumes of her memoirs. He is set on publishing them himself and making a killing. I strongly advise you to avoid any mention of Bonaparte. Once her tales start there will be no stopping the flow until the carriages arrive!"

"Oh Émile," said Coco, fluttering her eyelashes and turning her exquisite heart-shaped face to his, "that is exactly what I am hoping for. I am so much looking forward to hearing more of Madame the Duchess's adventures with the Emperor! How clever of you to arrange this evening. I am so grateful." She reached up to plant a kiss just below his ear. More than grateful: the promise of infinitely more. Émile promptly banished the threat of a dull interval in the evening with the prospect of an excellent night ahead and strode on with a spring in his step.

The brilliance of the interior of Le Grand Véfour was overwhelming. For the eye it was a vision in gold and white, its exquisite pastel frescoes set off and echoed by the profusion of gilt-edged neo-classical mirrors lining the walls. Likewise every other sense was swept off its feet. The air rang with excited noise and clatter and was heavy with a confusion of smells and smoke as customers sank into the plush upholstery and competed in lavishing extravagant praise on the divine food. By some tables Turkish tobacco overlaid the luscious aromas of meats, fish and wines, and as they passed the women, clouds of competing perfumes rose in the air. King of all: *Les Parfums de Lubin*, favoured since the fall of Napoleon by the returning aristocracy of the old regime. Despite the Marquis's regular gifts from this house, Coco had resisted it, wearing only a light floral from the new Guerlain shop, which she had trained him to buy for her. She had learned that it was unwise to be too easily pleased.

The restaurant was packed and the Marquis followed the waiter's lead in searching out their party.

"The Duchess does not have a regular seat these days," he said, leaning close to Coco and raising his voice above the hubbub. "She could be anywhere!" He smiled, excited to show off his contacts and pointing to a corner table. "There are government men in tonight. Look!"

Coco looked over and quickly scrutinised the serious men in dark frock coats. She immediately recognised the Comte de la Ferronnays, Minister of Foreign Affairs, and Louis de Caux, Minister of War, the one dark-headed, the other white and distinguished, both leaning towards their guests in rapt attention. Two men, seemingly foreigners from the cut of their coats, though oddly similar, with piercing blue eyes and dark hair, were similarly intent. The older one was speaking in faultless French, the younger listened.

"Oh really!" she said. "How exciting, Émile. Is one of them the Prime Minister? Is it that naughty Monsieur Martignac you were so cross about yesterday?"

"No darling, not Martignac," he said fondly, "just some of his Ministers. Now look over there, literary lions my dear! You should recognise Monsieur Victor Hugo. I have his work in my library. See he bows to us!"

Coco nodded briefly over the heads of the diners to a young man sporting a broad velvet collar, he seemed little older than herself, romantic, not quite foppish but with his hair brushed theatrically to the side. She spent no time on comment and hurried the Marquis forward, for there, at the next table, numbering about a dozen and in the midst of their dinner, was the party of the Duchesse d'Abrantès.

"Madame la Duchesse!" said the Marquis, kissing his hostess's hand and taking the empty seat by her. "A thousand pardons for our unconscionably late appearance!"

"My dear Marquis," said Laure, her mouth smiling, her eyes suspicious beneath her intricate piles of curls and girlish floral head-piece. "I knew you would be here as soon as you were able. But all is not lost! You have arrived in time for the *poulet marengo*."

The Marquis blenched slightly at the prospect, never having been a fan of crayfish, but he smiled gamely whilst serving dishes as big as shields and loaded with the restaurant's iconic dish approached their table, carried shoulder high by a line of waiters.

"A treat indeed. But Madame la Duchesse, before we begin, may I present again Mademoiselle Colette Montrachet? I believe you two ladies had no opportunity to speak at your *soirée* last week."

"Coco, the Duchesse d'Abrantès."

"Madame," said Coco, "I could hardly wait to have the pleasure of speaking with you since I heard that you have been tempted to write about your remarkable adventures with the Emperor."

Laure was at a late stage in her life and a particularly dire period in her finances, so any flattery was welcome, particularly when coming from a guest of the Marquis. He was known to be a generous man and had a substantial fortune founded on Caribbean sugar interests, so the girl's friendship might prove useful. He was obviously enthralled by her, and her choice of opening gambit allowed Laure to bring dear Honoré into the conversation.

Honoré de Balzac was a fleshy, ruddy young dandy. Wildly ambitious, and like

Laure herself, willing to utilise any contact in his relentless drive for self-advancement. He had secured his *entrée* into society *via* the Duchess, who was old enough to be his mother, but nevertheless kept herself smart and was a cheerful and adequate bed-mate. She matched him in spite, and her work not only fascinated him because of her youthful closeness to his current idol, the Emperor, but also might very well provide a much needed cash boost for his fledgling career as a publisher. He set about showing off to the Marquis's new doxy by enlarging on his successes and plans, but before the *poulet marengo* had been dispatched, his conversation had turned to dalliance and he had decided he had fallen, just a little, in love with her, as he was meant to.

As the conversation drifted, as it inevitably did, to the weighty matters of the Duchess's doings with Napoleon, the Marquis made his excuses and moved off to join the table with the two ministers and the foreign visitors. At the same time, Balzac was suddenly monopolised by Madame de Girardin on his left, leaving Coco a clear field. She slid over into the seat abandoned by the Marquis and wasted no time.

"Duchess, did you eat a *poulet marengo* in the company of the Emperor? Please say you did!"

Laure relaxed into her seat and raised a languid hand to her chin. "Oh my dear, so many times. On innumerable occasions, some grand, some," she paused for further effect, "some intimate."

Coco managed a squeak of delight, which encouraged Laure to embark on a version of her recitation that would fit neatly into the pause before the arrival of the meringues and fruit. It ranged over Napoleon's youthful appearances at her mother's *salon* and his great affection for them both, her husband's affair with the Emperor's sister Caroline, the effort it had taken herself to escape the clutches of the great Prince Metternich and the abiding love the Emperor cherished for her dear departed husband. Coco had already acquainted herself with the realities of Napoleon's despair over the mental degeneration of the Duke, his *aide de camp*, with the mad extravagances of both Duke and Duchess resulting in her being packed off home to France from Spain, then expelled from Paris by Napoleon for disloyalty. The Duke's suicide seemed to be an event in some doubt. He had certainly disappeared. After spending longer with Laure, Coco could see the value to the old boy of a swift exit.

As the meringues and fruit began to make an appearance, Laure eventually touched on an issue which gave Coco the break she needed.

"And now you see," she said, her eyes tragic, heavy with kohl and brimming with unshed tears, "after such a life, after such privilege, it is my duty to commit my memoirs to the page for the benefit of others. I have four children, Mademoiselle Montrachet. They must be provided for, and my expenses, even in my modest *hermitage* far from the centre of the city, are considerable."

"How well I understand your predicament," Coco replied, returning Laure's gaze, her own liquid gold-brown eyes obediently welling up in sympathy. "I too need an independent income. I do not wish to depend on dear Émile, but need to harness my own resources. I am from an ancient lineage Madam, but all was lost in the Revolution. My family did not obtain compensation in 1815, and though I could never be a talented writer in your league, I aspire to writing a history of my family and a treatise on the design of our family jewels, which were famous in their day."

Coco watched Laure very carefully at this point, it was vital not to threaten her self-satisfaction or appear as a rival, yet she must give a plausible excuse for pursuing the gems. "Your closeness to the Emperor during the Iberian Campaign might have enabled you to hear of them or even to see them, as I gather that the Emperor himself acquired them all as a *suite entière*."

"The Emperor acquired many gifts, bought many things," said Laure evasively, "but from what I heard when I was back in Paris, a very large cache was lost just before our great victory at Corunna. Let me think, the winter of 1808 it must have been. A quantity of baggage was on its way overland to the Emperor's brother in Madrid. Maybe it was lost in the mountain snows, or maybe the English had it." She seemed to tire of the subject, "Who knows? It was wartime."

"But, Madame," persisted Coco, "at your *salon* last week I saw an English woman wearing one of the set and I would dearly love to meet her so that I may ask about the origin of her jewels."

Coco reached for her cloak and showed Laure the miniature.

"Yes," said the Duchess, peering closely then letting the cloak fall through her fingers onto Coco's lap. "The same unusual setting, but hers were emeralds, yes? I cannot remember her name, she came with other guests, but I do know they were bound for Ireland and then on to the port of Bristol in England."

"Ladies, ladies," boomed Balzac, leaning in to join their conversation and resting his head on Laure's shoulder. "Why so secretive? What was being shown? Do tell!"

It suited Coco very well to see the Marquis threading his way back to their table.

"Émile, darling," she called, as she rose to close her conversation with Laure, "what a wonderful time we have had, despite the fact that the Ministers robbed us of your company!"

"Ah ladies, here I am, here I am," he said, well-suited with himself as he reclaimed his seat beside the Duchess. "I needed a word with them, I'm afraid, times being as they are." He looked over to where the older foreigner, pale now and somewhat haggard, was making his way out with the Ministers. "Talks will be continuing into the night for some I'm afraid, though not for all."

They followed his gaze to see the younger foreigner make his way to the clutch of writers carousing at a side table. "Whilst the British father attends to duty, the son makes his way over to young Hugo and his friends, to crown the evening with poetry no doubt!" Émile smiled broadly, slipping his hand round Coco's waist. "Now, have I missed all the meringues?"

Concerned by his father's ill health, but reassured that he would make his way to the hotel after a final session with the Count; Nathaniel Parry had decided to stay at Le Véfour and give himself up to pleasure for the rest of the evening. The two bottles of claret he had already had would now be followed by numerous noggins of cognac in the entrancing company he had ear-marked earlier in the evening. He waved his swordstick as he negotiated his way through the crowded tables and called a greeting.

"Victor, *mon ami! Ça va?* "

"*Salut, Nathaniel! Je vais bien, merci, merci!*" replied Monsieur Hugo, leaping to his feet and greeting him with his customary bear hug. "Now meet another friend of mine." He propelled Nathaniel round the table to meet a lounging young man with a shock of dark hair, thin sensitive face and a goatee beard. "This is Alexandre Dumas. At present clerk to the Duc d'Orléans but threatening to outshine me as a literary luminary as soon as he possibly can. Is that right! Alex, here is Nathaniel Parry of his Britannic Majesty's staff."

"Pleased to make your acquaintance, sir," said Dumas, shaking Nathaniel's hand readily. "As for you Victor, as you say, sharpened pens at dawn. Despite your name, it remains to be seen who shall triumph!"

Nathaniel took a seat, shutting out the uncertainties of the day and the dire warnings of the Ministers. He wanted to abandon himself to a night of drink and talk, in the magical company of Victor, doyen of French Romantics, and the new man Dumas, who looked interesting. But as he sat back and glanced round the table it was obvious that both of them had expensive women in tow. Dumas was examining his prize through an eyeglass he kept round his neck on a ribbon and Hugo, despite his wedding band, was exchanging smiles with a showy young woman in red. Nathaniel suddenly felt bereft, and thought of his widowed father returning to the hotel alone. He ran his fingers round the silver pommel of his stick, extravagantly engraved with Owen's initials and presented to him on his twenty-first birthday. Their work and the constant travel abroad in the service of their country had sacrificed family life, such as it was. He could not remember exactly when they had last been to their home in Wales. For years they had lived in a series of rented rooms and hotel suites without even regular servants to call their own. The sight of complacently happy matrons with white-haired spouses at nearby tables did nothing to lift his mood, but reminded him that he could barely remember his own mother's face. He drank his cognac, sombrely watching his reflection in the giant mirror before him, a still dark figure against a restless backdrop of talk and music, glaring light and colour.

# Chapter 1

**The early hours: 26th January, 1833.**
**The York House Hotel, George Street, Bath.**

Sir Giles Mortimer-Buckley Bt MP did not particularly like hotels, especially provincial ones. His body ached after being jolted down from London in the mail coach and he had heartburn after overindulging at dinner. Cursing briefly for leaving his valet behind, he dropped his evening clothes onto the floor, struggled into his nightshirt and threw himself into the unfamiliar bed. Most surprisingly, it proved to be comfortable and within minutes he had descended into a deep pit of tangled dreams.

The first vision started well. He was tumbling the most willing of the servants, a cheeky, hefty piece called Maisie Trickett who was officially employed as his granddaughter's nanny, but had also become his regular choice for bed-sport. Considering his age he had been going well, a veritable steam engine, when without warning Maisie reared up and flicked him over, her great red mouth roaring with laughter as she landed her fleshy bulk on top of him, her vast rolling bosom crushing his face, suffocating him as he lay helpless. He struggled to move but was powerless.

Groaning, he woke and turned over, but the image was stubborn, as the reality of Maisie was even more disturbing than the dream. He sat up, rubbing his hands over his face but he could see her still. Unlike the compliant servants who had been treated to his attentions over the years, she did not play to the rules of the game. The others had meekly accepted economical settlements when his enthusiasm waned, or when his wife, the Lady Leonora, had objected to them, or when they were vulgar enough to advertise a pregnancy. Maisie had announced she was breeding, demanded to keep her position, and the baby, and to be set up for life. She was adored by his wife, daughter and granddaughter, and was offensively confident that she could dig in for the long term. Her attitude reminded him unpleasantly of Johnathan Swift's: *Directions to Servants*, where employed females were reminded to be pert, rude and saucy and to charge for every accommodation they allowed their employer, from a friendly squeeze all the way to what he delicately referred to as "the last favour", which should net them a one hundred guinea prize, or twenty pounds a year for life. Maisie had refused to see the reliable doctor he had used before, and when he had tried to get her to drink a draught of pennyroyal to "return her system to normal", she had refused outright and accused him of trying to do away with her.

He thrust himself under the covers again and closed his eyes, but unwelcome thoughts of the trollop would not disperse. She was the primary reason for him being in the West Country. His predicament had encouraged him to accompany a parliamentary colleague and his wife to a house party at Mr Edwin Ravenswood's mansion on the outskirts of Bristol, where he hoped to solicit a solution to his problem. The Ravenswoods were old family friends, and though he had not visited them for a number of years, he had kept up a connection through the current Mr Ravenswood's infrequent visits to London. Edwin's father had been a legitimate and successful Bristol slave trader before the 1807 ban and the family sugar plantations in the West Indies still ran at a profit. But Edwin had diversified into other businesses, some more legal than others, and by all accounts was more astute and ruthless than his father had ever been. His advice and spider's web of contacts should help to curtail Maisie Trickett's career with minimum fuss.

But every benefit has a price.

He slid again into a troubled sleep, this time haunted by a kaleidoscope of nightmares from the past, of war service in Spain, of bayonets and burning bodies and of a man swinging on the end of a rope, screaming his innocence. Mercifully, the last scene acted as a grand finale and yanked him awake again, soaked with sweat and panting for breath.

Thinking of the Ravenswoods had reminded him of the war. His father's friendship with Ravenswood Senior had first tied him to them when, as a young man returning from Spain laden with loot, it had been the Ravenswood connections which enabled him to make the most of it. Not that he normally dwelt on that.

21

Buckley encouraged his thoughts to wander down less problematic byways. His elder brother's fortuitous riding accident had allowed him to inherit the family pile in Gloucestershire and a canny marriage to the dull but moneyed Leonora had set him up in a life of ease, culminating in him landing a county seat in the 1832 election. He liked to describe himself as a self-made man.

He rolled over to the other side of the bed to see if a fresh pillow would help him nod off to sleep, but instead found himself thinking of his travelling companions. Mr John Drake from the Foreign Office, and his wife Charlotte, had caused him to be quartered in the hotel for the night rather than the new Ravenswood mansion, as they needed to break their journey in Bath to attend a wedding. It had suited him to remain with them. Officially he and Drake were on a diplomatic mission to consolidate links with Ravenswood concerning his involvement with the China trade so it was wise to arrive together, but also Mrs Drake, or Lottie, as she preferred to be called, had proved to be a desirable piece in her own right. She had sat next to him in the coach from London and whiled away the miles by flirting and pressing herself against him most agreeably. He had managed a little squeeze of her waist as the coach rocked and just one casual brush of his hand over the side of her breast. Drake had not seemed disturbed by her performance and it probably would not have mattered to her if he had been. Lottie was obviously the one with the power in the relationship, as well as the status and the money. It had been annoying when Leonora announced that she was too unwell to accompany him on the trip, but perhaps it was a happy coincidence which would provide him with the leeway to get to know Lottie rather better. Buckley cheered up at the thought and sank into a few hours of uninterrupted sleep.

A modest tapping at the door brought him round, and once fully conscious he perked up even more at the prospect of the arrival of a chambermaid.

"Come," he called.

For a moment, a jaded twinkle lit his eye, but it was soon extinguished by the sight of a matronly rear reversing into the room.

"Good mornin' to ye, sir. 'Tis Dorcas 'ere. Oiy 'ave yer breakfast for ye," she said, redundantly, as she landed the laden tray on his bedside table. "Would you loike me to open yer drapes whilst Tabby sees to the fire?"

A juvenile of about ten years of age had struggled in behind her with a jug of hot water, which she clattered to its rest in the washstand bowl.

Buckley glowered, but accepted that it was for the best. "Yes," he snapped, as he hoisted himself higher against the pillows to inspect the provisions on the tray. "Get on with it."

As Tabby rattled the fire into life, the velvet drapes were twitched back to reveal a sullen sky and a sparkling white layer of frost riming the roof of the building across the street.

"Will that be all, sir?" enquired Dorcas, who on closer inspection bore a remarkable resemblance to a bulldog. He glanced at the juvenile answering to the name of Tabby, who turned her pasty, sullen face and one eye towards him, the other being wayward had rolled to the wall.

"That will most definitely be all," he said impatiently, waving them both away.

He gazed, unseeing, at the rolls, butter, jams and coffee, the nodding ferns and flower buds in the crystal vase, but then remembered that he had a day to play with in the old spa. Being a resort city, foul-tasting warm water should not be the only diversion on offer. Feeling marginally more optimistic, he set to work on the rolls.

Later that morning, another meal was served at the York House, a more convivial one. It was a wedding breakfast to celebrate the marriage of Mr Nathaniel Parry, from Llanddaniel on the Isle of Anglesey and Carlisle Lane, Lambeth, to Miss Emma Peterson of Marlborough Buildings, Bath, daughter of Captain Oliver and Mrs Lydia Peterson. They had been driven to the hotel in Captain Peterson's carriage after a service in Bath Abbey. The bells had rung out behind them and a vocal knot of well-wishers had scattered rice and blessings as they had been borne away up Broad Street. Drink had been taken and food eaten; it only remained for the formalities to be concluded. Nathaniel was looking over the assembled guests before making his groom's speech in response to the efforts of his new father-in-law, waiting for the guests to resume their seats and the rattle of applause to wear itself out. Captain Peterson had managed to bark out a gruffly emotional welcome and propose a toast before taking everyone by surprise and abruptly dropping back into his seat as if shot. A tear stood in the Captain's eye though he beamed still on Emma, his second and favourite daughter. Oliver Peterson was embarrassed to find himself overwhelmed by the occasion, a state of affairs he put down to advancing age and more happiness than was probably good for him.

"Too much fuss, damn it!" he blustered to himself.

He blew his nose volcanically and reflected on his good fortune. The ship of family relations was holding a steady course, a welcome relief for which he gave silent thanks. His son remained at sea with his vessel, which he now commanded, and his eldest girl was busy producing another child in Cirencester. His wife Lydia was in a state of unconfined delight, having seen Emma safely married off to the dashing young Parry, who had seemed frustratingly elusive in the early days of their acquaintance. Four girls had seemed a daunting responsibility in those lean days after the war, when far too many young women had buzzed around the reduced cohort of eligible young men.

"Two down and two to go," he reflected thankfully. "Half-time as it were."

The twins, in a high state of excitement, had giggled and flounced about all morning in their bridesmaid's gowns, unregulated by their mama, who had been occupied in overseeing the bridal preparations, entertaining honoured guests from London and greeting aged aunts and uncles, cousins, and a profusion of nephews and nieces. Oliver had seen the twins knock back at least two glasses of champagne each, but had chosen to ignore it.

Nathaniel winked at his father-in-law as he surveyed the tables of guests. He had been able to muster only one local relative and his family for the bridegroom's side in church, one Dr Charles Parry a cousin of his late father, a few times removed, so he had extended the invitation to new friends and a colleague, John Drake. This last gesture had shown how far their toleration of each other had grown since they had first met in the autumn of 1831, though Nathaniel trusted Drake little more than on first viewing. Captain Peterson had also wanted to invite Drake, as he knew him through connections with Lord Melbourne, and Nathaniel had been interested to see them conversing earlier, obviously on very familiar terms. It was still a matter of some surprise to Nathaniel that Oliver had neglected to take him into his confidence in the early days of their friendship, or even to drop a hint of warning about his continuing role with the Office. But he really should have guessed the truth of it, as he had known of Oliver's work with his own father, Owen, which had been clandestine and undertaken during the dangerous days of the war. Captain Peterson, though bluff and honest, was a man adept at keeping secrets, which could only be to his credit. He had also been charming to Lottie Drake, who had reciprocated and even succeeded in suppressing her metropolitan boredom and been pleasant in turn to Mrs Peterson. This attention had driven the mother of the bride into transports of delight. London connections were as gold dust in Bath society, especially when associated with the government.

Nathaniel was more pleased to see that his fencing club friends had taken the time to attend, Captain Charles Wilkins of the Yeomanry doing him the honour of serving as his best man. Half a dozen of Charles's officers from the Bath volunteers were there in uniform, giving the occasion a dash of martial grandeur. Fairfield and Cruttwell were there with their wives, in the company of Howard Dill, who was, as usual, escorting Tilly Vere. All six were in a jovial huddle raising their glasses again for some additional private toast. Nathaniel noticed this with great relief, as until this day he had always had an uncomfortable feeling that at some distant point in the future he might wake up and find himself married to Tilly, a victim to misplaced sympathy, or guilt, or maybe even lust. Tilly was still luminously beautiful, though after the mysterious disappearance of her husband she had an odd position in society, hovering on the edges of widowhood but not quite qualifying. Luckily, she seemed to get about town and lived high without attracting too much comment by attaching herself to Howard and his friends.

It was with more mixed emotions that he caught sight of Coco Montrachet and Diarmuid Casey. He had not seen them in the Abbey, but that was no surprise, as once there he had been preoccupied with the ceremony. He looked again at his new wife. She looked pretty, but strained in her finery, the tightly fitting wedding gown of gold embroidered ivory muslin and foaming blond lace, the net of sparkling diamante flowers taming her chestnut hair. Despite his successes as an agent for the government, his years abroad, his easy popularity with women, his had not been a charmed life. He had made a decision to join the Peterson clan to acquire a wife and a family to fill the void where the centre of his life should have been. It had been a calculated choice and there was a price to pay. He now had others to consider, a wife and household he had to protect in an unpredictable world. He glanced back at the officers in full dress uniform, sabres at their sides. Involuntarily he shrugged his shoulders. He was surprised to be enjoying the day as much as he was. It had been quickly planned to coincide with a pause in his business affairs after a meandering year-long engagement and was proving to be a strangely unreal experience, an insubstantial bubble quite separate from normal life. On her wedding band he had commissioned an engraving: *For Emma, my Bright Star*. It had seemed right at the time, in homage to their shared love for Keats, and she had been pleased. But perhaps it should have been something from Shelley. Keats always brought with him a sense of impending doom.

"Our man's gathering himself up to speak," said Diarmuid, on top rakish form as he returned to a table by the door to join his companion. His green eyes glinted with mischief as he sank the rest of his champagne.

"So I see," said Coco, smiling fondly at Nathaniel, who was as usual running a hand through his thick black hair to tame it and focus his thoughts before he spoke.

She enjoyed looking at him as much as she had enjoyed exploring his body. His eyes were arctic blue, his winter skin a bleached Celtic white, but he smelled always of warm summer. Emma should have the first of many enjoyable evenings once they made their escape from the reception. She rather liked Emma and wished her no harm, but that did not affect her views on Nathaniel in the slightest. She had enjoyed getting to know him, and making herself useful to him in a number of ways. And he in turn was not without his usefulness.

Her mission in Bath had almost stalled before the tasty little episode generated during his first investigations in the city at the time of the Reform Riots. Thanks to him and the events of 1831, Ravenswood and his wife had been tempted to come to Bath and she had caught sight of her very own El Dorado in the shape of Mrs Ravenswood waltzing round the Guildhall wearing the same Montrachet gold-mounted emeralds that she had spotted round her scrawny neck at the Duchesse d'Abrantès' *salon* in Paris three years before. It had taken time to determine the best way to close in on her quarry, but it had been worth the wait. Her relationship with Diarmuid was still casual in terms of commitment, but it had prospered modestly, as had he, and news from her surviving brother in France was encouraging. She had the makings of a plan, which had reasonable hopes of success.

"I bumped into Sir Giles Mortimer-Buckley in the foyer," continued Diarmuid, lowering his voice as Nathaniel began his thanks. "You know who I mean, sweetheart? The county member who's coming to the dinner with us tomorrow: entering the lion's den! But he reckons he's known Ravenswood man and boy, so he should realise what he's getting into."

"Do you still mix with him in the House, Diarmuid?" asked Coco, leaning closer to whisper in his ear. "Any information I can get on the Ravenswoods before tomorrow will be welcome."

"Sure, and it's a conniving hussy you are, my darling," said Diarmuid. As his arm encircled her waist, he planted a kiss on her cheek and squeezed her tight. There was always an element of danger in being close to Mademoiselle Montrachet, which he enjoyed. They continued to rent the same suites of rooms in Queen Square, a floor apart, close enough for dalliance but still separate. When they had first met in Bath and wanted to step out together in respectable society they had put about the tale that he was an old family friend chaperoning her on behalf of her brother. Surprisingly it still seemed to pass muster. He sometimes gave her money, but only as a casual present as he knew she had other men and was not short of funds. It suited Diarmuid not to ask for details as he loved her mysteries and found her tantalising.

They both found it amusing that they had managed to infiltrate most circles of society despite the irregularity of their relationship, but Diarmuid was clearly more welcome to attend alone at some events, and the cold wind of moral disapproval was blowing more fiercely as the century progressed. He had also noticed that its increase had a proportional effect on the numbers and repellent qualities of undergarments favoured by women. There might come a day when his career demanded the banishing of the delectable Coco from public view, but it was not yet. He craned his neck to make eye contact with a serving maid and motioned her over to re-charge their glasses.

Dairmuid Casey had entered parliament at the same time as Sir Giles Mortimer-Buckley after the 1832 elections, and the new reforming members had spent useful time together, forming alliances in the bars and tearooms, making themselves known to the Ministers. Diarmuid knew exactly what kind of man Mortimer-Buckley was: a ladies' man and a wastrel with irregular appetites. He seemed wealthy, and would need to remain so. He lived fast, whereas Diarmuid gave the impression of being a man about town without sacrificing his hard won resources to pleasure. Diarmuid had worked his way up, acting for Daniel O'Connell throughout the late 1820s, and he had achieved a great victory in winning a seat previously known for its Tory loyalties. Buckley had come in unopposed after extensive bribery had rendered the staging of an election unnecessary. The Great Reform Act might have given the vote to more men, but voters were still few enough in number to allow wealthy candidates to buy their way into many constituencies. Corruption had simply been tidied up round the edges rather than removed.

"He's said nothing to me about Ravenswood. But really, Coco my love, what more do we need to know? He'll trade in anything and anybody to turn a profit; he's a dangerous bastard and I vowed I would never get within striking distance of him. He would probably have done away with the both of us if he ever knew we had lifted a finger against him. I suggest you are simply grateful that I've wangled us an invitation to his dinner and try to behave whilst you are there in my company. He is rather beloved of Lord Palmerston. So remember that, and no monkey tricks or you might damage my brilliant career."

"We did not exactly raise a finger against him personally," said Coco pouting, as she knew he liked it.

"We got close enough and I would rather you wanted to pick anyone else's pocket rather than his! You had better be sure his wife's still got your family trinkets."

Coco patted his knee consolingly. "That is rather the point of the visit. Now, shush. Listen to the groom."

## On board the *Zhen Tian Lei* , London Docks, Wapping.

Two figures stood together, deep in conversation on the foredeck of the junk as it prepared to sail down the Thames on the receding tide. The Dutch crew handling the unfamiliar sails made sure they stayed at a respectful distance from the two men, well out of earshot and far enough away not to attract attention. One of them was known to them, a Mr Kizhe, the emissary of their employer, the Count. Kizhe had become a regular passenger on their own merchant ship over the last few months and had ordered them to sail his vessel to Amsterdam. Few were willing volunteers and some still bore the scars of his attentions. He was not a man to cross or one to be close to when displeased and the word was that the interview with the Londoner would not go well.

"So, Tiler," said Kizhe, turning his massive head from his scrutiny of the quay and fixing the other man with a searing, reptilian glare. "The problem stemmed from my scouts taking girls for the trade as part payment for gambling debts."

"Yes, sir," said Tiler, his eyes darting over Kizhe's rectangular frame, the bludgeon of a hand at rest on the weapon in his belt, his trademark "helmet breaker". He was new to Kizhe's employ and needed to be wary, but his master was unreadable, his closed face frozen long before in the wastes of the Russian-Mongolian borderlands. Tiler plastered an approximation to honesty onto his rat-like face and continued. "The man who calls himself Smith directed them, he's waiting below. They would've failed to meet your quota if they hadn't used more versatile methods. There weren't enough people ready to sell unwanted kids." He swallowed nervously. "The problem came as the men didn't explain the situation to their wives. Next minute the women are runnin' to the London police bawlin' that their girls are kidnapped and attractin' too much attention from the authorities. The papers are reportin' a wave of kidnappin' and the police are stickin' their noses in everyone's business round the docks. An' there's plenty to find out if they sniff for it. Quite a tidy few of the last consignment were taken off the streets, mudlarks and the like. Some of 'em had families or friends and they went to the police as well."

Kizhe nodded briefly. "The scouts must be more selective or my men will pay them a visit. I will make sure Smith understands this. And we need better quality stock. I know we have taken women and harlots from debtors before as part payment for debts, but they are not valuable prizes, Tiler. They are second hand goods." He paused to think, cracking his knuckles and flexing his massive shoulders. "Now, on another matter, I will return shortly to see a Mr Ravenswood of Bristol, he has two vessels at dock here. Watch them, discreetly. Be my shadow. Look out for a Chinese man called Lee, Cornelius Lee. He was working for me but left a job unfinished some time ago. Others have tried to locate him but failed and I have some new intelligence that he has left China and sailed for Europe. My man Qiang will be your contact until I return."

"Yes, sir," said Tiler. "See it as done."

They fell silent as Captain van der Linde strode up to them.

"Excuse me, sir. The cabins are ready for you to inspect."

The Captain led the way below decks but once there left Tiler and Kizhe to their own devices. So it was Tiler who led the way past the locked doors, sliding each inspection hatch open as they negotiated the narrow passageway. The atmosphere was cloying; heavy with the stench of perfume and drugs. The rooms were occupied by children and young women, all ominously silent, slumped semi-conscious on the bunks or asleep, ready to be transported to their fates at the hands of the highest bidders.

Kizhe nodded his head as they progressed, well-satisfied. After they left the cargo hold they made their way to the Captain's cabin, where Kizhe's men waited for their master to interview the second visitor. Kizhe settled in with his back to the porthole and ordered the Englishman to be summoned, but he was not the most urgent matter for consideration. A letter from China rested in his pocket with news from Canton. His operatives had sent word that the Emperor was tightening his grip on the criminal underworld at home and that the Count was now a person of interest. Kizhe's mouth set in an iron line. His patience with the scout would be short.

The Englishman ushered through the door was a slick, over-dressed rake of thirty years or so, puffed up with self-importance and heading for a fall.

"Mr Kizhe, you know my worth. Your quotas have been met in every particular and well within the time limit." He leered round the room, thumbs in his waistcoat pockets, his head cocked at an angle. "Double my pay or you lose my services!" He flung the ultimatum grandly, but had addressed it to Qiang who sat in the Captain's chair close to the door. It was his second mistake and an easy one to make, but it was a costly one, given the inaccuracy of the first.

"Mr Kizhe is seated at the head of the table," said Qiang, gesturing to his master. "You'd be well advised to make your pitch to him."

"Come closer," said Kizhe. "Sit by me." He patted the chair by him, and the Englishman, disconcerted and with a sudden sweat beading his brow, worked his way round the table to take the seat. "So you feel you deserve more rewards, Mr Smith? It is as Mr Smith you prefer to be known, I gather?" said Kizhe.

"Yes, Smith," said the man, reviving as he spotted Tiler in the shadows to Kizhe's right. "That is as I'm known, ain't it Tiler!"

But Tiler was wise enough not to say one word.

"I think you deserve more than you have," said Kizhe, placing a line of sovereigns on the table between them. "Do you think you deserve these as a start?"

Smith's face relaxed and his lips drew back in a grin, but even as he made a move to claim his prize, Kizhe drew a dagger with lightning speed and impaled the grasping hand before it closed.

Unmoved by the agonised howls, Kizhe said quietly. "This is only the beginning of what you deserve, Smith." He gestured to the quaking man's pocket watch chain and its dangling crucifix, "Do you read your Bible? Though not to my taste it is instructive. The wages of sin should be death. You have been spared today for your sins against the Count. Your stupidity in stimulating the rash of kidnappings has alerted the authorities and attracted unwanted attention to our business. Any future experimentation will be done only with my explicit permission. Do you understand?"

Ignoring the rambling assurances of his victim, he tore the dagger from Smith's hand and its anchorage in the table beneath. He signalled to Qiang. "Get him out of my sight. And Tiler, before you go back on shore, bring the woman from cabin number two to my quarters. The creature will have little retail value and I have some time to kill."

As Smith was dragged away, and Tiler disappeared to do his bidding, Kizhe surveyed the line of coins and the pool of blood. The prospect of meeting with Ravenswood again was a welcome one and would be lucrative. He hoped that the meeting with Lee would be equally rewarding but in a very different sense. As the ship pitched in the wash of a passing vessel, he watched the blood spread its gore further and his seamed face crinkled involuntarily into the harshest of smiles.

### Afternoon: Saint James's Square, Bath.

Captain Peterson's carriage, heavily loaded with the new Mrs Parry's trunks and boxes, had first laboured up the hill earlier that day. It had made the short journey from her family home in Marlborough Buildings to her new married quarters in Saint James's Square whilst the marriage ceremony took place in the Abbey. Nathaniel had bought the house well before Christmas and had had time to prepare. The most tired parts of the paintwork had been given a fresh coat, basic furniture had been acquired and, since the previous week, staff had been put in place. This was the first time he had assembled a cohort of retainers, as the rent for his rooms in Lambeth included domestic service and the family home he had inherited on Anglesey had a farm attached, which provided servants in the shape of the farmer, his wife and numerous off-spring.

The Bath contingent had been assembled at speed, but the boot *cum* knife boy, Tobias, he had known for some time and had originally employed as an informer. Nathaniel now planned to train him as manservant and general *factotum*. Em knew the boy and liked him, so that was good. Similarly she was kindly disposed towards Frances, a newly-promoted parlour maid whom she wanted to train as her lady's maid. Nathaniel had rescued this particular waif from criminal clutches some time ago and had been pleased to see her placed in the Peterson's kitchen. Em had resolved to bring Frances with her when she left home and saw her as a project in progress, which was also good. The aspect that might not be so good resided in the unknown quantity of the lynchpin of the staff. Since their household was small, he had hired a woman to be cook and housekeeper combined, the formidable Mrs Rollinson, whose expression in repose resembled that of a hippopotamus disturbed at dinner. She would have to oversee the comings and goings of the daily and weekly staff: the cleaners, the laundresses and the gardeners, and deal with any problems they generated. Her references were impeccable but unless Em could manage her there might be trouble on the home front. Mrs Rollinson had been issued with a scullery maid, one Harriet Pullen, and the whole troupe was out on the pavement, ready and waiting to greet the new master and mistress, as the carriage made its second appearance of the day in the square and the new owners were handed out onto the pavement.

Emma Parry stepped out in her wedding finery, still holding a spray of greenery and white roses but with the addition of a white velvet cloak around her shoulders, which flapped wide and billowed away from her in the bitter January wind. Her eyes shone with an unnatural brightness and she did not feel the cold. Being practical she put this down to the champagne, but it was also because of a delirious dose of happiness, which was for her very unusual and proving to be uncomfortable. During the speeches at the reception she had had too much time to reflect. To be realistic, and she was nothing if not brutally honest with herself, Nathaniel Parry was an extraordinarily good catch who attracted women wherever he went. She had seen his effect on them; some of them she readily admitted had the edge on her in looks, though she gave place to none in devotion. She had been even more relieved than Nathaniel to see Tilly Vere so securely latched on to Howard Dill. It seemed a lifetime ago that she had entertained a real anxiety about Tilly's designs on Nathaniel. Fortunately he had not been wealthy enough for her to make a determined play for him. Coco, however, was an entirely different matter and she really did not want to know the full details of his relationship with her.

But despite the current reality of her happiness, she had wasted time constructing mantras of insurance to protect herself against future disaster. She had repeated to herself foolishness such as: "Even if everything goes wrong tomorrow, this morning has happened. It's real. It can't be taken away." And a treacherous tear would roll down her face in sympathy with the foolishness. If she were unlucky someone would see it. Her mother had spotted one and said she should not be frightened and that marriage was normal. She must follow her husband's instructions and all would be well. Her father had seen one whilst Nathaniel was making his speech and asked if she was all right and she had told him they were tears of happiness, which in part they were, for she was happier than she had ever thought possible. It was a strangely ominous feeling.

So she stood, hesitating in the rising wind, trying to shake off her thoughts and return to reality by greeting the servants, when Nathaniel suddenly bent down and swept her off her feet, lifting her in his arms and striding forward to the open door.

"You shall be carried across the threshold, Mrs Parry," he declared. "Welcome to your new home! And look, here's Caradoc waiting for us! Here, sir! The new mistress is moving in, come and say hello."

"Oh Mr Parry, watch 'im!" yelled Tobias from the path, losing all the carefully tutored aitches he had built up painstakingly over the last year. "'E 'as bin in the old quarry and is all over mud!"

It was, of course, too late. Caradoc, Nathaniel's black and tan Welsh terrier, had at first resented being left behind by his master, who had looked unusually well-groomed that morning and was wearing new clothes trailing foreign scents; the strongest being tailor's shop and cologne water. Magnanimously, Caradoc had not complained but had abandoned the servants and spent the morning excavating a fox hole in a nearby park. He was now in a better mood and ready to pay his respects. With one enterprising leap he managed to land on top of Emma and her bouquet, whilst both were still bundled in Nathaniel's arms, in order to set about licking a ferocious welcome. It was not so much the additional weight but the velocity which toppled the lot of them onto the hall floor in a confusion of gold muslin, feminine squeaks, manly bellows, yaps and mud.

Emma wriggled free of Nathaniel, gasping with laughter, and attempted to struggle to her knees whilst fending off Caradoc. She did not mind the fall and was surprised to realise she did not care that there had been an audience.

"Good to see you too," she said, rubbing the dog's head before letting her new husband and staff rescue her and set her on her feet.

"Are you all right, my dear?" said Nathaniel, guiltily brushing her soiled sleeve. "Sorry about Caradoc, he was excited."

"Me too," said Emma. "It doesn't matter about the dress. I rather liked the welcome, but it was a baptism of mud! I need to change. Frances, could you lead me to my dressing room?"

Nathaniel kissed her before she went, which stimulated a ragged burst of applause from the domestic staff; a phenomenon brought on by the excitement of the wedding day and never again repeated. He then bent down, scooped up the wriggling and grimy Caradoc and bore him off to the outhouse.

Frances had helped her mistress out of the frothy gown, which was now additionally decorated with blotched paw prints, and laid it on the chaise longue.

"And the corset, if you please, Frances. I can't wait to get rid of it. You will soon discover in your new role as my maid that I am not a regular wearer of stays. I am no fashion plate I'm afraid. Now the head-dress, that's better, and brush my hair."

Emma sat before her dressing mirror in her petticoats and chemise, scrutinising her reflection. She felt back to normal and much calmer, as if the fall had shaken some sense into her.

"How are you getting on with Mrs Rollinson?"

"Well, Miss. Sorry, Madam, I should say," said Frances, pausing in her vigorous brushing of Emma's mass of glinting chestnut hair. Newly released from the netting, it fell over the back of the chair to her waist. "She's a powerful woman and no mistake. I'm right glad I'm parlour and bedrooms and not scullery no more. That little Harriet will have to jump to it."

"Well, since you are sharing a room with Harriet, keep an eye on her and let me know how she fares. What is your room like? I've not seen it myself yet."

"It's on the back, nice view of the garden, Madam. Mr Parry chose everything in it. It's unusual. It's good though," she said hurriedly.

Emma resolved to put on a plain gown and explore the house. They had just two days' grace in their new home and then they would pack and drive to the manor farm on the Isle of Anglesey for their honeymoon. It was a journey she had never made before, up the Wye Valley, by the mountains of North Wales, a great distance of over two hundred and fifty miles, so Nathaniel said. Her spirits soared at the prospect of a month of dallying there, Nathaniel free from work and she free of everything and everybody except him.

Whilst Emma was setting about her new role as mistress of the household, Nathaniel had summoned Tobias to receive his instructions for the rest of the afternoon. He was to go to the York House to collect and distribute a consignment of wedding cake.

"Take it to Mrs Spence's family," said Nathaniel, struggling to hold down a reluctant Caradoc in the tin dog bath. "Send them all my best wishes and spend some time with them, they will want to hear all about the wedding."

Tobias left willingly enough. A walk through town and a cup of tea at his old lodgings was a pleasant way to spend the rest of the afternoon. He made his way by the mews behind Royal Crescent, along Rivers Street and then turned down Lansdown Hill and made for the London Road. The York House was a large coaching inn on a corner site, dominating the crossroads and much of the coaching trade from the capital. Half a dozen servants were busy outside the front entrance dealing with two coaches full of travellers and their luggage, lately arrived from London. A third coach was turning into Broad Street, making for the stables' entrance at the rear and Tobias followed on behind it, weaving his way through the waiting ostlers and teams of fresh horses to make his way to the kitchen entrance. Nothing seemed to have changed since his brief stint there as a boot boy and it gave him a thrill to swagger in sporting his frock coat and striped waistcoat, playing the man, giving his instructions to the potboy like a regular gent. He took delivery of the cake box and within the quarter hour presented himself at Martha Spence's house in the trim Georgian terrace in Walcot, only just remembering to run the soles of his shoes over the boot scraper before she opened the door.

"Master Tobias Caudle," she said, rubbing her hands on her apron and stepping back theatrically to survey him. "Look at you in your finery! What have you got there?"

"Wedding cake for us all, Mrs Spence, from Mr Parry!"

He followed her down the dark hallway to the kitchen and was surprised to find it thronged with people in full flow. As expected Old Tom was in his place by the fire with the Johnty close by him, no longer a babe creeping round Tom's feet but a sturdy toddler, jumping, clapping and babbling his way through a high-pitched tale at his great-grandfather's knee. He was accompanied by coos, whistles and squawks from Jimmy Congo, Matthew's grey and red African parrot, who was shackled by the foot to his corner perch. Johnty's parents, Mary and Matthew, were also there, both on a shift off work and sitting at the table deep in talk with a weather-beaten old soldier. Tobias had never seen him before and stared, taking in the Waterloo medal hanging awry on his worn coat, his bowed back and the scanty grizzled beard, not thick enough to disguise a burn scar, livid white on the left side of his face.

"Mr Prestwick is our new lodger, Tobias," said Martha, with surprising warmth and stilling all other talk in the room as she did so. "He was an old friend of Mr Spence, my dear late husband." Smiling fondly at him as she placed the kettle on the fire, the severe lines of her face softened. "He came to us this week after too many years away. Sit you down. We'll all take tea shortly and eat this fine cake to celebrate Mr Parry's marriage!"

"Afternoon to all," said Tobias, taking a seat. "Pleased to make your acquaintance, Mr Prestwick."

"And Oiy yours, young man," replied the visitor, rising to attention and shaking Tobias by the hand.

"Hello, hello! Sit down, sit down damn you!" squawked the parrot, his greyish-yellow eyes glinting evilly.

"'Ee do be a caution to be sure, do old Jimmy," declared Old Tom, delighted by the bird and breaking into a cackling laugh.

"Ignore him, Father," ordered Martha, setting out the tea cups and fixing them both with her customary glare. "He's showing off and we want no more of it."

"Foine bird 'e do be!" grinned the old soldier. "Matthew 'ere told me 'e brought 'im back from the voyage when 'e lost 'is fingers! Oiy seen some things at sea 'twould make yer 'air curl," he added confidentially, eyeing Tobias to gauge which tale to offer next. "Once on the India run we 'ad a man overboard and 'e was eaten by a shark before our very eyes."

"What do sharks look like, sir?" said Tobias, thrilled.

"Like monstrous fish with jaws the size o' this table!" declared Ben. "Ripped into 'im they did and left just one boot complete with foot a-floatin' to mark the spot!"

Mary's squeak of alarm caused him to try a change of tack.

"And on land 'twas stranger still, as if the cursed heat weren't enough, widows threw 'emselves alive on their men's funeral pyres, wailin' and howlin'."

"Never! Don't say it!" said Mary, clapping her hands to her cheeks.

"Piece of cake, Mr Prestwick?" said Martha briskly. "We need to talk of happier events."

Reluctant to displace the old soldier, Tobias had to be coaxed to tell some tales of the wedding. Most were vague and at second hand as he had not attended but he gained enthusiasm and authority when he started on Caradoc's reception for the bride.

"So over they went, but she didn't turn a hair, not she! Proper good sport is Missis." The visitor had sat in silence as he listened to Tobias, but his brow furrowed as a slow realisation dawned on him.

"You say yer employer is a Mr Parry and a government man? Welsh you say?"

"I do say so."

"Would 'e by any chance have a father by the name of Owen?"

"I believe so, sir."

"Martha, bless me if 'e ain't likely to be the son of the self-same officer as Phil and me served before Phil's untimely death. Fine man was Owen Parry. He bein' the one who gave us leave to take our prize money in Spain, as Oiy told you all they years ago."

"So you knew my master's father," said Tobias, leaning forward, keen to learn more.

"Oh Ben, you must meet young Mr Parry," exclaimed Martha. "Fine young man he is and a model tenant here a while back. He would welcome a kind word regarding his father as I reckon he was devoted to that gentleman."

"He surely was," added Mary. "His father's death struck him to the heart. About four years past, wasn't it Mother? Tell us about the prizes, Mr Prestwick, and the part Mr Parry played, for I know Mother had great cause to be grateful. Why," she said, smiling round the room, "we do owe this house to the Spanish prize!"

Ben's eyes clouded as other memories surfaced.

"Well, well, terrible toimes, better left lie," he muttered, but immediately sensed the disappointment in the party, and Mary's embarrassment. He had to give more. "But Oiy must say that Mr Parry brought us all three a great stroke o' luck. Without 'im we'd 'ave 'ad no sniff of Napoleon's treasure. For such it was, from the Emperor 'imself bound for King Joseph in Madrid. Sacks of gold and jewels we seen, mounds of 'em! Napoleon's gold we called it! But before we redirected it to Old England, Mr Parry saw to it that we all 'ad our due share, dear old Phil, me and the Captain. 'Tis sad though that my fortunes have now fallen lower than they were. Cheated out of moiy business Oiy was and all Oiy 'ave now is what Oiy stands up in!"

"Napoley's gold!" squawked Jimmy Congo. "Napoley's gold!" flapping his wings wildly and following up with a piercing whistle to draw attention away from the newcomer and back to him where it belonged. As the company clapped and petted Jimmy Congo, Old Tom shot a suspicious glance in the direction of the new tenant. His eyesight was very poor and his legs were letting him down, but over ninety years of living had made him wise.

"As long as ye pays the rent at the month's end ye will be given the respect of a king, Ben Prestwick," he said. Memories of Prestwick as a youth were surfacing. He had led Philip into plenty of scrapes not of his choosing. Perhaps the leopard had not changed its spots.

"More cake?" asked Martha warningly.

"Aye, Mother," said Matthew. "And now, Mr Prestwick, more tales of my father, if you please!"

"And of my master's sire," said Tobias, pushing the cake plate nearer to the shabby man and drawing his chair closer.

**Evening: The Parry Residence, Saint James's Square, Bath.**

Free at last from the relatives, the guests and the staff, the newly-weds had gone up to their bedroom and stood before the open fire, which was locked in an unequal struggle to keep the chill of the room at bay. Nathaniel put his hands round Emma's waist and kissed her, running his hands over her hips and her breasts as he started to unhook her gown. Putting her arms around his neck she felt unsteady, her body answering his touch with a dizzying surge of pleasure.

"Shall I help?" she whispered shyly in his ear.

He smiled and stepped back as she took off her day gown.

"And the rest," he said, slipping off his jacket, waistcoat and stock, pulling his shirt over his head.

Emma stood uncertainly. "All of it? Do I put on my nightgown?"

"No, my darling Em, you do not," said Nathaniel. "And take off your chemise, and your stockings, every last stitch!"

He watched as she dropped the layers of silk to her feet to stand naked and vulnerable before him. It was his first sight of her body and it was a relief to see it was as comely as her face. He dropped the rest of his wedding finery to the floor and took her in his arms, pressing close to her, feeling her tremble, he hoped with desire rather than fear and the creeping cold.

"Come on Em, it's freezing," he laughed, "Let's get warm."

Under the mounds of sheets and blankets they could relax and explore. Her skin felt smooth and firm, like the silk of her gown to his touch and as he buried his head in her, she smelled of roses. Nathaniel was in no hurry as he had known many women. He could afford to be gentle and he knew the ways to make their first love last, which he did, hour on hour, and far into the night.

They woke early, locked in each others' arms and Emma ran her fingers gently over his chest, finding again the scars she had felt in the darkness. The exhausted anxieties of the wedding day had receded and she felt a profound peace, her body pleasantly a-fire and triumphant, as if she had passed a test, which in part she had. From eavesdropping on women's conversations since she had been a child she had some idea that the marriage bed might bring not just joy, but also pain and abject humiliation. Young ladies were not meant to have the slightest idea of what a husband might do, with what, and where, but her sister had been useful on that score. It had made up for the hours of boredom she had inflicted by boasting of her Cirencester farmer before Emma had a man of her own. A little knowledge was power indeed, but her sister had been wrong about never taking off your chemise.

Reluctant to go down for breakfast, they decided to look through the neglected

37

wedding correspondence they had brought up with them the night before. Nathaniel sat up, wrapped himself in his Damascus dressing gown and started to work through the mound of cards and letters. Most were brief good wishes, quickly read, and the pile was almost finished when he stopped abruptly.

"Change of plan required, Em," he said frowning. "We need to go to a dinner with the Ravenswoods tonight. There's a command from the Office and apparently an official invitation from the host will follow. We have a day in hand so our honeymoon in Wales will not be delayed."

"So be it," said Emma, snuggling closer under his arm, "I've never been to Arno's Tower, but I met Mr Ravenswood and his wife at a few events in the Assembly Rooms when I attended with my parents. The Ravenswoods started to come to the Reform Balls here after the Bristol Riots and we occasionally sat in their company. I know that Father, Mr Dill and Dr Parry have invested in Mr Ravenswood's shipping ventures, but I don't remember my parents ever dining with him before."

She paused, wondering if she should mention the unease she always felt in Mr Ravenswood's company. As Nathaniel remained silent she hurried on.

"The mansion is rumoured to be very grand. What exactly does the letter say?"

"Apparently Ravenswood has been informed that we are coming. No doubt an invitation is lurking somewhere in this pile of mail, or it will arrive at some point today. I am not sure how thrilled he will be about having to issue it. Apart from seeing him in the Rooms, I only met him once to speak to privately and I would not say that that either of us was particularly keen to repeat the experience."

Nathaniel leaned over to kiss Emma, who looked troubled.

"It seems that your father will be there with all of Ravenswood's other principal investors from Bath with their guests, which means Howard Dill and Tilly and my cousin Parry and Mrs P. But Drake will be there as well, so there's government business to keep warm. There will be some MPs, a county MP called Mortimer-Buckley and Diarmuid Casey, definitely. General Palmer isn't available. Melbourne wants me there, which now means us. He likes me to be his eyes and ears when business includes Ravenswood and the Office. So my dear, now that you are in my confidence, make sure you also watch our host carefully, he's a dangerous customer. Your father is aware of this now through his links with Lord Melbourne, but please don't discuss it with him."

He looked down at her and was immediately distracted. He ran his hands over her and kissed her again. "Are you content about this?"

"Very," she breathed, her mouth opening to his.

38

Nathaniel pulled back. "And about limiting what you say to your father?"

She smiled back into his eyes. "Of course. I wouldn't share our confidences. As for the evening, it should not be too much of a chore. I like Diarmuid, and Coco of course, no doubt she will be there as well," she risked a glance at Nathaniel, but he seemed unmoved to hear her name. "But I must say I am not eager to spend long in the company of the host."

"So you still like Diarmuid, do you, Mrs Parry. Then he's one I shall be keeping a particularly close eye on."

"Well there's no need," she smiled again and pulled him back to her for another kiss.

But neither of them joked about Coco.

Pleased to change the subject, Emma sat up and began to collect the discarded envelopes.

"Oh look here, we missed this."

She rescued a sealed letter that had been re-directed.

"It has been sent from the Office in London," said Nathaniel, scrutinising the scrawled script, "but it looks like it started off in Paris." He smoothed out the single sheet and read aloud.

*My dear friend,*

*I hope you received my letter that I sent last spring informing you of the successful conclusion of the trip I undertook in late 1831. I am in France to attend to some further business connected with that trip and discovered through contacts in Paris that you were still in England and had plans to marry.*

*Congratulations to you and your bride whenever your wedding may be! I wish you good luck and hope to see you both in the near future. This will be sooner than I thought, as I have business in the Port of Liverpool where I can be contacted at the Golden Fleece Inn. I am sorry to say that the enterprise we were able to inconvenience after our last meeting has flourished despite our attentions, especially in Liverpool and London.*

*Perhaps we may discuss these matters together.*

*I remain, your faithful servant,*
*C.L.*

"Who is C.L. Nathaniel?" asked Emma, but instantly thought better of it. "No, sorry, I should not have asked. I do understand that parts of your job are not to be discussed."

"Well said, Em," said Nathaniel thoughtfully. "But it looks as if you might meet this particular part so you need to know a few things. His name is Cornelius Lee and his permanent home, if he still has one, is in China. I regard him very highly and I know him to be a good man. I would not have been able to rescue Frances without him. However, having said that, it is important to know that he is connected with the Chinese government so his loyalties cannot lie with Britain. Will that do?"

As Emma nodded and sat up to gather together the rest of the scattered envelopes and packaging, Nathaniel put his hands behind his head and stretched out on the bed. The sight of his old friend's name had reawakened the sense of kinship and respect he had felt during their first meetings. He resolved to ensure that he would meet with his Chinese friend. At seventy odd miles from Liverpool to Anglesey it was only a matter of a day's travel on the mail coach. He grinned at the prospect and determined to write to Mr Cornelius Lee, care of the Golden Fleece.

### The previous evening: The Saracen's Head, Broad Street, Bath.

Sir Giles Mortimer-Buckley had had a strenuous and satisfying evening after a congenial day and was ensconced for a final drinking session in the smoke room of the Saracen's Head. He had started with an early session in the Pump Room where he had taken the waters, a full pint of it from the spring. It had been steamily hot and, in line with its reputation, was far from moreish, having an odd, metallic taste. He had quickly overlaid it with hot chocolate and Bath Buns. To follow there had been some gentle walking on the parades fuelled by regular meals in various restaurants, before he moved on to some successful play at a couple of gaming establishments. From the last of these, and following the advice of a fellow backgammon player, he had allowed himself to be led to a rather superior brothel. Though it was in the lower town, Madam Shadwell's was located in a terrace of substantial houses in Green Park and offered an imaginative array of services. It had been something of a slow evening in the house, and he had been able to choose from a bevy of assorted prostitutes, which paraded before him as he lounged on a striped sofa in the first floor drawing room.

To the tinkling accompaniment of the grand piano, he listened to the Madam offer an explanation of the catalogue of talents available and, waving aside some frankly alarming offers from a dominatrix in a leather carnival mask and another sadistic piece wielding a whip, he settled for a more conventional option.  His companion for the evening, a statuesque hussy called Clari, had proved to be totally exhilarating and he had resolved to be back for more of the same before the end of the week and his return journey to London. The combination of her yokel's accent, her overflowing, bounteous bosom and the sway of her rolling hips transported him into a rural fantasy of peasant girls and hayricks. She was a far more glorious version of Maisie Trickett and with no strings attached. He toyed with asking her to wear a frilled cap next week. Innocent pleasures!

He had strolled back to the upper town with Babcock, his comrade from the backgammon club, and they had made their way to the Saracen's Head, a small gable-fronted hostelry in the centre of town. Settled in the smoke room and well attended by the waiters, they had attracted more of their own kind. By late evening they had formed a loud company, their booming conversation dominating the room and, depending on their tastes, entertaining or irritating the rest of the customers.

As ill luck would have it, it was to the Saracen's that Matthew Spence brought his mother's new lodger, Benjamin Prestwick. This was the venue for Matthew's usual Saturday night entertainment: an hour or two in the company of his employer, a barge owner by the name of Declan O'Dowd. This night they would have the novelty of Ben to vary the usual desultory talk of horses, barges, steam engines and the merits of competing local ciders. Matthew looked forward to a few more stories of Philip Spence, the father he could not remember, and his famous adventures in Spain. These had been provided by Ben throughout the day, suitably embroidered to please his old friend's son and calculated to make him well-disposed towards the visitor. Ben was unlikely to be able to pay more than one month's rent, despite his assurances to Old Tom, and Martha's good nature was going to be imposed upon for as long as she would stand it. The last years had not been kind to Benjamin Prestwick. As he had admitted to the company in Walcot Street earlier that day, his business ventures, financed by his share of Napoleon's gold, had failed, as had his marriage. He found himself alone in his old age, his only prospects being parish relief followed by a pauper's grave. As his miserable wanderings brought him back to the West Country he had started to think again about Martha and view her as something of a last hope.

They jawed until they had finished their third mugs of cider, all of Ben's having been at Matthew's expense, and then, reluctantly, they made a move to leave. Their path led them past the voluble group of swells by the smoke room door.

"So your people are still in Gloucestershire!" brayed one. "Name again, Sir Giles! Must know 'em!"

"Mortimer-Buckley, old chap," drawled a voice.

It was unmistakable. Perhaps Ben was more attuned to his old life than he usually was after telling the tales of Spain all day. Perhaps it was also the freak coincidence of hearing again the name of Parry when the boy brought the cake from the wedding. Whatever it was, he stopped in his tracks and turned to that voice. It was him: there was the Captain, older and plumper, his features coarser, but still handsome. Stunned by the sight and sound from the past, Ben seized Matthew's arm.

"By God, there's moiy old Captain!" he gasped, causing Matthew and Declan to hold up and turn to gape at the gentlemen seated round the side table.

"Sir," said Ben, advancing to the group. "Captain Buckley, sir! Oiy last saw ye on the retreat to Corunna. The start of 1809 'twas! Moiy respects to ye, sir!"

Buckley surveyed the bent and bedraggled figure with horrified astonishment and quickly rose from his seat. He blundered round the chairs in his haste, excusing himself as he went, swiftly isolating his new chums from any exchanges he might have to make.

"Upon my soul," he said. "Private Prestwick. I did not know you survived the retreat."

More words were impossible.

Fortunately Benjamin Prestwick filled the void. He introduced Matthew, son of his old comrade Philip Spence, who he was certain Captain Buckley would remember from those old days. He introduced Mr Declan O'Dowd, Matthew's employer and proprietor of barges on the Bath run to Parker's Wharf in Bristol. He also, and in retrospect most unwisely, advertised his current status as tenant in the Walcot home of Matthew and the Widow Spence and expressed a firm desire that he should have the honour of speaking with the Captain at greater length some time in the very near future.

As their eyes locked, Buckley and Prestwick experienced the same vision, but took from it conclusions which were diametrically opposed. They were back on that westerly road to Corunna, night had fallen and a wicked wind blew. Cold and hungry, their small platoon of men had chanced on a village as yet unspoiled by the retreating army. At once and without leave they had fed on whatever could be found, to the bitter fury of the inhabitants, and followed up by draining the wine and spirit stores of every cottage. The night had disintegrated into carnage. Opposition was met by slaughter and the women suffered cruelly at the hands of the British soldiers amongst whom none had conducted themselves more despicably than Captain Giles Mortimer–Buckley. As dawn had broken, Ben had been in a shack with Buckley and another private, the family lying dead at Buckley's hands after his clumsy assault on the daughter and their desperate attempts at revenge, the other private reduced to a comatose bundle on the floor, sodden with drink. They had been discovered by a troop of redcoats sent by Sir John Moore to scour the rearguard for acts of villainy and summarily execute the perpetrators. Ben could see the drunken private now in his mind's eye, swinging on the end of a rope, accused and convicted on Buckley's

42

word, and taking his place on the scaffold.

"Terrible toimes, Captain!" said Ben, slyly.

He saw before him a far better meal ticket than Martha could ever be. Concerning the sacking of the village, his silence had saved Buckley's life. Concerning the sustained looting of the gold and jewels, it had saved his reputation. Mr Parry would not have looked kindly on Buckley's appropriation of the additional shares.

"Terrible indeed," agreed Buckley, reading in Ben's survival and poverty as severe and present a threat as had ever menaced his wellbeing since the end of the wars. He would have made it his business to ensure Prestwick had never survived the retreat if he had known that he had lived. He managed a smile.

"We must indeed meet again my good fellow. I will pass through Bath again in a few days. Shall we say next Wednesday evening? Here at eight o'clock?"

"Oiy look forward to it, sir," said Ben, shaking Buckley's hand energetically, hardly able to believe his good fortune.

Buckley's reactions were not so sanguine. He made his excuses and toiled up Broad Street to his hotel, head bowed, suddenly exhausted by the prospect of what he now had to arrange. The difference between this ignominious return and his sprightly swagger into town that morning was profoundly depressing. On turning the corner he arrived at the front entrance of the York House, chilled to the bone and shivering, he passed the hall porter, ignored the servant's respectful greeting and retired to his room for the night. He tore off his clothes and threw them onto the carpet, fumbled into his flannel nightgown and jammed his nightcap onto his head.

"A drink," he muttered. "Need to warm up."

He poured himself a generous slug of whisky from the decanter he had wisely requested for his room that morning and sank into his armchair. Resolving that another one could not hurt, he drank another three glasses swiftly and, beginning to feel slightly better, he abandoned the glass and crept into bed. Warm at last beneath the blankets and an eiderdown, he dozed off fretfully into a disturbed sleep, crowded by dreams of dark nights on frozen mountains, the rattle of gunfire, blood and the sickly stench of bodies. He passed again through burning villages and saw the ravaged dead. Crying aloud he awoke briefly then sank again into sleep. As a blessed relief, instead of horror his dreams conjured up a vision of the buxom Clari, kneeling up above him in the bed on the second floor at Madam Shadwell's. He saw again her red lips and dark hair, heard her throaty chuckle as she rolled back her head, but instead of her strong arms reaching for him, well-muscled and supple, there came a creeping white cloud, sinuous and wreathing into the shape of other arms and of another face, the skeletal arms of a white sister with black cavernous eyes and a gash of a smile. He screamed in his sleep and woke lathered in sweat, reaching convulsively for his talisman, his Saint Christopher medal which had seen him safe through worse toils than this. But even as his grasping fingers closed on it, he sank again into the morass of nightmare. He saw a twitching figure on the gallows, and by its side the next condemned man, it was himself, and in the front row of the crowd were Izar and Amaia, crowing in victory, reaching out across the years.

"No, no!" he cried in anguish, and opening his eyes to look up he saw a woman and a child. "No, Maisie, damn you, I told you that you could not have a child! This cannot be!"

As his focus sharpened he became aware of the cold morning light, which allowed him to recognise the matronly chambermaid and her assistant, both wearing the conventional uniform of the York House.

"Oiy be Dorcas, sir, with Tabby," said the maid, peering at him with interest.

So great was his relief and shame he knew not whether to laugh or cry.

# Chapter 2

**Six o'clock in the evening: 27th January, 1833.**
**The carriage drive to Arno's Tower, Arno's Vale, near Bristol.**

The wheels crackled over the frozen gravel of Ravenswood's drive as Captain Peterson's *Berlin* rounded the last bend before they reached the house. All four horses in the team were blowing hard after the run from Bath; their breath flying behind them in steaming clouds and their coats glistening with sweat in defiance of the piercing cold. Gas flares illuminated the dark road at intervals, flooding it with pools of light which caught the heaving flanks of the horses as they passed and lit the faces of the passengers with a fleeting pallor. The four inside passengers were tightly packed, sitting two by two on the bench seats facing each other, knees carefully positioned to the side to avoid collisions. The Captain and his wife had their backs to the horse and driver, favouring the newly-weds with the best view.

"It is bitterly cold in here, Oliver," complained Lydia Peterson to her husband, as she retreated still further into her fur-lined cloak and pulled the lap robe higher. "You ought to have had the foresight to order warmed bricks for our feet."

"Yes my dear, that would have been a damned good idea," agreed her husband. "It's even colder now that we've left the city. Dashed isolated, what! Good duck shooting though, I believe."

"Look! There is the house," said Emma, pointing ahead excitedly. "What are those huge stone figures? They look quite sinister."

"Surely not! Whatever do you mean?" snapped her mother, determined to quash any negativity which might mar the evening. She had warned her husband repeatedly over the preceding week about the doubtful look he had taken to assuming at the mere mention of Edwin Ravenswood's name. She had been looking forward to the dinner enormously and it had been too bad of Oliver to entertain any reservations concerning their host. He and Mr Ravenswood had been such friends until quite recently. The praise for the shooting was a very good sign and she would not have Emma casting aspersions which might fuel the estrangement. "I am sure that they will look quite splendid in the daylight, my dear. Now, remind me again Oliver, where are the other Ravenswood properties?"

Captain Peterson and his wife exchanged polite celebratory gossip about their hosts until the coachman reined in the team at the main entrance to Arno's Tower and all four visitors were handed out by footmen in the Ravenswood livery. Nathaniel glanced away from the flunkeys, and as he expected, he could just make out the shapes of more men guarding the wings of the house, their dark coats hardly distinguishable from the shadows. He looked back to the black mass looming above them, the door framed by stone griffin sentinels. Lit from below by gas flares, they seemed to leap up before him: gothic colossi, black in tooth and claw, investing the pillared doorway with a macabre grandeur. Emma had been quite right. Designed to alarm, they were part of a stage-set for Ravenswood's own *Divine Comedy*.

"Abandon hope all ye who enter here!" muttered Nathaniel to himself, taking advantage of the covering chatter provided by Mrs Peterson.

"What's that?" whispered Emma.

"Dante. We are passing through the vestibule to the underworld, or at least that's what he seems to be hinting at. Don't be intimidated, sweetheart."

"I'm not. Which particular circle of hell do you think would best suit our host?"

"He is greedy and adept at violence, fraud and treachery, which are the fourth, seventh, eighth and ninth circles."

Emma smiled thinly and followed her parents up the steps.

Whilst the Petersons and the Parrys were being shown to the drawing room, three more carriages were approaching Arno's Tower for the dinner appointment. The first was a private coach belonging to Dr Parry and housed not only that genial medical man, but also his wife, and their friends Howard Dill and Tilly Vere. The mood in the coach was buoyant as Dr Parry's anecdotes were flowing well and their guests were not only making all of the right noises, but also topping some of his tales with outrageous ones of their own and generally earning their seats. They were followed by a hired vehicle conveying John and Lottie Drake and Sir Giles Mortimer-Buckley where the mood had turned sombre after John Drake had admitted that they might be joined by the colleague whose wedding he had attended the previous day.

"You say his name is Parry," said Buckley querulously. "Are you sure? The son of Owen Parry who served under Castlereagh in the wars?"

"The very same," said Drake bitterly. "Not my choice old boy, nor Ravenswood's I might add. Melbourne particularly wanted him to attend as he and I worked together down here in '31. Melbourne valued his contributions, which were in fact damned undiplomatic in view of some business developments I was negotiating with Ravenswood. However, he will likely have left already for his honeymoon. He didn't mention the dinner when I spoke to him yesterday." Seeking to make the best of it, he added, "And even if he does dine, we four are definitely the only guests who have been invited to stay."

"I would have thought that your presence would have been sufficient as far as the Office was concerned," persisted Buckley. "We have important trading issues to discuss. He isn't a shareholder in Ravenswood's business is he?"

"I doubt it."

There seemed nothing more to be said, and Sir Giles Mortimer-Buckley turned his face resolutely to the rushing black void outside the window.

Rocketing along half a mile behind the London visitors and pulled by a sleek black cob, was Diarmuid Casey's brand new *Tilbury* gig. It was small, fast, sporty and dangerous and as such appealed to both Diarmuid and his guest, Mademoiselle Colette Montrachet, who were both set up on the single seat under the hood, cocooned in blankets and taking turns to drive. This allowed Diarmuid to show off his talent and his possessions, and helped Coco to relax and work off nervous energy.

"So you have never been here before?" she said, as she passed the reins to Diarmuid for the final stretch down the drive.

"I have not," said Diarmuid, taking in the extravagant gas flares, broad greenswards and deep woods. "'Tis a grand estate. It surely is. Crime pays, Coco. But I don't have to tell you that do I?"

Coco smiled. "I haven't the slightest idea what you mean. All my transactions are transparently virtuous. I cater for important needs and am given rewards for my efforts. As for tonight?" she shrugged her shoulders. "I am on a mission to view my family's property. Nothing criminal there, darling."

Diarmuid planted a gentle kiss on her cheek as he reined in at the entrance. "Here we are. And remember, discretion is the better part."

Coco looked at him and kissed him back hard on the mouth. Her strange amber eyes, gold flecked and brilliant, were alight with mischief. "It may be so, but it is not the only part I intend to play."

After a welcome interlude of warmth and drinking in the drawing room, Amanda Ravenswood had acted the grand hostess to perfection and transferred her guests smoothly to the dining room. She allowed her footman to slide her seat forward and she settled into it. As planned, Sir Giles had led her out and seated her at the table, exchanging amiable pleasantries, pressing her arm confidentially, and flattering her. He was handsome enough, early fifties she supposed; he had ten years on Edwin and lacked the sculpted rigour of his body, but he had kept a debonair swagger, still quite the "dasher". It had amused her that Lady Mortimer-Buckley had cried off. Perhaps the West Country had no appeal when one lived in Mayfair? It certainly would not have had any for Amanda. She had only been to London a handful of times, Paris twice and Dublin once. It was a matter of continuing annoyance that Edwin had resisted all of her attempts to arrange more trips. But she dared not ask again.

The absence of Sir Giles's wife, without notice, had caused a gap to open at the bottom of the table and Edwin had brought up the rear of the dining party alone as they processed from the drawing room. He now sat opposite Amanda at the far end of the table with a space to his right, where a footman was busily clearing the place setting. Edwin was talking animatedly to Captain Peterson, who she knew socially as a principal investor in the Ravenswood shipping interests. Her husband looked stunningly handsome as he worked on the Captain, a bluff, ruddy customer who had been unaccountably distant of late and needed softening up. She liked to look at her husband, especially from a distance. Living with Edwin was rather like dancing on the edge of the abyss.

She glanced round the rest of the table and felt very satisfied with her arrangements. The dining room was at its magnificent best: richly warm and heavy with the scent of flowers and fruits. Golden candlelight flickered from the wall sconces and the table candelabra, showing everyone to best advantage. Behind every seat was a footman: silent, white-wigged and extravagantly liveried. Fortunately Edwin had been too preoccupied with other matters and she had been allowed to arrange the formalities of the evening. It had given her great delight to construct her table, based not purely on social convention and business interests but also her own needs. Some rules had to apply. She had to be led in by Sir Giles, as the principal guest. Apart from his title and existing family connections, from well before her time as a Ravenswood, Edwin was particularly keen to tap him over the next couple of days for investment in the company, so his position was not negotiable. She still regarded Lottie Drake as a friend of sorts, or at any rate a good contact, but the relationship had soured in the face of Lottie's persistent play for Edwin. She had been shameless in her pursuit and Amanda was in the midst of a campaign to bring her down. When Amanda had written the cards pairing the couples for dining she had taken particular delight in joining Lottie with the rotund and jolly Howard Dill, whose besotted attachment to Tilly Vere made him invulnerable, even if Lottie were bored enough to set about him.

John Drake recognised Lottie's enthusiasm for Edwin and had become something of a partner in misery for Amanda. He deserved some pleasurable distraction, so she had paired him with Tilly Vere. This choice had just a little touch of malice to spice it, as she had gathered that Tilly and John had known each when young and attended the same Assemblies in Frome. If John were to be particularly gallant to Tilly, Lottie might be jealous and taste a little of her own medicine. Amanda homed in on Tilly's fluting little voice whilst still smiling at Sir Giles and nodding approval of his story about a triumphant grouse shoot in Scotland. Tilly was pretty, frothy and superficial, attributes which were clearly appealing to John Drake.

"But you were by far the handsomest young man in Frome, Mr Drake!" Tilly said in conclusion, after a particularly extravagant run of compliments, whilst continuing to pat his arm affectionately. "We all missed you frightfully when you left for London. You say you worked in France, how exciting! Do tell me what you enjoyed most."

Amanda could not bear to hear any more of the same, and looked further down the table to John's handsome subordinate, foisted on them by an official letter from the office of Lord Melbourne himself. She understood that his marriage had taken place only the previous day, and it had amused her to link the new couple with tempting partners. The dashing Nathaniel Parry had been paired with the French harlot that the Irish MP Casey paraded around with, whilst Casey himself entertained the little wife. There had been gossip about Nathaniel Parry and Coco Montrachet and they seemed to be getting on well. Emma in her turn seemed to be listening, entranced, to Diarmuid, yet Amanda was piqued to note that the newly-weds still took the opportunity to exchange glances, full of love and deep joy: quite tiresome for an observer. She also noticed with some bitterness that Emma Parry was no ordinary "little wife". Apart from being statuesque, a good head higher than Amanda herself, Emma had presence, a ready laugh and plenty to say. This was rather a shame, as Nathaniel Parry had appealed to Amanda from first sighting. The rest of the table had afforded less opportunity for amusement. Dr Parry and Mrs Peterson were old friends, as were Captain Peterson and Mrs Parry, and they partnered each other with pleasure. The only comfort gleaned was to punish Edwin by corralling him at the end of the table with that respectable quartet, well away from the sexual allure of the predatory Lottie and the pretty faces of the rest of the young women.

Amanda sat up poised and elegant in her chair as she surveyed her guests and waited for the white soup and sherry. Despite trivial set-backs, she felt oddly victorious, a rare feeling over the last few years after those first few months of marriage. If she squinted down at her chest she could just see the pendant of her heavy gold necklace, the emeralds flashing in the candlelight, and on her brow was the light touch of her new diamond tiara. No jewels rivalled hers around her table. Not even The Honourable Mrs Lottie Drake was wearing anything remarkable. She was pleased that Edwin had reminded her to wear the emeralds; as Sir Giles had originally presented them to her mother-in-law. That would create a pleasant talking point. Things really could not be better. She felt perfect, though at a cost, as her corset was laced viciously tight to show off the sleek lines of her new white satin gown and serve up maximum breast cleavage to be admired. Dairmuid's gaze had certainly lingered and Sir Giles had barely been able to keep his eyes off her chest. She had even caught a flash of envy in the eyes of Mademoiselle Montrachet. As the soup made its way round the table she reminded herself severely that one spoonful was her limit. It was a pity; as she loved almond soup, so exquisite and wildly fashionable, she could have made a whole meal of it, but there were other courses to consider. The tighter the corset, the more soup was left in the bowl. It was instructive to see that she, Lottie, Tilly, Mrs Peterson and Sir Giles left the most.

By the time the turbot had been finished Edwin Ravenswood was certain that Captain Peterson had discovered something unpalatable about his business but realised he was too closely tied through his investments to sever connections. It was also plain that Peterson still had government links and must know that Lord Palmerston supported his swashbuckling narcotics trade with China, would encourage more of it when the East India Company's monopoly lapsed and would keep a blind eye turned to any of his other endeavours, provided that they were not brought to his attention. The most discreet of these, the trafficking of women to the east, had suffered a set back over a year ago and Edwin suspected that the Captain had had wind of it. Despite this, the host felt more relaxed. Peterson was in check, virtually checkmate, and Ravenswood Enterprises was in no danger of losing that particular source of investment.

Whilst Edwin and the Captain had talked, Lydia Peterson and the senior Parrys had enjoyed their food and drink, blissfully unaware of the tensions at the end of the table. Diarmuid Casey, as Amanda had hoped, had made himself most agreeable to Emma Parry, as had John to Tilly Vere. He had been totally won over by her blue eyes, wide as saucers, and her drifts of blonde corkscrew curls: she had the happy knack of making any man feel that he was the most eligible creature in the world and John Drake was basking in the attention like a bull seal. However, Amanda had not foreseen that Lottie too would have an enjoyable evening. She had underestimated Howard Dill, who was as charming a man as one could wish to meet, and had overestimated Lottie. Once she realised the extent of Howard's wealth and linked it to his good nature, being attended by him was nothing short of delightful. At any lull in that attention, Lottie happily transferred her gracious appreciation to Sir Giles.

Another reaction, which would have surprised Amanda if she had known of it, was the agitation she caused for her principal guest. She could not miss the fact that Sir Giles seemed mightily impressed by her. They talked a great deal and he clearly admired her as a woman. What she was ignorant of was the consternation caused by her necklace. As he stole regular furtive glances at the display on her bosom she decided to open the batting on that topic.

"I see you recognise my emeralds, Sir Giles! I was so delighted when my husband presented them to me after his mother's death and I know their history!"

Sir Giles's stomach turned over at the thought of what was to follow. Quickly, he glanced over the table, hoping that Nathaniel Parry was engaged elsewhere to give him a chance to close the subject down, but it was too late. His heart lurched as his eyes met Parry's; the blighter had heard every word.

"Mrs Ravenswood," said Nathaniel smoothly. "I could not help but overhear your remark about the emeralds. I must confess that they had caught my eye earlier as they are in precisely the same setting as my mother's sapphires! Those curious links and the double chain are unmistakeable!"

Emma had looked up, smiling, as she heard his voice rise to reach Amanda at the top of the table. He drew her in.

"My dear! You see Mrs Ravenswood's emeralds? It was to be a surprise but I must tell you now. When we arrive in Wales I am going to retrieve my mother's necklace from the bank and present it to you as a wedding gift! You have a preview of the setting. It is an exact match and Mrs Ravenswood tells us that she knows some details of their provenance."

He looked encouragingly at Amanda, who was happy to oblige and, unlike Nathaniel, entirely missed the collapse of Sir Giles Mortimer-Buckley's features. They had crumpled like a rag as he foresaw what might develop into a third torment to add to his other two.

"Yes, indeed," said Amanda, smiling coyly. "Sir Giles brought them back from Spain during the wars. He was in the retreat to Corunna, weren't you Sir Giles? After most distinguished service. These emeralds are French and were part of his reward. He was a close family friend and gave them to my late mother-in-law as a gift. In fact," she added, looking up to see a procession of footmen arriving with the next course, "we have introduced two courses this evening to celebrate Sir Giles's war career. Here is the *poulet à la portugaise*, and later we shall have *aubergines à l'espagnole*. Two dishes from the Iberian Peninsula, specially created in your honour by our French chef!"

Sir Giles mustered a faint smile as the chicken arrived in its lurid red bell pepper sauce. It reminded him of blood. He felt nauseous and looked away from the table, beyond the food and his hostess, to the burning fire and the rising smoke which bloomed and curled as it lifted. And in it he saw the dark shapes of his nightmares: the cavernous eyes, and beneath, a gash of a smile. The room seemed to swirl away and in his throat he tasted again the raw Basque spirit. Horrified, he turned his head back to the table and fixed his eyes on Drake who sat opposite him, busily sniggering into the ear of the little blonde. He must not let his mind wander; must not let his imagination run away with him. But as he marshalled his wits, a hoarse voice whispered in his head.

"Keep sharp, Giles. You can do it."

It was not his voice, not his thought. He felt a twinge of fear but dismissed it. The advice was sound. There was no need for Parry to make any unfavourable links. Buckley shook his head clear and turned to look past Drake and Tilly to Nathaniel Parry, who was innocently occupied with the chicken.

"For God's sake, Buckley!" He rebuked himself sternly. "Parry was a mere child at the time. His father would never have shared intelligence information then, or later, he was a man of integrity. And he knew nothing of the second division of the spoils. We parted south of San Sebastian. He knew nothing of the road to Corunna." He had said it slowly, willing himself to believe it and accept that the damage could be limited. He rallied, permitted himself to smile again, complimented his hostess on her impeccable taste and began a lengthy monologue on Iberian cuisine.

But Nathaniel was not the only diner to have heard Amanda's announcement. Coco's eyes were glinting as she assessed the new situation. Perhaps Nathaniel also needed to be relieved of his ill-gotten gains. She had had a pleasant evening thus far, being entertained by Nathaniel on her right and Dr Parry on her left. There had been plenty of time, as she turned politely from one to the other, to inspect the Ravenswood assets. The dining room was vast and stately, the walls hung with expensive last century oils, mainly portraits and pastoral scenes, many of which were clearly European, a room stressing wealth and possession. The whole mansion was designed to inspire, and not just feelings of envy, but also of awe, and the discomfort of foreboding. Coco saw in Edwin Ravenswood's bleak good looks all the warning signs which would make her reject his attentions. She did not envy Amanda, but rather pitied her. Before she had felt jealousy and had scorned her starved looks and her harshness. Now she had some idea of the hell of her private life, but it would not alter her purpose. The emeralds were from the Montrachet collection and Amanda would be relieved of them.

A champagne sorbet cleansed their palates and was followed by a rich duck course, which allowed free rein for the French chef's national loyalties. Ravenswood had concluded his assessment of Captain Peterson and Coco had attracted him.

"Mademoiselle Montrachet," he said, catching her eye. "You might find this dish more to your taste. It's French, *canard à la rouennaise*. I can vouch for the meat, I shot it myself."

"Do you like shooting birds, Mr Ravenswood," said Coco, meeting his glance.

"Of course. I am a hunter, Mademoiselle. Now tell me about yourself, are you familiar with Rouen?"

The bottom of the table fell quiet, not just out of respect for the host but also in curiosity.

"I'm afraid not. I have lived in Paris most recently and know the south quite well."

"Do you have family there, Mademoiselle?" enquired Mrs Peterson, unable to stop herself, despite her usual reluctance to converse with Coco. If her host deigned to speak with her so freely, it was only good manners to do likewise.

"I have a brother in the Medoc, Madam," said Coco, but regretted it instantly. The desire to show she was not alone in the world had clouded her judgement. For reasons of her own, Jules and all his doings should have remained unknown.

"And this is a *bordelaise* sauce, if I am not mistaken, but with the addition of duck liver. Both variations will be popular in the Medoc, I would imagine," said Mrs Parry.

"You are absolutely right, Madam," said Amanda. "Our chef is from the south-west of France."

"And is your brother connected with the Bordeaux wine trade, Mademoiselle Montrachet?" enquired Dr Parry, beaming down at Coco.

"Ah well, Doctor," she said evasively, "few who live in the Medoc are not."

"You must know that one of our Bath MPs owns a number of vineyards in that area," said Dr Parry, warming to his theme. "General Palmer I mean of course, not Mr Roebuck. Ha! Ha! What a thought, "Tear 'em" Roebuck concerning himself with the cultivation of vines! Not quite his style, what! I'd be surprised if there were a rural side to that gentleman. Too busy haranguing the House! However, as I was saying, the General has had property there since the end of the wars. Palmer's Claret is still a famous drink and it was quite the toast of London at one point! Should have been here tonight, shouldn't he Ravenswood? But he's too busy in Town. The General owns vineyards next to Margaux and also on the right bank of the Garonne. Do you know them, Mademoiselle?"

Surprisingly, Ravenswood himself rescued Coco, first as he introduced the distinguished 1814 Chateau Palmer, which had been provided in the expectation of Charles Palmer's attendance, and then at greater length as he launched into a spirited description of his wine collection. This side-tracked Dr Parry and attracted the attention of all the guests. This was a favourite topic of Ravenswood's and it saw them through to the serving of the *aubergines à l'espagnole*, when Buckley had another difficult phase as the conversation turned inexorably to the war in Spain.

"My father also served in the Iberian campaign, Sir Giles," said Nathaniel amiably. "Isn't it remarkable that you both had trophies from the same collection! Did you ever meet? His name was Owen Parry. He served the Office in Constantinople and had travelled in the Far East."

Buckley pretended to think deeply. "You know, Mr Parry, I do think his name strikes a chord. But it is such a long time ago! Forgive me, I cannot say more."

John Drake shot him a glance, doubting he could carry off the bluff, but incredibly, he seemed to have done just that. Buckley dared to relax and started to believe that he was off the hook, unaware that Nathaniel continued to observe him, watching the man struggle with a wave of relief and the growing heat in the room, watching his face turn as red as the wine and his fingers tug surreptitiously at his collar for more air. Nathaniel was convinced that neither the high-banked fire nor the excessive feeding and drinking explained all of Sir Giles's discomfort and continued to observe him as general conversations broke out and moved the focus of attention away from 1809.

The evening wore on without further indiscretion and dinner continued successfully past the Spanish style aubergines to the desserts, the finale being the *iced bombe*, 1820 style, with maraschino flavouring. Immediately after the barrage of praise died, Amanda rose to lead the ladies out to the drawing room.

"Gentlemen," she smiled, "if you will excuse us."

"Now, gentlemen," said Ravenswood, as the footmen closed the double doors and the men resumed their seats, "first to our port. Again, an offering selected in honour of Sir Giles and his adventures against the French." He allowed himself a satisfied smile of self-congratulation as a decanter was borne in on a silver tray by one of the footmen. "May I present the 1815 Porto Ferreira, Waterloo vintage."

In the respectful silence that fell at the mention of a treat so sublime, Buckley winced and Drake ran his tongue over his lips in greedy expectation.

Ravenswood continued. "You may also smoke and, forgive me, but as you know we must also now turn to business."

The gentlemen moved to Ravenswood's end of the table as another footman removed the cloth and others brought an additional array of *digestifs*: madeira, various brandies and *eaux de vie*, offerings provided merely to reinforce the image of the generous host rather than with any thought that they might be of interest after the majestic port. Ravenswood dismissed the servants, as tradition demanded, and filled Dr Parry's glass, then his own, before passing the decanter to Captain Peterson. Its progress past Dairmuid and Howard was swift, but when it reached Buckley it became marooned. Ravenswood's steely glare bored into him impatiently.

"The port stands by you, Sir Giles."

"Indeed, indeed. Thank you, Ravenswood," blustered Buckley, rapidly filling his glass and allowing the decanter to renew its progress. Once John Drake and Nathaniel had provided themselves with full glasses the host was able to proceed.

"Your good health, gentlemen!" he said, re-assuming the role of genial host and raising his glass. "And also, if I may, a toast to our mutual enterprises." The glasses landed back on the table, spills were held to the candle flames, cigars were lit, and all eyes turned again to Edwin Ravenswood. He raked the company with a penetrating glance and made a snap decision to dispatch the business very quickly indeed. Apart from treating his principal investors to dinner, assuring himself of government support *via* Drake and wooing the MPs, his biggest concern had been to assess Peterson's attitude, which had caused him some concern. He was a major investor who had also been shaping up as an enemy. In theory, they should have been even closer allies as Lord Melbourne the Home Secretary had encouraged the Lord Lieutenant to secure both their appointments as magistrates, but he knew that it had been Lord Palmerston's insistence that had secured his position in the first place. His shipping activities and successful opium trade with China had impressed the Foreign Secretary, but by some means, Melbourne had been apprised of his other activities and the business had been seriously damaged. He was satisfied now that Peterson was not going to be obstructive, but the attitude of Peterson's new son-in-law was more difficult to gauge. Young Parry had not been on the original guest list and Edwin had no intention of discussing more business than was necessary in his hearing. It had been disappointing that the only Members available for the dinner had been Sir Giles and Casey, but he would make the most of a bad job.

"It is a pleasure to welcome Mr John Drake and Mr Nathaniel Parry, who represent the views of the noble Lords. Please assure them that my businesses will be delighted to take up some of the slack when open season is declared on the Chinese tea trade. In conjunction with that new business, my opium runs from India are poised to expand in the very near future. As you will know, I've profited substantially since the Company monopoly expired there in 1813." He smiled without mirth, his eyes implacable. "My new vessel, like the rest, custom built in America, is in the final stage of commissioning for her first voyage to the East and I am actively pursuing additional investment. As most of you will be aware, extensive repairs are still being carried out on the *Mathilda* which was burnt out by rioters in '31. Honourable Members, Sir Giles, Mr Casey, perhaps you would like to join our syndicate at some point?"

Nathaniel felt the familiar flood of relief that his part in the destruction of the *Mathilda* remained undetected. This house was not a place for discoveries or confessions. The men he had seen outside would not be the only ones in Ravenswood's entourage and he sensed that retribution would be illegal, unpleasant and swift. He watched the responses narrowly. Sir Giles seemed to have regained his *sang froid,* and become effusive, promising much, which he looked forward to discussing in detail before he returned to London. Diarmuid blustered about his capital being tied up in extensive investment in French vineyards after a few long evenings with the persuasive General Palmer. Nathaniel had to suppress a smile and wondered if Diarmuid was drunk and simply hung his excuse on the last bit of table conversation he could remember, or if there really was any truth in it. Knowing the turbulent state of Diarmuid's finances he doubted it.

"Couldn't recommend you putting much his way, old chap!" said Howard, his glasses flashing at Diarmuid in the candlelight. "You know Charles Palmer has sunk thousands into his new vines, with no pay-off to date. It's not going as well as it was. I urge you to consider Mr Ravenswood's suggestion. My family has had money in Bristol shipping for generations and never looked back. Sugar's down and the western run's had its day, but for an up and coming young man you cannot better the Far East trade and we are on the crest of that wave, wouldn't you say, Ravenswood!"

"Certainly: and will remain so."

John Drake knew that Ravenswood needed to shield any further discussion from Nathaniel Parry and moved in swiftly.

"So, Mr Ravenswood, on behalf of His Majesty's Government I can assure you and your investors that you will be given every assistance in the pursuance of your trade. The next phase in the development of the eastern market and the anticipated opportunities in tea trading are ideal for your business, as you say, in line with your current enterprises, and all your endeavours will be supported. Gentlemen, may I propose a toast to the future!"

The rest of the hour spent apart from the ladies was measured out in port for the majority, though Buckley, Drake and Diarmuid Casey were tempted to diversify and moved on to brandy, after which Drake coaxed Buckley into a boisterous mood. Soon he and Casey were taking turns to tell increasingly audacious tales. These stimulated ready guffaws from John Drake, Howard Dill and Dr Parry, coaxed reluctant chuckles from the Captain and Nathaniel but attracted only stony indifference from their host.

The ladies first withdrew to the white and gold drawing room where the guests had been received and Amanda served coffee with the help of a footman. The two matrons and Tilly set the pace, admiring the *décor* and giving Amanda opportunities to show off, whilst Lottie entertained herself by examining her hostess, Coco and Emma. She was pleased that there would be no embroidery session that night, she knew Amanda well enough to be able to rely on that. The tyranny of the needle ruined many an evening and the absence of such annoyance at Arno's Tower was one of its many attractions. It had been unfortunate that Amanda had taken exception to her little game with Edwin. Her master plan was for Amanda to entertain herself with John until she tired of Edwin, but it had not been working out well. Perhaps they were too alike. She looked again at Amanda; avaricious, jealous, anxiously thin, yet also ruthless with those strange pointed eyeteeth. So like John, who was foxy yet also insecure. He was good for the long term as his ambitions were paying off, but she needed variation, a little danger and excitement. She smiled to herself, reflecting on what the night might yet bring.

Emma Parry, the new bride, was of less interest, as were her connections. Lottie always saw Nathaniel Parry as a rather worthy subordinate of John's, upright and depressingly strong on moral rectitude, though she knew Amanda was taken by his looks. By all accounts he should not have been invited and was here on sufferance because of some ruling from Melbourne. However, Coco Montrachet was altogether more interesting. Lottie had spent time in Paris in the 1820s and recognised in Coco the same effortless elegance which had fascinated her there. It was rumoured that she had been a high-class courtesan. Perhaps she could learn a few things from Mademoiselle. Amanda obviously had the same idea, tiring of the subject of drapes she had turned to Coco for some light relief.

"So, Mademoiselle Montrachet, you know Paris well?"

"Oh yes," said Coco. "I believe we attended the same *soirée* in the winter of 1828. The Duchesse d'Abrantès was the hostess and I was in the party of the Marquis de la Blanquefort."

Amanda and Lottie drew visibly closer, leaning in towards Coco as she spoke.

"How fascinating!" said Amanda, smiling, eyebrow raised at Lottie, to signal revenge for the hours of torment she had previously endured. Amanda's failure to penetrate high society on her trips to Paris had entertained Lottie hugely and encouraged her to annoy the provincial Mrs Ravenswood with tales of aristocratic revelry at Versailles. If only Amanda had known that the Marquis was at the Duchess's gathering, she could have scored that particular point much earlier.

"Yes, quite diverting," said Coco, radiating charm, "but I am having a marvellous time in England. And this is the most wonderful house I have visited since I arrived! I gather it has been constructed recently and I have also heard that the design is exceptional. I have spent much time in older buildings in France but am longing to see innovative architecture, especially that which re-imagines the Gothic so splendidly. The Marquis himself was able to reclaim a number of his properties when Louis XVIII returned to the throne so at present he has to concentrate wholly on restoration." As the men were missing and it was a time to exchange confidences she risked another reference to her family. "My dear brother is renovating and extending a *château* in the Medoc. He sees it very much as a family project and often asks for my views on design. Mrs Ravenswood, would it be too much to ask to be allowed to see the upper floors here?"

"By all means, it would be a pleasure," said Amanda. "Would anyone else care to join us for ten minutes?"

"I'm happy here, thank you," said Lottie quickly. As a house guest she had plenty of time for snooping.

Coco, Tilly, Emma and Lydia Peterson had already risen to their feet but the senior Mrs Parry declined.

"I noticed your impressive staircases, Mrs Ravenswood," she said gravely. "I will remain with Mrs Drake, if I may."

Coco could not believe her luck. A brief idea of the lay-out of the house, the design of its shutters and the extent of its security was all she needed and it was to be handed to her on a plate. "Altogether," she reflected to herself, whilst smiling amiably at her hostess, "quite remarkable progress." It was the icing on the cake, as it had already been a very satisfactory evening. The matrons had been forced to be gracious to her, Amanda Ravenswood had proved astonishingly amenable and she even sensed some fellow feeling in the haughty Lottie. Emma had been on sparkling form and good company. Coco exchanged a glance with the new Mrs Parry as they moved to the door.

"Marriage suits you, Emma," she said.

"Thank you," said Emma warily, but liked the twinkle in Coco's eye and added smiling, "Does it show?"

Amanda led the way from the brilliant drawing room to the wide hall with its sweeping staircase circling round in a great arc to the grand first-floor landing. As the visitors followed Amanda up the marble stairs, Lydia Peterson looked about her in such a state of reverential awe that she missed her footing and would have slipped if Coco's arm had not darted out to save her before she went down.

"The music room, ballroom, library and art gallery are all on this floor," Amanda was saying. "They all have beautiful views. Let's start with the music room."

"What a superb collection of instruments, Mrs Ravenswood!" exclaimed Coco, relinquishing her grip on Lydia and flitting from harp to piano, to the instruments mounted on stands and then to the windows, inspecting the balcony and shutters as she did so. "Do you lock any of these violins away in safes to protect them?"

"No need," said Amanda with a short laugh. "My husband's men patrol the grounds at night, we have no security worries!"

"Do you play?" said Coco. "I confess I would want to be in this room all the day!"

"I do, but have little time to devote to music," said Amanda, leading them back to the landing. "As you see, the bedroom and dressing room floors above all look down on the hall from the circular balconies."

"And do the upper floor rooms all have the wonderful balcony views that the music room has?" inquired Coco innocently. "I would want the room in the very centre of the second floor I think. It seems larger than the others."

"That is mine," said Amanda triumphantly. "And yes, the balcony is marvellous. You can see right over to the wood. Come into the gallery now with the lights out and the shutters open."

They trooped into the darkened room and made for the French windows which could be opened onto the stone balcony. Standing close and quietly, looking into the night, they saw a sloping green and in the distance, the tree line, misty and indistinct.

Suddenly Emma caught her breath. "Oh look!" she gasped. "Someone is running by the edge of the trees! He's carrying a heavy bag."

"Where?"

Amanda pressed closer to the window, and the rest peered out in the direction of Emma's pointing finger.

"I can't see anyone," said Coco.

"Just mist my dear, do not cause consternation," cautioned Lydia.

Emma dropped her hand. "He's gone," she said, puzzled. "Just there towards the sundial, he disappeared."

"It must have been one of the men," said Amanda dismissively. "Now come with me." They followed her, but not before Emma looked out once more across the cold garden, and saw four of Ravenswood's men talking in a group, well away from the trees and the gathering mist.

"If you look up you might see a feature with which my husband is particularly pleased, but our view rather depends on the moon."

The moon was obliging, for when the women looked up towards the skylight at the top of the central tower they saw its stained glass brightly illuminated by a ghostly white lunar glare, which spilled down icy splinters of coloured light.

"Oh!" squeaked Tilly. "It's a dragon! Is there a Saint George?"

"No," said Amanda. "It's part of my husband's homage to the East. He has a suite of rooms dedicated to his collection on the ground floor of the west wing, but this keeps its eye on the whole house."

The women surveyed the green and silver scales, the licking flames gushing from its mouth, the leathery wings. Despite the beauty of the work, the malevolence was palpable.

"I see now," continued Tilly, quite unaware of any threat. "It has blue eyes like the *Blue Dragon* itself, Mr Ravenswood's ship!"

"Yes," said Amanda. "Mr Ravenswood tells me that this isn't like the dragon Saint George kills. That is a monster, but this one is the eastern dragon, it symbolises health and banishes evil spirits. Rather like the Welsh dragon."

"He still looks," Emma struggled for the polite word, "formidable. He is a force of nature."

Amanda laughed shortly. "Yes, he is, rather like my husband."

Shortly after they returned to the drawing room, the gentlemen joined them. Amanda played the piano and Lottie was persuaded to sing, which exhausted the matrons in the audience, and within another hour carriages were called. The two Bath bound vehicles were quieter on the return. In one, Nathaniel and Emma saved their deconstructions of the evening until they had privacy, and allowed Lydia Peterson to enlarge on the excellence of the event. Tucked into the *Tilbury,* Coco drove and kept her discoveries to herself, allowing the drunken Diarmuid to entertain her. Meanwhile, as the night wore on and the hostess and the guests turned in for the night, silence fell in Arno's Tower. The host remained in the drawing room in solitary state, stoking up the dying embers of the fire. But he did not remain alone for long, as a steady snore sounded from the second floor rooms allocated to the Drakes, Lottie slipped out onto the landing. Barefoot and wrapped in a silk dressing gown, she closed the door considerately on her sleeping husband and made her way to her rendezvous by the drawing room fire.

**Morning: 28th January, 1833.**
**The Parry Residence, Saint James's Square, Bath.**

Nathaniel and Emma had left the drapes open so they would wake early. Emma had looked pale and exhausted after the coach ride home with her parents, so Nathaniel had postponed any discussion of the evening at Arno's Tower to the morning. He had chosen to lie awake for an hour or two to review the intelligence gained and decide how much he wanted to discuss with her. He had no intention of burdening her with the full details of Ravenswood's Asiatic contacts and his lucrative line in kidnapped women and girls for the overseas flesh trades, but he was sure that her growing attachment to Frances would lead to her finding out eventually. Sadly, it seemed that Ravenswood was still prospering and poised to expand in all directions. The *Mathilda* was to be refurbished despite his best efforts and the new vessel would soon be afloat. He had no doubt that he was not yet trusted by Drake and Ravenswood as he had been pointedly excluded from the appeal for additional investment in Ravenswood Enterprises.

What would he need to convey to the Office? Officially all was well. The small sector of the opium trade run by Ravenswood would continue to prosper in common with the rest of the industry, ensuring a steady stream of silver out of China into British hands, which would then be exchanged back again for the purchase of tea; which was all very convenient for the British balance of payments. He still found it difficult to condemn the opium trade, despite his friend Cornelius Lee's sober warnings about addiction levels in China. Drake had not committed any glaring indiscretions in public, apart from the over solicitous pawing of Tilly when they rose from the table and recklessly encouraging Sir Giles to ever cruder reminiscences over the fourth round of *digestifs*. Both were not reportable offences. Drake's oblique assurance that all of Ravenswood's businesses would receive government support meant that a blind eye was still being turned to the unsavoury side of Ravenswood's trade, but there was no fresh evidence.

He awoke to find that the same thoughts were still circling in his mind, but was soon disturbed by a sustained yelping and scratching on the door.

"All right, Caradoc," said Nathaniel, yawning. "I'll let you out, but don't go far, we will be off for the wild north by mid-morning and you'll lose your seat in the coach if you're late!"

Caradoc shot him a withering look before bolting down the stairs to find the garden.

"Good morning," said Emma, rubbing her eyes and looking through the window. "No snow, that's good for us! How far will we get today?"

"Let's see how ambitious we feel once we are on the road," said Nathaniel, leaping back into bed. "But first, you have five minutes maximum to give your post mortem on yesterday evening, Mrs Parry!"

Emma folded her arms behind her head and considered. "The Parrys, Senior Branch, and my parents all seemed to have had a good time except I didn't like the look on Father's face when Mr Ravenswood interrogated him at the start of dinner. Something is not right there. Mr Dill still loves Tilly Vere, which is good and she seemed to have a fine time. Neither of them minded Mr Drake's zealous attention to her which everyone must have noticed, though Mrs Drake didn't seem to care! Diarmuid was fun, as usual, but Coco was a little different I thought. She asked to be shown around the house when we ladies went out to the drawing room. I wouldn't have thought she would be interested. Also, I had not realised how nimble she was or how strong. Mama slipped on the stairs and Coco saved her. She was so quick that Mama did not even touch the floor!" Emma fell silent for a moment.

"Go on," said Nathaniel. "I sense there is more."

"One really odd thing happened. I saw a figure, a man with a bag running through the grounds. He seemed to be trying to escape from something, or someone, but it was misty and no one else caught sight of him. Mrs Ravenswood said it must have been a guard, but I'm sure it wasn't. I saw a group of them talking together quite a way off. No one else was running." She looked perplexed.

"Never mind, darling, there must be a simple explanation. What about Mortimer-Buckley?"

"I have to say Sir Giles made rather familiar remarks, but it was later in the evening and I think he had had too much wine. At the table I thought he might say more about the emeralds he gave to Mr Ravenswood's mother, as he seemed to like talking about himself." She paused, "It was odd that he didn't, especially as Mrs Ravenswood had gone to so much trouble to celebrate his war experiences with … the Iberian selection at dinner."

Emma offered the last phrase in a spot-on perfect imitation of Amanda Ravenswood's pinched accents and Nathaniel hooted with laughter.

"You are right, dear one: on all counts. Interesting observations of Coco: she has hidden depths, and she bites, metaphorically speaking. I agree about Mortimer-Buckley, he seems a shady cove. Now for the finale: what about our hosts? Be frank."

"I think we would do well to spend as little time in their company as possible," said Emma gravely. "Mr Ravenswood has a chill about him. You were right, he seems dangerous, and Mrs Ravenswood does not seem to bear anyone goodwill, except for herself. But in a way, I felt sorry for her. I wouldn't like to be stranded out there in that forbidding place with him."

"Impressive analysis," said Nathaniel.

"And what was your verdict?" she laughed, pleased at the praise.

"Oh, I agree with you," said Nathaniel, pulling her close to plant a lingering kiss on her lips. And with the first thrill of desire she lost all interest in his verdict on last night's dinner.

After breakfast, they returned to their room to prepare for the journey. Nathaniel always packed his own trunk, one habit from his bachelor days he intended to keep. He checked his medicaments, home remedies for everything from cuts and bruises to fevers, put in some more clothing, though he knew he had a heavy coat and scarf waiting in the Welsh house, provided the moths had not got to them first. Most importantly, he needed to check the secret compartment. There were his silver-handled swordstick, pistols, ammunition, and his makila, the Basque walking stick with the concealed knife; indispensable for rural use. He selected the swordstick for the journey, hesitated and then took the pistols as well. Handling the weapons reminded him of another duty. He reached into the compartment again and took the makila.

"Em, I'm just going to have a word with Tobias. How long will you be? We need to catch the mail coach to Cheltenham."

Emma looked up from the mound of garments she had spread on the bed.

"How cold will it be in Wales?"

"Very," replied Nathaniel as he made his way downstairs.

"Send Frances up, darling," she called after him. "I'm ready for her help now, and I need to leave her instructions about unpacking the rest of the boxes whilst we are gone."

Nathaniel loped off down the stairs to the basement, sent Frances to wait on Emma, avoided Mrs Rollinson and caught Tobias shining boots in the garden.

"Mornin', sir," said Tobias, standing to greet Nathaniel.

"Good morning. Excellent job, Tobias! I'll take those riding boots with me, don't let me forget them."

"You leavin' soon, sir?"

Tobias looked forlorn at the prospect and it occurred to Nathaniel that the boy might have hoped to be included in the trip. "We'll be back by the start of March at the latest. Meanwhile, you will be the man of the house. Help out where you can but remember you must set aside time each day for training. I'll make sure Mrs Rollinson knows you will be out running and you must make time for some practice with your stick. Go and get it now."

"Yes, sir!"

Tobias needed no second telling. Nathaniel had taken it upon himself to train Tobias and work up his slight frame into something more substantial. Regular meals, warm clothes and a comfortable bed were not enough and Nathaniel had enjoyed working out a training schedule for the boy. He had presented him with a walking cane and taught him a few basic self-defence moves which had to be practised and perfected before he returned from Wales. They went to the bottom of the garden where there was a small paved area hidden behind the shed and vegetable plot and sheltered by the high stone walls.

"Right," said Nathaniel, "let's see what you remember. Take your stick in your left hand."

"I'm right-handed, sir," said Tobias, alarmed.

"That's the point. If you injured your right hand would you ask an enemy to wait for it to heal! I am also right-handed, but I will attack you holding my stick in the left."

Tobias blushed, uneasy, and took his stick in his left hand.

"Now keep still, trust that I won't split your pate."

Before the blush had faded Nathaniel had shifted his weight to his right foot, swung his stick in a swingeing arc, slid the right hand to support his hold and brought the weapon down to within a fist's height of Tobias's head. The boy yelped in shock, feeling the rush of air and a shiver of fear and excitement down his back.

"Your turn, but I'll use my replacement head!"

Nathaniel disappeared briefly into the shed and emerged with a post, on the top of which he had impaled a small pumpkin.

"Don't hit the pumpkin, Tobias. Swing and stop. You need control."

Tobias gloried in the attention. He started slowly, the technique slowly flowing to perfection. They tired his left hand and then moved on to the right, then back to the left, but faster.

"Well done. Now one more variation," said Nathaniel, his eyes shining like a boy's. "Body blows. Remember, left, then right. Let's start with the left."

After both sides were tried to the limit, and the pumpkin had shed more pulp than was good for it, Nathaniel called a halt.

"Excellent. You are allowed one new head a week so tell Mrs R I said so. See if you can perfect the moves by the time I return. Put these things away now. The next important task is to locate Caradoc. Has he gone to the park?"

"Not he," said Tobias, as he returned from the shed. "He be under the table in the kitchen catchin' scraps. Mrs R's bakin'."

"Flush him out," said Nathaniel firmly. "Then I would like you to be on call to help Captain Peterson's coachman with our trunks. He's driving us to the posthouse and he'll be here soon, so look lively."

## Early Evening: The George and Dragon, Walcot Street, Bath.

After an early supper with Mrs Rollinson, Frances and Harriet, Tobias wrapped a scarf round his neck and set off for Walcot Street. He had his walking cane with him and showed off his new moves, beating down imaginary foes whenever he had a clear stretch of pavement. He laughed to himself as he swaggered along, remembering Frances's jokes at the table; they had been funny and she had been put in her place by Mrs Rollinson. Harriet was a little rabbit but Frances was sharp as a pin and always made him laugh, though she was younger than he was. He wondered if he shouldn't have encouraged her, for after all he was fifteen next birthday. He shrugged his shoulders and moved on. Life was good, and he was looking forward to the evening's meeting in the George and Dragon. Matthew Spence and his new lodger would be there and maybe Matthew's grandfather, Old Tom. Matthew had fixed wheels on a chair so he could push the old man down the road to the Dragon to give him a change.

The sky was clear and glittering with cold starlight; under his feet, ice had made the pavements treacherous. Already, he had slipped once, so he slowed down as he neared the pub, not wanting to be seen on his backside. The door was tightly shut against the night and he put his shoulder to it to make sure it closed behind him after he entered, spluttering and coughing, his breath taken by the fug of heat. The meeting was in the front parlour as usual and he pushed in, craning his neck to see his friends. There by the fire was Tom on his throne, with Ben sticking close to him as a limpet, sat in a wooden captain's chair and leaning over to shout into the old man's ear above the roar in the room. Matthew was on the settle next to them and beckoned for Tobias to come over.

"Ale, young 'un?" said Matthew, as he poured Tobias a full mug. "Arthur's gone for another jug. He's been reading powerfully with no break for an hour. We've news of Mr Hetherington from *The Poor Man's Guardian* and also a lot on Cooperative Living and Unionism from Mr Owen's *Crisis* paper."

Matthew said the words slowly, he had listened but he not really understood all that he had heard. "Mr Hetherington's still in Clerkenwell Gaol, but spreading his good words from his cell. John Doherty, the spinners' union man from Manchester, is working with Mr Owen."

"Anythin' more on the Labour Bazaars and them using their own notes for money?" said Tobias, agog for more.

"London branch is in sore trouble," said Matthew, shaking his head. "I must say that using notes of labour hours for money sounds very rum. Their hearts are in the right place but I can't see it catching on. But Mr Owen keeps on preaching that if we only follow his way we'll leave error and misery behind and swap it for truth and happiness. God bless him!"

"Robert Owen 'ee lives in a fairytale land!" cackled a reedy voice. "Gave up on Old England and went to Amerikey 'ee did. Set up a co-operatin' community for Yankees! Crept back with 'is tail between 'is legs! Now 'ee's thinkin' 'ee can get printers loike old Arthur and Robert to unite with every other workin' man from carpenters to plasterers. 'Tain't natural! Young Doherty tried up north and failed good and proper."

"O' course, you 'ave seen all this afore, Mr Spence," said Ben encouragingly. He was keen to increase his stock with Old Tom, who of all the inhabitants in the Spence household would probably be the first to throw him out on his ear if he defaulted on the rent.

"That Oiy 'ave, young Benjamin Prestwick," said Tom.

"Grandfather," said Matthew, "we are in new times. You cannot deny that parliament was reformed last summer. We've a new-broom of a government under Lord Grey and they are set to pass some grand new laws."

Old Tom wheezed in delight. "Aye, young Matthew. Mighty impressive. 'Ave 'ee got the vote then? 'Ave Oiy? 'As any bugger round this 'ere table? No they ain't! And mark my words, this 'ere Factory Law for to protect little 'uns will be as weak as maid's water no matter what Mr Sadler says."

"We don't know yet what it will do, Mr Spence. And the slavery law is going through," said Tobias, unwilling to lose his good cheer. "There's no two ways about that one. If it wins the vote there will be no more slavery in the British Empire! Full stop!"

"Just loike there's no more slave trade in the Atlantic!" mocked Old Tom triumphantly.

"Aye," said Ben. "We barred that back in 1807 and it flourishes to this day when 'Is Majesty's West Africa squadron don't catch 'em at it."

"Look Grandfather, here's Arthur and Robert," said Matthew, tiring of Ben playing up to the old man.

Arthur Jamieson collapsed into his seat with a fresh jug, breathing hard, closely followed by Robert Turner, red in the face and frowning.

"Arthur, ye be the oracle of this 'ere pub," chuckled Tom. "Ye be a champion reader and ye keeps the peace!"

"Hello, young 'un," said Arthur to Tobias. "Oiy wondered where you was!"

"Wouldn't miss the meeting, Mr Jamieson," said Tobias eagerly. "Sorry I was late for the reading. Evening, Mr Turner."

"Nothing joyful to report as such," said Arthur. "More snippets from Mr Sadler's enquiry into children's work in factories. What's good is that what 'e found is so shockin' bad that government's bound to cut the little 'uns day to ten hours, what with the beatin' and the cruel wheels turning relentless, and no natural breaks as God intended."

"Aye," said Robert Turner, breaking his gloomy silence. "It's not the hours that's wrong, it's the unnatural state of being in a factory. That's what needs attention. Children away from their parents, worked too 'ard or running wild and getting thrashed by strangers. Any farmin' child will toil just as many hours, and do 'arder work, and no 'arm done. But when they're tired, they takes a nap, then up and off again scaring the birds away for Father! White slaves they do be in factories. Unnatural work can rightly be called slavery."

"Nobody's forcin' 'em to stay, Robert Turner," yapped Old Tom, revived by another slug of ale. "Slaves be damned, ye don't know the meanin' of the word! Their parents clamour for the chance to get 'em into the factories. Lining up for the jobs they be! Oiy think no black man's keen to be a slave."

Dyed in the wool reformer as he was, he liked to play devil's advocate and give young Bobbie Turner a run for his money. There was too much slack ale-talk as the night wore on. It was not often he had the chance to chaff the young lads these days and he relished it. He hadn't felt as well in years.

## Brooks's Club, Saint James's Street, London.

The gaming rooms upstairs were crowded and raucous. Some members were betting on card games at the tables, mainly faro; some were carousing in corners; some were crowded round an aspiring conductor who was lashing out the time with his walking cane as they roared their way through an obscene version of "William and Dinah". A couple of younger members, drunk as boiled owls, were slumped on a sofa, one offering noisy, slurred challenges to the other who was laboriously trying, but failing, to write up the wager in the betting book.

All of this was a mere distant buzz of irritation for Lord Melbourne as he sat alone in the comfortable Members' Room downstairs. He felt melancholy. Naughty Caro Norton, his lovely young companion, was pregnant, and entertaining herself far away from London on endless house party jaunts. On some of these she was accompanied by her boorish husband, and on some she was not. The last letter had suggested that she was alone and had sought to be amusing by taunting him with her casual flirtations. One of these had blossomed and caused her to bolt her bedroom door at nights to keep the bounder out. George Norton could not have been there or fist-fights would have ensued, bloodily.

Melbourne was owed a letter by his ex-mistress, Lady Brandon, and yearned for it to raise his spirits, but a more prosaic distraction materialised by his side in the shape of a club servant checking to see if he needed anything.

"Yes, Chis-lett, I do," drawled Lord Melbourne. "Another bottle. Taylor's 1811. There are a few cases left, I trust?"

"Yes, mi'lord," said Chislett with a slight bow.

"And bring a glass for Lord Palmerston. He will be here presently."

Despite the warm fire, he was feeling the cold. He wondered if it might be fatigue. Deuced chilly of course, being January, but it was not just the season, he had too much to do and it was sapping his strength.

It became even colder as the door opened to admit his fellow Minister and Club Member, the Foreign Secretary, Lord Palmerston.

"What-ho, Melbourne!"

"What-ho, old chap."

"Russell wants to play faro tonight. We arrived together. Coming up to the tables?"

"Presently, but I've just ordered another bottle of 1811. Fancy sharing a glass or two before we go?"

Palmerston strode over to the fire and turned his rear to it, flicking up the skirts of his frock coat.

"That's better! Damned cold out there, Melbourne."

Chislett returned with the port. At a signal from Melbourne he poured it and then retreated noiselessly from whence he came.

Palmerston was tempted back to the armchairs and lifted his glass. "To us! To the Whigs. Long may we reign!"

"Amen to that," said Melbourne, washing the port round his teeth. "We are going well. Tories dead in the water! Who would have thought it?" After considering the unlikely situation he continued. "Thank the Lord that Wellington's leadership remains decidedly dull for the young fellows, and what with their Evangelicals setting the pace for all this damned reform, we are sitting pretty to be credited for doing rather little!"

"Strange world."

"And getting damnably stranger. Sadler's report on the factories is poor stuff. Don't know if you've read any of it yet. Ghastly overwrought "penny blood" style horrors. Years out of date most of it. He seems to have dragged out a collection of human derelicts to wail over their ill treatment donkeys' years ago. Damned lucky to have had any jobs at all I would have thought. Also he's leading them by the nose. You know the form: "So my poor sad creature, tell me of your childhood, tell me about the beatings. How often were you beaten? How much did it hurt? Are you crippled? Oh dear, so you are." He never lets the wretches just talk. Always makes them sing to the same tune."

"Damned bore and you are obviously tired of it! I suppose you wish you were Foreign Secretary now?"

"Not at all, you seem to be filling the role most capaciously. And actually," said Melbourne, a slow, cynical smile lighting his face. "Sadler has played into our hands. The report is so exaggerated, we are obliged to follow up with a Royal Commission to check it, and I know just the man to steer that, taking a back seat of course, but hand firmly on the tiller."

"Would that be the *sehr effizient* Edwin Chadwick by any chance? I gather that he is referred to as *The Prussian* for his ferocious statistical efforts."

"Yes, the very same, my sober bureaucrat! He will, quite rightly, be brisk and businesslike, allowing the factory owners their right of reply, which Sadler of the bleeding heart did not. He will quietly, perhaps over dinner, ascertain the working conditions from the proprietors. He will repeat the interviews of the workers in a fairer manner, allowing each witness free rein."

Palmerston grinned broadly. "Enough rope to hang themselves by any chance?"

"I have no idea what you are talking about, my dear fellow."

The port flowed again, lusciously.

"I am more concerned about the slavery bill," said Palmerston, frowning suddenly as his thoughts returned to an angry exchange in the Lords with a plantation owner.

"Our friends in the West Indies will need generous compensation if we interfere with their business." He poured another large port. "Generous compensation Melbourne, and to a fault, depend upon it."

"Any thoughts on the scale?"

"Well, clearly, it will need to be a goodwill gesture," said Palmerston, "which is acceptable to all."

"And an overall figure? I've done some preliminary calculations. Well over ten million pounds will be needed."

"Absolutely. Double that perhaps."

"It would not do to inconvenience the West Indian lobby."

"Certainly not," agreed Palmerston, shaking his jowls vehemently.

"Nor," continued Melbourne, "can we afford to alienate the owners of our cotton factories. They are the men of the future. They dominate our export market don't forget. Cotton has been king for over thirty years and every year the trade grows. Confound it, sometimes you are so immersed in the regulation of foreign imports it seems to have slipped your mind!"

"Don't let my kindly exterior fool you, dear boy. Nothing gets past Pam!"

Melbourne sank the rest of his port and rose to his feet. "Is that so? Well let's see if you can get a few cards past Johnny Russell tonight."

"No problem even on a bad day."

Palmerston paused before entering the hall. "Speaking of domestic matters, can't you accelerate the enquiry into the Poor Law? It costs too damned much."

"All in good time," said Melbourne, now thoroughly warm and restored. "Chadwick has some ambitious ideas for the development of workhouses. He wants them in every town, city and county. Believe me, they will not be comfortable, no one will be keen to move in and Chadwick believes there should be no poor relief for the able-bodied unless the paupers live in a workhouse. That will make the claiming of relief an unattractive prospect. You can see that I don't want him rushed. He will pilot the factory enquiry through before summer and complete the work on the Poor Law next year. Then there will be a fine uproar no doubt. Let sleeping dogs lie for now, Pam: sufficient unto the day is the evil thereof."

**Morning: 29th January, 1833.**
**The Ravenswood Residence, Arno's Tower, Arno's Vale, near Bristol.**

Edwin Ravenswood had been down for an early breakfast, as he did every morning. Small talk over the rolls and coffee was not to his taste. He had eaten sparingly and in silence and then gone straight to his suite of rooms in the west wing.

He knew that Sir Giles was anxious to have a word with him in private and he expected him shortly. It might have been better to deal with him earlier in the visit, but yesterday had been busy with the house party and it had not been possible. In the morning they had walked over the estate and after lunch had been on a shoot. Before dinner, as planned, they had driven down to the wharf at Redcliffe to see his ships, but there he had been obliged to stay to speak with Captain Trevellis to finalise contracts for the next sailing. The rest of the party had been sent back for dinner without him, so it was on the final morning of his visit that Sir Giles managed to share his miseries.

The west wing was a place for confidences. They would not be disturbed in the Oriental Salon which served Ravenswood as an office and den, isolated from the main house by a separate corridor which was lined with wooden mannequins wearing suits from his extensive collection of armour. It was an eclectic mix, ranging from fourteenth-century European chain mail and the full brutality of sixteenth-century plate armour, to the elaborate equipage of a Japanese samurai warrior. In his suite of rooms there were other costumes, eastern confections of painted wood, feathered wings and gaping masks, shelves and cabinets of exotic weaponry, assorted treasures and macabre curiosities. Amanda rarely ventured into the west wing unless she was invited.

He glanced up from his papers to look through the French windows and saw her at a distance with Lottie and John Drake, strolling across the park towards the wood. She was still attractive, elegant and fastidious, still diverting, but there again, they had only been married for four years. The gloss should not have worn off quite yet. She suited him in many ways so why had he let Lottie into his life? It had surprised him when he had done so, as he was not a man who needed a variety of women. Lust was a weakness which he knew he did not have, but he was acquisitive. He bared his teeth as he smiled, without mirth. The Honourable Mrs Drake was a hunting trophy like the mounted animal heads on the wall, though he was quite well aware that she viewed him in exactly the same light.

A quiet knock was followed by the entrance of his butler.

"Sir Giles to see you, Mr Ravenswood."

Buckley walked in hurriedly and took a seat by Ravenswood at his table. He was anxious and had skipped breakfast, his eyes bulged, watery and sore after an unwise late night drinking session with Drake, and his heart beat unpleasantly hard. Though superficially handsome and urbane, he had let his body go to seed. An indulged life had taken its toll and he was now unable, as well as unwilling, to fight his own battles. He clasped his hands on the table top and laid himself on the mercy of his host; pouring out the details of his two torments: the London problem, the blowsy Maisie Trickett who could turn into a very expensive embarrassment, and the Bath problem, the unwelcome re-appearance of Ben Prestwick, whose indiscretions could lead him to the gallows.

Ravenswood listened in silence, toying with a jewelled paper knife as he did so. He had three options: the first, and easiest, being to close the issue down by disposing of Buckley for bringing the possibility of prosecution to his door. The Ravenswood family had helped launder money and jewels which were rightly the property of the Crown. Secondly, he could refuse to help, which left a desperate and incompetent Buckley floundering and it was clear to Ravenswood that Prestwick was likely to turn to blackmail, which could last a lifetime. Thirdly, he could resolve the problems of this long standing family ally, who was now not only a Member of Parliament, but also in possession of a fortune, some of which he was willing to invest in the business. Self interest would be best served by option three.

By the time Buckley had finished Edwin Ravenswood had devised two plans.

"Sir Giles, I have known you all my life and our families have been close for much longer than that. I can solve your problems but my methods will bring about final solutions."

"Edwin, my dear man," said Buckley, trembling under Ravenswood's penetrating gaze. "I understand what I have asked of you and I am entirely at your disposal in these matters. I will follow your suggestions to the letter."

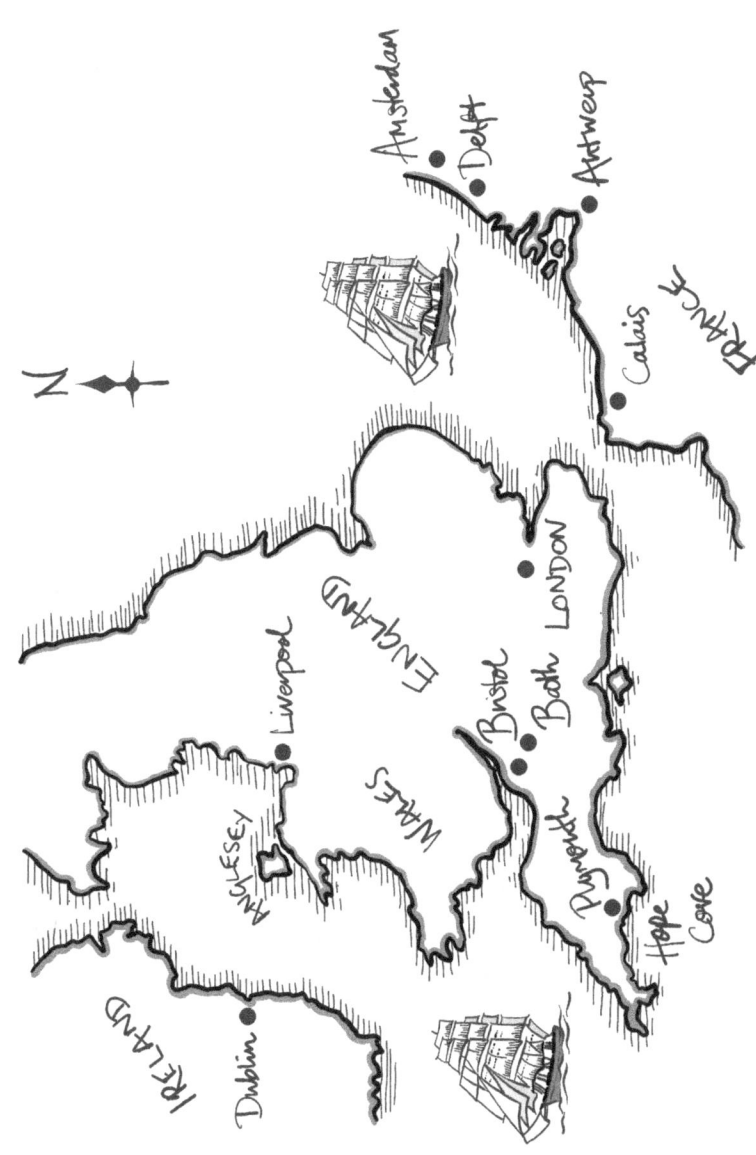

Great Britian: the location of the Isle of Anglesey

# Chapter 3

**Late afternoon: 1st February, 1833. Beaumaris Castle, the Isle of Anglesey.**

They stood side-by-side, arms linked against the wind, as they looked out over the ruined battlements. Beyond the white-capped rushing water of the Menai Straits the wild mountains of Snowdonia reared up before them, etched against the darkening sky, their peaks iced and scattered with a light snow. The air was clear, but buffeting, searching and bitter. A feeling of otherness grew upon them as they stood together; separating them from the world they had left. It was not the otherness of alienation, but the addition of another dimension of themselves. The low, rolling fields of Anglesey spread out behind them in the gloom of the gathering dusk and they were a part of it, cut off from their other lives by the swirling air and water, and the curtain wall of mountains.

The harsh croak of a raven drew her eyes down to the ivy grown wall of the tower. There he was, folding his wings as he settled on his stone perch, hunched up against the cold, glaring and baleful. He seemed to have called to her and Emma felt a threat shivering up her spine at the sight of him. The bird appeared to consider, inspected her more closely, and then made a decision. He put his head to one side and changed his tune to a high interrogatory: "Toc, toc, toc!" She smiled at him, her alarm melting away. Even in the failing light his plumage was captivating, sleekly blue-black, steely and iridescent. He preened his thick neck feathers and nodded his head.

"I think he wanted to know why we are here," she said. "When I looked at him he seemed to know that we belong here too."

"You feel part of it then, Em?" said Nathaniel.

"Oh, yes."

To her surprise and relief, she did. She had not wanted to play the part of an outsider. The language, the customs and the hostile climate: she had looked forward to all of these, but as challenges, not as gifts or punishments. She would not take them for granted.

"I'm glad," said Nathaniel.

He had not worried about bringing her to Anglesey as it was not in his nature to do so. But in his dreams of the mountains and the island she had not been there. He had hoped she would like it, but if she had not, he would have continued to come alone. As they looked at each other, still learning, a crazed barking broke out from below them, over towards the beach, and a flock of seabirds scattered into the sky. Nathaniel smiled broadly. He would not have been alone.

"Caradoc seems to be in his element. Do you think he remembers it? He probably does as he was full-grown when I took him from Llanddaniel."

"He knew where he was as we crossed the bridge," said Emma. "Remember, he was up at the window and yapped his way across. Maybe he could smell the sea air. Perhaps he recognised the scent of the land. Do you think it's possible?"

The other passengers had left the coach as they had entered Wales and she had spent their last day on the road encouraging Nathaniel to tell her more stories of the island. Her head was full of them; partially woven threads of magic and tales of holy wells, druid groves and standing stones. The stories had matched the lonely road in strangeness and now they had arrived she felt a flood of relief to be at one with it. It had been important to her, and important for them, though he might not know it.

"I am glad that you like the raven," he said, pulling her closer. "Some say they are birds of ill omen but I don't feel that."

"I know the superstitions," said Emma. "But the old wives' tales say the same about seeing just one magpie instead of two. It must be to do with their dark looks."

Nathaniel smiled at her, pleased. "Maybe it's because they are scavengers, they prey on dead meat."

She looked at the raven closely. "He looks stern but he is curious and lively, unlike his namesake!"

"What do you mean?"

"Edwin Ravenswood! The thought of him makes me uneasy, Nathaniel," she said, suddenly serious. "There's something dark as Hades about him."

Nathaniel changed the subject. "Well, this feathered friend here is linked to the gods above not below. In Welsh his name is Bran. In the old days there was a god called Bran the Blessed and there is also a tale of an Irish Celtic goddess who takes the form of a raven. She is Morrighan. And did you know that in the myths the ravens were messengers to other worlds?"

Emma smiled encouragement so he pressed on, happy to steer the conversation away from all thoughts of the mainland and the troubles of their ordinary lives. "Odin had two ravens called Huginn and Muninn: thought and memory. They travelled the world for him and told him of men's deeds."

She looked at the raven, who suddenly flapped his wings and whistled. They laughed and whistled back, then turned together to make their way down the broken steps.

"Do carriages ever blow off Mr Telford's bridge? I swear I felt it sway as we drove over," she said, moving carefully, feeling for the edges of the stone treads as they descended into the black hole of the spiral stair.

"There is movement," said Nathaniel, leading her down, out of the closeness of the stairwell and onto the cobbled path. "But no one has been blown away to my knowledge. The biggest injury it has done is to the ferrymen. They are ruined."

They crossed the empty moat and walked by the courthouse to the beach where Nathaniel whistled up Caradoc. He soon bounded into view, lugging a stick heavy with a sodden garland of kelp, and followed them as they turned to make their way back through the deserted town to the warmth of the Old Bull's Head. It was a cold walk, their feet ringing on the iron hard road, Caradoc labouring behind with his prize. They had almost made it to the door when the wind rose to a sudden howl behind them, tearing down the Strait and funnelling the length of Castle Street.

"Leave it, Caradoc," shouted Nathaniel above the shriek of the blast, as the terrier rammed the stick broadsides across the entrance. "Put it round the corner for tomorrow."

Caradoc was not pleased but could barely keep on his paws in the mounting gale and saw the sense in it. He disappeared round the side of the inn towards the dark archway leading to the stable yard, and returned, tail up.

They opened the parlour door at the Old Bull's Head to be met by a wall of sweltering heat and noise, so they made instead for the calmer dark of the dining room and a meal before an early night. On Nathaniel's recommendation, they ate well on *cawl eildwyn*, twice heated leek broth, and melting slabs of honeyed lamb. Afterwards, warmed through, they made their way up the creaking stairs. The maid had stoked up the fire in their room and piled the blankets high on the ancient four-poster. All other assistance had been refused. They undressed hurriedly, each

76

helping the other, laughing at their haste, struggling into nightgowns. As Emma moved away and slid under the covers, watching him, Nathaniel drew the curtains round the bedposts, leaving just one candle burning on the ledge by the bed, and followed her in.

Always drawn to the comfort of a fire, Caradoc had made a bee-line for the hearth and flung himself down before it. He had learned that any early attempt to move onto the bed for the night would be hopelessly premature and doomed to failure. Stifled giggles and the creak of the bed ropes from behind the curtain confirmed his decision. He would bide his time.

Presently, the pair fell quiet. Warm and content, with Emma in his arms, Nathaniel began to plan: "Bank first tomorrow, sweetheart. I will collect my father's remaining boxes, including mother's jewellery for you. And I'll check the accounts. The manager is an old family friend and will want us both for luncheon. We'll meet the solicitor too. You'll be all right on your own after that for a while? As you see the shore is five minutes away, there is much more of the castle behind the barbican entrance. Apart from being blasted in the Civil War, it was Edward I's last castle and never finished in the first place, but there is still plenty to see. I can arrange for a short drive for you if you want it. Penmon Priory is worth a visit, there's a holy well, a church and some romantic ruins. It's about three miles down the coast. I will ride to the house at Llanddaniel in the afternoon; it's only about ten miles and I'll be quicker on horseback than in a gig. I'll see Jones and get Mrs Jones to make everything ready for us. All being well, we will have Sunday here then travel to the house together on Monday."

Emma pulled away in alarm.

"Nathaniel, please let me ride with you," she felt a sinking in the pit of her stomach and knew she needed to make a successful strategic move, not just for now but also for the future.

He looked uncertain. "Sweetheart, it will likely be raining, definitely cold. That's twenty miles in the open air, plus lengthy talks with the Joneses, who speak not one word of English. And," he added, frowning, "the house will not look as I wished for you. It is over a year since I visited and I intended to instruct them in how to prepare it for us, which rooms to clean …," he hesitated as he also realised he had been looking forward to a fast hack over the fields with Caradoc and a long talk with Dafydd Jones over a pot of ale, probably ankle-deep in mud, whilst they inspected the beasts' stalls.

Emma took a gamble and reached for his face so that she could hold it in her hands, pushing back his trademark mane of hair to look him full in the eyes. She had not long had the right to do this and despite their other intimacies, it still felt bold, presumptuous. She swallowed down a stab of anxiety and steadied her voice.

"Nathaniel, darling, because of your work I know there'll be many times you will have to leave me behind. I know you will travel abroad and go to London when I won't be able to be with you. Whenever we can, I want to be by your side. I so much want to go tomorrow and have that first sight of Llanddaniel with you. It doesn't matter what it looks like. I can listen to the Joneses or take a walk on the farm whilst you talk business if you prefer. I want to help you; talk to you on the road, especially if it's miserable travelling weather. I want us to walk to Penmon together on Sunday. Especially if it is romantic!" She was relieved to see his frown lift and be replaced by amusement. "I've brought my riding habit with me and I am competent," she said. "And it is our honeymoon."

"Right then," said Nathaniel, taking both her hands and planting a kiss on each. It was novel to remember that he did not need to be alone again, there were different pleasures now. "So be it, my dear, *fy nghariad*, as we are in Wales. We ride together."

Emma kissed him in relief and gratitude. She had a fleeting vision of Edwin Ravenswood and Amanda's deference to him. No, it was more than that; she had sensed Amanda's fear of that grim man and thanked God she did not have to suffer the same.

"Tell me again about the stones," she said as she relaxed, exhaustion flooding through her body, which she now admitted to herself, ached in every inch after the five days on the road and would be immeasurably worse after the ride tomorrow. She moved closer, enfolding him in her arms, rested her head on his chest and closed her eyes.

Absent-mindedly he breathed in the scent of her and stroked her shoulder, but saw again the long low manor house he had inherited but never lived in: a few nights now and then, business and burials. It was stone built and strong, butting up against the elements, and beyond the house, enduring, was Bryn Celhi Ddu, the Mound in the Dark Grove. Beneath, he was sure; other bodies remained, not those of family who were laid to rest in the trim little churchyard but the pagan remains of the ancients. To his knowledge no one had dug it out to see what was hidden inside. It slumbered still. Boulders from the stone circle survived and guarded a ritual enclosure. A passage grave led into the hillock that for eons of time had survived as witness to the lost days. The Roman Army had destroyed the oak groves of the Druids, but some trees grew again by the stones, a small copse bordered the fields, which were now filled with his beasts and Jones's sheep and cattle. In his misery and loneliness after his father's death he had stretched out on the mound and drunk himself free of thought, only to be plunged in his dreams into a chaos of violence, poetry and songs howled to the moon.

"They are old, Em," he whispered, feeling the regular rise and fall of her breast against his, "as old as man."

He quietly disentangled one arm, reached over and snuffed out the candle.

By the fire, the terrier heard the sheet rustle and raised his head. Now, even for him uncomfortably hot, Caradoc took the darkness as a signal, padded silently over to the bed, nosed under the curtains and crept soundlessly under the eiderdown for the night.

## The Ravenswood Townhouse, Redcliffe Parade, Bristol.

Eli Trevellis stood uncomfortably before his employer, eyes focused away from Ravenswood's relentless gaze and fixing instead on the lines of masts swaying against the dying light above the moorings on Redcliffe Back. It was better not to catch Ravenswood's eye unless absolutely necessary, it could be seen as an impertinence, a challenge. No one in their right mind would upset Mr Ravenswood, and Eli was sane enough to know it. He had bided his time with his news as instructed, checked and double-checked the men and their stories, read the news story on the coroner's report. All ship-shape and Bristol fashion. He smiled cynically to himself to keep up his spirits, which narrowed his eyes unpleasantly to crafty slits. He smoothed his shock of brindled hair and shifted uneasily.

Then a good sign: Ravenswood gestured to him to be seated at the central table which served for dining and board meetings. To be taken to his master's desk at the window and made to stand would have been a poor start. Ravenswood had clearly had a successful couple of days in London. Eli noticed he was wearing a new waistcoat, canary coloured silk, cream striped with a leaf pattern on the stripe: an unusual choice for the master.

"So, Captain Trevellis," said Ravenswood, "let me hear your report on the events of Wednesday night."

"It's done, sir, the soldier's dead. Burial Monday. No trouble," said Trevellis: business-like, curt, as his master preferred and looking at him straight now, level to the eyes.

Ravenswood nodded, but he had not finished. "Good. Now the details."

Trevellis shifted in his seat and brought his fists onto the table, clenching and unclenching them to help order his thoughts as he recounted the events.

"That morning I went to Joshua Shadwell's brothel in Green Park and picked up his two men, Billy and Jabez. Paid 'em 'alf in advance and slipped a royalty to Shadwell. By the way, Sir Giles was 'avin' an hour with the whore called Clari when I got there. 'E 'ad not gone straight to London as planned."

Ravenswood nodded, noted the discrepancy.

"I went to the York House and paid one of the footmen to come to the Saracen's after eight with the message that Sir Giles was ill and had gone back to London. I planted myself in the Saracen's away from Billy and Jabez and watched for our men. In comes the footman, regular as clockwork and asks for Prestwick, which picked 'im out for me. Soon as I eyeballed 'im I was over and stood 'im some drinks. The old cove was downcast and ready to be cheered up. We jawed for an hour, swapped stories about the war and Spain, so 'e was 'appier. Then I left, barman saw me leave. I waited by the wall of Saint Michael's next to Saracen's. Billy slipped out the back through the stable yard and Jabez come out the front, walked up the street and waited in Gracious Court, up from Saracen's. Prestwick come out the front and set off up Broad Street so I went through Michael's churchyard and round the back of Saracen's to tip off Billy to go and wait on the passage steps between Bladud's Buildings and the Paragon."

Trevellis allowed himself a self-satisfied nod as he detailed the pincer movement: he was particularly proud of it.

"Then I cut back and caught up with Prestwick as 'e rounded Broad Street. Jabez was trailing 'im close. Just passed Bladud's Buildings, comin' up to the steps, Jabez stoved 'is skull in. 'E 'ad a crowbar. 'E then shoved Prestwick and he went down the steps like a ninepin. Billy was 'alf way down in the dark and finished the job, then rolled 'im down to Walcot Street ."

Trevellis paused. "I didn't need to pretend to chase Jabez off as it were deserted on the road. Billy came up the steps and we all made our way separately to Shadwell's. I paid 'em off. Prestwick was laid out in the George and Dragon by Thursday morn and the coroner ruled death by misadventure in the *Chronicle* that night. Like I said, funeral's on Monday."

Ravenswood reflected on the tale. It seemed secure: an improvement on the shambles which would have ensued if he had instructed Shadwell to deal with it. A few years ago he would not have had to send Trevellis on such a mission. He glowered at the memory. Shadwell was a spent force. He had noticed that Shadwell's wife, Rosie, seemed to be taking charge of the Green Park brothel and the Avon Street businesses. Joshua Shadwell had never been the same after the stabbing. Some mad whore and a gang of men taking revenge had ambushed him in his own yard. Shadwell had been reluctant to speak of it. Fortunately Ravenswood's business interests in human cargo had shifted focus to London, and Shadwell was no longer needed for the supply chain. This had been fortuitous in many respects. Ravenswood's days in London had been very well spent. Lottie's property portfolio was impressive and included a secluded suite of rooms in Mayfair that they had made very good use of. He suddenly felt expansive, took out his purse, and slid five sovereigns over the table.

"You have done well," he said with a rare smile of satisfaction. "Progress is being made. My new vessel in London dock is almost ready. You are still on target to leave next week, I take it?"

"Yes, sir," said Trevellis. "We'll quit Bristol by Wednesday."

"Drink, Captain?"

"Yes please, sir," said Trevellis, trying to sound unmoved and stifling his alarm. Ravenswood's rare shows of generosity were always unsettling and he cursed inwardly to see that his hand shook as he reached out for the coins.

Fortunately for him, Ravenswood missed the sign of weakness. After ringing for the footman he strode over to the window and stood, arms folded, watching the pale moon shine on the waters of the Floating Harbour. Buckley's first problem had been eliminated, and after the instructions he had given in London, the second was poised to go the same way. Sir Giles would be extremely grateful, in perpetuity. Ravenswood's fleet was growing. He had berths in London, vessels on the high seas and his various trades were rising exponentially. Normally, he had no time for poetry but something Drake had said came back to him.

*"Look on my Works, ye Mighty, and despair!"*

He liked it.


## Morning: 4th February, 1833. Saint Mary's Burial Ground, Bathwick, Bath.

The small group attending Benjamin Prestwick's funeral stood hunched against the intermittent gusts of wind like gaunt black birds, resigned and silent round the empty grave. They stood in the lee of the little mortuary chapel, so had a modicum of shelter as they listened to the curate gallop his way through the service. He knew nothing of Benjamin Prestwick but had some sympathetic feeling for old soldiers and, generally speaking, Martha said to herself, had made a brave show. As, she reflected with tight lips, had she. The fees had been paid out of her own pocket and she had made arrangements with a church she had always viewed with the greatest suspicion. Saint Mary the Virgin indeed: little better than Papists they were, to keep such a name. The worship of saints she deplored as particularly sinful. To add to the

81

annoyance, the fees were higher than they should have been, being as they were not regular parishioners. She had made sure there was no profligacy, no adding of insult to injury. With parish fees, burial service, clerk and sexton, who also tolled the bell, she had been charged two pounds and three shillings. Ben was buried with no stone or wall, his resting place was unmarked and shallow dug, near the freshly turned line of paupers' graves, but she would be providing refreshments when the time came.

She stole a glance around the unfamiliar churchyard. The chapel had only stood for fifteen years and she remembered it being built from the stones of the old Saint Mary's church itself, a squat, crumbling place left over from the old dark days before the blessed light of the Reformation had dawned. The march of progress, she thought to herself, satisfied. But then a sour thought, it had been demolished in an outbreak of road widening and new building encouraged by the Lord of the Manor, the Earl of Darlington. Martha's frown deepened at the thought of him. Only last month he had been made up to be His Grace the Duke of Cleveland. Everyone knew he chose the title in memory of his ancestor and notorious trollop, the first Duchess of Cleveland. Some duchess! Martha felt her blood boil. More of a doxy: that's what she was, one of bad old King Charles's harlots.

She tossed her head and glared at the unfortunate curate, who mistakenly assumed his address had missed the mark and gabbled all the faster. Martha forced her mind back to the business in hand. It was a duty to her late husband Philip to bury his friend decently, which meant in the ways of his family, and the old Prestwicks had been Anglicans. It was also a duty for her class of family to attend the service. Old Tom had stayed by the fireside with the Johnty, who had developed into a noisy and ebullient child, unsuitable for a funeral congregation, but her son Matthew and his wife Mary were there. She nodded her head in approval as she caught sight of Tobias Caudle slip through the iron gate to join the mourners. He had met Ben many times whilst the old soldier had been in Bath, it was right that he attended. It was a duty for him. She inspected him critically: he looked clean, well-clothed and was broadening out. He even had a gentleman's walking cane; that was new. Not so much of an urchin these days but a young man, though she knew his mother had spent plenty of her days in the poor house and on the wrong side of the law. No ornament to the city that one. She sniffed disapprovingly but caught Tobias's eye and beckoned him to join the family. He smiled nervously and made his way round the clutch of habitual funeral attendees who had turned up and swollen the numbers to a dozen: the obligatory scattering of dames and spinsters of the parish, two skeletal old men in greasy coats and battered hats. They would all expect a glass or two and a bite to eat afterwards.

Martha totted up the cost again, carefully, but only from habit. She did not mind it, though Ben had died owing a week's rent and would probably have sunk deeper into her debt if he had lived. She would have tolerated that too, for a while. What irked her still was the manner of his passing. She fixed her eyes back on the curate, who smiled. It was a brave grin, rather disarming, but she did not see it or hear him. Benjamin Prestwick had not fallen down the Paragon steps to Walcot in a drunken stupor, she was sure of it. He had not been out long enough for one thing, for, according to the watch, he had been found before ten that evening. She had seen him drink over the weeks of his stay as her lodger and knew his capacity.

Might he have been merry? Oh yes, and talkative too, even before taking a drop, but drunk before midnight? Never!

He was an old soldier and a good sailor, steady on his feet and tough as old rope. The suggestion that he might have been struck by a thief was possible, but he did not look a good prospect for a footpad. Apart from these nagging doubts, there was more. She recalled his last night and his mood. He was cock-a-hoop. Shaved and washed, his shabby coat with his Waterloo medal brushed almost clean, his eyes alight; he had taken her hands and danced her round the kitchen before he left.

"Martha," he said, "tonight's the night. Oiy be off to meet moiy salvation!"

"Salvation!" she'd said. "What salvation!"

"Moiy crock o' gold at the end of the rainbow! Yer rent will be paid and Benjamin will be in clover."

"Who are you seeing?" she'd said, "a magician?"

"A gentleman," he'd said. "An old officer of mine 'e was, from the Spanish wars. 'E'll see me roight."

And with that he had pranced out of the door and she had never seen him alive again. For her next sighting of him he was stretched out on the table in the parlour of the George and Dragon, with the watch and the coroner in attendance asking her to identify the body. He had been carried in there dead and the landlord remembered that he had seen him with Matthew and Old Tom at the reform meetings. The knock had come to her door before she had locked up for the night.

A sad end.

She had seen Ben's old eyes regain some of their youthful sparkle as he had taken her hands and they had vamped round her kitchen and she had thought of her husband Philip, long dead. She had been powerless then, but she was not now.

Who had Ben seen that night? An officer he'd said. Perhaps Philip would have known him too. Would such a man have done away with Ben? Ben's optimism now became ominous, grotesquely misplaced. It had ill-wished him.

They made their way out down the short gravel path to congregate on Henrietta Road, waiting for the gate to clank shut behind the curate and the rest of the party. Matthew and Mary linked arms with her for the walk home and Tobias trotted along at Matthew's side, keeping in step and beating time as he did with his cane. He felt a release in quitting the churchyard. Though many stones had recorded the deaths of old people, some even in their eightieth year and over, he had seen some sad records of dead children. He was just pleased he had not seen anyone his own age, or with his name, even part of his name, it would have been a bad omen.

"There's something not right about this death," said Martha. "I know I've said it before but I'll say it again. We need to find out who he was to meet in the Saracen's Head last Wednesday night. Someone did him a mischief!"

Matthew gestured to Mary to keep silent as they exchanged glances over Martha's grey head. They thought they had exhausted this subject over interminable discussions together, and with Martha, over the weekend. It seemed more than likely to them that an old man would fall down a steep run of dark steps after a skin-full of drink and break his head on the way. Furthermore, they had already agreed, privately, that the removal of the garrulous and poverty stricken Benjamin from the house was not a wholly bad thing. In fact, Matthew had already persuaded his mother to replace the impecunious Benjamin with a new lodger in the shape of a Mr Finn O'Malley, a friend of Matthew's employer, Declan. She had vetted him on the Saturday, decided he was not a drunk and could afford the rent, and had agreed he should move in at the start of next week, thus allowing a "decent interval".

"I'll look into it, Mother," said Matthew smoothly. "I'll talk to the landlord next time I'm in the Saracen's Head and find out who he met: see if there was any trouble. Though I'm sure he would have told the watch if there had been."

Martha looked up sharply. "Tonight, Matthew. Ask tonight."

"I can ask for you, Mrs Spence," piped up Tobias earnestly, keen to help. He had liked Benjamin, and his tales. "I can go tonight if Matthew cannot."

"Good," said Martha, glaring at Matthew for his hesitation, she did not like her son to be slow in showing obedience to his mother.

They had tramped along for a while, letting the offer rest, crossed the river and turned down Walcot Street, before Martha had another and even better thought. She stopped in her tracks.

"Tobias, when are Mr and Mrs Parry returning from their honeymoon?"

"By the start of March at the latest," said Tobias, well pleased with himself, his tone giving them to know of his importance in knowing his master's movements.

"Too late for my needs," said Martha dismissively.

84

"I know why you ask, Missis," said Tobias, suddenly excited. "Mr Prestwick said he knew my master's father from the days of soldiering in Spain. Mr Parry is a righteous man and he'll want to help you find out the truth. I know it! I've not had the right opportunity to tell him what Mr Prestwick said, but he'll hang on every word when I do. His father's memory is that precious to him, y'see. And I've another idea," Tobias paused for effect. "Do you remember Mr Prestwick's tales? He said that my master's father sailed away from Spain on the *Renowned* when he and the other soldiers went on to Corunna." He shot an anxious glance at Martha. "Sorry to mention the place, Missis, as I know it was fateful for Mr Spence, but I also know that the *Renowned* was Captain Peterson's ship!"

"Captain Peterson!" exclaimed Martha. "Well I never!"

"I used to visit Frances when she was a kitchen maid at the Captain's. Just now and then." He flushed and hurried on. "There's pictures of all the Captain's ships along the below-stairs corridor. I sat and looked at 'em a few times." He also remembered the gruesome discomfort that had accompanied the looking, as he struggled to read the captions, but he managed to keep that thought to himself. Time after time he had stared at those letters as he waited for a few words with Frances, eating his way through the raw pastry parings that he had begged from Cook in the kitchen after she had run her knife round the pie plate. He had sat, chewed, and raked his memory through the gleanings that remained from his weekly reading lessons. Then one day, he had read the names straight off.

"And apart from that, I've heard Mr Parry mention that his father knew the Captain. And he is himself firm friends with him, as his new father-in-law. Captain Peterson will help I'm sure. And he is not just connected with Mr Parry's family; he is also a magistrate," added Tobias grandly. There was a stunned silence, so he added, "Of the court."

"Yes, Tobias Caudle, we know what a magistrate does," said Martha briskly. "I shall see him. Tomorrow."

Matthew shot a dark and meaningful look at Tobias, who weathered it and basked in Martha's gratitude. She fairly beamed at him.

Now the Captain really was a gentleman and no mistake. He would listen. Feeling more positive and a touch victorious, she smiled tartly at the glum faces of her son and daughter-in-law, drew their arms more tightly under hers and stepped out with a will. She was now more than equal to providing the cold collation of funeral meats, the expected cordials and even, perhaps, the glasses of sherry that the guests would have despaired of, hers being a Methodist home.

## Afternoon: 5th February, 1833.
## The Peterson Residence, Marlborough Buildings.

Martha Spence was not feeling quite so combative by the time she had dressed herself the next morning, carefully buttoning herself into the unfamiliar mourning gown. She had bought it second hand from a Walcot Street clothes trader and the bombazine was a touch rusty, even moth-eaten in some well disguised parts of the skirt, but it had to be worn. The hat likewise with its trailing veil was not the most flattering. She had excused the rest of the family from mourning dress, apart from some decent black ribbons. Anyway, Matthew's best coat was black, so it served well and Mary's cloak was dark. Ben had not been family, any more would have been a needless expense, but she felt she had to show willing, for a month at least, as you might for a cousin, and especially on the mission she had given herself for that day.

She had seen Tobias in the morning when he had brought some news from the Saracen's Head, most of it discouraging. The barman who had worked the previous Wednesday had been there again and he had remembered Ben, as he had seen him a few times before; he especially remembered the Waterloo medal, just like his own father's. It had been only moderately busy in the smoke room early that evening and Ben had taken a seat by the door. He remembered that there had been some locals and a few strangers. It seemed that a footman from the York House had come looking for Ben, the barman had pointed him out and heard that a gentleman who was to come was taken ill and so was not coming after all, but had returned to London. That had been a blow. The "officer" and "gentleman" had never been there at all. Ben's tryst with him had not taken place. One other thing had transpired though. One of the strangers had bought Ben some drinks, more than a stranger normally would. The barman had heard snatches of the talk and some of it had touched on Spain and the wars. Before nine o'clock a few men had left, including the stranger, and Ben had made his way out, sober, that was telling, some little time afterwards. All the barman could say about the stranger was that he was a Somerset man to be sure, likely Bristol, but not a native of that city. Not: "Bris'le born and bred", said he.

She presented herself at the Peterson's door in Marlborough Buildings, late enough for even a tardy luncheon to have been concluded, and pulled on the bell. She allowed herself one glance up at the gracious facade towering above her and stretching out in a mighty terrace down the length of Marlborough Lane, facing the open parkland. She also turned, just once, to survey the magnificent vista of the

Royal Crescent behind her and to her right, which arched perfectly round its private green, separated from the common grass of the park by the stone wall of the ha-ha. No beast would be permitted to stray onto the hallowed turf. And, she reflected uneasily, not one person wandered along the pavement. All was still. How unlike the crowds on Walcot Street! Tom could sit at the gate and greet dozens in a morning, especially on market days. She felt suddenly awkward and steeled herself. Indistinctly, a maid's steps sounded on the marble tiles of the hall and the white door opened.

It proved easier than she had hoped. Mrs Peterson was evidently entertaining a group of ladies. She could hear their refined voices drifting down the stairs from the drawing room, restrained laughter, the chinking of tea-cups. From higher still she could hear the distant sounds of music practice, which suggested that the young twin daughters were gainfully employed and unlikely to distract. Surprisingly, Captain Peterson agreed to see her promptly and had her brought up to his study which overlooked the rear of the property. She felt relieved. The Captain had paid a visit to her home in Walcot Street when Mr Parry had lodged with her. That might have helped. It had certainly given her the courage to arrive uninvited, unannounced. She felt she could speak with him on a more professional footing without his wife there. He was, after all, a magistrate, who dealt with crime and injustice and there was a family link, of sorts, through the Parry connection.

The Captain smiled encouragingly at the shabby woman seated facing him at his desk. The low afternoon sun caught her face cruelly and he leapt up to twitch the drape over. Ever the gallant, it offered some shade for her eyes, and a kinder twilight for her care-lined face. He struck at his old tinderbox and lit the candelabra.

"Well, Mrs Spence, how might I be of assistance?"

Carefully, missing nothing, she told her tale. He would have welcomed her as a witness in court, so precise was she.

"So although the coroner declared it was a case of misadventure I fear someone did away with Benjamin Prestwick and I don't rightly know what to do next." She was horrified to feel a blush creeping up her neck. "I am sorry, sir, that I did not write to you to request this meeting. I would not have bothered you in person, but for the connection with Mr Parry's father and the mention of your ship. I feel there is need for haste."

Aspects of her tale intrigued him, especially as he had been running out of excuses for staying in his study and avoiding a tea session in the drawing room. Beautiful as the audacious Tilly Vere was, and charming as he knew the respectable Mrs Charles Parry to be, an hour of them and his dear wife Lydia dissecting the events of Emma and Nathaniel's recent wedding was more than he was willing to bear. He had been biding his time, in hiding, until forcibly winkled out.

He smiled again, expansively, letting his mind roll back to the events of the winter of 1808-9.

"I was indeed the Captain of the *Renowned* Mrs Spence, and conveyed Mr Parry's late father home to England, with a quantity of gold and gems. Now then, how shall we say he came by them?" His eyes twinkled conspiratorially, "Perhaps we can say, which he had liberated from the clutches of the Emperor Napoleon Bonaparte. All fair in love and war, what!"

Martha Spence was staring at him intently; she was not smiling, so the Captain smothered his usual bark of a laugh.

"I remember Mr Owen Parry and myself discussing the booty, as it were, and that three soldiers, a Captain, Mr Prestwick and your husband, had been recompensed for their efforts. They had been awarded prize money. Common enough in the army, and not set amounts, unlike the navy you know."

Martha Spence clearly did not know and continued to peer at Oliver Peterson, hoping for a solution. She struggled again for clarity.

"Benjamin Prestwick was going to meet an officer who he thought was going to give him so much money he would be set up for life, but the meeting did not take place and now he is dead. I smell a rat, Captain Peterson. It seems to me when poor folk think they are going to get possession of a money tree from rich folk they are usually mistaken or up to no good, sometimes both. Ben needed money, I know it. He was behind with his rent. So tell me, who was that officer in the Spanish war? The man who was to meet Ben has gone back to London according to the footman of the York House. This man had not been seen by Ben in Bath before so he must be a stranger."

Captain Peterson raked his memory and selected his next words carefully.

"I do seem to recall some adverse comments from Mr Parry's father about the officer in question. Nothing certain, just a general dissatisfaction I believe. I'm sorry, Mrs Spence, I am short of a name here, but I do remember the incident."

Martha Spence's reference to smelling a rat had the unfortunate result of tuning Captain Peterson's nose in to the stench of camphor emanating from her mourning dress. This was not too bad on its own, but more sinister aromas under-laid it and were drifting towards him in the heat of the room. The fire was extremely well banked up.

"What I propose," he said rising to draw the interview to a close, "is that I contact Mr Parry, who is at the family home on the island of Anglesey, acquaint him with your concerns and see if we can discover any further intelligence on the financial connections between Mr Prestwick and the anonymous Captain. I am sure that when Mr Parry returns he will speak with you on the matter."

He could see Martha's face fall.

"Mr Parry is a successful investigator you know," he said kindly. "Remember the part he played in bringing young Frances to Bath, and the other girls. Though, of course," he said guardedly, watching her closely and approving her brisk nod, "some aspects of that matter should still not be discussed."

A gush of renewed laughter from the drawing room reminded him of another mystery, not quite so well solved. Tilly Vere's husband was still missing, though presumed dead by most. According to Nathaniel, Vere had not been entirely blameless in an unpleasant case of murder and had been up to his neck in other unsavoury activities, so he was no great loss, though Tilly's anticipated marriage to Howard Dill was waiting on a solution to the conundrum of his disappearance. However, he reflected, she did not seem unduly distressed by the delay, judging from the silvery peals of glee she was busily venting next door.

Martha had risen to her feet and was finishing pushing the chair ruthlessly into place under the desk.

"So you will contact Mr Parry then, Captain? I am that grateful to you, sir."

"I shall do it this very afternoon, Mrs Spence," said Captain Peterson with a slight bow.

"It really is unlike the Captain not to join us, at least briefly," complained Lydia Peterson, perplexed. "His visitor left some time ago."

The women smiled, bonnet feathers nodding agreement that the ways of men, in particular husbands, were often unfathomable.

"The dear Captain must be longing for some company," said Tilly, sighing prettily at the prospect of the deprivation he suffered, cruel business having denied him a comfortable seat by her and the benefit of her charms. She was well aware that he found her rather beautiful and spent a pleasing amount of time admiring her physical assets, particularly when displayed by a low-necked ball gown. Mrs Charles Parry was also very fond of Oliver Peterson but was quite a different type of friend, in that she fully understood his reluctance to join them. She had the capacity to enjoy gossip, as long as it was not too regular and the personalities were varied, but she preferred to ration herself strictly to one dose of Lydia Peterson per month. Anymore was unnecessarily fatiguing.

Lydia had pulled the bell for the maid and sent her to chase Oliver out of his fastness in the study, but all this achieved was the briefest appearance from her husband, a flurry of hand shaking and bonhomie, after which he disappeared once more, pleading urgent and unavoidable business. Once back in his lair, he lit a cigar, smoothed out his headed writing paper, sharpened his pen nib and prepared to draft two letters, one a leisurely communication to his son-in-law and favourite daughter in the depths of rural Wales, the other, brief and much more formal, would be addressed to Lord Melbourne, Home Secretary, with reference to his noble colleague Lord Palmerston, Foreign Secretary. The second letter would be a duty, the conveyance of a nugget of intelligence.

**Early afternoon: 20th February, 1833.**
**The Mortimer-Buckley Residence, Park Street, Mayfair, London.**

The Honourable Charlotte Drake was not pleased with the progress of her call on Lady Mortimer-Buckley and her daughter. It had been convenient to visit, as the family lived across the road from her *pied-à-terre* in Park Street; her suite of rooms in her father's Mayfair mansion. But convenience was not everything: the Mortimer-Buckleys were not proving to be convivial. In fact, they were as dull as ditch-water. Lottie had only recently taken to exploiting her holdings in this corner of Mayfair and this call was her first one. Her affair with Edwin Ravenswood had prospered in Park Street, under the guise of Edwin being a visitor to her brother, an elusive rakehell who occasionally occupied the lower floors, either personally or by throwing it open to noisy groups of his fellow young bucks. She had spent more afternoons at the house of late and a friendship with Lady Mortimer-Buckley had seemed to be a shrewd move on two fronts. Firstly, it provided an excellent official reason for visiting Mayfair, apart from the necessary need to limit her brother's designs on her share of their father's house, and secondly it might provide entertainment in the shape of the louche Sir Giles. She had obviously entranced him at the Ravenswood dinner, and after spending a half hour in the company of his wife and daughter she could see why.

The female Mortimer-Buckleys had been pleased to entertain her, but only as a captive audience for the matron's rehearsal of the latest family drama. It really had been a waste of her new outfit. Lottie was resplendent in a dark green gown, viciously belted to twenty inches at the waist, with a row of bows down the front as big as chrysanthemums, billowing leg o' mutton sleeves, a white starched ruff and collar, and, the *pièce-de-résistance*, a green bonnet with iridescent peacock plumes. Really: quite sensational. Lady Mortimer-Buckley had not even had the grace to notice, though she herself was turned out, offensively, in enough ill-fitting burgundy satin to provide sails for a ship of the line. Of course she had heard the gossip about the nanny's scandalous disappearance, but had hardly expected it to dominate every moment of her visit.

Leonora Mortimer-Buckley's plump face was puckered with suppressed rage and disappointment as she continued to deliver her tale. This had had an unfortunate effect on the layers of powder adhering to it, particularly around the mouth, where they had cracked under the strain of her displeasure.

"My own granddaughter, left alone in the park! Unattended! And Nanny gone, vanished! She took nothing with her! Nothing! Is that not telling?"

Lottie managed a half-hearted smile of encouragement, though this was not the first time her hostess had drawn these facts to her attention.

"Nannies which match a child's needs precisely are not easily found, as you must know. You have a daughter, do you not? Miss Trickett, though in some ways a strident young woman, dealt with my granddaughter beautifully. She doted on the child and likewise the dear little one was devoted to her. Miss Trickett was a jewel! Though Sir Giles, unaccountably, felt she was becoming increasingly unsuitable, I will not have a word said about her! And neither will you, will you Prudence?" At this she shot a self-satisfied glance at her daughter and drew out a damp handkerchief with which she dabbed haphazardly at her watering eyes. "Oh dear, forgive me. But I really do not know what we shall do. Dear little Lulu, my granddaughter, is crying night and day for Nanny. My daughter is a shadow of her former self!"

Lottie rather hoped she was. Surely Prudence must have looked better at some point? The young woman drooped unattractively, her heavy white brocade dress, patterned with light brown, was insipid against her drained skin. Its heavy weave, scaly and gill-like, gave the appearance of desiccated fish skin. The limp black ribbon round her neck was also no ornament. Presumably it was a nod to the uncomfortable possibility that the absent nanny could by now be dead. If she had absconded, she would at any rate be dead to them. Lottie smiled again at that thought, but was now totally bored and glanced at the clock on the mantle-piece. She could reasonably conclude the conversation and leave within ten minutes. Her scrutiny took in the both of them: one last show of interest before the fond farewell.

"You said the child was found on a park bench. What did she say when the servants found her?"

Lady Mortimer-Buckley cut through her daughter's stammering effort to respond. "Shush Prudence, calm yourself. She simply said that men had come and Nanny had gone away with them. Maisie Trickett would never have done such a thing willingly. Who knows what pressure was applied! And as I said, her room is as she left it that morning. All her clothes are here, her trunk is full and her purse is left behind. Mrs Drake, she was kidnapped! What sort of world do we live in?"

Overcome by the possibilities, she let out a low, animal wail, bringing Lottie to her feet rather more quickly than she had intended. Fortunately action was not required, as Prudence relinquished her mother's hands and moved in to apply a full and tight embrace.

"There, there, Mother dear," she muttered, patting her mother's ample back.

"Well," said Lottie, capitalising on the break, "I must go and leave you to comfort your mother. I do hope that you have better news of your nanny."

The women reluctantly allowed her to stay on her feet and a servant was summoned to see her out. Lottie trotted downstairs from the drawing room with a spring in her step, as renewed sobs were muffled behind the closing door. Close to the foot of the stairs, her optimism was rewarded by a sighting of the man of the house. The front door was being hauled open by a footman to admit Sir Giles into the hall.

"Well met, Sir Giles," she said archly, posing on the bottom step. "I have just paid a call on your wife and daughter, but how lovely to catch you before I leave!"

In truth, Buckley was not looking good. Though spruce and clearly pleased to see her, he had a haggard look about him. His spirits rose marginally, as the company of Lottie would put off the unpleasant prospect of resuming relations with his family.

"Mrs Drake," he said, marching over to her swiftly, bowing and lifting her right hand for a lingering kiss, "how utterly delightful to see you. Do step into the library for a few minutes if you can spare the time."

Things were looking up. Within two minutes Lottie was in a comfortable leather chair, cherry brandy in hand, basking in the warmth of Buckley's appreciative gaze.

"May I say, Mrs Drake, that, as ever, you look wonderful," he purred, almost his old self, as he drank in the full effect of the dazzling green gown, framing the voluptuous curves beneath. The day had looked up for him too. "It is a treat to see you again, my dear lady. I realized that your father had a residence here, but did not know that you are now visiting in the neighbourhood."

A strangled yelp broke loose from above as a door opened, followed by the caterwauling of prolonged sobbing, then the sounds of footfalls and timorous servants bustling the ladies upstairs to the bedchambers.

"Oh dear," said Lottie, her eyes darting with mischief, "the ladies seem to have retired. The news of your nanny's disappearance is weighing heavily upon them."

Sir Giles's newly regained bonhomie seemed to deflate like a balloon, she noticed his hand shake and tighten on the glass.

"Yes," he said, faintly, "most distressing. She has probably run off, what?"

Lottie suddenly had a vision of her husband's face, urgent concern overlaying his usual expression which typically varied between cynical, greedy and facetious. "John has warned me that kidnapping is increasing. Mainly of unaccompanied women, lower class women, also children, apparently. Such perversion in the world isn't there!" She pulled a face. Their class and possible fates were both subjects which could not be discussed in mixed company. "Not that a lady would be out alone of course. Frightful bad luck if your nanny really was taken; she was clearly out with a child of rank, which should have served as a warning. Of course, it would have been so much worse if little Lulu had gone, wouldn't it? They might take children of rank, mightn't they, if they are planning to extort a ransom? John has warned our servants that they are not to take our daughter Lizzie out alone, but must be in twos, and one must be a footman carrying a pistol."

Sir Giles moved to pour her another cherry brandy. She noticed that he took a cognac for himself, a large one. His face was ashen.

"Are you feeling quite all right, Sir Giles?"

"Yes, yes, of course. Just not sleeping too well, to tell the truth. A little tired." He struggled to steer the conversation into safer waters but she kept him in danger of drowning.

"The last time we met was when we travelled to Bristol, wasn't it Sir Giles? Have you seen Mr Ravenswood since?"

At the mention of his name Buckley felt he was suffocating and gulped down a deep breath before the next strengthening draught of brandy.

"Yes, I have," he said. "He was in town last week."

How could he forget? Eating out with Ravenswood in the Strand he had been briefly elated to learn that his two problems had indeed been eliminated by the interventions of his host, but his food had turned to ashes in his mouth when he realized the scope of recompense to be exacted by Ravenswood. He now had fellow feeling with Doctor Faustus, as his soul was wrung in the cruel hands of his new tormentor. The first payment had already been made. He was now a principal investor in Ravenswood's new vessel, which was installed in a London dock. An intense weariness coursed through him, sapping his remaining energy.

She knew that it had been a risk to ask about Edwin, but really, the afternoon had been so tedious. And now she knew that Edwin had not been spotted in Park Street, though she would have been surprised if he had, they had been so careful. Sir Giles would presumably pull himself together, another nanny would be engaged and he would regain his *savoir-faire*.

"And you met did you? With Mr Ravenswood?"

The voice sounded in his head, hoarse yet insistent. "Giles! Pull yourself together. You can do it."

"Yes, Madam, we did meet," said Sir Giles. With a supreme effort he managed the ghost of his old smile. "Now, when might we have the pleasure of entertaining you and your husband?"

## Lord Melbourne's Office: Downing Street, London.

Lord Melbourne looked up from his dispatches and frowned at the sulky fire in the grate. "Percy, for Gawd's sake man," he drawled, "can't you see mi'fire's dwindlin' damn it?"

Percy could not see, as he was in the adjacent office, scribbling energetically to finish the last task issued by the noble lord. "On my way, mi'lord," he called, scraping the chair back as he leapt to his feet and bounded through the communicating door. He knelt before the smoking fire and set about it with poker, fuel, and shortly thereafter, bellows. Satisfied, he rocked back on his heels, waiting for judgement.

"Excellent, mi'dear fellow," said Melbourne, returning to his papers. "Excellent. Dashed long winter, what!"

He rustled through the documents most insistently drawn to his attention by Percy's coloured notation, until his gaze fixed on the report from the docks which had been eluding him.

"Bad business, Percy," he said, his customary cynical smirk briefly eclipsed by a shadow of genuine concern. "That spate of kidnappings in the parishes near the docks seems to be turning into something more serious. Damn it! Have you heard? A nanny on the staff of one of the Members has been snatched in Hyde Park!"

Percy stood to attention, pushing his round-rimmed gold glasses further up his nose. "Yes, mi'lord, the story's all over Westminster. The child was found in the park and the nanny was seen being hurried off by two men."

"Not that kidnapping is a rare occurrence, mark you," said Melbourne expansively, "but the current outbreak seems dashed sustained. I mention it to you as you will recall some paper work from the year before last. That business in Bristol at the time of the reform riots? You remember our man Parry, don't you Percy? He was onto some white slave trade out of the port. We dampened it down, if you remember. Lord Palmerston was keeping a weather eye on the personnel if you recall."

Percy did recall. He had personally retrieved the report from Nathaniel Parry which Lord Palmerston had discarded and drawn its battered contents to Lord Melbourne's attention. Pam had insisted on staying tight with his Bristol merchant, a Mr Edwin Ravenswood, who seemed to be up to his neck in the traffic. He was also a very useful informant and operator in the essential, and illegal, opium trade to China, which Pam was doing everything in his power to develop. Without that drain on their silver, the balance of trade with China would have been crushingly negative and Chinese tea, porcelain and silk had to be bought. The economic scales had to be tipped.

Melbourne fell silent for a moment, dredging up his memories of the affair. Not only had the merchant not been prosecuted, as Parry had advised, but he had been rewarded by an invitation to join the bench: Justice of the Peace forsooth!

"Contact Parry, would you," he rapped out at length. "Bring him in. Drake needs to be contacted as well. Lord Palmerston regards him as his principal agent for reporting on trade out of the West Country."

"Yes, mi'lord," said Percy, rubbing his hands on the sides of his trousers as he made for the door.

"Oh and Percy," called Melbourne, bringing him up short. "Speaking of the West Country, find me the recent letter from Captain Peterson, our man in Bath."

On a much lighter note and a rather fascinating one, he had been alerted by that particular contact that enquiries had been made touching on an old and beguiling mystery. Raising the name of Parry had brought it back to his notice.

"And have a rummage in the foreign archives. I am interested in the details of a consignment of treasure brought back from Spain in the winter of 1808-9. Owen Parry would have written the report on it and it was sailed back to Britain in the *Renowned* captained by Peterson. There was a question mark over the whereabouts of some of the consignment. One of the persons involved surfaced recently and very briefly as a matter of fact. He declared he was meeting an old army acquaintance and was about to become wealthy, then promptly got himself killed! It is a long shot, but there might be some connection with the missing goods."

Percy brought the Captain's letter, wrote the notes to Drake in London and Parry in Anglesey, then made his way to the archive vault. It was early evening before he emerged, looking the worse for his tussle with the dust and cobwebs, but triumphantly bearing a box of papers. Melbourne ordered veal pie and claret, cleared his desk and set about levering open the tin lid which gave way with a sharp crack. Blowing dust and grit off the bundle, he took it out and untied the string which held it. Smoothing out the roll of papers over the desk, he leaned closer to inspect the faded writing. The report confirmed that the mission to relieve Napoleon of a wagon of gold and assorted treasures bound for his brother Joseph in Madrid had been entirely successful. With just three soldiers to assist, and the useful offices of a French traitor, Parry had captured the goods and brought them to Britain. However, a question mark remained over the fate of one specific item. Parry reported that the soldiers had been awarded prize money in kind from the haul, but that he had noticed, once returned to Britain, that an artefact of particular significance was missing. He was sure he had seen it and it had definitely not been granted as a prize, though Parry had ensured he had not attracted attention to the piece by forbidding it or making any comment on its provenance. It could have been stolen on the ship, but more likely had been taken by one of the soldiers accompanying him on the raid.

Melbourne, the Honourable Member for Portarlington at the time, remembered something of the story concerning that artefact which, fortunately, had never reached the press. This particular treasure was more than the sum of its gold chain and jewelled inlays, as it was an antique pendant dating from the Middle Kingdom of Ancient Egypt. It had originally been stolen by marauding French troops early in 1799 during Napoleon's Egyptian campaign, only to be confiscated from them by the victorious British army in 1801. Along with countless other items, it had been taken to London and placed in the British Museum for the edification of the British public. What made this piece so very controversial was that Napoleon himself had been taken by it, and before he quit the country in the face of impending military defeat at the hands of the British, had ordered it be fitted with a new fastener in the shape of a gold and jewelled clasp bearing his initials: NB.

This adornment had sealed its fate. Within weeks of its arrival at the British Museum it had disappeared from view. Melbourne remembered the fanciful tales of occult power operating in connection with the disappearance, of dark mysteries and the displeasure of the pharaohs. Such stories were suppressed immediately, as was all mention of the piece, which he remembered had been stolen yet again, in an act of audacious larceny, presumably by a French agent. News of the theft had gone no further than Westminster but Parry would have known of it, and no doubt his eyes had lit up when he caught sight of it nestling in the miscellaneous bounty of Napoleon's gold! A special gift for his brother Joseph, calculated to inspire and strengthen him, it was more than a trinket; it was an ancient sign of power. The pendant, a full six inches in breadth, was a golden falcon inlaid with dark glimmering stones; blue lapis lazuli, green feldspar and red cornelian. The bird signified the god Horus, god of the sky, the sun and the moon, god of kingship, majesty, power and war. In its talons it gripped the Shen rings, the twined ropes of eternal protection, and above each claw, linking it to a mighty wing; there was a loop-tipped cross, the Ankh, the breath of life.

Melbourne sat back, deep in thought. To track down Napoleon's falcon and display it at the British Museum would be a triumphant piece of news, just the thing for these pedestrian days of endless drafting and redrafting of new pieces of unnecessary legislation. He sighed, windily. Surely to God, he declared to himself, we have enough laws already! Walpole had been right, bless him: let sleeping dogs lie. But, he reflected morosely, the dogs were no longer asleep and their order papers were as long as your arm. It really seemed that the public expected a government to be responsible for the welfare of every damned individual. Preposterous!

"Percy!"

"Yes, mi'lord?" The eager face, framed by lank overlong hair, shot round the door, the nose twitching up the glasses inquisitively, like a short-sighted squirrel.

"Jump to it. Write to Captain Peterson. Inform him that I am indeed most interested to hear that one of the party involved in ... well, just say, involved in the mission in question ... has been brought to his notice. The individual's unfortunate demise might just provide something of a lead on a very cold trail. Keep me posted. Yours, etc."

Percy jumped as required, but ensured that it was in His Lordship's direction before he headed for his own room.

"Shall I replace the documents, mi'lord?"

Melbourne had already transferred his attention to the veal pie, but managed to nod in assent and waved him away. Percy swept up the box and papers and made himself scarce, hauling his chair over to a side desk, out of his master's line of sight. Before he drafted the letter he read through the crucial documents left on top of the pile by his employer, and could barely believe his eyes. A tingle flashed up his spine and the back hairs of his neck lifted as he read of the strange adventures of the golden falcon. The office seemed to fade from view and he was transported to the sands of the desert, he felt the sweltering heat and saw in his mind's eye the waving palms and stone triangles of the mighty pyramids. All things Egyptian had been a grand European passion since Napoleon's soldiers and scholars had invaded a generation ago. Egyptology was all the rage and Percy was a demon for it. As if by an oasis he drank in the mysteries of the Nile, and as he daydreamed he suddenly had a rather good thought.

He had always liked Nathaniel Parry, saw him as, *sympatico*, a fellow Romantic who was shipwrecked on the same raft, adrift in the shark-infested waters of government service. He, Richard Percy, fixer *extraordinaire* of the Home Office, would make sure it was his friend and ally Nathaniel and not the detestable John

Drake who was on the inside track if there was any treasure hunting to be done. There was probably nothing in it, but the thought of it scattered a little magical dust and enlivened a dull day. Invigorated, he rifled through the correspondence he had prepared that afternoon, located the note to Anglesey, and, dipping his pen in the inkpot, set to work on a postscript.

# Chapter 4

**Late afternoon: 25th February, 1833.**
**The road to Llanddaniel, the Isle of Anglesey.**

The commercial traveller leaned round the door of the Old Bull's Head and shouted a last instruction to him as he rode away from the inn.

"You cannot miss Llanddaniel, Mr Lee! Keep to the coast road until you see the sign, then down the track to the village. Parry's farm is near an old burial mound by a copse. It's an ancient site with great stones at its mouth, guarding the bodies of the first men! You can't miss it!"

Cornelius Fu Lee rode out of Beaumaris and left behind the bustle of the town, the roaming dogs and the barefoot children, the cries of the fishwives and the shopkeepers touting for the last customers before closing time. In the cold twilight he covered a mile along the deserted coast road before he had more company. A harsh call sounded across the darkening fields and he looked up to see a raven sweep over the hedge and pause to wheel above his head. After catching his attention, the bird lit out towards the coast, patterning the fading sky with his soaring climbs and swoops before setting a straight course over the enamelled waves of the Strait to the mountains of Snowdonia. It was an auspicious sign to see such a bird at close quarters, a creature of wisdom and prophesy, and Cornelius paused to consider it. The raven was both a divine messenger of good news, and an omen of death. But though dark was falling, it was not yet late evening, so his call was lucky. Like the crow, the raven was a creature of harmony, embodying the light and the dark. He felt himself transported across time and space to the China of his youth and listened again to the strains of the *Wu Ye Ti*, "The evening call of the raven", a melody hundreds of years old, passed from teacher to pupil, and played for guests by shy girls in the small music room of his father's house.

He had already been lucky to arrive on the island of Anglesey in the company of an English speaker. The talkative commercial traveller from Liverpool had shared a bench seat with him in the mail coach and on arrival at the Beaumaris inn had insisted on negotiating his lodging and the hire of a horse. It became apparent that the traveller was an enthusiastic Evangelical Christian and leading light of his local anti-slavery society, so Cornelius was not surprised that the sight of a foreigner had intrigued him. The traveller was determined that the journey would be used for improving discussion, but he had not noticed that he was doing most of the talking and that the theme had shifted from him coaxing views from the stranger and preaching the ways of the just, to delivering his own life story. Cornelius was philosophical by nature, and on his travels in Europe enjoyed reading western literature on that subject. He often turned to Goethe's *Reflections,* which were instructive on the subject of conversation and the art of listening. Cornelius was a skilled practitioner of that art.

As they had left the straggling border towns and night had fallen, he had been obliged to demonstrate some of his other skills, which had cemented the bond between himself and the traveller. The horses had struggled to keep upright on a lonely stretch of icy road, pitch black and dense with evergreens on the verges. The passengers had been ordered out to ease the burden at the start of a sharp incline and, predictably, a couple of thieves had materialised from the shadows to confront them as the coach pulled on ahead. One faced Cornelius, waving two flintlock pistols erratically and demanding silence with an oath, whilst the other started to make a move towards the commercial traveller, an older, plumper target. They were both far too slow and standing together was their downfall. Before the oath was fully out of the snarling mouth or the other man had covered any ground, Cornelius had sprung forward, side-stepped the armed man and delivered a crashing left-arm block to sweep aside his outstretched arms. The shock caused both guns to discharge wildly, and the sharp retorts, smoke and sparks screened Cornelius's second blow, a lethal right-hander, which collapsed the gunman's throat, and his third, a side-kick to his left which dropped the other thief before he took a step. The commercial traveller had not even time to cry out before Cornelius had turned from one slumped body to the other. But it was another corpse. Amateurs to the last, one of the pistol balls shot in error had found a mark. The guard had rushed back on hearing the guns, bawling his intention to fire, but was only too glad to find his duties restricted to shovelling the bodies off the road and shepherding his passengers back to the coach. In fact, he decided to shepherd just the one plump passenger, as a glance at the bodies had persuaded him that the other one should be left to his own devices.

"God save us!" the traveller had stuttered, as they settled back into their seats. "Thank you, sir. I owe you my life!"

"You are welcome," Cornelius had said, with a slight bow of his head. He had decided not to add that it was "nothing". Would it have offended the man's self-worth? English manners were interesting, but labyrinthine to fathom. He left the challenge for another day and instead reflected briefly on the two footpads lying dead by the roadside. The loss of life was always regrettable and he had borne the men no particular ill-will, but the choice had been a simple one, their lives or his. And the application of a few basic techniques had not been without another advantage. He had had little time for training in Liverpool where he had rented an anonymous room, with, as the English said, barely the space to swing a cat. Also, despite his preference for discretion, he had personal reasons for defusing the situation. He had no intention of allowing his bag to be rifled. It had made the long journey from Paris unmolested and he was a visitor bearing gifts. He was determined that they would reach their destination.

Cornelius was used to surviving in strange lands and outwitting both assailants and the idly curious. It would not have been difficult for him to get what he needed from the innkeeper, Welsh speaker or not. But to have the deals done, and more than that, for him to arrive at this remote place, looking as outlandish as he did, with a sponsor and "friend" had been useful. Ports were cosmopolitan places, and in Liverpool the thin sprinkling of foreigners had allowed him a degree of freedom and anonymity. Once he had travelled into the countryside and crossed the border into Wales, he had become more conspicuous, much more than he cared to be.

The black horse hired at the Old Bull's Head was a powerful and stoical beast, not swift, but intelligent. It seemed to know its way along the deserted coast road, which gave Cornelius time for reflection. So far the mission had been moderately lucky. The journey from Paris to Liverpool had been easy, a horse-drawn diligence to the coast, then a steamer to the City of Liverpool. The port had been a rare sight, its vast wet dock filled with vessels. Fully one hundred were held at anchor and the quays were thronged with sailors and dock workers, travellers leaving and arriving, thieves and dealers all jostling together and moving like a tide round mounds of bales and barrels. The port rivalled London and put Bristol in the shade, though he knew it had not always been so. Cotton spinning and weaving had bankrolled the flowering of the North and one day, on a whim, he had taken himself off to Manchester to see its famous factories. These had proved to be vast brick-built blocks, their walls studded with blank windows. From each roof rose one tall blackened chimney, which together formed a forest of spires, piercing the gloom

101

above and belching out more poisonous black clouds to fuel it. It had been a bright day by the coast, but the Manchester sun glowed only as a grey disc, masked by the inky smoke. Beneath this Stygian canopy the air rang with the insistent metallic clatter of machines and the periodic shrieks of boiler steam which played counterpoint to the low incessant rumble of carts on the crowded roads. He could hear Manchester and taste it still in his throat when he was ten miles out on the return trip to Liverpool.

The journey to the cotton city had been remarkable as he had travelled on one of the new steam locomotives which ran independently on iron rails all the way from Liverpool to Manchester, a full thirty miles to the northeast. Never tired and rolling at a steady seventeen miles per hour, fuelled by the roaring furnace, the iron horses ploughed up and down the tracks, moving goods and people in ever growing numbers. It was the future, he knew it to be so, and imagined a world where all towns were linked, across hills and through forests, deserts and swamps. A vast endeavour of huge cost, but with profits to be made: the world would change.

Apart from the useful reconnoitring, and uncovering a lead which he would pursue in London, the trip to Liverpool had been productive mainly in a negative sense as it ruled out possibilities. He had hoped to track down his quarry, a savagely successful criminal, and also to forge links within the port for future work. He had failed to locate his man, and had been disappointed to see only half a dozen Chinese faces, none of which provided useful material for his purpose. At such a great port he had thought there might be more but he had drawn a blank. On his last visit to London he had found a few gangs of Chinese lascars working on the ships in the docks by Limehouse causeway, and two of his men were already placed in Ravenswood's crew, preparing another new American-built vessel for its first voyage to the East. Entrepreneurs in London and Liverpool were hungry for a share of the growing Chinese market and it was easy to guess which goods the merchants would favour. He frowned at the thought of the cursed opium run from India to China which beckoned to the English like a Satanic Grail. It was a trade he was sworn to destroy, under sacred oath to his Emperor.

His journeys in Europe had filled him with dismay. During his last stay in Paris the well-informed talk was all of entrepreneurs and their rights, of liberalism and free trade. The homespun philosophers traded the words of their hero Jean-Baptiste Say and of that grim Scot who had inspired him, the economist Adam Smith. Cornelius had come to know them both through the enthusiasm of their disciples, and it seemed to him that all they preached was the selfish pursuit of wealth. Wealth and profit: the twin towers of their faith were to him false gods, both entirely alien to his country, his faith and the dictates of his soul.

The horse shied suddenly and shook him from his thoughts as a growling roll of thunder sounded across the Strait from the mountains. Cornelius quietened him, checked the skies, and as he did so the rain started to fall. As he had been warned at the inn, it soon commenced to tear across the island in horizontal rods, drenching him, his pack and his stolid horse as they laboured on, down the narrow track towards Llanddaniel. A cloudy mist dropped, swathing the landscape and blotting out the sight of the sea. Wind and rain bit into him and, pulling his hat over his eyes, he turned to pleasanter thoughts to sustain him over the last few miles. He was looking forward to seeing Nathaniel Parry again. It was rare in his line of work to have any warm feelings for an acquaintance: rare and usually unwise. Nathaniel and he had been helpful to each other in the past and Nathaniel's steadfastness had surprised him. But more than that, he felt a bond with Parry, who seemed to be a westernised version of himself: not so much a brother, but a second self, an alter ego. Both worked for their own governments, had similar moral codes, were of an age and build and, bizarrely, both were born of American mothers. This discovery was also a sign. It had been a welcome one, in the solitary and precarious life of Cornelius Lee. But the match was not exact as the opium question separated them. It was the principal cause of distrust between their countries as the British ignored all pleas from his Emperor's government to cease their illegal trade in China, and the problem grew as the years passed. But that was for the future. For today, on this cold February day, Nathaniel's house beckoned to him as a haven. He looked forward to presenting his gifts to the newly-weds. These were the greatest of human pleasures: the giving and the taking, and as his study of Goethe had taught him, for contentment of the soul, nothing should be more highly prized than this day.

As he listened to the rhythmic, muddy squelch of his horse's hooves as it plodded on, snatches of the commercial traveller's tales returned to him. "Be warned, it always rains heavy in these parts in February. Do you know English sayings? February brings the rain, thaws the frozen lakes again! But sometimes it still snows. February is also called "fill dyke", black or white! This is a strange spot you've fetched up in. Oh yes: my, my. 'Twas the last stronghold of the Druids before the Roman army killed the lot of them: burned all their oak groves they did. It's always been a wild, pagan place and there are traces of the old days still." Then he had glanced furtively at Cornelius, "No offence," he had said, suddenly uncomfortable. "You are a good Christian I take it from your attire, sir?" Cornelius's smile had reassured him and he had rushed on. "No English spoken on Anglesey as a rule: be ready for that. I'm not a native of the place. Born on the mainland I was,

Welsh borders. Welsh mother. Most folk in the borders speak English and Welsh."

Cornelius spotted a faded sign by the wayside and turned his horse towards the village. As the traveller had said, he soon came to a hillock ringed with stones. Some stood sentinel, grey and lichen covered, some were toppled, and others framed the entrance to the ancient burial mound. Through that low portal, a stone-lined passageway could be seen; reaching into profound darkness. He felt the presence of the ancestors and of the earth as it once was: it was a place of power. He had not advertised the Taoism of his childhood to his Evangelical acquaintance as it served no purpose. Not that he was in any way a zealous pagan. His beliefs had been battered along the way, but he retained his spirituality: an unshakeable belief in harmony and a profound empathy for the natural world, times past and to come. He felt it overwhelmingly as he approached the stones, and reined in the unwilling horse.

And it was there that they found him.


Nathaniel and Emma had been sitting in the farm parlour when Caradoc first raised his head. Sensing the approach of a stranger the terrier bolted to the door and set up a ferocious barking. Nathaniel pulled on a cloak, picked up the old hunting rifle which always stood, primed and ready by the door, and let Caradoc loose. He smiled to Emma who had looked up, startled, from her reading. She was huddled into the corner, making the best of the pool of light shed by the oil lamp.

"What do you think it is?" she said. She had a town girl's fears of the swirling dark outside and her heart thumped unpleasantly.

"Probably foxes," he said.

Striding out into the yard, he saw no disturbance in the hen house, but heard a strange horse neigh to his mare in its stall and as he ran out to the fence overlooking the copse and the burial mound of Bryn Celli Ddu, he saw a gaunt figure clothed entirely in black, standing motionless in the driving rain. Nathaniel's face broke into a smile as he vaulted the fence to welcome the man he had not seen for well over a year, and once thought he might never see again, in this life.


Later, introductions done, pleasantries exchanged, and seated together in the farm dining room with their backs to the fire, there was a place and time for more than small talk. They had dined well on Mrs Jones's seaweed soup, the formidable *cawl lafwr*, followed by a substantial rack of mutton and a rice pudding. Emma had fretted about the pudding, which appeared Welsh style, sugarless, and flavoured with nutmeg and bay leaf. She had withdrawn from the table with a promise to have

104

Aberffraw cakes brought out with coffee after the men had finished with their brandy, but there were still three at the table.

Caradoc had recognised Cornelius immediately, he smelled the same, though he was thinner and his black hair had grown longer. The terrier had settled down, proprietorially, with his head on the visitor's feet. It was good to welcome an ally. The last weeks had been full of strangers and a revelation for Caradoc in many ways. He had met dogs exactly like himself for the first time since he was a pup and it had not been altogether pleasant. One in particular had arrived with a cowman and had swaggered about the farm as if he owned it. Caradoc had given him notice to quit, and still bore a few scars from delivering that message, but it had been heeded. The interloper had visited again, but under the cowman's orders. The dog was humbled, tail down, and stayed skulking at the entrance to the yard. Also on the plus side, the farm was a sound billet for food. The Joneses were as useful for rations, if not better, than Mrs Rollinson and the air was good, familiar, as was the soil. But he had to watch himself with the sheep. The temptation was sometimes too great. And there was the sheepdog to consider, a lean and intolerant collie by the name of Idris who lived in Jones's cottage. Idris was a force to be reckoned with, but they had an understanding. Caradoc lolled at ease as the voices of his master and the visitor continued, low, sometimes urgent, but comforting nonetheless. He was off duty and lost himself in dreams.

"The Welsh air suits you, Nathaniel," said Cornelius, "or perhaps it is your married state?"

"I am happy in both, I must confess," said Nathaniel, refilling Cornelius's brandy glass. "Though I doubted once I would ever marry."

Silence fell comfortably between them as they sat, their chairs close together, each retreating into their own thoughts as the fire cracked and settled in the grate.

When the grandfather clock in the hall struck nine, Cornelius took it as a cue to return to business. In a low voice, he took up the threads of their earlier talk. "So, I gather that you are not to play the contented Welsh squire for ever. Your news from London suggests we still have a mutual interest in the doings of Mr Kizhe and his English contacts. Their white slave trade continues to flourish and the recent disappearance of a servant connected with a politician has attracted the attention of your superiors. This is fortuitous, as my mission in England is to conclude Kizhe's activities." He looked steadily at Nathaniel, weighing again his worth, choosing his words with care. "I would welcome your help. I know that you and your masters are unconcerned by his involvement in the China opium trade where he is a powerful trafficker, but my masters view it as a grave matter, as does the Emperor himself."

105

Cornelius's face clouded with memory, and, uncharacteristically, he chose to speak freely. "Remember, Nathaniel, my own brother died an addict. The man I seek: Kizhe," he pronounced the word again, slowly, "Kee-jay: remember, it is just an alias for him, it means, "the others". He has many guises, and there are many such as he. He works for the Count, whose business interests in trading women outrage you. We too deplore this, but we also concern ourselves with the Count's other affairs, which extend beyond importing opium to robbery and extortion. His powers also allow him to influence the Triads, to stir up conspiracies which mask his trade and occupy the authorities. Only last year the Yao highlanders of Hunan rose up, led by Zhao Jinlong, their Golden Dragon King. They are simple mountain people, devout Taoists, but their ways of peace had been shattered by the local Triad society, descendent of the so-called Three Harmonies Society of heaven, earth and man, yet who know nothing of harmony. Once these societies were revolutionaries but are now simply criminals. They stole cattle from the Yao, whose vengeance has laid waste to the province. The Emperor's troops were so weakened by opium that the only way they could bring peace was by paying off the Yao, bribing them to go back to their homes. The Triads and the Count continue to wreak their evil on the land." Cornelius paused and looked directly at Nathaniel, his eyes like twin black pools. "In the words of the philosopher Lao Tzu, a journey of a thousand miles begins with a single step. So, my friend, with our first step, we tread on the Count's man, Kizhe."

Nathaniel raised his glass to Cornelius. "So be it," he said, and bowed his head briefly, confirming their understanding before he continued: "Emma and I return to Bath shortly, at the end of this month, and then I will leave for London directly. Shall we meet there? I have rooms in Lambeth."

Cornelius nodded. "We will meet, preferably close to the docks where our business will be. I will leave a note at your Office with details by mid-March."

They fell silent again, but looked up at the sound of feet approaching across the hall. The door creaked open to reveal a maid carrying the coffee tray, with a plate of tiny cakes like sugared scallop shells just maintaining a trembling balance on top of the milk jug. The youngest Jones girl was a novice at waiting-on and edged forward uncertainly, her eyes wide and fearful as she approached the master and the stranger. With relief, her shaking hands landed the rattling tray and she managed to scuttle out unnoticed, fleeing down the lobby to tell her tale in the kitchen, for Emma Parry had followed her into the room.

Cornelius had already been struck by the natural beauty of Nathaniel's bride. Her bright auburn hair was tied up in a sky-blue band, the same fabric as her gown, sprigged all in white flowers with green leaves. She was tall and straight, graceful, with a pleasing voice and a smile in her eyes. But there was more, he sensed it in her. She had a quietness of spirit that allowed her an acute perception if she cared to heed it. And tonight she was dressed for dinner in his honour. Though the gown was in character, restrained and gentle on the eye, for the occasion she had also chosen to wear a heavy necklace of curiously wrought golden links and great sapphires which flashed about her neck and white breast with a cold and alien brilliance.

"Are you ready for coffee, gentlemen? And perhaps you might like to try these cakes. They will taste sweeter than the pudding. Also, I think you might prefer to remain here, the drawing room is colder and the fire is smoking. You will be more comfortable out of it. I can leave you in peace if you have more to discuss."

The men rose to their feet, Cornelius dislodging Caradoc, who slouched away, half asleep, and flung himself down closer to the fire.

"Nathaniel," said Cornelius. "May I request that Mrs Parry does me the honour of remaining with us, if it pleases you both?"

It pleased them all and as they sat down together Emma set about pouring the coffee. The aroma revealed it to be overly pungent and slightly burned. She pulled a wry face as she passed the first cup to their guest. "Try this, if you would care to Mr Lee. We do not have many visitors here and our cook prefers to make tea."

"I hope to have the privilege of sampling it," said Cornelius smiling.

"You must. Do not let this be your only visit, Cornelius," said Nathaniel impulsively. "You will always find a welcome here." He glanced again at Emma and his eyes were drawn to his mother's sapphires. "What do you think of our family jewels? We have reclaimed this necklace from the bank vault for Emma."

"Spectacular," said Cornelius guardedly, "though not Welsh. European I would say. French, before the Revolution."

Emma unclasped the rope of gems and passed them to him. "On the back of each jewel setting there are tiny letters. One is a B," she said.

Cornelius examined one of the settings closely. "Yes. This is one of the marks used by Maison Bapst, the once and present court jeweller. They are survivors and they marry well. They are still trading on the Quai de l'École. Though Nathaniel will know that."

Nathaniel did know of the Parisian *atelier* but had never examined the stones closely. They had been locked away after his mother's early death and, apart from a brief viewing at the reading of this father's will, had remained undisturbed in the dark of the Beaumaris bank vault for over twenty years, too poignant to be disturbed without good reason. He smiled ruefully and hurried on.

"There is a tale connected with them, which is related to our earlier talk. My father brought them back from Spain during the wars and there are more in the set. Edwin Ravenswood owns one rope of emeralds. You probably saw them worn by his wife when you stayed in their house. They were given to the family by a man now known as Sir Giles Mortimer-Buckley. And," he said, his eyes now sparkling as hard and blue as the sapphires, "there is more. We dined with the Ravenswoods after our marriage and Sir Giles also attended as a guest. He deliberately misled me about the gems, disclaiming any knowledge of my father's presence on the expedition. I now have evidence from Percy at the Office that my father undertook the mission with a Captain and two men from the ranks. I have no doubt he will soon confirm that Sir Giles was that Captain. I have many volumes of my father's papers to check, which may shed more light on the incident. But apart from that, other matters have emerged which make the business of interest. I will not trouble you with the details, Cornelius, suffice to say there has been a death in Bath which seems linked to the mission, and according to Percy a mystery remains about another piece in that collection of jewels, which the government would dearly like to recover. When I return from London I intend to stay in Bath until the links there are clear."

Emma handed round the cakes as Nathaniel narrated the tangled tale of the gems, and as she did so the necklace seemed to weigh more heavily on her breast, warm now in the heat of the fire, suddenly oppressive. She took a deep breath and felt for the lowest stone, lifting it away from her body, and distracted herself by considering their unusual guest. She had enjoyed exchanging a few words with him, all quite polite but very measured, with nothing given away. Yet his restraint had encouraged rather than inhibited conversation. Cornelius was an impeccable dinner guest, but apart from his contributions to the talk, his presence also fascinated her. He had remarkable economy of movement and his body had the sleek power of the panther. She had seen drawings of them, shadowy creatures with a calm grace, watchful in deep green jungles. He was mesmerising. It was easy to understand why Nathaniel had taken to him, why anyone would. She cast her mind back to what she had read about the theories of Franz Mesmer, that a magnetic force exerted by an individual can be so attractive that you are as if spellbound by them. In truth she was hypnotised by his looks alone. She could not remember ever seeing a person from the East before, at least not at such close range, and had to be careful not to stare. But when she let her eyes slide back to glance at him he was already looking at her, and smiled.

"Did you see the burial mound as you rode here?" she asked before she could stop herself. "I have had such dreams after I walked into the heart of it, down the stone passage."

"Do the dreams alarm you?" asked Cornelius.

"No," said Emma, thoughtfully. "But they are vivid, rushing dreams of strange people and snatches of songs. They are confused, hard to explain."

"I have had dreams when I slept out on the mound," laughed Nathaniel. "But it was the brandy and maybe Mrs Jones's forest mushrooms to blame!" He did not add that the worst dreams were fired by utter misery and desolation after the death of his father. He spoke only from gallantry, from good manners, to disguise his discomfort.

"In your case, it is so," said Cornelius gravely. "But I think Mrs Parry is very open to hearing echoes of the past," he turned to her. "Madam, have you ever seen things in your waking hours which others have not?"

"I think I might have done. It was only once, last month, just after Nathaniel and I married," said Emma, suddenly realising how pleased she was to speak of it and allow the words to release a recurring worry about that night. Cornelius was skilled in asking, as well as in listening. "It was at Arno's Tower. Mrs Ravenswood was showing the ladies the upper rooms. It was evening, but the moon was bright. Over the lawn I saw a man running by the trees, he seemed to be dodging, evading something. I felt his fear. Then he disappeared. But the others didn't see!"

"Did he carry a bag?"

"Yes."

"Did he cross from left to right."

"Yes! How could you know this?" asked Emma

"It is just a suggestion," said Cornelius. "The figure could easily have been an intruder; the shadows could have given you a vantage point the others did not have. But it might be that what you saw was a shade of another kind: that of a poacher I saw die there two years ago." He neglected to add that Kizhe's shot had shattered the man's face, but it had been his own knife which had released his soul. "If I was there again," he continued, "it is possible that I too would see him."

"Remind me to stay with both of you to improve my vision," said Nathaniel, amused and also unsettled, looking from one to the other.

"Now," said Cornelius, rising quickly. "Please allow me to present you both with my wedding gifts! Too late for the wedding, but brought within the first month to bless your honeymoon."

He bowed and left the room.

Nathaniel looked quizzically at Emma. "Do you like him, Em?"

"Oh yes," she said. "I understand why he is important to you. Why he has become important."

"I wouldn't say important," began Nathaniel, but then realised she had seen far more than he had, and nodded.

Cornelius returned with a parcel and moved the tray aside to place it on the table between them. He pulled away the brown paper and tissue layers to reveal a bolt of midnight blue Chinese silk, embroidered with pink and russet blooms.

"For you, Madam: the new Mrs Parry."

"How beautiful," exclaimed Emma, her fingers tracing the swirling embroidery. "I thank you. These hues match my colouring perfectly!"

"They were chosen to do so." Cornelius laughed suddenly at their awestruck looks. "My contact in Paris described you to me. He had met you both in London," said Cornelius. "But I did not know then that the silk would match your family jewels so well."

Under the roll of fabric was a black box. "This is for you, Nathaniel," said Cornelius, presenting it with a bow. "Like your sapphires, it dates from before the Revolution."

The box was opened to reveal a gold pocket watch on a chain.

"Cornelius," said Nathaniel," you honour me indeed! A Breguet, by God!"

Cornelius knew of Nathaniel's attachment to Paris, the place where his parents first met, as well as his misery there when his father had died. It was a gift to acknowledge both extremes of experience and mark a new phase of life.

"Tell me about it!" said Emma, leaning forward to see the prize.

"Breguet's *atelier* in Paris has been open since the 1770s," said Nathaniel, opening the case reverently. "They made watches for the cream of French society, including the royal family, and still do. Breguet was rumoured to have spent over forty years making the greatest watch in the world for Marie-Antoinette. I don't suppose she got it in time to enjoy it."

He examined the treasure lovingly. "Look, Em! The Breguet trademark, blue hands and phases of the moon. Exquisite!"

He ran his fingers to the chain's end where there was something else; a golden medallion with a Chinese symbol picked out and fretted.

"What does it say?" asked Emma.

Nathaniel put down the gift and extended his hand to Cornelius. "It says friendship. Thank you, my good friend."

The handshake and the sudden silence were both sensed by the dozing Caradoc who snapped awake, shot over yapping and wormed between them to investigate the mound of paper on the table. Nathaniel grabbed him as he attempted to leap on it and hauled him away laughing.

"Down, sir! Nothing for you here!"

Cornelius remained standing as the others sat, Nathaniel pushing back his chair to accommodate Caradoc who now sprawled on his lap.

"Thank you for an excellent dinner," said Cornelius. "And your kind offer of a bed for the night. I will retire now, and leave in the morning, if that is convenient."

His face was closed, distant. It was important for him not to stay longer, not to give in to the temptation to sit down with them at the family table by the fire; to move out of reach of the creeping cold which seeped through the gaps in the shutters and stole round the edges of the room. Outside he could hear the wild winds and squalls of rain buffeting the house, tearing over the mound and rattling the bare boughs of the trees in the copse, raw reminders of that other, brutal world, which waited for them all across the narrow straits. He could not afford to lose touch with it.

**Late morning: 8th March, 1833.**
**Nathaniel's rented rooms, Carlisle Lane, Lambeth, London.**

Cross-legged on the floor, naked but for his favourite Damascus robe and surrounded by his personal arsenal, blackened rags and polishers, bottles of oil and unguents, Nathaniel selected a particularly soft cloth for the final polish of his percussion pistols. After a boisterous session of exercises which had brought the landlady rushing upstairs to investigate, he had whiled away the morning cleaning them, checking the mechanisms and stowing his ammunition. The ruinous cost of converting them from flintlocks had been worth every penny. His eyes shone with delight as he held up first one, then the other, admiring each at arm's length and then placing them down, precisely. Though only in the ranks briefly whilst on a mission, he took a soldier's pleasure in his weapons, never allowing a servant to clean or carry them. His life was his own responsibility and he took it seriously. He reached next for his makila, his Basque walking stick, checked the handle and then pulled it hard to draw its concealed blade from the shaft and rubbed it until it shone. Like the pistols, it would not be needed today. Westminster did not call for guns or a mountain stick, but he had the very thing. He leaned over and pulled his slim walking cane towards him. Perfect. He polished the silver handle and the ebony shaft and then drew the glinting steel, no ordinary sword in this stick, but a blade from the East. He held it up to catch the light and the watermark seemed to swirl along the edge with a life of its own, sinuous and deadly.

There had been a real pleasure in being in his Lambeth rooms again, returning to reality and taking up the reins of his previous life after the joyous but bizarrely over-heated experience of getting married, and the strange, magical limbo of the month on Anglesey. Earlier that week they had arrived back in Bath, where he had left Em, Caradoc, and all the luggage bar his small travelling bag before catching the next mail coach to London. His landlady had been forewarned and all was in order when he arrived. But it was quiet without Caradoc and after the first couple of nights of unconsciousness he had been restless in his empty bed. He had been mildly surprised that he had not wanted to find alternative company, as there was plenty to be had with little effort. Marriage seemed to be working out as it should. He pushed his hair from his eyes and shook his head, clearing his thoughts. To business: first, lunch in the nearest chop house, then to the Office for the afternoon meeting, and later, a rendezvous in Wapping at a tavern called the Prospect of Whitby. A letter from Cornelius had been waiting for him at the Office, in the safekeeping of Richard Percy. He would be in the Prospect at nine o'clock every evening this week, and it looked like tonight the coast was clear. Drake had been keen to let him know that he was occupied for the evening, so there was no possibility of a duty call Chez Drake to detain him. Nathaniel sprang to his feet and packed away the pistols and the Basque stick in his travelling bag. The walking cane he placed on the bed, quickly found linen, trousers, frock coat, top hat and put his mind to choosing a suitable waistcoat and cravat for the meeting in Downing Street.

By early afternoon he was making his way over Westminster Bridge, holding on to his hat as he glanced over the parapet to the teeming waterway below. The river was crowded with craft, mostly small and pushy; bustling about their city business, but the water by the bank was sluggish and putrid, the March wind lifting poisonous fumes from its slimy surface. An eddy from a passing boat rolled the paw of a bloated dead cat in a ghastly salute. He turned away, suddenly nauseous, pulled his scarf round his mouth and pressed on to Downing Street. Threading his way past the sight-seers who loitered by the Prime Minister's residence, he made his way to the buildings which housed the Offices of State. Once there, he reported to Richard Percy, whom he found at his usual post, scribbling away in the anteroom to Lord Melbourne's office.

"I appreciated your letter, Percy," he said quietly, as the secretary nodded an enthusiastic welcome, stowed his pen and gathered his papers together for the meeting.

"My pleasure, Parry," he answered, pushing his gold spectacles further up his nose. "And I made it my business to save your report which gave chapter and verse on the nefarious doings of a certain Bristol trader." He smiled primly and then suddenly a flash of excitement lit his earnest features and reduced his age by ten

112

years. "On a lighter note," he said, grinning broadly, "dashed fascinating news about the Egyptian falcon! Do you think you will get it back?"

"Unlikely," said Nathaniel. "But possible. Tell me, does Captain Peterson, Lord Melbourne's man in Bath, keep close contact with the Office these days?"

"Just the odd report, but regular I would say, maybe once a quarter."

Regular enough: Nathaniel noted he would need to bear this in mind in his conversations with the Captain.

"Speaking of Bath," said Percy. "Congratulations! I hear that you are married and have a home there now." He paused delicately. "In terms of my records for financial arrangements, will your account also be in Bath?"

"Thanks for the good wishes," said Nathaniel, breaking into a wry smile. "For your information, my new father-in-law is none other than Captain Oliver Peterson. So you will understand why his activities are of interest to me. As to my whereabouts, I do have a house in Bath, but I shall keep my London rooms, so there is no need for any change. Your records can stand easy as I will continue to do my banking in London."

"But of course," said Percy, grinning. "The case of Vere the disappearing Bath banker remains unsolved doesn't it?"

"In so far as that no body has ever been found."

Percy made a move to the communicating door. "We had better go through. Mr Drake is already in with Lord Melbourne."

"Of course he is," said Nathaniel, as he followed Percy into Melbourne's lair.


John Drake was looking confident, usually a sign that he had effectively promoted his own interests and skewered everyone else's.

"Sit down, Parry," said Melbourne, gesturing languidly to a corner seat. "This shouldn't take long, thank God. Not a great deal to occupy us here at the Home Office I am delighted to say. Drake and I have just reviewed the state of play. Am I correctly informed that you have been getting married and holidaying in North Wales for a month?"

"I have been on the island of Anglesey, my lord," said Nathaniel. He could see exactly how Drake had utilised his private session with Melbourne, took the opportunity to flash a stony glare in his direction as Melbourne glanced down at his papers, and resigned himself to enduring a lordly homily on the satisfactory state of current affairs.

"Quite so, dashed isolated. Out of touch, what! Oh, congratulations by the way Parry, I wish you well of your changed marital status. Now, briefly, in your absence Drake and I have pronounced ourselves a nation at peace; only the most extreme liberals and republicans are agitating for a further extension of the vote. That issue has been well and truly solved for all right thinking people and, since the disappearance of the cholera, public hysteria has ebbed. I envisage a few months of calm as voters await the imminent passage of the factory bill into law. Chadwick's work has ensured that most owners are sanguine about the loss of the under nine year old workers, and there will be flexibility elsewhere. Speaking of compensation, very acceptable terms will be offered to the West Indian sugar lobby after the impending abolition of slavery. Looking a little ahead, Chadwick's other current enquiry into the ludicrously high level of poor rate will return a verdict most advantageous to rate payers, probably by early next year. I suspect that, come the day, come the new Poor Law, there will be restlessness amongst the pauper classes who will find it far less attractive to apply for poor relief. Therefore, all in all, it is not a bad time for us to encounter an increase in unexplained disappearances, which as you know, has now impinged on the family of a baronet, Sir Giles Mortimer-Buckley. Drake will question Sir Giles on the matter, as well as another item which concerns us today, his close involvement with a valuable cache of loot."

He allowed a smile to crinkle his lips, but as usual it failed to reach his hooded eyes.

"As you will have gathered, it would be most advantageous if we could locate an item of missing treasure trove intended for the Crown, to whit, an Egyptian piece acquired when Napoleon was ousted from that land, and which was stolen from the British Museum shortly after it arrived. Egyptian pieces capture the public imagination, it would lift the mood. Now Parry, I gather you are to investigate a death in Bath which might link to that treasure trove. The connection with Sir Giles is crucial as it appears he was the officer involved with the mission to locate the treasure during the Peninsular War, under the command of your father." Detecting no change from Nathaniel Parry in response to this; Melbourne rolled his eyes over to his secretary who was busy taking minutes. "Well done for verifying that, Percy."

"Thank you, mi'lord."

As Percy was busy flushing with pride, Drake and Nathaniel for once shared an identical thought, a vivid memory of the dinner at Ravenswood's and Buckley's unconvincing denial of ever coming into contact with Owen Parry.

"Drake, you will discuss the matter with Sir Giles presently?"

"Tonight, mi'lord," said Drake.

"Parry, I also have your correspondence from a couple of years ago," said Melbourne. "It refers to your contact, Drake, a Mr Ravenswood, a merchant who remains most active in the China trade, and according to Parry has contacts with traffickers of," he paused, "shall we call them, white slaves? Some people do, don't they? Though one might perhaps see them as servants of a particularly intimate type. Laundresses, I am informed, often operate a side-line as common prostitutes. Some are keen to sell themselves abroad I gather. You might take the opportunity to question Mr Ravenswood, who might shed some light on who might be behind the current rash of disappearances. Of course, Mr Ravenswood himself, as a close ally of Lord Palmerston, will continue in his businesses unmolested."

"By great good fortune," said Drake, looking straight at Melbourne but horribly aware of Nathaniel's piercing scrutiny, ran his fingers round his collar as though he were short of space to breathe, "I dine not only with Sir Giles this evening but also with Mr Ravenswood." He risked an uneasy glance at Nathaniel. Drake had never been sure if Ravenswood had informed Parry of his involvement in the various activities of Ravenswood Enterprises. Cornelius he knew only as the sinister ally of Kizhe and Nathaniel was in no hurry to put him right.

"I will use the occasion to question them both."

Drake had been dreading the evening ahead even before he was lumbered with additional duties which might turn unpleasant. He did not like to see his wife in the company of her lover, Ravenswood. Not that he was a passionately jealous husband to the Honourable Charlotte, as she functioned for him mainly as a stepping stone into the highest ranks of society, but in matters of adultery, out of sight and thus out of mind was always the more comfortable option. Paraded in front of his face, and without Amanda Ravenswood to share his pain, it was a grim prospect. However, it would give him an opportunity to see Sir Giles and Ravenswood without Parry. That had to be a plus. The situation needed to be dampened down, and quickly, for everyone's sake, particularly his own.

Melbourne nodded lazily and turned to Nathaniel. "You will wait to see if Drake requires your assistance after his meeting tonight and profit from anything pertinent he might discover. Then return to Bath to enquire into the untimely death. It is highly unlikely, but if Sir Giles can shed any light on the victim, you might uncover a lead concerning the disappearing Napoleonic bauble."

He chuckled to himself and then barked out a short, brutish laugh. "Damned nonsense!" he muttered, before subsiding into a motionless reverie. When he looked up the three younger men were still sitting, waiting. Oh the joy of power! Melbourne waved them away. "It really doesn't matter one way or another but it is an interesting stratagem. Do your best." But then the clock on the mantelpiece chimed insistently and he was reinvigorated. "Good God," he exclaimed, standing abruptly to attention. "Brooks's calls! I'm due at my club! Away with you immediately my three wise men! I expect a full report by the end of the month. Percy, my coat and gloves there's a good fellow."

Nathaniel and Drake were soon stood out on the street together.

"I'll drop you a note, Parry," said Drake, dismissively. "Do you still have the rooms in Lambeth?"

"Yes," said Nathaniel, holding out his hand to Drake. "Good day to you then. I will delay my journey to Bath until tomorrow afternoon in case you need to discuss anything from tonight's meeting."

Drake shook his hand, reluctantly, and winced under the pressure: another reason to dislike Parry. "Hardly think it will be necessary. This whole affair is most likely a colossal waste of our time. But, as you like." Shoulders hunched and his mouth set in a hard line, he turned on his heel and marched away quickly, down the street and sharp left, to lose himself in the crowds of Whitehall.

**Early evening: The Mortimer-Buckley Residence, Park Street, Mayfair.**

In John Drake's view, it could have turned out a lot worse. The dinner party proved to be a small one and easily managed in terms of business. He was lucky to arrive at the same time as Ravenswood and before they had even crossed the threshold had given him a discreet warning about official interest in his oriental connections, as well as the proximity of Nathaniel Parry who would be following up links between Buckley and a recent death in Bath. He had been impressed to see that Ravenswood's footman had been dispatched to the docks immediately to put interested parties on alert.

Once indoors he found there were only half a dozen of them round the table: just the hosts, himself and Lottie, Ravenswood and Sir Giles's nondescript daughter, drafted in to make up the numbers as her husband was out of town. Drake had lost no time in looking her over but it had been a disappointing exercise. In the husband's place he too would have had urgent business out of town, and on a very frequent basis. Lottie was decked out in yet another new evening gown and topped off by some of her costlier diamonds but was corralled between himself and Sir Giles, whilst Ravenswood had Lady Leonora on one side and her daughter on the other. The contrast between the two Buckley women could not have been greater. Lottie had given him a spiteful and accurate description of the matron after an afternoon call so he was ready for the excess of flesh, the ill-chosen gown, and the twittering monologues. All of these were acceptable tariffs that Sir Giles had to pay for her wealth, but the daughter was a disappointment. Sir Giles had been a handsome man, and was attractive still, but their heiress was not, lacking even the ample proportions of her mother, she fluttered and simpered in Ravenswood's shadow like an etiolated weed. Perhaps it was for the best, taking petty revenge on Lottie for her misdemeanours was not a good choice. She would eventually tire of Ravenswood, he was sure of it. And she brushed up well. He reminded himself that he was in for the long game.

After the cloth was removed and the ladies left it was time for brandy and cigars, and for him to move into the second phase of his campaign.

"Excellent brandy, Sir Giles," he began affably. "It is good to get a chance to talk over such a superb Armagnac. I did not want to allude to the subject earlier, as your lady wife and daughter do now seem to be putting the incident behind them, but do you have any news on the mysterious disappearance of your daughter's nanny?"

Ravenswood's staff would have seen the warning signs, the tightening of their employer's jaw and the hardening of his eyes, but Drake ploughed on, ignorant and oblivious.

"As you know there were a number of kidnappings reported last month in the lower class tenements of the East End. All victims were female. Closer investigations by the police revealed that there had been even more, previously unreported incidents, and the disappearance of your servant has been linked to these cases."

"Haven't heard a word," said Sir Giles, his stomach somersaulting, his eyes fixed on Drake, studiously avoiding the brooding presence of Ravenswood.

"We have employed another nanny who seems quite acceptable. Time moves on. I suppose the young woman was lured away by men. It happens."

"But her belongings are all still here?"

"Yes," said Buckley, making a mental note that they must be called for in the not too distant future. Perhaps Ravenswood could make it happen.

Drake took a measured slug of his brandy and ran a nervous finger round his collar: the second subject would be trickier.

"Just one more question, in an official capacity I'm afraid," he glanced towards Ravenswood, then away again even more rapidly. "I recall our last meeting at Arno's Tower. We all talked of Mrs Ravenswood's emeralds which you presented to the family during the last war, and mention was made of a certain Owen Parry's role in the mission." No one was offering any help, so he soldiered on. "It has transpired that this man did in fact lead the operation and that there was a discrepancy in the contents of the haul when it returned to England. Parry recorded the presence of an Egyptian trinket, lately stolen from the British Museum, but when the haul was unloaded," he attempted a facetious grin. "Poof! It had disappeared like magic. And here is another interesting factor, apparently a man died in Bath recently who was very likely one of your men from that operation in Spain. His death was at first seen as misadventure, but new evidence has suggested a link to the mission. Isn't that interesting, Sir Giles! I wonder now, could you shed any light on this mystery? I might add that Lord Melbourne would very much like to retrieve any of His Majesty's treasure trove which has wandered. The Egyptology section at the British Museum is one of the most popular and the curators are already rubbing their hands in anticipation of its return."

Drake knew that Buckley had committed some misdemeanour on that mission. He knew it in his water, he knew as he would probably have done the same. But he was not prepared for the effect of his words on his host. Buckley seemed to diminish before his eyes, his hand shook and he drained of colour.

"You know, Drake," he said faintly, "after the dinner at Ravenswood's, I thought again about those old days in Spain, and I did just recall Parry. Yes, I believe I did. So long ago, he had slipped my mind."

He took a steadying breath as the voice, low and grating, sounded insistently in his ear. "Steady now. You are amongst friends, Giles. Be bold!"

He felt Ravenswood's eyes boring into him. He would say little but he would look the man in the eye. "As to the trinket. I cannot remember seeing it. No, I am afraid not." He smiled and reached for his glass.

"Good man," said the voice, steadying his hand, helping him grip the glass as though his life depended on it.

"And it had better stay forgotten," reflected Edwin Ravenswood.

Both he and Buckley were well aware that the Ravenswood family had benefited in many ways from their connections with him in his previous existence as Captain Mortimer-Buckley. It had not just been the receipt of a solitary rope of emeralds. There had been a purse of napoleons, there had been works of art from other sources, and from the robbery in the hills of Spain there had been, amongst other items, the falcon necklace. Edwin's father had requested it as a gift for his dear son, to add to his growing collection of artefacts from the Far East and the Middle East. And there it had remained, in a display case amongst the weapons, suits of armour and statuettes which adorned his Oriental Salon, one of the less sinister pieces, one which Amanda had often looked at, but was not permitted to touch.

"As I thought," said Drake, relieved to hear the denial. But even as his ears rejoiced, he remembered his visit to Arno's Tower, the guided tour of Ravenswood's collection. Thank God, that his host's enthusiasm for his swords had steered them away from the Egyptian cases. His new watchwords must be: out of sight, out of mind. He saw nothing, and neither did they. He looked from one to the other, confirming their stories. "I will inform Nathaniel Parry that you have never seen the item in question. I feel I should warn you, however, that he will be investigating the death in Bath and might want to speak with you about related incidents."

The voice tried to get him to tell Drake to go to hell, but Buckley did not trust himself to say more. He nodded and attempted a smile but had not succeeded in thoroughly launching it before a footman entered and announced that coffee awaited them, with the ladies, in the drawing room.

## Late evening: Wapping Wall, London.

Nathaniel had taken the precaution of packing his reversible frock coat, collapsible top hat and soft cap, as he had no intention of quitting his lodgings in Lambeth looking the same type of cove as he would appear in Wapping. He put both pistols in his belt and took the makila for good measure. He took a ferry down the river and made his way to the vicinity of the riverside tavern where Cornelius was waiting before he dodged into an alley, turned his coat inside out, stuffed the hat in his pocket and swapped it for the cap. Hunching his shoulders and digging his hands into his pockets, he sidled out and made for the Prospect. At eye level the streets were alive with drinkers, sailors swaggering and singing, women screeching, boys still trying to sell the final editions of the papers, and posses of children careering between them all, their bony fingers sliding into unwary pockets to relieve them of their silk handkerchiefs, purses and watches. As his glance dropped, he saw the detritus of the dock population, limbless beggars, many with tarnished campaign medals hanging forlornly on their chests, felled drunks, feral cats and stray dogs, all mired in the filth of the streets.

He passed ranks of warehouses and lodgings until he came to the ink-black passage of the Pelican Steps, where he looked up to inspect the tavern sign swinging above him. It showed a coal ship at anchor and the name painted on the bow was *The Prospect*, registered in Whitby. He glanced quickly down the steps, made out the glint of water and the dark shape of a ferry passing, and then entered the front bar, a foetid cauldron of heat and noise. Above him the ceiling shook with the stamps and jeers of the prize fight fanciers supporting a match and all around him crammed a press of drinkers, dogs and hoydens looking for business. But he knew where to look for Cornelius. He would be sitting in a shadowy corner, his back to the wall with an eye on the entrance, and one down-at-heel Chinese sailor fitted the bill. Sitting behind a couple of glasses and a jug was an unkempt lascar with matted hair and a tattered coat. But through the straggling fringe glinted two familiar dark eyes, sharp as razors.

"Porter?" offered Cornelius as Nathaniel took a seat next to him. "It is the usual drink in here."

"Then, yes, thank you," said Nathaniel, helping himself to a glass of the treacle-dark ale.

Cornelius dropped his voice but kept his eyes on the door.

"We will go down to Ravenswood's mooring in the dock, his new vessel lies there and it will be ready to sail in a day or two. It is being loaded, so the crew have been ordered to quit their lodgings and move into their quarters on board. I have not been able to locate my contacts."

"Are these contacts the men who helped me in '31?" asked Nathaniel, a vivid memory of two assassins flashing through his brain, masked men, responsible for torching Ravenswood's precious ship, *Mathilda*, reducing it to an inferno whilst puncturing his watchmen's throats with arrows. He remembered the steep climb up from Bristol's floating harbour with the four wretched prisoners, bundling them into the waiting coach and leaving those two grim men to the chaos as he drove away.

"No, not them," said Cornelius. "It was wiser for them to vanish, but the contacts I speak of have served Ravenswood for over three years with their heads down, biding their time and gathering information. They will remain so until I give them specific orders to act. I found out from some lascars on the dockside that another of Kizhe's vessels sailed last month, but only to the Hook of Holland, and will return shortly. No one mentioned Kizhe, but he might be on Ravenswood's vessel with the crew, or could be lodging locally. Whether he is or not, I need to find a way to get on board. I will give you directions to the berth and when the time comes, we will leave separately."

Cornelius poured himself another drink, and as he passed the jug to Nathaniel he pressed a sketch map of the location of the ship's berth into his hand.

Shortly before midnight they liaised near Ravenswood's elegant new clipper, keeping to the shadows by a stack of barrels with a good view of the vessel. Nathaniel noticed it was named the *Leonora,* no doubt as a sop to that lady's pride, and to acknowledge the extensive new role of the Mortimer-Buckley family in financing Ravenswood's activities. There was still a mountain of crates and tubs to be taken on board, an idle hoist, some ropes were hanging over the deck and a mass of fishing nets pooled on the dockside, but there was no sign of any sailors.

"I thought I might slip on board with the men if my contacts were working, but there is no chance of that," whispered Cornelius. "Stay here, I will see if there is another possibility of getting aboard."

Without waiting for an answer he slid away into the dark, avoiding the light from the lanterns strung along the quay, and visible only as a darker shadow moving over the nets towards the looming hull of the clipper. The stench on the dockside was foul and Nathaniel's eyes were stinging. It was hard to focus and he rubbed them with the back of his hand. In that one second, there was uproar, in a loud sliding rush of noise the idle hoist sprang to life and the ropes and nets snaked upwards, sweeping Cornelius off his feet and swinging him, a ball of struggling limbs, over the bow and onto the deck of the *Leonora*.

# Chapter 5

**Midnight: 8th March, 1833. On the deck of the clipper, *Leonora*, London docks.**

At a signal from the mate the swinging net, with Cornelius trapped and struggling inside, was dropped nine feet from the hoist to crash, suddenly motionless, onto the deck. It was immediately surrounded by a clutch of jabbering sailors, who had been lying in wait, cold and mutinous, since the message arrived from the owner. They had been put on alert to waylay any strangers attempting to board the vessel, particularly an English gentleman, tall, pale skinned and black headed. The mate turned on his heel and went below with the good news. With one in the bag as evidence of effort, the extra crew he had detailed for the night watch could get some sleep.

"'E's dead," said the cook, disappointed after kicking speculatively at the curled body in the roll of netting. "We'll get nought out of 'im."

"'Course 'e ain't," said another, an ox-headed midshipman, more used to brawls. "'E's out cold. Must 'ave taken a rap on the 'ead."

"And 'e ain't no English gent a-spyin' neither," said the cabin boy. "It's just one o' the lascars, poor devil. And I dunno why the mate wanted 'im bagged. It's a bit more than waylayin' if you ask me."

"Stow it," said ox-head. "Matey's comin' with Captain Vance."

The sailors fell back to allow their superiors to approach and inspect the prisoner. For his part, Cornelius had decided to continue playing dead. At the moment he was first swung up into the air, making a mental note never, ever, to fall for the jungle trap ploy again, he could not resist the fleeting thought that at least he had managed to get on board. But as Goethe observed, be careful what you wish for. His means of arrival had created plenty of challenges, but the situation had deteriorated further when the net was dropped from the hoist. Tangled in the mesh and unable to break his fall effectively, he had landed badly on his left side and his ribs were on fire with pain. Moving was excruciating and would remain so, at least until he had bound his chest, and even breathing was proving difficult, so he cut both to a minimum.

"Frisk him," demanded an authoritative voice. "And check he's alive."

He sensed bodies surging around him again. Hands tore away the net, rolled him over, felt his neck for a pulse and his heart for a beat, swarmed over and into his ragged coat and checked his legs, his ankles, his wrists.

"No weapons, Captain. In fact, nothin' at all, but he is breathin'." It was the voice of the kicker. Cornelius would not forget it.

"Well done, lads. Take him below and lock him in the grain store. Bar the regular watch, the rest of you can stand down. We've a busy day tomorrow."

Fortunately for Cornelius they did not take him by the arms and stretch his battered chest. One set of arms picked him up, hoisted him over a shoulder and carried him away.

Cornelius flicked his eyes open for a second as he was carried down a hatchway to the lower deck. He needed to get his bearings and prepare himself for a second unwelcome landing: but in the event it never came. A door opened onto a small, airless store room, which was to be his cell, but he was placed rather than dropped onto the floor. Another flicker of his eyelids explained why. The man who had picked him up was Fong, one of his own, last seen over a year ago in a meeting snatched on the dockside. At the sight of him, even the cracked ribs seemed more bearable.

"Tie him," ordered the Captain briskly. "We'll see if he sings when he comes round."

A length of rope was thrown to Fong, who knelt and leaned over Cornelius, his back turned to the others and their lantern light. Ankles tied, the rope looped up to secure his wrists, and trying to nurse his ribs, Cornelius managed to breathe a word of thanks, as a cold blade slid up his sleeve and the smooth knife handle slipped into his palm. As Fong rose from the floor, Cornelius risked another glimpse around the room. The sailors had been sent away and the Captain was about to leave with the lantern, when a massive figure appeared in the doorway: a rectangular, heavily-muscled man, with no discernable neck, and arms like tree boles. He pushed the Captain aside and moved towards Cornelius, eclipsing the light. It was a grotesquely familiar silhouette.

"Bring the light over," he rasped, amused, in his habitually harsh voice, ground down in the years of his youth by the desert winds of Mongolia. "Let me inspect your catch."

The man's silk coat fell open as he clasped his hands behind his back like an admiral and the light flashed on a brutal blade, the hooked hachiwari. Cornelius knew of only one man who carried such a weapon.

"Mr Kizhe, sir," said the Captain. "We caught this man stepping up to the ship, right under the bow. We were instructed to apprehend intruders."

Kizhe peered down at the figure, the matted hair and the filthy clothes. He gave a harsh snort of laughter.

"Your men have caught a stray lascar, Captain Vance. What's in his pockets?"

"Nothing, sir," said the Captain.

"Bring him round," demanded Kizhe. "Fetch a bucket of water."

Cornelius decided to risk consciousness. As the bucket of river water spewed over him he flicked his head forward so his hair stuck to his face, proceeded to roll feebly on the floor and set up a wailing cry.

"Where am I? Oh save me! Where am I? Never meant harm, my lords! I come in on a Company ship out of Calcutta and lost my billet. I was only after a place to sleep lords, but I got pulled up into the air and landed on your deck! I mean no harm!"

Kizhe lost interest. "Enough! You were trespassing and will stay here tonight and be dealt with in the morning. The men will jog your memory for you and you can tell them your life story." In an aside to the Captain he added, "I'm leaving now, we have no more to discuss. Mr Ravenswood will be here in the morning." His eyes gleamed with malice at the prospect of Ravenswood's fury. "You can display your sprat to him."

Cornelius let his head fall to the floor and moaned, which took little in the way of acting. The men withdrew, the door slammed shut and the lock turned. The leaping shadows of the storeroom, and his disguise, had saved him from discovery by Kizhe, but the light of day and interrogation by the crew would make him immediately recognisable to Ravenswood. He had once been a resident at Arno's Tower for months on end, and Ravenswood never forgot a face. It was imperative that he left before dawn. He knew that Fong would be back to slide the lock, and when he had torn his shirt and bound his chest, he would compose himself and make ready to do the rest. In the utter blackness of the store, he slid the knife down his sleeve and began to saw at the rope.

Meanwhile, Nathaniel had continued to watch from his vantage point behind the barrels until the commotion on deck had ceased and Cornelius had been taken below. He cursed to himself, barely able to believe what he had seen. There was no need for such preparations in the normal run of taking on provisions for a voyage. It was obvious that the crew had been tipped off to expect visitors and he had a shrewd idea as to whom the culprit might be. But that score could be settled later. Cornelius was in a dangerous place and he needed to get him out of it. It was unlikely that they would kill him before extracting information, but that would definitely be unpleasant and could start soon. Balanced against that, his disguise was good and his story would match it. Nathaniel thought quickly. Cornelius looked disreputable enough to be guilty of anything, so it should be child's play to set the dock police on him. Cheering himself up with that thought, he stole away from the harbour, turned his coat, swapped his cap for his top hat and donned an ostentatious white scarf for his visit to the office of the Marine Police Force in Wapping High Street.

It took longer than he had hoped, and a bone-white dawn was seeping up the slate-grey of the sky before he returned with a posse of dock police and a warrant coaxed out of a tetchy, yawning magistrate. The Captain ordered the dropping of the gangplank and they followed him to his cabin, passing two morose sailors with recent and impressive head wounds. Nathaniel allowed himself a degree of grim satisfaction, even if events had gone badly for Cornelius, the punishment had not all been one way.

"Captain," said the officer self-importantly, "this gent here, who is attached to the government," this last was added with due reverence, and followed by a pause. "Was robbed last night by a Chinese malefactor who legged it to your boat and was drawn on board sharpish by your men. I have reason to believe therefore that he is either one of your crew, or at the least is being harboured by them. I have a warrant to search your ship forthwith."

"You are too late, Officer," said Captain Vance wearily. "I was awoken not an hour ago by my first mate. We just passed him on deck; you cannot fail to have noticed that he has barely escaped with his life! The man you speak of was not of our crew but had been detained by them to be questioned for trespassing. In the night he escaped from the room where I had ordered him to be confined and fought his way off the ship. Two of my men are missing, presumed overboard and dead, five others are wounded. Four of these we had to retrieve from the water. You can charge him with murder as well as robbery when you catch him."

The dock police made a cursory search of the vessel whilst Nathaniel started to enjoy himself and extract intelligence. He chatted amiably with the Captain, commiserating and accepting a drink, brought by a cook with an open shirt and heavily bandaged chest. It was only as a carriage was heard drawing to a halt at the harbour side that a terrible realisation began to dawn on the Captain. An English gentleman, tall, white skinned and black headed? Oh God! And even worse, was it a conspiracy? Had a posse of bludgeon men come aboard last night for the lascar? And some "stray lascar" he had turned out to be!

His inward cursing of Kizhe was interrupted by the sound of Mr Ravenswood giving some terse instructions to his coachman. His guest, who had already risen, bowed and took his leave. Shouting words of encouragement to the police officers, he made his way across the gangplank and into the awakening hubbub on the quay.

**After lunch: 14th March, 1833.**
**The Parry Residence, Saint James's Square, Bath.**

Emma sat at her dressing table watching her maid's face in the mirror as she worked on the tangle of chestnut hair which still flowed down her back, defying the struggle to tame it into a bunch of seemly curls for the afternoon's bout of visiting. The girl was pre-occupied. Her usual stream of chatter had dried up and she was surprisingly clumsy. Emma's scalp was still burning after a rough raking from the comb and a reckless stab or two from the hair-pins.

"What is the matter, Frances?" said Emma, looking directly at the troubled blue eyes in the reflection, noting the flush as it ran up the thin white neck to the ears.

"Sorry, Madam," said Frances, smiling only with her mouth. "Nothing is the matter."

She had no intention of telling the Missis what had upset her, and cursed herself for letting her feelings show, declaring with a silent and bloody oath that she had gone soft in the head with too much good living. The last couple of years in service had been the best of her short life. She had food, shelter, clean clothes, some of them stylish, and for the first time, as well as the pity and care offered by the Parrys, she had the true affection of another human being. The love of another. As a slow tear rolled down her cheek she knew that the game was up, she had to give something and it had to give a nod to the truth in order to convince.

Emma turned round to face the girl, took the pins and comb from her hands and patted the seat by her. "Sit down and tell me, Frances. The hair can wait."

"I'm just a bit low about Toby, I mean Tobias, Madam," she started, watching Emma's face, gauging how much to say. She took a breath and started. "You know he likes to go to the George in Walcot with the men and listen to the reformers in the bar, well he goes pretty often now. And when we talk it's all of big affairs. I don't rightly understand the meaning of them. He seems that carried away with it, he's no time for the talk we used to have."

That would do, with no mention of the scene that morning when she had walked in on a shouting match between Tobias and the woman who came in to do the cleaning. Sweeping under his bed she had chanced on a package all done up with string and had dragged it out, just as he had nipped back to his room for his coat. Tobias had gone wild. As he tore the pack from her, cursing her for a nosey drab, it had opened and showered its contents over the floor. Frances had almost cannoned into the woman as she fled and found him gathering up the scattered papers from the floor in a panic. They were all the same, scores of copies of the new paper *The Destructive and Poor Man's Conservative*. Frances knew what it was, she had heard him quoting from it often enough, when he wasn't on about *The Poor Man's Guardian*, both Hetherington's rags, and this new one firmly linked to the trade unions: every copy unstamped and every copy illegal.

"Tobias, what the hell are you doin' with this lot?" she had asked, terror struck. "You're not fixin' to sell them are you? You'll be arrested! You'll lose your place. God Almighty, Toby, what were you thinkin' of!"

"No! I'm not, Fran," he had said, a cold sweat sheening his brow, "not sellin', just keeping hold of 'em 'til tonight, for Robert Turner."

But she did not believe him.

Emma watched the girl's face closely. She had joked with Nathaniel often enough about Tobias's dog-like devotion to Frances and his burgeoning interest in politics, both traits they had approved. She knew there was more, but it was enough for now.

"Well, Frances," she said, taking the girl's hands. "My best advice to you is to improve your reading, ask him about the things he is learning and show some interest. I happen to know that Tobias regards you most highly so I will help you myself. I too have an interest in politics. I've been to many meetings with my father."

"Thank you, Madam," said Frances, pleased to move away, re-plaster a compliant smile and renew her battle with Emma's *coiffure*. Frances was a survivor, the smile became more confident. If Madam was that interested in politics she might have an ally yet to help her keep Toby Caudle on the right side of the law.

For her part, Emma was pleased to see that no more tears dripped down. She had never known Frances to cry before; despite all her previous miseries and misfortunes. As the girl commenced to work on the rest of her hair Emma relaxed and allowed her thoughts to drift. The days of Nathaniel's absence in London had been busy ones as it was the first time she had ruled alone as mistress of the house. She had managed to diffuse the trial of strength between herself and Mrs Rollinson, who actually did know better on matters of household finance, ordering provisions, laundry, in fact almost everything. Emma felt quietly pleased with her progress. She had thanked and congratulated Mrs Rollinson on running the house so well in her absence and the gifts from Wales had been successful. Both the Welsh clover honey and the length of intricately checked woollen cloth had brought, if not a smile, at least a relaxation in the obstinate lines of Mr Rollinson's face. If she could keep her formidable housekeeper from bullying her, and harness her talents to run the house in the family's best interests, rather than in her own, it would be a victory indeed.

Emma had been busy with other matters since her return, visiting her parents, her friend Anna and her new baby, and mid-week, a most unexpected caller. The delivery of Mademoiselle Colette Montrachet's card had been followed by a visitation from the lady herself. Coco had provided entrancing company, especially in comparison with Anna who had provided an afternoon of surpassing dullness, tediously occupied by the exhibition of her offspring. But Emma could not meet with Coco without a tremor of anxiety. Coco's long-standing friendship with Nathaniel had caused her many sleepless nights before her marriage, and though she could love her as a friend and had almost convinced herself that Coco was setting her cap at Dairmuid as a husband, she was unsettled by her dangerous allure. Devastatingly charming and probably as duplicitous as the courtesan she was supposed to have been, Coco seemed capable of anything.

But the flawless oval face had been all smiles. She had been avid for tales of Anglesey and the sea, wishing Emma and Nathaniel well. She had been full of her forthcoming trip to France with Dairmuid, who had been spending more time with Charles Palmer, Bath's MP, and had become convinced that he needed to see the Medoc and its wondrous vines for himself. He had Irish friends there who were keen to host him and they would leave within the week. Delighted to learn of Emma's proficiency in French, Coco had prattled happily in her native language, allowing Emma the chance to practise and show off.

"*Formidable*, by dear," she had said. "You have quite the Parisian accent!"

128

Just before she had left she had recalled their evening together at the Ravenswood mansion, and in particular Nathaniel's announcement that Emma would be presented with his mother's gems when they arrived in Anglesey. How she would like to see them! And she had seen the sapphires. She had remarked politely on their beauty, and kissed Emma a fond goodbye.

How very lucky if one can transform rivals in love into friends, she thought. There was a time when she had also feared that Nathaniel might marry Tilly and now she was about to visit her for tea. She looked down to the ring on her hand and thought about the power of love, the elemental force which could bring even the toughest, like Frances, to their knees and stir up the most unruly emotions in everyone from ladies to drabs. The days might have been busy, but being separated from Nathaniel for all those nights after the passionate month in Wales had been purgatory. Her body had ached for him and his return from London had been a sweet relief. Before she had married she never had any real idea of what "wedded bliss" might actually feel like. To think of it sent a heady rush of desire coursing through her, a sensation completely unknown and unimagined during those lonely, empty nights in Marlborough Buildings.

The comparison of her position then, as a girl at home, and now, was as water unto wine. But her whole happiness was totally dependent on Nathaniel staying in her life. Without him it would be over. One error on his part, one enemy too many and she could lose him and all would fall into ruin. Her heart bumped unpleasantly at the thought of such a loss, of life's fragile thread. His story about Cornelius Lee, though carefully edited she was sure, still conveyed that Cornelius had been in danger in London and had escaped. Beside the possible threat to Nathaniel himself, she had also felt a measure of alarm for Cornelius Lee. He was a fascinating man and she was drawn to him, and more than to a friend, like Dairmuid Casey. She glanced at her needlework on the seat by the window. She was making a small reticule to match the blue silk evening gown made from the wedding gift Cornelius had brought to her. She hoped he might see her wear it someday.

She shot an encouraging smile to Frances and decided to share her plans. "The reason that I'm expected at my parent's before three o'clock is that my mother and I are going to Mrs Vere's. So we had better get on and make me fit to face Bath society! By the way, did Mr Parry take Caradoc to Walcot Street?"

"There was no stopping him, Madam," said Frances, deftly twirling a long curl and draping it over Emma's shoulder. "He was waiting over the road by the Crescent so he couldn't be shut in. And Mr Parry said they might not be back for dinner."

Caradoc had spent his time wisely during Nathaniel's absence. He had reacquainted himself with the garden and the park and been on the town in the company of Tobias. They often went to Walcot, either to meet the men, an excellent option, as the fire at the George was always well stoked and prowling under the tables provided more food than he could manage, or to visit the Spence household, which had been decidedly less pleasurable of late. He had many happy memories of the kitchen at the Spence's, the old woman, the ancient man, the fat baby and always a few other people, especially Mary, who treated him most befittingly, in fact, like a god. But there was an addition that had soured the experience, a squawking bird, coloured like a flag and flapping on a perch, high up out of reach. He knew birds and their noises, or he thought he did. But the creature was like no other. It had called his name and had him running round the kitchen. When he was wise to that it had whistled for him, and not like the shepherd when he had called for Idris, but in the self same whistle of his master.

On the subject of his master, this was their first walk out since his return. They had skirted round the back of the Crescent and crossed the steep slope of Lansdown Road, so it could have been an exceptional expedition, perhaps a left turn and up the hill to see the blonde woman in the big house, or even further, to the very top, with its tearing winds and sporting opportunities in the rabbit warrens. But they had not climbed the hill. They had crossed it, dodged the carriages on the London road and taken the dark steps to Walcot Street, a closed passage between dank and blackened stone walls where there was always a riot of smells, markers of threats and warnings. He kept his wits about him as he trotted behind Nathaniel. He knew where they were going, and he was ready.

When they arrived at the small Georgian terrace which housed the Spence family, Martha settled Nathaniel into the best armchair in the front parlour, Caradoc sat at his feet whilst his master waded through the essential tea drinking, cake eating and exchange of social niceties; the health of the Spence and the Parry families, the thanks for the cake, the wonders of the Parry trip to Wales and the happiness of the new bride, before getting down to business.

Martha still felt uncomfortably ashamed of her decision to visit Captain Peterson. "I felt I had no choice, Mr Parry," she said bluntly. "Ben's death was suspicious to me but no one else seemed to see it. I was that relieved when the Captain said he would ask you to help!" Her eyes glinted with determination. "He was no drunkard, though he liked a drink and if someone did away with him I want them to pay for it."

Nathaniel listened to the story again, jotting down the facts in his pocket book.

130

"So the man he was to meet was definitely a stranger staying in Bath. I have some ideas Mrs Spence and I intend to check the hotel registers, but first I need to go to the Saracen's Head to speak with the barman. You are sure of the date? The 30th January?"

"It is not something I would lightly forget," said Martha tartly.

Nathaniel rose to leave. "Indeed not, forgive me. I will get on then, Mrs Spence, thank you for your hospitality." He suddenly bethought himself of the Bristol connection. "Tell me, is Matthew still working on the Bristol barge?"

"That he is, Mr Parry," said Martha gratefully. "Having him at home has changed our lives. Mary works less now and she can see to the Johnty, who is a young rip I might add. And we have another tenant in your old rooms. He's a friend of Matthew's employer, a Mr O'Malley." She folded her arms defensively. "He is Irish Mr Parry, but not of the Avon Street stamp."

"I would never have imagined he would be if you allowed him under your roof," smiled Nathaniel.

"And I have some more good news, sir," said Martha, suddenly and oddly coy. "As well as Mr O'Malley I have the prospects of more lodgers with regular incomes. Other friends of Mr O'Dowd. So what with the prospects of more business, and with Matthew here now regular, I am going to move us all to a bigger house." She rushed on, "It seems everything has come together, just as one of my investments paid out, I've had enquiries for this place. So we're off. Not far though. Just across the way to Chatham Row."

"Congratulations, Mrs Spence," said Nathaniel. "And good luck. I am pleased you won't be leaving the city. It has been a pleasure to see you as always. Perhaps I could have a word with Mr Spence before I leave?"

Martha looked doubtful but led the way into the kitchen where Old Tom was seated in a chair by the fire, coddled in his blanket and slowly peeling turnips for the stew. Nathaniel took a chair and placed it within Tom's uncertain range of vision.

"Hello, Mr Spence," he said, cutting to the chase before Tom began a meandering tale. "I have come to see if we can find out more about the death of Benjamin Prestwick."

Tom's glazed eyes roamed uncertainly over the figure beside him, a powerfully built young man, with a familiar voice, and smell, he seemed to have brought a breath of fresh air in with him. "Oiy know ye, Mr Parry. Welcome. Oiy see ye're faring well. Now 'ere it is, Ben Prestwick was a fool, led our Philip into all sorts of scrapes as a lad. And 'ee squandered 'is treasure ye know." A claw-like hand dropped the knife and shot out to grip Nathaniel's arm. "Lost 'is gold and came 'ere to get a sniff of some of ours!"

"Napoley's gold! Napoley's gold!" squawked the parrot.

"Quiet Jimmy Congo, ye pert pest!" shouted Tom, but fondly and with a toothless smile. It crossed Nathaniel's mind that the bird might know more than Old Tom but forced himself to focus on the tale.

"Martha's a canny damsel, Mr Parry," he said confidentially. "Always was. Invested 'er winnin's from that partic'lar little adventure and saved enough to buy this dwellin', and now it's to be a flit to a grander one. Oiy 'eard 'er a-tellin' you the tale! Well, where was Oiy?" He recovered his knife and tapped it on the edge of the turnip basin to help him re-orientate his memory. It seemed to do the trick. He let out a wheezy cackle and pressed on. "Now, Ben met with 'is old Captain one night and 'ee reckoned 'ee was bound to be in clover ever after. Captain must 'ave taken a lion's share I'm thinkin' and Ben knew somethin' to encourage another sharin' out."

"I know that, Mr Spence," said Nathaniel as he rose to leave. "And I will make it my business to discover more. Good day to you, sir."

He made his way to the hall, followed by Caradoc, and as they were bidding farewell to Martha on the front step, Jimmy Congo delivered his final insult. The bird let out a torrent of barks, yaps and growls behind them, driving Caradoc to fury. He shot back to the kitchen and launched himself at the perch which over-toppled onto the back of Tom's chair and deposited Jimmy Congo, in a flurry of beating wings and ear-splitting caws onto the old man's back. It was lucky for them all that within minutes Matthew returned from a shift on the barge, calmed the bird and re-settled him on his perch. It gave Nathaniel space to pounce on Caradoc and haul him out as Martha ministered to Old Tom, shushing him in vain to stem the stream of raucous and fluent cursing he had set up as an accompaniment to the parrot, who had retrieved enough breath to damn everybody to hell. Matthew left them to it and caught up with Nathaniel at the gate.

"I don't know there's much to the story of Ben Prestwick's death, Mr Parry," he said doubtfully. "Mother is set on it, I know, and it's good of you to see about it."

"I'll do what I can," said Nathaniel, watching the man closely. He knew Matthew's job at the quay suited him and it was better for the family to have him home from the sea, especially for Matthew's gentle wife, Mary. But he knew that Matthew kept unsavoury company. The owner of the barge was one Declan O'Dowd. The man was previously employed by Joshua Shadwell, who not only owned a collection of brothels, but was also responsible for the attempted sale of Frances, amongst others, and was a Bath contact of Edwin Ravenswood's, this last being the one reason that Shadwell was still at liberty. That one of O'Dowd's friends was a tenant at the Spence's was not good news, and that others were set to follow was worse. Martha would be reliant on their money to help her with the new house and the damage was already done if Matthew was pouring cold water on his mother's fears at O'Dowd's bidding.

Uneasy about the news from the Spence family, Nathaniel made a mental inventory of the current state of affairs as he turned left up Walcot Street and walked towards the London road. On the plus side, always a good one to start with, Matthew Spence seemed a sound man and might even be useful through his connections with Declan O'Dowd; he had a good lead and a plan, of sorts; no news about Cornelius Lee was probably good news, he could very well be on Kizhe's tail by now and homing in; Tobias had been training in his absence as instructed, and was keen to play a bigger role in his service and Em, he smiled broadly as he walked, Em! His personal life had never been better. On the minus side, Matthew Spence could turn out to be a viper, Ravenswood was untouchable and profiting, presumably still with Drake in his pocket; Cornelius had disappeared and he had no proof that he had recovered from his ordeal on the *Leonora*; and Kizhe was presumably still on the loose menacing the seven seas. Optimistic by nature, he decided that the pluses had it, as the minus points only concerned work, whereas the plus points included work and his personal life, which is what really mattered. But then he thought again of Cornelius Lee, and there was nothing he could do for him but wait.

Squaring his shoulders against the rising wind, he held on to his hat and pushed on along the Paragon towards the York House. The manager was in the hall after greeting a coach full of important visitors from London and welcomed Nathaniel warmly, recognising him from his wedding celebrations, which he was eager to point out, had been his very great pleasure to provide for such a distinguished family and their highly esteemed connections. Such was the esteem, that there was no problem consulting the hotel register at leisure, ostensibly checking for the whereabouts of friends. Nathaniel turned the pages back to his wedding day, and there was Sir Giles Mortimer-Buckley, along with Drake and his wife, in two of the most expensive rooms. And there, the following week was Buckley again, taking his leave on Wednesday the 30th January. Nathaniel and Caradoc made their way to the stables and after some well paid conversations located the footman who had taken the message to the Saracen's Head on the night in question. He remembered the incident well, especially as he had heard that the old man died that very night. And much more interestingly, the resident had not given the note to him personally, but sent a stranger; a man from Bristol had handed it to him, and paid him handsomely to look lively.

The walk down Broad Street to the Saracen's Head was a short but also a thirsty one. Nathaniel settled himself at the bar with beer for himself and Caradoc and bided his time until the barman was ready to talk. His luck was in. Not only did the barman remember the night because of the excitement of the murder, but also as he had trotted out the details to the watch, the coroner and by the sound of it, also in response to the earnest questioning of one Tobias Caudle.

"I do recollect the man who died, as I have said a few times before," he said, pausing mid-way through polishing a glass. "Poor old devil, burned all down the side," he rubbed his own cheek in sympathy. "Waterloo veteran he was. He'd been here pretty regular over the previous weeks, since he moved into digs up Walcot. Sometimes he was with Matthew Spence and a blonde lad, and I've told him what I remember already," he sighed theatrically and then resumed. "Anyway, on that night the man in question was moping, as he had notice from the York that whoever he was waiting for wasn't coming. Then a stranger from Bristol way talked to him and bought him drinks. Like I told the others," another sigh. "They yarned about Spain then the stranger drank up and went. Mr Prestwick was left on his own, then he drank up and went, and it was the last we saw of him. The last anybody saw of him!" finished the barman, triumphantly.

"What about the others here that night?" probed Nathaniel. "Which local men did you recognise?"

Usual crowd," he said, "but a bit sparse, for it was a cold night. There was one pair we don't see much of, but they're locals, Jabez and Billy. They work for Joshua Shadwell."

It was all Nathaniel needed to know. He slid a sovereign to the barman and leaned over confidentially. "It has been suggested that Ben Prestwick was murdered. If you hear anything else at all let me know. There is more where this came from."

The barman shed his boredom on the instant, dropping it like an ill-fitting coat. "Yes, sir," he said, almost at attention. "Right you are, sir."

**Three o'clock in the afternoon: 14th March, 1833.**
**The Peterson Residence, Marlborough Buildings, Bath.**

Emma had arrived in plenty of time to meet her mother, but Lydia Peterson was far from ready. An afternoon visit to Tilly Vere's home in Lansdown Crescent was an occasion, but when the party included Mrs Vere's mother, Dr Parry's wife and also the fashionable and elusive Mrs Ravenswood, it was an event which required meticulous preparation. As hats were still being chosen and discarded, Emma had made her way to the schoolroom on the top floor and whiled away half an hour with Madame Junot who was supervising the twins as they laboured through a French grammar test. Emma's facility for French had made her a favourite with Madame. Smarter than her clodhopping elder sister and the young, giggling twins, Madame had singled her out for special attention and still fed her with reading to stoke the fire. Emma left the schoolroom with a slim volume under her arm and went to find her father. Captain Oliver Peterson proved to be in his study in order to avoid the possibility of being involved in the selection process for his wife's outfit, but he was pleased to welcome Emma.

"Come in, come in! Sit down. How beautiful you look, my dear!"

"Thank you, Papa," said Emma, brushing his ruddy cheek with a kiss and moving a chair close to his at the desk.

"What have you there?" he asked, reaching for the book, his eyes crinkled with good humour.

"Madame Junot has had it sent from Paris. See," she said holding it up for inspection. "It is called *Indiana* and though it says it is by George Sand it is written by a woman called Aurore Dupin, and Madame says it sheds much light on the human condition, in particular the female one." Emma leaned forward, excitedly. "Madame Dupin has written for *Le Figaro* in Paris and has published other books with a gentleman, Monsieur Sandeau, and she uses part of his name for her pseudonym. I'm not sure about the George part, Madame had nothing to say on it. Anyway, I can't wait to start it. Would you like to read it after me, Papa?"

"Perhaps," said Oliver, doubtfully, as vague memories surfaced of the scandalous career of the individual known as George Sand. Adultery came to mind, and a life occupied with writing whilst racketing around Paris in company with highly suspect intellectuals and smoking cigars whilst dressed as a man. He decided not to disturb any more vague memories; he had enough to be going on with. It had occurred to him before that Madame Junot was less conventional than her appearance suggested. He'd always thought her a dashed handsome woman. Not that he had ever felt inclined to get to know her better, he reassured himself. But she was his daughters' governess. There was a duty of care.

Madame Junot had come to the Peterson household, a very young, impecunious and grateful widow, towards the end of the wars with France, and she came by a most unlikely route: sponsored by her famous namesake and distant relative, General Jean Junot, Governor General of Portugal and Duke d'Abrantès. In the summer of 1808, after the British under Wellington had beaten the daylights out of the French at

Vimeiro, the Duke had had the unenviable task of surrendering Portugal *in toto* to the British forces. Thanks to the bungling deal signed at his Palace of Queluz Sintra, he had been conveyed, bag, baggage and army intact, to the safety of his own shores by the British fleet. Captain Peterson had sailed with the flagship and had found himself in company with the Duke during the strange limbo period before the evacuation. Addresses had been exchanged, goodwill had been extended. He had thought little about it until after the war, when he was prevailed upon at short notice to take on Junot's distant relative, who apparently, whilst being entirely suitable as a governess, was no longer welcome or happy at home in France. Some family squabble had come to a head and the family was unwilling to support her. Junot had volunteered to place her far away where she could no longer drain family coffers or irritate her nearest and dearest. Shortly after this, Junot, erratic and volatile since sustaining a head wound, appeared to have committed suicide, leaving his estranged wife widowed and thrown back on her own devices in Paris, deaf to all enquiries as to the likelihood of a distant relative being returned to France. He resolved to sound out Madame Junot's taste a little more searchingly, but for now it was enough to change the subject.

"I gather that Nathaniel's visit to London went well, my dear?"

"Moderately well I think, Papa. But not exceedingly well if you know what I mean. He has gone to Mrs Spence's to see what he can do for her. Has anything else come up about her poor tenant's death?"

Oliver could well guess that any meeting which included John Drake was unlikely to have been a resounding success. He had recognised the streak of self-seeking in the man on first sight and from fifty paces. Something was not right in the cut of the jib. But he would do all he could, he still had a little influence, a little weight, which might steady the ship for his son-in-law. He smiled at his favourite daughter.

"I rather think that nothing at all will come up unless Nathaniel digs it out, my dear."

Eventually her mother was prevailed upon to leave. Their *Berlin* had been brought round from the livery stables and after only two false starts, with the footman being sent back for the forgotten reticule, then the forgotten card case, she climbed in and the door was slammed shut for the trip up the hill and their invitation to tea with Mrs Tilly Vere. It was to the footman's credit that he managed to stand to attention on the pavement and smile, even as he cursed his employer to hell and back. The minute the *Berlin* turned the corner and passed out of view he bolted for the kitchen, just in time to catch the last wisps of steam rising from his own brew of tea and slap away the thieving paw of the boot boy as he reached for the very last jam tart.

Daintier fare was on offer in the gilded drawing room of Tilly's Lansdown mansion, and a great deal of it. Her ambitious mother, the corpulent Mrs Danby, had overseen the preparation of the menu and had proceeded to outstrip all comers in the speed with which she devoured the offerings as they were served. This was useful in so far as that it occupied her fairly comprehensively and prevented her from dominating the afternoon, as she had dominated most conversations since her arrival. Tilly was looking forward to her mother's return to the family home in Beckington, as her extended visit had become trying in the extreme. She had been supposed to go the previous day, but to Tilly's horror had insisted on staying for the tea party.

It was now well over a year since Tilly's husband had disappeared and her dalliance with the wealthy Howard Dill was going splendidly. Thus far she had managed to fend off her mother's visits and enquiries as to her plans, as she had a bevy of sisters who had all occupied her mother with their children and their various ploys, but nemesis was nigh. Her mother had taken to bewailing the fate of, "Poor, poor Tilly, left high and dry by the tragic disappearance of her dear husband", to all who would listen. Tilly objected to the infliction of martyr status and, free from her elderly, philandering and criminal husband, was happier than she had been for years. To lighten the afternoon Tilly contrived to saddle Mrs Peterson and the senior Mrs Parry with her mother. They were more of an age and once her mother was unleashed on the delights of Beckington and the magnificence of Howard Dill's holdings throughout rural Somerset, Tilly could focus more agreeably on Amanda Ravenswood and Mrs Parry junior who had chanced on the subject of Coco's impending trip to France.

"I remember you said you had been to Paris, Mrs Ravenswood," said Emma, who noticed that the chilly Amanda seemed more strained and preoccupied than before.

"Yes," she said snappily. "And we spent our honeymoon there. I would like to go again. Mr Ravenswood is much occupied in London at present and opportunities for travel are rather limited."

Amanda glared moodily at the assembled covey of women. Why on earth had she consented to come? As much as she now loathed Lottie Drake for poaching her husband, this provincial little crowd and their mealy-mouthed conversation was desperately dull. She tapped her foot angrily, and looked at the clock on the mantle shelf. Could she go in half an hour? Yes. But what would she do at home? She felt a rush of fury at the straits he had forced her into. She had never felt so rudderless and alone. And when Edwin came home she was often afraid. With a sinking heart she acknowledged that she was there because she needed some friends. She needed to be away from the oppressive grandeur of Arno's Tower and to be with some people who wished her no harm.

"Do you read French, Mrs Ravenswood?" persisted Emma. "I have been trying to improve my grasp of it. Today I collected a novel from home. Our governess, Madame Junot, recommended I read the work of George Sand. Do you know her? She is very popular in Paris."

"Junot you say," said Amanda, taking the chance to lift her spirits by showing off her contacts. "When we were in Paris we attended the *salon* of the Duchesse d'Abrantès, who is Madame Junot, widow of Napoleon's general."

"Well, what a coincidence," said Emma. "Our governess is a distant relative of that same Junot family who my father befriended during the war!"

Little by little, Amanda Ravenswood softened. Remembering the pity she had felt for her after the dinner, Emma worked hard and let Amanda shine. Tilly helped doing what she did best, which involved sitting close, stroking her shoulder periodically, offering her delicacies and trailing mounds of corkscrew curls over Amanda's arm, like an over-friendly dog. They were pretty, they were kind, and in her disordered and miserable state, Amanda realised that they gave her strength. It was as if she had withdrawn to a cave to lick her wounds. She could do without Lottie Drake, and maybe she could do without Edwin as well. She listened with half an ear to Tilly's contribution to the conversation about France, an excited and rambling description of the latest Parisian designs for summer, brought round only yesterday by her dressmaker. And as Emma tried more energetically to interest her in literature and tried out a few political ideas, Amanda smiled, parting her red lips and displaying her little pointed teeth.

### The Parry Residence, Saint James's Square, Bath.

Nathaniel had returned home with Caradoc whilst Emma was still out visiting. He had promoted Tobias from boot cleaning duties, told him to cast off his apron, collect his walking cane, hat and muffler and be at the garden gate directly. For his part, he ran upstairs for his additional clothes and his swordstick, got half way down and ran back again for one of his pistols, which he shoved in his belt, hurriedly checking his appearance in the mirror. He buttoned his frock coat over the pistol handle, took the stairs again, two at a time, and left through the back door, whistling up Caradoc as he did so. Tobias was waiting, and the three of them headed through the park to the Bristol road dropping down from the highway to the path which ran along the side of the river towards the quays.

"Where are we going, Mr Parry?" asked Tobias, slashing his cane at the bushes by the path as he went.

"Joshua Shadwell's place, Green Park," said Nathaniel. "I know his boys, Jabez and Billy, were in the Saracen's Head the night Ben died and I am going to try a little leverage. It is daytime Tobias, you are in the capacity of a footman and there should be no trouble, but be on your guard. I have had a run in with the two of them in the past and they might just remember me. Pull your hat low and wrap your muffler round your face."

"You can trust me not to let you down, sir!" said Tobias fervently, winding his scarf up to his nose and ramming his hat down hard.

"I do," said Nathaniel. "Remember, your training is for a purpose. You will not be the boot boy for ever." He looked Tobias over as they walked. The boy was shaping up, still slender, but developing strength, and growing tall. "I know you are friendly with Frances," he added, watching the boy colour up, shrug and avoid his eye. "I don't need to know what she has told you about her early life but it could well have included mention of the man we will see today. Remember, we had an agreement between us when I brought her and the others from Bristol, to leave some things unsaid. But now you and she are friends and it is natural that she will talk in confidence to you."

"I don't mind you knowing, sir," said Tobias earnestly. "I know Fran and Abi, the girl she came with, were tricked into going to Bristol by this man in Green Park. I know Abi worked for him, and Fran was made to go by her mother. And I know the name of the man who owned the ship."

"Do you now," said Nathaniel. "Well keep all those cards tight to your chest, along with our own names. We'll make this an anonymous call if we can."

They walked along the path in company with a few other pedestrians and horsemen. The traffic on the river was leisurely, the odd narrow boat hauled by a horse, one small steam barge chugging in from Bristol. As they tramped along Nathaniel became aware that Tobias was excited, but also increasingly on edge.

"Is something wrong, Tobias?" asked Nathaniel, for the boy had stopped in his tracks as the Abbey bells rang six.

"No, nothing," he lied, regretted it, and explained. "It's just that I was listening for the time. I promised to see Robert Turner in the George tonight sir. It's a meeting to read the papers."

"What time?"

139

"Eight o'clock."

"Shouldn't be a problem," said Nathaniel, intrigued. "I'm pleased to see you are taking the state of the nation seriously."

"Oh that I am, sir," said Tobias in a rush of enthusiasm, and suddenly he seemed to be inhabited by a different creature; he frowned with the effort and spoke the words of Robert Turner and the men of the George. "The working men have been abandoned by the middle classes. They got their votes in '32 with the help of millions of us ordinary folk. We were the ones who made the lords give in. But now, instead of spreading the vote to decent working men, even Earl Grey says: "Stay, enough!" And Lord John Russell who was a champion for reform now says what was done in '32 was final. The last word! It can't be right sir."

"So what now, Tobias?" asked Nathaniel, suppressing a smile.

"Mr Hetherington and Mr Owen's papers say we must build up the unions into mighty forces, but they must be peaceful, show the lords that we have power and we can use it well. They say there's laws ready to go through to stop slavery and to stop the owners working children too long. Change is still happening after '32!"

"I'm sure it is, Tobias, but do not expect too much from the law. There will always be bad men finding new ways to make mischief. Speaking of which, keep your wits about you, here's Green Park."

They turned off the river path and passed through a gate in the iron railings to a well-paved road, smooth greensward and elegant row of Georgian houses. As they had come within sight of the dens of Avon Street, the stench of the river had grown worse, but Green Park felt a world away from those once fashionable terraces, which now housed cheap lodgings, brothels and pubs, their crumbling facades masking stinking alleys, courts and pig sties. Green Park provided an oasis of calm down-river from that notorious slum, but all was not as it seemed. They walked the length of the terrace and passed the front of Shadwell's brothel, which nestled shamelessly amongst the respectable homes, then cut around the corner to the mews behind.

"Shadwell's office is in the stables," said Nathaniel as they approached the rear entrance. "Look, there's a light burning in the upper room."

In the falling dark, Joshua Shadwell could be seen by the window illuminated by his reading lamp, spectacles on his nose, peering at a folded copy of the *Bath Chronicle.* Nathaniel tried the gate, which did not budge. He checked swiftly, up and down, to ensure that the mews was free from watchers, then leapt at the wall, grabbed the coping stone and pulled himself up to snatch a view over it. "It's bolted halfway down Tobias, but the garden's empty. Shin over and open it."

He looked down at the terrier, who was busy nosing round a pile of wood.

"On guard, Caradoc," he whispered. The dog cocked one ear and continued in his work whilst Tobias put his foot in Nathaniel's hands and was hoisted over the wall. He landed silently and slid back the iron bolt. Within a minute they were both in the garden and padding over to the stable block. Nathaniel turned the handle and pushed open the door to reveal a flight of steps rising to Shadwell's office above, and also, in the corner of the entrance room, a small deal table, at which sat two men, frozen in the act of playing a hand of cards.

"What in damnation are ye a-doin' of 'ere?" demanded one, a bull-necked, swarthy individual, rising to his feet, whilst the other flung down his cards and drew a knife from his belt.

"I have come to see Mr Shadwell," said Nathaniel smoothly, as Tobias raised his stick and clenched it firmly in both hands. "He will be very interested to hear what I have to say."

"He said nought about a visitor," said the second man, who on closer inspection resembled a weasel who had done too many rounds with a fox. He made a sudden move towards them, brandishing the knife so it flashed in the light.

It was exactly the kind of split-second when training takes over. Without consciously deciding to do so, Tobias made a lightning short-circle swing with his stick, smashing it down hard on the knife arm. The weapon dropped, bouncing away on the flagged floor as the weasel-faced attacker yelped in pain and cowered on his knees, nursing his injured arm. Tobias raised his stick for a second blow, but held it high to one side of his head: "Stay still!" he commanded.

Simultaneously, Nathaniel had drawn his swordstick blade in a scorching forward thrust, stopping the tip two inches from bull-neck's throat.

"Not one move more," he hissed.

And into the shocked silence which followed broke the unmistakeable and menacing growl of an angry dog from behind the wall.

"I'm not alone, this time," said Nathaniel.

Jabez watched the eyes above the muffler warm in amusement. It was a treat for Nathaniel to see the progression in the shifty face before him. The righteous rage of the bodyguard was first baffled by incomprehension at the speed of the moves, and then swamped by a slowly dawning and horrid realisation.

"No, it cannot be," said Jabez, his eyes wild, fear clutching the pit of his guts, which had never fully recovered after his first brush with the man who now threatened to stick him with a sword. "You're Jack Drake, the same bastard who stabbed me in the vitals and smashed up old Billy 'ere, the bastard with the eyeglasses and the limp!"

141

"The very same," said Nathaniel, "but in better health. Now listen, I'm going up to see your master. I want some facts and it has to do with the death of an old man here in the city early this year. I want you two as well, so, Billy, get yourself off the floor. Both of you go ahead of me."

Motioning to Tobias to wait, Nathaniel sheathed the sword and drew his pistol to encourage Jabez and the snivelling Billy to climb the stairs.

Joshua Shadwell expected visitors. He had heard the footsteps on the garden path and the voices, low and guttural from his men, then more cultivated tones. He had heard the bedlam break out, blows, cries, growls, and then be stilled, to be followed by the expected tap on his door. Disappointingly, his men shuffled in first, Billy cradling his right arm, Jabez whole, but with a snarling fear etched on his face. Behind them came a stranger with a face partly muffled against the cold, prodding Jabez into the room at pistol point. Shadwell eyed the tall man uneasily. He was handy-looking, and apart from the pistol, had a stick in his other hand that was probably a blade. He had bright blue eyes emitting a steady glare, and looked ready for business.

Shadwell was usually confident in a situation like this, knowing his own pistols to be lying in wait in his desk drawer, primed and ready, and with Billy and Jabez, making a healthy three against one. But somehow the odds had become hopelessly skewed.

"You seem to have convinced my men that you mean no harm, so what business do you want with me?"

Nathaniel looked hard at the well-built figure before him, immaculate in a steel-grey coat, silk waistcoat and garnet pin in the gleaming white stock. His clothes did not proclaim his loathsome trade, a man who would deal in women, would sell children and probably even his own grandmother for profit, but this man would. The clothes spoke of a man of taste and discernment but his eyes betrayed him. Cruel and calculating, they raked over Nathaniel, assessing his threat and the scale of reprisals he might deserve. Nathaniel glanced quickly at Shadwell's hands: they were bunched into fists so he moved quickly onto the offensive.

"As I told your men here, I want to know more about the death of a man called Benjamin Prestwick. He died here in Bath on the 30th January this year, and he wasn't just any old soldier. He had information that some very powerful friends of mine need."

As Shadwell opened his mouth to discharge a stream of lies and abuse, Nathaniel raised his hand to silence him. "Save it. First understand that I know a great deal about you. The only reason that you and your men were not arrested for the villainy

142

on the *Mathilda* and the *Blue Dragon* was your link with their owner. The link stands. That man has friends in high places at present and his business will continue unmolested. I am not after you or your business."

"I've killed nobody," said Shadwell, struggling to control his voice as his stomach knotted in horror.

"I'm pretty sure you haven't," said Nathaniel. "But I know that these men, Billy and Jabez here, were in the Saracen's Head on the night in question. It was the last place Prestwick was seen. They know I haven't the patience to hear a pack of lies, so all of you, listen carefully. A stranger was there that night with Prestwick, a Bristol stranger, and I need to know his name."

Shadwell shot his visitor a look of pure malice and considered his position. He could not give Trevellis's name. Any linkage of the murder to Ravenswood was more than his life was worth. And closer to home, he had never told Rosie he had let Trevellis use the boys for the caper and the royalty payment had gone straight into his pocket. Who could blame him? It had never been the same since his injury at the hands of Abigail, the murderous drab! Rosie had run the business for months on her own whilst he recovered, and the bloody woman had a taste for power. The thought of her outrage made his scarred leg ache. Damn Ravenswood! He was safely away in Bristol, or London, or wherever he was spending his time these days, insulated from the sharp end of business. His wife would never dare challenge him. How would he manage if he had to share a bed with Rosie! But even as he let the comparison take shape in his mind, he had to acknowledge that Amanda Ravenswood obeyed her husband not so much for love but for the sake of her health. He had never knocked Rosie about, with her guaranteeing his living and running the girls it had never seemed worth it, and he could not let her even suspect he had lent the boys to Trevellis. Before he had to wrestle further with this particular difficulty, it was taken out of his gift.

"Cove never gave no proper name," blurted out Billy. "We were in the Saracen's that night, weren't us, Jabez? And we saw an old soldier talkin' to a man. We did talk to 'im ourselves now I recall. Man was called Eli. That's it," he finished defiantly, attempted to fix Nathaniel with a stare but gave it up and looked down at his boots instead.

That was all it needed to be, for the time being. Nathaniel knew that one of Ravenswood's most trusted henchmen was Eli Trevellis, Captain of the *Blue Dragon*, and that he could expect nothing further.

"Well, thank you for your help, gentlemen," said Nathaniel, backing out of the door and disappearing into the dark of the stairwell.

"Don't cross me again," growled Jabez, staying prudently out of reach as he shouted from the top of the flight.

Nathaniel emerged from the coach house just in time to see Tobias bid goodnight to a buxom young woman with a cloud of wild dark hair and her body wrapped in a shawl, who was making her way up the path to the house. They wasted no time in quitting the mews, whistling up Caradoc and heading straight up the hill to Queen Square then sharp left to the Circus, to blend in with the more salubrious crowds making their way to the Assembly Rooms. As Nathaniel turned towards Brock Street, Tobias stopped short.

"I'll go off to the George then, sir."

"Right then. And well done tonight, Tobias. We made progress and you played a good part."

"Thank you, sir!" said Tobias; still basking in the glow of his success. "Oh, I almost forgot. That woman in Shadwell's garden. You remember. She spoke to me when she was going back to the house from the privy. She's going to call on you at home on Wednesday morning next week."

"What for? And how the devil did she know who I was?" He stopped short, surprised. "So we managed to fox Shadwell and his clowns but not the whore! And Tobias didn't you mention I hadn't asked for any professional services? It wasn't that kind of business call."

"She knows that, sir. It was Clari, Clarissa Marchant" said Tobias, "she's the most popular of Shadwell's girls. Everybody knows of her round the quays. Anyway, she said she had listened to the row we had with Shadwell's men and she's got something to tell. Something you said must have given you away. She knew of you right enough."

Nathaniel watched the slight figure scud over the road and head towards Lansdown. How the devil had she known? He shrugged his shoulders. As long as he could reconcile his wife and housekeeper to the arrival of one of Bath's most notorious prostitutes on the doorstep, this could be very good news indeed. Putting that thought aside, he looked about him for Caradoc, convinced the terrier to abandon the innards of a dead bird, and set off for home.

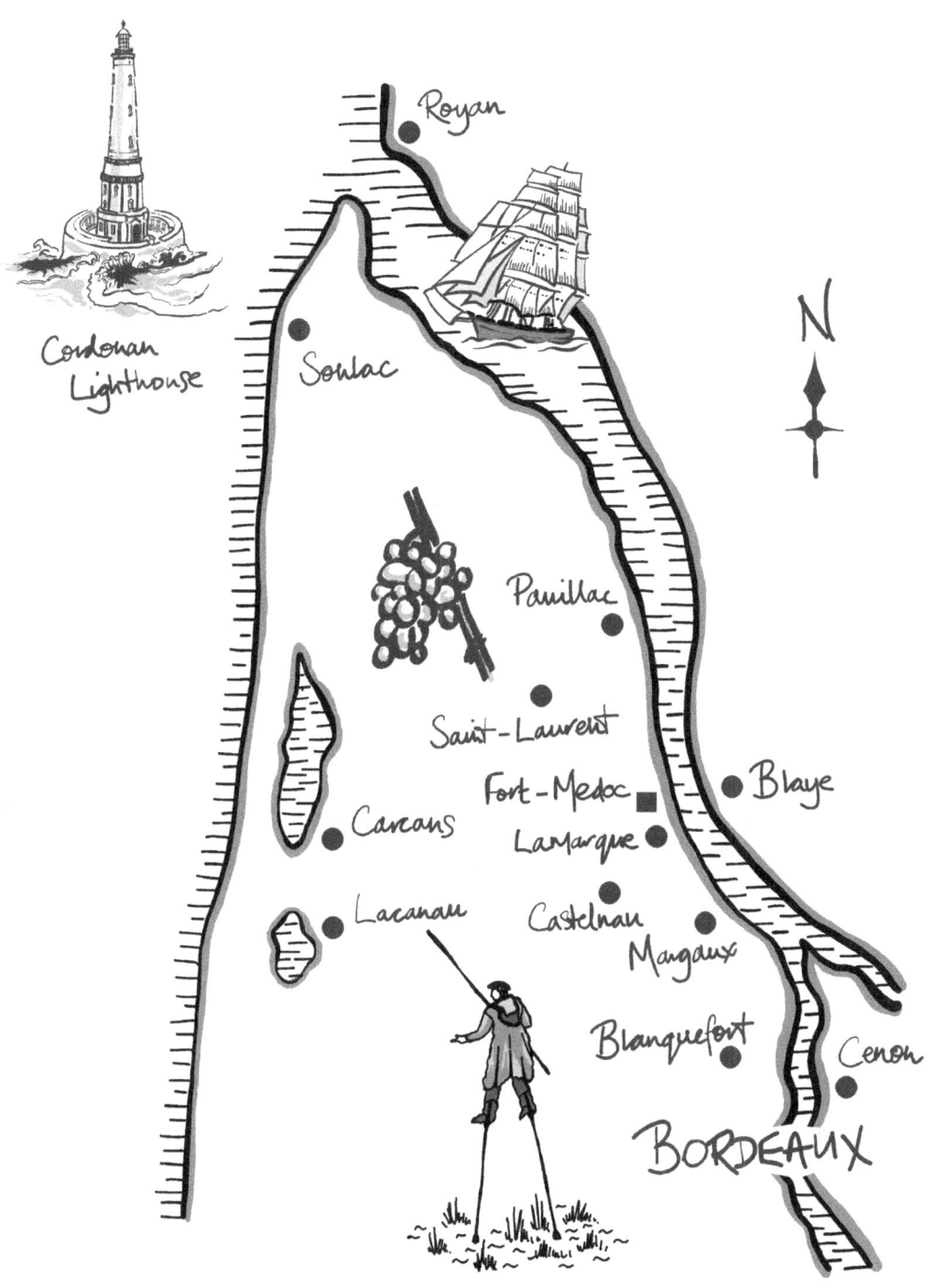

The Medoc: South-West France

# Chapter 6

**Dawn: 19th March, 1833.**
**Off the west coast of France, approaching the Gironde Estuary.**

"Can you make it out? It flashes then disappears. There it goes!" exclaimed Dairmuid triumphantly, gripping Coco even tighter and leaning further out over the rail of the clipper. His finger stabbed excitedly towards the faint twinkle which intermittently pierced the murk of first light. "It is herself sure enough! *Le Versailles de la Mer! Le Phare de Cordouan*! We're getting close to landfall in *la belle France!* What a beauty. Look at her would you now! The finest lighthouse in the world so she is, complete with all the trimmings. She's got royal chambers, and a chapel, in case himself comes a-visitin'. Damn fine!" He grinned, vastly enjoying the opportunity to show off his local knowledge, though truth to tell he could barely remember his last visit. He was sure he knew more than she did, and that was enough.

As bidden, Coco looked.

It was her first sighting of the lighthouse, but it seemed very familiar as she had listened many times to Émile's descriptions of it and the extravagant trips he had taken as a youth, up the estuary and south to Spain. She smiled tolerantly at

Dairmuid, allowing him his moment. He took her arm and pulled her closer. Their sails were full and the ship was skimming over the last choppy stretch of the Bay of Biscay before they entered the placid, muddy shallows of the Gironde. Once there they would hook up with a pilot to steer them through the sand banks to the safe haven of Pauillac. She inspected the lighthouse as it neared. The ghostly tower emerging from the mist was, as billed, a beauty. The lower floors rose in pillared tiers like a palace, the slender tower was studded with stone windows, each tricked out with a jutting pediment, and the whole was crowned by a revolving light, searching and brilliant as the pole star.

She had never made the sea journey before, though she had once visited her brother Jules by road after he had moved into the ruined *château* north of Saint Laurent. It had been a lengthy, uncomfortable haul from Paris; over a fortnight cooped up in a succession of stinking, oily carriages, every one of the stages packed and flea ridden, with only a makeshift bivouac for all of them at the end of it, hugger-mugger by the fire in the *château's* one habitable room. Now she was scudding over the water in one of the fastest sailing ships ever built with the graceful pinnacle of the lighthouse shining out a welcome. Its honey-coloured limestone was clear now in the daybreak: light and fair, like Bath stone, a good omen.

It was four days since they had left Bristol on the steam packet for Dublin where, courtesy of his old friends from Tipperary, Dairmuid had arranged their onward passage to France. This had turned out to be in conveniently adjoining cabins on a smart new clipper bound for the Medoc. It was only when they were boarding that she realised just how useful Dairmuid's connections were, for his friends were the Bartons, who not only owned the vessel but were also one half of the greatest wine growing and shipping partnership in Bordeaux: Barton & Guestier. She smiled to herself at the thought of Jules, mighty impressed, rolling his eyes, giving his long, slow whistle.

As they were on a working ship, Coco and Dairmuid were spared the annoyance of other passengers, with their attendant stench of vomit and the caterwauling of their seasick infants, both prime factors in the notorious discomfort of sea travel. The clipper was carrying an inert cargo of Irish wool, to be traded for claret and cognac, the weather had been tolerable, and they were both good sailors. Fine, cold days had allowed them to spend much of their time on deck and the nights had been whiled away pleasantly enough in the cabin, as Dairmuid was a familiar and congenial lover. Coco had been pleased when he had offered to arrange her trip to visit Jules, and even more so when he offered to finance it. Travel was much easier with an escort, and though she could have paid, she was pleased not to have had to. Also, she was glad he still needed her, as he was less keen on her company than he had been. His position as an MP, though his seat was in Ireland and far away from Bath, had made him more aware of his public image. He had ambition and was less disposed for sport, but he needed a partner for this trip and more particularly, a French speaker. His French was patchy at best, though he made the most of what he had. She smiled at him.

"As you say, the lighthouse is fine, *mon cher*. And this is altogether a wonderful trip. Thank you." She kissed him lightly, her gold-flecked lambent eyes burning directly into his: a warm fire in the cold morning.

"Oh, Coco," he breathed, wrapping his arms around her, reaching inside her cloak and pulling her close for a deeper kiss. "It's going to be a famous stay, so it is."

Invigorated, he pulled back, suddenly business-like, and held her round the waist at arms' length.

"Contacts, contacts, contacts! Make 'em and keep 'em!" he declared. "The party on Saturday week is the t'ing. Your mission is to stun 'em! You know General Palmer. He'll be hosting alone as the missis is sulking in London. He's lost a king's ransom on the vines already and she's pig-sick of it all, but she's no loss, he'll be a grand host and his place in Bordeaux will be worth a view. I'll be staying at the Château Langoa with mi'dear man Hugh Barton, like I told you. Remember now, we'll collect you in his carriage before noon on the day. He is a force to be reckoned with in Bordeaux, and so is his business partner, we'll meet him too and he'll probably have more of his kin in tow. And, Mademoiselle Coco, he's Baron Guestier, by the by!"

Coco raised an eyebrow, amused. "So when will you admit that you're not investing, Dairmuid?"

"Tscha!" Dairmuid waved a lordly hand. "The Bartons and their pals are the main targets. I'm there as a little touch of the blarney mi'darlin' to lighten the mood. I told you I had connections in Tipperary. Well I know young Barton, Hugh's son, Nat, that is. Like brothers we are. And I know the Phelans too from the old country, and Bernard Phelan himself will be there with his missis."

"And Mr Phelan is?"

"Another mighty Irish vineyard owner haling from Tipperary!" said Dairmuid laughing. "I know young Marie, his girl, and her man. I'm well on the inside track."

"Impressively so," she said, looking up at him, her eyes sparkling. "So am I there to make sure you make no promises?"

"Only partly. You're also there to tempt, to tantalise and, note this well, to translate when I need it: verbatim and discreet! I want nothing getting by me on the night. The men's talk after dinner will be in English in honour of the host, but earlier on there'll be French whispers a-plenty." Suddenly serious and more confidential, he continued, "The General is a good man in the Commons, Coco. He's a reformer and he's paved the way for me a few times. This will make sure he does so again. If I can help him keep his French adventure alive it's all to the good, for he's on his uppers at the minute. He's not just running the mansion and vines at Cenon, where we'll visit, he also has a packet of other places and the greatest of them all is just down the coast here," he gestured vaguely into the mist which was clinging to the left bank, "down there somewhere, bordering Château Margeaux. That was his first investment." He winked conspiratorially. "Bought on a whim from a lady on his journey home from the wars. Proper lady's man is the General."

"Had he any knowledge of the trade?"

"Not a jot. He first started losing money with wholesale replanting schemes. He was trying to suit his wine to the taste of old King George, fat jaded slug as he was and addicted to cherry brandy. You can guess what that had done to his palate! The General had been his *aide-de-camp* so the connection was there, and I suppose once he started experimenting he couldn't stop. More land, new vines, new methods, and all directed from London with no sound men here to keep it in check. Disastrous! He'll have to throw his hand in, and Palmer's famous claret will be no more. He needs cash and pretty damned quick."

Coco wrapped her cloak tighter round her neck, feeling for the familiar metal rim of her brooch. In her mind's eye she saw not the flash of the Cordouan light, but dazzling diamonds, emeralds and sapphires set in interlocking golden "Ms". The Wheel of Fortune was turning and Château Palmer was going down. With any luck at all, the house of Montrachet might be on the rise.

## Morning: 20th March, 1833. Chateau Pèlerin, the Medoc, France.

Birdsong woke Coco; though the shutters and the heavy, patterned bed curtains conspired to keep her room as black as pitch. She slipped out of bed, pulled her cloak around her, pushed her feet into her slippers and made for the window. The stone tiled floor made the room cold as a crypt and as she fumbled the casement catch, the chill struck up like a knife into the soles of her feet. Cursing as she wrenched the metal clip free, she folded the windows back to the wall, leaned forward and pushed open the creaking worm-eaten *volets*. No more Queen Square with its mannered terraces: no hackney carriages, sauntering crowds or crossing boys. The *volets* swung out and thudded to rest against the outside walls, letting in a

149

flood of pale golden light. She looked out on regimented lines of grapevines below, striping the fields as far as she could see, rank after rank, low, brown and skeletal, up and over the rise, off to the distant tree line. Shuddering suddenly in the cold, she closed the window and went back to bed, wrapping herself in the eiderdown and pulling her knees up under her chin. She felt victorious; the room was clean but otherwise as she had left it after her first visit when she had staked her claim. A watercolour of a lakeside scene still hung askew on the wall opposite her bed, the iron hooks remained behind the door: a chair, a washstand, a chest of drawers and an *armoire,* all in place. It was to be hers, forever, but she had expected to find it re-arranged by her sister-in-law, the dolorous and matronly Claudette, small and subtle changes made as markers to remind her that she was not the lady of the house. There was just one addition; a small wooden crucifix had been attached to the wall by the bed.

Claudette had not turned out to be a soul mate for Coco. If the *château* had run to a chapel Claudette would have been at Mass daily, and left to her own devices would probably have scuttled into a nunnery, taking the veil before she was twenty and staying there. But her father, M. Delgarde, had ambitions for her, both carnal and dynastic. Jules had figured prominently in M. Delgarde's dreams and was promoted from right hand man to son-in-law on the understanding that he took Claudette's name, coupling Delgarde with Montrachet in perpetuity. Rumours of Jules's activities amongst the local girls and disputed paternity suits had been a recommendation rather than otherwise, and Claudette's delivery of a son had cemented the bargain. Delgarde senior had been a well-fixed Bordeaux wine trader and the gift of the derelict *château* had been the bait to draw Jules into the family. He was expected to revive its fortunes without further help, but the pump needed to be primed. In exchange for permanent tenancy, Coco had promised Jules she would pay for the upkeep of one suite of rooms, including their rickety roof. But secretly, and if funds ever allowed it, she planned to pay for the renovation of the whole wing which contained them. Her rooms were located in an out-riding spur of the building on the side furthest from the farmyard and nearest to the road: the part least useful to Jules and his family. She saw the project as the creation of a sanctuary, a precious one in her haphazard life which was even more rackety than the *château.* The unfortunate circumstances of the Delgarde family had allowed her scheme to take root. The early death of Claudette's mother and the reluctance of M. Delgarde to remarry had limited the family to two. The second daughter, younger but barren, was married to a lawyer who had been energetically contesting his father-in-law's will for the last year. Claudette was deemed to have had more than her share already so the chances of inheriting enough to fund the entire refurbishment of Château Pèlerin were slim. For this reason alone, Claudette tolerated her sister-in-law's presence and financial contributions, which as she rightly guessed, were earned by methods entirely disreputable.

Coco had looked forward to her first sighting of Jules as she had waited in the foyer of the Pauillac hotel. She had had time to count, and it was fully six years since her previous visit. At twenty-three years, Jules had still had something of the young man about him, and his child was a mewling baby boy, clutched tightly to Claudette's bosom. Apparently there was another infant now to join him, and Jules had prospered. Her bags waited ready on the floor at her feet, and she had rehearsed careful plans with Dairmuid, who had been collected hours earlier by his friends' servants and rattled off in their coach to the *château* in Saint-Julien. She had sat uncomfortably on a hard settle, the air heavy with the lingering smell of lunch and sweat, time crawling by, ships docking and leaving, the hotel dogs already settled down to sleep off the afternoon. The sun was low and the room in deep shadow before he had arrived, roaring a welcome, his arms wide, filling the doorway and letting in a great gust of fresh air.

"Coco, *ma petite!*"

Stocky and powerful as a Pyrenean mastiff, bigger than before and becoming grizzled, he had shaken his great head in delight and kissed her soundly, crushing her close and squeezing her face between his calloused hands until she squeaked. Coco had pulled back to get a better look of him, holding his hands tightly in hers and a tide of faded memories had flooded through her, ambushing and embarrassing her: Jules as a boy; their dead brother, young and reckless; her parents' faces; their first home. Tears had pricked her eyes whilst her mouth worked, struggling for control. Wordless, she had occupied herself showing him the bags, allowing him to hurry her out onto the quay, listening, managing to smile, but by the end of the drive she had revived and was herself again, engaging and flirty, touching on nothing serious, preparing the ground work for what had to come.

Later, the meal with Claudette and the two children had been pleasant enough and the servants were clearly competent, taking the edge off Claudette's martyrdom. There had been some levity during the meal and much more after Claudette bustled off with the small fry; the nephew, Marc, named in memory of their late brother Jean-Marc, and the little niece, Simone, who had turned out to be bold. Coco had been pleasantly surprised by the child and *Tante* Colette in her turn, had been favoured by the girl.

"*Maman* has a new brooch!" Simone had cried, safe on Coco's lap and keen to entertain. "She doesn't like jewels but she likes brooches when they are shells. Look! There on the wall with the old one. She has polished it and will wear it to church."

On the wall above the fireplace, at the feet of the crucifix, were hung two scallop shell lapel pins. One Coco had seen before. It had given rise to the re-christening of the mansion as Château Pèlerin. The road by the fields was part of the old pilgrim route through France to Saint James's Spanish shrine at Santiago de Compostella and a battered metal badge, relic of some long forgotten journey, had been dug up by Claudette when they first began to work the vines. She had seen it as a sign.

"Papa was digging out the well and found the second one last week. It is treasure. Silver treasure!"

Claudette had given a rare smile. "It is indeed treasure, Simone. We treasure the pilgrim's badge of honour in our hearts. And it will come to the church with us on Sunday. As will *Tante* Colette I am sure."

"I look forward to it," Coco had replied sweetly, with a modest smile, avoiding even half a glance towards her brother.

After breakfast, which she had alone as the rest of the family had scattered to their daily tasks long before, Coco returned to her room and swapped her dress for a pair of men's trousers and a jerkin, the discarded set of riding clothes she had left mouldering in a bottom drawer. It was necessary to bide her time, make an impression, and not a pretty one, before presenting her scheme to Jules and she had gathered that mid-morning would usually find him in the barn. She crossed the farmyard to the side of the *château*, shooing a belligerent covey of hens before her as she picked her way through the mire and made for the vast out-building bordering the yard on its north side. Lofty as a church but derelict as the house had been, its tiled roof was in the final stages of drunken collapse. The high doors, wide enough to swallow a coach or a haywain, were sagging open, allowing the sounds of muffled thuds and sharp slaps to float out into the yard. As she had hoped, Jules was training, but he was not alone. She slipped in quietly, keeping to the dark walls, treading softly and using the cobbles as stepping-stones. Her brother was practicing kicks and punches with another man, similar in height, but even bigger in build, both well-muscled, stripped to the waist and glistening with sweat despite the cold. They traded blows, light taps, and then harder, focusing an inch into the flesh, then away, back again, now punching to the side and into the bag, full power. Punch bags hung from a beam on ropes, swinging out of synchrony, recalling long gone days with Jules and Jean-Marc. She had toddled in between them to join in with their efforts to perfect their French boxing, the *savate* of the streets, and they had howled with

152

laughter, tripping her up, tapping her head. But as she grew older, she had become a pet and they had wanted her to succeed.

She approached the men silently as they continued with their routine, aware of her presence, but not distracted by it. A front right kick from Jules was followed by a step forward and scorching left kick, skimming his opponent's head close as a coat of paint, a right punch followed up. She watched them, her fingers and feet tingling to join in. She padded closer, stretched her legs, her arms, her back, and warmed her limbs. Leaning forward to the ground she lifted her body onto her hands, walked a dozen steps upside-down, and then sprang back to her feet with a bounce. A quick glance exchanged with Jules and she had leave to join them.

A little demonstration was needed for the benefit of the other man, who was a stranger to her. She needed to lay down her own marker for the future. Facing the bag, she started to land front kicks lightly, feeling the hardness of the compacted straw, then harder. It had been a few years since she had practiced and it was not easy to make the bag swing, a useful reminder. Making moves in the air alone in her room had some value, but she needed to do more. The men stopped to watch her. Right kicks, then left, spinning kicks, front punches, blows from the elbow: warmer now, she felt her skills waking up and she showed them off. She would pay for it in aches and pains, but later and alone.

"Bravo, Coco!" said Jules. "May I present Pierre Valdez, the best labourer and bare-knuckle fighter in town: apart from me!" His sparring partner's face told the same story. A regular fighter's broad and crooked nose was crudely set in a battered chestnut-brown face; deeply seamed by a life lived outdoors. Grey streaked his dark shock of wiry hair, though he could not have been forty.

Coco took the outstretched hand which closed round hers like a bear's paw. "Pleased to meet you, Monsieur," she said, sidling up to him. "I'd go a long way to see you fight. When's your next bout?"

"You'll be the first to hear after I do!" said Pierre, looking her over appreciatively. "Unless your brother tells you first. He's the new manager of our little local entertainments. Meet the impresario of Saint-Laurent."

"Since when?" said Coco.

"Since very recently," said Jules, very pleased with himself. "I have a new friend, the Commander of Fort Medoc. We have a few shared interests."

"I need to go now," Pierre broke in, reaching for his shirt. "The men are waiting by the canal and we need to start if we are to finish digging the new drain this morning. Pleased to meet you, Mademoiselle."

Pierre marched out into the yard, struggling into his coat as he went. Jules turned to Coco, amused. "You have a new admirer. He could barely take his eyes off you. Perhaps I could lend you another shirt. With a more seemly fit!"

As Coco glanced down to check her buttons, Jules whooped with laughter, caught her round the waist and flung her over his shoulder into the hay bales.

It became their own morning routine, first sparring with Pierre, and sometimes half a dozen others from the gang of vineyard labourers. Then, Coco and Jules reforged their own bonds. After the first few days she had improved enough to catch him with a kick to his stomach and he had collapsed on the floor in a pantomime faint.

"You still kick like a mule! Lucky it wasn't my balls," he laughed, stretching back and groaning in the hay.

"The luck was yours, the judgement mine," she said.

Jules knew little for sure about her judgement or lack of it: nothing about the brief jail term, little about her patrons and clients, or the additional tricks up her sleeve, her use of poisons, her guns and her knives. It was all for her to know, and others to find out. But the bonds between them were re-made and she judged the time to be right. She flung herself down and snaked her arms around him to whisper into his ear.

"I suppose your little smuggling enterprise into Devon continues to run smoothly."

"It may well do," he said, amused. "What made you think about that?"

"No problems all these years?"

"No problems. Why? Are you here to offer a warning, Coco?"

"No, not a warning: a proposition."

And there it was, though the chatelaine of Arno's Tower did not know it, that plans were first laid to prise apart Amanda Ravenswood's grip on her emeralds. No stranger to a spot of larceny and game for the chance of redeeming his family's treasures, Jules was willing to enlist in Coco's scheme to give the Wheel of Fortune a helpful push.

**Mid-morning: 20th March, 1833.**
**The Parry Residence, Saint James's Square, Bath.**

As Coco was slipping into the Medoc barn to watch the men sparring, Nathaniel and Emma had returned to their bedroom in Saint James's Square. Emma was talking about paint and wallpaper, whilst Nathaniel was pulling out his father's strongbox from behind a camouflaging baffle of blankets that lay in a disorderly pile at the back of the wardrobe.

Over a mile away, in Green Park, Clari Marchant was closing the back door of Shadwell's brothel. She had put on her best boots and gloves, buttoned her coat up to the neck against the cold and was turning to make her way to the garden gate, when a voice bawled out above her.

"'Ere Clari, moiy love, don't forget mi'red laces for mi'busted stays! Oiy 'll be wantin' 'em for tonight."

Letty, or at least her grinning face under an untidy pile of bright auburn hair, was leaning down above her from a second-floor window.

"What did yer first servant die of, yer lazy baggage?" shouted Clari, but immediately regretted it.

A sharp tattoo of rapping on the windowpane by her ear was followed by the sash rocketing up and a furious Madam Shadwell sticking her head out.

"Trollop!" she hissed at Clari, eyes glinting behind her tiny gold spectacles as she twisted her head round, hoping to catch Letty before she dodged out of view. "And you, hussy!" she hollered above the noise of the window slamming shut above their heads. "What have I told the two of you about shouting in the open air? And now look what you've made me do!"

"Sorry, Madam," said Clari, shamefacedly.

"Manners maketh money. You'll be demoted to Avon Street if you can't behave."

Clari grinned. She liked Madam and felt sorry for her. Joshua might have recovered in a bodily sense, bar a slight limp, but he was still drained, enfeebled, and could barely keep a check on the men, who in their turn were not as effective as they should have been in running the riverside stews. Rosie Shadwell looked like she had the world on her shoulders.

"Will yer be a-needin' anythin' from town, Madam?" she asked.

"No Clari, but thank you. On you go," said Rosie, pausing with her arms raised to lower the sash. She still cut a graceful figure and had a harsh beauty, but the early sun caught a network of fine lines round her eyes and her mouth was tautly drawn.

Clari turned away from her, knowing that she would be watched until she closed the gate, and hurried off down the lane behind the Green Park terrace towards Kingsmead Square. Once there and sure she was unobserved, she veered away from the town centre and headed for Queen Square, then made the steeper climb to the Circus and the Crescent, on her way to the select residential enclave of Saint James's Square.

155

"Are you sure we need to keep the sapphires in the bank?"

Emma was sat on the bed with the jewels spread over her knee, idly tracing the golden links with her finger. She had up-ended the strongbox they were kept in and a pile of other necklets and bracelets had slithered to rest next to her in a haphazard mound, winking and flashing their charms.

"I think so," said Nathaniel, reaching for the box and inspecting its lock. "And whatever else you couldn't bear to lose must go too. Father never kept the best pieces at home. Anyway, this box is too much of a target if thieves ever come to call. It might as well have instructions carved on the front: Loot – Open Here."

He picked idly at the worn silk lining.

"I'd never get rid of it of course, being Father's."

Suddenly he stopped.

"Em, look here!"

As he had run his fingers along the back of the base, the silk had split.

"It's false: the bottom of the box is loose!"

She was over in a moment, excited, and watched him lift out the wooden square to expose a shallow void. Within it was a small, leather-bound pocket book.

Nathaniel picked it up and leafed carefully through the fragile pages. "It's Father's! Look, he's signed the first page."

He felt his heart beat faster, for it was more than a list of appointments. It was a journal: dates; people and places; thoughts and sketches; specimens of dusty herbs and grasses, some crumbling onto his lap as the pages turned, releasing a final breath of musky scent into the air. The sight of the familiar writing wrenched his heart and he ran his fingers over the script tentatively, feeling the irregularities in the ink.

But his exploration was cut short by a jangling pull on the doorbell, sounding up from the hall below. Emma ran onto the landing and leaned over the banister.

"Frances has let in a woman who is asking for you, Nathaniel," she said, pulling a face. "She is no lady. I'll put the diary back, shall I?"

Nathaniel had sent Frances off to bring coffee, shown Clari to the small front parlour and settled her into a chair.

"Tobias told me you were coming to speak to me on an urgent matter, Miss Marchant."

"That Oiy am, sir," said Clari, eyeing Nathaniel with professional appreciation. She particularly liked the look of his thick black hair, which was shoulder length and had a raffish look about it. He had an endearing habit of putting his hand to his forehead and pushing his hair back as he thought of what to say. He had done it twice, once as he spoke to her in the hall, and now as they were about to talk. She had noticed both times, and she would have liked to see a great deal more of Mr Parry, but men like him did not pay for company. He was tall and strong-looking with clean hands and sparkling linen, no tobacco marks or smell of spirits. His eyes were a curious bright blue and she looked into them directly, took a deep breath and started to tell him what he needed to know.

"This is confidential, sir. The people Oiy work with are 'andy with their fists, and Oiy need mi'looks, so this can go no further." She paused, checking his reaction, and went on.

"Oiy knew who you was straight off when Oiy saw you 'avin' the row at Shadwell's the other night and they called you Mr Drake. Oiy'd already found you out through Letty's brother Fred. She works with me and 'e's guard on the mail coach to Gloucester."

There was no need to say more.

"Then," said Nathaniel, "I would guess he has made the acquaintance of a servant at the Pelican by the name of Abigail and her story has now made its way via the brother to Letty and now to you. Remember Miss Marchant, the fewer who know of Abigail's history and her whereabouts, the better for her health."

"Oiy'd never tell on 'er, Mr Parry, sir! And neither will Letty, nor 'er Fred. Oiy knew Abi was in trouble in Bristol and you saved 'er life, prob'ly twice, as Joshua Shadwell would wring 'er neck if 'e caught 'old of 'er now and that's the truth. She told Letty's brother you called yerself Mr Drake, and Oiy 'eard you talkin' to Billy and Jabez 'bout the old soldier dyin'. Prestwick wasn't 'e? Oiy want you to know Oiy think one of moiy customers 'ad something to do with the poor old sod. Moiy customer was a gent called Mortimer-Buckley. 'E came for Oiy the night the old man died. Goin' at it hammer and tongs 'e was."

She took Nathaniel by surprise by abruptly throwing her head back and letting out a peal of laughter at the memory, slapping her knees and stamping her little boots. And he saw why she was a favourite. She had undone her coat as she had started her tale, revealing most of her large pair of white breasts, which were falling out of a plunging neckline and shaking with her delight at the memory of Buckley and his fancies.

"All sorts of ideas, has that gent," she said, wiping tears from her eyes. "Had me wearin' a flounced milk maid's cap of all things!"

A tap on the door was followed by Frances and the coffee. Frances, agog with gawping curiosity, could not take her eyes from Clari as she placed the tray on a side table.

"Shall I pour, Mr Parry?" she asked, but knew what the answer would be.

Nathaniel saw her off as quickly as he could, but it reminded him that the visit would have caused a stir below stairs. Explanations loomed. He shrugged off the thought and carried on.

"What's your evidence he has anything to do with it, Clari?"

"Well 'e was that done in afterwards," she said, with a measure of pride, "that 'e fell straight asleep. Done that before 'e 'ad and 'e dreams and talks in 'is sleep. That night 'e called out 'Prestwick! Prestwick!' quite a few times, no mistaking that, then 'e was mumblin' rubbish about jewels and Napoleon, all sorts of jumble. 'E seemed to be talkin' away to someone else, frightened loike. Then 'e started to roll and thrash 'is arms, sweatin' the while, and shouted somethin' foreign "*las tres hermanas!*" whatever the 'ell that is. But 'e knew about the old man roight enough. Oiy made that out clear and Oiy thought you should know, sir. I want you to know us girls are still grateful you 'elped Abi: one of our own. Not many would 'ave given 'er the time of day."

Emma had put the pocket book and jewellery away and allowed him ten minutes before she made her way downstairs. She lingered only briefly at the parlour door, as the voices were too subdued to repay eavesdropping, then continued down the next flight to the kitchen. She walked in to find the staff immobilised in a hostile stand-off. Tobias had paused mid-way through brushing a boot and was glaring daggers at Mrs Rollinson, who in her turn, was quivering with fury, floury arms folded and biceps on the bulge, squaring up to Frances. Harriet was likewise transfixed, but crouched over the table, her eyes rolled up fearfully to view Mrs Rollinson, knife in mid-slice over a turnip. Only Caradoc, hunched by the fire and locked in a growling battle with a bloodied leg bone, soldiered on with his task, oblivious.

"Now everyone," said Emma briskly. "What's amiss?"

"Do you know who's in the parlour, Madam," exploded Mrs Rollinson, glaring at Frances and Tobias in turn. "These two know who she is all right. I caught them talking of her and Master Caudle here gave me a mouth full of cheek, I might add, when I challenged him. She is a common bawd and they know more about her than is decent! She has no place in a respectable house and Master's on his own with her! It's not right."

Tobias stood up, ignoring Mrs Rollinson and dealing directly with Emma. "Madam, the woman has information Mr Parry needs. Mrs Rollinson was making to call you but the woman won't talk if anyone goes in."

It was a chance Emma knew she had to take. Though at first things had gone tolerably well between them, recently Mrs Rollinson had made it clear in many ways, small but unmistakeable, that she thought little of her. The tight lips and the

158

shake of the head after they discussed the weekly menu had moved onto the substitution of Emma's choice of dishes for a favourite of her own. She had become bold enough to interfere with every domestic decision Emma made, almost on principle; and meanest of all was her continuing petty cruelty to the miserable Harriet in the name of "training", despite Emma's mild attempts to shield the girl.

"Thank you, Tobias," said Emma, with all the regal chill she could muster. "I see you all have work to do. Please return to it. And Mrs Rollinson, yours does not include remarking on Mr Parry's visitors."

As Emma strode back into the lobby and made her way to the stairs, she could not suppress a silent huzza of triumph. Though with her mouth open to give it full vent, she did not cut quite the figure she had hoped as she met with Nathaniel and his visitor in the hall.

## Evening: 30th March, 1833.
## General Palmer's Château, Cenon, Bordeaux, France.

Coco stood by the bedroom window in General Palmer's mansion, looking out over the park and the ranks of vines lining the steep decline to the river. The Garonne shone like steel in the distance under the white moonlight, and up-river on the far bank she could pick out buildings on the outskirts of the old city of Bordeaux. By daylight it was a ravishing view and her room for the night was luxurious, impeccably appointed in the latest style, and in view of his dire financial situation, provided another example of the General's profligate extravagance. Charles Palmer had proved to be a charming host: generous and ill-advised, both faults making him the best of company. And the rest of the evening had provided far more of interest than it might have done. She had accepted the invitation to do Dairmuid a good turn, a *quid pro quo* for helping her visit Jules, but it had blossomed into much more, and might even dose the Wheel of Fortune with a little more oil and encourage it to turn in her favour.

Dairmuid's hosts, the Bartons, despite being extremely elderly had proved to be excellent company. During the long journey in their coach to Cenon, which included embarking the whole equipage on the ferry at Lamarque, Mrs Barton had proved to be a raconteur.

"It was in 1794, before the two of you were born," she had declared fiercely to Dairmuid and Coco, her head on one side, peeking out from under a lace cap as big as a bucket, "when this land was a hell on earth. There we were, Mr Barton and myself, all in the flower of our youth, imprisoned and like to have our heads sundered from our shoulders by the scoundrel rogues of the Revolution. All foreigners were doomed!" She fixed them all with a scything glare and delivered a lengthy tale honed to perfection. "And don't talk to me of the Emperor Napoleon!" she had ended triumphantly. "A lamb he was in comparison with the devils in the Reign of Terror but I thwarted their evil purpose! I disguised himself here in a woman's petticoats and wrap, and we were out through the gates in quick sticks, onto the ship and sailing back to Ireland!"

"It was exactly so, Mrs Barton," agreed her husband fondly. "You were ever a woman of remarkable resource." Squeezing her hand affectionately, he transferred his twinkling smile to Dairmuid and Coco, "And you young folk will shortly be meeting another man who kept his head as well as keeping our business afloat during all that terrible time."

But Hugh's business partner, Baron Guestier, had failed to put in an appearance at the dinner, which in the event did not surprise, for at almost eighty he was even older than the Bartons. However, his debonair and imperious son Pierre, and his wife, had been at the table, along with Pierre's sister Eliza, and her husband, the same Bernard Phelan whom Coco remembered from Dairmuid's stories. It was a heady company of Bordeaux's wine Czars. General Palmer could not have hoped for more and Dairmuid's work in arranging the evening would presumably not go unrewarded.

To her delight, matters of more immediate interest to herself had been touched upon towards the end of the evening when the talk had veered towards construction. The Bartons did not spend much of their year at the *château* in Saint-Estèphe and were more regularly to be found in Ireland. Hugh Barton enlarged on the details of a palatial spread he planned to build in County Kildare and Eliza Phelan had not missed the opportunity.

"Mr Phelan and I might well build in the Medoc. Mightn't we, Bernard?"

"Indeed, indeed," said Bernard Phelan, smiling expansively. "I wouldn't give up the Bordeaux house, but a *château* by one of my vineyards is a likely possibility as you say, my dear, probably Ségur de Cabanac."

"You will not regret it!" Pierre Guestier had declared. "I have had Beychevelle for over seven years now. Depend upon it, on my watch it will be the Versailles of the Medoc again! And I hear that the Marquis de la Blanquefort has some interesting plans. He's back with a wife and is making moves to resume his residence here in the Medoc. He's started on some landscaping at a site he has acquired on the outskirts of Blanquefort. Not the old white fort itself but a better situation altogether, the ruins of the mansion at Fort du Lac."

"So lovely to see the Marquis happily settled at last," said Madame Guestier

160

generally, then as an aside to her sister-in-law Phelan. "She is extremely wealthy: older than him," she raised an eyebrow and then added generously, "but altogether delightful. *Très élégante.*"

"So the Marquis has returned," said Eliza Phelan. "And in transports of delight by the sound of it."

The tide of talk had moved on, but not for Coco. In her mind's eye she was back to Paris and remembered his careless warmth, his slow mocking smile. So, the Marquis had surfaced, and married to a rich woman, an older woman.

"Has he now," Coco thought to herself, and not for the first time, as she watched the moon glide behind a bank of smoky cloud. "Has he by God. Well perhaps his life could be even more delightful if he renewed his acquaintance with one of his dearest old friends."

### Late morning: 2nd April, 1833. Mayfair, London.

Nathaniel had left his rooms in Lambeth, crossed Westminster Bridge and concluded some swift business at the Home Office in Downing Street. Drake had been loitering by Melbourne's door and they had made arrangements to dine together that evening at the Travellers' Club in Pall Mall. After a brief word with Percy, Nathaniel scooped up his mail and made for Birdcage Walk; skirted Saint James's Park and then headed straight over Green Park to Mayfair. He hoped to catch Sir Giles Mortimer-Buckley and confront him at home before he left for the House, or to his club for luncheon. Nathaniel was alone as he had planned only a brief visit to London, and decided to leave Caradoc in Bath. The dog had seemed more than happy with the arrangement. With age, Caradoc was proving to be increasingly pragmatic and independent. Ever since Mary Spence had befriended him he had shamelessly exploited the females of Bath. Tilly Vere had been an early convert, as were all the Peterson women and he was a favourite with Em, obviously. At home, Harriet and Frances also competed in plying him with extravagant attention, and most surprisingly, Caradoc's recent ratting exploits in the larder had won over the hard heart of Mrs Rollinson. He had laid down the bloody corpses of his kills at her feet as tribute, and now had a guaranteed lounging space in front of every fire in the house, not excepting the kitchen range.

But Nathaniel had not had spare time on his hands to dwell on Caradoc's absence. He had brought his father's journal with him and been occupied in reading through all the entries for the winter of 1808/9. They included confirmation of Buckley's participation in the raid on Napoleon's baggage train, which he had denied, as well as the unexplained disappearance of some of the loot, which had not been reported publically at the time. Likewise, it corroborated the fact that Buckley knew Philip Spence and Ben Prestwick from the mission. Furthermore, his father's distrust of Buckley was made plain. Owen had concluded that he was a rogue, and in his dealings with women, a cad. The entries made on his father's return to Britain made more mention of the missing pieces of jewellery and included a brief report of what he had learned about the shambolic retreat to Corunna: the crippling cold and disease, the atrocities inflicted on the Spanish villages and the sorry toll of executions which followed. But his father's sketches were of even greater interest. As well as a set of drawings of the jewels from the loot, which were architectural in their accuracy, there were others, done impromptu and out of doors, which brought the beating heart of the Montes Vascos to Nathaniel's cosy digs in Lambeth. Wild cats and wolves, leaping chamois, vultures and ravens decorated the margins of the notes and there were portraits. Two he noted most particularly: the faces were mesmerising, proud and hawkish. Below it said 'Izar and Amaia': *Las dos hermanas.* Again, the mention of Spanish sisters, but this time just two, not three. At the sight of those words he had a vision of Clari Marchant struggling to get her tongue round them. It seemed that Buckley was familiar with an additional Spanish *señorita.*

On his arrival at the Park Street mansion, the butler showed Nathaniel into the hall, and reappeared almost immediately to hurry him into the front parlour. He entered to find Giles Mortimer-Buckley looking as if he had just sprung guiltily to his feet, his pre-luncheon drink still quivering in his hand and his eyes bulging in alarm.

"Mr Parry!" he exclaimed, over heartily. "Welcome! Lady Leonora is lunching with our daughter, so do join me, take a seat. Will you have a drink?"

Nathaniel accepted, judging it to be a quick route to relaxing his prey.

"Bristol Milk! Hope sherry is to your taste," said Buckley nervously. "Appropriate, as we last met in Bristol if I remember correctly. How may I be of service?"

Nathaniel placed his drink down silently and looked straight into Buckley's eyes and down to the depths of his lost soul.

"Sir Giles, although you sought to hide it from me I have received confirmation that you knew my father and were recruited by him to join a mission in northern Spain during the French Wars. You and the other members of the group profited from the success of the mission and one of the men, Ben Prestwick, reacquainted himself with you the week before he met his death. On the night he died, rather than keep an appointment to meet him, you attended Shadwell's establishment in Green

Park and then left Bath." Nathaniel ignored the rising tide of bluster that was almost choking Buckley and pressed on. "Edwin Ravenswood's employee, Trevellis, was connected with Prestwick's death and I put it to you that, at the very least, you were well aware that Prestwick was in danger."

The room swam before Buckley as if he had been struck by a pole-axe. He had not slept soundly for weeks, since that cursed rat Prestwick had turned up in Bath to haunt him. And Prestwick was not the only ghoul to terrorise his nights. No, no! He must not think of them! He focused hard on the man sitting opposite him, on his pale face and piercing eyes, his right hand resting lightly on a silver-handled stick. Undoubtedly a weapon and the bastard could no doubt put it to deadly use.

"Think, Giles, think!" hissed the voice.

He managed to gulp down a shuddering breath and tried to compose himself. He drank his sherry in one swallow and slammed the glass down hard on the side table.

"Yes, Mr Parry, I misled you. The mission was secret you see, long time back, but old loyalties die hard." He smiled warily, treading like a man on a tightrope. "The drunken old fool had a loose tongue. I admit, I asked for help to frighten him off. I wanted him away from Bath, away from me. He was a man of no discretion and it was clear that he needed money. All manner of unpleasantness might have arisen."

"So you asked Ravenswood for help?"

Buckley nodded violently.

See, he said to the voice, so far, so good, no mention of gold or jewels; of the burning village and the girl or of blasted Maisie Trickett.

He dared to hope. "Yes, but I'm sure he did nothing rash. I had no idea that Prestwick would come to any harm and surely Ravenswood would do him no mischief. Damn it the man's a Justice of the Peace! Though I cannot speak for his servant. Trevellis, you say? Contacts might be dangerous, what!" he said, daring to relax and warm to his theme. He risked an olive branch. "And speaking of which, be warned Mr Parry, I know he is your colleague, but John Drake means you no good. He warned Ravenswood that you intended to investigate his new ship, the *Leonora*. Named for my wife, you know. Now if that is all, will you stay for luncheon?"

"I could not impose, Sir Giles," said Nathaniel, preparing to take his leave. "And I sense we will make no further progress today."

Buckley stood at the window as the front door closed behind his visitor, his lips working as if deep in conversation, his eyes staring bleakly at Nathaniel's retreating back. Another drink was already in his hand and his knuckles showed white as he steadied his hand on the ledge.

**Early evening: The Travellers' Club, Pall Mall, London.**

It was Nathaniel's first visit to the new incarnation of the Travellers' Club and he was pleasantly surprised to find that his membership still stood; financed by some labyrinthine means on an old account of his father's. Owen Parry had been a founder member of the original Club, which had been set up after the war, and had taken Nathaniel there countless times, but the current new and splendid building had only been finished the previous year. It was the natural habitat of diplomats and their distinguished foreign visitors, a facility supported from the start by Lord Castlereagh, the legendary Foreign Secretary during the French Wars, and by Lord Palmerston himself. Drake's ambition to join Brooks's had been side-lined of late as he had found membership of the Travellers both congenial, and more importantly, extremely useful in terms of the advancement of his career. This being the case, Nathaniel was surprised by Drake's appearance as he caught sight of him crouched in an armchair by the fire and staring moodily into the flames. He was clearly in low water, glum-faced and absently rubbing his old neck wound, a sure sign of anxiety, his brow furrowed and back bowed. Nathaniel had noticed that Drake had been preoccupied and strained when he had spoken with him briefly that morning at the Office but had put it down to the discomfort of having to wait upon the pleasure of Lord Melbourne, a notoriously lengthy business.

Drake looked up, eyes hollow and dull. "Hello, Parry. Have some port?"

Nathaniel caught the slight slur in his voice, noted the careless pouring of the drink and exaggeratedly careful replacement of the decanter on the table. Drake had been there some time. Nathaniel nodded and settled down quietly, letting Drake take up the slack when he felt equal to it.

"Any progress with the death of the old soldier?" said Drake finally, draining his glass and reaching again for the port. "Any more progress, what!"

"Oh yes," said Nathaniel. "I know that Sir Giles Mortimer-Buckley was involved with the consignment of treasure from France, that he knew the soldier by the name of Prestwick, who introduced himself and seemed ready either for a spot of blackmail or to divulge details of the mission. I also know that Sir Giles sought help from Edwin Ravenswood to remove Prestwick from Bath."

At the mention of Ravenswood, Drake's brow furrowed even deeper and he slammed down his glass, leaning over the table towards Nathaniel. "Ravenswood!" He spat out the name in a rasping whisper. "Ravenswood has much to answer for Parry. You do not know the half! He is an evil man."

"I am aware of that, Drake," said Nathaniel carefully. "As you know, I am also aware that you were obliged to work closely with him by our superiors. I know that

164

you had to keep his trust by informing him of my interest in the *Leonora*."

Drake's eyes glinted, still sharp enough to recognise dangerous ground, he struggled to steer the conversation to safety.

"I'd no choice; you know that Parry, had to work closely with him for the Office. With Pam's ambitions for the opium trade, I'd no choice. The independent merchants will be running the show by next year." he paused, overwhelmed by other memories. "But the business with the trade in girls, that bad business…." His voice trailed off.

Nathaniel smiled. "I know. You did what you had to do."

Nathaniel was certain that Drake remained ignorant of his connection with Cornelius Lee and that Cornelius had informed him of Ravenswood's affairs. For Drake, if he thought of him at all, Cornelius was just another treacherous member of Kizhe's staff, an operative who had unaccountably abandoned last year's voyage at his first chance after landfall in China, risking the wrath, not only of Kizhe, but also of Ravenswood himself. Drake was still unsure as to whether Ravenswood had informed Nathaniel of the details of the illicit trade in girls and Drake's readiness to take a cut. There seemed nothing further Drake wanted to discuss about last year's cargo or its fate. But there was clearly some other issue bearing heavily on him. Nathaniel refilled Drake's glass and waited.

"Thanks, Parry," said Drake, and with Nathaniel's words of reassurance still sounding in his ears, and with that final port slackening the last bonds of distrust, the light of caution died in his eyes and Nathaniel Parry seemed suddenly to be a friend. "I suppose you know that Ravenswood is conducting an affair with my wife," he blurted out, adding bitterly, "I am sure all London knows. I don't like it, Parry! Didn't think she meant that much to me, damn it. Of course I knew the value of her family. Thought that was enough. Seems it isn't. Feeling damned sorry for myself to tell the truth. And for Mrs Ravenswood, Amanda, pretty woman that. I can tell you she has been dashed open in her comments to me. The man's a monster."

Nathaniel's mind had wandered back to the docks and his last sighting of Cornelius. Amongst the pile of correspondence waiting for him at the Office had been the long-awaited note from his friend. Cornelius would be waiting for him at the same riverside pub they had used before, the Prospect of Whitby. He would be there each Friday night in April, waiting. Perhaps he could take something worth hearing to repay Cornelius's patience.

"Yes indeed, Drake," said Nathaniel easily. "Mrs Ravenswood does not deserve such neglect. I am sure you can be a great comfort to her. A problem shared lightens the load."

"Quite," said Drake, confidentially, seeing the possibility of a nobler role for himself: not the cuckold, but the rock, the manly shoulder for her tears. His head rose, he sat straighter in the chair.

"In fact, your conversations with Mrs Ravenswood could be of great use," said Nathaniel. "She will be less loyal to her husband in view of his treachery and I would like to know more of the whereabouts of the man you dealt with in connection with Ravenswood's more disreputable trading interests. A Mr Kizhe if I remember correctly." Nathaniel took a gamble; it was extremely unlikely that Drake was still ignorant of the extent of his role in foiling the shipment of girls last autumn. He could have read Captain Peterson's reports to Melbourne, which would undoubtedly have spelled out the details. Also, the presence of Frances in his house, and his connections with another victim, her friend Abi in Gloucester, were becoming more widely known. He needed Drake to feel he was being taken into his confidence. "As you will know, I was involved in frustrating Kizhe's dealings in a minor way. He will not have been impressed by my work and I like to know where my enemies are."

"Leave that to me," said Drake, suddenly lordly. "If Mrs Ravenswood has any knowledge of his movements, I am well placed to find out."

**Evening: 5th April, 1833. The Prospect of Whitby, Wapping Wall, London.**

It was Friday night and Nathaniel had packed his bag with the few clothes he had brought and his swordstick, to be ready to catch the mail coach for Bath at dawn. Before that, he had business to attend and had dressed for it in black, and shabbily. As on his last visit, he chose to take the makila, which did not mark him out as a gentleman, checked the hidden blade and practised a few swings before he left. Almost out of the door, he had returned for a pistol and loaded it, before tying a muffler round his face and catching the river ferry to Wapping. He found the pub easily as the Prospect could be heard before it was seen and was heaving with customers. He worked his way through them to take a seat by the wall, kept his eye on the door, ordered a jug of porter from the potboy and settled down to wait for Cornelius.

The crowd in the bar was rough and as the night wore on the volume of the banter rose to a thunder, the air was hot as a furnace and thick with the stench of bodies, tobacco and spilt ale. Most customers were English and Irish sailors keen to spend their money, but there were a few lascars in a knot by the door, some African deck hands playing dice and half a dozen whores scattered round the tables, squawking like Matthew's parrot and chaffing the men. Nathaniel was busy catching the eye of the barmaid when Cornelius materialised silently from the crowd and slid into the seat by him.

"More porter, if you please," ordered Nathaniel, as a barmaid bustled by, her hands full of empty glasses.

They sat in silence until the drink stood before them, the barmaid had moved off and the crowds had surged back, a solid mass, isolating their corner and shielding them from view.

"It is good to see you," said Nathaniel, "but I was pleased to find you gone from the *Leonora* when I got back with the police." Nathaniel smiled, remembering the weary state of some of Ravenswood's men, "You seem to have made an impression on the crew before you left."

Cornelius bowed his head briefly in acknowledgement. "I have to say they made themselves known to me also. I needed a while to recover and luckily I had some assistance on the night. Two of my men, Fong and Chen, had been sent to join the *Leonora* when the *Blue Dragon* returned for refit to Bristol. They are still here with me in London and they are the reason I was delayed. We were instructed to stay here longer so they resolved to make themselves some money on the local boxing circuit. I just stood as Fong's second. There is a competition going on in the yard at the side of the pub and Chen's turn is in about half an hour. It earns them a living, which they prefer, rather than being reliant on me, or depending on government pay. They also get sparring practice. Such as it is."

"Won't Ravenswood's crew recognise them, or maybe Kizhe's men?"

Cornelius laughed. "Englishmen are easily confused by Chinese sailors of average height. Different clothes, longer hair, moustaches and beards: the slightest change and we are unlikely to be recognised. Even you can confuse your countrymen without too much trouble, Nathaniel! And they do not have to try too hard as Kizhe and his men planned to sail with the *Leonora*. The crew who knew Fong and Chen well are on their way to Africa. So, unfortunately for me," he continued, suddenly grave, "Kizhe is out of reach."

"I might be able to help you find him," said Nathaniel. "It seems that Drake has taken against Ravenswood for having an affair with his wife and that he and Amanda Ravenswood have struck up a friendship. As revenge, she might be persuaded to tell Drake of her husband's business affairs that are of interest to us. Drake owes me some favours and has promised to find out all he can about Kizhe's whereabouts."

"Good," said Cornelius. "We have a start." Though, he reflected to himself, he had not mistaken Amanda Ravenswood's looks in his own direction. She might have warmed to Drake as to a fellow sufferer, but her signals to him were not of suffering. He resolved to renew his acquaintance with Mrs Ravenswood and investigate her new thirst for vengeance more closely.

"Have you ever wanted to get married, Cornelius?" asked Nathaniel, relaxing back against the wooden panelling and sinking more porter. "Ever wanted someone to go home to?"

Cornelius looked up, intrigued. Nathaniel was not usually given to asking personal questions. "There are places I think of as homes," he said. "There are people there, but no wife. My life's work excludes a personal dimension: for now. I am different people in different places. The still centre of my world is within me."

Nathaniel fell quiet. Perhaps he also was two different people, at least two, and each with an entirely different life. He loved Em but had thought of her only fleetingly over the last few days. He had been consumed by his London life and had slipped into it as into an alternate reality.

"Emma is a woman of beauty and awareness, of unusual emotional depth," continued Cornelius.

Nathaniel looked at him, surprised. "I was just thinking of her."

"Of course, you mentioned marriage; she must be in your mind. Emma is unlike most English women I have met. Time spent with her will never be wasted. I could be happy to go home to a woman like her. "

Nathaniel felt no jealousy, no petty annoyance at the suggestion and noted that Cornelius had known how he would take such a remark before he made it.

Cornelius glanced at his pocket watch.

"Time for Chen's bout," he said, and they made their way out into the yard and the bawling scrimmage of men under the swinging lamps.

They pushed their way round to where Fong and Chen stood waiting by the river wall for Chen's turn. Both men were watching the contest animatedly, and as Nathaniel turned to look at the make-shift ring, he realised why. Half naked, oily with sweat and mud, panting for breath and locked in a grappling hold were two fearsomely powerful women. Roughly-muscled and liberally insulated by rolls of fat, they careered round the ring, struggling for a throw, until one lost her footing and they both collapsed in a shouting ball of filthy petticoats and flailing arms and legs. The mood of the crowd was generous and uproarious; the two fighting prostitutes had given light relief, a spicy novelty turn before the serious bout; time to laugh, size up the slatternly charms on show and take the chance to empty their bursting bladders against the yard wall. Some had chanced a bet, but most were already turning their attention to Chen, who had stepped forward to face a brutish

168

local fighter, twice his size, thick-necked, sponge-eared and gap-toothed.

"It is good training for Chen as your male fighters are not allowed to use their feet," said Cornelius. "He would win too quickly otherwise and attract too much notice."

The umpire had started the match when Nathaniel looked back at the ring, marked only by the thick sawdust coating the cobbles of the yard to give some grip and soak up spilt blood. Chen was in the centre, his pivoted fists up, but still and watchful whilst his adversary bobbed and weaved in front of him. Big as a haystack, the man jeered and cursed him for a coward until he lost patience and flung a swingeing punch. Chen dropped into a low stance and with one blow took the wind out of him. He let him recover and then surgically landed a blow, then another, but not too hard as the bout must not end too soon and disappoint the crowd. He allowed his man to catch him once, then again in the ribs. Chen automatically raised his knee to prepare for a retaliatory kick but managed to lower it again in a second.

"Well done," breathed Nathaniel, whilst Cornelius observed it without comment, and no one else seemed to have noticed at all. The betting took its normal course; the crowd hollered encouragement and chose their champion. But at an upper window, the curtain twitched.

Nathaniel reckoned that Chen would let the bout run for at least five minutes more and took the opportunity to glance round the crowd. In the shadows away from the competition one of the prostitutes was slumped on a chair, winded but bloodily triumphant and cradling her prizes for the night, a wool coat and a bottle of gin. An old woman in a filthy cap was busy pouring brandy over a jagged claw mark on her neck whilst the other fighter was squinting in the smoky light of a lamp, threading a needle with twine and preparing to draw the wound together. Otherwise, the crowd was largely male and very mixed. High beaver hats bobbed above the caps, voices of privilege carried above the tumult and fine wool coats rubbed shoulders with fustian jackets. Some men had barrel-shaped fighting dogs with spiked collars, growling and snarling on their short leads. A thought of home: it was good to know that Caradoc was probably spread-eagled by the fire in Saint James's Square. It occurred to Nathaniel that he enjoyed his two lives: the comfort of the one and the knife-edge of the other; it was right to keep them separate.

The crowded scene in the yard burned like a watch fire, the bundled scrum of humanity enjoying the frantic blaze of life and light corralled by the makeshift screen of low walls and tumbledown buildings. Above was the vast black night with its wheeling stars and, below the wall, the dark river flowed fast and treacherous. Standing out up river at low water mark, now deep in the tide and skeletal in the moonlight, was the abandoned gibbet of Execution Dock, wreathed round with swirling rags of mist, silent and by most, unheeded. But for those alive to such things, it emanated an unmistakable warning that hissed, sibilant over the water, and crept with the mist over every inch of exposed skin. The warning was of the wolves which prowled still, circling the flickering warmth. Cornelius raised his head, looked and listened.

Isolated from the dark and deep in the boisterous crowd, Nathaniel was attracted by a change in mood round the bookmaker's table, voices were raised and betting slips were waving high in the air. He caught sight of Cornelius motioning to Chen, who promptly knocked out his man, raised his arms in triumph and backed out of the ring. Fong was ready with his coat and the three of them went to collect Chen's winnings. The timing was tight, as the shouts by the table had been succeeded by bellows and a couple of blows had triggered a brawl. Nathaniel raised his makila as a quarter-staff and cleared a way for himself through the high hats who were rushing for the gate in panic. He worked his way round to join Cornelius and his men who had cut through the crowd, done their business swiftly and were making for the exit. As Nathaniel moved in behind them as rearguard, a burly seaman broke from the pack and was almost upon him, a couple of followers on his heels. Nathaniel floored him with a stunning head blow from the makila, stepped in and swung the stick in a wide arc. As the followers paused, uncertain, he drew his pistol, persuading them to give him the space he needed to back out smartly from the yard. Once out on Wapping Wall he kept close to Cornelius and his men and they allowed themselves to be swept away on the tide of the crowd towards the ferry.

As they neared the mooring, Cornelius leaned closer and spoke urgently above the gabble around them and the drumming of feet. "We were watched from an upper window. Beware. We will separate now and I will contact you in Bath before the end of next month."

Nathaniel nodded and made for the boat without looking back. The pavement had become more spacious as the crowd thinned out. Between him and the ferry there were just half a dozen men and a gang of small children with famished faces, hovering mudlarks waiting to jostle passers-by and frisk their pockets. Nathaniel smiled to himself, tightened his grip on the makila and strode purposefully past them to climb aboard.

As the boat pulled away up river, a figure in a heavy cloak detached itself from the shadows of the buildings, watched the progress of the ferry for a moment, and then turned to plunge back into the dark.

# Chapter 7

**Noon: 10th May, 1833. The harbour, Hope Cove, Devon.**

The two Frenchmen stood on the sandy foreshore, muffled up to their eyes in scarves to keep out the blustery wind. The cold air was searching, shot through with the scents of iodine, brine and fish. Clouds scudded across the grey sky and the air rang with the noise of the gulls. Some were wheeling high above their heads whilst others stalked over the beach picking at worm casts. Half a dozen were fighting over mackerel heads on the slipway.

"It's cold as charity here, *mon frère,*" grumbled Pierre, thrusting his hands deep into his pockets. "We've waited over a week already. Are you certain she's coming?"

Jules was climbing onto a rock, placing his feet with care to avoid the slick greening of the sea and the brown swag of seaweed that crowned it and clung to its sides. He was watching the progress of a three-masted lugger which was tacking into the cove between the headland he now knew to call Bolt Tail, and the Shippen Rock. The vessel was heaving in the heavy swell, struggling against a contrary wind to make a safe landfall and join the knot of boats already at anchor. The sheltered harbour was busy with fishermen working on their catches between piles of crab and lobster pots and pyramids of coiled nets. From the main street, women's voices carried over the beach from where they stood at their front doors, some gossiping, one calling her man home to eat, and a dozen children scurried amongst the tide

171

wrack, circling and squawking like another flock of birds.

The boat was coming in bravely enough but Jules knew enough of the coast, and this cove in particular, to know it had teeth. Dodging the wrecks was as much a skill as skirting the rocks. He glanced over to Bolt Tail and caught sight of a wiry figure standing out black against the horizon. Antoine had been a good choice for the trip, young and adventurous, an expert seaman and strong as whip cord; but a man who said little and followed orders. The fewer involved in Coco's little caper the better, but he had needed at least a three-man crew to handle his boat, *La Coquille Saint-Jacques,* and bring her safe into this harbour. The trip needed more discretion than the usual smuggling run, which normally involved a deal in Roscoff and a sea anchorage off the Devon shore where the sealed kegs were lowered overboard in the night, marked with buoys and left to bob innocently on the tide, waiting for collection.

Jules had never had cause to land at Hope Cove before, but he had known the welcome would be warm. He had left the arrangements to his usual contact, a mop-headed fisherman called Pascoe, superficially affable and slow of speech but cunning as a monkey. He had proved his worth a dozen times over the years and for this visit had arranged for a room to be made ready for them with his brother-in-law Jarvis, the landlord of the Hope and Anchor. Jules had brought a case of claret for Pascoe and one for Jarvis, with a collar of *Alençon* lace for Esther his wife: these considerations had made the room very ready indeed.

Jarvis, though not yet thirty years of age, was garrulous and expansive. Each night in the bar he had entertained them with tales, some of which might even have been true. Last night it was the legend of the "galleon timbers" which framed his fireplace.

"Salvaged from the *San Pedro el Mayor* they were," he had declared, rolling his eyes upwards. "As God's my witness she was the only Armada ship wrecked on an English coast in that terrible autumn of 1588, after Captain Drake and the weather had done for the rest of 'em. Stripped bare she was, down to every last spar."

Jules had inspected the fireplace, running his hands over it, admiring it. It was a good story. The wooden lintels looked like ship's timbers and they were of great age. Altogether the tale fitted well with what he knew of the men of Devon who were notorious wreckers, scavengers and smugglers, and now, especially the last of these. Devon and Cornwall were united in their hatred of customs men. It was common knowledge that no local jury would convict a smuggler as anyone risking their liberty to thwart the Revenue was a hero. He had heard of men in gangs of up to a hundred strong unloading a cargo by moonlight despite the gathering strength of the King's officers, the preventive boats, the watchtowers planted on the headlands and coastguards prowling round every coast and creek. They well knew that smuggling, like privateering, which was common and profitable in times of war, was illegal and the penalties, if a man were to be convicted, could be fearsome. Despite this, here they persisted in the old ways; their women provided cover and aid, helping run teams of donkeys and Dartmoor ponies up the steep cliffs with the children as look-outs. Wine, brandy and French lace, at reasonable prices and tax free, were seen as the birthright of Englishmen. Any French man conniving to supply them was welcomed with open arms.

"She will be here one day, Pierre," said Jules absent-mindedly, still keeping track of the little boat as it zigzagged home. "We have a month to spare. *Tu es en vacances*! Once she's here there will be more then enough to do."

It had been a good time to indulge Coco as there had been little to keep them at Château Pèlerin. Though some called it summer and it was easier to sail, the work on the vines had not yet really begun. The buds were out and the frosts were over, though they rarely amounted to much in the sheltered Medoc, insulated from the gales of Biscay and far from the bitter cold of the Pyrenees. There was little new growth needing to be tied, and the men left behind could deal well enough with what there was. The flowers had yet to bloom and it would be June before the fruit started. He was even at a lull between his boxing competitions at the Fort. It could not have been a more suitable time for a little foreign enterprise and he was enjoying it. It was the chance to enter a different life for a few weeks, a rest from Claudette, though she had become dear to him, and the children, though he had surprised himself by being a doting father. Jules rarely made the sea trip with the contraband these days but let his men deal with it whilst he played *le grand seigneur* at home. The trip was a novelty and he felt suddenly younger, invigorated.

"Mornin' to ye."

Jules turned to see a short, squat figure standing by him, eyes crinkled and gazing out to sea.

"Hello Pascoe, *mon vieux*! How long do you think that ship will tarry in the bay?"

"Not long," said Pascoe, slowly. "No, she will not tarry long. She be the *Lively*, skippered by Shadrach Hollis who do know every tide and every rock in the bay." Pascoe then sucked in his breath, short and sharp for emphasis, just in case the foreigner had missed the point. "Every last rock 'ee do know."

"Has the Salcombe mail cart come in yet?" asked Pierre.

"Full an hour ago," said Pascoe with relish. "There were no passengers on 'im."

173

He paused, allowing them time to accept that fact before adding, "But there do be a beautiful young wench asking after the two of ye. Came in a carriage she did. Jarvis and Esther settled 'er into a room d'reckly. Though she may 'ave taken off for a saunter to stretch 'er legs by now."

"Why didn't you tell us?" said Jules, as he took off from the boulder, landed hard in the gravely sand and set off at a trot.

"Yer didn't ask!" called Pascoe, smiling broadly at his retreating back. "I be a-tellin' ye now."

Jules and Pierre strode up the shore and turned left into the high street, striking out for the thatched cob cottages that clustered round the Hope and Anchor. Coco was waiting for them in the dark of the front bar. It took their eyes a moment to adjust to the gloom before they saw her in a quiet corner, lit by the filmy rays of light slanting through the mottled bull's eye glass of the windowpanes. Pleased with herself, and smiling, her honey-brown eyes glinted gold as she stood up to greet them, turned out like a lady in shimmering oyster silk, as if the dust and fatigue of the road had never been.

"Coco, *ma chérie!* It does my eyes good to see you," said Jules, kissing her soundly.

"We thought you'd never come," said Pierre, taking her hand and kissing it, holding on too long.

She squeezed his hand then pushed it away, laughing and excited. "Well, here I am. I see you are favourites already and so am I. They welcomed me like a long lost cousin. I've eaten already and recommend the mutton pie. But for now, sit down and have a drink." Coco sat down and poured them each a glass of wine as the men took their seats, expectant, before her.

"I caught the mail coach to Exeter," she said, delighted to be able to tell her tale, "and then hired a *Berlin* and driver to bring me down here to the edge of civilisation! He is waiting with the team in the stables and will take us all back to Exeter tomorrow. Once there we will travel on to Bath separately, and then have a few days to finesse our arrangements quietly in my rooms. I live in the centre of town, it is easy to find and there are crowds of people there. Strangers are common in Bath and you will not be noticed. We will return here to Hope Cove after our business is done and I will drive us from Bath in a carriage I have on a long lease. It's a four in hand I am keeping in a private stable, so we can use the horses for our business trip, then ride back to Bath, pick up the carriage, and as I said, I will drive you back here. The job itself will be done on Friday 24th May and theoretically I will be in London from the previous Wednesday until the following Monday. I have a busy friend who will

174

be taking me to the races but will sadly have to let me occupy myself with sightseeing for a few of my days with him. No one will know that I am back in Bath."

Both men, stunned to silence, took deep drafts of their wine.

"We will hear the rest on a full stomach," said Jules, walking over to the bar. "Esther! Two mutton pies, *s'il vous plaît!*"

Coco had laid her plans well. This spring had been chosen for the burglary, as the Ravenswoods had embarked on a lengthy building project at Arno's Tower that would continue until the autumn. Two more gothic towers were to be added to the wings and on the back of the building at ground level a palm house was to be constructed, a glass conservatory heated by stoves to exhibit not only exotic plants but also the immense wealth of Edwin Ravenswood. Heedless of both glass and window taxes, he was creating an object of awe, and focus of envy, for friends, enemies and competitors alike. Builders arrived in a cart on a daily basis and it was to be their misfortune that they were excellent time-keepers. Interception of the builders and their cart would not be difficult. Friday 24th May was the day that the Ravenswoods were to attend an exclusive luncheon party in the City of Bristol at the new Mansion House in Great George Street and Amanda had unwisely advertised that fact widely to her circle of lady friends in Bath. The new mayor, His Worship Mr Charles Walker, was to entertain a prestigious gathering of Councillors and Aldermen, Justices of the Peace, Members of the Society of Merchant Venturers, the Dock Company and the West India Association. The Ravenswoods would drag themselves from their death-beds to attend. The event would be lavish and well victualled, but it would be a serious gathering. The main topic of conversation was likely to be the impending abolition of slavery and the urgent necessity for the slave owners to extract maximum compensation from the government for their loss. It would be a hot topic, as many of Bristol's finest examples of that class would be present and Ravenswood was one of them.

It was too good an opportunity to miss. Amanda would not be wearing her emeralds, as it was a luncheon party and not dinner. The house was in disarray and infested by strangers in the shape of the builder's labourers, who were ubiquitous and anonymous. As an added bonus, most of the indoor staff had been given the afternoon off. The Ravenswoods had a pack of guests arriving within a few days and all leave for domestics would therefore be temporarily cancelled. The Friday off in *lieu* could not have been better timed.

Somehow, when Coco talked, it sounded an easy business. Disguised as builders, with Coco in men's clothing and passable as a youth, they would feign attention to the building of the palm house, but Coco and Jules would steal indoors to remove the jewels and any other items which took their eye. Antoine would watch the horses nearby and they would be off to Bath before the alarm was raised.

Jules poured himself another drink. "How many men do the family employ at the house?"

"They would have taken the coachman and two footmen to Bristol so, ignoring the rest of the indoor staff, who will be unlikely to be at home, that would leave six of Ravenswood's guards. There are four of us Jules. They are no match."

"Three if we leave Antoine with the builders and the horses. Are they armed?" asked Pierre.

"Yes."

"Dogs?"

"Two. But I can provide you with something tasty for them if they appear," said Coco. "I assume you have brought handguns and rifles?"

"I was not planning on murder," said Jules.

"Neither am I," said Coco. "But have you brought your weapons?"

"Of course."

"And I see you have not left your hands and feet at home so all should be well."

Coco raised her glass. "*À votre santé*! And as the English enjoy saying: Confusion to our enemies."

## Morning: 24th May, 1833. The outskirts of the City of Bristol.

Cornelius had spent a useful week based at the Crown, the coaching inn on the main road running through the town of Keynsham. He, together with Fong and Chen, had quit London as they had had no more sightings of the man who shadowed them at the boxing match and Kizhe's trail was cold. They had made for the West Country so he could renew ties with Amanda Ravenswood. Once there, Cornelius had assumed the role of a merchant with time to kill, travelling at leisure with his servants whilst his vessel was taking on supplies in Bristol. He had stationed his men in a tavern by Redcliffe Back where they could sound out the crews and dock workers whilst he spent his first few days watching the Ravenswoods and reconnoitring the fields and woods of Arno's Vale. Edwin Ravenswood's daily routine was not difficult to predict. He spent most days and some nights at his townhouse on Redcliffe Parade, overseeing work on his vessels, terrorising his men, and using it as a base from which to attend court and discharge his duties as Justice of the Peace. Cornelius was in no doubt that the sentences handed out in his court would be as savage as the law could possibly permit. He watched Ravenswood's

176

guards from the safety of the woods and recognised most of them from his weeks spent at the Tower as Ravenswood's guest. They tended to double as gamekeepers and carried shotguns, but when the master was out the patrols were cursory and usually ended with lengthy stops in the lodge house where two of them lived: feet were put up on the fender and drink was taken.

He had also taken the opportunity to visit the lady of the house one morning when her husband was out. Amanda had been more than pleased to see him; within minutes he had been seated in the drawing room, welcoming drink in hand. At liberty to observe, he had been struck by the change in her. Though sharp featured and too spiteful for his taste, she had previously had an astringent elegance, a minx-like cleverness and self-possession which could be admired. Those attributes were all but gone. She was as if blunted by anxiety and desperation. Nathaniel's story of her husband's philandering could be read on every strained new line on her face. She had willingly given up her freedom to become the possession of a ruthless man in exchange for a life of luxury and the thrill of living dangerously, but the awful realisation seemed to have dawned upon her that there was more to pay.

Cornelius had dallied away the morning with her, accepted sherry, flattered and listened. Within the hour he had extracted all he needed to know about the imminent return of Kizhe, who was apparently not continuing with the *Leonora* but would spend time in Holland and then return to England. Next he had learned of her loneliness, of Ravenswood spending increasing amounts of time in Bristol and London, and of her distrust of many of her house staff, which had grown since the Bristol Riots and the burning of their vessel in the harbour. Apart from incompetence, she also sensed their contempt and disloyalty. Every one of them had been appointed according to their suitability to serve her husband and any she formed attachments to were dismissed. Chivalrously, as he took his leave, Cornelius had expressed a hope that he may be of service to her, stressed how much he looked forward to seeing her again and, of course, meeting with her husband. He had expanded on how much he also looked forward to seeing Mr Kizhe and taking the opportunity to explain exactly why he had not travelled north through China as planned after the *Blue Dragon* had docked there the previous year.

Within days of his visit, Amanda had persuaded Ravenswood to entertain Cornelius at dinner and he had received a letter at the Crown inviting him to Arno's Tower the following week. No doubt Ravenswood was keen to question him closely about his absence, but Cornelius also knew that his old master had a high opinion of him and his skills, and had valued his presence at the Tower. As in his favourite game of strategy, the encircling art of Wei Ch'i, Cornelius felt his first stones were placed wisely on the board. Now was the time to consolidate, to reflect on the significance of what he had done and wait for his adversary to make his move.

That morning, mindful that the Ravenswoods were going out for a lengthy lunch, he had decided to run to his old training ground by the ruins at Saint Anne's Well and spend a few hours practising before having another close look at the Tower. An hour before dawn he crossed the Bristol Road and struck out over the fields towards the woods. After a brisk few miles, and without seeing another soul, he recognised the abandoned workshop buildings, and near them in the clearing, the stony rim of the well-head which was all that remained of the old shrine. He bowed briefly in respect, then knelt, silent and still, to be at one with the wood and its music, to feel the gentle lift of the tree branches in answer to the low west wind, and once, to be aware of a dry rustle of paws in the undergrowth.

Then, flowing slow and faint, a familiar stream of echoes ran through his consciousness, an awareness of the place that had been before: shuffling lines of penitents with their tributes, sheaves of grain and flowers, prancing horses' hooves raising dust before the grand entourage of a king. Then all were prostrate before the altar and the image of Saint Anne, her circling arms cradling the Holy Mother and the Christ Child. Above her hung a golden crucifix encrusted in gems and, all around, he heard the shrouded choirs of holy sisters. Cornelius let the vision wash over him, the alien strangeness of the chanted Latin prayers for the dead, the flash of medieval glitter. It was there for a space, then before his gaze it disappeared, dissolved in fire, wails and cries, to be replaced by men with carts and spades, the dry scratch of pens on parchment. He let it go and his own world emerged. The spirits of the place rose up again to fill his soul: the earth, the trees and the wind, the first rays of the sun.

On these things he meditated, gave thanks, and his mind cleared. Rising to his feet he began his training regime. Slowly warming every limb he worked through the first dozen of his patterns of movement: each move designed to destroy his imaginary enemy, each move a battle with himself for perfection. By six o'clock he felt ready to move on. Already he had heard working men making their way along the path behind the wood, their feet and carrying voices breaking into the quiet. He bowed a farewell to Saint Anne, ran four short steps, dropped his hands down into a stand, somersaulted once, twice, glanced round once more, then slipped away into the woods. He kept to the dark ways, avoiding the road, and built up his speed to an easy loping run.

Within half an hour he was trespassing on Ravenswood land, jogging along behind the hedge that shielded the long drive to the house, when he heard the

178

grinding wheels of the builder's cart bringing the labourers to work on the new palm house. The driver was keeping up a shouted conversation with a man and a boy sitting behind him on a sack of sand and Cornelius paused to listen as they passed. The voices grew in volume as the cart approached, spoke of mortar and mixes, then faded, overtaken in volume by the turning of wheels and the steady clop of the horse's hooves. He was poised to move on when all those noises came to a rude halt in a confusion of blows, strangled cries and crashes. He sprinted forward and knelt by a low gap in the hedge. Three powerful looking men and a youth had bundled the builders out of the cart, knocked them all but senseless, and were making short work of tying and blindfolding them, stripping them of their jackets, waistcoats, hats and neckerchiefs, and man-handling them through the opposite hedge to the shelter of a copse. From the sound of it, Cornelius guessed that the gang had lashed the builders to the trees and covered them. He heard a rapid exchange in French and one voice amongst the four was different, lighter and higher. Soon three figures emerged from the hedge, took charge of the cart and drove on to the Tower.

Curious, Cornelius shadowed them as they trundled round to the building site at the rear where they commenced, slowly and deliberately, to unload the sand and a collection of building tools. He circled the park, found a convenient tree with a dense cloak of foliage and climbed up until he had a full view of the back of the house and an opportunity to watch the morning unfold. The little charade was of interest as the gang would probably make a move as soon as the family left for the luncheon, and that move, undoubtedly criminal, could very likely do him some good. If Ravenswood's current cohort of guards proved unequal to the challenge he could become a valuable addition to the staff, so he resolved to smooth the way for the enterprising French and spent the next few hours monitoring the movements of Ravenswood's men.

Coco's heart was banging in her chest as she sidled round to the stables to check if the carriage had really gone. The morning had progressed as planned but the suspense was almost choking her. It had been essential for the plotters to catch the builders early, just as they were arriving for work, so they could ride up to the house on the usual cart. Antoine would watch over them in the copse as they lay blindfolded, gagged and bound under a tarpaulin. His knife was sharp so any attempt to move or cry out would be discouraged easily. She was not worried on that score, but still, the hours had crawled by. As planned, most of the indoor staff had disappeared early for their rare day off and the builders had been left to muddle on unmolested. Just before eleven o'clock she had crept round to the front of the main house and heard a brief and bitter exchange between the Ravenswoods by the entrance before they left. Fortunately, it was not serious enough for the trip to be called off and she had lingered to hear carriage wheels on the drive. A glance round the stables assured her that the only family carriage had disappeared and she doubled back to Jules and Pierre.

"They've gone. Are you ready, Jules? We must go in now," she said, her eyes feverishly bright.

"I am ready. Take care, *ma petite*," said Jules. "Check your weapons."

"It's done."

She and Jules stole into the house whilst Pierre set up a busy tapping on a cornice stone to provide some extra cover. Coco's instructions had been precise. Jules made straight for the dining room, slipping his knife into his hand as he went. Closing the door behind him, he scoured the paintings she had described to him. One was certainly familiar. If it was not his grandmother's landscape it was close enough. He pierced the canvas and slid his knife round the frame, excised the oil in seconds, rolled it and dropped it into his sack. His eyes roamed the room at the ranks of art works lining the walls. No time to choose. He took another, then another, then headed for the oak buffet where he swept up silver caviar dishes, epergnes, extravagantly worked silver bowls, one with crouched lions as handles, and most stunning of all, a solid gold Renaissance salt cellar, a full foot high, in the shape of a ship in full sail, nestling delicately on the curved back of a miniature golden mermaid. Shouldering his sack, he retraced his steps through the hall and made a silent escape to the terrace unobserved.

Meanwhile, racing up the stairs two at a time, Coco had been inside Amanda's bedroom within the minute, rifling through the drawers. Top, middle, bottom: nightgowns, petticoats, stays, stockings, letters, diary, no jewel boxes. Her hand shook slightly as she moved to the tall drawers. Top drawer, yes! Pearls, diamonds, semi-precious: no emeralds. She took two handfuls at random and shoved them into her pockets, then froze as she heard a light step on the stair. The bed was made up, no fire was set, maybe a maid seeking out mending to occupy herself? Coco dropped like a stone and rolled behind the bed. The steps receded, a door opened, a pause, it closed again, steps trotted downstairs. She tried to breathe, struggling as her chest constricted. Perhaps there was a strongbox? Rattled now, she checked behind the paintings for hidden cupboards, behind mirrors: nothing, no panelling, no bookshelves. Her eyes raked round the room and rested on the mahogany nightstand by the bed. She knelt before it and pulled on the handle of the pot cupboard. Locked: a good sign. She took out her pocket knife and broke in, the door swung wide and there it was, not a chamber pot but a strongbox, small and perfectly formed. She pulled it out, closed the cupboard, and as she stood to leave, arms tight around her prize, the door opened to admit not a maid but a manservant, levelling his handgun at her head.

In the same second that the door swung wide she flung the safe at her assailant, and herself after it, rolling over the floor towards him as his deafening yell of surprise and cracking retort from his gun rocked the house and sounded out, muffled but unmistakeable, to the back terrace and beyond.  Her hand was in her pocket by the time she jumped to her feet before him, her pipe was out and she blew a stinging spray of burning pepper into his eyes. Blinded and staggering, she floored him with a blow, seized the safe, tore the key from the lock and was on the landing, locking him in before he lifted his dazed head. As she fled down the stairs with her heart pounding, thanking God for the extra training she had done with Jules, she heard raised voices and running feet in the direction of the passage leading to the back terrace. Her fastest exit was blocked. She skidded to a halt and then bolted down the west wing corridor towards Ravenswood's private suite.

Outside on the terrace Jules and Pierre's eyes met in despair at the sound of the commotion above. Earlier, Pierre had seen four of the outdoor staff making their rounds in the distance, armed and watchful with the gun dogs frisking alongside them, taking the odd potshot at game for their dinner at the lodge. They had not re-emerged from the woods but two others rounded the corner of the house, guns cocked, looking up as the yells redoubled from the bedrooms above and Coco ricocheted out behind them through the west wing door, her jacket bulging, a metal box under one arm. As Jules and Pierre dropped low, drew their handguns and fired at the legs of the guards, she flung herself flat to the wall. Guns discharging wildly, they were both brought down and she sprang at them, smashing the strongbox down hard on the nearest head, Jules and Pierre were already by her side, crouched over the second man, and in one bloodied minute both had been silenced and bound tightly.

"Drive the cart over," ordered Jules to Coco. "*Vite! Vite!*"

He staggered slightly, unbalanced by the weight of his sack whilst Pierre, pausing only to gather up the guards' guns, flew on ahead. Chests bursting, they flung themselves in the cart and rattled off down the drive, the old horse lashed to full gallop and the empty cart careening left and right behind them. Once round the bend they pulled up, set the horse loose and scrambled through the hedge to where Antoine waited, having readied their own horses at the sound of the racing cart. Astonishingly, with no sounds of pursuit, they were free to mount, secure their haul and ride off at a trot towards the Bath road.

But in the woods behind Arno's Tower, four bodies lay insensible. Two dead birds had been delivered to them by the dogs, who lay panting in the grass, tongues lolling, whilst half a mile away a figure dressed in black flitted through the trees, silent as a shadow, setting his course for Keynsham.

## Late-morning: 26th May, 1833.
## Abbey Churchyard, by the Great West Door, Bath.

The Petersons were out first, but were soon joined by Nathaniel and Emma, closely followed by Dr and Mrs Charles Parry, Tilly Vere, Howard Dill and Mrs Danby. Lydia Peterson had been grossly inconvenienced as she had failed to corner the party before the service to apprise them of all the grisly details of last Friday's outrage at Arno's Tower.

"Have you heard?" she demanded, cutting into Mrs Danby's continuing monologue to Howard about her recent martyrdom at the hands of her portrait painter. He raised his head eagerly, never to his knowledge having been so very keen to hear from Mrs Peterson.

"Heard what, Madam?"

"About poor Mr and Mrs Ravenswood!" she obliged him, pausing briefly, eyelids fluttering, hand lightly placed on her bosom to still her racing heart. "I was so shocked to hear! They have been burgled in broad daylight. All her jewellery gone, the silver, paintings, his Oriental Salon turned up-side down, his builders kidnapped and his servants shot! Beaten senseless!"

Nathaniel had sensed that the Captain had news, but he and Emma had been on the last minute for the service and had been seated too far away for a word. "Is anyone dead?" he asked quickly. "Are the builders still missing?"

Lydia shot him a suspicious glance. "No. They were found tied up in a field by the drive and no one was killed. Thank God!" She added quickly and piously. In the shadow of the Abbey she could not even admit to herself that reporting bloody murder would have been even more delicious than audacious robbery. But what she had was meat enough.

"Mrs Ravenswood was to pay me a call yesterday but instead up rode Mr Ravenswood himself, explaining all. She is too distraught to leave home. Poor Amanda! And Mr Ravenswood so exercised by all this unpleasantness."

Nathaniel exchanged glances with Captain Peterson and the two stepped back from the circle as the clamour rose. The manly chorus of, "By Gad!", "Scoundrels!" and "Dashed impertinence!" competed with Tilly's wails of commiseration for Amanda and Mrs Danby's demands to be told exactly which paintings had gone and how much the jewellery had been worth. Mrs Charles Parry stood by, watchful and amused, noticing how the Peterson twins took advantage of the noise to renew a heated personal squabble behind the backs of their parents and Emma contrived to move towards her father and Nathaniel to hear exactly what was being said.

"Ravenswood's in a cold fury," said Captain Peterson, lips pursed at the memory, bushy eyebrows drawn up tightly to meet each other. "Came round demanding I rouse every watch in the city! No stone unturned, what! He's already got the Bristol constables scouring the countryside." He shook his head at the memory. "He'll have the perpetrators flayed alive if he ever gets his hands on them. And I wouldn't have liked to be in the shoes of his ground staff. They are all laid up and not fit enough to make themselves scarce, two shot in the legs and the others nursing broken bones and sore heads."

"So no one was killed," said Nathaniel thoughtfully. "It sounds like a professional job to me. How many does he think were in the gang?"

"There were three impersonating the builders, but four of his men were attacked in the park. They don't seem to know what hit them."

"Do you mean by the woods at the far side of the lawn behind the house?" said Emma suddenly. "Because that is where I saw a figure running in the dark when we went to the Ravenswood's for dinner after our wedding." She looked quickly to Nathaniel. "Do you remember?"

He did, and he remembered an evening round the fire in Anglesey with Emma and Cornelius. He smiled to himself. "Well enough," he replied.

That afternoon Nathaniel decided to walk over to see the Spence family. Matthew's continuing employment with Declan O'Dowd could have brought him into contact with some of Ravenswood's men or O'Dowd himself might have spread some inside information about the burglary. He was sorry that his last visit to Martha Spence had not been a happier one. He had been able to support her theory that Ben Prestwick had been murdered but was still unable to bring her the good news that the perpetrators were in custody, or better still, were already paying the price for their crime. She was a stoic and had accepted that powerful men were involved and it would take considerable time to bring them to book. He whistled up Caradoc, leaving Emma to prepare next week's menus and her plan of campaign for imposing them on Mrs Rollinson. He kissed her on the head, jammed on his top hat and strode off in the direction of the Crescent.

As they neared Walcot, Caradoc's hackles rose at the prospect of his continuing trial of strength with Matthew's bird, the infuriating and despicable Jimmy Congo. It had been a while since his last visit but he had smelled the creature on his master once or twice, a vexatious reminder of unsettled scores. He could almost taste the feathers and vowed to make them fly. They had crossed Lansdown at Guinea Lane and made their way to Walcot Street, but just as they neared the house and he was fully prepared, growling to himself, rehearsing his opening barrage, they crossed again. He stopped bewildered.

"No lagging, sir!" shouted Nathaniel. "Come on! They've moved."

He trotted on behind as his master turned left into Chatham Row and stopped before a different terrace of houses, taller and more commodious than the Spence family had occupied before. Regular rents from both tenants, coupled with Matthew's wages and the maturing of the larger of Martha's investments had combined to elevate them in the world.

"Stay," said Nathaniel. "You're on guard, Caradoc, 'til you and the bird are on cordial terms."

A disappointment.

Caradoc cocked his leg on the railing, turned his back and spread-eagled himself on the pavement.

"I won't be long," said Nathaniel, as the door closed behind him.

"Good to see you, Mr Parry," said Matthew Spence, looking fuller in the face and more content than Nathaniel remembered. "Mother's in the dining room with our guests if you need to see her. They are still yarning after their meal."

"It is you I want to see," said Nathaniel. "Could I have a word?"

"Yes, indeed. Come into the front parlour," said Matthew. "But will you say hello to Mother first?"

"With pleasure."

Nathaniel put his head round the dining room door and interrupted a jovial party in the final stages of a Sunday dinner, collars loose and chairs pushed back. Martha was on her feet, red in the face and directing Frances and Mary's removal of the dessert plates. At the sight of Nathaniel, old Mr Spence set up a cackling cry of welcome whilst the Johnty continued to flail around on his lap, jumping up to lean precipitously over his shoulder and feed seeds to Jimmy Congo perched behind him on his stand. Tobias, earnest and animated, was caught in the middle of a tale and two men seated by the wall were hanging on to his every word. These last he was not familiar with but was introduced to them as Martha's new lodgers, the bargees Mr Declan O'Dowd and Mr Finn O'Malley, who looked shifty but declared themselves delighted to make his acquaintance and were at his service. Tobias sank lower in his seat and coloured up at the sight of his employer.

"Good day, everyone," said Nathaniel with a bow. "I am sorry if I have

184

interrupted your meal." He smiled easily at Tobias and Frances. "I am glad to see you have been fortunate enough to have such a kind invitation on your day off."

"No interruption at all, Mr Parry," said Martha. "I wish we saw more of you, though it is a tonic to see these two young ones thriving."

Tobias, puce with discomfort, managed a sheepish grin.

"Thank you, Mrs Spence. Good day, Mr Parry," said Frances, bobbing a curtsey.

"Mr Parry wants a word with me, Mother," said Matthew. "We will go into the parlour."

"You will want tea," said Mary.


Nathaniel and Matthew stationed themselves in the front room, which was chilly despite the season, and exchanged pleasantries until the tea was brought and the door closed.

"I hear that the Ravenswoods were burgled," said Nathaniel, watching Matthew closely.

Matthew's eyes blinked wide at the memory and stood out from his head like the hat pegs at Martha's chapel. "Burgled! That they were, sir! Last Friday, and in the morning if you please! All the men were knocked about and the blackguards got clean away. Though how anyone dared do that to Mr Ravenswood beggars belief," he muttered, running a nervous hand over his face before rushing on: "Declan, Finn and me have been asked to work up at the house while the men get back on their feet, but I doubt he'll keep them much longer when they do." He grinned suddenly. "We are pretty well placed there Mr Parry. We've been doing a few bits for Mrs Ravenswood, and after the thieving she's determined to see off all the outdoor men. Says she can't sleep easy in her bed with such as them keeping watch. And she's been kind to us, showing us favour. Extra pay all round and a brace of game birds last week for Mother." He paused, watching Nathaniel's reactions, sensing he was not convinced of the virtue of the new situation.

"Mr Parry, Mother was grateful you came round to tell her she was right about Ben Prestwick's death being no accident. She went to his grave, just to let him know, and she's confident you will get to the truth if anybody can."

"As I told your mother," said Nathaniel. "It might take some time before the law lays hands on the guilty parties. But she knows her Bible well. If she asks again, tell her to remember that the mills of God grind slow but exceeding small. We are not finished yet."

Matthew smiled. "Right-ho, Mr Parry. The mills of God. She will like that."

Nathaniel glanced at his pocket watch, preparing to go. "Is there anything else you can tell me about the burglary, Matthew? Have any strangers called recently or any odd events occurred?"

"Yes," said Matthew. "Though it seems an age ago with all the fuss at the end of the week. Your acquaintance, that man I met in Bristol when I came back from overseas, the man from China, he came to call on Mrs Ravenswood. He's at the Crown at Keynsham and he's to dine at the Tower with both of them."

Nathaniel looked down at his watch again. "Is he now?" he said with a smile.

"And what of Captain Trevellis and the *Blue Dragon*?"

"Still at sea," said Matthew. "And do you know, Mr Parry, no one ever talks of Captain Trevellis, no one at all."

Nathaniel took his leave of the Spence family quickly, though leaving Chatham Row was not quite so swift. Caradoc had obviously ceased to sulk and made off on a mission of his own.

"Caradoc! Show yourself, sir! Caradoc!"

Nathaniel strode off down the road towards the river, checking the railed off deep-set areas of the houses, a favourite haunt of Caradoc's as they gave access to the subterranean kitchens. The dozen plots of Chatham Row ran down a gentle incline to the River Avon, so Nathaniel followed his nose and made for that. Before he reached the water he was rewarded by a sighting of Caradoc clearing the boundary wall and racing towards him with a dead rat clenched between his teeth.

"Well done," he said. "Is that for me?"

Normally it might have been, but even those most highly esteemed must bear some disappointments in life. Caradoc gave him a look, at once mournful and resolute, and passed his master by to deliver the corpse to the doorstep of the family Spence. A double-edged sword, it was not only tribute to his friends but also a warning to the evil bird whose day of reckoning was yet to come.

Jobs done, they sauntered down Walcot Street, crossed the bridge and made their way to the livery stables of Moses Pickwick at the White Hart where Nathaniel had kept his horses and carriages since Tasker's had closed. He had decided to drive over to Keynsham and seek out Cornelius without delay so he had his two-wheeler made ready, a new green and gold gig, took his fastest horse, and within half an hour they were bowling through town for the Bristol Road.

Cornelius was easily found in his room at the Crown.

"Matthew Spence told me you were back," said Nathaniel, settling into a window seat opposite his friend, whilst Caradoc leapt up beside Cornelius.

"He hasn't seen you for a while but he doesn't forget."

Cornelius smiled. "We three are not the forgetting types. Your information about

186

Mrs Ravenswood turning against her husband was very interesting and I decided to pre-empt Drake's efforts on our part to extract information from her. My moves so far have paid off. I intended to contact you when I had firmer news of Kizhe's return but it is good that you have sought me out. I assume that you know about the break-in at Arno's Tower?"

"It is the talk of the town."

"I was fortunate enough to observe the events at first hand and ensure that the outcome was satisfactory."

"For the burglars?"

Cornelius bowed his head briefly. "Of course," then continued: "It was a bold plan, imaginative, and unduly optimistic. The group of four, who spoke together in French, were taking a risk as they were so few in number. That said, they moved well and disabled the builders effectively, but they were all very soft targets. I took it upon myself to reduce the odds in favour of the French against the more effective opposition, with the effect that the Ravenswoods are very interested in improving their security. Ravenswood knows my skills and soon it will suit him to re-instate me in the house. Doubtless he will take the opportunity to try to extract details from me of my movements after the *Blue Dragon* docked in China in '31. Mrs Ravenswood seems disposed to make overtures of a different kind."

"And how will you respond to them?"

"As effectively as seems necessary."

Nathaniel laughed. "Is there anything else that struck you about the burglars, Cornelius?"

"Oh yes," he said. "One of the two who entered the house was smaller and younger than the others, and undoubtedly a woman."

Nathaniel's eyes clouded. "I rather feared that might be the case."

## Afternoon: 31st May, 1833. The Ravenswood Residence, Arno's Tower, Arno's Vale, near Bristol.

In the wake of the events of the previous week, a grand house party that the Ravenswoods had planned was called off and only one couple had been encouraged to make the journey to the Tower. At the insistence of Edwin Ravenswood, John and Lottie Drake had arrived for the weekend, wisely leaving their daughter with her nanny in London. Drake had not had high hopes for the weekend and even those had not been met. The conversation thus far had been limited to a detailed post mortem of the daring and successful robbery, the intricacies of Ravenswood's plans for the detection of the culprits, the subsequent exacting of revenge upon them, and how

Drake could make himself useful to those ends. It was fortunate for the burglars that execution for theft was rarely sanctioned in these enlightened times, but Drake had no doubt that transportation for life to the most unattractive of Australia's prisons would be guaranteed for anyone that Ravenswood managed to lay hands on. They had been even luckier that a clumsy blow had not accidentally killed one of the staff, or it would have been the noose for at least one of them.

Ravenswood's handsome face, always on the edge of sinister, had developed a new quality of menace and the only one of the party keen to look him in the eye was Lottie.

"I shall examine the lists of all criminals I have dealt with since taking office as magistrate. Every one shall be tracked down, as will each and every visitor to this house since the building project began," continued Ravenswood relentlessly. "Alert all your London contacts, Drake. If the wretches intend to sell, some of the gems will need to be fenced on the London market to realise their value, unless of course," he added bitterly, "they are out of the country already. With that in mind I have sent notification to my contacts in Amsterdam to watch for the pieces and they will contact their men in the Paris markets. As for some of my personal treasures, the net needs to be cast even further afield than Europe. I will soon meet again with my Far Eastern partner and he will do what he can to track down any attempts to sell my property."

The partner in question had to be Kizhe. Drake blenched at the thought of him, remembering the massive bulk of the man, the reptilian eyes, his preference for carrying a brutal short sword, his "helmet breaker".

"They invaded my Oriental Salon," Ravenswood added, almost to himself. "My collection of *tanto* daggers alone is priceless. Most unusual early medieval examples, small, neat, so perfectly formed. They stole one, threw the rest on the floor, then snatched up the objects easiest to hide," he paused, still barely able to contemplate the enormity of the crime. "They forced the door of one of the seventeenth-century cabinets. The cost of repairing the inlays will be almost as great as the value of some of the curiosities they stole. What in God's name was it all about? A handful of coins, some Egyptian beads?" For a moment words failed him. "Some items I can understand," he said at length. "The greatest value was in the gold and silver ware from the dining room, and one of the paintings they took was particularly valuable. Of course, my wife's jewels were also of considerable importance. But, thank God, they had no time to plunder my collection further."

During the silences between Ravenswood's outbursts Drake had allowed his mind to wander. He was picturing one of Ravenswood's cabinets of curiosities, a vast piece of furniture in black walnut with gold decorations, which housed sets of drawers and cupboards for the more miscellaneous, bizarre and macabre pieces in his collection. Mummified bats, finger bones of saint and sinners, preserved organs, a pitch-black obsidian mirror which Drake fantasised could reflect back into the black pits of his eyes the evil spirit in Ravenswood's soul.

"Remember, Drake," said Ravenswood, whose eyes were now no longer dead pools, but glinted dangerously. "If you have any luck in tracking down the criminals, they must be handed over to me. I will have every last shred of evidence extracted from them, the time taken will be no object."

Amanda stirred uneasily and made herself busy pouring tea. The last few days had been a living nightmare with the extent of Edwin's rages, truly terrifying. She had suffered only a few bruises during his conversation with her about the losses from her room but she doubted that some of the injured men would be better before autumn after their interrogation at his hands, and if it suited his purposes, they might not survive. Not that she cared less about them or her loss. Her stolen pieces of jewellery were the least of her worries, though once she had taken pride in their grandeur and worn them with pleasure. Every single piece had been his choice; all were symbolic of her servitude and could have easily been shackles for all they meant to her now. Keeping them in the box had been by way of a silent protest. But she had resented, deeply resented, the intrusion into her room. She felt no pity for the burglars despite the baroque excesses of her husband's wrath. Unmoved, she could watch them dangle at a rope's end. In fact, she thought to herself, she would like that very much. A vision from the aftermath of the 1831 riots flitted through her memory: bodies twitching their last above the door of Bristol's New Gaol. No, she would not mind that at all.

She forced herself back to the business of serving tea and ensured her smile was still in place: it was.

"For you, Lottie, my dear," she said, placing a cup just out of the Honourable Charlotte's reach and returning to her own thoughts.

On the positive side she had continued her campaign for freedom in other small ways, making sure that the most objectionable amongst the servants took most blame for the burglary. She had started to nurture the careers of others and best of all, had ensured that Cornelius Lee was welcome in the house. He had come to dinner and it had gone well. Soon, when Edwin was next away from home, she would suggest he came back into the house to improve security, perhaps with a few of his hand-picked men. And it was not all he might be good for. She looked up to see Lottie watching Edwin, her lips parted in excitement at his rage. Then over to Drake who looked horribly discomfited, looking anywhere but at his host, their eyes met. Perhaps, thought Amanda, though not a first choice, maybe a second. Perhaps the mysterious Mr Lee might not be her only possibility.

"Your cup, Mr Drake."

## Afternoon: 1st June, 1833. The Parry Residence, Saint James's Square, Bath.

Encouraged by their host to explore the countryside before dinner whilst he attended to some shipping business in Bristol, the Drakes had borrowed a coach and pair and gone for a drive to Bath. Drake wanted to get out of the house and make contact with Nathaniel, whilst Lottie was disinclined to spend the afternoon in Amanda's company. The previous night she had managed her usual illicit session with Edwin, and really, the liaison was still quite thrilling, definitely in the category *dangereux*: the anticipation, having to make the delicious choice from the array of silk nightgowns she had brought, the silent tip-toeing down stairs in the dark to meet him by the fire. John had not drunk as much as usual at dinner and been tiresome before he went to sleep, but she did not really begrudge him his rights. It was not that she had completely tired of their marital arrangements, but they were readily available and they were simply not enough. Occasional bouts with Edwin were breath-takingly exciting, though, she had to admit, they were becoming increasingly violent. There might come a time when she had to move into quieter waters. As it was, he had used her so roughly on the previous night that she had been obliged to cover the bite marks on her neck and shoulders. She had not yet had the courage to inspect her aching limbs but already she could feel the bruises blooming under her skin. It was some consolation that he would not have escaped unmarked.

John and Nathaniel had disappeared into the study whilst she had been ushered into the drawing room to find a ladies' tea afternoon in full swing.

"How lovely to see you, Mrs Drake," said Emma, rising to greet her and show her to a seat. "You will remember Mrs Vere and Miss Montrachet? Ladies, the Honourable Mrs Drake."

"Oh, how absolutely wonderful to see you again!" gushed Tilly, leaning over to pat Lottie on the arm. "We heard you were at Arno's Tower but we never thought we would have a sighting of you this weekend. You have come just in time to hear that our little circle is to be reduced! Coco is returning to France: permanently! Aren't you, darling!"

Coco managed a sad little smile, a sigh, and a resigned shrug.

"I have enjoyed my few years here," she said wistfully, "but my family and friends in France are demanding my return. So, my belongings are packed and I leave on Monday." Caradoc was draped over her feet, a few stray crumbs in his beard providing evidence of a successful afternoon. She stroked his head affectionately as she spoke. "As I said, I shall go first to Paris."

"It is all too exciting!" squeaked Tilly. "Can we write to you there? What will be your address?"

"I will let you know where I am, depend upon it, once I am able to receive mail," said Coco evasively.

"You will keep up with dear Mr Casey, won't you?" said Tilly. "He knows where your family live in the Medoc doesn't he?"

Coco's face hardened. "I will be nowhere near the address he knows, but I'm sure we will keep in touch. Though not through his Bath address," another regretful smile. "Mr Casey is giving up his rooms in Queen Square as he is too busy in London to make it worth his while to continue maintaining a base in Bath."

"Especially with you gone," said Tilly.

"Quite."

Emma made herself busy during this exchange, serving tea and observing Lottie Drake who looked tired and abstracted. Emma made a move to include her in the conversation.

"Mrs Drake, it must be a rather traumatic time for the Ravenswoods after that frightful burglary. How is Mrs Ravenswood? We have heard that she is distraught."

"Really? I would not say so. She is well enough, considering," said Lottie, though at the same time reflecting that, in her brazen refusal to show guilt, she had taken almost no notice of Amanda. In retrospect, her hostess had behaved oddly, perhaps she was in shock? There had been some indignation, but no anger, no tears, no real regret at her loss. "She is resigned to the reality of the situation," said Lottie blandly, "whereas Mr Ravenswood, as you would expect, has a more robust view. My husband and he have discussed the matter and John will do all in his power once we return to London. Some of the gems were quite remarkable and the villains might seek to dispose of them in the larger markets there."

"Excellent idea," said Coco. "I remember that Mrs Ravenswood had an interesting collection. London would definitely be the place to start a search."

"I must confess it has made us even more determined to take my few pieces to the bank," said Emma thoughtfully. "We have talked of it before, but never made time to arrange it."

"Emma," said Coco suddenly, "has Mrs Drake seen the wonderful new curtains you showed us? My dear, your taste is absolutely *impeccable*! I am so pleased I saw your changes to the house before I leave tomorrow."

Shortly after Lottie's guided tour of the new soft furnishings and Tilly and Coco's final giggles and declarations of undying regard, the men emerged from the study and the party broke up. Frances waited by the hallstand ready to help Tilly into her outdoor coat and Coco into her cloak. As she waited, she put out her hand tentatively to stroke the velvet collar of the cloak. It was sumptuous and silky to the touch; she crushed it lightly between her fingers, rolling it against the grain, then on an instant let go as a searing jab pierced her thumb. Suppressing a squawk of pain she inspected the damage and saw a trail of oozing blood. Sucking it clean she looked at the back of the collar more closely and found the culprit, a brooch pin sticking proud, and holding a delicately painted miniature firmly in place. The image was of a woman; white-faced and white-wigged, dressed in a ball gown. Frances was entranced by the beauty of it and held it closer for a better view. The gown was oyster silk and sprinkled with tiny gemlike flowers, the neckline was edged with gauzy net, fine as a butterfly wing, and round the lady's neck was a rope of diamonds, intricately cut and held on a heavy gold chain of interlocking letter "Ms".

## Evening: 4th June, 1833. The Guildhall, High Street, Bath.

Captain Peterson, Emma and Nathaniel had secured good seats for the debate on social reform. The Guildhall was full and they were just two rows back from the dais where the speakers were taking their places.

"So," said Emma, "enjoy Mr Casey's speech because he will rarely be here in the future." She looked up to the platform and caught his eye. He needed no more of an invitation, bounded down the stairs, wrung the men's hands and lavished kisses on Emma's kid gloves.

"Well now, Mr Casey," said the Captain, "I gather we shall lose you in the near future. Our provincial meetings will be the poorer!"

Dairmuid bowed. "Grand of you to say so, Captain! But I'm preaching to the converted here sure enough. The keeping of slaves throughout the British Empire will soon become an evil consigned to the past! And before this summer is out we'll get the majority in both Houses on a short-time bill for our own factory children, at least for those in the cotton trade to reduce their working day, and very likely we will secure a consideration to promote their learning."

"I will look you up in the House when I'm next in London," said Nathaniel.

"And don't you dare be forgetting, sir!" said Dairmuid.

"Please explain, Mr Casey," said Emma, reluctant to let him go. "Government money for the schooling of cotton labourers? Are you sure?"

"Almost, my dear Mrs Parry," said Dairmuid indulgently. "The nine to thirteen year olds are likely to have short-time and specified hours for learning in the day. Money is likely to go to the Anglican and Nonconformist education societies to help provide more places."

"What about the Catholics?" said Emma.

Dairmuid raised his eyebrows. "How could they be helped, dear lady? There might be Catholics in Parliament but there aren't enough to make a play for that."

"And will the children pay for the schooling?"

"It will be taken out of their wages if the factory owners are involved in provision, but otherwise they'll pay their school pence," said Dairmuid, sad to see Emma's frown deepening, and her father's warning hand on her arm.

Nathaniel had also noticed. "Well then, Mr Casey," he said. "I look forward to hearing your speech and seeing you again, perhaps in London?" He glanced over to the dais. "We should take our seats. I see General Palmer is preparing to open proceedings."

As they settled down and looked up expectantly at the Honourable Member for Bath, across the city in Saint James's Square a slim figure dressed in dark trousers and buttoned jerkin climbed over the wall of one of the houses backing onto the park. Dropping to its knees, the figure patted a black and tan terrier which had rushed over, growling and belligerent from its hiding place behind a tool shed. After a few pats and explanations, its tail commenced to wag and when a handful of meat was offered it was wolfed down. For a few moments they stayed together, the figure bent over the dog, whispering and stroking, until the creature's legs suddenly gave way and it collapsed to the ground. Just one last caress of the dog's head, then the figure crept soundlessly up the path, leapt up onto the wall and started a careful ascent of the climbing shrub which wound around the drainpipe and reached up to the bedrooms. The climbing ceased at the second floor, a knife flashed in the moonlight, silently, a window sash was pushed up and the figure disappeared inside the house.

Downstairs in the kitchen, Mrs Rollinson and Harriet were mending before the fire.

"Sounds like the wind's getting up," said Mrs Rollinson, pausing to re-thread her needle. "And I thought I heard Caradoc a few minutes back. Hunting again!"

She nodded sagely to herself. "He is a champion amongst dogs, and with a better temperament than most humans." She stuck the needle back into the linen with renewed ferocity. "And speaking of temperament, that Tobias Caudle had no business taking young Frances into town for that meeting."

"No, Missis. That he had not," said Harriet, her head down and her bottom lip

193

thrust out as she mechanically repaired a stocking.

"Did he ask you to go?" demanded Mrs Rollinson.

"No, he did not," said Harriet out loud, then mouthed a soundless, "More's the pity."

By the time the Guildhall speeches were over, the applause had died away and Captain Peterson and the Parrys were sauntering up Milsom Street, a bedroom in Saint James's Square bore traces of a thorough and successful search. Drawers and cupboards had been opened, their contents ruffled, then closed. Nightstands had been minutely investigated, and lastly the great wardrobe had been opened, the blankets moved aside and the strongbox taken to the bed.

Relieved by the sight of it, the burglar decided to risk a light. From a pocket came a pair of pliers and a small glass capsule. A sharp crack and the Promethean match hissed into life, illuminating the contents of the box. A hand darted in and drew out a string of faultless sapphires, the gold links winking in the dying flare of the match. Just one gasp of delight, then the prize was tucked into the breast of her jerkin. Totally unmoved by the possible consequences of the night's work; Coco Montrachet allowed herself a satisfied grin of triumph, replaced the box and stole out the way she had come. Down the pipe she went, across the garden, past the slumped figure of Caradoc and away across the park to her stable, where her carriage was waiting. For the second time within the month, she led out the team, checked the reins and then whipped up her four in hand towards the Exeter road.

# Chapter 8

**Early evening: 21st June, 1833. The Saint-Laurent to Pauillac road.**

Nathaniel's head was pounding and his eyes burned. He had not quite shaken off the low fever he had caught on the boat from London, though he had already been obliged to waste two days recuperating at General Palmer's mansion at Cenon. His genial host was in London with no immediate plans to leave, but had been pleased to equip Nathaniel with a letter of introduction and put the *château* at his disposal on learning of the plan to visit Bordeaux. The generous offer had been made in the Travellers' Club at three in the morning during one of Dairmuid's "famous nights".

"Feel free, dear boy!" Palmer had said, scribbling a note to his housekeeper in erratic French whilst Dairmuid, with super-human effort, successfully waved over a club servant.

"Just one more," he had managed to say, very deliberately. "Just one more. One more bottle of your excellent brandy, my very good man."

"National business, what!" General Palmer had continued, signing off with a flourish. "Pleased to be of service. Least I can do for a member of Lord Melbourne's staff and my constituent, by God! Privilege! Dashed coincidence meeting you here, my dear boy!"

Over the night, as well as agreeing with them on all questions of reform, denouncing their opponents, pulling the world by the ears and setting it to rights and, by way of a finale, encouraging Dairmuid to croon his way through a selection of Irish ballads, Nathaniel had managed to extract from them what he needed. He knew the details of their Irish contacts in the Medoc, had a full report of Dairmuid's last visit to the Bartons and had ascertained the exact whereabouts of Château Pèlerin, which turned out to be situated just outside a town by the name of Saint-Laurent. He had learned that it was the estate of that relatively new owner, Monsieur Jules Delgarde-Montrachet. He had also investigated Coco's alibi for the thefts at Arno's

195

Tower and learned just how little time Dairmuid had had for Coco when she was supposedly visiting him in London and attending the Epsom races at the time of the attack on Ravenswood's property.

After his talks with John Drake, Matthew Spence and Cornelius Lee, Nathaniel had been in no real doubt about the identity of the burglars at Arno's Tower, but the break-in at his home in Saint James's Square was less clear-cut. Supposedly, Coco had left Bath before the event, but the work had her hallmarks all over it. That she might be a sneak thief was no surprise and Frances had made an interesting connection, which could provide her with a possible motive. The maid had come up to their bedroom in some distress, not to attend to Emma, but to report that Tobias had just found Caradoc laid out in the garden. Frances had arrived moments after they had discovered that the sapphires were missing, as it was that very morning that Nathaniel had planned to go to the bank and deposit the best pieces of jewellery. When he had opened the strongbox, he had realised that he was too late. A cursory inspection of the windows overlooking the garden had provided all the evidence he needed of the burglar's progress.

"It's really strange," Frances had said. "Madam's necklace was so unusual, but last week I saw one that might have been its sister. I seen Miss Montrachet's brooch when she visited. Under her cloak collar it was: a miniature of a woman in a ball gown with a string of brilliants round her neck, mounted on a heavy chain just like Madam's. I never did see such a setting before." Frances had hesitated, biting her lip. "Such a coincidence, isn't it Madam, Miss Montrachet calling so often, and she has been in this room. Once she was left on her own whilst you called out for me. Do you recall, Madam?"

Emma had recalled and sent Frances away.

It had surprised him that Emma was not more enraged by the theft. The violation of their privacy had seemed to move her more than the material loss and after Frances had gone she had even tried to rationalise why Coco might have committed the crime. "Even people we think we know have secrets from us, Nathaniel," she had said. "We know nothing of her real circumstances. She cannot live on fresh air and her sources of income," she paused delicately. "Well, they might have run out. The gems are French and so is she." She shrugged resignedly. "And she's gone back for good, or so she said."

But Nathaniel was not reconciled to the loss of his mother's necklace, and the poisoning of Caradoc rankled. He had to admit that it had been better to find him out cold than with his throat cut, but the terrier had been in a poor way afterwards, vomiting steadily for days and was still dragging himself round, whining. So, it was for various reasons, not all of which he admitted even to himself, that Nathaniel resolved to leave for London, ascertain a few facts and try to pick up Coco's trail.

After the successful evening at the Travellers' he had taken a travel bag from Carlisle Lane and boarded the steam packet for Calais. It had proved to be a pleasant trip. The steam engines always reduced the incidence of sea-sickness and in the benign midsummer weather they also made excellent time. Within fourteen hours he had landed and was on the fast coach to Paris. On arrival he transferred to a hackney cab and made straight for the Quai de l' École and the *atelier* of Maison Bapst to see if he could nail the provenance of the sapphires.

Though the court jewellers had travelled a dark road during the 1790s, when it was a capital crime even to sympathise with aristocrats, never mind be one, it had re-emerged, formed a new partnership with the Ménière family and was thriving. Nathaniel was in luck as his outfit for the day and Parisian accent marked him out as a potential customer, the shop was not busy and the assistant had time to kill. He was taken to the workroom and introduced to an ancient man, bent and crabbed over his work, but he was also talkative, and remembered the old days very well. A glass of wine shared during his break, a perusal of Owen's sketches in the battered journal, and stories of the great collections began to flow. Yes, he remembered the interlocking "Ms" of the chain links favoured by the Montrachet family, and their bespoke suite of gems, from the hours he spent in a corner studying the pattern books as a boy. There had been necklaces, and much more, tiaras, ear-rings, bracelet cuffs and the brooches, what he could not tell of them! And there was silver plate. There was no time for that, but he had said enough.

Nathaniel had travelled through the night to the coast and boarded a merchant ship leaving for Bordeaux. The journey could not match the Channel crossing on the steam packet for smoothness, and proved to be exhausting. Not one fellow traveller was sorry when they reached the smooth waters of the Gironde Estuary and made their way to the Bordeaux quays. On arrival he had left the city centre behind and travelled to Cenon where he found the mansion of General Palmer, built on a commanding ridge above the river valley. Though much of the house was closed up, there was a handful of permanent staff and the housekeeper had helped him weather the worst of the fever that had tightened its grip on him even before he left the ship. He had also needed the time to tune his ear to the local dialect. His Parisian French had been fluent since childhood, but in most of the provinces he might just as well have broken out in Greek. He had learned passable Gascon, Basque and Spanish from his father and, combined, they gave him the tools to cope with the assortment of Bordelaise servants: the housekeeper, maids and outdoor staff.

As soon as he was able, he made ready to track Coco down. The odds on retrieving any of the stolen goods were low and he was no longer feeling particularly lucky, but he did feel driven to reach some sort of conclusion, some closure, and perhaps it was not all to do with what was lost. He felt too ill to delve into his motives more deeply. He had risen before dawn, been pleased to find himself steadier on his feet, dressed as a gentleman, complete with swordstick, borrowed General Palmer's new *Stanhope* from the stables and driven down to the river to take the ferry to Lamarque. Though the gig had handled well, the General's stallion had not proved to be a good sailor and despite the break at the port, he was skittish and the journey had been heavier work than it needed to be. Once they had passed through Saint-Laurent, Nathaniel pulled on the reins and brought the gig to a halt. Despite the scorching heat of the last few days, the drainage ditch by the roadside was still brimming with water so he loosened the harness, led the horse down the bank to drink and sat down beside him on the grass verge.

The lines of grape vines, decked with blossom and alive with bees, stretched out on either side of the deserted road, their symmetry relieved only by occasional clumps of trees and on the horizon, a low stone tower. On its dome perched a bird, a smudge of black behind the heat haze. Sweating in the heat but with a shaking hand, he fumbled in his pocket for his flask and drank some of the wine, tepid now and souring; not a good choice. Too late he realised that he should have brought some laudanum but he had left his stock behind in his travel bag at Cenon. He shook his head to clear it but the world swam around him. Slowly, he brought himself to his knees and after a moment's pause, was back on his feet. He harnessed the horse and pulled himself up into the driver's seat.

Within the quarter hour he had come upon a newly painted sign announcing the boundary of the estate of Château Pèlerin, passed its fields of vines and was approaching the high stone wall surrounding the mansion, which basked serenely in the sunshine beyond the open gate, surrounded by dusty trees. A flight of steps led up to the balustraded terrace that ran across the front of a single-storied building. Two slate-roofed wings rose at either end, both dilapidated and one half-smothered in ivy. Away to the right was a farmyard, an abandoned cart standing at its entrance. Nathaniel pulled up the horse and became aware that he was observed. A young woman dressed in black with two small children at her skirt, was standing behind the balustrade watching him. He managed to climb down from the carriage and make his way unsteadily to within hailing distance of her, but it was as far as he got. His legs buckled beneath him, the house and sky slewed round above his head and the ground rushed up.

**The Parry Residence, Saint James's Square, Bath.**

It was early that morning when they had first missed Tobias. Mrs Rollinson had started by stamping around the kitchen as she prepared breakfast, periodically shouting for him to come to the table and taking out his non-appearance on the porridge pot which she had commenced to stir with the brutal energy of a steam engine.

"Though," she said, above the drumming of the spoon and at a theatrical volume in order to annoy Frances, "I suppose he's no better than he should be, seeing as what he is. He should never be going out and taking drink on a Thursday night. I wouldn't have allowed it if I'd been Madam. Slack, that's what it is. There's a duty to the young and foolish," she continued relentlessly, casting a meaningful and venomous glance to the door leading to his room, which remained stubbornly closed. "If they are not taught the error of their ways they will soon be doing the devil's work! Mark my words."

By half-past six, with all other staff breakfasts eaten and cleared away, it had been Harriet's task to beat on his door. She got no response and when she finally summoned enough courage to push it open, she discovered a bed as smooth as a flat iron and the day's clean linen, folded and ready on his bedside chair.

Emma first heard of his disappearance as she pulled herself up in bed to greet Frances but instead of chirruping round the room, opening the curtains and laying out her clothes, the girl had remained at the door, wide-eyed and tear stained.

"Oh, Madam!" she blurted out, choking down a sob. "Tobias has disappeared and Mrs Rollinson's fit to murder him when she catches hold of him!"

Oddly, and she was ashamed to realise the truth of it, the shock of the news brought some relief to Emma and energised her. It was something new to think about. Since Nathaniel had left for France she had felt oppressed, as if a band had tightened around her heart. She had thought that her old jealousy of Coco was dead and buried, but it had just been sleeping. Now it was awake, tightening its coils and preparing to crush the life out of her. The new friendship between them, which she had foolishly encouraged, she now saw as a sham, and it seemed more plausible for that.

At first, the bizarre possibility that Coco had been involved in the burglary then migrated to France for good had been of some comfort. It stood to reason that anyone using Caradoc cruelly, then violating their home and stealing precious memories of his mother, should be unforgivable in Nathaniel's eyes. Let it have been her! Emma could put that misdemeanour to great use in her campaign to neutralise the threat from Coco. But later, after he left, and of course returning ten-fold in the darkness of the night, she had realized the danger. Though she had never visited the Medoc or the city of Bordeaux, she could read and she could imagine. And in that dream of heat, of wine and soft air, of lapping waters and sandy lakes, what spell could not be cast by a woman like Coco?

Why had she ever allowed him to go without her?

How often had she resolved to be with him whenever she could?

But she did know, deep down she knew. She had not wanted to see their eyes meet, had not wanted to see their reconciliation and endure the forgiveness. And now he was far away, pursuing the beautiful, the dazzling Colette Montrachet. Oh, she could imagine the lakes, the lazy rivers and roaring seas. She could drown in them.

So, fired with new purpose, she had dressed quickly and swept down to the kitchen with Frances in tow to check the facts and make a plan. But her moment of sublime control was short lived, for even as Mrs Rollinson was denouncing Tobias for the feckless young scoundrel that he was, simultaneously reducing Harriet to a cowering jelly by the fire and Frances to wringing her hands ever tighter in misery, events had overtaken them. Police officers had arrived, officious, grim faced and in possession of a search warrant.

The rest of the morning had been both miserable and disturbing. Tobias's room was searched because he had been followed whilst hawking unstamped papers around the town the previous night, and he had been arrested outside the George and Dragon. They were not burdened by the officers of the law for long as it took less than ten minutes for brown paper packages to be discovered beneath his mattress. They had proved to contain not only copies of Hetherington's *Poor Man's Guardian* and *The Destructive*, which brazenly advertised that it was published *"contrary to the law of the land"* but also, beneath those copies, a stock of the notorious Richard Carlile's republican rag: *The Gauntlet*. The victorious search party took itself off to Grove Street police station, complete with the incriminating evidence, leaving Emma free to send word to her father. Captain Peterson had acted swiftly, first taking both Emma and Frances to Grove Street to visit Tobias, then insisting that Emma come home to luncheon.

"Obviously you must dismiss the boy," said Lydia Peterson, opening the conversation disapprovingly as soon as desserts had been finished and the twins had been banished to their music practice. "Really, Emma, I do not know why Nathaniel was so generous to him in the first place. There are respectable young people seeking domestic employment, one does not need to resort to urchins like Tobias Caudle. And, I might add, as he has now shown himself to be dishonest, I hope you are considering the possibility that he might have been the thief who took your jewellery?"

Emma made sure she paused before answering, folded her hands and reined in her temper. To lose control was to lose the bout, but her mother was no ordinary opponent. She had made it a career choice to be uniquely infuriating and was an expert in the field.

"I will not be dismissing him." Emma managed to reply calmly, holding steady eye contact. "And there is no question of him having been involved in the theft. Please do not suggest that again, Mama. Nathaniel has spent considerable time training Tobias and he is fond of him, as am I. If you remember the poor boy was sleeping at the back of the stable at the White Hart when Nathaniel first employed him. He was an illiterate orphan with no one in the world to care for him. He has positively blossomed over the last few months and …"

"And this is how he repays his master!" cut in Lydia triumphantly. "Breaking the law, deceiving you and using his new talents to acquaint himself with treason! Anyone reading such publications should be ashamed of themselves. And not satisfied with corrupting himself he was seeking to spread the contagion to others!"

First blood: Lydia one, Emma nil.

"He is young and he has offended us by breaking the law," replied Emma, regretting making the emotional appeal, which had clearly been a poor move. "But I cannot see that helping poor people to read the news is so very bad if it helps them to understand how their country is run and how they can help themselves, through their unions and on their own. They can become better subjects by reading. In my view spreading information can be seen as a noble cause."

"But surely," said Lydia, as sweetly as she could, as she had seen the warning signs. The umpire was becoming restive. Her husband's bushy brows had drawn together, preparing to call time. He was unlikely to leave her uninterrupted for long. "Surely, my dear, you see that the material he was trying to sell is seditious. *The Destructive* if you please! Also, a publication rejoicing in the title: *The Gauntlet*! I have read of it in my newspaper. It is against the King, it is republican! Its very title is a crude challenge and a call to arms. It is seeking revolution and Richard Carlile is an evil man. Isn't he otherwise known as 'The Devil's Chaplain'?" she said with a shudder.

"I really have no idea, Mama!" said Emma, successfully hiding the fact that she had a very clear idea indeed after nipping into Madame Junot's schoolroom before luncheon and exchanging a few hurried words. And she hoped to be even better informed after reading the dog-eared journal edited by Carlile's notorious mistress

Eliza Sharples, which the French governess had slipped inside a poetry book and pressed into her hands.

"I have not researched Mr Carlile, or his ideas."

And she had not, at least not yet.

"And I do not think Tobias has either. He was trying to sell *The Poor Man's Guardian* and he did not know that *The Gauntlet* was included in the batch. It was crucial for the working men to know the latest about the new law for short time working in the cotton mills. He was doing it as a favour to his friends. They were being watched, and they were family men. They could not risk prison."

"And neither should he have," said Lydia bitterly. "The shame of it! Having one of your own staff in the hands of the law!"

"It is unlikely that he will be imprisoned on a first offence if his fine is paid," said her husband, trying his best to fix his two volatile women with a masterful glare. It really played gip with his digestion to have dispute at the table, though at least they had had the grace to wait until he had cleared his plate. "Hundreds have been imprisoned in London it is true, but I have some influence here and I will ensure he avoids gaol."

Emma flashed a grateful smile to him. She felt flustered and had lost count of the score but felt certain that Lydia had been pulled back to a draw.

"I gather that a man called Mr Lovett has set up a Victim Fund in London, Father," said Emma. "Five shillings a week is provided for the prisoner and his family during his sentence. Though I think most of those selling are boys like Tobias, or young men in their twenties with no families to care for. They are like soldiers in their way. It is called a war, a war of the unstamped press! Are there others arrested here like poor Tobias? We could do with a fund in Bath."

"Fund! Fiddlesticks!" exploded Lydia. "The publishers should pay their stamp duty as their respectable colleagues do. That is the law."

"My dear," said Oliver Peterson, putting a restraining hand on her arm in an effort to distract her. "If they did, no poor person could afford to buy the papers. If they are more than a penny they are out of reach, which was the intention of the government when they raised the tax in the first place. And I must say that public opinion seems to be moving in favour of a repeal of the duty. I don't think the Whigs will be long before they support a change in the law."

"Do I sense that you are applauding the movement, Oliver," said Lydia, twitching her arm away. "As a magistrate you must uphold the law."

"I have every intention of doing so, my dear," said Oliver firmly.

"You know what it says on *The Poor Man's Guardian* Mama?" said Emma.

202

"Knowledge is power. And a symbol the reformers use is the beehive to represent the workers. Poor men and women should understand the world they labour in."

"They labour," said Lydia tartly, stung by Emma's attempt to instruct her, "on the instructions and in the establishments of their betters. Look to France, young lady. Can you see the destruction that comes from letting the masses rise? Well, can you?"

"One day, when the poor are educated and wiser they should be allowed to vote. Mama, you must have looked at the papers this week! The new Factory Act states that child workers in the cotton factories will have compulsory instruction each day."

"They will be able to follow instructions more easily, my dear," said Oliver. "That will enable them to keep pace with the demands of working with the new machines. They will hardly be equipped to vote."

Lydia had tired of the discussion. Her husband's interest in politics was understandable, especially now that he was a magistrate, but her daughter's enthusiasm was simply bewildering, as well as being unedifying in the extreme.

"Perhaps it is better to wait until Nathaniel returns before making a decision about the boy," she said. "No doubt he will know absolutely the right thing to do. When is he returning home?"

Emma looked hard at her mother. She and Nathaniel had agreed that no one would know about his journey to France, not even her father, until he was back with some answers.

"No date as yet, Mama."

At least Nathaniel's line of work closed down idle enquiries. Lydia had to leave it at that, sensing a defeat on points but lacking the resolve to slug it out to another round.

"Well," she said, as she rose, exasperated, from the table. "At least take our footman for the afternoon, he can help in Saint James's Square whilst you are operating with a reduced staff." She raised her head, conscious of the nobility of her generous offer, and as a final touch to reinforce her image as martyr added. "I shall now listen to Maddy and Ginette's scales." With an acidic parting smile for her daughter, she swept out and Emma was left with her father.

"Come into my study, my dear," he said, kindly, as he led her out. "I'll have some coffee brought in for us."

Once safe in his den with the door closed, Emma relaxed.

"Do you think Tobias will be released on bail, Papa?"

"He could be. But it might be wise to leave the young rip to stew for a few days: for his own good, you understand. Nathaniel can pay the inevitable fine, since he is so attached to him. But be prepared for young Caudle to have to endure a few hours in the stocks."

"Must he, Papa?"

"I'm afraid so. The borough justices will take a dim view of him supplying Carlile's blasphemous scribbling. They won't want to be seen as lax in their duties, my dear."

Emma's face clouded with concern, she had seen the victims often enough, exposed for all to abuse in Orange Grove, humiliated and showered with missiles, rotten vegetables and dead cats if they were lucky, stones if they were not. At least the pillory was not used as freely as in the past, but she had seen men stripped to the waist and flogged until they were bloody, and once when she was a small child, a woman too, screaming, cursing and terrified.

"Papa, Tobias looked so afraid and so alone. I want to see him again, take him something."

"Take him some food, and a change of clothes. But do not stay long. He needs to be left alone. It will concentrate the mind," said Oliver. "Let him learn a lesson early, Emma. It is right for young men to be passionate and reckless, but they must learn to temper their recklessness or they will become men without judgement who are dangerous to everyone about them."

She heard and she understood, but as she sat quietly she was nurturing the beginnings of a plan.

"I agree with you. May I take up Mama's offer of the loan of your footman? He can escort me to Grove Street."

### Morning: 22nd June, 1833. Château Pèlerin, Saint-Laurent, France.

Nathaniel had been aware that he had been lifted, his head raised from the white dust of the drive and his body carried by at least three men, up steps, through a dark doorway and into the *château*. Deciding it was a wise move, he had allowed his removal to take its course, kept his eyes virtually closed and his body relaxed. He had achieved an entry to the house and attracted a degree of sympathy, or so it appeared. It was more than he had expected.

"Take him to the drawing room. Put him on the *chaise longue*."

A man's voice: rough edges, but a proprietorial one, probably the brother.

"Bring a basin of water and a cloth."

A woman, a lady: perhaps the one watching his arrival from the balustrade.

"And bring some wine," she commanded. "Go now! Hurry!"

Pattering steps receded.

His memories of the evening were sketchy. He had managed to produce his card and offer some garbled apologies for the imposition of his presence. As he had gained strength and sat up in the chair, drinking his wine, he had put in place a barricade of contacts which could prevent the brother from murdering him in his sleep. Heavy names were dropped: General Palmer, friend and host, whose staff, even now, were aware of his destination and anticipating his return to Cenon; Monsieur Barton and his partner, Baron Guestier, and closer still, their mutual friend Dairmuid Casey, Member of Parliament and close confident of Mademoiselle Colette Montrachet, to whom Nathaniel wished most earnestly to pay his respects, which was the sole purpose of his unannounced visit. It had been enough. He had been helped to a bedroom, where, once assured that his horse and gig were stabled, he allowed himself to fall into a deep sleep.

On waking he found himself in a plain white room, the darkness pierced only by dazzling needles of white light shafting through the fixings of the shutters. Heavy mahogany furniture roosted anonymously in the shadowy corners, but on the wall facing him, a metallic shimmer flashed off a brass crucifix which rose up, starkly erect, above a wooden *prie-dieu*. He dressed quickly, checking his pockets: money, watch, some personal papers, all there, even his hat and swordstick were on a chair by the door. So far, apart from the fever, it could not have gone better, but he was under no illusions. If Coco, her brother and some of his men had risked their lives and reputations for the attack on Ravenswood's home, then he was by no means in safe hands. He slipped out onto the corridor to search for his hosts, but it was Coco he found. Rounding the corner, she came to an abrupt halt at the sight of him, stock-still and radiant in a pale blue gown, her lips parted in surprise, her body framed in a glowing nimbus of gold by the morning light streaming in behind her.

"Nathaniel," she said, a catch in her breath, running lightly to him, arms wide. "Have you recovered? What a wonderful surprise to find you here last night!"

In a moment she was pressed against him, kissing him a welcome, smiling into his eyes. He could not help but smile back. Blame it on the fever, the heat or her beguiling smile, he took her in his arms and kissed her again, and not in welcome.

"Coco, we need to talk," he said, pulling away.

"I am so much looking forward to it," she said, too quickly. "I could not believe it when I came home to hear that you were laid-up in the guest room. How extraordinary of you to turn up here like this! But come to meet my brother and his family. Have breakfast then he can show you the vineyard. He is very proud of it."

The hot day slipped through his hands like sand. First breakfast, where he got nothing out of the massive and taciturn Jules, engaged in polite conversation with

Claudette, managed to make her smile and successfully amused the pair of chattering children. For the rest of the morning he was marched round the estate by Jules who had moved on to a transparent assessment of his level of threat, which after Nathaniel's sustained charm offensive he seemed to rate as low. The heat and brilliant sunlight had lifted his mood, but as he felt physically better he felt even more frustrated in his purpose. Jules introduced him to a gang of labourers, the leader of which was a man called Pierre who was built on similar lines to Jules, powerful and heavily muscled as a carthorse, but with a touch of melancholy about him which made him even less amenable to small talk. According to both of them, they had never been to Britain and knew nothing of Bath. Their words told him about the vines, the wine and the *terroir* whilst their battered faces and Pierre's cauliflower ears spoke of other enthusiasms. At the lengthy luncheon Coco managed to be evasive, express proper regret concerning the Ravenswood's misfortunes and act out a pretty show of surprise and sorrow when she heard of the burglary at Saint James's Square. Luncheon was followed by a *siesta* which engulfed the afternoon, but on the plus side, after swallowing a draft of Claudette's own narcotic remedy, Nathaniel slept off much of the remains of the fever. This was even more fortunate than it might have been, as the early evening required him to accompany Jules and Pierre to their next fight at Fort Medoc.

The three of them climbed into the farm wagon and set off down the dirt track to the old fort, Jules and Pierre in the front, Nathaniel behind and able to keep an eye on them, which he preferred. Lit by the moon and stars, and to their left, the distant glimmer of the Gironde, they rode through the velvet midsummer night. If the occasion had been different Nathaniel would have been enjoying himself. The perfumed air was alive with the soft burr of the cicadas and the swooping flutter of bats' wings. Once or twice a pair of bright, feral eyes burned out at them from the undergrowth of a copse in answer to their swinging lamp.

"Pierre is our champion tonight," said Jules over his shoulder as he flicked the whip over the horse's head. "We have a team and we are fighting men from over the river, from Blaye, but there's room for strangers as well. You might like to join in." Nathaniel could sense his crafty smile; saw the wink exchanged with Pierre as the words were left to lie.

"Do you think so, Monsieur?" he said.

"I am sure of it," replied Jules.

They crossed the shallow moat and entered the fort through a great triumphal arch.

"What is this place?" asked Nathaniel, looking up at the stone face of the sun below the pediment, its carved white rays of greeting picked out by the moonlight.

"It was one of Louis XIV's forts," said Jules. "This is *le porte royale* just in case the Sun King ever paid a visit, but of course, he never did."

They passed through the tunnel of the entrance below the guard-house and emerged into a vast square surrounded by low buildings, some derelict and few with lights burning. Ahead, in the dark and fronting on the river, Nathaniel could make out the back of the cannon emplacements. Closer to the gate there was a makeshift ring marked out in the centre of the parade ground and a small crowd milled around it: otherwise the place was echoing and deserted.

"How many soldiers are based here?"

"Just a couple of dozen now," said Jules. "Marshal Vaubon built it to guard the estuary and the route to Bordeaux but the cannon have never been fired in anger. After the defeat of the Emperor the place was more or less given up. The men have nothing to do except survive their posting, do a bit of training and scratch their arses. I rent out some storage space in some of the empty buildings, sell them wine, on reasonable terms of course, and organise our little sessions of *savate.*"

It was then that Nathaniel realised what he was in for. It was not to be sticks, swords or a bout of prize fighting with men's rules, but a free for all. *Savate*, the street fighting of Marseilles, was more suited to Cornelius's fighting style than his own. It had the makings of a difficult night.

Their wagon was taken to the stables and they joined the crowd of soldiers and local men by the roped-off ring. A lean, swarthy man advanced on them, his lined face pock-marked, his jacket off and shirt sweat-stained, but with his sword buckled by his side and an aura of authority.

"*Ici le Chef!*" announced Jules delightedly. "Monsieur Parry, here is the Commander-in-chief, Colonel Lesparre, who so graciously provides us with a venue for our little shows."

Introductions made, they pushed their way to the front and the fighting began almost immediately, giving Nathaniel some thinking time. Jules obviously had a nice little deal going on with the Colonel. Assuming he was involved in smuggling, as virtually all sailors and fishermen he had ever known were, he would have a convenient storehouse here, well away from his own property with no questions asked. From the state of the soldiers and the barracks he guessed that Paris would have only the vaguest notion that this place existed and left the skeleton staff to its own devices. This was a place you could easily die in and leave not one trace behind.

The first bout was innocent enough, a lengthy brawl between two youths, farm boys with their forearms scarred from the crops, short lads, but rock˙hard and sinewy. What they lacked in finesse they made up for in speed and audacity, raining down indiscriminate punches and kicks on each other with their horn-hard hands and rough-booted feet until one caught a blow full in the face and was dragged out of the ring insensible. Betting was proceeding freely at a trestle table, and next to it sat Colonel Lesparre, enthroned on an armchair, worm-eaten, but high-backed and elaborately carved. Jules was on a seat by him and it was clear they were fast friends, sharing jokes at the expense of the fighters and the platoon. Nathaniel stayed on his feet, weighing his options. Generally the mood was good and as the night progressed some of the soldiers brought out fiddles and others sang to while away the pauses between bouts. Nathaniel moved over to stand by Jules and the Colonel.

"A pleasant spot, Colonel," he said. "Did you live here before you took this post?"

"I'm from the Pyrenees, born and bred. But this billet could be worse," said the Colonel suspiciously. "Jules tells me that you have travelled from England and are visiting his sister. Beautiful woman, beguiling, no? *Très belle!* I also hear you have other interests; maybe you would like to try your luck against one of the men here. You think you are their equal perhaps, maybe their superior, Englishman?"

"I am not English, Colonel," said Nathaniel quietly, changing to Euskara, the language of the Basques. He was pleased to see a change in the Colonel's face, a dawning of greater respect. "I am Welsh, perhaps you, who are from *Euskal Herria* know the importance of such a difference?"

The Colonel bowed his head briefly, his eyes never leaving Nathaniel's.

"And I would not presume to spar with an expert *tireur*," continued Nathaniel. "I have not the skill. It would be an insult."

Quiet had descended on the crowd as they heard the pure Basque replace the faultless French. The stranger was of interest and they gathered for the spectacle.

"Perhaps you would like to test your weapons skill?" suggested Colonel Lesparre, his eyes now gleaming with malice. "*Canne de combat* perhaps?"

He spotted a soldier loafing by the storehouse at the back of the crowd. "Bring a stick for the visitor!" he shouted and then turned to Nathaniel. "Are you a swordsman, Monsieur? Jules told me you had served in the military, so you could regard a bout with the sticks as a little light sabre training."

Nathaniel bowed and took hold of the wooden stick. It was heavy, but with good balance and a basket hilt. He swung it round in his right hand and whistled it through the air. This was safer ground, as he was no stranger to practising with sticks. His father had encouraged him to train with a makila when the stick was taller than he

208

was and if all else failed he could take it in both hands and use it as a quarter-staff. Nathaniel threw two gold napoleons on the table.

"I accept with pleasure. My own stake, winner takes all," he said.

After a hurried huddling of the men, shuffling of feet and searching of pockets, a lieutenant stepped forward into the ring, his hands cupping a mound of silver which he threw down on the table.

"A match for you, stranger."

The man's upper body was bare except for his braces, greasy with sweat and smeared in dust, as were his raw-boned calloused hands, and his chin, blue-grey with dirt and two days' growth.

"Shirt off," commanded the Colonel. "It will be easier to count the hits if you run to a draw."

Nathaniel unbuttoned his shirt and hung it on the back of Jules's chair. He was ready, one slight knee flex, then totally still, waiting, watching. He needed to finish it quickly but with maximum spectacle, as he was still weak from the fever and lacked stamina. His opponent had the best part of a bottle of brandy inside him and expected to bludgeon him to his knees, first blood within two minutes and then back to the unfinished bottle.

He allowed the man first swing and side-stepped, no point losing his strength too early. Then the second, another and another, Nathaniel danced round him lightly, driving him to fury. The man let out a bellow and hewed forward again. Nathaniel side-stepped again, then parried with all his strength. The man stumbled, almost toppling over, but recovered and hacked forward. Nathaniel countered five blows and on the sixth deftly turned his weapon, flicking the lieutenant's stick out of his hands to bounce away over the dirt to the feet of the audience. In two strides he was on his man, the stick across his throat and the crowd in a roar.

Nathaniel stepped back to bow but as he did so the lieutenant rushed forward, his face flushed and working in fury.

"Come on," he yelled, out of control. "Let's see what else you are made of, Welshman!"

Jules and Pierre exchanged glances. The heavy names the stranger had dropped still rang in Jules's ears. He half stood, nudging the Colonel and whispering in his ear, when to his surprise Nathaniel caught the soldier's blow even as it cannoned towards him, wrenching the arm back and flooring the man in a tearing arm lock. Nathaniel released him, but the fight was still just about in him. The man lunged again and Nathaniel stopped him with a right hook, landing it square on the man's cheek and followed through with a left-handed undercut to the jaw, scouring his

209

throat on the way. Fighting for breath and spitting blood, the man doubled-over and sank to the ground. His friends rushed out, took him by the underarms and dragged him away.

Nathaniel looked round the ring, holding the men's eyes. "I look forward to the rest of the bouts. My stake and his go towards the rest of tonight's brandy."

The acclaim echoed round the barrack square, a chair was brought and as Pierre took to the ring, Nathaniel took his seat by Jules and Colonel Lesparre. He had survived the test, but as yet, with the prospect of, at most, one more day before he had to leave, that might be the sum of his achievement.

**Late afternoon: 23rd June, 1833, the Eve of the Feast of Saint John. The road to Carcan, the Medoc, France.**

"Coco, I need to leave tomorrow."

"I know."

Nathaniel rode alongside her as they made their way to the lake through the marshes and sheep pasture that lay between the vineyards of the estuary and the ocean dunes. The burning heat of the day had slackened and was now languorous and heavy with the scents of summer. Wild ponies grazed undisturbed, giddy midges hung in clouds by the small clumps of trees and, on the horizon, he had caught sight of a shepherd, raised high on his stilts above the plain, resting, triangulated on his crook, like a painter raised on his easel.

Today he had stayed, and she had insisted that it was necessary to ride out to the water.

"We shall be *en fête*, Nathaniel," she had smiled. "The fires have to be lit, and the best place is by a lake."

"The fires?" he had enquired. He had lived in cities for too long.

"It is the Eve of the Feast of Saint John! What were you thinking of in church when you should have been listening to the priest?" she had laughed. "We must light the fires of purification!"

She had stood before him in men's breeches and boots, with an open-necked white shirt like a farm boy's, her skin golden-brown, her hair plaited down her back. Before leaving, she had slung a bag over the pommel of her saddle.

"We've got bread, some cheese, a flagon of wine and a cake, and I have the herbs and flowers. It's what we have to do," she had said.

That morning, under a sky of cerulean blue and past the ranks of flower-decked vines, he had driven into town with the family to attend Mass, retracing his journey along the Saint-Laurent to Pauillac road until they reached the crumbling church of

210

Saint Laurentus, which squatted uncertainly in the centre of town. Claudette said it had stood there since the twelfth century and it crossed Nathaniel's mind that the stones thought it was long enough. They looked ready to subside back into the earth from whence they came, though the carved gargoyles still clung gamely to the walls, to watch and to warn.

Crossing from the white glare of the town square into the shadowy nave, they had passed through the arched doorway under the eyes of a line of stone heads. Nathaniel had returned their gaze as he walked beneath them, and realised he was looking into the eyes of the seven deadly sins personified; each capital vice was featured above the door; each vice a corruption of a natural passion. He sat in the pew, sunk in thought. What was life but a search for balance, a walk along a tight rope between vice and virtue? Each reflected the other, was its alter ego, so knowledge of each must be equally necessary. The seven provided an allegory of the human heart. Take self-hood and ambition, both so necessary for survival, they exist also in corrupted forms as hubris and selfishness. Our bodily needs, our appetites, also necessary for life and bringing such pleasure, when indulged to excess brought degenerate addiction. He had continued to think idly of such things during the priest's address, most of which he had managed to filter out, including, so it seemed, all the pious recollections of the saintly John and his works. His mind had wandered to thoughts of Cornelius and his Taoism, of balance and harmony, of the rich duality of life, the inter-connectedness of good and evil, of God and of Lucifer, his fallen angel.

And he had looked at Coco. He remembered his first sighting of her in Bath, two years back or so, once in the Pump Room, on Dairmuid's arm, with her knowing smile, her brown eyes shining gold, her skin like almond milk. Then he revived an image of her mourning her murdered lover in the Abbey; her customer, the lost ticket to a life of ease. She had been a friend, a reliable one, and he remembered too that once, for a few hours, she had been something more. There was pride in her for certain, but never wrath or sloth. And the sins of desire and appetite? Lust, envy, greed and gluttony? He watched her breast rise as she breathed, the white fichou softening her neckline, auburn curls escaping her bonnet and glinting in the coloured lights of the stained-glass windows. Her whoring was a means to an end, a practical solution to social and financial needs, but there was still a joy in her for lovemaking. If she was his thief, he could not believe it was just for naked greed. There would have been another reason. There was a feral and reckless love of life in Coco, like the wild eyes that burned from the thicket in last night's twilight.

All this Nathaniel recalled as they rode together through the golden afternoon

211

and his heart was heavy. Oddly depressed by the necessity for him to break the spell of the day and speak of thieving, deceit and betrayal, he had put off the inevitable, but it could be evaded no longer. He brought his mind back into focus and listened again to Coco's chatter.

"Jules said there is often a gathering tonight by the Hospitallers' Commanderie at Benon. The villagers light their fire by the stream and dance through the night. But we are going to the lake. There is said to be stronger magic there, and the odd prowling wolf," she said, her eyes alive with mischief. "We shall have our own celebration, we two."

Nathaniel made no answer, so she continued. "You must have Saint John's fires in England. Though I must say I never heard of them in Bath."

"No," he answered abruptly. "You wouldn't see them in the towns. In the villages they have the fires still. The people jump over them for luck and some roll flaming cartwheels downhill to the streams. The longer the flames last, the longer the luck and the better the fruit." He shrugged his shoulders and then turned to her, his eyes searching her face. "So Coco, have we had enough of this? Have we exhausted our reasons for the ride? I need some answers about burglaries before I return to England."

She looked over to him but barely heard his words. The preliminaries were over, he had tired of the sport and moved to the end game, but it did not seem to matter any more. She felt a sudden rush of longing, more ambushed by desire than anything he had said. She turned her gold-flecked eyes on him hungrily. Nathaniel rode as he walked, with an easy elegance and dishevelled glamour. His shoulder-length black hair, blue-black as a raven, was pushed back from his eyes by a broad-brimmed hat he had borrowed from Jules. Unusually, a light tan lit his pale skin, which further accentuated the brilliant blue of his eyes, watchful and more grave than usual, but looking as always into her soul. Her breath came faster and she felt her heart pound.

"I have made some enquiries about a certain set of family jewels, made by Maison Bapst before the Revolution. They were unmistakable; the gems were set in heavy gold with the family initial repeated in the double chains. The makers' mark tallied exactly with the string of sapphires I knew as the property of my mother, a gift to her from my father when I was a small boy. They came as prize money from a cache of jewels and he gave them as a symbol of their love and his safe return from the wars. In their present life they are a gift from me to my wife, to Emma, your friend."

He paused, watching her. She rode by his side, silent and expressionless, but now she was listening.

"My father's prize also included gold coins. The jewels and the money were all taken from the Emperor's stores towards the end of the war. Now, I think you know that the jewels were not the only losses suffered by the family who had commissioned their making. Their property was confiscated during the early stages of the Revolution and the senior members of the family were executed. Very unjust wasn't it, Coco? Very sad for the Montrachet family. You share their name, don't you? You might even think you should share more than that."

She looked him full in the face, defiant, and achingly beautiful.

"Officially, I admit nothing, Nathaniel, and explain nothing. I am no fool. But yes, together as we are now, whilst we are on the road and alone, we can speak of injustices; they suffered the same fate as many other great families. Only a few scraps are left to mark the passing of my grandparents. Yes, my own grandparents, I share more than a name. There is no doubt. I remember my father and my mother, and all their stories. We were close, Nathaniel."

Just for a moment, she lowered her eyes, hesitated, then ploughed on. It was the time for confidences.

"All I had left was a brooch. It is a miniature of my *grandmere*."

She felt, without looking, for the familiar metal rim beneath her collar and turned it to him.

"When I was last in Paris, in 1828, I was with Émile, the Marquis de la Blanquefort at the Palais Royale. We were dining at Le Grand Véfour in the company of a Duchess, Madame Junot. It was an important night, politicians were there, and foreign diplomats. That night she helped me find the start of the trail which eventually led to my discovery. Later, I found it was the Ravenswoods who owned the Montrachet emeralds. Whether they were stolen or purchased was irrelevant to me. Do you understand at all, Nathaniel? I wanted to retrieve something of my life which had been lost. It became an obsession or a pilgrimage perhaps." At this she had the grace to laugh at herself.

"I left Paris, followed them first to Ireland and then to the south-west of England, but the trail went cold. I settled in Bath until I could track them down. It was later that I found out about your sapphires."

The intelligence he had travelled to discover now seemed of little worth. His eyes had lit up as he was transported back to Paris. He saw before him the crowded restaurant, and his father.

"Coco, I was there! I met the Marquis de la Blanquefort. I was at the table with the ministers, and then I stayed on with the *literati*. I knew Hugo from an earlier visit."

He took off his hat, rubbed his eyes and ran his hand through his hair, a despairing gesture.

"It was the week my father died."

He was unable to say more and she was unwilling to disturb him, so for a further mile, they let their horses find their own way along the path, hooves padding softly in the sandy earth. They passed a small farm, wooden and white-washed with its sheep-fold thatched and its hen-houses built tall enough to escape the attentions of nimble foxes. Before one wooded corner, the tinkling of sheep bells warned them of an approaching flock, which poured onto the path before them, driven by a boy and his dog. They let the woolly flood surge round them and then ambled on.

"I have no interest in fighting Edwin Ravenswood's battles for him," said Nathaniel when they were alone once again on the track. "And I do not want to take from you anything which is rightfully yours. But you might be able to help me. The jewels and the gold were not the only things taken from Napoleon's carts the night my father led the raid. There was also a stock of treasures looted from Egypt. One item is a matter of some importance, a necklace of gems bearing a representation of the falcon headed god, Horus. You wouldn't know anything about that, would you?"

Coco pursed her lips. "Unfortunately not. It sounds like a trinket I would enjoy owning. I did go into Ravenswood's private suite but I was in a rush and only had chance to look in one cupboard. I took one handful of bits and pieces, a dagger and a few coins, gold napoleons. *C'est tout.*"

"I have some too," said Nathaniel, "my father's."

They rode on, the silence now easy and companionable; she stole a glance at him.

"How is Emma?" she asked. "I do like her and I see why you do. She is unusual."

"So are you."

She put her head to one side, and smiled, half to herself.

"I love her, Coco. I have married her." He looked at her and paused as if seeking affirmation. "She is my *Bright Star.*"

"You are a Romantic, Nathaniel," said Coco with a laugh. "But never mind Keats, what about Shelley? Have you heard his views on having only one love, one mistress or one friend? He could not understand why it should be necessary to forsake all others to "*commend to cold oblivion*" someone you care for. The cruelty of it! How can love be only for one? There are many loves. You must know what Shelley said: "*to divide is not to take away*". And speaking of loves, I have met Émile again, Nathaniel. He has started to build a new house at Blanquefort. He has such plans. The landscaping will be a fantasy of grottoes and fountains. He too is such a romantic, though not in a literary sense! And his wife is a nice old thing, we get on famously."

They looked at each other and Nathaniel laughed out loud.

"Coco, I wish you well, though you did abuse my friendship. Your little charade with Emma was despicable and, I might add, Caradoc has not yet recovered."

"Sorry for that, *mon cher*. Needs must. Tell Emma I love her and I am sorry, and tell Caradoc too. I mean it, Nathaniel. I love them both, and I love you."

They skirted the small village of Carcan, once a small fishing port, now miles from the sea, distanced by the rolling dunes and marsh, just one in the dotted string of coastal settlements now sheltered from the bay, becalmed behind the lakes. They dismounted and took a sheep path through the bushes and stunted trees, heading for the small sandy beach by the glittering water. They tied up their horses in the brown shallows, tiny fish teeming about their feet. A solitary heron stood on a fallen trunk by the water's edge, white and graceful, but otherwise they thought themselves unobserved. He set about collecting brushwood and lighting the fire whilst she took from her bag a wreath of soft leaves, crushed from the journey, exuding the headiest perfume: Saint John's wort, rue, rosemary, lemon verbena and fennel, bound crown-wise around the circled stems of three white lilies. She placed the circlet on her head, peeled off her breeches and let them fall. Her shirt followed so she could stand naked, feeling the soft evening breeze caress her body.

Then she turned to Nathaniel. "Come with me," she said.

He shrugged off his jacket and shirt, watched her walk into the water, then, with decision, he shed the rest and followed her.

By twilight, a striding shepherd, high on his stilts behind the tangle of gorse bushes and marsh grass, heard the soft whinnying from their horses as they grazed by the trees, saw the discarded clothes of the lovers by the fire and passed on his way to his cabin by the stream. They did not see him, though Nathaniel heard his rapid stride as he passed and looked up from where they lay by the water.

"We need to go back," he said. "Tomorrow morning I will return to Cenon and I will not visit again, Coco. It will be goodbye. I wish you good luck with your Marquis."

She rolled over towards him, laughing. "We have lit the fire of purification so we will have at least one whole year of luck. It is a good night for saying farewell."

And she kissed him again, a kiss of melting sweetness, and he pulled her to him for one last time by the dying flames and dallied there until the fire went out.

They rode back, mostly in silence, and after stabling the horses went to their rooms. Nathaniel sat on his bed and set to winding his watch by the light of the candle. The sight and feel of the exquisite Breguet timepiece always brought pleasure, and that night it also conjured up a vision of Cornelius Lee. As his mind roamed back to a dark, cold Anglesey night and the ties of friendship, the door opened and there she was, holding two glasses of brandy.

"A nightcap? The last one?"

He shrugged in agreement, for friendship's sake.

They took a deep draught each and exchanged a last kiss, but before the glasses were drained a tide of weariness coursed through him. She pushed him back, carefully, onto his bed, and drawing a pair of scissors from her pocket, cut off a lock of his hair and wound it round her finger. She unfastened her brooch; pulled open the golden back plate, curled her prize round in the small empty space behind the miniature and snapped the case shut. She covered his sleeping body, ran her hands over him for one last time and pressed her lips to his.

In the morning, after a dreamless sleep, Nathaniel woke late and had breakfast in the dining room alone. The maid told him that Coco had left before dawn, Claudette had taken the children to town and the men were in the fields. When he returned to his room he opened his bag to pack for the drive to Cenon, and there on top was a small leather pouch. Inside were six perfect sapphires, smaller than the great central drop and lower gems of the necklace, three stones had been taken from each side near to the fastening, each clipped away from its housing on the golden Montrachet chain: a peace offering and a farewell.

## Morning: 24th June, 1833. Hyde Park, London.

The Honourable Lottie Drake and her daughter Lizzie had left the house in Mayfair with two footmen trailing behind at a respectful distance. They made their way along Park Lane and entered Hyde Park by the Stanhope Gate. Lottie walked quickly towards the Serpentine, hiding her face behind her lace parasol and avoiding the crowds, especially a bevy of a dozen young women whom she knew. Apart from the captive Lizzie, whose presence gave her a reason for being out, she did not want company. Quite the reverse, as she had had rather too much of it of late and her main ambition was to be rid of it. She chose an empty bench under a shady tree and arranged herself to cover as much of it as possible, spreading her wrap and reticule around her like a barricade and dispatching Lizzie to the waterline with a substantial bag of crumbs for the ducks.

It was essential that her affair with Edwin be concluded, which was annoying as it had been extremely good sport until very recently. It was after the burglary at his home in Bristol that he had changed and become past tolerating, which was odd, as she had never thought that such a trivial matter would have bothered him in the slightest. Of course there might be other problems with his mercantile pursuits, business affairs of unspeakable tedium and vulgarity. She sighed, but wished she had not as she jarred her jaw as she did so. He had actually struck her, in anger. The affair was no longer amusing and when she told him she would never see him again he had laughed, rather horribly, and said that she would do exactly as she was told. Her stomach turned over merely at the memory of his cold anger and her throat constricted in fear.

It had all seemed so exciting at first. Edwin was so broodingly handsome and undoubtedly dangerous, all rather thrilling. But the sport had become increasingly rough. Fortunately John had not noticed her bruises; she had always changed alone in her dressing room, or in the dark. Not that he could have prevented her from doing as she wished. He had warned her off Edwin, which had made her all the keener, and to have him know she had made such a dire mistake would have been unbearable.

She had also lost Amanda, who had been a friend of sorts, an excellent sparring partner, in a verbal sense of course. It had been rather fun at first to think that Amanda was afraid of her husband, but now she was not so sure. She had also been visiting Sir Giles and Lady Leonora more frequently of late. They continued in low water, with the nanny issue unresolved, although she had been replaced. Sir Giles seemed almost to cringe at the mention of Edwin's name, all of which was most odd. Lottie shivered despite the growing warmth of the day. Edwin's grip on her was debilitating, and becoming terrifying. As she gazed, unseeing, at the murky water of the Serpentine, she became aware that Lizzie was busily watching. She was enthralled by a small boy baiting a fish-hook with a worm. He skewered it and cast it adrift on the water. All three of them watched as the line floated over the surface, but they had not long to ponder its fate. Within a minute there was a convulsive jerk and the worm disappeared beneath the surface.

**The Prospect of Whitby, Wapping Wall.**

Whilst Lottie shifted uncomfortably on the bench, tormented by how she might make her last encounter with Edwin Ravenswood the final one, the man himself was sitting in the back room of a tavern by the docks. He was in the company of a sparely-built local man in a dark cloak and two formidable Asiatics whose frames occupied the whole of the wooden settle. One of the foreigners was finely dressed and appeared to be a gentleman, though his eyes flickered with forensic precision over Edwin Ravenswood, appraising him like a hunter whose skinning knife was already drawn.

"My men have not been idle whilst I was in Holland," said the foreigner. "After the unfortunate episode before the *Leonora* sailed I left them with instructions to seek out the Chinese man who so much enjoyed his little charade, which he played out at our expense, and also to find the gentleman who pursued him so self-righteously and boarded the ship with the marine police. It is plain now that they were accomplices. The two sailors, Fong and Chen, whom we mistakenly believed to have been drowned, are also in the pay of the Chinese man, whom I believe to be none other than Cornelius Lee. All four have been seen together, in the yard of this tavern, by this man." He waved his massive paw of a hand to the man in the cloak. "He acts as my shadow and knows every by-way of the docks. He sees a great deal, and reports to my associate, whom you may call Mr Qiang."

The man on the settle bowed to Ravenswood.

"His name means: The Strongman. You will find it is so!"

"I will take your word for that, Mr Kizhe," said Ravenswood smoothly, noting only that Qiang seemed to have been cut from the same cloth as his master. No one in their right mind would knowingly cross either of them without a brace of guns to hand, primed and loaded.

"The gentleman," said Ravenswood. "Would he be black-haired with eyes of bright blue? Tall, strong, about six and twenty in years?"

"He was," said the man in the cloak, the leering smile of recognition on his ratty face baring a full set of yellow teeth.

Ravenswood sat very still and then nodded, his mind made up.

"Gentlemen, accompany me to Somerset. It is time for the brightness of those eyes to be extinguished. And I think, Mr Kizhe, that we both have questions that Mr Lee needs to answer."

Edwin Ravenswood was not one to dwell on reverses but preferred to right them. The task of neutralising Parry would not be a simple one, but he had effective help. Lee he hoped to utilise in other ways and had postponed a decision on his fate. The man had delivered the payment from China reliably enough, but probably had other secrets that he needed to be persuaded to disclose. The Honourable Lottie's usefulness was almost over. There were places she could go, many fates might await. She may yet look back at her nights with him as the mildest of diversions, veritable walks in the park. And at that thought he flashed his cold smile round the table and raised his glass.

"To Somerset then," said Kizhe. "Mr Qiang and I are at your service."

218

# Chapter 9

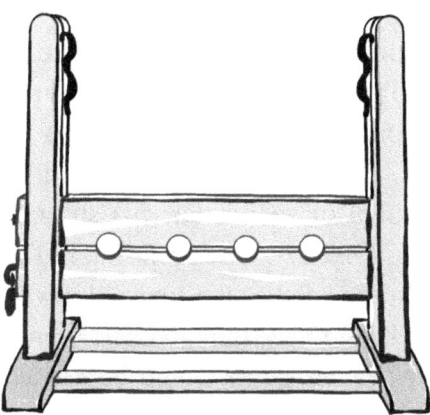

**Morning: 28th June, 1833. The Police Station, Grove Street, Bath.**

The metal cover on the spy-hole in the cell door snapped open and a beady eye peered through.

"Tobias Caudle?"

"You know very well who I am, Silas Monkton."

The eye swivelled round the cell, creasing in delight as it settled on the slight figure standing by the window.

"Time to show yourself to your public!"

Tobias straightened his back, tried to take a deep breath to steady his racing heart, and made for the door. He had two things to do and he hoped he could do them both that day. He would try not to think any further than the doing of them and getting through to the night without disgracing himself. But even as he resolved that it would be so, his stomach betrayed him and turned over at the prospect of what might come. He swallowed down a rush of bile and forced his mind onto the well-trodden and narrow path that he had made for his thoughts during the miserable days and nights since his arrest. First, he would do his time in the stocks without flinching: no matter what. He would not call out for mercy, God help him. He had seen the town drunks wailing for help like babes after the crowd tired of pelting them with rotten fruit and moved on to more imaginative missiles which usually included bleeding gobbets of offal from the nearby butchers' stalls. He vowed he would never sink to their level, but despite the heat of the day a clammy shiver ran through him as Monkton snapped a cuff on his outstretched arm, dragged him down the dark passage, past the desk sergeant and out through the studded front door onto the street. Tobias struggled to ignore the creeping fears that clawed at his belly and focused on the second thing he had to do.

Two things: he could only permit himself to think of two things.

The second one was harder than the first as he had to face Mr Parry and hear the verdict on his future and all his dreams, which were probably now doomed and rattling off to hell in a handcart. His decision to sell the papers might have lost him the best job he had ever had, and the trust of Master and Madam, and the daily sight of Frances. At the very thought of such a fate his stomach threatened to turn over again, so he dragged his mind back to his second task. He had to see Mr Parry and apologise to him, but he also had to act the man, like Mr Parry had told him, over and over again. Madam had been to see him and had been very kind, but she was not Master. Not that he knew when Mr Parry would be home. He just prayed to God it would be today so he could get everything over at once. Only then would he allow himself to think of other things, of what to do with what was left of his life if he found himself back on the street.

The officer strode ahead of Tobias, his long legs eating up the distance as he hauled his shackled prisoner behind him at a trot. They rounded the corner of Grove Street, crossed Pulteney Bridge and made their way to Orange Grove and the stocks. As the Grove came into view Monkton gave an additional yank on the cuffs.

"No laggin' Caudle. Regular criminal like you shouldn't be affrighted by yer just desserts!"

If only it had not been him.

Tobias had known Monkton from his days as a boot boy at the York House Hotel, but Monkton had not been an officer of the law then, far from it. He had been a stable lad, a brawny, rough customer, with a broad streak of cruelty to match, and as idle and shifty as he could manage without getting the sack. A speciality of his had been to terrorise the younger boys and, like the rest, Tobias had kept out of his way as much as he could. It had been a relief for all the small fry when Monkton had tired of life in the stables and taken a job as a police officer. Sadly for Tobias, a few crumbs of authority had done nothing to improve Silas Monkton. He remained brutal, small-minded and peevish, and worse than all of these, he had a vague memory of Tobias and singled him out for special treatment. He recalled a destitute child employed as a Christian duty by a pious housekeeper, a popular boy, whip-thin and eager to please. In the York House days, Monkton had despised Tobias, but now he resented him for his fine clothes, for his visits from Madam and Frances, and he resented the gifts, the tid-bits the women brought for Tobias at every visit. Always a

220

greedy hog, Monkton had been quick to pilfer the food as soon as the visitors turned their backs, but before they did, it had amused him to make himself agreeable to them, chatting about the weather and bringing chairs so they could sit.

"Oh thank you, sir," Frances had said to him. "So kind of you, sir."

That hateful memory had a use: it made his blood boil and you don't feel afraid if you're itching to strangle somebody.

He stumbled as they rounded the corner to the green and for the thousandth time wondered how he had come to this. It all seemed so right at the time. Just sell a couple of parcels of papers to help the cause, just once or twice until the new boys were ready to take over. And the cause was a grand one. There was no doubt about that. No doubt at all. What had Mr Jamieson and Mr Turner said? Unstamped papers were - now what was it? - "an instrument of civilisation", that is what they were, bringing knowledge to working men which would bring happiness to all! He was a hero, they had told him that, and there were hundreds like him, the numbers growing every day. They were heroes like those who smuggled the papers from London, like Mr Hetherington himself and Mr Carlile, the great publishers, both still locked away in London gaols. Not that they cared! Mr Hetherington had said if he had twenty thousand lives he would sacrifice them all for the cause!

Tobias held himself straighter as they approached the crude wooden stand near the stone obelisk. No one was going to kill him today. He had committed no hanging offence and he would not even go to gaol, Madam had told him that, and she had said she would pay his fine. He could think on that. It would help with jobs one and two.

Officer Monkton unlocked the cuff from his own wrist, transferred it and Tobias to the wooden upright and shoved him roughly towards the bench behind the stocks. Tobias sat down, stretched out his legs through two holes of the wooden yoke and glanced round the Grove. It was almost deserted: a good start. A hackney carriage picked up a fare at the stand, moved off the line and rolled by. Two couples were sauntering along taking the morning air, the odd working woman scurried past and two men in silk top hats marched on a mission to the Guildhall, looking neither left nor right. Perhaps the first task would pass easier than he had feared.

Feeling bold, he shouted out: "The red stamp is the mark of the beast, a blood mark of might against right! No tax on knowledge!"

Almost before he finished the back of Monkton's hand split his lip and bounced his head off the wooden upright.

"Shut yer mouth, Caudle. Save yer breath."

The advice was good as far as it went. He lifted his head to offer one more challenge to Monkton and the Grove, deciding it would probably have to be the last, as the blow had been a hard one and he did not want much more of the same, but it was too late. Tobias's heart sank and the brave words died on his lips, for round the corner of High Street pranced a trio of urchins he knew of old. They used to be some of his boys, his neighbours, fellow guttersnipes and thieves from Little Corn Street, but he had left them behind and bettered himself. After the first few months of working for Mr Parry he had given them nothing, not even his friendship. There had been neither a wink nor a nod about the best houses to rob in Saint James's Square; he had not made them one visit, nor shared one drink with them. Some would barely have noticed he had gone; some would have wished him luck, but not these three. They would not have forgiven his neglect.

Attracted by Tobias's shouts, the boys recognised him and set up an answering cry of their own. Obscenities streamed through their bared teeth, their eyes turned hard in their sallow faces, pinched by drink and putrid food, their fingers pointed accusations and crude gestures to shame him. Two doubled back to the market for ammunition; one picked up stones, stole a bucket and filled it from the steaming pile behind a horse at the carriage stand. Tobias steeled himself, head down for the onslaught.

"Caudle!" yelled one.

He looked up. Should he try talking to them?

From every hand the missiles rained down. He tucked his head into his breast, squeezed his eyes tight shut and prayed.

"Been a bad boy, Caudle!"

"Breakin' the law don't pay, Caudle!"

Dollops of stinking manure hit his defenceless head, along with decayed fish heads, fly-blown fruit and mildewed vegetables from under the market carts. Before he could catch his breath they were sharply followed up by stones. Two hit him square in the face and he spat out blood as it coursed from his nose into his mouth and from behind his closed lids, watery rivers of shock and pain flowed to follow it.

"Stop it!" he yelled. "Stop it, you cowards!"

But it did not stop. Hyena laughs rose to a demented crescendo around him, his head was buffeted left and right, blow followed blow until he felt he was slipping away, the noise closing in on him.

"You don't look so good now, Caudle!"

"Nor smell so good neither!"

The torment continued as the morning dragged by. At times his persecutors disappeared, only to return with more ammunition and fresh taunts, or, tiring of the sport, they sat by the stocks and were content simply to watch him suffer. At length, when the onslaught resumed after just such a pause, Tobias felt he could take no more. In a despairing gesture he lifted his head for one final time, dragging his burning eyelids back from his eyes, and was rewarded with the best sight in the world. It was his salvation, in the shape of a black and tan tornado with a head like a brick, flying at his gaggle of tormenters like a thunder ball and scattering them in a furious maelstrom of barking, growling, teeth and claws.

"Caradoc!" he cried with relief. "Oh Caradoc, you beauty!"

And behind the terrier came Madam, and Frances. His head fell forward, but he heard a lady's voice raised to Monkton.

"Were you planning to let those louts kill Mr Caudle?"

"No, Madam," blustered Monkton. "Just letting him have a taste or two of chastisement before I sent them on their way."

"The purpose of the punishment was not to have this young man murdered! Your superiors will hear of this."

Tobias lifted his head again and heard himself trying to splutter out words of thanks. Frances was on her knees by him.

"Don't try to talk, Toby, you idiot."

She wiped his face and made him wince.

"Sorry! Oh Tobias Caudle, what a state you are in! Now don't worry. You have to stay a while longer, but Madam says we shall be back to collect you in the carriage when it's done and there will be no more a-showering of you with filth. Look there!"

As his eyes struggled to follow her instructions, he managed his first grin of the day, albeit lopsided and giving him as much pain as pleasure. There, rounding the corner of the High Street was not another gang of louts, but a smiling crowd led by Arthur Jamieson. Most of the men were printers, with some from other trades, and all from the radical reading group of the George and Dragon. He even caught sight of some women, two he knew as working wives he had seen in the bar, but one was dearer and the sight of her warmed his heart. There was Martha Spence, and alongside of her was Robert Turner, pushing a chair with four wheels cunningly attached to better convey the oldest man in Walcot Street, Mr Thomas Spence

"Sit steady, young'un!" called out Arthur. "We're all here to see you through your 'ardship. We shall be as a shield wall with umbrellas at the ready and woe betide any rascal who tries to assail ye!"

**Nine o'clock in the evening: The Parry Residence, Saint James's Square.**

After bringing Tobias home and seeing to his injuries, Emma had insisted that there would be no more discussion of the incident that day and no work for him until tomorrow. He had been anxious that Nathaniel had not yet returned home, and she was with him on that, but had swept aside his concerns, seen him fed and watered and told him to go to his room and rest. He had hesitated, unwilling to give in, his conscience heavy with thoughts of the work left undone during his wasted days in Grove Street, until Caradoc forced his hand. The terrier had sat by Tobias all the way home in the carriage and stayed by his side during the lengthy cleansing session in the kitchen. When Emma ordered Tobias to his room, Caradoc jumped up to accompany him and when he made no move, bolted down the corridor to the boy's room, dived onto the bed and set up a persistent bark. It was a rare mark of favour for him to quit the comforts of the kitchen when Nathaniel was away and he meant everyone to know it.

"Well go on then!" Frances had ordered. "Before we are all deafened."

Exhausted by the day and keen to have some time to herself, Emma chose to retire early, which also released Frances from duty. Once she was alone in her room, she wrapped herself in Nathaniel's Damascus dressing gown, held its folds to her face to breathe in the scent of him, then propped herself up in bed on a mound of feather pillows, preparing to read unobserved.

In a drawer of her nightstand, discreetly hidden from view, she kept the journals which Madame Junot had lent to her. The French governess was now much more to Emma than her parents' employee: she was Céline, a friend and *confidente*. Emma still saw Tilly Vere occasionally, and more rarely still, the haughty Amanda Ravenswood. Anna, her old friend from Portsmouth, was less of a pleasure to meet than she had been, as she was now obsessed by talk of babies to the exclusion of all else. She was not close to any of them, any more than she was to Lottie Drake who deigned to drop in occasionally on an infrequent visit from London. Céline was different, as her conversation fed Emma's soul. Her political awakening had taken place at reform meetings with her father and she still accompanied him when she could. It was part of their relationship; part of their conspiracy. Her mother never came to the meetings, and neither had her elder brother or sister when they lived at home. It had given her an outlet for her thwarted ambition, allowed her to have her father all to herself and, miraculously, the rest of the family seemed to understand and let them be. But her new friendship with Céline had brought her face to face with a more extreme world than that inhabited by her father.

She took out the well-thumbed copy of the *Isis*. It would soon be a collectors' item, no doubt of it. Céline had ten issues in her collection and had been pleased to inform her that the magazine was created not by a man but by an *editress* by the name of Eliza Sharples, and had been published by her imprisoned partner, Richard Carlile.

The copies were precious as the magazine had only run briefly in 1832, collapsing before the year's end. Carlile had moved on to other publications like *The Gauntlet,* which she had seen in Tobias's bundle, but his relationship with Eliza was far from over. According to Céline, his wife had left him to set up her own radical bookshop and Eliza had given birth to his child. This, along with the notorious scope of his republican views and his abuse of the church, was the scandal that her mother had vaguely heard of, though mercifully she was ignorant of the details. If she had known more, and also of the extent of Céline's admiration for Eliza Sharples, the Peterson residence would have been short of a French governess in quick time.

Emma turned to the page where she had left Eliza's philosophising. She smiled to see Céline's jottings in the margin and the fierce underlining of the passages she particularly wanted to be read. Amongst other matters the piece dwelled on the injustice of the newspaper tax, which Emma now understood on a personal level, and the undue submission of women, which had never been anything other than personal. Eliza said women should have equal rights in law with men. She believed that the cause of the child worker and the cause of the slave were both worthy but were well rehearsed and supported by all liberals, whilst the repression and servitude of one half of the population, the female half, was one which had few supporters. Her voice seemed to be the only female one raised on a public stage to plead the case.

Céline's attachment to Miss Sharples had started in early 1832 on one of her regular trips to London and she had entertained Emma with a breathless account of attending one of Eliza's famous lectures at the Blackfriars Rotunda. A handsome and striking woman at any time, Eliza had appeared on the stage in a sumptuous evening gown against a theatrical backcloth of Egyptian and Greek symbols and over a floor strewn with laurel and whitethorn. She was at once posing as Isis, the Egyptian goddess of health, marriage and wisdom, friend of the down-trodden and mother of Horus the falcon headed, and also conjuring up the image of Hypatia the Greek philosopher. Eliza was a latter day "Pythoness of the Temple" and at the same time another Eve, daring to pluck the fruit from the tree of knowledge. It was heady stuff. In another age Miss Eliza Sharples could have been burned at the stake, but after careful cross-questioning of Céline, Emma found that her current fate seemed to be bankruptcy and ridicule.

Despite the failure of Eliza's public career, Emma drank down the strange words like nectar. Some were too sweet for her taste, but all stimulated her senses. Perhaps a woman had to play the showgirl to attract attention and had to work under the cloak of a male protector to capture even a few months of attention from the world before she disappeared again from public sight, back to acceptable obscurity. Perhaps that was the way the world was always going to be, but just for today, Emma felt that even she had not been obscure. She was proud of Tobias and his war wounds, his misguided attempt to help his friends. On the ride home he had been touchingly anxious to share his beliefs and justify what he had done. It was now clear to her that she had misjudged him to a degree. Not all his nights out had been spent at the George, as after a full day's work the boy had often taken to attending lectures at the Mechanics' Institute in Chandos Buildings. Yes, there were reasons enough to take pride in him. She was also pleased with herself. Using her parents' footman as chaperone she had been able to make the house call she needed without attracting attention. She had sought out Matthew Spence in Chatham Row and he had made himself useful at the George and Dragon, getting the men in the reading group to rally round and give up their break to protect Tobias.

She smiled to herself. It had been a good day, though little was settled and there was much to do. She had exchanged a few words with the demonstrators from the George about their campaigns and learned that the general feeling on reform of the press was combative and optimistic, they seemed sure that the government would relax the newspaper taxes before too long. But other campaigns, once thought won, had turned out to be hollow victories. The new Factory Act might be of as little use to the working child as last year's Reform Act was to the working man. Though the middle class men in towns had gained votes, the few poor men who had votes had lost them, and the rules for child labour, though protecting workers of less than nine years of age, applied only to those in cotton factories, whilst the rest could slave round the clock, unregulated and unobserved. The elusive ten hour day for all, long desired and long sought, was as far away as ever. The men had joined in a chant before she had left them.

"We will, we will, we'll have the Ten Hour Bill!" But it was a token performance with no real fire in it.

Those thoughts were sad, but thinking of the wider world had helped her today and would help her tomorrow. It preoccupied her and stopped her haunting the hall, waiting for every morning and afternoon post, it clouded her longing for Nathaniel to come home and her dread of hearing the news that he had found Coco. The thought of their meeting and possible reconciliation was too painful to be borne.

Like Tobias, she had also given herself just two things to do that day. First task accomplished; Tobias had been rescued and now she was going to finish reading the article she had started the previous night. Pushing aside all other thoughts, she reached over and turned up the lamp.

**Three o'clock in the morning: 29th June, 1833.**
**The Shadwell Residence, Green Park Buildings West.**

"Oiy thought Oiy saw a light!" said Letty, roguishly, sticking her head round the kitchen door and beaming at the back view of a young woman seated at the table clad only in a petticoat and fringed shawl, her thick brown hair loose and tumbling down over her bare shoulders. Letty bustled in, wrapped her arms round the woman's neck, popped a smacking kiss on her head and thudded down into the chair next to her.

"I guessed it was you! Not seen you all the day, Clari. What've you been doing moiy girl?"

Clari giggled and waved her arms over the random collection of left-over food she had assembled. "Oiy've taken too much brandy and Oiy'm moppin' it up with some supper. Want some?"

She took up the kitchen knife and set about slicing into the remaining half of a high-raised mutton pie.

"Make it a fair size. Oiy be starvin'," said Letty. "And while you're at it, Oiy'll brew some tea." She jumped up to poke her nose into the kettle, find the poker and rattle up a blaze amongst the dying embers of the fire. "Shouldn't be long it's still warmish. 'Ow's business?"

"At it since nine, moiy love," said Clari as she hewed off another piece of pie and shovelled the fall of crumbs into her mouth with her fingers. "Mmm, is this the best pie in Bath? Well yes, Oiy do believe it is!" As the fresh assault of dry pastry coincided with this declaration her chest convulsed. "Damn," she spluttered. "Cold drink, Letty, moiy love. Quick! Oiy'm gettin' the hiccups!"

Letty slopped a draught of small beer into a glass from the jug on the shelf.

"Get it down, Clari."

"Thanks, better. Now what were we sayin'? Business you said? Well, moiy last customer wouldn't go without buyin' a bottle and draining it dry. Oiy 'ad to 'elp the daft old sod with it, specially as Madam's started chargin' over double the rate on brandy and 'e wanted to see it off. We need 'im to come back! And you?"

"Good enough. Better'n last week," said Letty, moving to the window and pushing up the sash. She leaned out to breathe in the night air. "God, it's that 'ot!

Who would 'ave thought it at this time of a mornin'. It's like livin' in the tropics!"

She checked the kettle again. "It'll do," she said doubtfully. "Now where's that caddy to?" She searched the cupboards, found the tea, scattered a few leaves into two cups and filled them with the lukewarm water.

"Come and sit!" commanded Clari. "Oiy didn't tell you who Oiy seen this mornin'!"

"'Oo's that then?"

"Well," said Clari, in a carrying voice, designed to be confidential but suffering from a lack of judgement brought on by the half bottle of brandy, the numerous beers and the bottle of wine she had taken over the evening. "Oiy was in town this mornin' and who do Oiy see clamped in the stocks but that lad who was 'ere with, well, shall we call 'im Mr Drake!"

Guffaws of laughter rang out from the two of them at the table and carried well, out through the window, into the dark and down the garden path .

"What 'ad 'e done, Clari?"

"Sellin' papers with no stamp."

"Don't 'e work for that gent now? That "Mr Drake" moiy Fred found out about in Gloucester?"

"Course 'e do. Tobias Caudle, the lad is called, 'e 's training up as Mr Drake's valet, Mr Parry that is. Does all sorts in the 'ouse and follows 'im round as a manservant."

"What's 'e like that Mr Parry, when 'e 's not actin' as someone else that is!"

Clari rolled her eyes. "Letty, up close 'e 's as 'andsome as ever Oiy seen! And strong too. As ye know, Oiy seen 'im myself 'ere with young Tobias gettin' the better of Joshua and the men out the back. Remember like Oiy said before, 'e was the one who sorted Billy and Jabez out good and proper a couple of years back!"

"You're roight," said Letty, hacking off another piece of pie. "And Abi said 'e was a marvel gettin' her out of that toil in Bristol docks when poor Babs died. God rest 'er!"

Behind their backs, as they paused respectfully and took another mouthful of tea, the kitchen door swung back on its hinges.

"Having a little recreation, ladies?" The tall figure of Joshua Shadwell, black against the hall light, stepped into the kitchen. He drew back his thin lips in a cheerless smile. "Don't tire yourselves out."

They exchanged terrified glances, plastering on smiles as they desperately tried to remember what they had said, and when.

"Join us for some tea, Mr Shadwell?"

"Not tonight, Clari," he said. "I had enough of your talk as I walked up the garden. And yours," he said, with a venomous glare at Letty.

He limped over to the table and struck Clari a blow across the face, leaning over to her as she froze in her seat.

"Your information about the enterprising Mr Parry was interesting and I am disappointed you kept it from me for so long. You're drunk, you're careless and you are too stupid to keep secrets from me so don't try it again."

He straightened up and served Letty the same, the flat of his hand leaving her face burning red.

"And you. Don't you ever deceive me again." He glowered at the two of them, his harsh voice rising to fill the kitchen and batter their ears. "Anything to do with this house, or any girl in this house, is my business. You speak to me first or I'll make you wish you'd never been born!"

Without another word he turned abruptly and left them transfixed in misery. The door slammed behind him and they sat listening to his retreating steps, uneven and dragging on his injured side, as he made his way upstairs.

"Oh Letty," whispered Clari. "What 'ave we done! Oiy wish to God Abi 'ad made a better job of stickin' that knife in 'im!"

**The Parry Residence, Saint James's Square, Bath.**

Later that morning, the bell jangled in the Parry's front hall and Frances trotted down the stairs from Madam's bedroom to answer it.

"There is no point waiting for Mrs Rollinson to go," Madam had said with a smile. "From what you said she's at a crucial stage with the seed cakes so she won't have much patience with visitors."

Frances was humming to herself, preoccupied with her own happiness. Tobias was on his feet despite his bruises and his swollen face, the sun was up and she was looking forward to an exchange in the fresh air, probably with one of Madam's lady friends, or maybe the post boy. She opened the door with a flourish, smiling a welcome, only to sustain a shock cruel enough to knock the breath out of her. Horrified, she stepped back gasping, her hand flying to her mouth, as she stared into a face that was terrifyingly familiar. The man before her was foreign, an Asiatic, tall and powerful looking, with thick black hair and expressionless eyes. He was also a spectre from the darkest hours of her short life, from a foetid cell in the Redcliffe caves where he had visited with other men, and worst of all with the terrible dark man who owned the ship that was to have taken her away.

"You must be Frances," said the man quietly whilst watching her intently,

229

holding her still in his gaze. "I know you saw me once in unpleasant circumstances and you are alarmed, but think carefully, you must also remember the other Chinese men who helped you on the night you escaped. They had been sent by me. They are my friends and I am a friend of Mr Parry. He is the reason I am here. I need to speak with him urgently, Frances."

"He's away, sir," said Frances uncertainly, but feeling calmer as she looked back at him more closely, listened to him speak and ran over her memory of him again. He had not been the one who had frightened her, or made her stand before him like a beast at an auction. He had not touched her, or even approached her, but had remained like a statue at the door, then left without a word. She realised she had bunched her hands into fists, took a breath, and allowed them to uncurl.

"But he will be back any day now, sir. Madam expected him before now."

The man reached into his pocket, brought out a silver case, heavily engraved and with a miniscule silver pencil attached. He set about writing a note on the back of a visiting card.

"Frances, this is important. Take this and ensure that Mr Parry receives it the moment he returns." He made a slight bow: "Please convey my respects to Mrs Parry."

He left her staring after him on the doorstep, untied his horse from the railing and mounted up.

Half-dressed, Emma had walked out on the landing to lean over the banister and see if she could catch more of the conversation below. As she heard Frances closing the door, she shot back to her bedroom and lifted the curtain. Her heart gave a thump as she recognised him: there, riding a chestnut mare down the hill towards the Bristol Road, was Cornelius Lee. Hearing Frances running upstairs she moved away from the window, embarrassed, and took up a position by her dressing table.

"Madam," said Frances breathlessly, holding out an embossed visiting card in ivory white. "There's a message for Mr Parry on this, but I thought I should bring it to you straight away. The visitor was a foreigner, Madam, and I think he's part of Mr Parry's business. I didn't want to leave it on the hall table."

She did not need to say more. Open messages on public display were fair game for domestic staff. Emma smiled at her, for Frances would know all about that. She was without doubt the canniest servant Emma had ever known. Even after being acquainted with her for nearly two years and having some sketchy details of the trauma of her early life, Emma sensed she had little idea of who Frances really was, or who she had been, other than that she was a born survivor. Luckily for Emma, the life of an unwanted child in Avon Street, who had been sold on by her mother to the first offer, was as alien as the life of the poor in Timbuktu. Her mind wheeled back to Cornelius and the tales he had told them of the sad wretches in his own land. Round the fire that night on Anglesey he had urged Nathaniel, and not for the first time it seemed, to realise the scale of the menace of opium addiction in the coastal towns of China, fuelled by smugglers from British India and abetted by native criminals who defied the Emperor's laws. Degradation and squalor: always just a step away from gentility. Alien worlds, but some souls moved between the two and become wise enough to have lived twice over.

"You did right, Frances," she said. "Now, I may have other callers, so bring the cream gown with the sprigged flowers. We need to hurry."

As Frances helped her into the day dress Emma tried to recall Nathaniel's exact words about Cornelius before he left. He had mentioned that his friend had returned to Bristol and that they had met, but the robbery and Tobias's problems had driven the details from her mind. Then she remembered. Cornelius planned to take up residence again in Arno's Tower. Looking down at the card in her hand it was plain that he was not at the Tower today. The note announced that he was returning to the Crown at Keynsham throughout the next week, every afternoon, at five o'clock. She had a vivid memory of him and his striking looks, but more than that, the magnetism of the man, his prescient understanding which was so piercing it was almost a second sight. And she remembered his gift to her, the bolt of embroidered blue silk. Today at least, he would not wait alone.

Later that afternoon Emma had Frances prepare her for a drive. She was feeling expansive, and if she had admitted it, on the border-line of reckless. On an impulse she had summoned Tobias from his labours on a neglected pile of boots and Caradoc from guard duty by his side. He had seen her order as a mark of favour, which made her all the more glad for having thought of it. She knew he was still anxious about Nathaniel's return and found it touching to see him strive to impress her.

"Right away, Madam," he had said, rushing to wash his hands in the bowl before doubling back to his room to brush his hair, and even more important for the boy, to collect his stick. Every spare minute since returning home he had spent perfecting the techniques that Mr Parry had taught him and he was keen to play the bodyguard. It was another step down the road to redemption. As it was another fine day she had walked with them to Pickwick's Livery at the White Hart to pick up Nathaniel's post chaise and both of his horses.

"Thank you," she said, as the hired driver handed her up to the seat and Caradoc bounded up beside her. "And I have a request. I would like my boy here to sit up in front with you. It is time he learned to drive."

231

The two half-crowns she slipped into his hand made him a patient teacher, and for the trainee, there could not have been a better gift. Tobias, blushing under his bruises, his clear eye shining with excitement, climbed up eagerly and as they left Bath, was transported not just out of the town but also, for a while, out of himself and his worries.

They bowled along the toll road, over the New Bridge on the outskirts of Bath and on through the village of Saltford, all in the brilliant golden blue of a mid-summer afternoon. The fields swooned in the heat and not a breeze ruffled the bulrushes in the water meadows by the river. She let her eyes flow along the scene as they passed at a brisk trot and had a moment's view of a heron rising lazily from the river's margin, flapping his great white wings and trailing spindly legs in the water as he gained height and lit out over the sparkling Avon. A sudden thought intruded: a thought of other rivers and warm lakes. She looked away.

"Well done, Tobias!" she called, seeing the boy had taken the reins on the easy straight. "Have you ever ridden a horse?"

"No, Madam," he called back, not daring to take his eyes from the road.

"Well you shall today. Driver, put him on one of the horses as we slow down in the Keynsham traffic."

### The Crown Inn, Bristol Road, Keynsham.

Within the hour and close to five o'clock, they arrived at the Crown and drove round to the stables. Emma, with Caradoc at her heels, had Tobias and the driver escort her inside and was relieved to spot Cornelius by the window as soon as she entered the front parlour. Whilst the dog made a bee-line for him and settled at his feet, she pressed a florin into Tobias's hand and sent him and the driver into the tap room to wait with the other servants and coachmen. She struggled to ignore the fact that for the first time in her life she was entirely un-chaperoned, and furthermore she had chosen to arrive unannounced to meet a man in a public house. Confronted by the extent of her indiscretion, the remnants of her euphoria evaporated and she felt excruciatingly exposed. To give her courage she thought of Eliza Sharples standing proudly on the stage as Isis, mother of Horus, posing as a new Hypatia, another Eve.

"Mrs Parry," said Cornelius, standing to greet her, noting the blush of discomfort rising up her cheeks. "Thank you for making the journey to meet me. I gather by your presence that Nathaniel is not yet home. And by the presence of his fellow," he said, ruffling Caradoc's head, "I assume he is away on business."

Immaculate as usual, and in black with a severe white stock at his neck and gold stitching on his waistcoat to relieve it, Cornelius cut an exotic figure. She could feel

232

the eyes of the other customers turning to them.

"May I order some refreshment for you?" he was asking. "There is a coffee room here, and it is quiet."

They quit the busy parlour, Caradoc pausing only to lift a chop bone from a discarded plate, and she followed Cornelius to take a seat in a shaded room away from the road. As they waited for the waitress to finish unloading their order from her tray and sneaking curious glances at Cornelius, he took the chance to observe Emma. She was as beautiful as when he had first seen her in the cold of the Welsh winter, highly strung and ready to run like a roe deer, her fine skin glowing, and tendrils of red-gold hair framing her face. On his second sighting of her, she remained an unusual woman. Her lavender gown and pelisse were cut close to her body, restrained and in the classical style, still resisting the swags and flounces of the fashion plates with their bizarre sleeves billowing ever larger like hot air balloons. But her eyes were troubled now. Whatever her motive had been in coming to him, he needed to make time to listen.

"I thought it would be helpful if I came to see you," she started hesitantly, "to let you know of some problems we have had. You see, after the robbery at Arno's Tower," she paused, feeling horribly awkward, and then began again. "I think you know that there was an incident, you spoke with my husband shortly afterwards, I believe? Well, before long we were also visited by a thief. The sapphires were taken, those we showed you which Nathaniel's father brought from Spain."

He noticed she did not lay claim to them, she did not call them: "My sapphires".

"Nathaniel has travelled to France."

How much to say? How much to leave unsaid?

Cornelius resolved her dilemma.

"Following the woman? It was I who told him that the robbers were French and I know there was a French woman in Bath who knew of the wealth of the Ravenswoods. I know also that the sapphires were in an identical setting to a piece owned by Mrs Ravenswood. There was a clear link, especially as you mention no other loss from your collection. A long shot perhaps, but it is natural he should seek to recover the property."

"Yes," said Emma carefully. "It is natural."

"Mrs Parry," he began.

"My name is Emma. Please feel free to use it as you did at our last meeting. I hope you regard both Nathaniel and me as friends."

"Yes I do, Emma." He watched her closely, gauging how much he should disclose to make her able to unburden herself of whatever troubled her. "I called on you this morning as I need Nathaniel to know that events are moving to a possible conclusion in my pursuit of the man known as Kizhe. It is a priority for me to track him down, and Nathaniel also has an interest in this. I now know that he is in Bristol with at least two others and he has a ship, fully crewed, docking there from London. For now he is staying at the Ravenswood town house in Redcliffe Parade. The reason I left Arnos' Tower this morning was that I heard this news and furthermore I learned that he is accompanied by Edwin Ravenswood himself, a man with whom Nathaniel and I also have unfinished business. It is imperative that Nathaniel speaks with me before he has any further dealings with any of these men. Certain matters came to light in London which compromised our position."

He watched her deal with the threat. She would be prudent in her use of the information and she would be efficient, of these things he was sure. It was unnecessary to burden her further with the fact that Ravenswood, Kizhe, and his henchmen, were looking to eliminate Nathaniel and make his own life as difficult as possible. She was not informed that Fong had accompanied him to Bath and had stayed there for her protection, watching the house in Saint James's Square until Nathaniel returned. He also kept to himself the details of Amanda Ravenswood's desperate flight from Redcliffe that morning. She had attended a dinner there last night and heard all she needed to know about the aims of her husband and his conspirators. To compound the news, Shadwell had arrived early that morning with information that hammered the final nail in the coffin for Nathaniel, proof of his involvement in the release of the girls who Ravenswood had been hoping to sell in the autumn of 1831 and therefore also in the burning of Ravenswood's ship, the *Mathilda*. And Amanda had become another counter on the board. He had allowed her to come closer to him, to become involved, and so now she cared, clutching at straws of comfort from him, a stranger and potentially a very dangerous one. The relations had paid off, as now she feared for his life and had warned him. He had been able to leave the Tower without a confrontation and well before Ravenswood returned.

"Nathaniel must know of these developments immediately upon his return," he said, closing the subject. "But I sense there is more to your visit, Emma. What troubles you?"

Again, as it had happened the night in Anglesey when she first met him, almost involuntarily she spoke to him frankly, with no blush or embarrassment, though not this time of dreams and ghosts.

"I am afraid of the consequences if Nathaniel finds the French woman, Colette Montrachet. They were friends before he loved me, probably more than that, and

234

perhaps they are again."

Cornelius's eyes searched her face.

"Emma, be surer of yourself and take strength. You are a lady, and a beautiful one, if I may say so. You love Nathaniel and he is deeply attached to you. From what I gather she is a fortune hunter ready to go with any man who suits her purpose. Who is he likely to prefer? And think on this, would it not be strange if such a successful man, such a man of talent, had no other friends or had not had other lovers?"

"Yes, of course. But I fear he will be tempted away and our love will be ruined. The life I have would be lost, Cornelius. I do not think I would recover easily."

Tears slowly welled up in her eyes. "I am sorry," she said, looking away in confusion. "I should not have spoken. I should go, and I will make sure Nathaniel has your message as soon as he returns."

"It was not wrong to come to me with this Emma, but be sure, none of what you fear will come to pass," said Cornelius gently, taking her hand. "There is something between them for certain, as there was before, and probably always will be. But it is not what he has with you."

"Should he not forsake all others? We are married Cornelius we have made promises."

Cornelius shook his head dismissively. "In my country the rules and the promises are different from here, but neither code is superior and in the end neither is designed to cater for the strangeness of each individual life. Our Emperor makes promises to his Empress, but he also has responsibilities to his Noble Consort." He smiled at her surprise. "And the ordinary Consorts, and of course the Concubines, and the Noble Ladies, and of less importance, the ordinary ranks of female attendants. Emma, they number in thousands. Such rules are not limited to the Emperor; successful men have their concubines too. It is simply a matter of scale."

"And of course," said Emma. "It goes without saying that noble women will not have the same rights!"

"There is a saying in my homeland. One teapot is usually accompanied by at least four cups, but one cup does not need four teapots."

She nodded. "Women as receptacles: it's a familiar image."

"It is, but what is familiar is not necessarily wise or harmonious. Emma, irrespective of social conventions we have to make our own path in this world and the next; we must all find our own way of being. Say little when Nathaniel returns. His journey will be at an end and he will be back with you, which is as it should be. If he met with her and wishes to speak of it, then listen, otherwise, do not pursue it.

There are many kinds of love, Emma, deep and abiding love for a lifetime is just one of them. You seem to have found it, though I suspect I never will. Physical love can be many things; it can be a welcome and a farewell. It can be a convenience, or used to cloak another purpose, but even then it is not always without pleasure. Life is cruelly short; we should always consider that before passing judgement on another."

"Do I ask too much?"

"You fear too much."

Emma sat in silence for a moment, feeling the warm pressure of his hand on hers and strangely, an overwhelming sense of peace.

"It is a relief to discuss such things, though I am unused to it, and certainly not with a man who is not my husband. Thank you, Cornelius."

He took her hand and pressed it to his lips.

"Know that Nathaniel loves you and that he will return to you. Others are like the moon to your sun. Be strong, believe in yourself."

She stood to leave.

"Will I see you again?"

"I am sure of it," said Cornelius.

**The Parry Residence, Saint James's Square, Bath.**

Emma was quiet on the journey back, tightly wrapped in her own thoughts, but no one noticed, as the driving instruction continued from where it had left off on the outward journey. She had them take her home to Saint James's Square leaving Tobias with the driver to enjoy a final ride through town before walking back from the livery stable with Caradoc. She took dinner alone and retired to her room as the sun was setting. The room seemed the same, but things had changed, she still felt at peace and could still feel the warmth of Cornelius's hand on hers. She had been mistaken to think of her marriage as a sacred relic, to be kept in aspic as it was on the day they exchanged vows. They were living and breathing creatures, with patchwork emotions from the past, old friends, and for Nathaniel, old loves as well.

Perhaps concern for our relationship is rather like concern for our bodies, she thought, perhaps we should not fear challenges or disease and dread them coming to corrupt us, but rather see that what we fear is probably within us already. We live with it and through it, and we must gain strength with every new experience. She found she could think of Coco without dread or resentment and admit that, despite her suspicions and jealousy, she had enjoyed her conversations with the vivacious French woman. She also found room in her heart for gratitude. Coco had once been of great service to Nathaniel, sheltering Frances's wayward friend and taking the trouble to place her in employment, out of harm's way. Emma took off her wedding ring and held it to the lamp light to read the engraving. On that freezing January day when they married she had been his "*Bright Star*".

She walked over to the curtains and opened them wide. Looking up, above the sinuous curve of the Royal Crescent, she saw the limitless bowl of the heavens scattered with thousands of stars, millions of pin-pricks of light, some indistinct, woven in the swirling translucent skein of the milky way, some placed precisely in their ancient patterns, studding the impenetrable darkness as they always had and always would do: but brighter than the rest was the pole star, brighter than them all. Let them all guide him home. She slipped the ring back on, climbed into bed and took Eliza's journal from the drawer.


Caradoc heard him first. Spread-eagled on the floor by Tobias's bed, he raised his head and just one ear. There it was again, an unmistakeable voice sounding low in conversation outside on the road, a carriage door slammed and a trunk dropped heavily onto the pavement. The terrier jumped up and scratched his way out of the door, ran through the kitchen, his claws skittering on the flags, up the stairs, into the hall and in one flying bound leapt straight into the arms of his master.

"Good to see you too," laughed Nathaniel, dodging the barrage of yapping and the wettest of the welcoming licks. "Quiet, sir! You'll rouse the house."

"I should think he has already."

She stood for a moment at the top of the stairs, pausing to tie his Damascus gown more securely around her, then with a laugh ran down to them.

"Em, darling!" said Nathaniel, struggling to plant Caradoc on the floor. "Down, you hooligan!"

She flung herself into his arms and kissed him, burying her face in his neck with Caradoc capering around them in a frenzy of excitement.

"My love, how I have missed you," she whispered. "How did you fare?"

She pulled back to look at him. He was tanned, but thinner than when he left; his cheeks gaunt, his eyes smudged with dark shadows.

"Are you well?"

"Yes," he said. "Don't worry. All's well. We will talk of it later." He reached into his pocket and drew out a small pouch. "For you," he said. "To have strung as you wish."

She emptied the pouch into her hand and six perfect blue stones tumbled out.

"So these are to be mine," she said with a wry smile. "I take it that the excess has been discarded?"

237

**Evening: 30th June, 1833. The Crown Inn, Bristol Road, Keynsham.**

Cornelius had not risked signing in as a resident at the Crown, so had taken Nathaniel and Caradoc to a back room where they could dine well away from the front parlour and its regular influx of coaching trade.

"I hear Emma visited you yesterday," said Nathaniel.

"She did. She was lonely and she missed you."

"Was that all?"

"No. She feared you would leave her for the French woman."

Nathaniel nodded. "I see. But there was no need to consider that a possibility."

"So I told her."

They sat in silence by the empty fireplace as an evening breeze crept through the open window and stole round them, relieving the torpor of the summer night.

"Did you recover the jewels?"

"It turns out they should have been hers in the first place. They had belonged to her family, so I felt there was no call to recover them, but she made me a present of some of the sapphires. Emma can have them made up as she sees fit."

"And did you recover your French friend?"

"I bade her farewell," said Nathaniel.

"And Emma, was she in good spirits on your return?" asked Cornelius, observing his friend closely, noting the exhaustion and the familiar gesture, the hand raking through his long hair, pushing it back from his face as he gathered his thoughts. He noted also the absence of anxiety, and of guilt: the reunion must have been satisfactory for both parties.

Nathaniel smiled. "She certainly was. She seems to have been well occupied whilst I was away. One of our servants had a brush with the law and she saw him through it. His recent passion for reform had prompted him to sell unstamped papers." Nathaniel shrugged. "I was pleased to see him cope with the experience, and learn from it. It is what youth is for."

"This boy is a protégé of yours? You have plans for him?"

"Yes, I do," said Nathaniel. "And he shows promise."

"In life we only truly know ourselves, and understand our potential, when we are faced with a severe threat," said Cornelius half to himself, and then paused, lost in thought, before continuing. "Our Masters only know if we are capable of facing such challenges and profiting by them if we are put to the test. I remember a time in my youth when I too was imprisoned. You know that I lived in a temple as a child where I trained in the fighting arts. In my country, such training is usually done in secret, outside the law, as our Manchu overlords are few in number and fear rebellion. I had

238

been on an errand for my Master, taking a message to a village a day's journey away, but I walked into a trap. I was arrested and held prisoner in an animal shed for five days. They beat me to try to make me reveal the name and whereabouts of the sender of the message I carried. I tell you, I suffered more from the shame of capture than the treatment, which I was trained to withstand. I should not have walked into the house like a lamb to the slaughter but as I had done so, I tormented myself with the thought that it might have been better to fight back. But as the days passed, I came to realise that my first reaction was the better one. Fighting would have revealed my skills, and as my life was not in danger I could not let that happen but had to endure the test. So I continued to play the frightened farmer's boy, but all the time fearing what my Master would say. I kept to my story that a man on the road had asked me to deliver the message to his sick family, but my captors were not convinced and would not let me go."

"So how did you escape?" asked Nathaniel.

"I drew on my training and started to watch the pattern of the guards' movements. The room was dark, lit only by a crack of light from the window. Every morning two soldiers would unlock the door and come in to me, one carrying a jug of water, the other a lamp. They would walk directly to the corner where I slept. Every other day the job was done by a man and a youth of about my build. I targeted them. One day the jug was held out as usual, but only to a bundle of my clothes stuffed with straw, whilst I lay motionless and half naked behind the door, covered in the filth from the floor. As the other guard raised his lantern to inspect my rags, I struck. In the temple we learn the ways of many creatures. Some are mythical like the dragon, some real and ferocious like the tiger and the leopard, but some are more humble, like the crane and the snake. Did you know that this is the year of the black water snake?  It is a good time for this story, and in the darkness of the shed it was also a time for the snake. I rolled over the floor, keeping low and fluid, swept the legs from under them and struck them both as they hit the ground. The village was surrounded by a forest and I knew I would be safe there once I escaped from the hut, so I took the clothes from the smaller guard and slipped away through the trees."

"You were lucky that neither of them saw you by the door."

"The eyes often see what they expect to see and my disguise worked. As you know, it is important to blend in with your surroundings."

"If possible," laughed Nathaniel. "Especially when you are in a net on Wapping Wharf!"

Cornelius grinned. "The blend there was not so good: but there was a lesson to be had. A sacrifice was needed in order to get on board the ship and it turned out to be me."

They laughed together, feeling their renewed bond of friendship.

"What did your Master say when you returned?" asked Nathaniel curiously.

"I tried to explain what had happened, but I sensed he already knew. He did not ask me to explain my delay but just said that lessons are learned in various ways, experience is gained on which we can build. The next day he moved me on to a different type of training. At the time, I thought it was some form of punishment, but later I realized that I had progressed to the next level."

Nathaniel nodded, he felt that he too had progressed in the process of understanding his friend, but there was a long way to go.

Cornelius glanced round the room. The nearest customers were still a good way off and out of earshot, a group of three men, commercial travellers locked in their own buzz of conversation. "To business, our enemies have gathered at Redcliffe Parade," he said quietly. "Kizhe's war junk, the *Zhen Tian Lei,* arrived yesterday and the *Blue Dragon* is also in port."

"*Zhen Tian Lei!*" exclaimed Nathaniel. "Does that mean something about thunder shaking the heavens?"

"Yes, as in thunder crash bombs. Kizhe doesn't like mixed messages."

"You were very fortunate to be given warning," said Nathaniel. "Emma passed on your message and I have written to Drake in London. He has a personal interest in Ravenswood's career so I told him to come if he wants to help make it less profitable. I have advised him to bring Home Office authorisation to call out a platoon of troops. We might need them and I don't want to involve the Yeomanry. We need regulars if we are to attempt to arrest Kizhe when he has the backing of an entire crew and I want Captain Trevellis for the murder of Ben Prestwick. We will have the crew of the *Dragon* to deal with when we go after him."

"Amanda Ravenswood travelled from Redcliffe alone to warn me," said Cornelius.

"She is now your ally then?"

"We have an understanding. Her suffering as Ravenswood's wife has been extreme and it has grown to hatred because of his affair with Drake's wife. She turned to me for consolation, and has returned the favour. Unfortunately she has also found other means to lift her pain."

"Other men?"

"No, laudanum, and it has made her reckless. Not to say she is without other friends. The new men employed at the Tower are more hers than Ravenswood's. In particular, the two Irish, and Matthew Spence, the man who used to sail in

Ravenswood's crew, all three are loyal to her. She favours them and keeps them close to the house. I know she has gained access to duplicate keys and has searched Ravenswood's study. She has plans of her own, but tonight my friend, we must finalise ours. We have a small window of opportunity to settle some old scores."

# Chapter 10

**Evening: 5th July, 1833. The Ravenswood Residence, Arno's Tower, Arno's Vale, near Bristol.**

It had become habitual for Edwin Ravenswood to choose to sit at the opposite end of the dining table from his wife and so far this had proved to be a night like any other. He surveyed her bleakly across the long run of cloth, cluttered at each end by the remains of the last course, each set of glasses, plates and cutlery corralled round its diner like a barrier of circled wagons. He could barely remember the last time they had dined close enough to touch each other during a meal, for his hand to hold hers, or brush her back; for her feet to twine themselves round his. Not much of a loss, but it irked him that she appeared unmoved by the change.

His jaw tightened in annoyance. After spending a relaxing hour in his Oriental Salon adjusting the face mask on his Japanese samurai armour, she had managed to irritate him within minutes of her arrival in the dining room. His temper was unusually short as he had had an intense week of negotiations with Kizhe and his officers at Redcliffe Parade. His visitor had been as demanding as he knew he could afford to be, testing Ravenswood's patience and pushing the boundaries to breaking point. As the right-hand man of the Count, the facilitator of the clandestine routes into China and grand master of the human trafficking which enhanced his income from the opium trade, he was an important cog in the wheel of the Ravenswood fortunes, one which must be well-oiled, feted and indulged. It had been a trying week. Apart from the drain on his personal time, there had been collateral losses, in particular the injuries suffered by a couple of the prostitutes sent to the visitor. They had been lent by a contact who expected them back and earning the next night but their experiences at Redcliffe Parade had made that impossible.

During their meetings Kizhe had outlined ambitious plans. His trips to Holland and regular meetings in London had not been part of his trafficking endeavours as Ravenswood had first thought, but a new and lucrative branch of the Count's business in the shipping of stolen art and jewels. His hand-picked forgers were at their creative work, making pieces to plant in the place of stolen goods and Kizhe had brought a trunk full of gems and very superior paste for Ravenswood to compare. It was not a trade of interest to Ravenswood and his dilemma had been to keep Kizhe committed to the existing side of the business without extracting a promise from him to contribute to the new schemes. This was his first night at the Tower since returning from London and he had expected it to be more congenial than it was proving to be.

He surveyed his wife with distaste. She had arrived late for dinner and distinguished herself only by drinking too much and keeping up a stream of inconsequential chatter; a pathetic attempt to stave off the questions she needed to answer when they found themselves alone. But answer she would.

"More wine," demanded Amanda, raising her empty glass to a footman, her eyes glassy and her cheeks flushed.

"I think, Madam, that you have had more than enough," said Ravenswood, waving the staff away. "Leave us. I will take brandy presently in the west wing."

She had been ordered to join them at Redcliffe Parade for the welcome dinner on his return with the guests from London. The evening had passed well enough, but she had claimed to be unwell and returned to the Tower the next morning, shortly before he dispatched his men there to pick up Cornelius Lee. Ravenswood had been distracted by a visit from Joshua Shadwell whose news made the detention of Lee even more desirable. But far from supervising security at the Tower, Lee was nowhere to be found. His men interrogated the staff and checked in local inns but at every turn they drew a blank.

"Still no sign of our Chinese security guard I see," said Ravenswood, leaning back in his chair, dangerously quiet. "How very strange, was it not, that your return coincided with him disappearing into thin air? One might almost think that you rushed back to warn him to make himself scarce, which suggests he is a person of some interest to you."

Amanda's flush drained from her face and her eyes flashed with anger.

"A person of interest! My God, yes! How unusual it has been to have a man in the house who concerns himself with my needs! A cultivated man, a gentleman!"

And unsaid: also a thrillingly imaginative lover, capable of appearing unannounced in her room in the night and transporting her to a much better place.

Attack was her only defence.

"And do not think Edwin, that I am unaware of your own extramural interests: in particular your liaison with Charlotte Drake. I am sure there are more, though once I thought you were immune to such temptations. Such a cold fish with such particular appetites! There must be plenty of women who enjoy the punishment you like to give, especially when they are paid to do so."

Ravenswood stood, furious, his hands gripping the edge of the table as if he prepared to launch it at his wife and slam them both to fragments against the wall. Her mention of Lottie infuriated him. It was a reminder of more unfinished business.

"So," he countered, "you dally with the hired help whilst I am negotiating the fortunes you would like to spend. Are you so different from the harlots in Shadwell's brothel, Madam?"

He surprised her by following up with a swift move towards her and she leapt to her feet.

"Damn you, Edwin! Damn you to hell where you belong!" she screamed, flinging her glass wildly at him, to fall just wide and smash like a shrapnel shell into the wall behind his head.

"Predictably unbalanced, as well as disappointingly barren, Amanda," said Ravenswood with distaste as she stood, head bowed and gulping down air, her body starting to shudder with raw, racking sobs. "Are you of any further use at all?"

He covered the remaining ground between them before she looked up, grabbed her by the arm and pulled her to him. She struggled to push him away but his grip on her left arm tightened whilst his other hand tore the gown from her shoulder and pushed up her skirts. Always aroused by fear, he pulled her to him, pinioning her arms and burying his face in her neck.

"No, no!" She struggled, twisting her body away from him and rolling her head out of reach, but he held her tighter still as he pushed her back onto the table.

Her body flat, but with her legs still free, she took a desperate chance and brought her knee up hard between his legs. She wriggled from under him as he gasped and doubled-over in pain, but his hold on her arm never faltered. He straightened up and struck her twice across the face. All the frustrations of the last week were in the blows and Amanda fell to the floor choking, her mouth full of hot blood and her arms circling her head in defence as she curled up in a ball on the floor.

"Get up," he said curtly. "There might just be a few more uses for you. Go upstairs and get ready, perhaps you can redeem yourself before morning."

She rolled onto her knees, cradling her jaw. "You've broken my back teeth, you

244

bastard."

"You heard me. Go and clean yourself up. You are marking the carpet and it is worth considerably more than you are."

She heard her husband stride away, the sound of his footfalls retreating towards the west wing. Shaking, she rose unsteadily to her feet, wiped her eyes on the back of her hand and walked slowly out of the dining room and up the stairs. As she stood on the landing she looked up. The moon was out, its pale beams illuminating the dragon window in the roof. Despite her sad state, she smiled at the memory of standing below it in the arms of Cornelius Lee, bathed in the green and silver of its scales and the yellow fire of the flames which gushed from its mouth. He would not be far away, and from that thought she gained strength. She went to her dressing room, crouched on the stool before the mirror and rinsed out her swollen mouth. Wincing in pain, her hand automatically reached for the laudanum bottle and she took a deep draught, but then she paused and put it back on the shelf, looking instead at her reflection in the mirror. She sat up straighter and stared deeply into her own eyes. There could be someone new, a life force not dulled with drugs or the pain of rejection, and not her old self, sharp, catty and trivial, but someone different, someone capable of much more. It was within her power to conjure that person from the depths of her misery and she would do it.

Leaving no time to think any further she kicked off her shoes and ran quietly down the stairs. All the staff had gone to ground, wisely staying clear of the fracas in the dining room. It suited her. Edwin would be in the Oriental Salon with his brandy, and with any luck he would be standing at the window looking out on the completed palm house which overlooked the garden, illuminated now by gas jets for his evening pleasure. She slipped across the hall towards his territory, a walk which usually made her nervous: but not tonight. Tonight would be the last time and it would be different. As she stole by the disembodied sentries in the dark entrance corridor, the ghoulish empty suits of armour with their hollow heads and limbs, their metal hands and scabbards bristling with weapons, she stopped abruptly at the masked figure of the Japanese samurai. She had listened to Edwin's proud descriptions of his collection so many times that she could name each part and even conduct a tour herself. The warrior wore two swords, the long katana at his left hip and cross-wise in his belt, and to his right, a short wakasashi. She reached out to the smaller weapon, grasped the handle and pulled. It slid soundlessly from its shark-skin scabbard; she touched the blade and saw a fine line of blood start from her finger.

There was no going back. She gripped the handle tightly in her hand, held the wakasashi above her head and crept through the open door of the Salon. Ravenswood was standing, brandy glass in hand with his back to the door, looking out, as she had hoped, towards the side window of the palm house. Sensing her movement he whipped round as she closed in on him, but he was too late. The raised sword slashed down through the air at his neck as he dropped the glass, dodged away and clawed at her with both hands to deflect the weapon as the blade bit into his shoulder, cutting through his jacket to the flesh. She slashed again, catching his defending arm and hand.

"Stop it, you mad bitch," yelled Ravenswood in an agony of pain, as she screamed a volley of curses at him, then backed away, swivelling her head round, searching for an escape. Sobbing now with fear she bolted for the door to the garden and fled into the night, zigzagging over the green towards the dark line of trees.

Ravenswood paused only to grab a pistol from his desk drawer before chasing after her. Despite his wounds he picked up speed over the short dry turf, visibility was good and she was an easy target in the moonlight. As they neared the trees he was within ten feet of her but she reached cover just ahead of him and plunged into the undergrowth.

"Come out!" he shouted, ploughing in after her and coming to a stop as he emerged into a clearing, his pistol raised, his eyes raking the darkness. As the silence grew around him, he forced his voice to soften. "You are ill, darling. Come out and we'll have a drink together. No harm done."

As he raised the gun, his hand and body start to tremble. He glanced down and saw the dark bloodstain from his shoulder had spread, soaking his jacket. The glade was strangely quiet as he turned painfully, struggling to focus in the shadowy moonlight. In the distance beyond the trees, the sundial and the sloping green, the house reared up black against the night sky, lit along the back by the flaring jets of the palm house. He turned again to a surge of cold air, and felt rather than saw the dark shade of a man rush by him, a heavy bag dragging at his shoulder, his breath painful and ragged. Confused he staggered after it and in the distance saw a light bobbing in the wood. He raised his pistol and fired wildly, but before the cloud of smoke cleared a searing pain scorched through his neck from behind. Amanda brought down the wakasashi and felled him to his knees. She struck again and again, without mercy, until he lay slumped on the grass, blood pooling around him.

"Madam, Madam! What in God's name is happening?"

She looked up, disorientated, the dripping blade in her two hands. Matthew Spence was standing on the edge of the clearing, holding a lamp high. "I was doing the rounds with Selwyn, the new man, and we heard voices. He's shot back there in

246

the wood, Madam! He's not movin', either. Bit like Master."

Amanda dropped the blade as though it burned her. Her next move could dictate the rest of her life, and the length of it.

"Matthew," she said slowly. "Matthew, thank God it's you." She searched for words, her mind racing. "Mr Ravenswood heard noises in the trees and came out." Again, a pause: she gathered her wits. "I followed him and found that," she pointed to the wakasashi at her feet, its steel still wickedly bright, but streaked and livid with blood. Her eyes roamed around the clearing, seeking inspiration.

"Did you see a figure pass you?"

Matthew dragged his eyes from the body crumpled at their feet and looked into her eyes. There was no need to struggle further, there was an unspoken agreement. She was his employer and his benefactress: he put a protective arm around her.

"Can I help you to the house, Madam? There's been a lot of talk about folk seeing things just here in the wood. I reckon intruders get in. Thieves probably, like the last time. Come away. I'll have these bodies taken to the house and send for the magistrate. There's nothing we can do for them. Master mistook Sel for the intruder." He looked at her; they both nodded in silent agreement and turned towards the house.

Matthew had never touched Mrs Ravenswood before. She was shivering despite the warmth of the night, like a sparrow he had once caught in his hands, its wings beating on his palms, its heart pounding fit to burst. He glanced down at her as they neared the lights of the house. Her dress was torn from her shoulder, the fabric lying limp over her breast, her feet were bare and scratched, the side of her face was swelling and it was smeared with blood. He was in little doubt about the identity of her attacker, or what deed she had done that night. But for now he would keep that knowledge close. He led her back through the open door to the Oriental Salon and closed the door on the night.

### Late afternoon: 17th July, 1833. The Church of Saint Mary Redcliffe, Bristol.

The widowed Mrs Amanda Ravenswood sat demurely in the front pew of Saint Mary Redcliffe Church. The heavy black veil draped over her hat and face fell in gauzy folds to her shoulders, obscuring every expression, and to the minds of the congregation every bitter tear, from the prying eyes of the public. The funeral of Mr Edwin Ravenswood had attracted many sight-seers and the nave was full. By Mrs Ravenswood sat a distinguished figure: Mr John Drake from the Foreign Office in London, proof of the national standing of the late Mr Ravenswood and close friend of the bereaved widow. There was also an array of important men of Bristol, the

247

social elite and business magnates, resplendent in the front pews with their wives. The Mayor, Aldermen, Councillors and Members of the Bench were in attendance, also a group of foreign business men, Asiatics, seated away from the rest in the aisle, their dealings with the famous Mr Ravenswood cut tragically short.

No close relatives were left alive to attend and the few distant ones were occupied on the family plantations in the West Indies. It was just as well, as there was nothing for them. Mrs Ravenswood had inherited all of her husband's possessions: the businesses, the houses and all their contents, as well as the distant sugar plantations with their complements of slaves. The loyalty of the staff had been established quickly, once they realised that their new pay-mistress guaranteed the security of each job and that compassionate leave, without pay, was available for all who might need it. Gratifyingly, none did, and Matthew Spence had been as good as his word when the time came for him to give evidence. The tragic events which led to the deaths of two men, one a pillar of society and invaluable magistrate, the other his loyal servant, were blamed on misadventure following the pursuit of a brutal intruder. Though Ravenswood's profile demanded continuing enquiries, the coroner agreed that the funeral could be arranged without delay. And there was one other who had been invaluable over the difficult days. She had sent a message in search of Cornelius on the morning after Edwin's death and he had been at Arno's Tower by nightfall.

As the funeral party made its way to the burial, a hectic, and for some a very satisfying scene was playing out on the wharf below Redcliffe Parade. A detachment of dragoons dominated the quay, mounted and with drawn sabres, their horses skittish and prancing. Huddled before them, rounded up and trapped between the troops, was the crew of the *Blue Dragon,* with Captain Eli Trevellis singled out and bound in chains before a magistrate.

"Eli Trevellis," snapped Captain Peterson. "I ordered your arrest in my capacity as Justice of the Peace concerning the death of Benjamin Prestwick in Bath on the 30th January of this year."

Trevellis scowled and struggled, making to pull himself free from the men who held him. "I never did 'im in. There's no true proof in the world could pin that on me."

"I have heard evidence linking you to the death, Trevellis," said Captain Peterson.

"Who the devil from?" snarled Trevellis.

"Evidence gathered at Joshua Shadwell's brothel ties you very tightly to the crime. You may not have landed the blows but it appears that you were the puppet master in the sorry affair. You won the poor man's friendship and delivered him to his killers. Take him away!"

As Trevellis was dragged towards the ramped walkway leading to Redcliffe Parade he caught sight of Nathaniel and Cornelius waiting by the troops.

"Lee!" gasped Trevellis. "I heard a rumour you'd surfaced but I didn't believe it. By rights your bones should be bleaching by the Pearl River after you jumped ship."

"Expect the unexpected," replied Cornelius drily.

"And this ship is impounded until further notice," declared Captain Peterson. "A word gentlemen!"

He motioned Nathaniel and Cornelius over, out of earshot of the troops.

"Mr Lee, you clearly know a considerable amount about Trevellis. If the charges do not succeed I may need to speak with you on this matter in the near future."

"I may be of even greater assistance," said Cornelius quietly. "I saw Trevellis assault Mr Raphael Vere of the New Bank in Bath. He intended to drown him on Ravenswood's orders."

"Good God!" exclaimed the Captain.

"But," cautioned Nathaniel, "that intelligence should only be used if Trevellis appears to be escaping conviction. It is in the national interest, as you know, for the Ravenswood businesses to continue for the present and a resurrection of the Vere enquiry might place them in jeopardy."

Captain Peterson puffed out his cheeks, thwarted. "Indeed. Thank you Mr Lee, your information stops with me for now."

As Cornelius bowed the Captain turned from him abruptly. "Well, Nathaniel, a successful caper so far. For my part I'm going aboard the *Blue Dragon*. It's a while since I've been on a deck and theoretically I own a share in her, so I have a mind to inspect my property!"

With a spring in his step, Oliver Peterson made for the gangway.

"Nathaniel," said Cornelius urgently. "I need to leave now and ride to the church before the burial is over. The *Zhen Tian Lei* has not only quit this wharf but is not in any of the boatyards for refit as some of the crew claimed. It has left Bristol and my men have reported that it is idling at anchor below Clifton Rocks. It will be waiting for the evening tide and I suspect that Kizhe and his party may not return to Redcliffe Parade for the funeral reception as planned, but go straight to the ship. I need to complete my mission with regard to this man and I need to do it alone."

"I can come with you," said Nathaniel.

"Cornelius shook his head. "Thank you, but it is better not to involve any British government official in this. Nathaniel, I assume that you and Drake will need to be in London to see your masters next week. Shall I see you there?"

"You will," said Nathaniel. "In London then: Carlisle Lane, Monday night." He held out his hand. "Good luck."

Cornelius bowed, clasped his hand and then made off through the ranks of dragoons to where his horse was tied by the locked doors to the red caves. Nathaniel watched as he swung himself up into the saddle, galloped up the steep path to Redcliffe Parade and was lost to view.

As the funeral party left the graveside, Amanda took Drake's arm and prepared to lead the procession for the short walk through the churchyard back to Redcliffe Parade. As they moved off she heard hurried footsteps behind her and turned to see a servant approaching from the group of Asian businessmen.

"Madam," he said with a bow. "Mr Kizhe sends his respects. As Mr Lee has not attended as he was told to expect, he is leaving now. He will contact you with regard to pressing business matters at a more suitable time in the near future."

"I see," said Amanda. "How unfortunate. I am sure that Mr Lee will be waiting at the house. Perhaps he was unable to attend church. Do tell Mr Kizhe that he is very welcome to join us."

"It is too late, Madam," said the servant, turning away and disappearing amongst the crowd.

"I see Kizhe's coach," said Drake. "Look there!"

Down the road and ready to head to Bristol Bridge, was the garish red coach Kizhe had hired in London.

"I see it. And he will be safely stowed in it already!" said Amanda, annoyed, but then she laughed. "But look who is behind them!"

Cornelius, astride Ravenswood's fastest chestnut mare, rode by the church railings from the Parade as the servant made it to the coach and climbed up to the driver's seat.

"He will not be the only one," said Drake, waving a signal to a horseman at the gate. "My man will shadow our foreign visitors."

And, he thought, but left unsaid, with luck will see them all off the premises. He took Amanda's black-gloved hand and looked down fondly on her pale face, shadowed and indistinct behind the folds of her veil. Their alliance forged in the worst days of Lottie's infidelity with Ravenswood had not lapsed with the cooling of the affair. "Don't rely too much on your new right-hand man, Amanda. He is not just an enterprising associate of the opium traders. I believe that Mr Lee may be quite a different person from what he has led us to believe."

"Yes, John," she said meekly, her expression conveniently masked behind the filmy net of her veil. "I think you may well be right."

Cornelius kept well back in the press of traffic approaching the bridge but never let the red coach out of his sight. Kizhe had planned his exit strategy well, baulked of his chance to settle with Cornelius he had packed his belongings at Redcliffe Parade and had his war junk waiting on the tide down-river from the city. Chen and Fong were already in position, hiding in the rocks overlooking the anchorage to make sure that Kizhe did not give him the slip again. He shadowed the coach through the city and out on the road towards the coast. The fashionable village of Clifton which clung to the rocks overlooking the river had been left behind and the road became lonely.

Cornelius unwrapped his bow and quiver from their carrying cloth, placed the bow across his back and the quiver by his side. He rode closer to the scrubby trees overhanging the road, crouching low on his horse, feeling the body and gait of the animal to move with her as one. Round the next bend in the river he saw the *Zhen Tian Lei* at anchor and the coach coming to a halt at the bank. His quarry leapt out and stood by the horses, a mountain of a man, rectangular, with his massive head rising from his shoulders, the hachiwari thrust in his belt. He heard a guttural order barked out: a heavy chest was carried from the interior of the coach by two servants whilst the driver and one other unloaded the trunks from the back.

Still a hundred yards from his target but with the two men holding the chest in plain view, Cornelius urged his horse forward to a gallop, drew his bow, and fired at one of them. Sliding from the horse and letting it run, he dropped into the bushes for cover, shot again and dropped the man left standing. At the sound of the approaching horse Kizhe had wheeled round, saw the slumped bodies on the road and rolled under the coach bellowing orders. The remaining two men struggling with the rest of the luggage instantly ditched the trunk they were carrying and drew their percussion pistols, scouring the road and the rocks above their heads as they backed closer to the coach. For a moment, silence, as Cornelius waited for a clear shot at Kizhe, then an ominous hiss as fused missiles flew down from high above them on the rock face. Four consecutive explosions rocked the coach and smoke filled the air. Fong and Chen scrambled down into the thick of the confusion and ran through the choking smoke towards Kizhe's guards. They opened fire, felling them both in a precise fusillade of arrows.

But the crewmen on the boat were already out on deck. Their enraged shouts floated over the water accompanied by the unmistakable sound of the launching of a jolly boat to bring a gang of them to assist on shore. Under cover of the explosions Cornelius knew that Kizhe would have taken the chance to slip away in the smoke and had run up to a terrace on the rocks to get a higher vantage point. As the smoke started to clear his adversary materialised on the terrace not ten feet in front of him, levelled his two pistols and opened fire with his right. Dropping to his knees Cornelius dodged the shot, drew an arrow from the quiver at his side as if it were a sword in a sheath and flung it at Kizhe's head, following in quick succession with another, and another. As his target dodged and deflected, Cornelius narrowed the distance between them, closed in on his foe and parted Kizhe from his remaining loaded pistol with a high sweeping kick.

As the two men squared up to each other in the clearing gloom Kizhe drew his hachiwari, the helmet breaker, and launched himself at Cornelius, the weapon scything round and down, aiming to bury itself in his head. The weapon missed its mark, but despite his size, Kizhe's body followed its circular path, flying towards the ground, rolling over on his free arm, and snapping back onto his feet like a monstrous mountain cat, weapon still in play. Cornelius remembered the move, had anticipated it, and waited for the next. Again, the scything blow came, but now as a feint, stopping short and pulling back, raking Cornelius's arm with the hook as a kick powered through to deliver a glancing blow to the side of his head.

A surprise. Cornelius shook his head clear. The last time they had fought, Kizhe he had never used his feet, and also this time, as the hook of the hachiwari had bitten into him, he had looked at it. There was a discrepancy, but only a split second to register it. Sounds of the oarsmen on the jolly boat drew nearer. He had only moments and used the first to clear his mind. He must respond to the attack and not to the individual. He exhaled, coordinating his body, mind and spirit. The advancing sounds from the water faded away and time slowed. He summoned his whole being and delivered a lightning left-fist thrust to his opponent's throat, followed up by a right-hand punch to the chest so fast that it had landed before the eye could catch it in flight and so deadly that it collapsed the lung and pushed a rib into the heart. He bent down swiftly and put his hand to his opponent's neck. It was finished. He glanced around, gave a shrilling double whistle of confirmation, heard the same in distant response from Fong and Chen, thrust the fallen hachiwari into his belt and pushed the body over the edge of the terrace to roll down to the road.

By the time he was half-way up the hill, working low through the overhanging trees, the boat had reached the river's edge and a dozen men poured over the side onto the path. Ragged cries floated up as the men swarmed over the scene, some checking the road fearfully, most helping up the injured and lifting the fallen, taking them on board to be ferried to the ship. He made more height and gave a low bird-call. An answer from even higher up by a small cave led him to the eyrie of Fong

252

and Chen.

"Thank you, friends," said Cornelius and then looked down at a locked chest at their feet. "What is this?"

"We came down just after the explosion," said Fong, grinning. "We couldn't leave a strongbox lying on the road. There are too many thieves about!"

Cornelius did not answer, but he could not begrudge them their prize. He had more on his mind as he looked back to the abandoned coach and watched the distant figures rowing away from the shore. He thought instead of his adversary and the way he had moved, he glanced down at the helmet breaker, then looked up to watch the sails of Kizhe's ship billow out on the early evening breeze, catching the tide to the open sea.

**Late morning: 22nd July, 1833. Downing Street, London.**

Drake and Nathaniel had first met in the Foreign Office and gone up to the junior clerks' attic to while away the time before Lord Palmerston condescended to join them for their meeting. The Foreign Office ranged over four rickety houses at the far end of Downing Street, on the left of the cul-de-sac as one entered from Whitehall. The accommodation for the juniors, though shabby, was informal, comfortable, and in their opinion had an excellent view, which was of Fludyer Street and its gin shops. A few youths were tinkling on a piano, trying out some new tunes and from the wall hung some moth-eaten boxing gloves. Neither activity was enticing. They settled on a hand of cards, swept aside an abandoned game of backgammon, and took over the table.

"You deal," said Nathaniel.

"Mi'noble Lord will not be pleased to hear the details of the loss of Ravenswood," said Drake, dashing out the cards.

"Never thought he would be," said Nathaniel, swiftly rearranging his hand.

"With no Company monopoly he would soon have been all legal and above board," said Drake opening the play.

"Apart from the slaving, murder and extortion," said Nathaniel, sweeping up the trick.

"Well, yes, obviously."

Drake's finger strayed to fiddle with his collar, that old nervous tic was so nearly extinguished, just like old "John Company", but it could still rear up in moments of stress. It did so now at the thought of his close shave with Ravenswood's business empire. He played his next card.

"No more "*sneer of cold command*" from that "*shatter'd visage*" what!"

"How's that?" asked Nathaniel.

"You know, Shelley's *Ozymandias*. Ravenswood fancied himself as a King of Kings: "*Look on my works, ye Mighty, and despair*!" Drake sniggered, well pleased with himself. "I had a man trailing Lee along the river road by Clifton. It looks like he saw off that devil Kizhe and I gather he is helping Mrs Ravenswood keep the business on an even keel."

Nathaniel watched Drake carefully. Cornelius was no longer seen by him as just another henchman, but it was important to keep Drake in ignorance with regard to the full scope of his friend's mission. To the same end, additional clever footwork had been required to cool the Captain's enthusiasm for interviewing Cornelius about Vere's death.

"Yes," he said casually. "It is useful to leave Cornelius Lee in place for now. He might be helpful to us. My trick I think."

Drake stuck out his bottom teeth in frustration. "I suppose it is, and I suppose he will. I warned Amanda. I don't want her relying on his support for her business."

He paused before playing his next card.

"Damned relief for me that Ravenswood's gone though. And that scoundrel Trevellis!" He smiled. "Made my life a bit smoother at base camp I don't mind telling you. You must come up to town and stay with Lottie and me. Bring Emma. We could go to the theatre. London shows will knock your provincial offerings into a cocked hat." He looked down. "Damn it! Yours again!"

"I was pleased to collar Trevellis," said Nathaniel. "And I heard that his two henchmen from Shadwell's have disappeared. They caught wind of Trevellis's arrest and guessed he would give them up to save his own skin."

Nathaniel had been pleased to hear that the unwholesome presence of Jabez and Billy had disappeared from the streets of Bath. Tobias had reported the news after seeing Clari Marchant in Kingsmead Square. She had been in high good humour and was delighted to tell the tale of their replacement, Letty's amiable brother, Fred, who had abandoned coach driving and moved into Green Park West as Rosie Shadwell's right-hand man. Joshua would be spending more time than ever in his office at the bottom of the garden. He might have to move into it permanently.

"Mine! At last!" Drake smirked.

As he swept up the cards a servant entered.

"Mr Drake, sir, Mr Parry, sir, Lord Palmerston is detained at Brooks's and you are invited instead to report to Lord Melbourne's office. I'd be sharp if I were you," he added as an afterthought. "He's got Percy putting all the papers away and he just said he could eat a horse."

They descended from the clerks' "Nursery" and made their way from the Foreign Office quarters to the luxury of the Home Secretary's rooms to find that the servant was spot on. Melbourne was hovering by the window, shooting his cuffs and muttering to himself, clearly ready for the off.

"Excellent to see you both," he said. "Splendid, splendid. Don't sit down gentlemen. Just a word will do. Just a word. Ha! Ha! Now, the news! That blasted pirate in Bristol has had his come-uppance I gather as well as some foreign rascal! What!"

"Yes, mi'lord," said Drake levelly. "Edwin Ravenswood was killed in an incident with an intruder. Investigations are ongoing but no arrests as yet. His firm's business capability for engaging in the opium trade is unaffected so Lord Palmerston will be gratified. Other less acceptable activities are more likely to cease, especially as his Captain has been arrested on suspicion of conspiring to murder. Your contact, Captain Peterson, remains connected with the business as you will be aware and will exercise more influence as required. He is acquainted with the widow who has inherited the business in its entirety."

Melbourne nodded vigorously. "Good, good, case closed. That's the ticket. I must say it is also most edifying to see the spate of kidnapping in the city reduced. Perhaps the removal of Mr Ravenwood's unsavoury associate is not unconnected with that." He clapped his hands twice to emphasise his approval, lost his thread, and then resumed. "Oh yes! A bit of good news on that score. Remember the Honourable Member whose servant disappeared? Well, the woman's turned up! Most pleasing for the morale of the House. And the other business? Murder of the old soldier settled?"

"Yes, mi'lord."

"No Egyptian jewels I take it? No Napoleonic loot? Damned wild goose chase. Percy will be disappointed. Won't you, Percy?"

Richard Percy poked his head round the door. "Yes, mi'lord."

"Very taken by romance of the Nile weren't you, my boy!"

"Very, mi'lord."

Percy retreated to his desk and continued packing up the papers. It had been a short day and he was not complaining. He felt pleased to note the improvement in relations. Drake's attitude had mellowed and he seemed on positively cordial terms with Nathaniel Parry. He was grateful for the improved atmosphere as, apart from that, the year had been an unrelieved slog and it was only half done. It was common knowledge that Earl Grey was worn to a frazzle and the continued rise of Lord Melbourne's star was inevitable. The punishing legislative programme would not be letting up any time soon, the Whigs were on a roll whether they deserved the credit or not, and his lord and master was limbering up for the premiership.

The dulcet tones of Melbourne boomed through the open door. "So there we are. Done and dusted. Written reports on my desk before tomorrow morning, gentlemen. Then back to Bath with you, Parry. Keep your ears open for reactions to the new Factory Act in the clothing towns. Put yourself about in the Political Unions. The Act has no teeth whatsoever in terms of their adult workers so the owners should not be too vexed even if the operatives are. And the Slavery Bill should be through very soon to lighten the mood round Bristol. Compensation for owners will be fair, to be frank, more than fair."

### Evening: Nathaniel's Rooms, Carlisle Lane, Lambeth, London.

"What is it?" said Nathaniel, looking up from the table and his preoccupied labours over the Ulrich pistols which involved ramrods, assorted wire brushes, soap, boiling water and grease.

Caradoc had been stretched out on the floor by his feet, growling periodically in his dreams and deaf to the evening serenade of bird song which floated sweetly through the open window from the Bishop's gardens, but without warning his head had shot up, and just one ear. Even before the footfalls on the stairs announced the arrival of the housemaid and a guest, the terrier was at the door barking a welcome to Cornelius Lee.

"It is tranquil here, for London," said Cornelius, pausing in the doorway as Nathaniel strode over and took his hand.

"It is," said Nathaniel. "Close enough to the centre, but as you say, tranquil. Come in, be seated. Brandy?"

They sat in the fading light and Caradoc contrived to spread himself equidistantly between the two of them. The heat of the night made it an unattractive prospect to sprawl on their feet or favour one of them with his head on their lap. He had given a decent welcome, drunk his bowl dry and now needed to focus on finding a pitch with the maximum draft.

"Cornelius, my friend, you rarely give much away, but your face shows not even a flicker of the conquering hero."

Cornelius smiled wryly. "No. The ambush of Kizhe's coach went according to plan. Fong and Chen played their parts. And they rewarded themselves." He took a string of brilliants from his pocket and threw them to Nathaniel. "A sample for you."

Nathaniel turned them over in his hands. "Beautiful," he said.

"Look closer."

Nathaniel went to his table, rooted out a magnifying glass from his cleaning kit and took the gems to the window.

"Astonishingly good paste!" he said.

"It looks as though Kizhe might be developing another side line."

Nathaniel looked up at him sharply. "Present tense?"

"The man I killed on the river road may have looked like Kizhe, but he did not move like him. I also took the hachiwari so I could inspect it later. Do you remember that he carried a helmet breaker like the ones some Japanese officers carry? They are heavy and blunt on the side with a pointed end and a hook to trap a sword thrust. I had seen Kizhe's weapon close up before, this one did not have the same detail on the lacquer. It was a replica, a replacement, as was the man. I have no doubt that my foe sailed with his vessel. I will return to China in the spring once I have put in place all the contacts I need in the Ravenswood business."

"So Amanda Ravenswood will continue with the trade?"

"With some aspects of it. The drug trade outside the East India Company monopoly will be legal within months, though it still contravenes Chinese law. My mission is incomplete."

"And are your dealings with Mrs Ravenswood concluded?"

"Not quite," said Cornelius. "I shall advise her on the trade to suit my ultimate purpose, and as that is diametrically opposed to the wishes of your government I had better keep that advice to myself."

"And your dealings which are not concerned with trade?"

"It is in our mutual interest for me to return briefly. I will help her gain strength. One of my duties," he said with a smile, "has been as her instructor. She has developed an interest in weapons training, in particular the use of the short sword."

"Has she become a formidable woman, Cornelius?"

"All people can have the capacity to be dangerous, Nathaniel, men and women alike. Take your French friend for instance. Training is an essential in life; it makes us aware of our weaknesses as well as our strengths. We need to know ourselves before we can ever know another."

For a while they sat together without speaking and listened to the last soft notes of the evening chorus, until at length just the voice of a lone nightingale remained to drift between them through the growing dark of the room.

"We trained together for years. But now I feel I know my father better than I did before," said Nathaniel. "This year has resurrected ghosts from his wars and most of them have been laid to rest with poor old Prestwick. I was glad to leave the fate of the jewels for Coco to decide. It seemed the right thing to do. She had more claim on them than I had. And the strangest thing happened, Cornelius! When I spoke with her in France, we discovered she had seen me before, when I visited Paris with my father, the year he died. She is taking up with a wealthy old lover of hers, a Marquis. I met him too that night. And so the world turns. She sees life like that: as a capricious turn of the wheel, a random spin from Lady Fortuna."

He poured another brandy for them both and lifted his glass, swirling the spirit round to cling to the sides and slowly recede like waves from a shore.

"Life isn't just linear, is it? It has a circularity about it. I found my father's journal of the Spanish campaign in one of his old strongboxes. He had the measure of Sir Giles when he was plain Captain Mortimer-Buckley. From what Lord Melbourne said today, his missing servant has returned and it also appears that he has escaped all blame for Prestwick's death. So his reckoning will have to wait, but I am sure his turn will come."

"Consider that life is not linear or circular my friend but an eternal present, an everlasting paired and balanced existence of the dark and the light, an inseparable whole."

Nathaniel stretched out his glass. "Here's to the delicate balance. Long may it hold!"

As the glasses clinked in agreement they fell silent, each lost in his own thoughts until Caradoc sensed a change and ambled over to his master for an explanation.

"Visit us in Bath before you leave," said Nathaniel, scratching the terrier's ear. "This fellow will not forgive you if you don't, and Emma will be pleased to see you. We both will. She is keen to entertain you and show off the gown she made with the silk you brought from China."

"I will not leave before making that visit," said Cornelius.

**Evening: 1st August, 1833.**
**The Mortimer-Buckley Residence, Park Street, Mayfair.**

Sir Giles Mortimer-Buckley had dared to believe that his life was starting to return to its customary ease. Ravenswood was dead. As far as he knew there was no record of his role in Prestwick's death, or the abduction of Maisie Trickett, and his lawyers were busy claiming back his investment in the Ravenswood businesses. With the little widow left in charge that could hardly prove to be a difficult manoeuvre. There was just Parry's knowledge of his connection with the raid in Spain, but he was a busy man with no proof. The future had indeed started to look bright. But one ring at the door had reduced that hope to ashes.

Last week, Maisie had returned like a bad penny. Stupid and venal she may be:

she had also proved to be a survivor, slipping away from her captors in Holland and working her way home to London. There she had stood at the door, her pregnancy grossly advanced, the return of the lost lamb. Leonora and Prudence had welcomed her with open arms and installed her again in triumph. Everyone had been told of the brutal treatment she had received at the hands of her captors, the assaults and the obvious violation of her person, the subsequent mortification of a pregnancy. She would, of course, be cared for by the Mortimer-Buckley family in perpetuity as an old and valued retainer. Her position with Lulu would be restored and the unwanted child adopted. The nightmare had returned. Maisie seemed to be running with the explanation of her plight and had not yet linked her abduction to him but was starting to complain about the disappearance of her trunk, which she claimed she never did send for, as Sir Giles seemed to think. And so she paved the way for relentless extortion to come.

Buckley had taken to retreating to his dressing room for brandy after dinner, always French these days, never Spanish. It was August but it was an unaccountably cold day. He had demanded the fire be lit for warmth, and had taken himself off to be in the company of his own dark thoughts, and of that low, grating voice. It always had some ideas, some suggestions for his next move. He locked the door, pulled his chair close to the flames and soon dropped off into a troubled sleep, wrapped in his trailing dressing gown, his glass and bottle cradled slackly in his lap.

The nightmares were not slow to intrude upon his dreams. As always, the two sisters: both darkly beautiful, Izar with her whore's eyes and behind her the graceful Amaia, silent and so bizarrely named: The End. Their fair faces lasted only moments, eclipsed by a fiery chaos of murder, sundering timbers and the crashes of collapsing buildings, a naked woman sprawled dead on a cabin floor, Prestwick's burned face lolled before him, growing ever larger, incongruously superimposed on the head of a hanged man dangling from a gibbet.

Sir Giles woke; howling in anguish, to find himself lurched forward towards the fire. His glass of brandy spilled over his lap as he looked directly into the smoke billowing gustily from the hearth, and there wreathed in its toils was the third sister with her empty eye sockets, her gash of a smile, reaching out with skeletal arms.

"Get away from me, witch!" he screamed. "Damn you! Damn you all!"

"Now! Throw it!" The voice, no longer low, rose to a wild shriek. "Blow her back to hell where she belongs!"

And he flung the bottle into the fire.

The sound of shattering glass and a muffled explosion, thudding crashes and cries of pain sounded out above the drawing room where the women sipped their coffee, and reverberated down the stairs to the servants' quarters. None of them could have run any faster, the footmen clearing the steps two at a time, the women pattering and puffing behind.

"Giles! Giles! Lord preserve us, I smell smoke! Look, look through the door. Fire! Fire!"

"Sir! Open the door! Sir!"

But it was all too late; the roaring flames fuelled by the exploding spirit had him in a death grip, consuming him as he writhed, screaming by the toppled chair, pains locking his chest in a grip of iron, his fingers clawing his neck for air, tearing his silver chain asunder and sending his lucky medal spinning away across the floor, rolling away from him and the blazing hearth, to a place of safety.

# Epilogue

**Early evening: 7th December, 1833. The Grand-Théâtre, Bordeaux.**

As the claret-coloured carriage came to a skidding halt outside the theatre, the horses champing and blowing hard in the glittering dark, two liveried footmen sprang down to open the doors for their employers. Pierre and Anna Guestier, and their guests, Bernard and Eliza Phelan, were bundled out with some difficulty, encumbered by winter layers topped by fur-lined cloaks, their fingers clumsy in padded gloves. As Pierre issued orders to the driver, Anna stamped her feet in a vain attempt to accelerate the circulation and beat down the numb cold rising from her toes. She looked longingly up the steps to the light and warmth streaming out from the theatre doors, then rolled her eyes in barely concealed impatience until they lighted on a couple who had not been seen in the city since the summer, but who had been the target of malicious gossip at every day call and evening *soirée* since.

"Eliza!" she gasped, grabbing her sister-in-law's arm and inclining her head vehemently in their direction. "Look who's coming! It's the Marquis de la Blanquefort and he's with that woman he went away with directly after his poor wife passed away. You know who I mean! She came to dinner at General Palmer's with the Irish politician, that friend of the Bartons." She pursed her lips and raised her eyebrows. "He does not appear to be in mourning."

"My dear," said Eliza Phelan authoritatively. "Why should he be? The Marquis was never one for convention and he has married the hussy already. You can see

261

why!"

Coco held her Marquis's arm as she picked her way daintily over the slippery pavement. She did not seem to suffer from the cold and allowed her cloak to blow wide, revealing a sparkling necklace of emeralds set in heavy gold above a green velvet gown with white fur trim. The dress was not cut as tight as fashion demanded, so as to allow accommodation for her swelling breasts and the rising mound of her unborn child.

"Well, I never!" exclaimed Anna.

"Bernard, look who it is!" exclaimed Pierre, orders now issued and the carriage rattling off down the road. "The Marquis is back! I need to catch him."

"Pierre," squeaked Anna. "Don't bring him over! He is with that woman, that Jezebel!"

"Be that as it may, darling," he said over his shoulder as he strode towards the pair. "They are married, therefore she is also a Marquise, and I have business with her husband."

So, despite Madame Guestier's orders, they all climbed the steps together and gathered briefly before stepping into the warmth and going their separate ways. For the Marquis there were rushed commiserations for his loss, congratulations for his gains, and rendezvous were agreed, for both gentlemen and ladies, for the very near future.

As they passed through the doors Pierre added, "Monsieur le Marquis, I rode by your landscaping at Blanquefort last week, it is progressing magnificently. The grottoes by the lake are quite magical."

"Spellbinding!" said Eliza.

"Yes, indeed," added Anna, looking hard at the new Marquise, "Utterly bewitching."

Coco smiled, inclining her head in a graceful bow to her new neighbours, her hand holding the edge of her cloak collar to her face. Out of sight, she rubbed her thumb along the hard metal surface of her hidden brooch, a talisman strong enough to re-kindle the midsummer fires of Saint John on a cold December night.

## The Adelphi Theatre, The Strand, London.

Five hundred miles away, in another city, another quartet prepared to enjoy an evening's entertainment. John Drake and the Honourable Charlotte, with their guests, Nathaniel and Emma Parry, were settling into their box at the Adelphi.

"I haven't been here since September when the place was entirely refurbished," said Charlotte, excited. "I love the gold on the boxes; the blue silk was tired out."

"I have never been here before," smiled Emma. "And it all looks wonderful to me. This is such a treat, Lottie. Thank you!"

"Our pleasure."

Quite a different Lottie Drake, thought Emma, from the one I first met at Arno's Tower. It seemed a lifetime ago. The frisson between Lottie and Mr Ravenswood had been obvious for anyone with eyes to see, though by all accounts it had withered even before his ghastly murder that summer. John looked happier too, more relaxed. Apparently they had made something of a new start, sold in Mayfair and re-invested in one of the new squares in Belgravia.

Emma had been concerned when she had heard they were to see John Buckstone's new burletta: *The Rake and his Pupil; or Folly, Love, and Marriage.* She had feared it was rather near the bone, for everybody involved, given Lottie's indiscretions and major roles in the play being that of a Marquis, a Marquise and a certain Madame de Lignolle. This last, a flighty French minx played for all she was worth by the celebrated Mrs Laura Honey. But the play's fame had spread, it had been playing to full houses for a fortnight and the men swore they would not miss it. They had all come a long way.

As Lottie caught sight of friends in the stalls and started to tell Emma their life stories Drake shared a quiet word with Nathaniel.

"I entertained Lottie's brother at my club last week. He bought her share of the Mayfair house just down the road from Sir Giles's place. The widow has sold up apparently and gone to Gloucestershire to their country pile. Don't blame her in the slightest. Terrible way to go for Sir Giles."

Nathaniel nodded. "Indeed," he said, but thought instead of the interconnectedness of life, of circularity and of reckonings. He looked at Drake, leaning over to watch the arrival of the orchestra in the pit. The man was quite boyish tonight and at one with himself. In some ways he could even be seen as a friend: though one to be kept at arm's length. Nathaniel had decided not to disabuse Drake of his belief that Kizhe had died on the river road, but to let him enjoy the cheerful prospect of closure on that particular problem, at least for the time being.

As the lights dimmed he looked over to the ladies and his eyes met Emma's. She looked radiant, three sapphires sparkling in the jewelled *aigrette* fixed in her hair, three mounted on a pendant hanging from a fine chain around her neck. The gems sat lightly on her now that she wore them on her own terms, fashioned to her design and freed from the heavy Montrachet settings. As Lottie continued to talk, Emma exchanged a smile with him. The autumn months had passed fruitfully for her in many ways. She had the house running like a well-oiled machine and had spent more

263

time in the company of Céline Junot, who was now a regular visitor, as were other new friends. He often returned from London to find the drawing room full of ladies, a hand-picked collection of Bath's blue stockings, debating anything from religion to reform and putting the world to rights. He felt a pride in her. There she sat, her auburn hair shimmering in curls over her shoulders and the collar of her new loose gown of midnight blue, and lying in her lap, a reticule, a silk one, the fabric exotic and glowing, exquisitely embroidered in pink and russet blooms.

## Morning: 9th December, 1833. Saint Mary's Burial Ground, Bathwick, Bath.

Matthew, Mary and the Johnty accompanied Martha to old Saint Mary's burial ground whenever Matthew was home on a Sunday. Since Ben's death it had been an occasional custom for her to visit his grave and share a few words with him, but after the court case and the transportation of Trevellis it had become a weekly observance. She had gloried in the retribution meted out to that sinner, though she would have liked someone to have swung at a rope's end for the deed. That could yet come to pass.

"The mills of God," she had said, repeatedly and triumphantly. "They grind slow but exceeding small. Praise the Lord!"

The old lady also said that talking to Ben was the closest she got to having a word with her late husband. But there was no resting place for Father, Matthew had thought, but left unsaid. Philip Spence's bones were far away and likely scattered, left to rot on the road to Corunna. He folded his arms and clamped his hands in his armpits. He was growing to dislike the cold more passionately with every year. The hand with the missing fingers throbbed and the stab of pain transported him back to his years aboard the *Blue Dragon* and Ravenswood's other vessels.

Was a broken hand and recurring fever all he had got from working for that cursed slave driver? He smiled to himself. Not by a long shot. Without the years before the mast he would never have had his present job and Mrs Ravenswood's favour: a couple of days a week at the Tower, a fair wage to keep Mary and the boy and help pay Mother back for the years of his absence. He stood higher with Mrs Ravenswood than the other new men; he knew that, especially after the night he had found her in the wood. Nothing would ever change that. Though he did not stand the highest, that was certain.

He would also never have had Jimmy Congo.

Matthew looked over to the far side of the cemetery at the sound of sustained barking and a shriek of laughter from the Johnty. Caradoc had come with Tobias and Frances, who walked out together on a Sunday when the Parrys were not at home. If he was left behind they usually brought Caradoc with them, who always took it upon himself to secure the perimeter of the cemetery and rid it of the two resident cats. With the Johnty as rearguard he seemed to be succeeding in his mission, which was more than could be said for his vendetta with Jimmy Congo, whose whistles and barks still drove the dog to the edge of insanity. His most successful move against his enemy was always a well-timed leap at the perch, up-ending both perch and parrot, but a recent use of this manoeuvre had caused him, once again, to be temporarily barred from the kitchen. Matthew's grandfather and the parrot were inseparable. As well as the baiting of Caradoc, Old Tom encouraged Jimmy Congo to maintain his extensive vocabulary of oaths, to squawk on demand "Napoley's Gold" as taught by Benjamin Prestwick (God rest his soul!) and extend his repertoire to broadest Somerset. The two of them comprehensively tormented everyone unwise enough to tangle with them in the kitchen, which was their stronghold. Not that they were always there these days. On occasions they came with Martha to the cemetery, Tom in the chair and Jimmy on his shoulder, but today the cold air had kept them indoors.

"Time to go, Mother," said Matthew. "Mary, I'll get the Johnty before him and Caradoc get us barred from the graveyard with their racket!"

He made his way round the mortuary chapel but did not have to search further. Tobias, looking taller and broader than ever, was walking towards him, arm in arm with Frances who had the Johnty hoisted on her hip. All were following on behind a swaggering Caradoc, crowned with the whitened stalks of dead bindweed and leading them out under the baleful glare of the two defeated cats, who now balanced, in the interest of self-preservation, on the extreme end of the boundary wall.

## Morning: 10th December. 1833. The Pump Room, Abbey Churchyard, Bath.

The pumper applied himself with his usual energy, and also as usual, the rush of the waters surging into the glasses could barely be heard above the cacophonous tide of gossip generated by the morning crowds of Bath society, the visiting travellers and the prowling packs of fortune hunters.

Dr and Mrs Parry, Captain and Mrs Peterson, plus the two Miss Petersons were corralled in a tight group by the window overlooking the King's Bath, which mitigated Mrs Parry's claustrophobia to some degree. As the men had launched into a deep and exclusive discussion on shipping she was obliged to listen to Lydia Peterson's family news unrelieved by support or distraction. The continuing joy of Emma's pregnancy had been covered satisfactorily as had the immense importance of her son-in-law, who was at present, and even as they spoke, about business in the national interest in the capital city. Mrs Parry had been under the impression that the younger Parrys had gone up to town to see a play, a rather fast one, but let that go. Lydia had already moved on to the prospect of the two Miss Petersons continuing their education in Paris.

"Madame Junot will be chaperoning the girls," declared Lydia triumphantly, drawing an unusually subdued Maddy and Ginette into the circle from where they had been attempting to skulk behind her. "Marvellous opportunity. Though it took considerable effort to persuade the Captain to agree! One cannot imagine why. Paris is as calm as Bath these days."

She stopped suddenly as a trio approached.

"Oh, how lovely! Look, my dear! Look, Oliver! Dr Parry! Mrs Vere's party cometh!"

Captain Peterson's jovial face fell. How much he would have liked to give the beautiful Tilly Vere even a hint of comfort about the mysterious case of her disappearing husband! On Nathaniel's advice he had not pursued the startling evidence offered by Mr Lee about Raphael Vere's likely fate, and in the event Trevellis had been shipped off to Australia months ago on the strength of Nathaniel's evidence alone. Oliver Peterson blew out his cheeks in frustration, but made a mental note to keep a weather eye on the informative Mr Lee.

For her part, the elder Mrs Parry was even more delighted than Lydia to see the new arrivals and set about a fulsome greeting of Tilly Vere, Howard Dill and Mrs Danby, skilfully manoeuvring herself between her husband and Mr Dill to gain maximum relief from Lydia's relentless news.

"Hello, hello, hello!" sang Howard.

"How do, old boy!" boomed Dr Parry. "Haven't seen you for an age, Dill, but I gather we shall meet again before the end of the week. I take it you have had notice of the meeting scheduled at Redcliffe Parade?"

"Certainly have," said Howard, his eyes twinkling. "Splendid job Mrs Ravenswood's making of affairs, wouldn't you say?"

"Indubitably!"

"Poor lady!" exclaimed Mrs Danby suddenly. "Such a terrible blow to lose her husband so early. I know only too well myself of the miseries of widowhood!"

Tilly observed her mother glumly.

"At least she has the satisfaction of knowing where he lies, Mother," she said. "And I am sure Father rests easy in Beckington."

The spectre of Tilly's missing husband rose once again to sour the day for more than Captain Peterson. A brief, respectful hush fell on the party as Tilly's pretty mouth turned down in self-pity and annoyance.

What she would give to have news of his vile body resurfacing! Her marriage to Howard could take place without delay, babies of her own would surely follow, and of more immediate importance, she could pack her mother off to her own home in Beckington on the next coach. Mrs Danby's visits to Lansdown Crescent were frequent and protracted. There seemed barely a week's respite between one and the next and she did not know how much more she could stand. Her mother's portrait, undertaken by her distant relative, the acclaimed Francis Danby, had finally been finished to her satisfaction and was the current focus of her mother's attention. To Tilly's horror she realised that it was to be discussed yet again as her mother re-launched the conversation.

"Yes, yes, my dear. We all know how you suffer and you deserve to have a little gift!" She treated the company to a self-satisfied smile. "My portrait you know. Dear Francis has finished it at last and we have been vexed to decide where the best possible place would be for such a work to be hanged! But I have a solution: at Lansdown Crescent in the hall! I think I have convinced you of the wisdom of that thought, haven't I dear? I could keep you company and welcome you home every time you open the door."

"Mrs Danby," said Howard. "The idea is a capital one. It's as good a place to be hanged as any."

## The Ravenswood Townhouse, Redcliffe Parade, Floating Harbour, Bristol.

Matthew, Declan and Finn were shown into the first floor room overlooking the wharf for the morning briefing. It looked very much as it had done in the days of the master, with the grand table in the centre, the fine wood cabinets by the walls, the shelves of leather-bound books, his jewelled paper knife lying on the desk. Mrs Ravenswood had made it her habit to speak to the men here in small groups every Monday morning to give the orders for the week and sometimes to announce changes.

The African and Far Eastern clipper trade continued to run, including the unofficial smuggling of Indian opium, but there had been no extra passengers. No more women had been shipped out since the day Madam took over. There had been extra wages for all, with promises of much more, as the compensation for the loss of the Ravenswood slaves on the West Indian plantations was to be considerable and Madam was one for sharing the joy. As she began to talk, Matthew looked at her closely. Controversially, she had abandoned her widow's black weeks ago and was wearing a red silk dress, extravagantly beribboned, with tight cuffs, and sleeves blossoming out about the upper arms. Round her shoulders she had a fur wrap, as she liked to sit by the window, despite the cold drafts, keeping an eye on the dock. Her face was pale, but her eyes sparkled and she was amused, her lips drawn back in a foxy smile to reveal her tiny pointed eyeteeth.

As he watched her re-arranging the wrap, loosening it round her neck, his eyes strayed down to her throat where a new piece of jewellery caught his eye, an intricate gold piece of many coloured stones, blue, red and green with a large bird in the centre, a full six inches across. Looking more closely still he saw it was a bird of prey holding rings in its talons and above each claw, looped crosses. A distant memory: he had seen such a bird before, tattooed on dark brown arms on the North African run. Another image came to him: the black-rimmed eye, the eye of Horus. He looked again. Yes, there it was: the falcon's eye.

With a start he felt other eyes on him and looked up directly into the penetrating gaze of Mr Lee, dressed as always in sombre black and now, as usual, close by her side. In confusion, Matthew looked away, over Madam's shoulder and out of the window to the wharf below. It was alive with men working on two ships. One, the *Leonora*, had recently arrived from London and a new vessel was in the final stage of its commissioning. He could see the sign writer painting the name on the bow: she was to be called the *Amanda*.

## Authors' Notes

The first book in the set is called *Riot and Retribution*. The main plot is set in the autumn of 1831, and the epilogue in the autumn of 1832. In *Napoleon's Gold* Nathaniel Parry continues to collaborate in secret with Cornelius Lee, and the themes and characters develop in this second book, which is set mainly in 1833. *Napoleon's Gold: The Wages of Sin* can be read without prior knowledge of the first book.

In the second book, as in the first, real locations, some of which still exist today, are used in the plot. The Old Bull's Head Inn and the Castle in Beaumaris on the Isle of Anglesey, the Prospect of Whitby in Wapping, the Hope and Anchor at Hope Cove in Devon, the medieval church of Saint-Laurent with its stone carvings of the seven deadly sins, Fort Medoc on the Gironde estuary, the Paris restaurant Le Grand Véfour in the Palais Royal and the Grand-Théâtre de Bordeaux all remain. General Palmer's mansion at Cenon can still be seen, though it now serves as a community centre. The prestigious Château Palmer in Margaux, on the left bank of the Gironde, was built after the General had descended into bankruptcy and sold all of his vineyards.

Current Bath locations are also used. Saint James's Square and Marlborough Buildings remain as fashionable residential areas. The Spence's home in Chatham Row also still stands, though much gentrified over recent years. The burial ground of Old Saint Mary's Church can be visited, beautifully tended by volunteers. The Ravenswood townhouse is placed in Redcliffe Parade, Bristol, a terrace where many powerful Bristol merchants lived in the nineteenth century. The Bristol-Bordeaux link has been a close one since the medieval period and the port cities remain twinned today.

Edwin Ravenswood's mansion in Arno's Vale is fictional, though the Neo-Gothic design is typical of the period. Similarly, Château Pelèrin is an invention, though its location is based on an existing vineyard to the north of Saint-Laurent and its appearance is inspired by Château Beychevelle, located in Saint-Julien, the Medoc, which was originally constructed in 1565 and rebuilt in 1757. In 1825 it was bought by Pierre Guestier, who appears as a character in the book and was also Mayor of Saint-Julien. The Marquis's new mansion at Blanquefort was inspired by Chateau Dulamon, built in 1865, and the landscaped park and gardens of Majolan, which still exist in the town of Blanquefort. The entrancing network of waterways, paths, caves and grottoes were constructed in 1870 and reflect the earlier eighteenth century passion for the construction of follies.

Whilst most major characters and their adventures are fictional, some figures of national and local significance appear in the story for example, Lords Melbourne and Palmerston, the Home and Foreign Secretaries, Caroline "Naughty" Norton and Laure Duchesse d'Abrantès, who play parts which have been created to reflect their characters. Also, General Charles Palmer, the Bath MP at the time, was a reforming politician who invested heavily and ultimately ruinously in Medoc vineyards. His ill-luck stemmed in part because of the criticism his wine received from the Prince of Wales. General Palmer had been part of the Prince's high society set, until they fell out over a military dispute. Seeking to suit his wine, the famous "Palmer's Claret", to the Prince's palate, he undertook continual costly changes in the vineyards, which proved to be uneconomic. The details on his holdings, as well as the careers and characters of the Irish owners are based on research. Barton and Guestier joined in a partnership in 1802. Their company continues to trade and is the oldest wine merchant in Bordeaux. Bernard Phelan left Ireland at the end of the eighteenth century and married into the Guestier family. The family *château* was built by their son in the later nineteenth century.

In terms of the political background, the efforts to reform labour laws and abolish slavery were dominant issues of the time. The Factory Act of 1833 was a disappointment to campaigners, but as it included the appointment of inspectors it was the first of its kind to achieve even a modicum of success. The abolition of slavery in the British Empire in 1833 was a landmark act and reinforced the image of Britain as a pioneer of the abolition movement. No action was taken to prevent the exploitation of women at this time. Married women were unable to own property in their own right until 1870, but in 1839, after intense lobbying, Caroline Norton secured improved access to their children for divorced mothers. The age of consent varied between 10 and 12 years of age before 1875 and child abduction was only tackled more effectively after the 1880s.

The "War of the Unstamped" was an important issue in the early 1830s and took the form of a ceaseless campaign to repeal the newspaper tax. Real characters from that struggle, for example Henry Hetherington and Richard Carlile, feature in the novel. In 1836 they won a partial victory when the Whig government reduced the stamp duty from 4d to 1d (d was the symbol for penny before decimalisation and was worth 2.4 new pence), though penalties increased in severity for evasion of the duty. It was finally abolished in 1855, which stimulated the founding of the first penny paper, *The Daily Telegraph*, and in 1861 the remaining duty on paper was repealed. Punishment by humiliation remained and although the use of the pillory was banned by the late 1830s, the stocks remained in use until mid-century. In Bath, punishment in the stocks was last ordered in 1840. Transportation to a penal colony in Australia was favoured above imprisonment if detention was required, and by the 1830s execution was limited to crimes of murder, attempted murder, treason, piracy and arson in a royal dockyard. The Prospect of Whitby has a model gallows on its balcony overlooking the Thames to serve as a reminder that the Execution Dock was located close by. This was used for the hanging of pirates convicted in the Admiralty courts and stood below the line of low tide where the Admiralty jurisdiction began.

Smuggling also continued until mid-century despite the increase in numbers of revenue officials. It was a life style choice for those living in the coastal settlements of the south-west until Britain became the free trade centre of the world and the incentive to avoid duties was drastically reduced. After 1840 the British government began systematically to shed duties on foreign goods and the first international free trade agreement, the Cobden-Chevalier Treaty between Britain and France, was signed in 1860. The early 1830s saw an escalation in the illegal smuggling of opium into China by the British. Though other nationals were involved on a small scale, the British dominated and until 1833 the East India Company monopolised the China trade with Britain. After this time, the merchants who had worked for them, as well as others, were openly trading despite the banning of such trade by the Emperor. The situation continued to deteriorate and culminated in the First Opium War which broke out in 1839.

The references to Egyptian treasure reflect an obsession of the period. The birth of Egyptology in France and a craze for all things Egyptian in Europe followed Napoleon's Egyptian campaign of 1798-1801. Though the Emperor himself left Egypt in 1799, he had set up a headquarters in Cairo and 167 savants, scientists and scholars occupied themselves with local research. In 1802 the British confiscated looted antiquities from the French, for example the Rosetta Stone, and they were all taken to the British Museum. During the mid-1820s, British travellers brought back more antiquities and added to the collection.

Detail concerning the weapons is also accurate. Nathaniel's swordstick with spring loaded quillons forming a hand-guard was based on nineteenth-century examples, though his version has a special Japanese blade. The makila, a Basque walking stick, is still manufactured. In the nineteenth century it was common for one variety of makila to have a short concealed blade. The hachiwari referred to in the story is believed to be the forerunner of the jutte weapon and was used for law

271

enforcement in Tokyo. Expertise in savate, French kick-boxing, was current in the early 1830s. This allowed Coco and her brother Jules to have experience of this style of fighting. The male and female bare knuckle fighting described in the novel is also based on examples from the time. The fighting skills demonstrated by Cornelius reflect the well-respected Chinese martial styles, known as Wu Shu, which were often taught in secret. During the reign of the Manchu Qing Dynasty (1644-1911) the indigenous Chinese (Han people) were officially forbidden to practise the fighting arts. In the west, these skills are usually known under the generic heading of Kung Fu and can occasionally be seen in traditional form on stage, for example in "The Wheel of Life" performed by Shaolin monks from China. These fighting methods underpinned and influenced further developments of martial arts and weaponry on what is now known as the island of Okinawa.

*Acknowledgements*

The details concerning the locations, the political situation, the characters of the politicians, the Bristol Riots and the disturbances in Bath were written as accurately as possible based on research conducted by Alex over many years. The staff of Bath and Bristol Reference Libraries and Colin Johnston and his staff at Bath Record Office were extremely helpful, as was Graham Snell, who worked as Secretary of Brooks's Club in London and was most kind in sharing his expert knowledge of the history of the Club. We extend our grateful thanks to them all. We would also like to take the opportunity to thank James and Claire Kolaczkowski, Chris and Sue Simpson, Sarah Sawyer, Diane Chorley, Alan Mather and Marina de Rementeria for their time spent in reading the draft chapters, for their comments and their encouragement.

We would also like to thank: Ana María Espiñeira Luksić for the original preparation of the background art on the cover and cameo image; Stan Kolaczkowski for his advice on martial arts and his contribution to the plots, as well as for the preparation of the outline sketches in the chapters and maps, and finally, Hilary Strickland for using her artistic skills to turn these sketches and the cover lay-out into high quality images.

Bath, October 2017
Dr Alex Kolaczkowski
Professor Robert Hayes

# The Authors

The nominal author of the book, Alex E. Robertson, is a pen name, incorporating the names of the creators of the work. The text was written by Alex Kolaczkowski, based on an overarching plot from Robert Hayes, who also collaborates on research and contributes to the evolving story-line.

**Dr Alex Kolaczkowski** has taught history at schools in Bath and Bristol, as well as in Wiltshire, Oxfordshire and Surrey. Her B.Ed degree was awarded by the University of Bristol and her Ph.D by the University of Bath. A dedicated teacher, passionate about all aspects of her subject, she took her pupils on frequent field trips, making ancient, medieval, early modern and modern topics alike come vividly to life. Bath and Bristol are cities very well known to her having lived, studied and worked in both of them. Her expertise in Bath history stemmed from her years spent researching the city as a case-study for her doctoral topic on the development of municipal socialism and the civic ideal in the nineteenth century. By invitation from the Dictionary of National Biography she provided the entry for Sir Jerom Murch who was Mayor of Bath on seven occasions, and wrote a paper on aspects of Bath Non-Conformism in the Unitarian Journal. These research activities helped to provide her specialist background knowledge of the period and places in which the novel is set.

**Professor Robert Hayes** is a full-time academic at the University of Alberta in Canada. Apart from his distinguished research and teaching in chemical engineering, he is a calculating thinker with an interest in mystery and intrigue within a historical context. As a Ph.D student at the University of Bath in the early 1980s, he developed an interest in the game of Go (which originated as Wei Ch'i in China), often travelling to Bristol to play at the Go Club in Hotwells, and later was a founder member of the Bath Go Club at the Crown Inn, Bathwick Street. During the 1990s he was a frequent visitor to Bath and Bristol. In addition to his passion for historical mysteries, he is a lover of fine wines, single malt whisky, and of course whiskey.

# Brief introduction to the use of local dialect

To convey the atmosphere of the region, in some sections of the story conversations with people native to the area are expressed in a phonetic version of a south-west English accent. There are many different varieties of this gentle rural accent, and the version used in this novel is typical of the accent which could frequently be heard in Bath well into the twentieth century.

You will notice, as with many regional accents, the south-west style of speech tends to exclude letters at the beginning and ends of words, to shorten words, and alter grammar. Some speakers also lengthen vowels. In the nineteenth century it was normal for the lower classes in all areas to exclude the "h" at the start of words, and if they wished to sound very polite to include an "h" at the beginning of words where there was no such letter. Below we have provided the equivalent in standard English for a few examples of the accent as it features in the story. This has been included to help foreign readers and those unfamiliar with the south-west of England to identify and appreciate the local accent, which can still be heard occasionally today.

**Chapter 1:**
'Ee do be a caution *means* He is one who needs to be watched
terrible toimes *means* terrible times
Moiy *means* my
Oiy *means* I

**Chapter 6**
'E come for Oiy *means* He came for (I) me
Done that before 'e 'ad *means* He had done that before

**Chapter 9**
Where's that caddy to? *means* Where is the tea caddy?
'E's as 'andsome as ever Oiy seen *means* He is the handsomest (man) I have ever seen